GOTHIC

SWORDS &STEAM SHORT STORIES

ANTHOLOGY OF NEW & CLASSIC TALES

Foreword by S.T. Joshi

FLAME TREE PUBLISHING

FANTASY

This is a FLAME TREE Book

Publisher & Creative Director: Nick Wells
Project Editor: Laura Bulbeck
Editorial Board: Catherine Taylor, Josie Mitchell, Gillian Whitaker

FLAME TREE PUBLISHING
6 Melbray Mews, Fulham,
London SW6 3NS, United Kingdom
www.flametreepublishing.com

First published 2016

16 18 20 19 17
1 3 5 7 9 10 8 6 4 2

ISBN: 978-1-78361-997-9

The cover image is created by Flame Tree Studio
based on artwork by Slava Gerj and Gabor Ruszkai.

A copy of the CIP data for this book is available from the British Library.

Printed and bound in Turkey

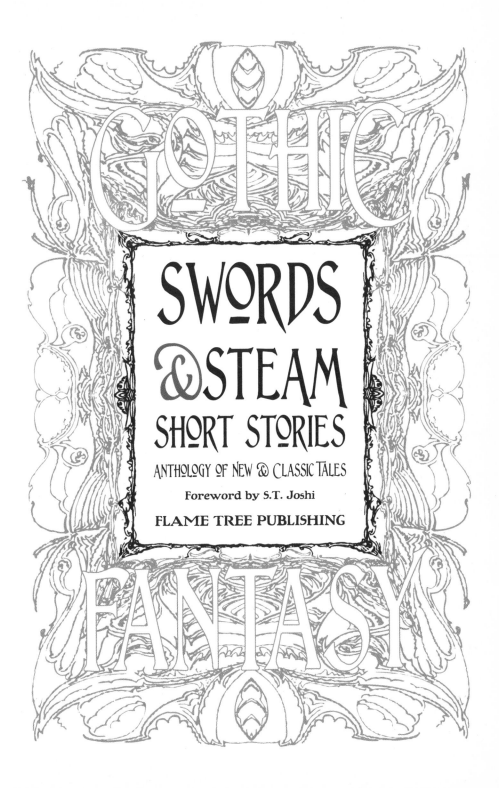

GOTHIC

SWORDS
&STEAM
SHORT STORIES
ANTHOLOGY OF NEW & CLASSIC TALES

Foreword by S.T. Joshi

FLAME TREE PUBLISHING

FANTASY

Contents

Foreword: Swords & Steam

IT IS OFTEN THOUGHT that the genres of weird fiction, fantasy, and science fiction are recent products of popular culture. It is true that these genres (as well as others, such as the detective story, the western, and the romance) came into organised existence by way of the American pulp magazines of the 1920s. But all these genres had antecedents that extended back decades if not centuries; and they also attracted the attention of some of the most acclaimed writers of their time. In his masterful study, 'Supernatural Horror in Literature', H.P. Lovecraft wryly notes the tendency of mainstream writers to dabble in the weird and fantastic. Cosmic fear, he wrote, 'has always existed, and always will exist; and no better evidence of its tenacious vigour can be cited than the impulse which now and then drives writers of totally opposite leanings to try their hands at it in isolated tales, as if to discharge from their minds certain phantasmal shapes which would otherwise haunt them.'

Many of the motifs used by the Gothic novelists of the late eighteenth and early nineteenth centuries, and by later writers, were drawn from ancient European folklore. Long before the brothers Grimm codified many of these motifs in their various collections of fairy tales, beginning in 1812, writers found them full of inspiration. The German writer Friedrich de la Motte Fouqué's novella *Undine* is an exquisite mingling of love and death, as it tells the delicate story of a water nymph who marries a human being. Sigmund Freud used E.T.A. Hoffmann's enigmatic 'The Sandman' as a springboard for his discussion of weird fiction in his essay 'The Uncanny'.

In Great Britain, Sir Walter Scott drew heavily upon Scottish folklore in his several tales of ghosts and spectres, while in America Washington Irving created an imperishable modern fairy tale in 'Rip Van Winkle'. Mary Shelley's *Frankenstein* may be the first true work of science fiction, but in several shorter tales she expanded on the ideas in that pioneering novel. 'Roger Dodsworth: The Reanimated Englishman' is an interesting mix of scientific verisimilitude and political satire.

Edgar Allan Poe revolutionized weird fiction by restricting it to the short story and by relentlessly focusing on the psychology of fear. His 'The Unparalleled Adventure of One Hans Pfaall' may perhaps be a satire or parody, but it was one of several tales that laid the groundwork for the genre of science fiction. His older contemporary, Nathaniel Hawthorne, generally looked to an older tradition in his pensive tales of Puritans and moral temptation; but in 'The Artist of the Beautiful' he may have written the first known story of a robotic insect.

Jules Verne became famous throughout Europe for his novels of trips to the moon or voyages under the sea. As such, he became the ultimate source for the entire genre of science fiction, and his focus on advances in technology makes him a revered ancestor to the related genre of steampunk. Toward the end of the nineteenth century, Sir Arthur Conan Doyle exhibited facility in several different genres. While he may be best known today for his Sherlock Holmes stories, which set the standard for detective fiction for all succeeding generations, he also worked extensively in horror fiction and even in science fiction. 'The Horror of the Heights' makes use of the very recent invention of the airplane to depict the bizarre terrors that hapless aviators may encounter in the mysterious realm of our atmosphere.

The later nineteenth and early twentieth centuries might be considered a 'golden age' of horror and fantasy fiction, with many towering writers emerging, including the Scotsmen Robert Louis Stevenson and John Buchan. One of the most unusual was the American novelist Robert W. Chambers, whose *The King in Yellow* has become something of a cult classic by virtue of the fact that elements from it were cited in the first season of the popular television show *True Detective*. Chambers was able to work as well in ethereal fantasy as in supernatural terror, and 'The Demoiselle d'Ys' is a hauntingly beautiful tale about a man who is supernaturally transplanted into the mediaeval age while hunting in the Breton countryside.

With the dawn of the pulp era, such writers as A. Merritt and Robert E. Howard were able to find many venues for their tales of fantasy. Howard is the virtual inventor of the genre of sword-and-sorcery, although some antecedents can be found in the work of William Morris and Lord Dunsany. Howard's Conan the Cimmerian (the basis for the *Conan the Barbarian* films) is his most iconic creation; but in 'Skulls in the Stars' he has invented another memorable figure – Solomon Kane, a seventeenth-century Puritan who travels the world in search of adventure. This tale is only one of several in this book to focus on historical fantasy, a genre that has exploded in popularity in recent decades.

Readers who only know contemporary examples of fantasy, horror, and science fiction owe it to themselves to delve into the origins of these genres in the literature of the past two centuries. They will see how these genres were shaped by the hands of some of the most distinctive writers in European literature, and they will also find that their tales, although seemingly remote from present-day concerns, offer imaginative thrills and supernatural chills rivalling the best of recent work.

S.T. Joshi
www.stjoshi.org

Publisher's Note

OUR LATEST short story anthologies delve into new realms, with the topics of *Swords & Steam* and *Dystopia Utopia*. We received such a great response to our call for new submissions that choosing the final stories to include proved to be incredibly tough. Our editorial board thoroughly enjoyed discovering the multitudes of different worlds on offer – from supernatural pasts to clockwork inventions – and ultimately we feel that the stories which made the final cut were the best for our purpose. We're delighted to publish them here.

In *Swords & Steam* we're whisked away to historical settings and arcane escapades, with classic adventures by Walter Scott, mysterious encounters by John Buchan, and sword and sorcery grounded in our own world by the master Robert E. Howard. We also journey into steam-powered worlds, seeking the predecessors to the Steampunk genre through the pens of Jules Verne, George Griffith and Nathaniel Hawthorne. Some of these stories will be familiar, but we hope to have uncovered seldom-read gems too.

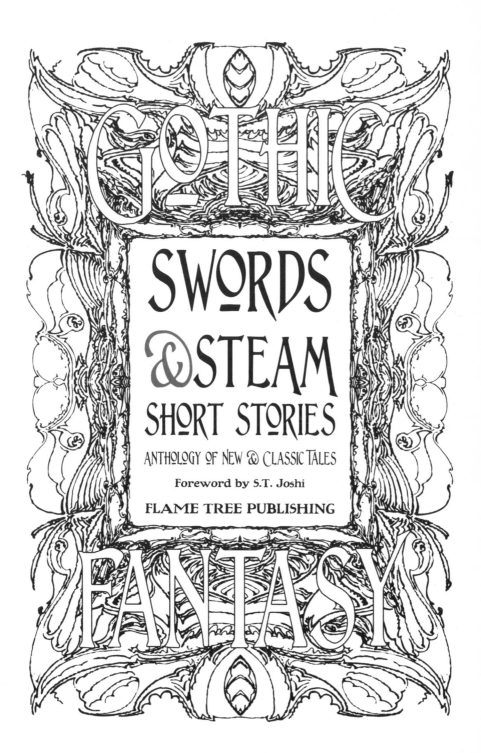

GOTHIC

SWORDS
&STEAM
SHORT STORIES
ANTHOLOGY OF NEW & CLASSIC TALES
Foreword by S.T. Joshi
FLAME TREE PUBLISHING

FANTASY

Little Healers

Andrew Bourelle

JESSICA STEPPED through the gate of the graveyard and began walking among the tombstones. Her breath came out in nervous bursts, white in the darkness. Her wool cape was pulled tight around her, but she still felt chilled. The cold came through the seams of her clothes, icy tendrils so tiny that they wormed their way through the threads of the fabric. Her hands trembled, but she thought this might not be because of the cold. She had journeyed into the graveyard to look for her husband.

She could see quite clearly, with the moon casting a bluish-white light on the frosted ground. She saw a feral cat sitting atop a stone cross, and in the distance she could hear the faint howling from what she hoped was a dog and feared was a wolf. She reached involuntarily into the deep pocket of her cape and wrapped her hand around the grip of her husband's gun. Henry had shown her once how to load it – how to measure the powder and ram the ball down the barrel, tamping it to make sure it was in place – and she had remembered the instruction well. There had been no real purpose to the lesson. He was target shooting – practicing for a fox hunt he'd been invited to – and she'd asked him about the gun. He then showed her how to use it. He let her shoot once, and when she hit, on her first attempt, the target he had missed his previous three tries, he had snatched the gun away from her and told her to leave him be. He had the steadiest hands of any person she'd ever known, but he was a poor shot with the pistol because he flinched when he pulled the trigger. She had been secretly proud that she could shoot better than him. She had never dreamed that she might need the gun to protect herself from him.

In the distance, Jessica saw the faint glow of a light: a lantern. She crept through the grass and could hear each step pressing down on the stalks, frozen stiff from the cold. She used the trees and the headstones for cover, and as she drew closer to the light source, she heard the scrape of a shovel against frozen dirt and an occasional muffled voice. She finally came to a point where she could see them, and she knelt behind a large marble headstone and spied. Her husband was in the grave, his waist level with the ground, tossing shovelfuls of dirt into a pile. Her husband's assistant, James, stood above, holding the lamp. Henry wasn't wearing his top hat – it sat atop a nearby grave marker – and the lamplight illuminated his face. Even at this distance, she could see his eyes were wide and crazed, like a lunatic escaped from the asylum.

She realized her fears were warranted – he was doing exactly what she'd dreaded – and she felt rage swelling from within, so powerful she wanted to rush into the lamp light, gun drawn. But she restrained herself and continued watching from her remove.

How could he do this? He was digging up the grave of their son.

* * *

Henry had begun to sweat underneath his shirt and trench coat. His chest rose and fell, pulling cold air into his lungs and exhaling smoky bursts. He thrust the shovel again, biting into the black soil, and then swung the dirt up and out, dumping it upon the growing pile. James, his protégé, stood above the hole with the lamp. Only one of them could fit in the grave at a time. Henry was tired, but he felt this work – digging up the grave of his own child – was his responsibility. He had brought James along only for … for what? he asked himself.

But he knew the answer: in case he found what he was looking for.

Finally, the blade of the shovel struck wood, and the two men looked at each other. The hole was five feet deep now, and Henry was buried almost to his shoulders. He scraped and shoveled more, clearing the top of the coffin lid. He tossed the shovel out, and his assistant handed down the pry bar. The space in the hole was tight because the coffin was only four feet long, and he kept bumping into the walls with his shoulders and elbows. His coat was mud-caked, and his gloves were blackened and stiff. He pried the lid at its edges, the wood creaking loudly in the black night. But he couldn't pry up the lid because he was standing on the coffin.

"Damnation," he growled.

He stopped working, closing his eyes and breathing deeply. His specialty was working in close quarters, working with the tiny, the miniscule. If he could build the inventions he had, using magnifying glasses and instruments smaller than sewing needles, then he could find a solution to this problem.

He climbed out and instructed James about what he wanted to do. James set the lamp down at the edge of the hole. Henry, holding the pry bar in one hand, lay chest down on the ground, his arms hanging over the edge. His assistant grabbed his legs, lifting him forward, lowering him head-first into the open grave.

The lid of the coffin shrieked as Henry pulled it away, and then he was face to face with his son. Both of the coins that had been laid across the boy's eyelids had slipped off in burial, and Anson's eyes were wide and staring. Sitting in dark, sunken sockets, the whites of the eyes had begun to turn yellow, and the irises – once a brilliant blue – were softening into a milky gray. The boy's skin was yellow and already tightening against his skull.

No father should have to see such a sight, Henry thought.

And then the stench crawled up his nostrils, and he shouted to his assistant to pull him up.

* * *

Jessica watched as James pulled Henry out of the grave by his feet. Her whole body was trembling. That was the grave of her son they were defiling, and it didn't matter that the one doing the defiling was her husband. In fact, that made it worse.

She hadn't wanted to believe he was capable of something like this. He had always been obsessive, but that's what gave him his genius. And he was a genius; this was no exaggeration. He was the son of a watchmaker, taught at an early age to examine the inner workings of machinery. By the time he was a teenager, he was more skilled than his father, able to design and assemble the gears and pins to build clocks large and small. It was widely known that he helped his father build the town's clock tower, which had run without slowing for twenty years. However, Henry had confided in her – and she believed him – that he had done the majority of the work, and his father had actually been the assistant. Each night, from their home, she and Henry could hear the distant ringing of the clock at each hour – its long, slow cadence of chimes was soothing to her – and she always felt a swelling of pride that her husband had created such a marvel.

His real specialty, however, was in smaller machines. He built complex time pieces no larger than a coin, with intricate gears virtually invisible without the use of a magnifying glass. This had begun his fascination with the miniscule. "There are other worlds just out of our sight," he had told her when he began his courtship. He was a student at the university then, studying chemistry and biology and trying to understand the worlds that he said were there even if you couldn't see them, worlds of cells and molecules.

Teaching others about this invisible world of science became his profession, but watch-making continued as his hobby. He loved to toil for hours in his study, using hair-thin needles as instruments, staring through magnifying glasses, and making the inner workings of his timepieces smaller and smaller. Then he extended his inventions beyond watches and clocks, making elaborate and strange metal machines. He built mechanical figurines, foot-high toy soldiers, who could be wound up just as a pocket watch and walk and move their arms. Then he invented an elaborate pair of goggles, with multiple lenses he could move in and out of his view, allowing him to work on an even smaller scale. Afterward, he made smaller versions of his figurines as chess pieces – knights, rooks, kings, and queens no taller than an inch, with microscopic inner-workings – and created a game where the pieces played against each other without the aid of human participants. Once wound up with a turnkey, the pieces moved themselves. No strategy was duplicated no matter how many times the figurines played.

"How did you do it?" she had asked, amazed.

"It's a mixture of my two passions," he said. "Science and engineering."

He explained that this was his true calling: to invent and to build.

Through all of his studying, his teaching, his inventing, he had been a charming courter and remained a devoted husband. He genuinely enjoyed life and was exuberant about his discoveries. His cheerfulness extended to their carriage rides along the river, their evenings reading by the fire, their Saturday mornings having a cup of tea on the veranda. In those first years, she had wished he would come home earlier from his laboratory or spend less time in his study, but she wasn't ignored. He would arrive with a bouquet of roses or surprise her with tickets to the opera. In the darkest months of winter, when she was melancholic, she was always able to convince herself that life was as it should be and she shouldn't ask for more.

But life did give her more: a son. He was a beautiful healthy baby boy whom her husband doted over as much as she did. And for five years, their life together was even happier. Her husband spent more time at home, his son being his most interesting project yet. With their son, she finally felt complete. But then young Anson became ill. They fretted over him as he lay feverish and unresponsive. They called in doctors, and when those doctors couldn't give her husband a clear diagnosis, he wrote for other doctors to come, regardless of expense. While their frustration mounted, Jessica became her son's nurse. Henry retreated to his study and his laboratory, spending more time than ever away from the family. He saw his assistant, James, more than he saw his ailing son. Only then had she really become angry: their son was dying and Henry's response was to escape the family?

But then one day, as if by a miracle, Anson's fever broke. He sat up in bed. He smiled. He ate soup and laughed, and both she and her husband were there to watch the boy's return. Whatever illness had taken hold of him, he was healing now. And her husband was back. From the moment Anson's recovery started, Henry didn't so much as set foot in his study or leave for his lab at the university. She could forgive Henry and allow life to return to normal.

But then they awoke two nights ago to Anson's screams. Running to his room, they found him writhing in his blankets. He was bleeding from his mouth and nose, his ears and eyes, even from the pores of his skin. She held him as he screamed. Her husband shouted, "No! No! No!" and then moments later the boy's shrieks simply stopped. He was limp in her arms. His temperature – so hot during the illness – faded, and his body became chilled.

When the physician and the funeral director came to remove Anson, Henry went mad, shouting that they must not take him, that he needed to inspect the body. She realized that her husband might have gone insane. The constable and two deputies had to restrain him. And he remained quiet, barely speaking, through all of the funeral arrangements.

Jessica wanted nothing more than to retreat, as her husband had before, and lay in bed weeping all day. But she'd had to collect herself and construct a strong face for family and friends. But her strength was a façade – she wasn't tough enough to shoulder the death of her son, certainly not compounded with the lunacy of her husband.

And now the situation had grown even worse. After the funeral, she had come to his study to deliver a cup of tea. Outside the door, she heard voices and listened to Henry speaking to his lab assistant. They spoke about shovels and digging utensils and an agreed time to meet after dark. She couldn't believe it. He meant to examine the body still, even after it was buried.

So she feigned going to bed and waited until Henry peeked into the room to make sure she was asleep. The covers were pulled to her neck, but she was fully clothed underneath and wide awake. She crept to the door to see her husband walking along the cobblestones under the orange glow of the street's oil lamp. She moved to follow him but then stopped at the threshold. She turned back to retrieve his pistol from its mount above the fireplace, trying to convince herself it was simply an extra precaution.

And now Jessica knelt in the graveyard, hiding behind a headstone, spying her husband and his assistant as they stared into the newly dug grave of her son. The world, it seemed, was going mad around her, and she was clinging to her own sanity as she clung to the pistol in her pocket.

* * *

James asked, "Do you want me to do it?"

"No," Henry said, standing on weak legs. "He's my son."

He'd brought a toolkit with him, and now he turned to it. He opened it on the ground and quickly found what he was looking for: a large scalpel, with an eight-inch handle and two-inch razor-sharp blade. The metal gleamed in the moonlight like a silver flame.

He stepped down into the grave, his feet balancing on each side of the coffin. He tried to kneel but there wasn't enough room. He set his foot down inside, his ankle brushing his son's shirt. Now he knelt. The smell was rank, and he feared he might retch. He brought out his kerchief and held it to his mouth and nose. With his other hand, he tried to cut open Anson's shirt. He couldn't do it one handed. He put the kerchief into his pocket and tried to breathe shallowly.

He yanked open his son's shirt, tearing off the buttons and exposing the boy's yellowing flesh.

"Dear God, help me," Henry wailed.

He stabbed the scalpel into the boy's abdomen and, quickly, so he wouldn't lose his nerve, he cut upward. The blade stopped when he hit the breastbone. Henry, holding his breath from the fresh stink emanating from the cut, changed positions, giving himself leverage, and cut upward, opening the boy from navel to neck.

Henry leaned back and ordered James to move the light. The assistant changed positions, illuminating the incision. Henry could see the gray meat of the boy's organs.

"Perhaps it wasn't –"

Then he saw movement inside the boy's chest cavity. A mass of what looked to be tiny insects poured out. Individually, they were barely large enough to see with the naked eye – much smaller than any ant – but they swarmed out in a heap, thousands of them, growing like an eruption of thick black foam.

Henry gasped, dropping the scalpel, and scurried out of the hole.

"The oil!" he shouted. "Get the bloody oil!"

His assistant hesitated for a moment, looking into the grave, and then his face turned pale, and he scrambled backward. He pulled a flask out of the toolkit. Henry snatched it from his hand and ran over to the hole. He began dumping the oil out onto the mass of tiny creatures. He splattered the oil over his son, trying to douse him from forehead to shoe tip. The creatures were now piled several inches high, with the pile growing and spreading with each second. He couldn't believe how many of them there were.

"Get the matches," he shouted at James.

The young man reached into his coat and drew out a box of matches.

Henry emptied the bottle and then tossed the flask into the grave. It landed in the growing mass of insects and immediately it was covered.

"Set fire to them!" Henry yelled.

His assistant stepped forward and struck the match. He held it high, over the grave, allowing the flame to grow to a healthy, vigorous height.

"Burn them!" Henry shouted. "For the love of God, burn them a–"

* * *

Jessica squeezed the trigger, and flames jumped from the barrel, lighting the darkness around her. Her husband's assistant grabbed his chest with his free hand, inhaled loudly, the sound constrained and wet, and then he fell face forward into the grave, bringing the match with him. Flames erupted from the hole in a flash of bright white light. She heard the man's shrieks and saw the flames twisting up out of the grave, orange and red and yellow. This wasn't what she'd wanted – she'd hoped he would fall backward, the match falling with him into the extinguishing chill of the icy grass.

She lowered the gun and opened her mouth to scream. But no sounds came out.

Next to the cauldron of fire, she saw her husband staring toward her.

* * *

Henry could see nothing in the darkness. The lamp stood next to the pit, and flames reached up out of his son's grave, making the immediate vicinity as light as if it were day.

But the light also had the effect of blinding him beyond its reach, and past a few gravestones, he could only see blackness.

He looked down into the hole and saw that James had stopped moving. Flames engulfed his son and his assistant and, he hoped, the creatures that he'd come here to destroy.

He stared back in the direction the shot had come from. He thought perhaps he was now in the sniper's sights. He turned and fled. As he ran, the headstones of the dead stood like sentinels driving him away.

* * *

She approached her son's grave, moving slowly. The fire had begun to die, but her husband had left the lamp and she could see clearly within its circle of light. She lifted the lamp and peered down into the grave. Tentacles of smoke undulated from the blackened remains of her son and the assistant. She looked carefully and thought she saw movement amidst the charred flesh, a blob of darkness among the coals that seemed to shift and writhe.

She turned in horror and ran into the night.

* * *

She found him in his study, sitting in front of his work bench, his head in his hands. The room was filled with microscopic lenses, magnifying glasses, and spectacles with glass of varying dimensions and thicknesses. Tools and gears and mechanical pieces – made of brass and copper and iron – lay scattered among the benches as well, but the dominance of the lenses made her feel as if she was being watched, surrounded by glass eyes.

She walked to the other side of the table, lifted the reloaded gun, and said to her husband, "What have you done?"

He raised his head, looked at her at first with an expression that suggested he didn't recognize her. Then his face changed to a look of recognition followed by a look of confusion.

"You?" he said. "It was you?"

"Tell me what you've done!" she yelled.

He leaned back in his chair, hunched in defeat. "You can lower the gun. I will tell you."

Hesitantly, she lowered the pistol. Her chest heaved with each breath.

His hand reached for a glass jar on the table, clear glass tapered at the top and sealed with cork coated in melted wax. He slid it toward her.

"Look inside," he said. "Don't open it."

She picked up the jar with her free hand. She thought it was empty, but then she held it close to her face and saw that inside were a few tiny black dots, perhaps a dozen, no bigger than grains of soil. They were moving, rolling around the bottom and up and down the sides of the glass, as if of their own volition.

"Here," he said, holding up a magnifying lens the size of a saucer.

Hesitantly, she holstered the gun in her cape pocket and took the lens. She held it before the jar and looked through it. The black objects were still small, but now she could see with more clarity. Each dot was a tiny centipede, with shells and hinged legs made of what looked like metal. They raced around the glass like insects, but she could see with enough detail to know that they were mechanical not biological.

"My masterpiece," her husband said, but he spoke the words with irony. "My greatest achievement."

She set the glass down and slid it back across the table to him.

"What are they?"

"I call them my Little Healers," he said. "They eat germs, microbes of disease, only the bad. Or so I thought."

Now she was beginning to understand. During Anson's illness, Henry had retreated to his laboratory and his study, and she had thought perhaps he didn't care that his son was dying. But all along he was trying to create some new invention that would cure Anson.

"I tested them," he said. "But only on dead animals. When they consumed the dead flesh, I thought it was because they took the rot for disease."

She stared at him. His face was white.

"And you unleashed them on our son?"

"I did not know they would multiply as they did," he said. "I only administered three: one in his mouth, one in his nose, one in his ear. I thought they would eat the disease and then die. Or perhaps stay inside him, bolstering his immune system. I did not think they would eat the bad and the good."

She thought of her son's final minutes.

"You killed him," she said.

"He might have died anyway," he said absently, as if more to himself than to her. "I wanted to make the world better. Starting with our family."

"Don't you remember his screams?" she said.

He lifted the glass jar and looked in at the mechanical insects.

"I still hear his screams," he said.

Then he set the jar down and stood quickly, moving so abruptly that she reached for the gun, startled.

"I'm going to the constable," he said. "I plan to confess everything."

She looked at him and remembered the man she'd fallen in love with. He had been overly obsessed with his work, but he had been a good husband. A good man, with good intentions.

She had forgiven him his imperfections before, but now ….

In the distance, the clock tower he built with his father began its midnight ring.

* * *

The sound of the clock tower made Henry think of the potential he had once had. And of the happiness he had once shared with Jessica.

He looked again at his wife, remembering how beautiful she always was. Her face was stern now, expressionless. Her complexion was flushed, her eyes narrowed, her lips pressed into a thin, straight line. He had never seen her look this way. He hoped she could forgive him. He had acted for the sake of helping their son, not killing him. Surely she must understand. She was always very smart. She would understand, perhaps even try to talk him out of turning himself in.

He took a step, and she said, "Wait."

He stopped – as the clock tower chimed again – and he turned to Jessica, longing for a loving look, an expression that said she forgave him.

"Before you go," she said, "you must do something."

"Yes," he said. "Anything."

She motioned toward the glass jar.

"Swallow them," she said.

He looked at the jar and gulped. "But," he said, "they are evidence. I must –"

She raised the pistol, cocked the hammer back, and pointed the gun at his face. The gun was steady in her hand, the black circle at the end of the barrel staring at him like a dark eye.

He sighed. "A bullet would be more merciful," he said.

"Do you deserve mercy?" she said.

He lifted the jar and looked through the glass at his Little Healers. He looked back at her and saw hate in her eyes.

"Forgive me," he said. "I cannot forgive myself."

"Then you shall not be forgiven."

He pulled the cork off the top of the jar.

In the distance, the last of the clock tower's midnight chimes was followed by a long empty silence.

The Grove of Ashtaroth

John Buchan

C'est enfin que dans leurs prunelles
Rit et pleure-fastidieux
L'amour des choses eternelles,
Des vieux morts et des anciens dieux!
Paul Verlaine

WE WERE SITTING around the camp fire, some thirty miles north of a place called Taqui, when Lawson announced his intention of finding a home. He had spoken little the last day or two, and I guessed that he had struck a vein of private reflection. I thought it might be a new mine or irrigation scheme, and I was surprised to find that it was a country-house.

"I don't think I shall go back to England," he said, kicking a sputtering log into place. "I don't see why I should. For business purposes I am far more useful to the firm in South Africa than in Throgmorton Street. I have no relations left except a third cousin, and I have never cared a rush for living in town. That beastly house of mine in Hill Street will fetch what I gave for it – Isaacson cabled about it the other day, offering for furniture and all. I don't want to go into Parliament, and I hate shooting little birds and tame deer. I am one of those fellows who are born colonial at heart, and I don't see why I shouldn't arrange my life as I please. Besides, for ten years I have been falling in love with this country, and now I am up to the neck."

He flung himself back in the camp-chair till the canvas creaked, and looked at me below his eyelids. I remember glancing at the lines of him, and thinking what a fine make of a man he was. In his untanned field-boots, breeches, and grey shirt he looked the born wilderness-hunter, though less than two months before he had been driving down to the City every morning in the sombre regimentals of his class. Being a fair man, he was gloriously tanned, and there was a clear line at his shirt-collar to mark the limits of his sunburn. I had first known him years ago, when he was a broker's clerk working on half-commission. Then he had gone to South Africa, and soon I heard he was a partner in a mining house which was doing wonders with some gold areas in the North. The next step was his return to London as the new millionaire – young, good-looking, wholesome in mind and body, and much sought after by the mothers of marriageable girls. We played polo together, and hunted a little in the season, but there were signs that he did not propose to become a conventional English gentleman. He refused to buy a place in the country, though half the Homes of England were at his disposal. He was a very busy man, he declared, and had not time to be a squire. Besides, every few months he used to rush out to South Africa. I saw that he was restless, for he was always badgering me to go big game hunting with him in some remote part of the earth. There was that in his eyes, too, which marked him out from the ordinary blond type of our countrymen. They were large and brown and mysterious, and the light of another race was in their odd depths.

To hint such a thing would have meant a breach of his friendship, for Lawson was very proud of his birth. When he first made his fortune he had gone to the Heralds to discover his family, and these obliging gentlemen had provided a pedigree. It appeared that he was a scion of the house of Lowson or Lowieson, an ancient and rather disreputable clan on the Scottish side of the Border. He took a shooting in Teviotdale on the strength of it, and used to commit lengthy Border ballads to memory. But I had known his father, a financial journalist who never quite succeeded, and I had heard of a grandfather who sold antiques in a back street in Brighton. The latter, I think, had not changed his name, and still frequented the synagogue. The father was a progressive Christian, and the mother had been a blond Saxon from the Midlands. In my mind there was no doubt, as I caught Lawson's heavy-lidded eyes fixed on me. My friend was of a more ancient race than the Lowsons of the Border.

"Where are you thinking of looking for your house?" I asked. "In Natal or in the Cape Peninsula? You might get the Fishers" place if you paid a price."

"The Fishers' place be hanged!" he said crossly. "I don't want any stuccoed, overgrown Dutch farm. I might as well be at Roehampton as in the Cape."

He got up and walked to the far side of the fire, where a lane ran down through thorn-scrub to a gully of the hills. The moon was silvering the bush of the plains, forty miles off and three thousand feet below us.

"I am going to live somewhere hereabouts," he answered at last.

I whistled. "Then you've got to put your hand in your pocket, old man. You'll have to make everything, including a map of the countryside."

"I know," he said; "that's where the fun comes. Hang it all, why shouldn't I indulge my fancy? I'm uncommonly well off, and I haven't chick or child to leave it to. Supposing I'm a hundred miles from rail-head, what about it? I'll make a motor-road and fix up a telephone. I'll grow most of my supplies, and start a colony to provide labour. When you come and stay with me, you'll get the best food and drink on earth, and sport that will make your mouth water. I'll put Lochleven trout in these streams – at 6000 feet you can do anything. We'll have a pack of hounds, too, and we can drive pig in the woods, and if we want big game there are the Mangwe flats at our feet. I tell you I'll make such a country-house as nobody ever dreamed of. A man will come plumb out of stark savagery into lawns and rose-gardens." Lawson flung himself into his chair again and smiled dreamily at the fire.

"But why here, of all places?" I persisted. I was not feeling very well and did not care for the country.

"I can't quite explain. I think it's the sort of land I have always been looking for. I always fancied a house on a green plateau in a decent climate looking down on the tropics. I like heat and colour, you know, but I like hills too, and greenery, and the things that bring back Scotland. Give me a cross between Teviotdale and the Orinoco, and, by Gad! I think I've got it here."

I watched my friend curiously, as with bright eyes and eager voice he talked of his new fad. The two races were very clear in him – the one desiring gorgeousness, and other athirst for the soothing spaces of the North. He began to plan out the house. He would get Adamson to design it, and it was to grow out of the landscape like a stone on the hillside. There would be wide verandas and cool halls, but great fireplaces against winter time. It would all be very simple and fresh – 'clean as morning' was his odd phrase; but then another idea supervened, and he talked of bringing the Tintorets from Hill Street. "I want it to be a civilised house, you know. No silly luxury, but the best pictures and china and books ...I'll have all the furniture made after the old plain English models out of native woods. I don't want second-hand sticks in a new country. Yes, by Jove, the Tintorets are a great idea, and all those Ming pots I bought. I had meant to sell them, but I'll have them out here."

He talked for a good hour of what he would do, and his dream grew richer as he talked, till by the time he went to bed he had sketched something more like a palace than a country-house. Lawson was by no means a luxurious man. At present he was well content with a Wolseley valise, and shaved cheerfully out of a tin mug. It struck me as odd that a man so simple in his habits should have so sumptuous a taste in bric-a-brac. I told myself, as I turned in, that the Saxon mother from the Midlands had done little to dilute the strong wine of the East.

It drizzled next morning when we inspanned, and I mounted my horse in a bad temper. I had some fever on me, I think, and I hated this lush yet frigid tableland, where all the winds on earth lay in wait for one's marrow. Lawson was, as usual, in great spirits. We were not hunting, but shifting our hunting ground, so all morning we travelled fast to the north along the rim of the uplands.

At midday it cleared, and the afternoon was a pageant of pure colour. The wind sank to a low breeze; the sun lit the infinite green spaces, and kindled the wet forest to a jewelled coronal. Lawson gaspingly admired it all, as he cantered bareheaded up a bracken-clad slope. "God's country," he said twenty times. "I've found it." Take a piece of Sussex downland; put a stream in every hollow and a patch of wood; and at the edge, where the cliffs at home would fall to the sea, put a cloak of forest muffling the scarp and dropping thousands of feet to the blue plains. Take the diamond air of the Gornergrat, and the riot of colour which you get by a West Highland lochside in late September. Put flowers everywhere, the things we grow in hothouses, geraniums like sun-shades and arums like trumpets. That will give you a notion of the countryside we were in. I began to see that after all it was out of the common.

And just before sunset we came over a ridge and found something better. It was a shallow glen, half a mile wide, down which ran a blue-grey stream in linns like the Spean, till at the edge of the plateau it leaped into the dim forest in a snowy cascade. The opposite side ran up in gentle slopes to a rocky knoll, from which the eye had a noble prospect of the plains. All down the glen were little copses, half-moons of green edging some silvery shore of the burn, or delicate clusters of tall trees nodding on the hill-brow. The place so satisfied the eye that for the sheer wonder of its perfection we stopped and stared in silence for many minutes.

Then "The House," I said, and Lawson replied softly, "The House!"

We rode slowly into the glen in the mulberry gloaming. Our transport wagons were half an hour behind, so we had time to explore. Lawson dismounted and plucked handfuls of flowers from the water-meadows. He was singing to himself all the time – an old French catch about Cade Roussell and his *trois maisons*.

"Who owns it?" I asked.

"My firm, as like as not. We have miles of land about here. But whoever the man is, he has got to sell. Here I build my tabernacle, old man. Here, and nowhere else!"

In the very centre of the glen, in a loop of the stream, was one copse which even in that half light struck me as different from the others. It was of tall, slim, fairy-like trees, the kind of wood the monks painted in old missals. No, I rejected the thought. It was no Christian wood. It was not a copse, but a 'grove' – one such as Artemis may have flitted through in the moonlight. It was small, forty or fifty yards in diameter, and there was a dark something at the heart of it which for a second I thought was a house.

We turned between the slender trees, and – was it fancy? – an odd tremor went through me. I felt as if I were penetrating the temenos of some strange and lovely divinity, the goddess of this pleasant vale. There was a spell in the air, it seemed, and an odd dead silence.

Suddenly my horse started at a flutter of light wings. A flock of doves rose from the branches, and I saw the burnished green of their plumes against the opal sky. Lawson did not seem to notice them. I saw his keen eyes staring at the centre of the grove and what stood there.

It was a little conical tower, ancient and lichened, but, so far as I could judge, quite flawless. You know the famous Conical Temple at Zimbabwe, of which prints are in every guide-book. This was of the same type, but a thousandfold more perfect. It stood about thirty feet high, of solid masonry, without door or window or cranny, as shapely as when it first came from the hands of the old builders. Again I had the sense of breaking in on a sanctuary. What right had I, a common vulgar modern, to be looking at this fair thing, among these delicate trees, which some white goddess had once taken for her shrine?

Lawson broke in on my absorption. "Let's get out of this," he said hoarsely, and he took my horse's bridle (he had left his own beast at the edge) and led him back to the open. But I noticed that his eyes were always turning back, and that his hand trembled.

"That settles it," I said after supper. "What do you want with your mediaeval Venetians and your Chinese pots now? You will have the finest antique in the world in your garden – a temple as old as time, and in a land which they say has no history. You had the right inspiration this time."

I think I have said that Lawson had hungry eyes. In his enthusiasm they used to glow and brighten; but now, as he sat looking down at the olive shades of the glen, they seemed ravenous in their fire. He had hardly spoken a word since we left the wood.

"Where can I read about these things?" he asked, and I gave him the names of books.

Then, an hour later, he asked me who were the builders. I told him the little I knew about Phoenician and Sabaean wanderings, and the ritual of Sidon and Tyre. He repeated some names to himself and went soon to bed.

As I turned in, I had one last look over the glen, which lay ivory and black in the moon. I seemed to hear a faint echo of wings, and to see over the little grove a cloud of light visitants. "The Doves of Ashtaroth have come back," I said to myself. "It is a good omen. They accept the new tenant." But as I fell asleep I had a sudden thought that I was saying something rather terrible.

* * *

Three years later, pretty nearly to a day, I came back to see what Lawson had made of his hobby. He had bidden me often to Welgevonden, as he chose to call it – though I do not know why he should have fixed a Dutch name to a countryside where Boer never trod. At the last there had been some confusion about dates, and I wired the time of my arrival, and set off without an answer. A motor met me at the queer little wayside station of Taqui, and after many miles on a doubtful highway I came to the gates of the park, and a road on which it was a delight to move. Three years had wrought little difference in the landscape. Lawson had done some planting – conifers and flowering shrubs and such-like – but wisely he had resolved that Nature had for the most part forestalled him. All the same, he must have spent a mint of money. The drive could not have been beaten in England, and fringes of mown turf on either hand had been pared out of the lush meadows. When we came over the edge of the hill and looked down on the secret glen, I could not repress a cry of pleasure. The house stood on the farther ridge, the viewpoint of the whole neighbourhood; and its dark timbers and white rough-cast walls melted into the hillside as if it had been there from the beginning of things. The vale below was ordered in lawns and gardens. A blue lake received the rapids of the stream, and its banks were a maze of green shades and glorious masses of blossom. I noticed, too, that the little grove we had explored on our first visit stood alone in a big stretch of lawn, so that its perfection might be clearly seen. Lawson had excellent taste, or he had had the best advice.

The butler told me that his master was expected home shortly, and took me into the library for tea. Lawson had left his Tintorets and Ming pots at home after all. It was a long, low room, panelled in teak half-way up the walls, and the shelves held a multitude of fine bindings. There were good rugs on the parquet floor, but no ornaments anywhere, save three. On the carved mantelpiece stood two of the old soapstone birds which they used to find at Zimbabwe, and between, on an ebony stand, a half moon of alabaster, curiously carved with zodiacal figures. My host had altered his scheme of furnishing, but I approved the change.

He came in about half-past six, after I had consumed two cigars and all but fallen asleep. Three years make a difference in most men, but I was not prepared for the change in Lawson. For one thing, he had grown fat. In place of the lean young man I had known, I saw heavy, flaccid being, who shuffled in his gait, and seemed tired and listless. His sunburn had gone, and his face was as pasty as a city clerk's. He had been walking, and wore shapeless flannel clothes, which hung loose even on his enlarged figure. And the worst of it was, that he did not seem over-pleased to see me. He murmured something about my journey, and then flung himself into an arm-chair and looked out of the window.

I asked him if he had been ill.

"Ill! No!" he said crossly. "Nothing of the kind. I'm perfectly well."

"You don't look as fit as this place should make you. What do you do with yourself? Is the shooting as good as you hoped?"

He did not answer, but I thought I heard him mutter something like "shooting be damned."

Then I tried the subject of the house. I praised it extravagantly, but with conviction. "There can be no place like it in the world," I said.

He turned his eyes on me at last, and I saw that they were as deep and restless as ever. With his pallid face they made him look curiously Semitic. I had been right in my view about his ancestry.

"Yes," he said slowly, "there is no place like it – in the world."

Then he pulled himself to his feet. "I'm going to change," he said. "Dinner is at eight. Ring for Travers, and he'll show you your room."

I dressed in a noble bedroom, with an outlook over the garden-vale and the escarpment to the far line of the plains, now blue and saffron in the sunset. I dressed in an ill temper, for I was seriously offended with Lawson, and also seriously alarmed. He was either very unwell or going out of his mind, and it was clear, too, that he would resent any anxiety on his account. I ransacked my memory for rumours, but found none. I had heard nothing of him except that he had been extraordinarily successful in his speculations, and that from his hill-top he directed his firm's operations with uncommon skill. If Lawson was sick or mad, nobody knew of it.

Dinner was a trying ceremony. Lawson, who used to be rather particular in his dress, appeared in a kind of smoking suit and a flannel collar. He spoke scarcely a word to me, but cursed the servants with a brutality which left me aghast. A wretched footman in his nervousness spilt some sauce over his sleeve. Lawson dashed the dish from his hand, and volleyed abuse with a sort of epileptic fury. Also he, who had been the most abstemious of men, swallowed disgusting quantities of champagne and old brandy.

He had given up smoking, and half an hour after we left the dining-room he announced his intention of going to bed. I watched him as he waddled upstairs with a feeling of angry bewilderment. Then I went to the library and lit a pipe. I would leave first thing in the morning – on that I was determined. But as I sat gazing at the moon of alabaster and the soapstone birds my anger evaporated, and concern took its place. I remembered what a fine fellow Lawson had been, what good times we had had together. I remembered especially that evening when we had found this valley and given rein to our fancies. What horrid alchemy in the place had turned a gentleman into a brute? I thought of drink and drugs and madness and insomnia, but I could fit none of them into my conception of my friend. I did not consciously rescind my resolve to depart, but I had a notion that I would not act on it.

The sleepy butler met me as I went to bed. "Mr. Lawson's room is at the end of your corridor, sir," he said. "He don't sleep over well, so you may hear him stirring in the night. At what hour would you like breakfast, sir? Mr. Lawson mostly has his in bed."

My room opened from the great corridor, which ran the full length of the front of the house. So far as I could make out, Lawson was three rooms off, a vacant bedroom and his servant's room being between us. I felt tired and cross, and tumbled into bed as fast as possible. Usually I sleep well, but now I was soon conscious that my drowsiness was wearing off and that I was in for a restless night. I got up and laved my face, turned the pillows, thought of sheep coming over a hill and clouds crossing the sky; but none of the old devices were of any use. After about an hour of make-believe I surrendered myself to facts, and, lying on my back, stared at the white ceiling and the patches of moonshine on the walls.

It certainly was an amazing night. I got up, put on a dressing-gown, and drew a chair to the window. The moon was almost at its full, and the whole plateau swam in a radiance of ivory and silver. The banks of the stream were black, but the lake had a great belt of light athwart it, which made it seem like a horizon, and the rim of land beyond like a contorted cloud. Far to the right I saw the delicate outlines of the little wood which I had come to think of as the Grove of Ashtaroth. I listened. There was not a sound in the air. The land seemed to sleep peacefully beneath the moon, and yet I had a sense that the peace was an illusion. The place was feverishly restless.

I could have given no reason for my impression, but there it was. Something was stirring in the wide moonlit landscape under its deep mask of silence. I felt as I had felt on the evening three years ago when I had ridden into the grove. I did not think that the influence, whatever it was, was maleficent. I only knew that it was very strange, and kept me wakeful.

By and by I bethought me of a book. There was no lamp in the corridor save the moon, but the whole house was bright as I slipped down the great staircase and across the hall to the library. I switched on the lights and then switched them off. They seemed a profanation, and I did not need them.

I found a French novel, but the place held me and I stayed. I sat down in an armchair before the fireplace and the stone birds. Very odd those gawky things, like prehistoric Great Auks, looked in the moonlight. I remember that the alabaster moon shimmered like translucent pearl, and I fell to wondering about its history. Had the old Sabasans used such a jewel in their rites in the Grove of Ashtaroth?

Then I heard footsteps pass the window. A great house like this would have a watchman, but these quick shuffling footsteps were surely not the dull plod of a servant. They passed on to the grass and died away. I began to think of getting back to my room.

In the corridor, I noticed that Lawson's door was ajar, and that a light had been left burning. I had the unpardonable curiosity to peep in. The room was empty, and the bed had not been slept in. Now I knew whose were the footsteps outside the library window.

I lit a reading-lamp and tried to interest myself in Cruelle Enigme. But my wits were restless, and I could not keep my eyes on the page. I flung the book aside and sat down again by the window. The feeling came over me that I was sitting in a box at some play. The glen was a huge stage, and at any moment the players might appear on it. My attention was strung as high as if I had been waiting for the advent of some world-famous actress. But nothing came. Only the shadows shifted and lengthened as the moon moved across the sky.

Then quite suddenly the restlessness left me, and at the same moment the silence was broken by the crow of a cock and the rustling of trees in a light wind. I felt very sleepy, and was turning to bed when again I heard footsteps without. From the window I could see a figure moving across the garden towards the house. It was Lawson, got up in the sort of towel dressing-gown that one wears on board ship. He was walking slowly and painfully, as if very weary. I did not see his face, but the man's whole air was that of extreme fatigue and dejection.

I tumbled into bed and slept profoundly till long after daylight.

* * *

The man who valeted me was Lawson's own servant. As he was laying out my clothes I asked after the health of his master, and was told that he had slept ill and would not rise till late. Then the man, an anxious-faced Englishman, gave me some information on his own account. Mr. Lawson was having one of his bad turns. It would pass away in a day or two, but till it had gone he was fit for nothing. He advised me to see Mr. Jobson, the factor, who would look to my entertainment in his master's absence.

Jobson arrived before luncheon, and the sight of him was the first satisfactory thing about Welgevonden. He was a big, gruff Scot from Roxburghshire, engaged, no doubt, by Lawson as a duty to his Border ancestry. He had short grizzled whiskers, a weather-worn face, and a shrewd, calm blue eye. I knew now why the place was in such perfect order.

We began with sport, and Jobson explained what I could have in the way of fishing and shooting. His exposition was brief and business-like, and all the while I could see his eye searching me. It was clear that he had much to say on other matters than sport.

I told him that I had come here with Lawson three years before, when he chose the site. Jobson continued to regard me curiously. "I've heard tell of ye from Mr. Lawson. Ye're an old friend of his, I understand."

"The oldest," I said. "And I am sorry to find that the place does not agree with him. Why it doesn't I cannot imagine, for you look fit enough. Has he been seedy for long?"

"It comes and goes," said Mr. Jobson. "Maybe once a month he has a bad turn. But on the whole it agrees with him badly. He's no' the man he was when I first came here."

Jobson was looking at me very seriously and frankly. I risked a question. "What do you suppose is the matter?"

He did not reply at once, but leaned forward and tapped my knee.

"I think it's something that doctors canna cure. Look at me, sir. I've always been counted a sensible man, but if I told you what was in my head you would think me daft. But I have one word for you. Bide till tonight is past and then speir your question. Maybe you and me will be agreed."

The factor rose to go. As he left the room he flung me back a remark over his shoulder – "Read the eleventh chapter of the *First Book of Kings*."

After luncheon I went for a walk. First I mounted to the crown of the hill and feasted my eyes on the unequalled loveliness of the view. I saw the far hills in Portuguese territory, a hundred miles away, lifting up thin blue fingers into the sky. The wind blew light and fresh, and the place was fragrant with a thousand delicate scents. Then I descended to the vale, and followed the stream up through the garden. Poinsettias and oleanders were blazing in coverts, and there was a paradise of tinted water-lilies in the slacker reaches. I saw good trout rise at the fly, but I did not think about fishing. I was searching my memory for a recollection which would not come. By and by I found myself beyond the garden, where the lawns ran to the fringe of Ashtaroth's Grove.

It was like something I remembered in an old Italian picture. Only, as my memory drew it, it should have been peopled with strange figures – nymphs dancing on the sward, and a prick-eared faun peeping from the covert. In the warm afternoon sunlight it stood, ineffably gracious and beautiful, tantalising with a sense of some deep hidden loveliness. Very reverently I walked between the slim trees, to where the little conical tower stood half in the sun and half in shadow. Then I noticed something new. Round the tower ran a narrow path, worn in the grass by human feet. There had been no such path on my first visit, for I remembered the grass growing tall to the edge of the stone. Had the Kaffirs made a shrine of it, or were there other and stranger votaries?

When I returned to the house I found Travers with a message for me. Mr. Lawson was still in bed, but he would like me to go to him. I found my friend sitting up and drinking strong tea – a bad thing, I should have thought, for a man in his condition. I remember that I looked about the room for some sign of the pernicious habit of which I believed him a victim. But the place was fresh and clean, with the windows wide open, and, though I could not have given my reasons, I was convinced that drugs or drink had nothing to do with the sickness.

He received me more civilly, but I was shocked by his looks. There were great bags below his eyes, and his skin had the wrinkled puffy appearance of a man in dropsy. His voice, too, was reedy and thin. Only his great eyes burned with some feverish life.

"I am a shocking bad host," he said, "but I'm going to be still more inhospitable. I want you to go away. I hate anybody here when I'm off colour."

"Nonsense," I said; "you want looking after. I want to know about this sickness. Have you had a doctor?"

He smiled wearily. "Doctors are no earthly use to me. There's nothing much the matter, I tell you. I'll be all right in a day or two, and then you can come back. I want you to go off with Jobson and hunt in the plains till the end of the week. It will be better fun for you, and I'll feel less guilty."

Of course I pooh-poohed the idea, and Lawson got angry. "Damn it, man," he cried, "why do you force yourself on me when I don't want you? I tell you your presence here makes me worse. In a week I'll be as right as the mail, and then I'll be thankful for you. But get away now; get away, I tell you."

I saw that he was fretting himself into a passion. "All right," I said soothingly; "Jobson and I will go off hunting. But I am horribly anxious about you, old man."

He lay back on his pillows. "You needn't trouble. I only want a little rest. Jobson will make all arrangements, and Travers will get you anything you want. Goodbye."

I saw it was useless to stay longer, so I left the room. Outside I found the anxious-faced servant. "Look here," I said, "Mr. Lawson thinks I ought to go, but I mean to stay. Tell him I'm gone if he asks you. And for Heaven's sake keep him in bed."

The man promised, and I thought I saw some relief in his face.

I went to the library, and on the way remembered Jobson's remark about *First Kings*. With some searching I found a Bible and turned up the passage. It was a long screed about the misdeeds of Solomon, and I read it through without enlightenment. I began to re-read it, and a word suddenly caught my attention –

For Solomon went after Ashtaroth, the goddess of the Zidonians.

That was all, but it was like a key to a cipher. Instantly there flashed over my mind all that I had heard or read of that strange ritual which seduced Israel to sin. I saw a sunburnt land and a people vowed to the stern service of Jehovah. But I saw, too, eyes turning from the austere sacrifice to lonely hill-top groves and towers and images, where dwelt some subtle and evil mystery. I saw the fierce prophets, scourging the votaries with rods, and a nation penitent before the Lord; but always the backsliding again, and the hankering after forbidden joys. Ashtaroth was the old goddess of the East. Was it not possible that in all Semitic blood there remained, transmitted through the dim generations, some craving for her spell? I thought of the grandfather in the back street at Brighton and of those burning eyes upstairs.

As I sat and mused my glance fell on the inscrutable stone birds. They knew those old secrets of joy and terror. And that moon of alabaster! Some dark priest had worn it on his forehead when he worshipped, like Ahab, 'all the host of Heaven'. And then I honestly began to be afraid. I, a prosaic, modern Christian gentleman, a half-believer in casual faiths, was in the presence of some hoary mystery of sin far older than creeds or Christendom. There was fear in my heart – a kind of uneasy disgust, and above all a nervous eerie disquiet. Now I wanted to go away, and yet I was ashamed of the cowardly thought. I pictured Ashtaroth's Grove with sheer horror. What tragedy was in the air? What secret awaited twilight? For the night was coming, the night of the Full Moon, the season of ecstasy and sacrifice.

I do not know how I got through that evening. I was disinclined for dinner, so I had a cutlet in the library, and sat smoking till my tongue ached. But as the hours passed a more manly resolution grew up in my mind. I owed it to old friendship to stand by Lawson in this extremity. I could not interfere – God knows, his reason seemed already rocking – but I could be at hand in case my chance came. I determined not to undress, but to watch through the night. I had a bath, and changed into light flannels and slippers. Then I took up my position in a corner of the library close to the window, so that I could not fall to hear Lawson's footsteps if he passed.

Fortunately I left the lights unlit, for as I waited I grew drowsy, and fell asleep. When I woke the moon had risen, and I knew from the feel of the air that the hour was late. I sat very still, straining my ears, and as I listened I caught the sound of steps. They were crossing the hall stealthily, and nearing the library door. I huddled into my corner as Lawson entered.

He wore the same towel dressing-gown, and he moved swiftly and silently as if in a trance. I watched him take the alabaster moon from the mantelpiece and drop it in his pocket. A glimpse of white skin showed that the gown was his only clothing. Then he moved past me to the window, opened it, and went out. Without any conscious purpose I rose and followed, kicking off my slippers that I might go quietly. He was running, running fast, across the lawns in the direction of the Grove – an odd shapeless antic in the moonlight. I stopped, for there was no cover, and I feared for his reason if he saw me. When I looked again he had disappeared among the trees.

I saw nothing for it but to crawl, so on my belly I wormed my way over the dripping sward. There was a ridiculous suggestion of deer-stalking about the game which tickled me and dispelled my uneasiness. Almost I persuaded myself I was tracking an ordinary sleep-walker. The lawns were broader than I imagined, and it seemed an age before I reached the edge of the Grove. The world was so still that I appeared to be making a most ghastly amount of noise. I remember that once I heard a rustling in the air, and looked up to see the green doves circling about the tree-tops.

There was no sign of Lawson. On the edge of the Grove I think that all my assurance vanished. I could see between the trunks to the little tower, but it was quiet as the grave, save for the wings above. Once more there came over me the unbearable sense of anticipation I had felt the night before. My nerves tingled with mingled expectation and dread. I did not think that any harm would come to me, for the powers of the air seemed not malignant. But I knew them for powers, and felt awed and abased. I was in the presence of the 'host of Heaven', and I was no stern Israelitish prophet to prevail against them.

I must have lain for hours waiting in that spectral place, my eyes riveted on the tower and its golden cap of moonshine. I remember that my head felt void and light, as if my spirit were becoming disembodied and leaving its dew-drenched sheath far below. But the most curious sensation was of something drawing me to the tower, something mild and kindly and rather feeble, for there was some other and stronger force keeping me back. I yearned to move nearer, but I could not drag my limbs an inch. There was a spell somewhere which I could not break. I do not think I was in any way frightened now. The starry influence was playing tricks with me, but my mind was half asleep. Only I never took my eyes from the little tower. I think I could not, if I had wanted to.

Then suddenly from the shadows came Lawson. He was stark-naked, and he wore, bound across his brow, the half-moon of alabaster. He had something, too, in his hand – something which glittered.

He ran round the tower, crooning to himself, and flinging wild arms to the skies. Sometimes the crooning changed to a shrill cry of passion, such as a maenad may have uttered in the train of Bacchus. I could make out no words, but the sound told its own tale. He was absorbed in some infernal ecstasy. And as he ran, he drew his right hand across his breast and arms, and I saw that it held a knife.

I grew sick with disgust – not terror, but honest physical loathing. Lawson, gashing his fat body, affected me with an overpowering repugnance. I wanted to go forward and stop him, and I wanted, too, to be a hundred miles away. And the result was that I stayed still. I believe my own will held me there, but I doubt if in any case I could have moved my legs. The dance grew swifter and fiercer. I saw the blood dripping from Lawson's body, and his face ghastly white above his scarred breast. And then suddenly the horror left me;

my head swam; and for one second – one brief second – I peered into a new world. A strange passion surged up in my heart. I seemed to see the earth peopled with forms not human, scarcely divine, but more desirable than man or god. The calm face of Nature broke up for me into wrinkles of wild knowledge. I saw the things which brush against the soul in dreams, and found them lovely. There seemed no cruelty in the knife or the blood. It was a delicate mystery of worship, as wholesome as the morning song of birds. I do not know how the Semites found Ashtaroth's ritual; to them it may well have been more rapt and passionate than it seemed to me. For I saw in it only the sweet simplicity of Nature, and all riddles of lust and terror soothed away as a child's nightmares are calmed by a mother. I found my legs able to move, and I think I took two steps through the dusk towards the tower.

And then it all ended. A cock crew, and the homely noises of earth were renewed. While I stood dazed and shivering Lawson plunged through the Grove towards me. The impetus carried him to the edge, and he fell fainting just outside the shade.

My wits and common-sense came back to me with my bodily strength. I got my friend on my back, and staggered with him towards the house. I was afraid in real earnest now, and what frightened me most was the thought that I had not been afraid sooner. I had come very near the 'abomination of the Zidonians'.

At the door I found the scared valet waiting. He had apparently done this sort of thing before.

"Your master has been sleep-walking, and has had a fall," I said. "We must get him to bed at once."

We bathed the wounds as he lay in a deep stupor, and I dressed them as well as I could. The only danger lay in his utter exhaustion, for happily the gashes were not serious, and no artery had been touched. Sleep and rest would make him well, for he had the constitution of a strong man. I was leaving the room when he opened his eyes and spoke. He did not recognise me, but I noticed that his face had lost its strangeness, and was once more that of the friend I had known. Then I suddenly bethought me of an old hunting remedy which he and I always carried on our expeditions. It is a pill made up from an ancient Portuguese prescription. One is an excellent specific for fever. Two are invaluable if you are lost in the bush, for they send a man for many hours into a deep sleep, which prevents suffering and madness, till help comes. Three give a painless death. I went to my room and found the little box in my jewel-case. Lawson swallowed two, and turned wearily on his side. I bade his man let him sleep till he woke, and went off in search of food.

* * *

I had business on hand which would not wait. By seven, Jobson, who had been sent for, was waiting for me in the library. I knew by his grim face that here I had a very good substitute for a prophet of the Lord.

"You were right," I said. "I have read the 11th chapter of *First Kings*, and I have spent such a night as I pray God I shall never spend again."

"I thought you would," he replied. "I've had the same experience myself."

"The Grove?" I said.

"Ay, the wud," was the answer in broad Scots.

I wanted to see how much he understood.

"Mr. Lawson's family is from the Scottish Border?"

"Ay. I understand they come off Borthwick Water side," he replied, but I saw by his eyes that he knew what I meant.

"Mr. Lawson is my oldest friend," I went on, "and I am going to take measures to cure him. For what I am going to do I take the sole responsibility. I will make that plain to your master. But if I am to succeed I want your help. Will you give it me? It sounds like madness, and you are a sensible man and may like to keep out of it. I leave it to your discretion."

Jobson looked me straight in the face. "Have no fear for me," he said; "there is an unholy thing in that place, and if I have the strength in me I will destroy it. He has been a good master to me, and, forbye, I am a believing Christian. So say on, sir."

There was no mistaking the air. I had found my Tishbite.

"I want men," I said – "as many as we can get."

Jobson mused. "The Kaffirs will no' gang near the place, but there's some thirty white men on the tobacco farm. They'll do your will, if you give them an indemnity in writing."

"Good," said I. "Then we will take our instructions from the only authority which meets the case. We will follow the example of King Josiah." I turned up the 3rd chapter of Second Kings, and read –

> "*And the high places that were before Jerusalem, which were on the right hand of the Mount of Corruption, which Solomon the king of Israel had builded for Ashtaroth the abomination of the Zidonians ...did the king defile.*
>
> "*And he braise in pieces the images, and cut down the groves, and filled their places with the bones of men,*
>
> "*Moreover the altar that was at Bethel, and the high place which Jeroboam the son of Nebat, who made Israel to sin, had made, both that altar and the high place he brake down, and burned the high place, and stamped it small to powder, and burned the grove.*"

Jobson nodded. "It'll need dinnymite. But I've plenty of yon down at the workshops. I'll be off to collect the lads."

Before nine the men had assembled at Jobson's house. They were a hardy lot of young farmers from home, who took their instructions docilely from the masterful factor. On my orders they had brought their shot-guns. We armed them with spades and woodmen's axes, and one man wheeled some coils of rope in a handcart.

In the clear, windless air of morning the Grove, set amid its lawns, looked too innocent and exquisite for evil. I had a pang of regret that a thing so fair should suffer; nay, if I had come alone, I think I might have repented. But the men were there, and the grim-faced Jobson was waiting for orders. I placed the guns, and sent beaters to the far side. I told them that every dove must be shot.

It was only a small flock, and we killed fifteen at the first drive. The poor birds flew over the glen to another spinney, but we brought them back over the guns and seven fell. Four more were got in the trees, and the last I killed myself with a long shot. In half an hour there was a pile of little green bodies on the sward.

Then we went to work to cut down the trees. The slim stems were an easy task to a good woodman, and one after another they toppled to the ground. And meantime, as I watched, I became conscious of a strange emotion.

It was as if some one were pleading with me. A gentle voice, not threatening, but pleading – something too fine for the sensual ear, but touching inner chords of the spirit. So tenuous it was and distant that I could think of no personality behind it. Rather it was the viewless, bodiless grace of this delectable vale, some old exquisite divinity of the groves. There was the heart of all sorrow in it, and the soul of all loveliness. It seemed a woman's voice, some lost lady who had brought nothing but goodness unrepaid to the world. And what the voice told me was, that I was destroying her last shelter.

That was the pathos of it – the voice was homeless. As the axes flashed in the sunlight and the wood grew thin, that gentle spirit was pleading with me for mercy and a brief respite. It seemed to be telling of a world for centuries grown coarse and pitiless, of long sad wanderings, of hardly-won shelter, and a peace which was the little all she sought from men. There was nothing terrible in it. No thought of wrongdoing. The spell, which to Semitic blood held the mystery of evil, was to me, of a different race, only delicate and rare and beautiful. Jobson and the rest did not feel it, I with my finer senses caught nothing but the hopeless sadness of it. That which had stirred the passion in Lawson was only wringing my heart. It was almost too pitiful to bear. As the trees crashed down and the men wiped the sweat from their brows, I seemed to myself like the murderer of fair women and innocent children. I remember that the tears were running over my cheeks. More than once I opened my mouth to countermand the work, but the face of Jobson, that grim Tishbite, held me back.

I knew now what gave the Prophets of the Lord their mastery, and I knew also why the people sometimes stoned them.

The last tree fell, and the little tower stood like a ravished shrine, stripped of all defences against the world. I heard Jobson's voice speaking. "We'd better blast that stane thing now. We'll trench on four sides and lay the dinnymite. Ye're no' looking weel, sir. Ye'd better go and sit down on the brae-face."

I went up the hillside and lay down. Below me, in the waste of shorn trunks, men were running about, and I saw the mining begin. It all seemed like an aimless dream in which I had no part. The voice of that homeless goddess was still pleading. It was the innocence of it that tortured me. Even so must a merciful Inquisitor have suffered from the plea of some fair girl with the aureole of death on her hair. I knew I was killing rare and unrecoverable beauty. As I sat dazed and heartsick, the whole loveliness of Nature seemed to plead for its divinity. The sun in the heavens, the mellow lines of upland, the blue mystery of the far plains, were all part of that soft voice. I felt bitter scorn for myself. I was guilty of blood; nay, I was guilty of the sin against light which knows no forgiveness. I was murdering innocent gentleness, and there would be no peace on earth for me. Yet I sat helpless. The power of a sterner will constrained me. And all the while the voice was growing fainter and dying away into unutterable sorrow.

Suddenly a great flame sprang to heaven, and a pall of smoke. I heard men crying out, and fragments of stone fell around the ruins of the grove. When the air cleared, the little tower had gone out of sight.

The voice had ceased, and there seemed to me to be a bereaved silence in the world. The shock moved me to my feet, and I ran down the slope to where Jobson stood rubbing his eyes.

"That's done the job. Now we maun get up the tree roots. We've no time to howk. We'll just blast the feck o' them."

The work of destruction went on, but I was coming back to my senses. I forced myself to be practical and reasonable. I thought of the night's experience and Lawson's haggard eyes, and I screwed myself into a determination to see the thing through. I had done the deed;

it was my business to make it complete. A text in Jeremiah came into my head: 'Their children remember their altars and their groves by the green trees upon the high hills.' I would see to it that this grove should be utterly forgotten.

We blasted the tree roots, and, yoking oxen, dragged the debris into a great heap. Then the men set to work with their spades, and roughly levelled the ground. I was getting back to my old self, and Jobson's spirit was becoming mine.

"There is one thing more," I told him. "Get ready a couple of ploughs. We will improve upon King Josiah." My brain was a medley of Scripture precedents, and I was determined that no safeguard should be wanting.

We yoked the oxen again and drove the ploughs over the site of the grove. It was rough ploughing, for the place was thick with bits of stone from the tower, but the slow Afrikander oxen plodded on, and sometime in the afternoon the work was finished. Then I sent down to the farm for bags of rock-salt, such as they use for cattle. Jobson and I took a sack apiece, and walked up and down the furrows, sowing them with salt.

The last act was to set fire to the pile of tree trunks. They burned well, and on the top we flung the bodies of the green doves. The birds of Ashtaroth had an honourable pyre.

Then I dismissed the much-perplexed men, and gravely shook hands with Jobson. Black with dust and smoke I went back to the house, where I bade Travers pack my bags and order the motor. I found Lawson's servant, and heard from him that his master was sleeping peacefully. I gave him some directions, and then went to wash and change.

Before I left I wrote a line to Lawson. I began by transcribing the verses from the 23rd chapter of *Second Kings*. I told him what I had done, and my reason.

"I take the whole responsibility upon myself," I wrote. "No man in the place had anything to do with it but me. I acted as I did for the sake of our old friendship, and you will believe it was no easy task for me. I hope you will understand. Whenever you are able to see me send me word, and I will come back and settle with you. But I think you will realise that I have saved your soul."

The afternoon was merging into twilight as I left the house on the road to Taqui. The great fire, where the grove had been, was still blazing fiercely, and the smoke made a cloud over the upper glen, and filled all the air with a soft violet haze. I knew that I had done well for my friend, and that he would come to his senses and be grateful …But as the car reached the ridge I looked back to the vale I had outraged. The moon was rising and silvering the smoke, and through the gaps I could see the tongues of fire. Somehow, I know not why, the lake, the stream, the garden-coverts, even the green slopes of hill, wore an air of loneliness and desecration.

And then my heartache returned, and I knew that I had driven something lovely and adorable from its last refuge on earth.

Moon Skin

Beth Cato

BEULAH emerged from the river and into a brisk autumn night that made the waning moon shiver behind the clouds. Her vision, even with the color spectrum narrowed, was keen in the darkness, and she detected the movement of men amongst the few wooden buildings and tents near the shore. The vertical slits in her nose opened and she took in the ripeness of the swamp and the wretched stench of the *Dorchester*'s iron hulk.

With a tilt of her head, her seal skin peeled back to her shoulders. Smells altered, the marsh's rot more bothersome, the iron more annoying than appalling. She could see the *Dorchester* better now. The forty-foot submarine floated alongside a pier. Gray metal maintained a dull sheen beneath lit lamps. A few soldiers bobbed in a boat at the tip of the long spar where a torpedo would be affixed in place. If all went according to Papa's plan, tomorrow the submersible would engage the enemy.

"Miss Beulah's back!" a spotter called.

She sensed Papa's approach. His body glowed with innate magic, like a full moon that cast no shadows on the normal world. Annie's pelt, hooked to his waist, held a fainter glow tonight, like a lamp tucked beneath a quilt.

Oh, Annie. Her sister endured such agony right now. The dimmed pelt was proof of that.

Only her head above water, Beulah shimmied out of her pelt. She hunkered as she walked onto higher ground and obscured herself in the reeds. Her frail human skin pocked in goose bumps, she pulled on a thick robe she'd left hanging there and draped her long gray pelt over her arm. Her bare feet squished in mud as she walked onto land. Papa awaited her on the embankment. A glow behind him caught her eye. She stopped.

Amidst so many fellows in gray attire, the strange man didn't stand out at all but for his innate blue glow. He was a boy, really, close to her age. Skinny as a fence rail, his features plain. In water, she knew of everything around her by the current against her whiskers; the buzz of his magic was strong like that, the sense of it different than Papa or Annie. Like the difference between a wood fire and a gas lamp.

"Miss Beulah." Papa inclined his head, a dozen questions compounded into her name. He was never one to dither.

"Captain Kettleman, sir." She saluted. Even in private, she had not been permitted to call him 'Papa' for years. "Two Union sloops still off-shore, three civilian crafts aside. One a fisherman, the others smuggling."

If anyone spied her, they'd likely think she was a porpoise. Seals were uncommon along the North Carolina coast; she had never met one in the wild.

"They must know we're hidden in the vicinity. Let the Yanks linger. All the better for tomorrow. Won't need to sail far to find our target." Papa fidgeted with Annie's pale pelt.

He nodded at Beulah. "You're a good girl. You get adequate rest. Be ready for tomorrow." The words held a warning.

His care for her extended to her usefulness. As a child, she had been taught enough reading and arithmetic to manage as his secretary. Back then, she thought it was flattering, even if her literacy set her uncomfortably apart from the other house slaves. As if being the master's bastard daughter wasn't enough.

His treatment of Annie proved that anything of his blood was his property, to use as he will. Skin color had nothing to with it.

"Yes, sir." Beulah's teeth threatened to chatter.

She clutched her own pelt a little closer for both warmth and security as she walked past Papa. She caught the direct, wide gaze of the man behind him. It was pretty clear that he *saw* her, and not simply as a young woman in a robe. He appeared as skittish as a kitten in a dog kennel as he looked between her and Papa. He must have never seen magic in a person before. How peculiar.

"Miss Beulah?"

"Sir?" She stopped and faced her father.

"This man here, Chaplain ...?"

"Walsh, sir," said the stranger.

"Yes, Walsh. He will escort you once you're dressed."

"Not Lieutenant Groves, sir?" she asked.

"Lee believed a chaplain's presence would do the men well before we deploy, but we have no need of him yet." Papa's curled lip revealed he had no use for a chaplain, period, but Lee's word was akin to God's. "Lieutenant Groves has plenty else to do."

With that, Papa walked on, already bellowing an order to another soldier.

The man who glowed, a chaplain? Through thin lamplight, they stared each other down. His face was pale and pink, his nose blotched with freckles. Irish, then, like Papa's line. They'd carried a lot of old magic to American shores, though she'd noticed that glow in other folks, too. Most of them hadn't seen hers in turn, though.

"I be but a few minutes, sir," Beulah murmured, and scurried past him to her tent.

The tent had been her home for a brief while, until it became clear that she needed a quieter environment for sleep; shifting to seal and back left her drained, and if she was deprived she couldn't manage the change at all. Papa had begrudgingly arranged for her to stay with a loyal yet humble family nearby.

She emerged in proper clothes, hugging her coat close to her cotton dress. It was cold enough that she belted her pelt in place beneath her layers, girthing her like a saddle blanket.

Papa's soldiers nodded and sidestepped around her. She knew some made signs of the cross and muttered, but no one behaved cruelly with her secret known, and it wasn't simply because of Papa's command or that he was known as a selkie, too. She was respected in her own right – a peculiar thing, truly – for her service in the war. She'd scouted for the *Hunley* and more, and the *Hunley* had busted the Union blockade of Charleston. Until it recently docked for repairs, the submersible had prowled the South Carolina coast and sent Yanks fleeing northward.

A month after the *Hunley*'s first success, Sherman had been obliterated on his march from Chattanooga to Atlanta. Peace and independence might be possible by the dawn of 1865, God willing.

Peace for white folk, anyway. But if Beulah had to be a slave, she'd be with Annie and Annie would treat her as well as she could.

Chaplain Walsh awaited her with a wagon; he seemed afraid to look at her. She sat on the bench seat and tugged blankets onto her lap. The chaplain clicked his tongue, and the horse pulled the wagon onto the bumpy road.

Beulah waited until the camp's noise was replaced by the chirps and trills of the marsh. "No need to worry, sir. Captain Kettleman can't see your glow."

He shot her a nervous glance. "But he's a selkie, like you, if I understand correctly? That is, er ..."

"Yes, sir, he's my father, but men-selkies can't change form or use any magic they carry. You never met no one like us before?"

"You have?"

"A few times, yes, sir. Not that common, and not every person with magic can see or sense how it's carried in others. I got a sense that you're not of selkie blood, sir."

His grip on the reins tightened. "Can you sense what I am, Miss Beulah?"

What a strange conversation this was. She twined her hands beneath the blankets. The night was fiercely quiet. Back when the blockade was still in place and more Lincoln soldiers lurked close, Papa kept more guards around her. As if she'd run north and leave Annie behind, or even let soldiers steal her away.

She squinted at him. "I met some Indian spirits I don't know to name, and a dryad once. You glow like a pure drink of water, like nothing else I seen."

"Like a pure drink of water." He repeated it with a small smile in his voice. "The pelt the Captain carries. Who ...?"

"My sister. Annie." She noted the quick shift in subject.

"She's –"

"White, sir. His wife's child. She was a good woman, God rest her."

"I was 'bout to ask her age, the skin so small."

"Oh. She's seven, sir."

His brow furrowed. "It's hooked on his belt, too. Am I right to reckon ...?"

"She got a hole through her left hand. Size of a blueberry. Never heals. He keeps her pelt close here. For luck."

"God Almighty," he whispered. The horse snorted. An owl hooted from somewhere distant. "The other men say as much, that the skin's their lucky charm. That you're part of that, too, seein' as you made the *Hunley* succeed, and now you'll bless the *Dorchester* next."

Bless. She looked away to hide her revulsion. The *Dorchester* needed to succeed and then Papa would be promoted and then the bluebellies could blow it to kingdom come. Annie's pelt just needed to be away first, back near the rest of her flesh.

"I don't know what you expect me to say to that, Chaplain. I'm not particularly lucky, and my sister ..."

"No one can know their own luck, I reckon. I'm just ...still in awe that we see each other's magic in such a way."

The house was just ahead, a lamp on in the parlor window. Surrounding trees fringed the yard like dark lace. The woman of the house was likely peering through the curtains in wait. The wagon rolled down the drive and Beulah stood to disembark.

This man carried some kind of power and he was friendly to the point of foolishness. Maybe he could help her get Annie's pelt away from Papa. Beulah could run south, get her sister. How they'd make it north together, God only knew, but others had done it. *"Follow the north star,"* folks said.

"Everyone knows what I am," Beulah said slowly, "but no one knows 'bout you. You're the one with a secret."

His breath caught. "It's best they not know."

"What, you're not wanting to give everything for the cause? Sir?" She played a dangerous game, wielding power over a white man like this, but if it could save Annie, it was worth it.

"There's no givin' in this war. Just takin'." The door to the house opened.

"I tell you this. I won't tell no one, for now." Instead of feeling mighty with the words, the power, she felt all sour inside.

"Thank you, Miss Beulah," he said quietly. He didn't even sound mad. "I already been told I'm to fetch you 'bout midnight."

"Midnight," she murmured, and hopped from the wagon without looking back.

The missus greeted her with a scowl that'd scare away any soldier, blue or gray. A few minutes later, Beulah had cleaned off a whole plate of food, including the cold, cooked fish her human body craved so often now.

"Almost forgot," the woman said. "There's a letter on the desk. Reckon you can read?"

"Yes ...yes, missus."

Beulah murmured her thanks as she retreated to her room. A rain-marbled envelope awaited her on the felt mat of the desk.

The handwriting was Annie's.

It was dated a mere week before; blessed fast, compared to how things were when Charleston was under siege. Annie's fat pencil loops quivered across the page. Beulah's eyes scanned back and forth as she read the seven-year-old's words, read beneath pleasantries about how Annie rode her horse with old Rickery's help, about how the leaves had started to shift color and whirl away.

Beulah pictured Annie sitting in her bed like a doll propped against down-filled pillows. Her little lap desk against her knees, her mousey brown hair kept up in curlers. A week ago, her pelt was brighter, too. Now she likely hadn't the strength to write.

That child's gap-toothed smile lit up Beulah's world with a glow greater than any magic. Papa and most everyone else had scolded Annie, told her to not treat Beulah like a sister. The girl wouldn't heed. She had a stubborn streak wider than the James River, bless her.

And Papa was killing her, slowly yet surely.

Beulah closed her eyes and rocked. The paper crinkled in her grip. Annie's pelt was so far away from her body. That was bad enough, but far worse, it was so often in the *Dorchester*. Iron gnawed on magic like hungry termites. Beulah's own pelt had been taken aboard the *Hunley*. She had been left bed-bound and wretched, and for the first time, the *Hunley*'s mission was a success. The submersible had blown apart the *U.S.S. Housatonic* and gone on to sink or scare off the rest of the Union blockade.

Now it was Annie whose pelt was to be their lucky charm. Annie, who Papa was sure had stronger and purer magic, being white and all. If the *Dorchester* did its duty along the North Carolina coast, Papa said he was sure to be promoted. He wouldn't need to go out to sea no more.

Annie had to stay stubborn and strong. She'd have her pelt back soon enough. Beulah would make sure of that, one way or another.

* * *

The night was strangely balmy for late October. Too hot for Beulah to belt her pelt beneath her clothes. She climbed into the wagon with her glowing skin draped over her shoulder and lap. She caught Chaplain Walsh's double-take upon sight of it. He clicked for the horse to move forward. The wheels found the ruts of the road.

"It's strange, seeing the same glow twice over," he said.

"I suppose so, sir."

"You needn't 'sir' me out here."

"It's best to stay in the habit. Sir." She frowned, discomfited by his friendliness even after her hint of blackmail the night before.

All was quiet but for the grind of wheels. "I don't hold with slavery," he whispered, as well he should. Dangerous words. "I'm from up in Virginia, the hills. Didn't think to join. They made me."

"The western side of the state, the Union part?" She heard a lot of slaves ran up through there, headed to Ohio.

"Yes. I was riding my circuit when ..."

"You really are a preacher?"

At that, he smiled. "I am."

"Hardly seems smart to tell me this, sir, when I already know you hold some power inside."

"If anyone asks what I think, I tell them truth."

She snorted. Good grief. Here she hoped for the man's help, and he continued to prove himself a fool. "You won't have to worry 'bout Yanks shooting you then. Boys in gray will do it first."

"I'm not lookin' to die or be a martyr, but I ain't about to lie, either. God sees all."

"How do you judge my soul, then, with what I do? Directing these fish boats so they kill hundreds of men in a night?"

He looked surprised. "Why, I don't judge your soul at all. Not my place. That's between you'n the Almighty."

She stroked her pelt, an anxious habit. In the water, Beulah could taste rendered metal, munitions, the tartness of blood and flesh. She knew she didn't have a choice in her duty, truly, but guilt weighed on her all the same. She worried for her own soul, but even more, she worried for Annie's.

"I wonder, d'you think –" she began.

A tailed critter – fox, coon, something – darted across the road. The horse reared in the shafts and the wagon lurched forward. The sky rotated as Beulah flung over the low back rest. The underside of her noggin cracked against wood. New stars lit her vision as terrible heat flared in her ears. She rolled, dazed, the world blurred. Wood and metal snapped – the back hatch of the wagon, busting open. Everything turned black. Dust filled her nostrils. She blinked. Her head felt hot and wrong and her right leg hurt in an awful way.

She had to be able to swim tonight. Had to. If she couldn't scout, if she couldn't keep Annie's pelt safe ...

Beulah forced her body upright. The horizon spun around her and threatened to squeeze supper from her gut. She couldn't see the wagon, but even more, her seal skin wasn't right close by.

Gritting her teeth, she leaned on her knuckles and took several slow breaths to get her bearings. Her leg – oh Lord, her leg. Summoning all her gumption, she stood. Her other toes tapped for balance. Sheer agony almost melted her into the dirt.

Standing, she could see the wagon wasn't far ahead. A plume of dust still hovered in the air. The wagon was stuck in high grass along the road, and it rocked back and forth as the horse squealed and kicked. The beast sounded panicked more than anything. Where was the Chaplain?

Beulah scanned for his glow and found it out in the swamp, some twenty feet away. Dark as the night was, their ability to see each other was handy. He swam straight toward her, her pelt in hand. He staggered up the embankment and flopped to earth, gasping. He was wet as a fish, and it was impossible to tell if he was hurt.

Dear God, he had her pelt.

He could blackmail her now, or damage it, or do any number of things. Even if she wrestled it away, she couldn't run, not with her crippled leg.

Chaplain Walsh still wore a gun at his hip. If she could get that …but then what? Papa still had Annie's skin. Beulah couldn't escape. Couldn't do anything.

"Miss Beulah? How do you fare?"

She took several long breaths to mask her pain and panic. "Alive, sir. And you –"

"Your pelt. It is indeed blessed. It just saved my life."

"What?"

"I flew off the wagon and landed out there in deep water. I swim as well as a rock. I was like to drown, but I reached out, found your skin. It pulled me to the surface. I could feel magic in it, warmth. And, and there was an alligator out there, I was not a foot away from the beast. It …it left. Ignored me. Praise Jesus."

Beulah's toes tapped the ground for balance. She cried out, and Chaplain Walsh pivoted to look up at her.

"What the …? Miss Beulah?" He stood.

"It's my leg. It's not …"

"It surely is bad, so don't protest the contrary. Would it help you to change form?"

He held out the pelt to her. She stared at it. God forgive her. She'd thought to shoot him, and he handed her skin over with nary a mean thought. Beulah buried her face in the familiar gray and black fur. It smelled of dank water and saltiness and the comfort of her own self.

"No. I'd be a lame seal." Her voice was muffled against the skin. "I can't be lame, not tonight of all nights."

Chaplain Walsh looked toward the wagon. "I need to check on the horse. You – I wouldn't reckon you'd be so keen on the *Dorchester* succeeding."

"I hate that boat like nothing else." Agony loosened her tongue and her wits. "The iron's making Annie awful sick. The glow of her pelt, it's dimmer by the day. If Papa's promoted, he won't have to be on board, and Annie –"

Oh, blessed Annie, who'd hide handwritten copies of Elizabeth Barrett Browning poems in her Bible to read during her daily devotionals. The girl who had to be scolded to walk all ladylike, or she'd scamper like a crazed squirrel. Beulah knew just how Annie's little hand fit in her grip when they walked together in the far fields, their arms swinging.

Would Beulah know that touch again? She wavered on her feet.

Chaplain Walsh grabbed hold of her arms while keeping himself at a gentlemanly distance. "Easy, easy," he crooned as he helped her to sit. Her hands found lush grass about wrist deep. Agony jolted down her hip. She buried her face in the pelt and sobbed.

"I'll be right back," he said.

The wagon wheels rattled and groaned as Chaplain shushed the horse, just as he soothed Beulah. A moment later, Chaplain returned.

"Had to make sure the horse didn't cause further mischief. He seems well enough for now, and the wagon's back on the road. Can I see your leg? I'm not – I don't have improper intentions."

"Most men say such things. You ...you really do tell truth."

"I'm as much a sinner as any man."

She doubted that. She pulled up her skirt to tuck above her knees. By starlight, she could barely see the bulge of her thigh bone through her careworn, bloodied petticoats.

"Do you doctor, like some preachers do?" Her voice warbled.

His hands hovered over her leg, as if to warm them over a fire. "I do ...something."

In a span of seconds, splinters of bone dragged through her muscle, the femur's shaft tugging into place with an audible pop. Red spots of pure pain dappled the ebony night. Next she knew, she was flat on her back, her skull tingling as if it held a hive of bees. Chaplain Walsh leaned over her, his pink face skewed in worry.

"What'd you do?" Her voice was hoarse. "How long ...?"

"You slept a minute. It ...it was for the best. How d'you feel now?"

She raised a hand to her forehead first, then shifted both legs. "Sore, but not hurting like I was. This is what you do then, the magic in you?"

"Yes." He whispered. "It's at a cost. An awful cost."

She spanned her fingers into the grass. The lush, deep groundcover had turned brittle. It crackled at her touch.

"I can't control how it takes from anything and anyone living close by. I try not to use it, but ..."

"Why on me, then?" She clutched her pelt against her chest as she sat up. "Why give my skin back?"

Chaplain Walsh looked strangely old and tired. "You're the first person I met who uses magic – is magic, and who can see it in me. I ...I want to be friends. You bein' a slave, it don't matter to me. I don't desire for you or your sister to suffer. I got little sisters, too. No magic in them, just mischief and giggles."

How like Annie he was, in his defiance. "You don't know your kin ...?"

"My mother was grabbed by fae folk back in Ireland. She ...she fought to escape. She thought she'd been bound all of a night, but it'd been five years. She came to America, then I was born."

Beulah regarded him in silence for a time. "I won't tell no one about you, what you do. But you need to mind your own lips. You need to lie. It'll keep you alive."

"As you keep yourself alive, I reckon." It was simply stated. "You're a weapon for a cause in which you don't believe, you and your sister both."

She stood, pelt draped over her shoulders, and offered him a hand. He shakily stood and almost leaned against her.

"Pardon. Healing takes something outta me. You said ...you said before that you want the Captain promoted and off the *Dorchester* to keep your Annie safe. How d'you reckon?"

"Why – Papa wants to work in Richmond, he's said as much –"

"That's not what I mean. What makes you think the *Dorchester* would do without a pelt? Men swear by its luck. The *Hunley*'s in port for repairs, and it's failed every sea worthiness test of late." He staggered forward a few steps.

"I – I hadn't heard such." Her mouth went dry. "Much as my scouting helps, they could use the surface to use the periscope instead. I …" The Confederates would rather have two submersibles run, most certainly. That meant she'd be bed-bound again, sick as a hound dog, her pelt going as pale as Annie's.

Dazed, she glanced behind them. A yellow scar of dead grass marked where she had sprawled, extending twenty feet wide. It encompassed both sides of the road and into the water. Reeds draped over, limp. The water looked almost lumpy, too. Maybe the fish were all dead. Maybe that gator, if it swam close. She shivered and turned.

Chaplain Walsh was falling, his eyes rolled back to whites. She dove forward and managed to catch his shoulders before his head struck the ground.

* * *

By the time Lieutenant Groves and his men found them, Beulah had managed to drag Chaplain Walsh up to the wagon. They tended him from there. He was conscious now and murmured to soldiers who sat in back with him. His voice slurred. An off-kilter wheel made the carriage to lurch with each rotation. Beulah clutched the bench seat as she bounced forward against her folded pelt.

"Are you well enough to swim?" Lieutenant Groves asked, an eye on her bloodied clothes.

No, she wanted to say, but what did her health truly mean to these men? They would steal her pelt, store it in toxic iron, leave her bed-bound and writhing in misery. She wanted Chaplain Walsh to be wrong, but her mind traced his logic like a dog chased its tail. He was right. She and Annie, they'd never be free. It wasn't up to Papa. Their role was bigger than him.

"I need to do my duty, sir," she murmured. "I can clean myself up. I can swim."

He studied her for a moment before nodding. "Our last reports placed the Union sloop *Woolton* at the river's mouth. Direct the *Dorchester*, as we practiced."

"Yes, sir. What about Chaplain Walsh, sir?"

The lieutenant glanced over his shoulder. "Head injuries are fickle things. Seen a man strip off his clothes and dance naked in a fire once, after a blow to the skull, and he didn't recall nary a thing after. Chaplain can do his prayer with the men aboard and we'll drive him to town in the morn. Don't fuss over him. You got plenty to do."

"Yes, sir."

The tension at the dock was at an intense simmer, the kind where everyone spoke at a murmur, lights dim, birds mute. Men scurried around the *Dorchester*. A boat bobbed on the far side, near the twenty-foot spar with its attached torpedo. The vessel would attack by tapping the mine against an enemy hull. A battery and copper wire would enable Papa to detonate the explosive once they were a safer distance away.

Papa was nowhere in sight at the moment, likely in the iron belly of the beast.

Chaplain Walsh stood in the wagon bed and leaned on a soldier for balance. Beulah's eyes met his for an instant and she turned away. He'd set the sailors' souls right with a prayer, then maybe he could rest to recover from her healing.

What of Beulah's soul? Because of her, the *Hunley* had killed or captured over a thousand men. Now here she was, leading the *Dorchester* to its prey, all for the sake of Annie's pelt. No more. After tonight, she'd find a way to save her sister's skin. It was time for them to them to go north.

A few minutes later, Beulah waded into the river.

The warmth of her pelt settled on her shoulders, then settled deeper. Heat nestled in her marrows and viciously tingled down and back up the lengths of her arms and legs as they receded. Colors shifted. She wiggled her new tail, water embracing her like cool silk, then she dived.

Fifty feet away, the *Dorchester* wallowed, to her attuned senses more putrid than any cesspool. Its ballast tanks sloshed and echoed as they filled with water, and the submarine lowered into the depths. Reverberations carried from each rotation of the hand crank that propelled it forward.

She surfaced in the middle of the river. Her seal eyes showed her a world hued in blues and greens. Bubbles marked the submersible's wake.

At the end of the dock, a blue glow caught her eye. The figure waved at her.

" …pelt won't work!" she barely made out. "No glow!" Other soldiers surrounded Chaplain Walsh, gripping his arms, trying to calm him.

Beulah swam closer, her mind blank, her heart racing.

"No glow!" he shouted again. "She got no glow!"

No glow? Annie's pelt had no glow? No. Beulah sank into absolute darkness. Chaplain Walsh had to be lying. He just wanted to stop her, stop the *Dorchester*. He was a Yankee at heart, and a man of God. He had every reason to want this to fail.

Ripples slapped her whiskers as the *Dorchester* thrummed by. Beulah twisted in the water and swam alongside. She rested a flipper against the icy hull. The metal gnashed her limb as if with spiny teeth. In her mind, she heard her human self scream in agony as she struggled to stay conscious. Her senses fought through the accursed iron to find Papa within.

She knew his magic the way she knew the murmur of indistinct voices a room away. He stood five feet distant at command position. Metal groaned as the crew powered the crankshaft, but she could not discern the individual men with her magic. Nor could she find any other glow. The skin may as well have not been there, but she knew it was; the men wouldn't have sailed without it. Chaplain was right.

The submarine pushed past in a torrent of bubbles. She drifted, limp. She was scarcely aware of how her flipper ached and throbbed and how lingering convulsions rippled across her skin.

Annie's pelt was empty. She was dead.

Papa killed her.

You're a weapon for a cause in which you don't believe, you and your sister both. Chaplain's words pierced through the numbness. Papa's cause had killed Annie, and would kill Beulah, too. Her and so many more. The Union ship was out there, with hundreds more burdens on her soul.

Papa's good luck charm was dead. Without Annie's magic, the *Dorchester* would eventually fail, as the *Hunley* had. Maybe take its crew of ten with it.

Beulah couldn't wait. If she was going to be a weapon, this'd be the last time, on her terms. God have mercy on her soul.

She swam, her body a sleek torpedo. She surpassed the submarine, powered by pedaling men, and passed the wooden spar with its explosive. She knew the river's sinuous curves as it broadened into the Atlantic. By her whiskers and the flow of the water, she knew the channel's depth, the anxious and erratic paths of fish. She stopped to let the submarine catch up.

Beulah's flipper banged on the hull, fast enough that it didn't scald her. Tap-tap. Tap-tap-tap. Tap. An obstacle ahead, bear right. *You're a good girl*, Papa always said. He trusted her to be obedient, to do as she ought.

After a long pause, it began to turn, oh so slowly. It was a perfect maneuver, one they had practiced time and again. The new angle aimed the torpedo-laden spar directly at rocks thirty feet ahead. The submersible was at full speed.

Beulah swam hard, but not far enough. Not fast enough. Metal crunched and whined and not a second later the explosion shoved her through the water. She sensed shrapnel shoot past, and she dove deeper. Her tail, her every muscle pushed her forward. To what? A shore, swarming with Confederates who would want to know what happened? To a world without the brightness of Annie awaiting her back home? She swam by blind instinct until she could take it no more. She shot to the surface.

Her head craned from the water and she screamed. The hoarse bray echoed. The sound of the explosion had faded, though something still crackled in the distance. She didn't turn around to look. The dock was not far away, still adorned with the blue glow of Chaplain Walsh. Men scrambled and yelled from the shore and pier. Oars slapped the water.

"I see Miss Beulah!" called one of the men. "She's out there!"

"Miss Beulah?" echoed Lieutenant Groves, panting. He sat in the lead boat, not ten feet away. "What happened?"

She sensed Chaplain Walsh's gaze on her. He knew she had done this. Would he condemn her, as part of his honesty?

Still in deep water, she pulled back her skin to the shoulders. "Lieutenant!" she cried, hoarse from her scream. "Something went awful wrong. I tried to catch up, but I moved too slow. They plowed straight into them rocks down at the fork."

"God Almighty. All our hopes ..." Lieutenant Groves looked so weary and old as he gazed in the direction of her voice. "That Union sloop may send men in to investigate. Might be a battle here soon enough, but we can't let them get salvage. Get ashore, girl. The men'll get you inland."

"And Chaplain Walsh, sir?" she asked. "Is he well? I thought he yelled somethin'."

"He's to stay still. Ain't right in the head." Lieutenant Groves motioned a soldier to continue paddling. Boats hurried past. The other men on the pier had dashed away, readying for battle.

Chaplain Walsh looked directly at her. "Your sister ...I'm so very sorry, Miss Beulah."

"So am I, Chaplain Walsh, for so many things." Tears streamed down her cheeks. "I'm going. Before they use me as a weapon again. Before ...before I end up like Annie."

"Yes. Yes." He stared away and she wondered if he was about to faint again. "I'd swim away with you, if I could." The words were so soft, she barely heard them.

"No. You don't believe in their cause, but they made you vow to serve. Knowin' you, you'd still hold yourself to such a thing."

He snorted. "You know me so well, so quickly."

"Yes, and you ...you're gonna end up dead yourself. Battle or sickness or because of your own mouth. I wish you could lie. I wish you'd try. I wish you'd stay alive."

"Thank you for that." He paused. "I'll do what I need to do."

Beulah stared at him in dismay, emotion choking her throat. The fool. The wonderful, stupidly stubborn fool.

In the moonless blackness, his magic made his pale skin glow all the more. "I'll pray for you."

"Yes. I'd like that. Pray for me. Please. I need your prayers, Chaplain Walsh."

Beulah pulled herself deeper into her own skin, deeper than she had ever gone before. Water thrummed against her whiskers, her vision of dark colors, the human color spectrum a mere memory. She tucked her flippers flush against her sides and swam. The river flowed against her, but she'd fight it every inch of the way.

The Demoiselle d'Ys

Robert W. Chambers

*"Mais je croy que je
Suis descendu on puiz
Ténébreux onquel disoit
Heraclytus estre Vereté cachée."*

*"There be three things which are too wonderful for me, yea, four which I know not:
"The way of an eagle in the air; the way of a serpent upon a rock; the way of a ship
in the midst of the sea; and the way of a man with a maid."*

I

THE UTTER DESOLATION of the scene began to have its effect; I sat down to face the situation and, if possible, recall to mind some landmark which might aid me in extricating myself from my present position. If I could only find the ocean again all would be clear, for I knew one could see the island of Groix from the cliffs.

I laid down my gun, and kneeling behind a rock lighted a pipe. Then I looked at my watch. It was nearly four o'clock. I might have wandered far from Kerselec since daybreak.

Standing the day before on the cliffs below Kerselec with Goulven, looking out over the sombre moors among which I had now lost my way, these downs had appeared to me level as a meadow, stretching to the horizon, and although I knew how deceptive is distance, I could not realize that what from Kerselec seemed to be mere grassy hollows were great valleys covered with gorse and heather, and what looked like scattered boulders were in reality enormous cliffs of granite.

"It's a bad place for a stranger," old Goulven had said: "you'd better take a guide;" and I had replied, "I shall not lose myself." Now I knew that I had lost myself, as I sat there smoking, with the sea-wind blowing in my face. On every side stretched the moorland, covered with flowering gorse and heath and granite boulders. There was not a tree in sight, much less a house. After a while, I picked up the gun, and turning my back on the sun tramped on again.

There was little use in following any of the brawling streams which every now and then crossed my path, for, instead of flowing into the sea, they ran inland to reedy pools in the hollows of the moors. I had followed several, but they all led me to swamps or silent little ponds from which the snipe rose peeping and wheeled away in an ecstasy of fright. I began to feel fatigued, and the gun galled my shoulder in spite of the double pads. The sun sank lower and lower, shining level across yellow gorse and the moorland pools.

As I walked my own gigantic shadow led me on, seeming to lengthen at every step. The gorse scraped against my leggings, crackled beneath my feet, showering the brown earth with blossoms, and the brake bowed and billowed along my path. From tufts of heath rabbits scurried away through the bracken, and among the swamp grass I heard the wild duck's drowsy quack. Once a fox stole across my path, and again, as I stooped to drink at a hurrying rill, a heron flapped heavily from the reeds beside me. I turned to look at the sun. It seemed to touch the edges of the plain. When at last I decided that it was useless to go on, and that I must make up my mind to spend at least one night on the moors, I threw myself down thoroughly fagged out. The evening sunlight slanted warm across my body, but the sea-winds began to rise, and I felt a chill strike through me from my wet shooting-boots. High overhead gulls were wheeling and tossing like bits of white paper; from some distant marsh a solitary curlew called. Little by little the sun sank into the plain, and the zenith flushed with the after-glow. I watched the sky change from palest gold to pink and then to smouldering fire. Clouds of midges danced above me, and high in the calm air a bat dipped and soared. My eyelids began to droop. Then as I shook off the drowsiness a sudden crash among the bracken roused me. I raised my eyes. A great bird hung quivering in the air above my face. For an instant I stared, incapable of motion; then something leaped past me in the ferns and the bird rose, wheeled, and pitched headlong into the brake.

I was on my feet in an instant peering through the gorse. There came the sound of a struggle from a bunch of heather close by, and then all was quiet. I stepped forward, my gun poised, but when I came to the heather the gun fell under my arm again, and I stood motionless in silent astonishment. A dead hare lay on the ground, and on the hare stood a magnificent falcon, one talon buried in the creature's neck, the other planted firmly on its limp flank. But what astonished me, was not the mere sight of a falcon sitting upon its prey. I had seen that more than once. It was that the falcon was fitted with a sort of leash about both talons, and from the leash hung a round bit of metal like a sleigh-bell. The bird turned its fierce yellow eyes on me, and then stooped and struck its curved beak into the quarry. At the same instant hurried steps sounded among the heather, and a girl sprang into the covert in front. Without a glance at me she walked up to the falcon, and passing her gloved hand under its breast, raised it from the quarry. Then she deftly slipped a small hood over the bird's head, and holding it out on her gauntlet, stooped and picked up the hare.

She passed a cord about the animal's legs and fastened the end of the thong to her girdle. Then she started to retrace her steps through the covert. As she passed me I raised my cap and she acknowledged my presence with a scarcely perceptible inclination. I had been so astonished, so lost in admiration of the scene before my eyes, that it had not occurred to me that here was my salvation. But as she moved away I recollected that unless I wanted to sleep on a windy moor that night I had better recover my speech without delay. At my first word she hesitated, and as I stepped before her I thought a look of fear came into her beautiful eyes. But as I humbly explained my unpleasant plight, her face flushed and she looked at me in wonder.

"Surely you did not come from Kerselec!" she repeated.

Her sweet voice had no trace of the Breton accent nor of any accent which I knew, and yet there was something in it I seemed to have heard before, something quaint and indefinable, like the theme of an old song.

I explained that I was an American, unacquainted with Finistère, shooting there for my own amusement.

"An American," she repeated in the same quaint musical tones. "I have never before seen an American."

For a moment she stood silent, then looking at me she said. "If you should walk all night you could not reach Kerselec now, even if you had a guide."

This was pleasant news.

"But," I began, "if I could only find a peasant's hut where I might get something to eat, and shelter."

The falcon on her wrist fluttered and shook its head. The girl smoothed its glossy back and glanced at me.

"Look around," she said gently. "Can you see the end of these moors? Look, north, south, east, west. Can you see anything but moorland and bracken?"

"No," I said.

"The moor is wild and desolate. It is easy to enter, but sometimes they who enter never leave it. There are no peasants' huts here."

"Well," I said, "if you will tell me in which direction Kerselec lies, tomorrow it will take me no longer to go back than it has to come."

She looked at me again with an expression almost like pity.

"Ah," she said, "to come is easy and takes hours; to go is different – and may take centuries."

I stared at her in amazement but decided that I had misunderstood her. Then before I had time to speak she drew a whistle from her belt and sounded it.

"Sit down and rest," she said to me; "you have come a long distance and are tired."

She gathered up her pleated skirts and motioning me to follow picked her dainty way through the gorse to a flat rock among the ferns.

"They will be here directly," she said, and taking a seat at one end of the rock invited me to sit down on the other edge. The after-glow was beginning to fade in the sky and a single star twinkled faintly through the rosy haze. A long wavering triangle of water-fowl drifted southward over our heads, and from the swamps around plover were calling.

"They are very beautiful – these moors," she said quietly.

"Beautiful, but cruel to strangers," I answered.

"Beautiful and cruel," she repeated dreamily, "beautiful and cruel."

"Like a woman," I said stupidly.

"Oh," she cried with a little catch in her breath, and looked at me. Her dark eyes met mine, and I thought she seemed angry or frightened.

"Like a woman," she repeated under her breath, "How cruel to say so!" Then after a pause, as though speaking aloud to herself, "How cruel for him to say that!"

I don't know what sort of an apology I offered for my inane, though harmless speech, but I know that she seemed so troubled about it that I began to think I had said something very dreadful without knowing it, and remembered with horror the pitfalls and snares which the French language sets for foreigners. While I was trying to imagine what I might have said, a sound of voices came across the moor, and the girl rose to her feet.

"No," she said, with a trace of a smile on her pale face, "I will not accept your apologies, monsieur, but I must prove you wrong, and that shall be my revenge. Look. Here come Hastur and Raoul."

Two men loomed up in the twilight. One had a sack across his shoulders and the other carried a hoop before him as a waiter carries a tray. The hoop was fastened with straps to his shoulders, and around the edge of the circlet sat three hooded falcons fitted with tinkling bells. The girl stepped up to the falconer, and with a quick turn of her wrist transferred her falcon to the hoop, where it quickly sidled off and nestled among its mates, who shook their hooded heads and ruffled their feathers till the belled jesses tinkled again. The other man stepped forward and bowing respectfully took up the hare and dropped it into the game-sack.

"These are my *piqueurs*," said the girl, turning to me with a gentle dignity. "Raoul is a good *fauconnier*, and I shall some day make him *grand veneur*. Hastur is incomparable."

The two silent men saluted me respectfully.

"Did I not tell you, monsieur, that I should prove you wrong?" she continued. "This, then, is my revenge, that you do me the courtesy of accepting food and shelter at my own house."

Before I could answer she spoke to the falconers, who started instantly across the heath, and with a gracious gesture to me she followed. I don't know whether I made her understand how profoundly grateful I felt, but she seemed pleased to listen, as we walked over the dewy heather.

"Are you not very tired?" she asked.

I had clean forgotten my fatigue in her presence, and I told her so.

"Don't you think your gallantry is a little old-fashioned?" she said; and when I looked confused and humbled, she added quietly, "Oh, I like it, I like everything old-fashioned, and it is delightful to hear you say such pretty things."

The moorland around us was very still now under its ghostly sheet of mist. The plovers had ceased their calling; the crickets and all the little creatures of the fields were silent as we passed, yet it seemed to me as if I could hear them beginning again far behind us. Well in advance, the two tall falconers strode across the heather, and the faint jingling of the hawks' bells came to our ears in distant murmuring chimes.

Suddenly a splendid hound dashed out of the mist in front, followed by another and another until half-a-dozen or more were bounding and leaping around the girl beside me. She caressed and quieted them with her gloved hand, speaking to them in quaint terms which I remembered to have seen in old French manuscripts.

Then the falcons on the circlet borne by the falconer ahead began to beat their wings and scream, and from somewhere out of sight the notes of a hunting-horn floated across the moor. The hounds sprang away before us and vanished in the twilight, the falcons flapped and squealed upon their perch, and the girl, taking up the song of the horn, began to hum. Clear and mellow her voice sounded in the night air.

> *"Chasseur, chasseur, chassez encore,*
> *Quittez Rosette et Jeanneton,*
> *Tonton, tonton, tontaine, tonton,*
> *Ou, pour, rabattre, dès l'aurore,*
> *Que les Amours soient de planton,*
> *Tonton, tontaine, tonton."*

As I listened to her lovely voice a grey mass which rapidly grew more distinct loomed up in front, and the horn rang out joyously through the tumult of the hounds and falcons. A torch glimmered at a gate, a light streamed through an opening door, and we stepped upon a wooden bridge which trembled under our feet and rose creaking and straining behind us as we passed over the moat and into a small stone court, walled on every side. From an open doorway a man came and, bending in salutation, presented a cup to the girl beside me. She took the cup and touched it with her lips, then lowering it turned to me and said in a low voice, "I bid you welcome."

At that moment one of the falconers came with another cup, but before handing it to me, presented it to the girl, who tasted it. The falconer made a gesture to receive it, but she hesitated a moment, and then, stepping forward, offered me the cup with her own hands. I felt this to be an act of extraordinary graciousness, but hardly knew what was expected of me, and did not raise it to my lips at once. The girl flushed crimson. I saw that I must act quickly.

"Mademoiselle," I faltered, "a stranger whom you have saved from dangers he may never realize empties this cup to the gentlest and loveliest hostess of France."

"In His name," she murmured, crossing herself as I drained the cup. Then stepping into the doorway she turned to me with a pretty gesture and, taking my hand in hers, led me into the house, saying again and again: "You are very welcome, indeed you are welcome to the Château d'Ys."

II

I AWOKE next morning with the music of the horn in my ears, and leaping out of the ancient bed, went to a curtained window where the sunlight filtered through little deep-set panes. The horn ceased as I looked into the court below.

A man who might have been brother to the two falconers of the night before stood in the midst of a pack of hounds. A curved horn was strapped over his back, and in his hand he held a long-lashed whip. The dogs whined and yelped, dancing around him in anticipation; there was the stamp of horses, too, in the walled yard.

"Mount!" cried a voice in Breton, and with a clatter of hoofs the two falconers, with falcons upon their wrists, rode into the courtyard among the hounds. Then I heard another voice which sent the blood throbbing through my heart: "Piriou Louis, hunt the hounds well and spare neither spur nor whip. Thou Raoul and thou Gaston, see that the *epervier* does not prove himself *niais*, and if it be best in your judgment, *faites courtoisie à l'oiseau*. *Jardiner un oiseau*, like the *mué* there on Hastur's wrist, is not difficult, but thou, Raoul, mayest not find it so simple to govern that *hagard*. Twice last week he foamed *au vif* and lost the *beccade* although he is used to the *leurre*. The bird acts like a stupid *branchier*. *Paître un hagard n'est pas si facile.*"

Was I dreaming? The old language of falconry which I had read in yellow manuscripts – the old forgotten French of the middle ages was sounding in my ears while the hounds bayed and the hawks' bells tinkled accompaniment to the stamping horses. She spoke again in the sweet forgotten language:

"If you would rather attach the *longe* and leave thy *hagard au bloc*, Raoul, I shall say nothing; for it were a pity to spoil so fair a day's sport with an ill-trained *sors*. *Essimer abaisser*, – it is possibly the best way. *Ça lui donnera des reins.* I was perhaps hasty with the bird. It takes time to pass *à la filière* and the exercises *d'escap*."

Then the falconer Raoul bowed in his stirrups and replied: "If it be the pleasure of Mademoiselle, I shall keep the hawk."

"It is my wish," she answered. "Falconry I know, but you have yet to give me many a lesson in *Autourserie*, my poor Raoul. Sieur Piriou Louis mount!"

The huntsman sprang into an archway and in an instant returned, mounted upon a strong black horse, followed by a piqueur also mounted.

"Ah!" she cried joyously, "Speed Glemarec René! Speed! Speed all! Sound thy horn, Sieur Piriou!"

The silvery music of the hunting-horn filled the courtyard, the hounds sprang through the gateway and galloping hoof-beats plunged out of the paved court; loud on the drawbridge, suddenly muffled, then lost in the heather and bracken of the moors. Distant and more distant sounded the horn, until it became so faint that the sudden carol of a soaring lark drowned it in my ears. I heard the voice below responding to some call from within the house.

"I do not regret the chase, I will go another time. Courtesy to the stranger, Pelagie, remember!"

And a feeble voice came quavering from within the house, "*Courtoisie*"

I stripped, and rubbed myself from head to foot in the huge earthen basin of icy water which stood upon the stone floor at the foot of my bed. Then I looked about for my clothes. They were gone, but on a settle near the door lay a heap of garments which I inspected with astonishment. As my clothes had vanished, I was compelled to attire myself in the costume which had evidently been placed there for me to wear while my own clothes dried. Everything was there, cap, shoes, and hunting doublet of silvery grey homespun; but the close-fitting costume and seamless shoes belonged to another century, and I remembered the strange costumes of the three falconers in the courtyard. I was sure that it was not the modern dress of any portion of France or Brittany; but not until I was dressed and stood before a mirror between the windows did I realize that I was clothed much more like a young huntsman of the middle ages than like a Breton of that day. I hesitated and picked up the cap. Should I go down and present myself in that strange guise? There seemed to be no help for it, my own clothes were gone and there was no bell in the ancient chamber to call a servant; so I contented myself with removing a short hawk's feather from the cap, and, opening the door, went downstairs.

By the fireplace in the large room at the foot of the stairs an old Breton woman sat spinning with a distaff. She looked up at me when I appeared, and, smiling frankly, wished me health in the Breton language, to which I laughingly replied in French. At the same moment my hostess appeared and returned my salutation with a grace and dignity that sent a thrill to my heart. Her lovely head with its dark curly hair was crowned with a head-dress which set all doubts as to the epoch of my own costume at rest. Her slender figure was exquisitely set off in the homespun hunting-gown edged with silver, and on her gauntlet-covered wrist she bore one of her petted hawks. With perfect simplicity she took my hand and led me into the garden in the court, and seating herself before a table invited me very sweetly to sit beside her. Then she asked me in her soft quaint accent how I had passed the night, and whether I was very much inconvenienced by wearing the clothes which old Pelagie had put there for me while I slept. I looked at my own clothes and shoes, drying in the sun by the garden-wall, and hated them. What horrors they were compared with the graceful costume which I now wore! I told her this laughing, but she agreed with me very seriously.

"We will throw them away," she said in a quiet voice. In my astonishment I attempted to explain that I not only could not think of accepting clothes from anybody, although for all I knew it might be the custom of hospitality in that part of the country, but that I should cut an impossible figure if I returned to France clothed as I was then.

She laughed and tossed her pretty head, saying something in old French which I did not understand, and then Pelagie trotted out with a tray on which stood two bowls of milk, a loaf of white bread, fruit, a platter of honey-comb, and a flagon of deep red wine. "You see I have not yet broken my fast because I wished you to eat with me. But I am very hungry," she smiled.

"I would rather die than forget one word of what you have said!" I blurted out, while my cheeks burned. "She will think me mad," I added to myself, but she turned to me with sparkling eyes.

"Ah!" she murmured. "Then Monsieur knows all that there is of chivalry –"

She crossed herself and broke bread. I sat and watched her white hands, not daring to raise my eyes to hers.

"Will you not eat?" she asked. "Why do you look so troubled?"

Ah, why? I knew it now. I knew I would give my life to touch with my lips those rosy palms – I understood now that from the moment when I looked into her dark eyes there on the moor last night I had loved her. My great and sudden passion held me speechless.

"Are you ill at ease?" she asked again.

Then, like a man who pronounces his own doom, I answered in a low voice: "Yes, I am ill at ease for love of you." And as she did not stir nor answer, the same power moved my lips in spite of me and I said, "I, who am unworthy of the lightest of your thoughts, I who abuse hospitality and repay your gentle courtesy with bold presumption, I love you."

She leaned her head upon her hands, and answered softly, "I love you. Your words are very dear to me. I love you."

"Then I shall win you."

"Win me," she replied.

But all the time I had been sitting silent, my face turned toward her. She, also silent, her sweet face resting on her upturned palm, sat facing me, and as her eyes looked into mine I knew that neither she nor I had spoken human speech; but I knew that her soul had answered mine, and I drew myself up feeling youth and joyous love coursing through every vein. She, with a bright colour in her lovely face, seemed as one awakened from a dream, and her eyes sought mine with a questioning glance which made me tremble with delight. We broke our fast, speaking of ourselves. I told her my name and she told me hers, the Demoiselle Jeanne d'Ys.

She spoke of her father and mother's death, and how the nineteen of her years had been passed in the little fortified farm alone with her nurse Pelagie, Glemarec René the piqueur, and the four falconers, Raoul, Gaston, Hastur, and the Sieur Piriou Louis, who had served her father. She had never been outside the moorland – never even had seen a human soul before, except the falconers and Pelagie. She did not know how she had heard of Kerselec; perhaps the falconers had spoken of it. She knew the legends of Loup Garou and Jeanne la Flamme from her nurse Pelagie. She embroidered and spun flax. Her hawks and hounds were her only distraction. When she had met me there on the moor she had been so frightened that she almost dropped at the sound of my voice. She had, it was true, seen ships at sea from the cliffs, but as far as the eye could reach the moors over which she galloped were destitute of any sign of human life. There was a legend which old Pelagie told, how anybody once lost in the unexplored moorland might never return, because the moors were enchanted. She did not know whether it was true, she never had thought about it until she met me. She did not know whether the falconers had even been outside, or whether they could go if they would. The books in the house which Pelagie, the nurse, had taught her to read were hundreds of years old.

All this she told me with a sweet seriousness seldom seen in any one but children. My own name she found easy to pronounce, and insisted, because my first name was Philip, I must have French blood in me. She did not seem curious to learn anything about the outside world, and I thought perhaps she considered it had forfeited her interest and respect from the stories of her nurse.

We were still sitting at the table, and she was throwing grapes to the small field birds which came fearlessly to our very feet.

I began to speak in a vague way of going, but she would not hear of it, and before I knew it I had promised to stay a week and hunt with hawk and hound in their company. I also obtained permission to come again from Kerselec and visit her after my return.

"Why," she said innocently, "I do not know what I should do if you never came back;" and I, knowing that I had no right to awaken her with the sudden shock which the avowal of my own love would bring to her, sat silent, hardly daring to breathe.

"You will come very often?" she asked.

"Very often," I said.

"Every day?"

"Every day."

"Oh," she sighed, "I am very happy. Come and see my hawks."

She rose and took my hand again with a childlike innocence of possession, and we walked through the garden and fruit trees to a grassy lawn which was bordered by a brook. Over the lawn were scattered fifteen or twenty stumps of trees – partially imbedded in the grass – and upon all of these except two sat falcons. They were attached to the stumps by thongs which were in turn fastened with steel rivets to their legs just above the talons. A little stream of pure spring water flowed in a winding course within easy distance of each perch.

The birds set up a clamour when the girl appeared, but she went from one to another, caressing some, taking others for an instant upon her wrist, or stooping to adjust their jesses.

"Are they not pretty?" she said. "See, here is a falcon-gentil. We call it 'ignoble,' because it takes the quarry in direct chase. This is a blue falcon. In falconry we call it 'noble' because it rises over the quarry, and wheeling, drops upon it from above. This white bird is a gerfalcon from the north. It is also 'noble!' Here is a merlin, and this tiercelet is a falcon-heroner."

I asked her how she had learned the old language of falconry. She did not remember, but thought her father must have taught it to her when she was very young.

Then she led me away and showed me the young falcons still in the nest. "They are termed *niais* in falconry," she explained. "A *branchier* is the young bird which is just able to leave the nest and hop from branch to branch. A young bird which has not yet moulted is called a *sors*, and a *mué* is a hawk which has moulted in captivity. When we catch a wild falcon which has changed its plumage we term it a *hagard*. Raoul first taught me to dress a falcon. Shall I teach you how it is done?"

She seated herself on the bank of the stream among the falcons and I threw myself at her feet to listen.

Then the Demoiselle d'Ys held up one rosy-tipped finger and began very gravely.

"First one must catch the falcon."

"I am caught," I answered.

She laughed very prettily and told me my *dressage* would perhaps be difficult, as I was noble.

"I am already tamed," I replied; "jessed and belled."

She laughed, delighted. "Oh, my brave falcon; then you will return at my call?"

"I am yours," I answered gravely.

She sat silent for a moment. Then the colour heightened in her cheeks and she held up her finger again, saying, "Listen; I wish to speak of falconry –"

"I listen, Countess Jeanne d'Ys."

But again she fell into the reverie, and her eyes seemed fixed on something beyond the summer clouds.

"Philip," she said at last.

"Jeanne," I whispered.

"That is all, – that is what I wished," she sighed, – "Philip and Jeanne."

She held her hand toward me and I touched it with my lips.

"Win me," she said, but this time it was the body and soul which spoke in unison.

After a while she began again: "Let us speak of falconry."

"Begin," I replied; "we have caught the falcon."

Then Jeanne d'Ys took my hand in both of hers and told me how with infinite patience the young falcon was taught to perch upon the wrist, how little by little it became used to the belled jesses and the *chaperon à cornette*.

"They must first have a good appetite," she said; "then little by little I reduce their nourishment; which in falconry we call *pât*. When, after many nights passed *au bloc* as these birds are now, I prevail upon the *hagard* to stay quietly on the wrist, then the bird is ready to be taught to come for its food. I fix the *pât* to the end of a thong, or *leurre*, and teach the bird to come to me as soon as I begin to whirl the cord in circles about my head. At first I drop the *pât* when the falcon comes, and he eats the food on the ground. After a little he will learn to seize the *leurre* in motion as I whirl it around my head or drag it over the ground. After this it is easy to teach the falcon to strike at game, always remembering to *'faire courtoisie á l'oiseau'*, that is, to allow the bird to taste the quarry."

A squeal from one of the falcons interrupted her, and she arose to adjust the *longe* which had become whipped about the *bloc*, but the bird still flapped its wings and screamed.

"What *is* the matter?" she said. "Philip, can you see?"

I looked around and at first saw nothing to cause the commotion, which was now heightened by the screams and flapping of all the birds. Then my eye fell upon the flat rock beside the stream from which the girl had risen. A grey serpent was moving slowly across the surface of the boulder, and the eyes in its flat triangular head sparkled like jet.

"A couleuvre," she said quietly.

"It is harmless, is it not?" I asked.

She pointed to the black V-shaped figure on the neck.

"It is certain death," she said; "it is a viper."

We watched the reptile moving slowly over the smooth rock to where the sunlight fell in a broad warm patch.

I started forward to examine it, but she clung to my arm crying, "Don't, Philip, I am afraid."

"For me?"

"For you, Philip, – I love you."

Then I took her in my arms and kissed her on the lips, but all I could say was: "Jeanne, Jeanne, Jeanne." And as she lay trembling on my breast, something struck my foot in the grass below, but I did not heed it. Then again something struck my ankle, and a sharp pain shot through me. I looked into the sweet face of Jeanne d'Ys and kissed her, and with all my strength lifted her in my arms and flung her from me. Then bending, I tore the viper from my ankle and set my heel upon its head. I remember feeling weak and numb, – I remember falling to the ground. Through my slowly glazing eyes I saw Jeanne's white face bending close to mine, and when the light in my eyes went out I still felt her arms about my neck, and her soft cheek against my drawn lips.

* * *

When I opened my eyes, I looked around in terror. Jeanne was gone. I saw the stream and the flat rock; I saw the crushed viper in the grass beside me, but the hawks and *blocs* had disappeared. I sprang to my feet. The garden, the fruit trees, the drawbridge and the walled court were gone. I stared stupidly at a heap of crumbling ruins, ivy-covered and grey, through which great trees had pushed their way. I crept forward, dragging my numbed foot, and as I moved, a falcon sailed from the tree-tops among the ruins, and soaring, mounting in narrowing circles, faded and vanished in the clouds above.

"Jeanne, Jeanne," I cried, but my voice died on my lips, and I fell on my knees among the weeds. And as God willed it, I, not knowing, had fallen kneeling before a crumbling shrine carved in stone for our Mother of Sorrows. I saw the sad face of the Virgin wrought in the cold stone. I saw the cross and thorns at her feet, and beneath it I read:

*"PRAY FOR THE SOUL OF THE
DEMOISELLE JEANNE D'Ys,
WHO DIED
IN HER YOUTH FOR LOVE OF
PHILIP, A STRANGER.
A.D. 1573."*

But upon the icy slab lay a woman's glove still warm and fragrant.

Hilda Silfverling

A Fantasy

L. Maria Child

Thou hast nor youth nor age;
But, as it were, an after dinner's sleep,
Dreaming on both.
Measure for Measure

HILDA GYLLENLOF was the daughter of a poor Swedish clergyman. Her mother died before she had counted five summers. The good father did his best to supply the loss of maternal tenderness; nor were kind neighbors wanting, with friendly words, and many a small gift for the pretty little one. But at the age of thirteen, Hilda lost her father also, just as she was receiving rapidly from his affectionate teachings as much culture as his own education and means afforded. The unfortunate girl had no other resource than to go to distant relatives, who were poor, and could not well conceal that the destitute orphan was a burden. At the end of a year, Hilda, in sadness and weariness of spirit, went to Stockholm, to avail herself of an opportunity to earn her living by her needle, and some light services about the house.

She was then in the first blush of maidenhood, with a clear innocent look, and exceedingly fair complexion. Her beauty soon attracted the attention of Magnus Andersen, mate of a Danish vessel then lying at the wharves of Stockholm. He could not be otherwise than fascinated with her budding loveliness; and alone as she was in the world, she was naturally prone to listen to the first words of warm affection she had heard since her father's death. What followed is the old story, which will continue to be told as long as there are human passions and human laws. To do the young man justice, though selfish, he was not deliberately unkind; for he did not mean to be treacherous to the friendless young creature who trusted him. He sailed from Sweden with the honest intention to return and make her his wife; but he was lost in a storm at sea, and the earth saw him no more.

Hilda never heard the sad tidings; but, for another cause, her heart was soon oppressed with shame and sorrow. If she had had a mother's bosom on which to lean her aching head, and confess all her faults and all her grief, much misery might have been saved. But there was none to whom she dared to speak of her anxiety and shame. Her extreme melancholy attracted the attention of a poor old woman, to whom she sometimes carried clothes for washing. The good Virika, after manifesting her sympathy in various ways, at last ventured to ask outright why one so young was so very sad. The poor child threw herself on the friendly bosom, and confessed all her wretchedness. After that, they had frequent confidential conversations; and the kind-hearted peasant did her utmost to console and cheer the desolate orphan. She said she must soon return to her native village in the Norwegian valley of Westfjordalen; and as she was alone in the world, and wanted some-thing to love, she would gladly take the babe, and adopt it for her own.

Poor Hilda, thankful for any chance to keep her disgrace a secret, gratefully accepted the offer. When the babe was ten days old, she allowed the good Virika to carry it away; though not without bitter tears, and the oft-repeated promise that her little one might be reclaimed, whenever Magnus returned and fulfilled his promise of marriage.

But though these arrangements were managed with great caution, the young mother did not escape suspicion. It chanced, very unfortunately, that soon after Virika's departure, an infant was found in the water, strangled with a sash very like one Hilda had been accustomed to wear. A train of circumstantial evidence seemed to connect the child with her, and she was arrested. For some time, she contented herself with assertions of innocence, and obstinately refused to tell anything more. But at last, having the fear of death before her eyes, she acknowledged that she had given birth to a daughter, which had been carried away by Virika Gjetter, to her native place, in the parish of Tind, in the Valley of Westfjordalen. Inquiries were accordingly made in Norway, but the answer obtained was that Virika had not been heard of in her native valley, for many years. Through weary months, Hilda lingered in prison, waiting in vain for favourable testimony; and at last, on strong circumstantial evidence she was condemned to die.

It chanced there was at that time a very learned chemist in Stockholm; a man whose thoughts were all gas, and his hours marked only by combinations and explosions. He had discovered a process of artificial cold, by which he could suspend animation in living creatures, and restore it at any prescribed time. He had in one apartment of his laboratory a bear that had been in a torpid state five years, a wolf two years, and so on. This of course excited a good deal of attention in the scientific world. A metaphysician suggested how extremely interesting it would be to put a human being asleep thus, and watch the reunion of soul and body, after the lapse of a hundred years. The chemist was half wild with the magnificence of this idea; and he forthwith petitioned that Hilda, instead of being beheaded, might be delivered to him, to be frozen for a century. He urged that her extreme youth demanded pity; that his mode of execution would be a very gentle one, and, being so strictly private, would be far less painful to the poor young creature than exposure to the public gaze.

On the day of execution, the chaplain came to pray with her, but found himself rather embarrassed in using the customary form. He could not well allude to her going in a few hours to meet her final judge; for the chemist said she would come back in a hundred years, and where her soul would be meantime was more than theology could teach. Under these novel circumstances, the old nursery prayer seemed to be the only appropriate one for her to repeat:

> *Now I lay me down to sleep,*
> *I pray the Lord my soul to keep:*
> *If I should die before I wake,*
> *I pray the Lord my soul to take.*

The subject of this curious experiment was conveyed in a close carriage from the prison to the laboratory. A shudder ran through soul and body, as she entered the apartment assigned her. It was built entirely of stone, and rendered intensely cold by an artificial process.

The light was dim and spectral, being admitted from above through a small circle of blue glass. Around the sides of the room, were tiers of massive stone shelves, on which reposed various objects in a torpid state. A huge bear lay on his back, with paws crossed on his breast, as devoutly as some pious knight of the fourteenth century. There was in fact no inconsiderable resemblance in the proceedings by which both these characters gained their worldly possessions; they were equally based on the maxim that 'might makes right.' It is true, the Christian obtained a better name, inasmuch as he paid a tithe of his gettings to the holy church, which the bear never had the grace to do. But then it must be remembered that the bear had no soul to save, and the Christian knight would have been very unlikely to pay fees to the ferryman, if he likewise had had nothing to send over.

The two public functionaries, who had attended the prisoner, to make sure that justice was not defrauded of its due, soon begged leave to retire, complaining of the unearthly cold. The pale face of the maiden became still paler, as she saw them depart. She seized the arm of the old chemist, and said, imploringly, "You will not go away, too, and leave me with these dreadful creatures?"

He replied, not without some touch of compassion in his tones, "You will be sound asleep, my dear, and will not know whether I am here or not. Drink this; it will soon make you drowsy."

"But what if that great bear should wake up?" asked she, trembling.

"Never fear. He cannot wake up," was the brief reply.

"And what if I should wake up, all alone here?"

"Don't disturb yourself," said he, "I tell you that you will not wake up. Come, my dear, drink quick; for I am getting chilly myself."

The poor girl cast another despairing glance round the tomb-like apartment, and did as she was requested. "And now," said the chemist, "let us shake hands, and say farewell; for you will never see me again."

"Why, won't you come to wake me up?" inquired the prisoner; not reflecting on all the peculiar circumstances of her condition.

"My great-grandson may," replied he, with a smile. "Adieu, my dear. It is a great deal pleasanter than being beheaded. You will fall asleep as easily as a babe in his cradle."

She gazed in his face, with a bewildered drowsy look, and big tears rolled down her cheeks. "Just step up here, my poor child," said he; and he offered her his hand.

"Oh, don't lay me so near the crocodile!" she exclaimed. "If he *should* wake up!"

"You wouldn't know it, if he did," rejoined the patient chemist; "but never mind. Step up to this other shelf, if you like it better."

He handed her up very politely, gathered her garments about her feet, crossed her arms below her breast, and told her to be perfectly still. He then covered his face with a mask, let some gasses escape from an apparatus in the centre of the room, and immediately went out, locking the door after him.

The next day, the public functionaries looked in, and expressed themselves well satisfied to find the maiden lying as rigid and motionless as the bear, the wolf, and the snake. On the edge of the shelf where she lay was pasted an inscription: "Put to sleep for infanticide, Feb. 10, 1740, by order of the king. To be wakened Feb. 10, 1840."

The earth whirled round on its axis, carrying with it the Alps and the Andes, the bear, the crocodile, and the maiden. Summer and winter came and went; America took place among the nations; Bonaparte played out his great game, with kingdoms for pawns; and still the Swedish damsel slept on her stone shelf with the bear and the crocodile.

When ninety-five years had passed, the bear, having fulfilled his prescribed century, was waked according to agreement. The curious flocked round him, to see him eat, and hear whether he could growl as well as other bears. Not liking such close observation, he broke his chain one night, and made off for the hills. How he seemed to his comrades, and what mistakes he make in his recollections, there were never any means of ascertaining. But bears, being more strictly conservative than men, happily escape the influence of French revolutions, German philosophy, Fourier theories, and reforms of all sorts; therefore Bruin doubtless found less change in *his* fellow citizens, than an old knight or viking might have done, had he chanced to sleep so long.

At last, came the maiden's turn to be resuscitated. The populace had forgotten her and her story long ago; but a select scientific few were present at the ceremony, by special invitation. The old chemist and his children all "slept the sleep that knows no waking." But carefully written orders had been transmitted from generation to generation; and the duty finally devolved on a great grandson, himself a chemist of no mean reputation.

Life returned very slowly; at first by almost imperceptible degrees, then by a visible shivering through the nerves. When the eyes opened, it was as if by the movement of pulleys, and there was something painfully strange in their marble gaze. But the lamp within the inner shrine lighted up, and gradually shone through them, giving assurance of the presence of a soul. As consciousness returned, she looked in the faces round her, as if seeking for some one; for her first dim recollection was of the old chemist. For several days, there was a general sluggishness of soul and body; an overpowering inertia, which made all exertion difficult, and prevented memory from rushing back in too tumultuous a tide.

For some time, she was very quiet and patient; but the numbers who came to look at her, their perpetual questions how things seemed to her, what was the state of her appetite and her memory, made her restless and irritable. Still worse was it when she went into the street. Her numerous visitors pointed her out to others, who ran to doors and windows to stare at her, and this soon attracted the attention of boys and lads. To escape such annoyances, she one day walked into a little shop, bearing the name of a woman she had formerly known. It was now kept by her grand-daughter, an aged woman, who was evidently as afraid of Hilda, as if she had been a witch or a ghost.

This state of things became perfectly unendurable. After a few weeks, the forlorn being made her escape from the city, at dawn of day, and with money which had been given her by charitable people, she obtained a passage to her native village, under the new name of Hilda Silfverling. But to stand, in the bloom of sixteen, among well-remembered hills and streams, and not recognise a single human face, or know a single human voice, this was the most mournful of all; far worse than loneliness in a foreign land; sadder than sunshine on a ruined city. And all these suffocating emotions must be crowded back on her own heart; for if she revealed them to any one, she would assuredly be considered insane or bewitched.

As the thought became familiar to her that even the little children she had known were all dead long ago, her eyes assumed an indescribably perplexed and mournful expression, which gave to them an appearance of supernatural depth. She was seized with an inexpressible longing to go where no one had ever heard of her, and among scenes she had never looked upon. Her thoughts often reverted fondly to old Virika Gjetter, and the babe for whose sake she had suffered so much; and her heart yearned for Norway. But then she was chilled by the remembrance that even if her child had lived to the usual age of mortals, she must have been long since dead; and if she had left descendants, what would they know of *her?* Overwhelmed by the complete desolation of her lot on earth, she wept bitterly.

But she was never utterly hopeless; for in the midst of her anguish, something prophetic seemed to beckon through the clouds, and call her into Norway.

In Stockholm, there was a white-haired old clergyman, who had been peculiarly kind, when he came to see her, after her centennial slumber. She resolved to go to him, to tell him how oppressively dreary was her restored existence, and how earnestly she desired to go, under a new name, to some secluded village in Norway, where none would be likely to learn her history, and where there would be nothing to remind her of the gloomy past. The good old man entered at once into her feelings, and approved her plan. He had been in that country himself, and had staid a few days at the house of a kind old man, named Eystein Hansen. He furnished Hilda with means for the journey, and gave her an affectionate letter of introduction, in which he described her as a Swedish orphan, who had suffered much, and would be glad to earn her living in any honest way that could be pointed out to her.

It was the middle of June when Hilda arrived at the house of Eystein Hanson. He was a stout, clumsy, red-visaged old man, with wide mouth, and big nose, hooked like an eagle's beak; but there was a right friendly expression in his large eyes, and when he had read the letter, he greeted the young stranger with such cordiality, she felt at once that she had found a father. She must come in his boat, he said, and he would take her at once to his island-home, where his good woman would give her a hearty welcome. She always loved the friendless; and especially would she love the Swedish orphan, because her last and youngest daughter had died the year before. On his way to the boat, the worthy man introduced her to several people, and when he told her story, old men and young maidens took her by the hand, and spoke as if they thought Heaven had sent them a daughter and a sister. The good Brenda received her with open arms, as her husband had said she would. She was an old weather-beaten woman, but there was a whole heart full of sunshine in her honest eyes.

And this new home looked so pleasant under the light of the summer sky! The house was embowered in the shrubbery of a small island, in the midst of a fiord, the steep shores of which were thickly covered with pine, fir, and juniper, down to the water's edge.

The fiord went twisting and turning about, from promontory to promontory, as if the Nereides, dancing up from the sea, had sportively chased each other into nooks and corners, now hiding away behind some bold projection of rock, and now peeping out suddenly, with a broad sunny smile. Directly in front of the island, the fiord expanded into a broad bay, on the shores of which was a little primitive romantic-looking village. Here and there a sloop was at anchor, and picturesque little boats tacked off and on from cape to cape, their white sails glancing in the sun. A range of lofty blue mountains closed in the distance. One giant, higher than all the rest, went up perpendicularly into the clouds, wearing a perpetual crown of glittering snow. As the maiden gazed on this sublime and beautiful scenery, a new and warmer tide seemed to flow through her stagnant heart. Ah, how happy might life be here among these mountain homes, with a people of such patriarchal simplicity, so brave and free, so hospitable, frank and hearty!

The house of Eystein Hansen was built of pine logs, neatly white-washed. The roof was covered with grass, and bore a crop of large bushes. A vine, tangled among these, fell in heavy festoons that waved at every touch of the wind. The door was painted with flowers in gay colours, and surmounted with fantastic carving. The interior of the dwelling was ornamented with many little grotesque images, boxes, bowls, ladles, etc., curiously carved in the close-grained and beautifully white wood of the Norwegian fir. This was a common amusement with the peasantry, and Eystein being a great favourite among them, received many such presents during his frequent visits in the surrounding parishes.

But nothing so much attracted Hilda's attention as a kind of long trumpet, made of two hollow half cylinders of wood, bound tightly together with birch bark. The only instrument of the kind she had ever seen was in the possession of Virika Gjetter, who called it a *luhr*, and said it was used to call the cows home in her native village, in Upper Tellemarken. She showed how it was used, and Hilda, having a quick ear, soon learned to play upon it with considerable facility.

And here in her new home, this rude instrument reappeared; forming the only visible link between her present life and that dreamy past! With strange feelings, she took up the pipe, and began to play one of the old tunes. At first, the tones flitted like phantoms in and out of her brain; but at last, they all came back, and took their places rank and file. Old Brenda said it was a pleasant tune, and asked her to play it again; but to Hilda it seemed awfully solemn, like a voice warbling from the grave. She would learn other tunes to please the good mother, she said; but this she would play no more; it made her too sad, for she had heard it in her youth.

"Thy youth!" said Brenda, smiling." One sees well that must have been a long time ago. To hear thee talk, one might suppose thou wert an old autumn leaf, just ready to drop from the bough, like myself."

Hilda blushed, and said she felt old, because she had had much trouble.

"Poor child," responded the good Brenda: "I hope thou hast had thy share."

"I feel as if nothing could trouble me here," replied Hilda, with a grateful smile; "all seems so kind and peaceful." She breathed a few notes through the *luhr*, as she laid it away on the shelf where she had found it. "But, my good mother," said she, "how clear and soft are these tones! The pipe I used to hear was far more harsh."

"The wood is very old," rejoined Brenda: "They say it is more than a hundred years. Alerik Thorild gave it to me, to call my good man when he is out in the boat. Ah, he was such a Berserker **(footnote 1)** of a boy! And in truth he was not much more sober when he was here three years ago. But no matter what he did; none could never help loving him."

"And who is Alerik?" asked the maiden.

Brenda pointed to an old house, seen in the distance, on the declivity of one of the opposite hills. It overlooked the broad bright bay, with its picturesque little islands, and was sheltered in the rear by a noble pine forest. A waterfall came down from the hillside, glancing in and out among the trees; and when the sun kissed it as he went away, it lighted up with a smile of rainbows.

"That house," said Brenda, "was built by Alerik's grandfather. He was the richest man in the village. But his only son was away among the wars for a long time, and the old place has been going to decay. But they say Alerik is coming back to live among us; and he will soon give it a different look. He has been away to Germany and Paris, and other outlandish parts, for a long time. Ah! The rogue! There was no mischief he didn't think of. He was always tying cats together under the windows, and barking in the middle of the night, till he set all the dogs in the neighbourhood a howling. But as long as it was Alerik that did it, it was all well enough: for everybody loved him, and he always made one believe just what he liked. If he wanted to make thee think thy hair was as black as Noeck's **(footnote 2)** mane, he *would* make thee think so."

Hilda smiled as she glanced at her flaxen hair, with here and there a gleam of paly gold, where the sun touched it. "I think it would be hard to prove *this* was black," said she.

"Nevertheless," rejoined Brenda, "If Alerik undertook it, he would do it. He always has his say, and does what he will. One may as well give in to him first as last."

This account of the unknown youth carried with it that species of fascination, which the idea of uncommon power always has over the human heart. The secluded maiden seldom touched the *luhr* without thinking of the giver; and not unfrequently she found herself conjecturing when this wonderful Alerik would come home.

Meanwhile, constant but not excessive labour, the mountain air, the quiet life, and the kindly hearts around her, restored to Hilda more than her original loveliness. In her large blue eyes, the inward-looking sadness of experience now mingled in strange beauty with the out-looking clearness of youth. Her fair complexion was tinged with the glow of health, and her motions had the airy buoyancy of the mountain breeze. When she went to the mainland, to attend church, or rustic festival, the hearts of young and old greeted her like a May blossom. Thus with calm cheerfulness her hours went by, making no noise in their flight, and leaving no impress. But here was an unsatisfied want! She sighed for hours that did leave a mark behind them. She thought of the Danish youth, who had first spoken to her of love; and plaintively came the tones from her *luhr*, as she gazed on the opposite hills, and wondered whether the Alerik they talked of so much, was indeed so very superior to other young men.

Father Hansen often came home at twilight with a boat full of juniper boughs, to be strewed over the floors, that they might diffuse a balmy odour, inviting to sleep. One evening, when Hilda saw him coming with his verdant load, she hastened down to the water's edge to take an armful of the fragrant boughs. She had scarcely appeared in sight, before he called out, "I do believe Alerik has come! I heard the organ up in the old house. Somebody was playing on it like a Northeast storm; and surely, said I, that must be Alerik."

"Is there an organ there?" asked the damsel, in surprise.

"Yes, he built it himself, when he was here three years ago. He can make anything he chooses.

An organ, or a basket cut from a cherry stone, is all one to him."

When Hilda returned to the cottage, she of course repeated the news to Brenda, who exclaimed joyfully, "Ah, then we shall see him soon! If he does not come before, we shall certainly see him at the weddings in the church tomorrow."

"An plenty of tricks we shall have now," said Father Hansen, shaking his head with a good-natured smile." There will be no telling which end of the world is uppermost, while he is here."

"Oh yes, there will, my friend," answered Brenda, laughing; "for it will certainly be whichever end Alerik stands on. The handsome little Berserker! How I should like to see him!"

The next day there was a sound of lively music on the waters; for two young couples from neighbouring islands were coming up the fiord, to be married at the church in the opposite village. Their boats were ornamented with gay little banners, friends and neighbours accompanied them, playing on musical instruments, and the rowers had their hats decorated with garlands. As the rustic band floated thus gayly over the bright waters, they were joined by Father Hansen, with Brenda and Hilda in his boat. Friendly villagers had already decked the simple little church with ever-greens and flowers, in honour of the bridal train. As they entered, Father Hansen observed that two young men stood at the door with clarinets in their hands. But he thought no more of it, till, according to immemorial custom, he, as clergy man's assistant, began to sing the first lines of the hymn that was given out. The very first note he sounded, up struck the clarinets at the door. The louder they played, the louder the old man bawled; but the instruments gained the victory. When he essayed to give out the lines of the next verse, the merciless clarinets brayed louder than before. His stentorian voice had become vociferous and rough, from thirty years of halloing across the water, and singing of psalms in four village churches. He exerted it to the utmost, till the perspiration poured down his rubicund visage; but it was of no use. His rivals had strong lungs, and they played on clarinets in F. If the whole village had screamed fire, to the shrill accompaniment of rail-road whistles, they would have over-topped them all.

Father Hansen was vexed at heart, and it was plain enough that he was so. The congregation held down their heads with suppressed laughter all except one tall vigorous young man, who sat up very serious and dignified, as if he were reverently listening to some new manifestation of musical genius. When the people left church, Hilda saw this young stranger approaching toward them, as fast as numerous hand-shakings by the way would permit. She had time to observe him closely. His noble figure, his vigorous agile motions, his expressive countenance, hazel eyes with strongly marked brows, and abundant brown hair, tossed aside with a careless grace, left no doubt in her mind that this was the famous Alerik Thorild; but what made her heart beat more wildly was his strong resemblance to Magnus the Dane. He went up to Brenda and kissed her, and threw his arms about Father Hansen's neck, with expressions of joyful recognition. The kind old man, vexed as he was, received these affectionate demonstrations with great friendliness. "Ah, Alerik," said he, after the first salutations were over, "that was not kind of thee."

"Me! What!" exclaimed the young man, with well-feigned astonishment.

"To put up those confounded clarinets to drown my voice," rejoined he bluntly. "When a man has led the singing thirty years in four parishes, I can assure thee it is not a pleasant joke to be treated in that style. I know the young men are tired of my voice, and think they could do things in better fashion, as young fools always do; but I may thank thee for putting it into their heads to bring those cursed clarinets."

"Oh, dear Father Hansen," replied the young man, in the most coaxing tones, and with the most caressing manner, "you *couldn't* think I would do such a thing!"

"On the contrary, it is just the thing I think thou couldst do," answered the old man: "Thou need not think to cheat me out of my eye-teeth, this time. Thou has often enough made me believe the moon was made of green cheese. But I know thy tricks. I shall be on my guard now; and mind thee, I am not going to be bamboozled by thee again."

Alerik smiled mischievously; for he, in common with all the villagers, knew it was the easiest thing in the world to gull the simple-hearted old man. "Well, come, Father Hansen," said he, "shake hands and be friends. When you come over to the village, tomorrow, we will drink a mug of ale together, at the Wolf's Head."

"Oh yes, and be played some trick for his pains," said Brenda.

"No, no," answered Alerik, with great gravity; "he is on his guard now, and I cannot bamboozle him again." With a friendly nod and smile, he bounded off, to greet some one whom he recognised. Hilda had stepped back to hide herself from observation. She was a little afraid of the handsome Berserker; and his resemblance to the Magnus of her youthful recollections made her sad.

The next afternoon, Alerik met his old friend, and reminded him of the agreement to drink ale at the Wolf's Head. On the way, he invited several young companions. The ale was excellent, and Alerik told stories and sag songs, which filled the little tavern with roars of laughter. In one of the intervals of merriment, he turned suddenly to the honest old man, and said, "Father Hansen, among the many things I have learned and done in foreign countries, did I ever tell you I had made a league with the devil, and am shot-proof?"

"One might easily believe thou hadst made a league with the devil, before thou wert born," replied Eystein, with a grin at his own wit; "but as for being shot-proof, that is another affair."

"Try and see," rejoined Alerik. "These friends are witnesses that I tell you it is perfectly safe to try. Come, I will stand here; fire your pistols, and you will soon see that the Evil One will keep the bargain he made with me."

"Be done with thy nonsense, Alerik," rejoined his old friend.

"Ah, I see how it is," replied Alerik, turning towards the young men. "Father Hansen used to be a famous shot. Nobody was more expert in the bear or the wolf-hunt than he; but old eyes grow dim, and old hands will tremble. No wonder he does not like to have us see how much he fails."

This was attacking honest Eystein Hansen on his weak side. He was proud of his strength and skill in shooting, and he did not like to admit that he was growing old. "I not hit a mark!" exclaimed he, with indignation: "When did I ever miss a thing I aimed at?"

"Never, when you were young," answered one of the company; "but it is no wonder you are afraid to try now."

"Afraid!" exclaimed the old hunter, impatiently. "Who the devil said I was afraid?"

Alerik shrugged his shoulders, and replied carelessly, "It is natural enough that these young men should think so, when they see you refuse to aim at me, though I assure you that I am shot proof, and that I will stand perfectly still."

"But art thou really shot-proof?" inquired the guileless old man. "The devil has helped thee to do so many strange things, that one never know what he will help thee to do next."

"Really, Father Hansen, I speak in earnest. Take up your pistol and try, and you will soon see with your own eyes that I am shot-proof." Eystein looked round upon the company like one perplexed. His wits, never very bright, were somewhat muddled by the ale. "What shall I do with this wild fellow?" inquired he. "You see he *will* be shot."

"Try him try him," was the general response. "He has assured you he is shot-proof; what more do you need?"

The old man hesitated awhile, but after some further parley, took up his pistol and examined it. "Before we proceed to business," said Alerik, "Let me tell you that if you do *not* shoot me, you shall have a gallon of the best ale you ever drank in your life. Come and taste it, Father Hansen, and satisfy yourself that it is good."

While they were discussing the merits of the ale, one of the young men took the ball from the pistol. "I am ready now," said Alerik: "Here I stand. Now don't lose your name for a good marksman."

The old man fired, and Alerik fell back with a deadly groan. Poor Eystein stood like a stone image of terror. His arms adhered rigidly to his sides, his jaw dropped, and his great eyes seemed starting from their sockets. "Oh, Father Hansen, how *could* you do it!" exclaimed the young men.

The poor horrified dupe stared at them wildly, and gasping and stammering replied, "Why he said he was shot-proof; and you all told me to do it."

"Oh yes," said they; "but we supposed you would have sense enough to know it was all in fun. But don't take it too much to heart. You will probably forfeit your life; for the government will of course consider it a poor excuse, when you tell them that you fired at a man merely to oblige him, and because he said he was shot-proof. But don't be too much cast down, Father Hansen. We must all meet death in some way; and if worst comes to worst, it will be a great comfort to you and your good Brenda that you did not intend to commit murder."

The poor old man gazed at them with an expression of such extreme suffering, that they became alarmed, and said, "Cheer up, cheer up. Come, you must drink something to make you feel better." They took him by the shoulders, but as they led him out, he continued to look back wistfully on the body.

The instant he left the apartment, Alerik sprang up and darted out of the opposite door; and when Father Hansen entered the other room, there he sat, as composedly as possible, reading a paper, and smoking his pipe.

"There he is!" shrieked the old man, turning paler than ever.

"Who is there?" inquired the young men.

"Don't you see Alerik Thorild?" exclaimed he, point, with an expression of intense horror.

They turned to the landlord, and remarked, in a compassionate tone, "Poor Father Hansen has shot Alerik Thorild, whom he loved so well; and the dreadful accident has so affected his brain, that he imagines he sees him.

The old man pressed his broad hand hard against his forehead, and again groaned out, "Oh, don't you see him?"

The tones indicated such agony, that Alerik had not the heart to prolong the scene. He sprang on his feet, and exclaimed, "Now for your gallon of ale, Father Hansen! You see the devil did keep his bargain with me."

"And *are* you alive?" shouted the old man.

The mischievous fellow soon convinced him of that, by a slap on the shoulder, that made his bones ache.

Eystein Hansen capered like a dancing bear. He hugged Alerik, and jumped about, and clapped his hands, and was altogether beside himself. He drank unknown quantities of ale, and this time sang loud enough to drown a brace of clarinets in F.

The night was far advanced when he went on board his boat to return to his island home. He pulled the oars vigorously, and the boat shot swiftly across the moon-lighted waters. But on arriving at the customary landing, he could discover no vestige of his white-washed cottage. Not knowing that Alerik, in the full tide of his mischief, had sent men to paint the house with a dark brown wash, he thought he must have made a mistake in the landing; so he rowed round to the other side of the island, but with no better success. Ashamed to return to the mainland, to inquire for a house that had absconded, and a little suspicious that the ale had hung some cobwebs in his brain, he continued to row hither and thither, till his strong muscular arms fairly ached with exertion. But the moon was going down, and all the landscape settling into darkness; and he at last reluctantly concluded that it was best to go back to the village inn.

Alerik, who had expected this result much sooner, had waited there to receive him. When he had kept him knocking a sufficient time, he put his head out of the window, and inquired who was there.

"Eystein Hansen," was the disconsolate reply. "For the love of mercy let me come in and get a few minutes sleep, before morning. I have been rowing about the bay these four hours, and I can't find my house any where."

"This is a very bad sign," replied Alerik, solemnly. "Houses don't run away, except from drunken men. Ah, Father Hansen! Father Hansen! What *will* the minister say?"

He did not have a chance to persecute the weary old man much longer; for scarcely had he come under the shelter of the house, before he was snoring in a profound sleep.

Early the next day, Alerik sought his old friends in their brown-washed cottage. He found it not so easy to conciliate them as usual. They were really grieved; and Brenda even said she believed he wanted to be the death of her old man. But he had brought them presents, which he knew they would like particularly well; and he kissed their hands, and talked over his boyish days, till at last he made them laugh. "Ah now," said he, "you have forgiven me, my dear old friends. And you see, father, it was all your own fault. You put the mischief into me, by boasting before all those young men that I could never bamboozle you again."

"Ah thou incorrigible rogue!" answered the old man. "I believe thou hast indeed made a league with the devil; and he gives thee the power to make every body love thee, do what thou wilt."

Alerik's smile seemed to express that he always had a pleasant consciousness of such power. The *luhr* lay on the table beside him, and as he took it up, he asked, "Who plays on this? Yesterday, when I was out in my boat, I heard very wild pretty little variations on some of my old favourite airs."

Brenda, instead of answering, called, "Hilda! Hilda!" and the young girl came from the next room, blushing as she entered. Alerik looked at her with evident surprise. "Surely, this is not your Gunilda?" said he.

"No," replied Brenda, "She is a Swedish orphan, whom the all-kind Father sent to take the place of our Gunilda, when she was called hence."

After some words of friendly greeting, the visitor asked Hilda if it was she who played so sweetly on the *luhr*. She answered timidly, without looking up. Her heart was throbbing; for the tones of his voice were like Magnus the Dane.

The acquaintance thus begun, was not likely to languish on the part of such an admirer of beauty as was Alerik Thorild. The more he saw of Hilda, during the long evenings of the following winter, the more he was charmed with her natural refinement of look, voice, and manner. There was, as we have said, a peculiarity in her beauty, which gave it a higher character than mere rustic loveliness. A deep, mystic, plaintive expression in her eyes; a sort of graceful bewilderment in her countenance, and at times in the carriage of her head, and the motions of her body; as if her spirit had lost its way, and was listening intently. It was not strange that he was charmed by her spiritual beauty, her simple untutored modesty. No wonder she was delighted with his frank strong exterior, his cordial caressing manner, his expressive eyes, now tender and earnest, and now sparkling with merriment, and his "smile most musical," because always so in harmony with the inward feeling, whether of sadness, fun, or tenderness. Then his moods were so bewitchingly various. Now powerful as the organ, now bright as the flute, now *naive* as the oboe. Brenda said everything he did seemed to be alive. He carved a wolf's head on her old man's cane, and she was always afraid it would bite her.

Brenda, in her simplicity, perhaps gave as good a description of genius as *could* be given, when she said everything it did seemed to be alive. Hilda thought it certainly was so with Alerik's music. Sometimes all went madly with it, as if fairies danced on the grass, and ugly gnomes came and mde faces at them, and shrieked, and clutched at their garments; the fairies pelted them off with flowers, and then all died away to sleep in the moonlight. Sometimes, when he played on flute, or violin, the sounds came mournfully as the midnight wind through ruined towers; and they stirred up such sorrowful memories of the past, that Hilda pressed her hand upon her swelling heart, and said, "Oh, not such strains as that, dear Alerik." But when his soul overflowed with love and happiness oh, then how the music gushed and nestled!

"The lark could scarce get out his notes for joy,
But shook his song together, as he neared
His happy home, the ground."

The old *luhr* was a great favourite with Alerik; not for its musical capabilities, but because it was entwined with the earliest recollections of his childhood. "Until I heard thee play upon it," said he, "I half repented having given it to the good Brenda. It has been in our family for several generations, and my nurse used to play upon it when I was in my cradle. They tell me my grandmother was a foundling. She was brought to my great-grandfather's house by an old peasant woman, on her way to the valley of Westfjordalen. She died there, leaving the babe and the *luhr* in my great-grandmother's keeping. They could never find out to whom the babe belonged; but she grew up very beautiful, and my grandfather married her."

"What was the old woman's name?" asked Hilda; and her voice was so deep and suppressed, that it made Alerik start.

"Virika Gjetter, they have always told me," he replied. "But my dearest one, what *is* the matter?"

Hilda, pale and fainting, made no answer. But when he placed her head upon his bosom, and kissed her forehead, and spoke soothingly, her glazed eyes softened, and she burst into tears. All his entreaties, however, could obtain no information at that time. "Go home now," she said, in tones of deep despondency. "Tomorrow I will tell thee all. I have had many unhappy hours; for I have long felt that I ought to tell thee all my past history; but I was afraid to do it, for I thought thou wouldst not love me any more; and that would be worse than death. But come tomorrow, and I will tell thee all."

"Well, dearest Hilda, I will wait," replied Alerik; "but what my grandmother, who died long before I was born, can have to do with my love for thee, is more than I can imagine."

The next day, when Hilda saw Alerik coming to claim the fulfillment of her promise, it seemed almost like her death-warrant."He will not love me any more," thought she, "he will never again look at me so tenderly; and then what can I do, but die?"

With much embarrassment, and many delays, she at last began her strange story. He listened to the first part very attentively, and with a gathering frown; but as she went on, the muscles of his face relaxed into a smile; and when she ended by saying, with the most melancholy seriousness, "So thou seest, dear Alerik, we cannot be married; because it is very likely that I am thy Great-grandmother" -- he burst into immoderate peals of laughter.

When his mirth had somewhat subsided, he replied, "Likely as not thou art my great-grandmother, dear Hilda; and just as likely I was thy grandfather, in the first place. A great German scholar **(footnote 3)** teaches that our souls keep coming back again and again into new bodies. An old Greek philosopher is said to have come back for the fourth time, under the name of Pythagoras. If these things are so, how the deuce is a man ever to tell whether he marries his grandmother or not?"

"But dearest Alerik, I am not jesting," rejoined she. "What I have told thee is really true. They did put me to sleep for a hundred years."

"Oh, yes," answered he, laughing, "I remember reading about it in the Swedish papers; and I thought it a capital joke. I will tell thee how it is with thee, my precious one. The elves sometimes seize people, to carry them down into their subterranean caves; but if the mortals run away from them, they, out of spite, forever after fill their heads with gloomy insane notions. A man in Drontheim ran away from them, and thy made him believe he was an earthen coffee-pot. He sat curled up in a corner all the time, for fear somebody would break his nose off."

"Nay, now thou art joking, Alerik, but really" –

"No, I tell thee, as thou has told me, it was no joke at all," he replied. "The Man himself told me he was a coffee-pot."

"But be serious, Alerik," said she, "and tell me, dost hou not believe that some learned men can put people to sleep for a hundred years?"

"I don't doubt some of my college professors could," rejoined he; "provided their tongues could hold out so long."

"But, Alerik, dost thou not think it possible that people may be alive, and yet not alive?"

"Of course I do," he replied; "the greater part of the world are in that condition."

"Oh, Alerik, what a tease thou art! I mean, is it not possible that there are people now living, or staying somewhere, who were moving about on this earth ages ago?"

"Nothing more likely," answered he; "for instance, who knows what people there may be under the ice-sea of Folgefond? They say the cocks are heard crowing down there, to this day. How a fowl of any feather got there is a curious question; and what kind of atmosphere he has to crow in, is another puzzle. Perhaps they are poor ghosts, without sense of shame, crowing over the recollections of sins committed in the human body. The ancient Egyptians thought the soul was obliged to live three thousand years, in a succession of different animals, before it could attain to the regions of the blest. I am pretty sure I have already been a lion and a nightingale. What I shall be next, the Egyptians know as well as I do. One of their sculptors made a stone image, half woman and half lioness. Doubtless his mother had been a lioness, and had transmitted to him some dim recollection of it. But I am glad, dearest, they sent thee back in the form of a lovely maiden; for it thou hadst come as a wolf, I might have shot thee; and I shouldn't like to shoot my--great-grandmother. Or if thou hadst come as a red herring, Father Hansen might have eaten thee in his soup; and then I should have had no Hilda Silfverling."

Hilda smiled, as she said, half reproachfully, "I see well that thou dost not believe one word I say."

"Oh yes, I do, dearest," rejoined he, very seriously. "I have no doubt the fairies carried thee off some summer's night and made thee verily believe thou hadst slept for a hundred years. They do the strangest things. Sometimes they change babies in the cradle; leave an imp, and carry off the human to the metal mines, where he hears only clink! clink! Then the fairies bring him back, and put him in some other cradle. When he grows up, how he does hurry skurry after the silver! He is obliged to work all his life, as if the devil drove him. The poor miser never knows what is the matter with him; but it is all because the gnomes brought him up in the mines, and he could never get the clink out of his head. A more poetic kind of fairies sometimes carry a babe to Aeolian caves, full of wild dreamy sounds; and when he is brought back to upper earth, ghosts of sweet echoes keep beating time in some corner of his brain, to something which *they* can hear, but which nobody else is the wiser for. I know that is true; for I was brought up in those caves myself."

Hilda remained silent for a few minutes, as he sat looking in her face with comic gravity. "Thou wilt do nothing but make fun of me," at last she said. "I do wish I could persuade thee to be serious. What I told thee was no fairy story. It really happened. I remember it as distinctly as I do our sail round the islands yesterday. I seem to see that great bear now, with his paws folded up, on the shelf opposite to me."

"He must have been a great bear to have staid there," replied Alerik, with eyes full of roguery. "If I had been in his skin, may I be shot if all the drugs and gasses in the world would have kept *me* there, with my paws folded on my breast."

Seeing a slight blush pass over her cheek, he added, more seriously, "After all, I ought to thank that wicked elf, whoever he was, for turning thee into a stone image; for otherwise thou wouldst have been in the world a hundred years too soon for me, and so I should have missed my life's best blossom."

Feeling her tears on his hand, he again started off into a vein of merriment. "Thy case was not so very peculiar," said he. "There was a Greek lady, name Niobe, who was changed to stone. The Greek gods changed women into trees, and fountains, and all manner of things. A man couldn't chop a walking-stick in those days, without danger of cutting off some lady's finger. The tree might be--his great-grandmother; and she of course would take it very unkindly of him."

"All these things are like the stories of Odin and Frigga," rejoined Hilda. "They are not true, like the Christian religion. When I tell thee a true story, why dost thou always meet me with fairies and fictions?"

"But tell me, best Hilda," said he, "what the Christian religion has to do with penning up young maidens with bears and crocodiles? In its marriage ceremonies, I grant that it sometimes does things not very unlike that, only omitting the important part of freezing the maiden's heart. But since thou hast mentioned the Christian religion, I may as well give thee a bit of consolation from that quarter. I have read in my mother's big Bible, that a man must not marry his grandmother; but I do not remember that it said a single word again his marrying his *great*-grandmother."

Hilda laughed, in spite of herself. But after a pause, she looked at him earnestly, and said, "Dost thou indeed think there would be no harm in marrying, under these circumstances, if I were really thy great-grandmother? Is it thy earnest? Do be serious for once, dear Alerik!"

"Certainly there would be no harm," answered he. "Physicians have agreed that the body changes entirely once in seven years. That must be because the soul outgrows its clothes; which proves that the soul changes every seven years, also. Therefore, in the course of one hundred years, thou must have had fourteen complete changes of soul and body. It is therefore as plain as daylight, that if thou wert my great-grandmother when thou fell asleep, thou couldst not have been my great-grandmother when they waked thee up."

"Ah, Alerik," she replied, "It is as the good Brenda says, there is no use in talking with thee. One might as well try to twist a string that is not fastened at either end."

He looked up merrily in her face. The wind was playing with her ringlets, and freshened the colour on her cheeks. "I only wish I had a mirror to hold before thee," said he; "that thou couldst see how very like thou art to a -- great grandmother."

"Laugh at me as thou wilt," answered she; "but I assure thee I have strange thoughts about myself sometimes. Dost thou know," added she, almost in a whisper, "I am not always quite certain that I have not died, and am now in heaven?"

A ringing shout of laughter burst from the light-hearted lover. "Oh, I like that! I like that!" exclaimed he. "That is good! That a Swede coming to Norway does not know certainly whether she is in heaven or not."

"Do be serious, Alerik," said she imploringly. "Don't carry thy jests too far."

"Serious? I am serious. If Norway is not heaven, one sees plainly enough that it must have been the scaling place, where the old giants got up to heaven; for they have left their ladders standing. Where else wilt thou find clusters of mountains running up perpendicularly thousands of feet right into the sky? If thou wast to see some of them, thou couldst tell whether Norway is a good climbing place into heaven."

"Ah, dearest Alerik, thou hast taught me that already," she replied, with a glance full of affection; "so a truce with thy joking. Truly one never knows how to take thee. Thy talk sets everything *in* the world, and *above* it, dancing together in the strangest fashion."

"Because they all do dance together," rejoined the perverse man.

"Oh, be done! Be done, Alerik!" she said, putting her hand playfully over his mouth. "Thou wilt tie my poor brain all up into knots."

He seized her hand and kissed it, then busied himself with braiding the wild spring flowers into a garland for her fair hair. As she gazed on him earnestly, her eyes beaming with love and happiness, he drew her to his breast, and exclaimed fervently, "Oh, thou art beautiful as an angel; and here or elsewhere, with thee by my side, it seemeth heaven."

They spoke no more for a long time. The birds now and then serenaded the silent lovers with little twittering gushes of song. The setting sun, as he went away over the hills, threw diamonds on the bay, and a rainbow ribbon across the distant waterfall. Their hearts were in harmony with the peaceful beauty of Nature. As he kissed her drowsy eyes, she murmured, "Oh, it was well worth a hundred years with bears and crocodiles, to fall asleep thus on thy heart."

* * *

The next autumn, a year and a half after Hilda's arrival in Norway, there was another procession of boats, with banners, music and garlands. The little church was again decorated with evergreens; but no clarinet players stood at the door to annoy good Father Hansen. The worthy man had in fact taken the hint, though somewhat reluctantly, and had good-naturedly ceased to disturb modern ears with his clamorous vociferation of the hymns. He and his kind-hearted Brenda were happy beyond measure at Hilda's good fortune. But when she told her husband anything he did not choose to believe, they could never rightly make out what he meant by looking at her so slyly, and saying, "Pooh! Pooh! Tell that to my -- great-grandmother."

Footnote 1. A warrior famous in the Northern Sagas for his stormy and untamable character.
Footnote 2. An elfish spirit, which, according to popular tradition in Norway, appears in the form of a coal black horse.
Footnote 3. Lessing.

Dear George, Love Margaret

Amanda C. Davis

My Dearest George:

Only an hour ago I watched your train pull away from the station, and already I am compelled to send my words of love. How will I tolerate these long years without you? Already I miss your voice, your comforting presence. I will bear up. But, my love, I will count the days.

The automaton you bought me has made itself at home, it seems, and taken the liberty of commanding the household. It considers the maid inadequate and the cook barely tolerable. George, how can a machine judge such a thing as cooking? Lord knows what happens to the samples it ingests.

Forgive me – I know you think I am too often crude. Consider me distraught at your absence, and think kindly on my flaws.

The automaton is insisting that I help close up your room so that it may be easily prepared upon your return. This I can do gladly, although working so near to a bronze monster will try my nerves. (Do not think ill of my repulsion! I know you only meant well.) For the sake of my love for you, I will control my emotions. Let him be bronze. I will be steel.

> Forever yours,
> And terribly lonely,
> I remain
> Your wife,
> Margaret

* * *

My Dearest George:

Your letter filled my heart with joy – and not a little fear. To think of the dangers you face rattles me. When you described the men in your company I was forced to put down your letter and request the automaton to read it aloud for me. My only hope is that you return to me in two years. (Twenty-two months! I cling to the calendar!) I cannot bear the thought that you might be prevented.

The bronze man has invented a calculation regarding your chances of survival. When I told him, quite forcefully, that I did not appreciate his efforts, he grew still, in the manner of a chastened child. I am under no illusions *regarding his emotive capability (I deny them utterly) and yet he performs an unsettling simulation.*

Enough talk of metal monsters! I shall speak instead of fleshly ones. Your parents are thriving, and lavishing their favor upon your brother – the good one, who did not marry a schoolteacher's 'vulgar' daughter and did not head West for the promise of a better life – forgive me, the thought of them sets me to boiling. I stand strong with you, my love. We stand together, though many miles apart.

May we stand beside one another soon.

Your devoted
Margaret

* * *

My Dear George:

I will not tell you the bronze man's calculation of your survival odds. Such unseemly efforts benefit no one. Besides, I have no wish to encourage his ghastly mathematical hobbies.

The creature will not leave my side except by direct order – and oftimes, not even then. I fear his cognitive machinery may be calibrated for a more fawning servant than I care for. I wish to have him tuned to my preference; will you please advise me of a tinkerer who might perform a careful alteration? I promise I shall find the means in our household budget.

Your brother came calling, delivered his fill of insults toward my person, and left again carrying, I suspect, your grandfather's cufflinks. I make no formal accusations but I have not seen them since. How your father could prefer him to kind, reliable George is a vexing mystery!

These four months have been torment, George, but you would be proud at how I fill my days. I find comfort in the garden and in the church. I have founded and developed friendships amongst other women of our class. This city is not so cold as I thought it once.

I am proud of you, also, for the hardships you bear for our sakes.

Your flower,
Margaret

* * *

My Dear George:

When next you embark on a hunting excursion, I beg you to keep the details to yourself. Your description of the buffalo killing (and everything done to its poor corpse!) quite turned my stomach.

As you see no value in proper care of my bronze man, I have rolled up my sleeves and taken the steps that I must. Many of my friends and their husbands have some interest in automation; they were good enough to loan me several relevant books. After many long hours of study – and more than one grave mistake! – I have successfully altered the bronze man's persona. He is more independent, less critical. And to my great relief, he no longer samples the cooking. George, you might have warned me of his waste disposal methods. I would have learned eventually.

The summer grows long. The months pass without news of you. Please, my husband – remember me.

Loving and trusting,
Margaret

* * *

My Dearest George:

I beg you to forgive me for the impertinent tone of my previous letters. I fear the strain of your absence leads me to forget my place. If it is your wish, I will make no further adjustments to the bronze man, and I truly and humbly welcome any details of your adventures. You are risking so much for our sake, I can do no less.

I am pleased to hear of your successes out West. I pray daily for your safety. Every day brings us closer again.

Your brother has been by again, and this time I observed him pluck a figurine from the mantle and put it into his pocket! When I made it clear that I had seen, he claimed that it was his and he had been 'meaning to reclaim it'. I did not prevent him, but I write this so that you may confirm or more probably refute his story. If the figurine is in fact yours, I shall call on your brother and snatch it again from his mantelpiece. It is the ivory figure of a shepherd inlaid with gold. Please do reply, I am anxious to confront him.

Be safe, my darling.

Your contrite
and ever loving
Margaret

* * *

GEORGE STOP TERRIBLE ACCUSATIONS REGARDING FINANCES STOP PLEASE WIRE EXPLANATION STOP I DO NOT KNOW WHAT TO MAKE OF IT STOP POSTSCRIPT I LOVE YOU STOP MARGARET STOP

* * *

GEORGE PLEASE WRITE TO ME STOP VERY WORRIED STOP MARGARET STOP

* * *

George:

While I am still very anxious to hear what you have to say for yourself, I have ferreted out the truth and must – as a dutiful wife and a once-trusting woman – confront you with it.

After you accused your brother of theft, I of course visited him at once. I took the bronze man along – in case of trouble. I admit this was against your wishes. In light of what I learned, I do not regret it.

The figurine was not upon his mantle, as I had hoped, so I, very sweetly, inquired as to where he had it. He looked stunned. When I told him that I knew it was yours, and that he had boldly stolen it, he threw back his head and let out a hard laugh, the likes of which I had never heard from him.

He began to describe in wretched detail a slanderous story: a story about you, George. How you had sunk into debts by gambling and vices even more vile. How you had settled for a wife with a small dowry so that you might pay down enough to allow you to escape West, where your creditors might not reach you. How your brother had been slowly paying off your debts with things stolen from your own home – from our home! – so that I might remain unmolested and the family name untarnished. How you had little inclination to return to us.

I could not believe any of this, and said as much. I (and the bronze man) left in a fury. We went immediately to the telegraph office to wire you for an explanation, which you, of course, passed off with a blithe reply that I should not worry. I should not worry! Either our finances are ruinous or our family a den of treachery! This could not go unexamined, and I did not allow it to.

George, I have met with your creditors. I know all. Whether by my own charms or by the very significant presence of the bronze man, I have obtained detailed accounts of your debt. You will be pleased to know that a schoolteacher's daughter is well equipped to do sums. You will be less pleased to find that she can read, and can therefore discover where your wayward finances have gone.

By the time you receive this I will have begun selling your personal effects in order to pay your monstrous debt. I trust you will have little need of them until you return East, if indeed you do, and I will rely upon your brother to spare any family heirlooms from the pawnshop. No wonder your parents thought so ill of me, and so well of him! We are colored by your shadow.

If you have any wish to regain my affections or explain yourself, I encourage you to act with all haste.

Margaret

* * *

Dear George:

Forgive me for being indelicate. I find your declarations of love, unaccompanied as they are by admission of guilt or sincere regret, unconvincing.

As for your inquiry regarding our estate, you might as well be apprised of the mess you have left behind. To repay your debts and maintain a reputable house is a trying puzzle. Your finest clothes and articles are not worth so much as I had hoped. I maintain the staff – I must! For the sake of the future and the neighborhood – and am successfully paying down your interest, but little of the principle. If you ever cared for me, George, send money, that we might not lose all. Even the distasteful set of illustrations secreted in your mattress did not bring in enough.

I have again adjusted the bronze man (who I have taken to calling 'Samson' for his girth) to better serve his position as the man of the house; in this new situation I require him to be defender and protector, as well as servant. You cannot fault me for wishing to protect my person. Nor can you fault me the desire to save money by performing the adjustment myself!

I am considering a plan to offer my services to make ends meet. Were you by my side, we might discuss this as lovers and helpmeets; as you prefer the lonely West, I must decide on my own.

The season grows cold here. I can only assume it is the worse where you are. I wish you well.

Your wife,
Margaret

* * *

GEORGE STOP I AM APPALLED AT YOUR INSINUATION STOP I AM NOT SO IMMORAL AS YOU THINK ME STOP LET US WASTE NO MORE WORDS ON THIS THEY ARE TOO DEAR STOP MARGARET STOP

* * *

Dear George:

If I suspected you were suffering for your indiscretions, I would tell you that you may now rest easy: the last of your creditors has been paid. Your debt is gone.

Shocked as I am at the lengths you thought me willing to go, I admit proudly that I earned the difference myself – not through the scandalous means you suspected, but by nimbleness of a different sort altogether. In allowing Samson to accompany me on social calls, I was able to advertise my own talent for making alterations to his brand of automaton – a popular one, you will recall. My friends placed a few orders, and were happy to pass on my name to others with the highest recommendations. Now half the bronze men in the city have a sweeter temperament. And you and I are free.

Your brother has spoken to your parents on my behalf. They graciously hosted me last weekend. I hope to return their generosity soon. From them I heard stories of the gentleman you were before being overtaken by your vices. I wonder: though the new George went West, could the old George return?

In the meantime, I have made one additional alteration to Samson. I intend it to help me bear the cold winter nights. So far, he performs admirably. The neighborhood ladies have been intrigued and I expect a few more discreet orders *in the near future. So should your grand Western dreams fail, dear George, know that I shall be financially secure. And until you return to me, George, I shall not be lonely. I have my bronze man.*

These sixteen months shall not last so long. I pray that they pass as pleasantly for you as they are sure to do for me.

Dutifully, lovingly, I send you all my best.

Still yours,
Margaret

Pax Mechanica

Daniel J. Davis

AS SOON AS the machine stumbled in the river's current, Quintonius knew they were in trouble. The centurion silently prayed to the gods, naming everyone from Jupiter to Sol, but the heavy Roman war-walker only managed another three steps. Then it lurched and stopped, a sudden explosion of steam and shredded metal erupting from the rear quarter.

The other two legionnaires aboard the walker scrambled aft, their cloaks pulled up against the escaping steam. The engineer Varus covered his hands and worked a valve, slowly diminishing the flow, until at last he could see the extent of the damage. Almost immediately, Quintonius heard a string of curses uncharacteristic of the younger man.

Varus backed away from the mangled piping. "It's bad, sir."

Before he could stop himself, Quintonius glanced at the century's battle standard, the red and yellow banner that flapped on the war-walker's bow. A feeling of unease crept its way over him. *It was a mistake to bring the colors on this mission,* he thought.

He scanned the north bank. They'd made it more than halfway across. That put them closer to the barbarians' territory than it did their own men, the meager scouting detachment of forty legionnaires lined up on the southern bank. And while the Celts had abandoned their side at the war-walker's approach, they were still exposed and vulnerable here.

"Can you fix it?"

Varus doffed his helmet and ran a hand over his short-cropped hair. He let out a long grunt. "I don't think so, sir. I can swap out the burst section of pipe, but there's got to be a pressure problem somewhere down in the guts. She's going to need a magista to work properly again."

Quintonius swore. The magista were the Republic's miracle workers. Trained from childhood in the arts of thaumaturgy and alchemy, they were both magicians and engineers, skilled at transmuting iron into harder metals, and using them to create fantastic mechanisms. They maintained the airships, war-walkers, and other machines that had given Rome her supremacy over half the world.

Unfortunately, the nearest magista was Antonius, ranking Artificer to the Eighth Legion. And in his infinite wisdom, General Caesar had left the man across the sea in Gaul.

This is why I prefer war-elephants, Quintonius thought. He leaned on the walker's gunwale, peering over the side. Below, half a spear's length from the machine's iron belly, the river Tamesis churned around the walker's four motionless legs. He estimated the water to be no deeper than a man's neck.

Not ideal fording conditions for heavy infantry. Especially not if the barbarians returned.

He turned to Titus, his veteran standard-bearer. The man wore a slight mocking smile, one that fell just short of insubordination. Quintonius shot him a warning look. He wouldn't tolerate open disrespect.

Whatever Titus intended to say, he chose to keep it to himself. "Your orders, sir?"

"Get on the trumpet. Blow a signal to Galvinius. Get him to move two squads to the northern bank. I want to secure this crossing before these savages find their courage again."

The other man looked past his commander. His expression darkened. "It might be too late for that, sir."

On the northern bank was a single Celt. He stood at a break in the fir trees, up where the land rose away from the river. Even at this distance, Quintonius could tell he was a member of the ruling caste.

"I thought we'd seen the last of him," Varus said. "I would have bet a month's wages he was still running, the way he took off earlier."

Quintonius didn't respond. He couldn't remember seeing this man among the barbarians that had abandoned the hasty defenses. Unlike the rest of the rabble that turned heel, he appeared tall and well fed. He wore a shirt of mail and a crested helmet, and he had the drooping moustache and clean-shaven jaw of a Celtic aristocrat. In his hand he held a long sword.

He's a chieftain, Quintonius thought. *Maybe a king.*

The Celt pointed his weapon at the stranded walker. Then, with the flat of the blade, he began to beat a steady tattoo on the rim of his oval-shaped shield.

The hackles on Quintonius' neck went up. Reflexively, his hand went to his left hip, to the hilt of his gladius. "Varus, get this machine moving."

The young engineer looked from the ruptured steam line to his commander. "I – I don't know if I can, sir."

"If you value what's attached to your neck, you're going to damned well try." In Gaul, Quintonius had seen tribal chieftains decorate their walls with rivals' heads, hammering iron spikes through the eyes to hold them in place. If they committed such savagery against one another, Quintonius shuddered at what they might do to a Roman invader.

Titus leaned close. He spoke under his breath. "Worried you're about to earn the same glories as your father, sir?"

"Be silent!"

Titus gripped the pole of the battle standard. "I can just swim over and hand it to him, if you like."

Quintonius wheeled on him, ready to deliver a backhand to the insolent man, but the look of frustration in Titus' eyes stopped him. He'd carried the century's colors for years now, Quintonius reminded himself. He'd fought for and earned that privilege. The thoughts of losing it in battle – and the fear of the dishonor that came along with such failure – were written plainly across the man's face.

"We're not going to let the colors fall, Titus. And I'll ask you not to mention Praetor Simonius in my presence. Ever."

"Yes, sir."

Varus bent to the ruptured line. He pulled a leather satchel from a hidden compartment and dumped it. A set of tools and some short lengths of piping spilled to the walker's deck. The young engineer quickly snatched the ones he needed.

Quintonius returned his attention to the Celt. The man was no longer alone. Another clutch of warriors had joined him. These were bare-chested, as tall and well fed as their leader. All carried shields and spears, and wore the distinctive long moustache and clean-shaven jaw of the barbarians' ruling class. Blue symbols were painted on their bodies with woad. One by one, they joined the armored man's tattoo, banging their spear shafts against their shields.

Quintonius addressed Titus without taking his eyes from the shore. "Signal Galvinius. Tell him to hold position." The standard bearer hesitated but did as he was told, blowing three short blasts into the walker's mounted trumpet.

"But sir," Varus said. "Shouldn't we call them forward?"

The centurion shook his head. "We're within the barbarians' javelin range. The river would be clogged with their corpses before they reached us."

As Quintonius watched, more Celts emerged from the trees. Whatever tactical advantage he'd gained by showing the war-walker was rapidly disappearing. The barbarians were losing their initial fear of the iron monster. Twenty warriors became forty. Forty became a hundred. A hundred became two.

The Celts issued a thundering war cry, a rising scream more animal than human.

"Sir!" Titus grabbed his commander by the shoulder, pointing south.

Quintonius cursed. "What is that damned idiot doing?"

Galvinius had ordered a charge. The forty legionnaires were all in the river, wading towards the immobilized walker. Already knee deep in the water, they were rapidly pushing forward.

"Sound a retreat!" Quintonius ordered. "Get them back on that bank!"

Titus blew two short blasts. When the men didn't listen, he blew the signal again. Quintonius snatched a javelin from the walker's weapon rack and threw it, striking the river a few steps from Galvinius. The charging legionnaire drew up short.

"Get those men back!" Quintonius shouted. For emphasis, Titus sounded retreat a third time. In a tangled jumble of men, shields, and spears, the legionnaires reversed their charge, climbing out of the river and re-forming on the southern bank.

Stupid, Quintonius thought. Stringing the legionnaires across the river would only nullify their fighting strength. The Celts would have picked them off easily. Galvinius should have seen that. More importantly, he should have obeyed orders. Like Titus' insubordination, it was a breach of discipline that would have to be addressed.

If we survive.

A Celt's javelin struck the hull of the walker with a sharp, metallic ring. Quintonius spun. While his attention was focused on his own men, a dozen of the barbarians had made their way to the edge of the water. They took turns posturing for their comrades, raising their weapons overhead and shouting. Each time, they were met with a thunderous cheer. Their armored chieftain stood by the trees, looking on.

Quintonius unfastened his shield from its stowage hook on the gunwale. He passed it to Titus. "Cover Varus while he works. Quickly!"

No sooner had he spoken than another javelin streaked overhead. It clattered off the rear quarter of the walker. Titus took position, holding his shield up and at an angle over himself and the engineer. On the riverbank, the Celts jeered and taunted. Quintonius ducked low, reaching for another shield. He brought it up barely in time.

Javelins rained on them, striking shield, deck, and hull. The Celts cheered wildly every time one of the missiles hit home. Dozens of them struck, their metal tips clanging against the walker's iron hull. At last, after what seemed like minutes, the barrage tapered off. Quintonius lifted his head to peek at the shore.

Three of the Celts had gotten brave. They were in the river, wading towards the walker while their comrades took up the rhythm of a savage battle song. Quintonius dropped his shield. He seized the remaining pair of javelins from the weapon rack. He took aim at the Celt in the lead, a man still twenty yards distant and waist-deep in water. He waited for the natural swing of the man's arms to carry his shield just a hand's-breadth to the left. Then he made his throw.

It was an expert cast, and the javelin stuck the warrior's painted chest just beside the sternum. The force of the impact knocked him down, and he floundered in the river attempting to get his feet back under him. Then he went still, the water around him turning red before gently carrying him away.

Quintonius didn't waste a moment. He lined up his shot at the next man. Again, he timed it to the natural swing of the warrior's arms. But the Celt brought his shield back up, catching the javelin on its face. The warriors on the riverbank cheered. The Celt brought the shaft of his spear down across his shield, neatly snapping Quintonius' javelin off at the head. The useless shaft swirled in the river for a second, seeming to pause in place. Then it followed the dead barbarian downstream.

Quintonius glanced at the weapons rack. There were still three of the heavy pila spears, the legionnaire's famous primary weapon, but they were only suitable for fighting in close formation. They were next to useless for throwing.

Titus lowered his shield and looked to his commander. "Sir?"

"Keep protecting Varus," Quintonius ordered. "If he falls we're dead for sure." He took up one of the pila and prepared to repel boarders.

The lead warrior was much closer now, less than five yards away. The water was up to his upper chest. He held the spear and the shield overhead, keeping them dry. At last he reached the left front leg of the walker. Quintonius leaned against the gunwale, the pilum resting easy in his right hand.

The Celt worked his shield over one forearm to free his hand. He gripped the walker's leg. Quintonius waited for him to begin hauling himself upward. Then he drove the pilum into the warrior's face. The tip erupted out the back of the man's neck, and he spasmed and jerked before falling sideways. As his body sagged the pilum was ripped from Quintonius' grip.

Shit, he thought. The way things were going they'd be unarmed soon. And then …

And then you'll go down in history alongside your father. Quintonius, son of Simonius. The second generation of his family to lose a standard in battle.

Once again, he glanced at the banner flapping on the walker's bow. He'd nearly left it at the rear, with the men who'd remained as part Caesar's main body. But a desire to escape the stigma of his father's dishonor had compelled him to bring it, the only one of the scouting detachments to do so. If a Roman force was going to cross the Tamesis today, he'd thought, then let it be his century's colors planted in the barbarians' soil. Let the history books remember his name.

Stupid, he thought. It was nothing but stupid pride and a hunger to prove he wasn't his father. Now that stupidity had all but guaranteed he'd be forced to fall on his sword, sealing his legacy as Simonius' son forever.

He reached for another pilum.

The last Celt to reach the walker was smarter. He attempted to stab upward with his spear rather than immediately dropping his shield. But the barbarian was still fighting from an inferior position, on unsure footing and struggling with the river's current. Quintonius sparred back and forth with the man, easily faking, thrusting, and blocking with the shaft of his pilum.

At last, he saw his opening. He delivered a solid thrust that pierced the man's shoulder at an angle. The pilum grated against bone, a satisfying shudder travelling up the shaft into

Quintonius' hands. The Celt screamed and clutched at the weapon, his own spear drifting away on the river's current. The centurion leaned over the gunwale, driving his weight downward and pushing the pilum deeper into the man's body.

The warrior's scream abruptly cut off. Quintonius released the pilum, and the dead barbarian floated downstream after his friends.

"Varus, status report."

The engineer threw a mangled section of pipe over the side. "It's still not looking good, sir."

"It's going to look worse when they're bearing our heads back to their hill-forts. Get this machine working."

"Yes, sir!"

Quintonius watched the barbarians. They were still chanting war cries, still cheering the few that postured in front of the main line. He had seen similar displays in Gaul. The Celts had certain war rituals, intended to prove individual courage and prowess. They would send champions forward to engage in single combat before the battle. That was why the javelin barrage had stopped. It gave the three warriors a chance to approach alone, to test themselves before their peers. It was a game. The next step – once they tired of this display – would be a wave of screaming barbarians, one that would swallow the walker's crew before crushing Galvinius' men on the south bank. He envisioned the Celts then marching south to Caesar's line, carrying the torn and soiled battle standard with them.

He needed more time. He needed a way to delay the enemy's charge as long as possible.

Quintonius had a mad thought, then. *To forestall the charge, one could always prolong the game.*

"Engineer Varus," he said. "If you get this machine working again, reverse course and bring our colors back to Galvinius' line. Do not let it fall into enemy hands. Am I understood?"

It was Titus who spoke. "What are you going to do, sir?"

"I'm going to try the barbarians' style of warfare."

Quintonius doffed his helmet. He shrugged out of his mail armor and tunic, leaving only a pair of linen breeches. He reached into the space Varus was working, gathering some machine grease on his fingers. He used it to draw rough symbols on his chest. They were completely meaningless, but the intent wasn't to gain mystical protection, or courage, or whatever else these barbarians believed the woad-symbols did.

It was to issue a challenge. One that would easily cross the language barrier.

Quintonius stood on the bow of the war-walker. He drew his gladius and held it high, and did his best to mimic the wild-animal war cry of the Celts.

Several of the warriors on shore laughed. A few threw javelins. Quintonius stood firm, forcing himself not to flinch as they whistled close. One nicked the side of his face, white-hot pain searing its way up his cheek.

Quintonius pointed his gladius at the armored chieftain. Once again, he issued the war cry. Then he jumped into the river.

The cold water hit him like a wall. Quintonius gasped at the sudden shock, and as soon as his feet found purchase he began to work towards the shore. The flow of the Tamesis threatened to carry him away, to sweep his legs out from under him and deposit him downstream among the dead. He forged on, fighting the current, planting his feet, and pulling himself ever closer to the northern bank.

In Gaul, Quintonius had been present for the torture of a druid. He learned the Celts had no fear of death. They believed it was always nearby, that the veil between the Earth and the otherworld was thin. He dismissed it as barbarian superstition at the time. But now, charging the enemy alone and unarmored, he saw why they believed it. For the barbarians it was true. This was battle as they knew it. Not shield walls and formations, but the mad rush to the enemy's spear points.

Quintonius embraced it wholly.

The water was below his waist now, the river's current a gentle tug at his legs. Another of the Celts had waded into the shallows to meet him. Not the chieftain, but another of the woad-painted champions. The Celt drove forward, thrusting with his spear.

Quintonius knocked the strike aside with his gladius. He closed, grabbing the top rim of the barbarian's shield and pulling it downward. The Celt tried to hit him with the shaft of his spear, but Quintonius was too close for the blow to have any power. He drove his gladius into the man's unprotected breast, angling the blade so it slipped between the ribs just above the heart.

The Celt was dead before Quintonius pulled his sword free.

The warriors on the shore fell silent. Whether from shock or respect for the dead man, Quintonius couldn't say. It didn't matter. He pointed at the chieftain, seizing the opportunity to be heard.

"You!" he shouted. Quintonius' command of the barbarian tongue was awful. But like any soldier, he'd learned a handful of the more colorful phrases. "*Sugh mo bhod! Soith!*" He uttered a few more, throwing out half-remembered words for 'mother', 'whore', and 'goat'.

Like his approximation of the woad-paint and the mimicking of their war cries, he knew the meaning would transcend his butchery of the language.

It was only a moment before he saw the effect he was hoping for. Several of the warriors looked away from him, and instead looked to their chieftain.

The armored man stood silently for a moment. Then he handed off his shield. He walked down from the break in the trees. As he came he removed his helmet and his mail shirt, tossing them aside for retainers to pick up. All around him, the barbarians beat their shields, howled their war cries, and cheered. The warriors at the water's edged parted for him, and he waded into the river.

As the chieftain stood before him, Quintonius finally got the full measure of the man. He stood nearly a head taller than the centurion. The Celt was strawberry-haired and heavily built, with streaks of gray beginning to show in his hair and moustache. Old and new scars crisscrossed his body. Like the other warriors before him, the man's torso and face were covered in woad paint. His long sword rested in his right hand, the blade nearly a forearm's length longer than Quintonius' gladius.

Quintonius studied that blade. It was an advantage for the Celt. One he needed to negate if he were going to buy Varus more time.

He had a flash of inspiration then. It was a long shot. But if it worked …

He waited until the Celt got within a few paces of him. Then he tossed his gladius away. He kept his eyes on the barbarian, not bothering to look where his weapon landed. He spread his arms and smiled.

The Celt stopped. His eyes narrowed as he studied Quintonius, and they burned with a barely contained rage.

Quintonius' grin widened. From what he knew of the barbarians' social rules, cutting down an unarmed man wouldn't prove the chieftain's courage or recover his honor. Even in death, Quintonius would have unmanned him in front of his people. If the chieftain wanted to save face, he only had one choice left to make.

The Celt, to his credit, managed to insult Quintonius in the civilized tongue. "Roman dog." Then he drove the point of his sword into the river muck.

The centurion's satisfaction was short lived. With a sudden violence the Celt exploded forward, battering Quintonius with both his massive forearms. He swung them like clubs, landing powerful blows on Quintonius' head and shoulders. The centurion staggered under their force, maneuvering and covering. He tried to find an opening to counterattack, but it was all he could do to cover and roll with the strikes.

He disengaged just long enough to risk a glance at the stranded walker. Varus still worked feverishly. Titus still protected him. The battle standard still waved.

Come on, damn it!

The next time the Celt landed a blow, his hands snaked around Quintonius' head. Quintonius drove two hard punches into the man's midsection, but it was no more effective than hitting a stone wall. The barbarian heaved, jerking Quintonius off his feet and plunging him beneath the waist-deep water. Massive hands found his throat. They closed in an iron grip and began to squeeze. Quintonius tried to kick, to claw, but nothing had any effect. The barbarian drove a knee into his chest, forcing the air from his lungs in an eruption of murky bubbles.

Then Quintonius heard a rumbling, churning sound in the water. The Celt's grip slackened. Quintonius took advantage, slipping free and biting the first section of flesh his mouth touched. He wrenched back and forth, tearing skin and tasting blood.

When the centurion broke the surface he saw two things. The first was the war-walker, with Varus at the helm, plodding towards the Celtic line. The second was that the Celt no longer stood between Quintonius and the sword he'd driven into the river muck.

With a desperate cry, Quintonius dove for the weapon. The chieftain saw what he was doing and followed, but a split-second too late. Quintonius reached the sword first. He drew the weapon and spun, aiming a slash at the barbarian's neck. Iron connected with flesh, then bone. The Celt staggered and fell, his head rolling from his shoulders.

Quintonius did not pause. He spun to meet the next opponent from the barbarian side. But there was none. Once again, the sight of Rome's steam-powered monster had set them running. Woad-painted men fled into the trees, shouting oaths and curses in their Gaelic tongue.

Titus blew a single long blast from the walker's trumpet, the signal to charge. On the south bank Galvinius led the men into the river. It was another breach of discipline. But one the centurion just might decide to overlook, under the circumstances.

With an exhausted sigh, Quintonius fished the chieftain's head from the water. Caesar would no doubt see it as a useful tool for quelling further resistance. He'd present it to the General personally when the main force arrived. But first, he had to get to that break in the fir trees.

It would be the perfect place for the son of Simonius to plant his battle standard.

Fire to Set the Blood

Jennifer Dornan-Fish

Brodie, CA 1853

NAJA PUSHED aside the greasy blanket that hung over the doorway. The dim hall reeked of piss and sawdust. She tried not to let her medical bag brush against the peeling red wallpaper.

"This way, ma'am." The young man eyed Naja with clear suspicion. He led her through the old mine offices now taken over by his family of squatters. He held up his oil lamp to make sure she was keeping up as he ducked into a cramped room.

Naja gasped.

The girl on the cot was worse than she expected, nothing but bird bones held together by parchment flesh.

With practiced efficiency she set down her bag and pulled out what she would need – stethoscope, lancets, thermometer.

The man hovered, confused. "Thought you was a witch."

"I am, but I'm also a doctor. I need to make sure she isn't just sick."

"She fell feverish the same time as all the other kids. Hasn't moved since."

"Hum," Naja acknowledged softly. She'd just come from Linton Manor where both of the Linton girls were similarly ill. Far as Naja could tell, every single child in the town of Brodie, rich as the Lintons or poor as this girl, had fallen to the fever at the exact same moment.

Naja felt the girl's burning forehead. At her gentle touch the girl's eyes flew open, sharp with terror. Magic buzzed through Naja's body and she instinctively yanked her hand away.

"What's her name?" Naja kept her voice low.

"Sadie."

"Sadie, can you hear me?"

The girl's body remained relaxed, unmoving, eyes wide and unblinking. Naja lifted the false bottom of her medical bag and extracted her hidden gear – a shallow oaken bowl, amate paper, a satchel of corpse dust, a bone needle.

Naja paused, it'd been a long time since she'd cast a real spell. No one burned witches any more, but it was still dangerous, never knew when folks would turn on you. She spared a glance at the young man. Would he blame her if Sadie didn't survive?

Naja let herself picture the mountain cabin she'd spent the last five years building. Her small medical practice back in Seven Pines. Life out here on the edges of the world suited her just fine and it didn't take a divination for her to know things here in Brodie would be the end of that peace. If she wanted a quiet life she should walk away now, leave this little girl and all the other children of Brodie to die.

Damn it.

With a resigned sigh, Naja flattened a crackling sheet of bark paper onto the cot. She lifted the bone needle and pricked her finger. Using the bloody tip of the needle she wrote on the paper, dipping the needle again and again into the crimson ink flowing from her finger.

As she toiled, the young man backed slowly out of the room, fear radiating off him like heat.

Finally happy with the sigil, Naja put her finger in her mouth and let the slow trickle of blood coat her tongue.

She gently rolled the paper into a tight scroll and placed it in the bowl. Pulling flint from her pocket, Naja lit the paper.

As it burned, she sprinkled a pinch of corpse dust over the flame. Smoke poured from the bowl, filling the room with the scent of death like ancient creosote.

"Will this fix Sadie?"

"No, this will just reveal any magic being used against her. I need to know what we're dealing with before I can help."

Once the embers cooled, Naja took a calming breath.

"Don't let any of this get on you."

The young man nodded vigorously and stepped even further away till only his head peeked around the door.

She held the bowl up to her mouth and took a long breath in. Pulp, blood, and magic entered her lungs. Above the girl Naja blew out sharply. The ash swirled into the air and then floated down.

A figure emerged beneath the black dust – the sinewy corpse crouched over Sadie like an animal, bony hands around her throat, writhing body pressing her to the cot.

"What the hell is it!" the young man cried out.

Naja stumbled back, covering her mouth.

As the ash drifted to the ground the figure disappeared leaving only the girl, eyes wide open, heart fluttering her little chest like a butterfly.

"It's Sadie's own death come to claim her," Naja croaked.

"Can you …save her?"

The question snapped Naja out of her horrified reverie. Her medical training took over – analyze the problem, come up with a solution, implement the solution.

"Everyone's death is always with them," she said clinically, packing her gear. "It might brush up against you, but for most of our lives death hovers in the distance like an aura, getting slowly closer as your time approaches."

She hefted her bag.

"But this is no brush with death. Powerful witches can manipulate the dead around us, can call it up, control it."

"So how do we …?"

"How do we stop it? First I have to figure out who or what's doing this. To control the dead, you have to take a small piece of it inside yourself. The most powerful witch I've ever known could bring the dead onto one person. One. To fell all the children here at once … well that's got to be twenty kids. I've never even heard of someone that powerful."

"What do I do?"

"You stay here. Don't let anyone touch her." Naja strode past him, boots echoing on the rough hewn floor.

"And you?" he called after her.

Without glancing back she growled, "I'm going to hunt a monster."

* * *

Naja's long skirt dragged in the red dust as she walked up Main Street. She squinted in the hazy afternoon, thinking. Who hated these people enough to curse their children?

Skeletal horses nickered as she passed, hoping for a sugar cube. A woman glared from the window above the boarded-up general store. Two men sat out front of the saloon, eyeing her with open hostility. Suspicion fell over the town like a shroud and she was an outsider come just after their kids fell sick. For all they knew, Naja was to blame for that.

For all they knew, she was to blame for everything gone wrong in Brodie over the past few years – the dry mine, the dying town.

She straightened her back and tromped toward Angel's Rest Saloon. Maybe someone there could answer her question.

Inside, two groups of men hunched around pockmarked tables. They looked up, chatter dying off as she crossed the room.

A plump native woman nodded to her from behind the bar.

"Get you something to drink?"

"You have any cold beer?"

The woman snorted. "I'll make you a gin 'n ginger." She filled a gritty glass and slid it to Naja. "You the witch doctor the Lintons asked to come about the girls?"

Naja inclined her head in agreement and sipped the warm drink. Back when she started her practice, she'd sold simple charms to make extra cash. Seemed harmless at the time but now she regretted letting people know about being a witch. Dammed fool thing to do.

"I'm Naja."

"Genevieve, though most call me Genny. Run Angel's Rest for Mr. Linton, all that entails …"

The two let a moment of silence pass between them, the unspoken camaraderie of lone women like them living in places like this.

"Thing makin' those kids sick ain't natural," Genny said, more a comment than question.

"Agreed. I'm hoping to figure out who'd hate Brodie enough to curse their kids."

"Well, not many folks left here at all. The miners all gone. Just a few squatters in the old mine offices. All their kids'er sick too so can't be them. All the girls that worked here left last year. I stayed 'cause I got family nearby, plus there's still some blood to squeeze from this stone." She laughed, eyeing the men in the saloon with a mixture of amusement and malice.

"What about those three?" Naja raised her chin toward the closest group of men.

Genny frowned. "Tall one's Billy Linton, Mr. Linton's brother. Ran the hard-rock mine before it dried up. The two with him are Hence and Carl Cobb. Used to run the general store before it closed. Now they mostly run up tabs here." She smiled revealing nubby yellow teeth.

Naja considered Billy Linton and the Cobb brothers, men with the soft boyishness of those used to easy work and getting their way.

"And those two in the far corner?"

Two men silently sipped drinks in the shadows. Unlike Linton and his crew, the two men wore travel-worn clothes and wind-scarred faces.

"They weren't even here when the kids got sick. Just slave catchers chasing some caravan of escape slaves. Say they'll split the $2000 reward if we help nab all of 'em that got away."

Naja stared down at her drink and steadied her voice. "Thought California was freeland. Slaves made it here were safe."

"Used to be, but some new law passed few years back."

Naja had passed as white for so long she almost never felt nervous about her past, but the day left her defenses low. Her breath came fast, heart began to roar in her ears, hands began to tremor.

She stood up too quickly sending the stool shrieking across the floor. "The outhouse out back?"

"Yeah, you okay?"

"Fine, just need a moment."

She stumbled to the outhouse seeking privacy while the memories had hold of her.

It's just fear making you sick. Get it together. Naja tried to clear her mind. It'd been a long time since she'd had a flashback. Not even six years old, she hadn't fully understood what was happening as her family made their escape. But she'd understood the fear in her mother's as Naja was left behind with the white couple that agreed to take pale little Naja in and pretend she was their own.

What a terrible mistake coming to Brodie had been. Could she run back to Seven Pines?

Naja wiped sweat from her lip and stepped out into the evening light. Run or fight? What kind of woman are you, Naja?

Naja was about to head back in when the saloon door banged open. The Cobb brothers exited behind Billy to form a semi-circle. Testosterone and anger crackled in the juniper air.

"Hear you'se a witch."

Naja squared her shoulders. "I'm a doctor." Her voice sounded stronger than she expected.

"Nah, I heard you did some magic to Sadie. You know what happened out there at Brimstone, you bitch?" Billy took an unsteady half step toward her.

Fiery spikes of adrenaline clouded Naja's vision.

The saloon door banged open again.

"What's going on out here?" Genny stepped out with Valkyrie eyes.

"Just asking the witch what she done to our kids," Billy slurred.

"Now Billy, you know for a fact that your brother asked her here to help. She wasn't even in town when the kids got sick."

"Far as we know," he took another step toward Naja.

Naja smelled sour whisky on his breath.

Genny's voice sharpened. "Don't be a fool. You want to explain to Henry why you're bothering the doctor he brought to help the girls?" Her voice softened into a caress. "Listen, you lot are drunk. Let her do her job."

The men stopped their advance, lulled by gentle reason.

Genny gestured Naja inside.

Naja skirted the men and slid through the door. Fear shuddered and arced between the two women as the door swiffed shut.

"Thank you," Naja squeezed Genny's hand.

"Best go up to your room." She pressed a key into Naja's palm. "The Lintons paid for it, sent your bag up. The boys'll calm down once you're out of sight."

As Naja hurried up the stairs, Genny whispered after her, "You want to save the kids, you go see what Billy Linton's got in his barn. He's hiding somethin out there."

* * *

In her room, Naja stared at the vial in her shaking hand. One potion.

Damn it.

She held the vial to the candlelight and tapped the glass. Flakes of crimson cinnabar. Chunks of poplar ash. Thick black globs of menstrual blood. A protection potion that should shield someone from just about anything ...assuming it still even worked. She'd made the potion years ago.

Damn it all to hell. She'd fought her way into medical school to avoid this kind of thing.

Naja cinched the vial onto her belt and took a long swig of whiskey from the flask in her travel bag.

Night transformed her windows into black voids.

Time to see what Billy Linton was hiding.

* * *

Naja paused so her eyes could adjust to the maze of shadows. The barn smelled of barley and dried leather. Moonlight cut a silver streak across the hay-scattered floor.

Farm tools hung by her head and five stalls lined the back wall. The shuffling of hooves and horse breath came from the first four. Moaning echoed from the fifth stall – garbled sounds that built on each other like some fel orchestra tuning instruments.

One hand on the potion, Naja unlatched the gate and pulled.

Naja's breath caught. "Chloe?"

A small girl slept among the hay. No more than three or four years old, the girl's narrow lips parted in peaceful slumber. Her skin, dark as midnight, stood out against the yellow straw.

Black wisps roiled around the girl in knots of shrieking agony.

After a moment of wild longing, Naja realized the little girl was not really her dead sister.

Not Chloe then, but this girl was clearly at the heart of whatever was happening in Brodie. No way she was the witch. No child that young had so much power. Maybe some kind of possession?

Naja hugged her arms to her sides, contemplating what to do when footsteps approached.

She pulled up her skirt and leaped into the fourth stall, landing next to a grey stallion that snorted at her arrival.

Heavy boots thudded into the barn.

"It's still the same."

Billy Linton's boozy scent filled the stall.

"We got to do something, Billy. Henry'll kill you if he finds out what we done."

"Yeah, you might be right." Billy spoke a wood's-width away from Naja.

A shudder ran through her body. She balled her fists trying to still herself.

"You think the witch can really fix them kids?"

"Nah, she can't fix what we done out at Brimstone Gulch. We've got to kill this thing. Never should'a brought it here. So much for free merchandise."

"But, what if killin' that thing kills all the Brodie kids too?"

"Then we blame the witch and never tell anyone. You understand?"

"Billy, we can't just let all them kids die. Your nieces for God's sake."

"What choice we got? You want to be hanged for what we done? Plus, maybe it won't kill 'em. Maybe killing this thing's how we free 'em."

Silence stretched so long Naja thought for sure they could hear her heart pounding against the gate.

"God forgive us," one of the Cobb brothers finally whispered.

"Ain't no God here," Billy grunted back then cleared his throat. "It's decided. We can dump it down the mine later."

The three men left the barn. Naja collapsed to the floor, muscles quailing.

After a few shaky breaths she pulled herself up to contemplate the child.

"Analyze the problem, come up with a solution, implement the solution," Naja murmured trying to calm herself down.

The problem – she couldn't leave the girl here but couldn't pick her up without protection against whatever possessed her. Solution – she needed a sigil. Implement the solution …without pausing to overthink, Naja slid her finger along the blade of a rusty scythe. She sketched a protection symbol directly onto her cotton blouse, sticky blood soaking to her skin. With the flint from her pocket she lit a fistful of straw and pressed the burning clump against her chest.

Naja let out a low moan at the pain.

She scooped up the girl and paused to see what would happen. A shiver swept up her arms like pulling back a trigger to where the hammer's just about to fall, that sense of destructive potential in the tiniest movement, but then a tingling spread from the sigil at her chest, pushing it back.

"Well I'll be," Naja said surprised that the damned thing even worked.

Naja pulled them both onto the waiting stallion. Arms wrapped around the girl, hands tangled in the horse's mane, Naja kicked hard and they shot from the barn into the night.

They galloped toward Brimstone Gulch, a slot canyon not five miles west of Brodie. Naja would ride through the canyon, see what she could find, then continue on to the flats where she could circle back to Seven Pines. Get the girl far enough from Brodie and the curse would break, freeing the kids there. Maybe at home Naja could rid the girl of this demon possession.

She glanced back. In the distance three riders pursued them under the full moon. The dust they kicked up rose like a ghost lured home to the milky road of stars.

With saddles and no girl to keep ahold of, the men were gaining ground.

Naja leaned forward, legs quivering from riding bareback. The throaty huffing of the horse at full gallop replaced the sound of blood roaring in her ears. The cold snap of desert sage burned her nose.

They reached the base of the mountain and the sure-footed stallion slowed as the path climbed along narrow switchbacks. An opening appeared between two boulders and they entered Brimstone Gulch. Cold rock walls rose until the moon disappeared leaving nothing but a narrow band of stars to light the way.

Naja could no longer see the men but the sharp cracks of their reins echoed along the canyon until the sound folded back on itself. The staccato fugue triggered vivid flashbacks that took hold of her reason – running through the bayou, baying hounds and men on horseback running them down. Guns cracking. Papa crying out, white bone and red blood. The stench of stagnant water. Mama and aunt Cass dragging papa onward. Naja carrying Chloe, desperately trying to quiet her cries.

Like the little girl she was that night, Naja's world collapsed into one thought – escape.

They rounded a sharp curve. Lost in panic, Naja didn't see the rockfall until it was too late. The horse reared back but they still slammed into the rubble. Unseated, Naja cradled the girl as they crashed to the ground. The impact slammed her head to the ground.

Panting and dazed, she stared up at the rubble. Where the rocks had rolled away a flash of pale blue shone against the red rocks.

Some kind of cloth.

Confused, Naja crawled over to tug on the material.

A human arm flopped out of the debris, palm open to the sky.

Shuddering, she pushed aside more rocks. A torso emerged. Then the head of a woman, skull crushed, eyes closed. Naja wiped sand away from the dead woman's face revealing black skin. Naja's vision blurred and jumped. The face morphed into an image Naja conjured with the fragmented memory of a child.

"Mama?"

Tears running free, she clawed at the rubble. A woman's arm. Aunt Cass? A child's foot. Little Chloe? Body after body emerged, bone and flesh. Blood and stagnant water. Cracking guns.

"It's not them, it's not them," Naja bit her tongue to knock loose the hallucination. "It's the lost caravan."

Behind her, Billy and the Cobb brothers dismounted.

She stood to face the three men.

"Murderers." Her voice rumbled down the canyon like thunder. "You killed them."

The men stopped, hands resting on the guns at their hips.

"Why," Naja demanded.

"It was an accident."

"Shut up, Hence," Billy barked.

"No, maybe we can still fix this. We just meant to catch 'em ourselves. Why share the money with them bounty hunters? Could'a saved the whole town."

Hence stepped next to Billy. "We was gonna wait 'til they was in the canyon and blast the other end, trap 'em. Only they got caught in the rockfall. It was an accident."

"Liar!" A voice boomed from the shadows like two boards clapping together.

Naja and the men spun to face the girl who stood, body convulsing, eyes rolling.

"Tell the truth." Her words rang with the clangorous din of twenty voices. "Not all of us were dead. You left us to die." She jerked forward like a marionette, limbs akimbo.

"What else could we do?" Hence's voice spiked with panic. "We would've owed money for the ones we killed."

Watching the unconscious girl animated by death, Naja finally understood. When the canyon walls fell, she must have absorbed the dead of her loved ones. Rather than claim their own bodies, her terror and anger must have drawn the death inside her. Now she wielded power over death itself, fueled by the collective rage of a family destroyed.

The child's mouth spread into an impossible O and she vomited darkness.

A tempest of sinewy figures swirled into a funnel that ricocheted off the canyon wall like a twister out of control.

Billy Linton drew his gun.

The whirlwind pulled up sand and rocks in its vortex as it headed directly toward Naja. She yanked the protective potion free. Crush it on herself or save the girl?

The edges of the twister began to tear at Naja's flesh.

Billy Linton sighted down his pistol.

With a cry, Naja tossed the potion. It smashed with a whump onto the little girl's chest.

The bullet flew from Billy's gun and entered the puff of ash and magic. It slowed as if shot into molasses and fell harmless to the ground.

Naja closed her eyes with relief as the swirling death consumed her.

In the darkness, Naja heard screams. Gunshots. A small girl's voice.

Then nothing.

* * *

The promise of dawn glowed above the canyon when Naja opened her eyes.

The stallion nickered over her, gently nibbling her ear.

Bodies cluttered the canyon floor, most of them from the escape caravan, but Naja recognized Linton and the Cobb brothers crushed by rocks, bound forever to the dead they created.

Naja crawled over to the little girl. A faint haze of darkness still hovered around her. Naja felt for a heartbeat and found it, thready and fading. Only one thing could save a person who took in that much death – a piece of someone else's life.

She knelt by the girl as the rising sun raced up the canyon like a wildfire. Naja sang a desperate spell, scratching sigils in the dry earth with the blood that dripped from her fingers. The throaty chant came directly from Mama and Aunt Cass, from every woman that came before, from the earth and the sky and the girl's body beneath her hands. Her sonorous voice shook with tears as she sang for her own lost family.

She sang for all the lost children like her.

When she finished, Naja pressed her hands to the girl's chest.

"We'll forge something new," she whispered.

The sunlight hit them. In the blazing aura of dawn, the sigils began to smoke. Their blood mingled.

The girl let out a long exhale that Naja felt leave her own lungs. The cloak of death dissipated like summer dew.

The curse lifted and Naja imagined the children of Brodie waking from their fevered nightmare.

She struggled to her feet.

"Well, our blood's set now. Looks like we've found a new family, you and me."

With a grimace Naja picked up the child, stumbled to her new horse, and together they set off toward home.

The Horror of the Heights

Arthur Conan Doyle

THE IDEA that the extraordinary narrative which has been called the Joyce-Armstrong Fragment is an elaborate practical joke evolved by some unknown person, cursed by a perverted and sinister sense of humour, has now been abandoned by all who have examined the matter. The most macabre and imaginative of plotters would hesitate before linking his morbid fancies with the unquestioned and tragic facts which reinforce the statement. Though the assertions contained in it are amazing and even monstrous, it is none the less forcing itself upon the general intelligence that they are true, and that we must readjust our ideas to the new situation. This world of ours appears to be separated by a slight and precarious margin of safety from a most singular and unexpected danger. I will endeavour in this narrative, which reproduces the original document in its necessarily somewhat fragmentary form, to lay before the reader the whole of the facts up to date, prefacing my statement by saying that, if there be any who doubt the narrative of Joyce-Armstrong, there can be no question at all as to the facts concerning Lieutenant Myrtle, R.N., and Mr. Hay Connor, who undoubtedly met their end in the manner described.

The Joyce-Armstrong Fragment was found in the field which is called Lower Haycock, lying one mile to the westward of the village of Withyham, upon the Kent and Sussex border. It was on the 15th September last that an agricultural labourer, James Flynn, in the employment of Mathew Dodd, farmer, of the Chauntry Farm, Withyham, perceived a briar pipe lying near the footpath which skirts the hedge in Lower Haycock. A few paces farther on he picked up a pair of broken binocular glasses. Finally, among some nettles in the ditch, he caught sight of a flat, canvas-backed book, which proved to be a note-book with detachable leaves, some of which had come loose and were fluttering along the base of the hedge. These he collected, but some, including the first, were never recovered, and leave a deplorable hiatus in this all-important statement. The note-book was taken by the labourer to his master, who in turn showed it to Dr. J.H. Atherton, of Hartfield. This gentleman at once recognized the need for an expert examination, and the manuscript was forwarded to the Aero Club in London, where it now lies.

The first two pages of the manuscript are missing. There is also one torn away at the end of the narrative, though none of these affect the general coherence of the story. It is conjectured that the missing opening is concerned with the record of Mr. Joyce-Armstrong's qualifications as an aeronaut, which can be gathered from other sources and are admitted to be unsurpassed among the air-pilots of England. For many years he has been looked upon as among the most daring and the most intellectual of flying men, a combination which has enabled him to both invent and test several new devices, including the common gyroscopic attachment which is known by his name. The main body of the manuscript is written neatly in ink, but the last few lines are in pencil and are so ragged as to be hardly legible – exactly, in fact, as they might be expected to appear if they were scribbled off hurriedly from the seat of a moving aeroplane. There are, it may be added, several stains, both on the last page and on the outside cover which have been pronounced by the Home Office experts to be blood – probably human and certainly mammalian. The fact that something closely resembling the organism of malaria was discovered in this blood, and that Joyce-Armstrong is known to have suffered from intermittent fever, is a remarkable example of the new weapons which modern science has placed in the hands of our detectives.

And now a word as to the personality of the author of this epoch-making statement. Joyce-Armstrong, according to the few friends who really knew something of the man, was a poet and a dreamer, as well as a mechanic and an inventor. He was a man of considerable wealth, much of which he had spent in the pursuit of his aeronautical hobby. He had four private aeroplanes in his hangars near Devizes, and is said to have made no fewer than one hundred and seventy ascents in the course of last year. He was a retiring man with dark moods, in which he would avoid the society of his fellows. Captain Dangerfield, who knew him better than anyone, says that there were times when his eccentricity threatened to develop into something more serious. His habit of carrying a shot-gun with him in his aeroplane was one manifestation of it.

Another was the morbid effect which the fall of Lieutenant Myrtle had upon his mind. Myrtle, who was attempting the height record, fell from an altitude of something over thirty thousand feet. Horrible to narrate, his head was entirely obliterated, though his body and limbs preserved their configuration. At every gathering of airmen, Joyce-Armstrong, according to Dangerfield, would ask, with an enigmatic smile: "And where, pray, is Myrtle's head?"

On another occasion after dinner, at the mess of the Flying School on Salisbury Plain, he started a debate as to what will be the most permanent danger which airmen will have to encounter. Having listened to successive opinions as to air-pockets, faulty construction, and over-banking, he ended by shrugging his shoulders and refusing to put forward his own views, though he gave the impression that they differed from any advanced by his companions.

It is worth remarking that after his own complete disappearance it was found that his private affairs were arranged with a precision which may show that he had a strong premonition of disaster. With these essential explanations I will now give the narrative exactly as it stands, beginning at page three of the blood-soaked note-book:

"Nevertheless, when I dined at Rheims with Coselli and Gustav Raymond I found that neither of them was aware of any particular danger in the higher layers of the atmosphere. I did not actually say what was in my thoughts, but I got so near to it that if they had any corresponding idea they could not have failed to express it. But then they are two empty, vainglorious fellows with no thought beyond seeing their silly names in the newspaper. It is interesting to note that neither of them had ever been much beyond the twenty-thousand-foot level. Of course, men have been higher than this both in balloons and in the ascent of mountains. It must be well above that point that the aeroplane enters the danger zone – always presuming that my premonitions are correct.

"Aeroplaning has been with us now for more than twenty years, and one might well ask: Why should this peril be only revealing itself in our day? The answer is obvious. In the old days of weak engines, when a hundred horse-power Gnome or Green was considered ample for every need, the flights were very restricted. Now that three hundred horse-power is the rule rather than the exception, visits to the upper layers have become easier and more common. Some of us can remember how, in our youth, Garros made a worldwide reputation by attaining nineteen thousand feet, and it was considered a remarkable achievement to fly over the Alps. Our standard now has been immeasurably raised, and there are twenty high flights for one in former years. Many of them have been undertaken with impunity. The thirty-thousand-foot level has been reached time after time with no discomfort beyond cold and asthma. What does this prove? A visitor might descend upon this planet a thousand times and never see a tiger. Yet tigers exist, and if he chanced to come down into a jungle he might be devoured. There are jungles of the upper air, and there are worse things than tigers which inhabit them. I believe in time they will map these jungles accurately out. Even at the present moment I could name two of them. One of them lies over the Pau-Biarritz district of France. Another is just over my head as I write here in my house in Wiltshire. I rather think there is a third in the Homburg-Wiesbaden district.

"It was the disappearance of the airmen that first set me thinking. Of course, everyone said that they had fallen into the sea, but that did not satisfy me at all. First, there was Verrier in France; his machine was found near Bayonne, but they never got his body. There was the case of Baxter also, who vanished, though his engine and some of the iron fixings were found in a wood in Leicestershire. In that case, Dr. Middleton, of Amesbury, who was watching the flight with a telescope, declares that just before the clouds obscured the view he saw the machine, which was at an enormous height, suddenly rise perpendicularly upwards in a succession of jerks in a manner that he would have thought to be impossible. That was the last seen of Baxter. There was a correspondence in the papers, but it never led to anything. There were several other similar cases, and then there was the death of Hay Connor. What a cackle there was about an unsolved mystery of the air, and what columns in the halfpenny papers, and yet how little was ever done to get to the bottom of the business! He came down in a tremendous vol-plane from an unknown height. He never got off his machine and died in his pilot's seat. Died of what? 'Heart disease,' said the doctors. Rubbish! Hay Connor's heart was as sound as mine is. What did Venables say? Venables was the only man who was at his side when he died. He said that he was shivering and looked like a man who had been badly scared. 'Died of fright,' said Venables, but could not imagine what he was frightened about. Only said one word to Venables, which sounded like 'Monstrous.' They could make nothing of that at the inquest. But I could make something of it. Monsters! That was the last word of poor Harry Hay Connor. And he *did* die of fright, just as Venables thought.

"And then there was Myrtle's head. Do you really believe – does anybody really believe – that a man's head could be driven clean into his body by the force of a fall? Well, perhaps it may be possible, but I, for one, have never believed that it was so with Myrtle. And the grease upon his clothes – 'all slimy with grease,' said somebody at the inquest. Queer that nobody got thinking after that! I did – but, then, I had been thinking for a good long time. I've made three ascents – how Dangerfield used to chaff me about my shot-gun – but I've never been high enough. Now, with this new, light Paul Veroner machine and its one hundred and seventy-five Robur, I should easily touch the thirty thousand tomorrow. I'll have a shot at the record. Maybe I shall have a shot at something else as well. Of course, it's dangerous. If a fellow wants to avoid danger he had best keep out of flying altogether and subside finally into flannel slippers and a dressing-gown. But I'll visit the air-jungle tomorrow – and if there's anything there I shall know it. If I return, I'll find myself a bit of a celebrity. If I don't this note-book may explain what I am trying to do, and how I lost my life in doing it. But no drivel about accidents or mysteries, if *you* please.

"I chose my Paul Veroner monoplane for the job. There's nothing like a monoplane when real work is to be done. Beaumont found that out in very early days. For one thing it doesn't mind damp, and the weather looks as if we should be in the clouds all the time. It's a bonny little model and answers my hand like a tender-mouthed horse. The engine is a ten-cylinder rotary Robur working up to one hundred and seventy-five. It has all the modern improvements – enclosed fuselage, high-curved landing skids, brakes, gyroscopic steadiers, and three speeds, worked by an alteration of the angle of the planes upon the Venetian-blind principle. I took a shot-gun with me and a dozen cartridges filled with buck-shot. You should have seen the face of Perkins, my old mechanic, when I directed him to put them in. I was dressed like an Arctic explorer, with two jerseys under my overalls, thick socks inside my padded boots, a storm-cap with flaps, and my talc goggles. It was stifling outside the hangars, but I was going for the summit of the Himalayas, and had to dress for the part. Perkins knew there was something on and implored me to take him with me. Perhaps I should if I were using the biplane, but a monoplane is a one-man show – if you want to get the last foot of life out of it. Of course, I took an oxygen bag; the man who goes for the altitude record without one will either be frozen or smothered – or both.

"I had a good look at the planes, the rudder-bar, and the elevating lever before I got in. Everything was in order so far as I could see. Then I switched on my engine and found that she was running sweetly. When they let her go she rose almost at once upon the lowest speed. I circled my home field once or twice just to warm her up, and then with a wave to Perkins and the others, I flattened out my planes and put her on her highest. She skimmed like a swallow down wind for eight or ten miles until I turned her nose up a little and she began to climb in a great spiral for the cloud-bank above me. It's all-important to rise slowly and adapt yourself to the pressure as you go.

"It was a close, warm day for an English September, and there was the hush and heaviness of impending rain. Now and then there came sudden puffs of wind from the south-west – one of them so gusty and unexpected that it caught me napping and turned me half-round for an instant. I remember the time when gusts and whirls and air-pockets used to be things of danger – before we learned to put an overmastering power into our engines. Just as I reached the cloud-banks, with the altimeter marking three thousand, down came the rain. My word, how it poured! It drummed upon my wings and lashed against my face, blurring my glasses so that I could hardly see. I got down on to a low speed, for it was painful to travel against it. As I got higher it became hail, and I had to turn tail to it. One of my cylinders was out of action – a dirty plug, I should imagine, but still I was rising steadily with plenty of power. After a bit the trouble passed, whatever it was, and I heard the full, deep-throated purr – the ten singing as one. That's where the beauty of our modern silencers comes in. We can at last control our engines by ear. How they squeal and squeak and sob when they are in trouble! All those cries for help were wasted in the old days, when every sound was swallowed up by the monstrous racket of the machine. If only the early aviators could come back to see the beauty and perfection of the mechanism which have been bought at the cost of their lives!

"About nine-thirty I was nearing the clouds. Down below me, all blurred and shadowed with rain, lay the vast expanse of Salisbury Plain. Half a dozen flying machines were doing hackwork at the thousand-foot level, looking like little black swallows against the green background. I dare say they were wondering what I was doing up in cloud-land. Suddenly a grey curtain drew across beneath me and the wet folds of vapours were swirling round my face. It was clammily cold and miserable. But I was above the hail-storm, and that was something gained. The cloud was as dark and thick as a London fog. In my anxiety to get clear, I cocked her nose up until the automatic alarm-bell rang, and I actually began to slide backwards. My sopped and dripping wings had made me heavier than I thought, but presently I was in lighter cloud, and soon had cleared the first layer. There was a second – opal-coloured and fleecy – at a great height above my head, a white, unbroken ceiling above, and a dark, unbroken floor below, with the monoplane labouring upwards upon a vast spiral between them. It is deadly lonely in these cloud-spaces. Once a great flight of some small water-birds went past me, flying very fast to the westwards. The quick whir of their wings and their musical cry were cheery to my ear. I fancy that they were teal, but I am a wretched zoologist. Now that we humans have become birds we must really learn to know our brethren by sight.

"The wind down beneath me whirled and swayed the broad cloud-plain. Once a great eddy formed in it, a whirlpool of vapour, and through it, as down a funnel, I caught sight of the distant world. A large white biplane was passing at a vast depth beneath me. I fancy it was the morning mail service betwixt Bristol and London. Then the drift swirled inwards again and the great solitude was unbroken.

"Just after ten I touched the lower edge of the upper cloud-stratum. It consisted of fine diaphanous vapour drifting swiftly from the westwards. The wind had been steadily rising all this time and it was now blowing a sharp breeze – twenty-eight an hour by my gauge. Already it was very cold, though my altimeter only marked nine thousand. The engines were working beautifully, and we went droning steadily upwards. The cloud-bank was thicker than I had expected, but at last it thinned out into a golden mist before me, and then in an instant I had shot out from it, and there was an unclouded sky and a brilliant sun above my head – all blue and gold above, all shining silver below, one vast, glimmering plain as far as my eyes could reach. It was a quarter past ten o'clock, and the barograph needle pointed to twelve thousand eight hundred. Up I went and up, my ears concentrated upon the deep purring of my motor, my eyes busy always with the watch, the revolution indicator, the petrol lever, and the oil pump. No wonder aviators are said to be a fearless race. With so many things to think of there is no time to trouble about oneself. About this time I noted how unreliable is the compass when above a certain height from earth. At fifteen thousand feet mine was pointing east and a point south. The sun and the wind gave me my true bearings.

"I had hoped to reach an eternal stillness in these high altitudes, but with every thousand feet of ascent the gale grew stronger. My machine groaned and trembled in every joint and rivet as she faced it, and swept away like a sheet of paper when I banked her on the turn, skimming down wind at a greater pace, perhaps, than ever mortal man has moved. Yet I had always to turn again and tack up in the wind's eye, for it was not merely a height record that I was after. By all my calculations it was above little Wiltshire that my air-jungle lay, and all my labour might be lost if I struck the outer layers at some farther point.

"When I reached the nineteen-thousand-foot level, which was about midday, the wind was so severe that I looked with some anxiety to the stays of my wings, expecting momentarily to see them snap or slacken. I even cast loose the parachute behind me, and fastened its hook into the ring of my leathern belt, so as to be ready for the worst. Now was the time when a bit of scamped work by the mechanic is paid for by the life of the aeronaut. But she held together bravely. Every cord and strut was humming and vibrating like so many harp-strings, but it was glorious to see how, for all the beating and the buffeting, she was still the conqueror of Nature and the mistress of the sky. There is surely something divine in man himself that he should rise so superior to the limitations which Creation seemed to impose – rise, too, by such unselfish, heroic devotion as this air-conquest has shown. Talk of human degeneration! When has such a story as this been written in the annals of our race?

"These were the thoughts in my head as I climbed that monstrous, inclined plane with the wind sometimes beating in my face and sometimes whistling behind my ears, while the cloud-land beneath me fell away to such a distance that the folds and hummocks of silver had all smoothed out into one flat, shining plain. But suddenly I had a horrible and unprecedented experience. I have known before what it is to be in what our neighbours have called a tourbillon, but never on such a scale as this. That huge, sweeping river of wind of which I have spoken had, as it appears, whirlpools within it which were as monstrous as itself. Without a moment's warning I was dragged suddenly into the heart of one. I spun round for a minute or two with such velocity that I almost lost my senses, and then fell suddenly, left wing foremost, down the vacuum funnel in the centre. I dropped like a stone, and lost nearly a thousand feet. It was only my belt that kept me in my seat, and the shock and breathlessness left me hanging half-insensible over the side of the fuselage. But I am always capable of a supreme effort – it is my one great merit as an aviator. I was conscious that the descent was slower. The whirlpool was a cone rather than a funnel, and I had come to the apex. With a terrific wrench, throwing my weight all to one side, I levelled my planes and brought her head away from the wind. In an instant I had shot out of the eddies and was skimming down the sky. Then, shaken but victorious, I turned her nose up and began once more my steady grind on the upward spiral. I took a large sweep to avoid the danger-spot of the whirlpool, and soon I was safely above it. Just after one o'clock I was twenty-one thousand feet above the sea-level. To my great joy I had topped the gale, and with every hundred feet of ascent the air grew stiller. On the other hand, it was very cold, and I was conscious of that peculiar nausea which goes with rarefaction of the air. For the first time I unscrewed the mouth of my oxygen bag and took an occasional whiff of the glorious gas. I could feel it running like a cordial through my veins, and I was exhilarated almost to the point of drunkenness. I shouted and sang as I soared upwards into the cold, still outer world.

"It is very clear to me that the insensibility which came upon Glaisher, and in a lesser degree upon Coxwell, when, in 1862, they ascended in a balloon to the height of thirty thousand feet, was due to the extreme speed with which a perpendicular ascent is made. Doing it at an easy gradient and accustoming oneself to the lessened barometric pressure by slow degrees, there are no such dreadful symptoms. At the same great height I found that even without my oxygen inhaler I could breathe without undue distress. It was bitterly cold, however, and my thermometer was at zero, Fahrenheit. At one-thirty I was nearly seven miles above the surface of the earth, and still ascending steadily. I found, however, that the rarefied air was giving markedly less support to my planes, and that my angle of ascent had to be considerably lowered in consequence. It was already clear that even with my light weight and strong engine-power there was a point in front of me where I should be held. To make matters worse, one of my sparking-plugs was in trouble again and there was intermittent misfiring in the engine. My heart was heavy with the fear of failure.

"It was about that time that I had a most extraordinary experience. Something whizzed past me in a trail of smoke and exploded with a loud, hissing sound, sending forth a cloud of steam. For the instant I could not imagine what had happened. Then I remembered that the earth is for ever being bombarded by meteor stones, and would be hardly inhabitable were they not in nearly every case turned to vapour in the outer layers of the atmosphere. Here is a new danger for the high-altitude man, for two others passed me when I was nearing the forty-thousand-foot mark. I cannot doubt that at the edge of the earth's envelope the risk would be a very real one.

"My barograph needle marked forty-one thousand three hundred when I became aware that I could go no farther. Physically, the strain was not as yet greater than I could bear but my machine had reached its limit. The attenuated air gave no firm support to the wings, and the least tilt developed into side-slip, while she seemed sluggish on her controls. Possibly, had the engine been at its best, another thousand feet might have been within our capacity, but it was still misfiring, and two out of the ten cylinders appeared to be out of action. If I had not already reached the zone for which I was searching then I should never see it upon this journey. But was it not possible that I had attained it? Soaring in circles like a monstrous hawk upon the forty-thousand-foot level I let the monoplane guide herself, and with my Mannheim glass I made a careful observation of my surroundings. The heavens were perfectly clear; there was no indication of those dangers which I had imagined.

"I have said that I was soaring in circles. It struck me suddenly that I would do well to take a wider sweep and open up a new airtract. If the hunter entered an earth-jungle he would drive through it if he wished to find his game. My reasoning had led me to believe that the air-jungle which I had imagined lay somewhere over Wiltshire. This should be to the south and west of me. I took my bearings from the sun, for the compass was hopeless and no trace of earth was to be seen – nothing but the distant, silver cloud-plain. However, I got my direction as best I might and kept her head straight to the mark. I reckoned that my petrol supply would not last for more than another hour or so, but I could afford to use it to the last drop, since a single magnificent vol-plane could at any time take me to the earth.

"Suddenly I was aware of something new. The air in front of me had lost its crystal clearness. It was full of long, ragged wisps of something which I can only compare to very fine cigarette smoke. It hung about in wreaths and coils, turning and twisting slowly in the sunlight. As the monoplane shot through it, I was aware of a faint taste of oil upon my lips, and there was a greasy scum upon the woodwork of the machine. Some infinitely fine organic matter appeared to be suspended in the atmosphere. There was no life there. It was inchoate and diffuse, extending for many square acres and then fringing off into the void. No, it was not life. But might it not be the remains of life? Above all, might it not be the food of life, of monstrous life, even as the humble grease of the ocean is the food for the mighty whale? The thought was in my mind when my eyes looked upwards and I saw the most wonderful vision that ever man has seen. Can I hope to convey it to you even as I saw it myself last Thursday?

"Conceive a jelly-fish such as sails in our summer seas, bell-shaped and of enormous size – far larger, I should judge, than the dome of St. Paul's. It was of a light pink colour veined with a delicate green, but the whole huge fabric so tenuous that it was but a fairy outline against the dark blue sky. It pulsated with a delicate and regular rhythm. From it there depended two long, drooping, green tentacles, which swayed slowly backwards and forwards. This gorgeous vision passed gently with noiseless dignity over my head, as light and fragile as a soap-bubble, and drifted upon its stately way.

"I had half-turned my monoplane, that I might look after this beautiful creature, when, in a moment, I found myself amidst a perfect fleet of them, of all sizes, but none so large as the first. Some were quite small, but the majority about as big as an average balloon, and with much the same curvature at the top. There was in them a delicacy of texture and colouring which reminded me of the finest Venetian glass. Pale shades of pink and green were the prevailing tints, but all had a lovely iridescence where the sun shimmered through their dainty forms. Some hundreds of them drifted past me, a wonderful fairy squadron of strange unknown argosies of the sky – creatures whose forms and substance were so attuned to these pure heights that one could not conceive anything so delicate within actual sight or sound of earth.

"But soon my attention was drawn to a new phenomenon – the serpents of the outer air. These were long, thin, fantastic coils of vapour-like material, which turned and twisted with great speed, flying round and round at such a pace that the eyes could hardly follow them. Some of these ghost-like creatures were twenty or thirty feet long, but it was difficult to tell their girth, for their outline was so hazy that it seemed to fade away into the air around them. These air-snakes were of a very light grey or smoke colour, with some darker lines within, which gave the impression of a definite organism. One of them whisked past my very face, and I was conscious of a cold, clammy contact, but their composition was so unsubstantial that I could not connect them with any thought of physical danger, any more than the beautiful bell-like creatures which had preceded them. There was no more solidity in their frames than in the floating spume from a broken wave.

"But a more terrible experience was in store for me. Floating downwards from a great height there came a purplish patch of vapour, small as I saw it first, but rapidly enlarging as it approached me, until it appeared to be hundreds of square feet in size. Though fashioned of some transparent, jelly-like substance, it was none the less of much more definite outline and solid consistence than anything which I had seen before. There were more traces, too, of a physical organization, especially two vast, shadowy, circular plates upon either side, which may have been eyes, and a perfectly solid white projection between them which was as curved and cruel as the beak of a vulture.

"The whole aspect of this monster was formidable and threatening, and it kept changing its colour from a very light mauve to a dark, angry purple so thick that it cast a shadow as it drifted between my monoplane and the sun. On the upper curve of its huge body there were three great projections which I can only describe as enormous bubbles, and I was convinced as I looked at them that they were charged with some extremely light gas which served to buoy up the misshapen and semi-solid mass in the rarefied air. The creature moved swiftly along, keeping pace easily with the monoplane, and for twenty miles or more it formed my horrible escort, hovering over me like a bird of prey which is waiting to pounce. Its method of progression – done so swiftly that it was not easy to follow – was to throw out a long, glutinous streamer in front of it, which in turn seemed to draw forward the rest of the writhing body. So elastic and gelatinous was it that never for two successive minutes was it the same shape, and yet each change made it more threatening and loathsome than the last.

"I knew that it meant mischief. Every purple flush of its hideous body told me so. The vague, goggling eyes which were turned always upon me were cold and merciless in their viscid hatred. I dipped the nose of my monoplane downwards to escape it. As I did so, as quick as a flash there shot out a long tentacle from this mass of floating blubber, and it fell as light and sinuous as a whip-lash across the front of my machine. There was a loud hiss as it lay for a moment across the hot engine, and it whisked itself into the air again, while the huge, flat body drew itself together as if in sudden pain. I dipped to a vol-pique, but again a tentacle fell over the monoplane and was shorn off by the propeller as easily as it might have cut through a smoke wreath. A long, gliding, sticky, serpent-like coil came from behind and caught me round the waist, dragging me out of the fuselage. I tore at it, my fingers sinking into the smooth, glue-like surface, and for an instant I disengaged myself, but only to be caught round the boot by another coil, which gave me a jerk that tilted me almost on to my back.

"As I fell over I blazed off both barrels of my gun, though, indeed, it was like attacking an elephant with a pea-shooter to imagine that any human weapon could cripple that mighty bulk. And yet I aimed better than I knew, for, with a loud report, one of the great blisters upon the creature's back exploded with the puncture of the buck-shot. It was very clear that my conjecture was right, and that these vast, clear bladders were distended with some lifting gas, for in an instant the huge, cloud-like body turned sideways, writhing desperately to find its balance, while the white beak snapped and gaped in horrible fury. But already I had shot away on the steepest glide that I dared to attempt, my engine still full on, the flying propeller and the force of gravity shooting me downwards like an aerolite. Far behind me I saw a dull, purplish smudge growing swiftly smaller and merging into the blue sky behind it. I was safe out of the deadly jungle of the outer air.

"Once out of danger I throttled my engine, for nothing tears a machine to pieces quicker than running on full power from a height. It was a glorious, spiral vol-plane from nearly eight miles of altitude – first, to the level of the silver cloud-bank, then to that of the storm-cloud beneath it, and finally, in beating rain, to the surface of the earth. I saw the Bristol Channel beneath me as I broke from the clouds, but, having still some petrol in my tank, I got twenty miles inland before I found myself stranded in a field half a mile from the village of Ashcombe. There I got three tins of petrol from a passing motor-car, and at ten minutes past six that evening I alighted gently in my own home meadow at Devizes, after such a journey as no mortal upon earth has ever yet taken and lived to tell the tale. I have seen the beauty and I have seen the horror of the heights – and greater beauty or greater horror than that is not within the ken of man.

"And now it is my plan to go once again before I give my results to the world. My reason for this is that I must surely have something to show by way of proof before I lay such a tale before my fellow-men. It is true that others will soon follow and will confirm what I have said, and yet I should wish to carry conviction from the first. Those lovely iridescent bubbles of the air should not be hard to capture. They drift slowly upon their way, and the swift monoplane could intercept their leisurely course. It is likely enough that they would dissolve in the heavier layers of the atmosphere, and that some small heap of amorphous jelly might be all that I should bring to earth with me. And yet something there would surely be by which I could substantiate my story. Yes, I will go, even if I run a risk by doing so. These purple horrors would not seem to be numerous. It is probable that I shall not see one. If I do I shall dive at once. At the worst there is always the shot-gun and my knowledge of ..."

Here a page of the manuscript is unfortunately missing. On the next page is written, in large, straggling writing:

"Forty-three thousand feet. I shall never see earth again. They are beneath me, three of them. God help me; it is a dreadful death to die!"

Such in its entirety is the Joyce-Armstrong Statement. Of the man nothing has since been seen. Pieces of his shattered monoplane have been picked up in the preserves of

Mr. Budd-Lushington upon the borders of Kent and Sussex, within a few miles of the spot where the note-book was discovered. If the unfortunate aviator's theory is correct that this air-jungle, as he called it, existed only over the south-west of England, then it would seem that he had fled from it at the full speed of his monoplane, but had been overtaken and devoured by these horrible creatures at some spot in the outer atmosphere above the place where the grim relics were found. The picture of that monoplane skimming down the sky, with the nameless terrors flying as swiftly beneath it and cutting it off always from the earth while they gradually closed in upon their victim, is one upon which a man who valued his sanity would prefer not to dwell. There are many, as I am aware, who still jeer at the facts which I have here set down, but even they must admit that Joyce-Armstrong has disappeared, and I would commend to them his own words: "This note-book may explain what I am trying to do, and how I lost my life in doing it. But no drivel about accidents or mysteries, if *you* please."

The Fires of Mercy

Spencer Ellsworth

THE ASSASSIN, the mother, and the child fled into the desert.

* * *

The sandstorm had blanketed the world the night before. Sand hung still on the leaves of the palm trees; sand sat on a skim atop the water; sand pillowed against rocks. Grains swept the crevices of palm trees, shone like jewels in the sun.

The assassin emerged from the rocks and used her hand to sweep away the drifts that had piled against the cave entrance. She breathed through a light veil, as much to hide her face as keep sand out, and she prayed.

She praised the Thousand Names, the one and many, and she praised the Prophets, and she spoke the forbidden name of the Thirteenth Prophet, a heresy. She prayed for a guiding hand, and felt a fool.

She turned then, and motioned for the mother and child to emerge from the hollow in the rock.

They peered around the world. The mother's face was dark with stains; two days ago kohl had run with her tears and smeared the paint on her face. Sand clung to her face and bedraggled her hair. She still wore pearls around her neck, and bits of fine clothing showed through under the wool robe the assassin had given her. She cleared sleep from the child's eyes.

The child, for his part, was quiet. He had always been so, in the eight months of his life. He rarely cried, even when cold. He took only as much breast milk as he needed. He watched and listened.

And so the child watched while the assassin told his mother there would be no fire, and his mother made sounds of protest, but not many. The assassin was not tall, nor particularly strong. She was so thin and featureless she was often mistaken for a man. Her eyes, though, stopped speech. They were deep black wells rimmed with silver, like the sun on those wild days when it is covered by the moon.

The mother groaned. She wept a little. She often had, since the night of horror.

The assassin shared out dried meat. Her cold silver eyes scanned the horizon.

They crossed the dunes in the morning. The assassin timed their trip well. As the air began to shimmer around them, and the dunes wavered under the sun, and their tongues began to feel like lead weights, they sighted a familiar stand of rocks. The assassin topped a dune, looked back at the mother and child slowly wading up the mountain of sand, and wished she could see through the haze of heat to tell who waited in those rocks.

"Shade," the mother said. "Gods-blessed shade!"

"Slowly," the assassin said.

The child watched with interest, and a little trepidation. In the last few days the child had looked more and more on the assassin, and less on his crying, confused mother.

"Slowly," the assassin said, for lack of something better.

Slowly they walked toward the rocks.

An arrow struck the assassin's shoulder. She spun, threw the mother and child to the hot sand, and ran.

More arrows came. One, two, three. The child watched with interest, the mother with horror. The assassin spun around the second arrow, around the third. Knives, gleaming, left the assassin's sleeves. They caught the sunlight and shivered in the light. The mother and the child did not see the men who were found by the assassin's blades, but they heard bodies fall.

She went on running. After a time, she came back to the mother and the child. The arrow still emerged from her shoulder.

"These were just bandits," the assassin said. "They have not found us yet."

The assassin took the dead bodies into the desert, left them to desiccate in sand and be eaten by jackals.

She kissed their knife-marred bodies, for every act of war has, at its heart, an act of mercy.

Together, they waited in the cool under the rocks, waited out the worst of the days heat. The assassin extracted the arrow herself. She sat and rinsed it with what water she could spare. She drank a bit of henbane and dark potent liquor, but carefully. One could not choose which senses were dulled.

The arrow was buried in a black, swollen mess of meat and blood. It was a familiar wound, familiar and easily treatable – when the assassin was in her element.

Her lesser assassins, kept in sway by her fierce mind and blood oaths, could have treated it. Others like her, with flecks of silver in their eyes, could knit her together with a magic of blood and fire, stone and shadow.

But now she broke the shaft high, and carefully pulled the point from her shoulder, and it screamed pain at her, and her eyes swam, shuttered, like the heat.

Not enough. This is not enough!

She remembered being strapped to a post and whipped, remembered the flesh of her back hanging down in strips like stalactites. She remembered the sand in her fists as she crawled. She remembered her brother in a killing pit, remembered her knife at his throat, and she remained conscious.

She was a mind-eater. She would live.

She made a poultice and stuffed it inside the open wound. Despite her best efforts, grains of sand fell into the wound.

* * *

The mother dreamed. She dreamed of her childhood, before she came to the palace, and before the desert.

Little men came from far to the east to trade with her father. They brought fireworks. Her father called for pigs – not heretics, actual pigs! Since the Eighth Prophet had banned the eating of swine flesh hundreds of years ago, no one had seen the actual animal near her home.

These were the real thing; little snorting unclean monsters, spotted brown over pink skin. The little eastern men liked pigs, he said, and a wise man honors his guests before he honors his house. It seemed a foolish point of view. But he had the pigs slaughtered, and he fed them to the little men, and in return they sold him fireworks and put on a display that honored their house for a year.

Even then, she had been marked for marriage to wealth. Thus her mother wouldn't let her near the pigs. Warts, goiters, leprosy, sluttishness – all came from swine flesh.

She snuck in to the pens late at night, as a child, the night before they were slaughtered, and touched a pig. She was surprised by how much fine hair there was on that skin, hair just beginning to darken.

Her son had been born with light hair that soon darkened. She sometimes thought of the pigs, and thought of her son slurping at her breast, and was amused as he slurped at the breast milk.

This morning, in the desert, she managed only a trickle of thin, nearly clear breast milk. They kept walking.

Three nights ago, a carved door of rare wood had shattered. The dark figure had swept into the harem and cut the throat of one woman, and another. More figures came. They killed the concubines. They killed the children. Old faces, kind faces, bitter faces. The strong women, beautiful and tall, who turned the harem on the whims. Their weak, pale girls from the north who spoke little. Every soul in the king's palace had died under those blades.

She had hidden, shut herself, gasping, in a shed. Until the sun peered through the door, and the assassin tore that door open. And taken her by the wrist, and raised the curved knife …

The mother saw something else in the assassin's silver-flecked eyes, that bloody morning.

As night fell, the assassin's wound ached worse and worse for the walk they made to water.

She touched the pendant around her neck, ran her hands across the calligraphy. The simple Name, one of the Thousand Names, swept up into points, toward the sky, around the dots and curls of vowels. She traced the grooves. Dots and curves of vowels, grooves worn deep.

There were words, she thought. Words, carved in stone. Carved with blood that had dried before the seas dried up over this desert.

The language was that of air and fire, the words the keys to burning the whole world. It was a weapon, but one only a fool would dare. It was forbidden, in every text in every history, to call upon the children of air and fire.

She had taken the pendant from its secret place, as she embarked upon this most secret of missions. If the assassin and her subordinates had been caught by the emperor's soldiers, if the blood magic had been broken and secrets stripped from their minds, she would have called the children of air and fire to burn the world, for there were secrets in her Order that could not come to light.

But their mission had failed in a far different way.

The mother asked the question that night. "Why? Why did you save us?"

The assassin didn't answer. The mother didn't try a second time.

While the mother slept, the assassin lay against the rock and tried to ignore the ache from her wound. She had treated such, and deeper, darker wounds. She had worked with blood and silver, found the healing that balanced the killing, as the haft of a knife balances the blade. Another mind-eater could have healed her, but they would insist on weighting the action, balancing it with the mother and child's death.

The next morning, the mother asked, "Where are we going? How do you find water in this desert?"

The assassin looked at the horizon, a tangle of sand and rocks. She knew the trail of water here, strung out like the pearls the mother still wore. Scattered across a land better traveled than the assassin would have liked. "I know," was all she said.

They walked that day, to a small, filthy pool of water that left them belching sulfur. The baby cried when the mother washed his face with the water. In the middle of the night the baby woke screaming and flatulent; he soiled all the clothes and the mother and assassin washed what they could and tore new ones.

"The servants wound him with more rags than this," the mother said.

The assassin stroked the baby's cheek. "This is all we have."

* * *

The attack came the next day. The arrows recoiled, black, thin, like serpents, off the rocks around them. The assassin turned and shouted at the mother. The mother ran to shelter.

They were feeling her out, the assassin knew. Her men were still afraid of her. So they hung back, fired arrows from a distance.

These were her men, who had woken confused at the king's palace, finding her gone. They were still afraid of her, testing her resolve.

That was their mistake.

"We cannot run from the mind-eaters," the mother sobbed as they did just that. "We cannot run from them!"

The assassin didn't answer. She knew. All her former compatriots had to do was head the three off, send them deeper into the desert, and the assassin, mother and child would die.

She looked at the rocks where she knew her compatriots waited. She would go. She would go, and they would come at her, and her mind would be quicker. The fingers of her soul would reach out through the blood oath and wrap around one, two, three of them. Her knives would cut their throats while their bodies would not react. She would see the fear in their silver eyes, and then their eyes would fade.

Except she had no more knives. Her soul was weak and quavering from lack of food and water. And if she killed them, more would come. One step wrong, and death.

The assassin stared the other way, at the eastern horizon. Somewhere beyond that thousand thousand leagues of empty sand, that waterless abyss, lay the east. There lived little men who did not speak the Thousand Names. Not the name of the Thirteenth Prophet, nor any Prophet. There the mother and child would go unknown. It would not matter if the child was an emperor here; there he would be but a boy.

Somewhere beyond death.

The mother caught the assassin staring. "I've heard there's no water," she said. "No water, and ghosts, and monsters, and death."

The assassin stared into the dunes.

"We need to get to a town."

"Mind-eaters hide in towns," the assassin whispered. "The darkness does not guard against our knives, nor the light." The assassin thought of a firelit study, of old, old books bound in skin, of dark words. She thought of words in a tongue of fire, of a question that could not be asked. She thought of that knife, the balance, the haft and the blade. She touched the pendant around her neck.

"We can circle around to the south," the assassin said. "A few days in the dunes." She looked at their pitiful waterskins. "A few days without water; we can survive."

The mother wept. "No, no, no. I have no milk, I have no strength, I can't walk, I can't ..."

The assassin reached into the mother's mind, and stroked it, calmed it. It was much like giving calm to the dying.

They filled the waterskins and went back into the desert.

They went up dunes the size of mountains, sinking in sand to their knees, slipped down the other side. The mother slurped all her water the first day, tried to breastfeed the baby, but the baby slept now, slept all day and night, and breathed shallowly and whimpered.

The heat tore at the assassin's wound, seemed to scour it. She imagined it was boiling wine, cleansing the infection.

The dunes froze at night, cold emptiness rushing into what had been warm air, sucking life out of them. The assassin and the mother and baby huddled together. Now her wound raged with a cold, maddening pain, tearing at the assassin's brain. She thought of her life, buried in vengeance, of her order, and it seemed such a silly thing to be a part of such a foolish world.

The assassin stared into the desert. She saw ghosts, travelers long-dead, the shadowy caravans traveling across the lines of the dunes to the lands of the dead. Their jewels glittered, their clothes fine in long-gone suns, but she had eyes only for their bulging waterskins. The ghosts wandered, forever, to wells dried for centuries, to kingdoms swept into the desert.

She thought she saw herself, black-clad, forever leading the mother and the child deeper into the desert, another shade doomed to wander.

Morning came and with it, the heat.

The dunes went on forever, red waves, empty, burning. The assassin's arm flesh had turned black at the edges of the wound, red veins lancing outward from the rot.

They stumbled up dunes and down again. The assassin turned toward the towns of the south, looked for them in vain. The mother could hardly walk, sinking in sand, gasping. The baby lay too still in the mother's arms.

They were days from anywhere.

The assassin looked at the endless blue sky. It seemed beautiful, a great gem descending on the world, overwhelming them. She stared into the sky, and realized she had collapsed as well, fallen to the sand.

She closed her eyes.

She recalled that night, the knife in her hand, the close purpose. She had waited for the emperor of the whole world, behind a fine satin curtain. She had sprung from her place and slit his throat, and his words had come easy. "Die, by blood and fire, stone and shadow." His blood had run over her hands. She had laughed as it ran down her forearms, rich and dark like wine. The most precious vintage in the world.

The harem must die. They had agreed; every soul in the palace dead by midnight. Such was vengeance, for this emperor had burned their people and laughed, mocked the heretical pigs who believed in the Thirteenth Prophet. They were the shadows that took revenge, and this emperor's crimes were legion. It was time for war, in return.

The assassin had opened the door to the harem, and consumed their minds, quelled their resistance, and slit the throats. She cut perfect, soft, swanlike necks. She cut the fleshy throats of babes, and children, and the swarthy throats of servants.

She had been made for this, in fighting pits, in a place where she put her own brother to the knife. She had been put in the hands of justice, a blade in the hand of the Thousand Names. A blade could not question the hand that wielded.

Such a night of blood it had been, the night she killed the ruler of the world. Dozens of women. Scores of children, all by her knife. Blood running like rivers, across tiled floors, pooling with the bodies that lay in the fountains.

Enough to give even a mind-eater pause.

She had thought the business done when the sun rose. She had gone to the river to cleanse herself. Blood had come away from her in great scabby brown flakes, scrubbed roughly from her skin by river sand. No matter how she tried, it stained her – the cracks on her fingers, grooves of her fingerprints, the creases at her elbows, the soft hollow of her collarbone.

On her way back, she had heard them, gasping, shivering in hiding. She had taken out her knife again, and pulled back the curtain to see the mother and child.

And stayed her hand.

She had stared at them, and she thought not of the name of the Thirteenth Prophet, not of the crimes of the Faith, but of the Thousand Names she revered, and remembered, for the first time in years, that one of those names was Mercy.

As fire is tempered by air, and each act of war must have, at its heart, an act of mercy.

Her heart was full of blood, flooded and drowned with the blood of others, bound by oaths in shed blood, and her knife hand would not move. Was it the Gods' hand? The foolishness of a mind-eater who had too much fear? The end of her mission?

Questioning gave her no answers. She knew she could not kill them. This was the act of mercy at the heart of this war, and it simply was.

She had herded the mother and child from their hiding place, using her magic to quiet them, and gone to the river, found a pleasure boat, and rowed them far from the palace, then set out across the desert.

She looked at the mother and child now, lying collapsed on the sand, and the assassin pulled the knife from her belt. It was time. They would spend the rest of their lives in danger from those blades in the dark. The boy was an heir to the entire world, and no one would see him but as a tool. The dream of escaping to the east was just that: a dream. The mercy was her flaw.

She would kill them, and she would go back, and the mission would be complete, and she would forget her mistake. This was the blade; there was no need for balance here.

Her good arm was throbbing from the wound, so she switched her knife to her lesser hand, and raised it, looking down at the mother and child.

And then she dropped it.

One choice yet remained.

The assassin sat upon the sand, and drew out her pendant, and spoke the words inscribed on the pendant. They were written in a language few could speak, and none dared.

The assassin called out the forbidden words, the summoning words, in the language of flame in the darkness, wind in the dark of night.

They came.

The children of air and fire rose from the ground, shining in the sun, their seven-fingered hands wavering like tongues of flame. Their sharp teeth were black as coals, their eyes the blue of the heart of flame.

They surrounded the assassin and the mother and child in a circle. Their words rippled through the flame, burned the assassin's heart.

You have called us. You are the first in millennia.

"I wish to make a bargain," she whispered. "Take them across the expanse of sand, and go to the east."

What is the bargain?

The assassin laughed. "What do you wish?" The words felt hot on her tongue, a language only of exchange, of dark deeds for dark words.

The spirits spoke, their words rushing like flame. *We wish for your world. We wish to burn, to burn the forests, to burn the cities, to burn the people.*

"That is no fair bargain for three lives." She staggered to her feet.

Give us three to burn, then.

The assassin considered her subordinates, her enemies, her brother, who would now rule the order in her place. She considered the palaces of kings and emperors, who had burned her people. She considered herself.

Perhaps it was the heat, or the pain, but she spoke of nothing she had considered.

"The justice in the hearts of my assassins. The hatred in the hearts of the rulers. The fear ..." She wavered. "The fear of mercy."

The head of the creatures flickered, quavered. *We do not want that!*

"Then you will burn nothing. There will be no ash." She wavered on her feet, forced herself to stay standing. "This is no small burn. You will eat minds, eat souls, as they accuse us of doing. You will burn some men and women completely." For some had nothing left but hatred, and fear of mercy.

Was she one of those? She could not say.

They children railed and snorted, like fire crackling in high wind. *You have summoned us for foolishness.*

"I know," she said, and realized that they were the last words she had in her.

She fell to the sand, lay cold in it, and heard the spirits speak, the hissing, popping, deep-throated roar of flame as it ate wood. She heard them and almost she understood. Almost. *To burn at all is to burn enough,* one said. *And her soul will burn brightly.*

A smile touched the assassin's lips.

* * *

Shadows, shifting black whispers of fire. She thought she saw stars far above, heard strange music coming from the east. The mother and the child swept away, on the wind, saved. Seven-fingered hands closed around her body.

The assassin writhed, and thought she died.

She saw herself, as the Gods had made her, her soul made of intertwined branches, as perfect as a spun tapestry of calligraphy. The creatures of air and fire gathered around her soul. Their flame touched the edges of that tapestry, caught threads, bright with licking red tongues.

They took the justice from her, the hatred, and finally the fear. Threads of her soul broke away, embers floating into the Gods' great space, each one losing its light, its heat, and becoming cold, grains, fluttering like sand through the air.

The assassin woke in the sand alone. No, not alone. All around her, glass jars of a thousand shapes: bulbs, onions, flower petals, thorns. Each one glowing with a red light.

This was the bargain. And she knew.

The mother and child were safe in the East, now. But the assassin's mission was not yet done. She would take the creatures of air and fire, bottled up in these glasses, to the cities. She would take them to lords. To assassins of other stripes. Perhaps even to her own order. And they would be a weapon, to turn blood to water, swords to coins, to eat the minds of the mind-eaters.

For each act of war has, at its heart, an act of mercy.

Sisters

David Jón Fuller

SÖLVEIG DIDN'T WANT to be back in Bjørgvin. The coastal city where she had grown up and left as soon as she was able still looked much the same now, eleven years later, in the Year of Our Lord 1365. The winter cold and tang of the ocean reached through her cloak and clutched at her mail, chilling her. Salt and frost encrusted the buildings of the Bryggen, the busiest trading quays in Norway, especially now that the Hanseatic League had set up there. All so familiar. For a moment, as she stood on the dock with Mihr Nûsh, she thought: *actually, we aren't ashore yet. We can ask the captain where he is headed next, and leave.*

But no. They'd come for Lutz, damn him – that lovable, proud fool – and no trolls would stand in their way. She hoped.

The gulls' cries were piercing, she heard them clearly; but she had to read the captain's lips and expression carefully. The sloshing of the waves made so much indistinct to her.

She paid him and nodded to Mihr Nûsh, who shouldered her sword and shivered in her double-layered kazaghand. Sölveig was shocked at the deep familiarity of scents she'd not smelled in more than a decade: tar and oil, smoke from homes, inns and the occasional forge, and the ever-present stench of fish and seagull shit. Somehow the combination was never the same in other ports. Filling the eastern sky, the jagged, snow-covered peaks of the Seven Mountains to the east seemed to continue straight through the buildings and deep into the sound. Even the sea had always seemed to Sölveig a mere visitor in this place; the mountains owned it, and would stand long past Judgment Day.

All this must have been new to Mihr Nûsh, whose gaze lingered on the snowy mountains, so unlike her home in Iran. "Where to first?" she asked Sölveig.

"I know where you can get horses," said Lutz's squire, Max, who had hung back as they disembarked. "I returned the ones Sir Lutz and I used –"

"Oh, you're coming with us, never fear," said Sölveig, because she didn't like the way Max had used the word *you*. "But first, we'll need news on what has happened since you left."

"You have family here, don't you?" said Mihr Nûsh, delicately.

"I do, but they no longer have me," she said, frowning against the sleet. "We'll see the bishop. Everyone will have come to him for help. Especially if things got worse after …after Lutz."

She led the other two to the church, and, after waiting for His Excellency to complete an audience with the mayor, they were ushered into the bishop's office.

Bishop Gisbrikt looked about sixty, with dark circles under his eyes and a downcast mouth, and his hair was a steely grey. His gaze swept over them in a heartbeat and settled on Max. "So, young squire," he said, his Norwegian larded with an English accent strong enough for Sölveig to detect, "is there more you wish to tell me about the incident this time?"

Max coughed and Sölveig broke in. "We are here to investigate what happened to our comrade, Sir Lutz of Bremen."

The bishop's eyes narrowed and gave both Sölveig and Mihr Nûsh a harder look. "Are you, now? Then I fear you are too late. We have made our own excursions – at no small risk – up the mountain and found that he is dead."

The words hit Sölveig like a thunderclap; her heart stopped and she swayed. Then she gripped the back of a wooden chair and her pulse began to race, sending a roar of blood through her ears, making them hot. "What proof do you have? And who has seen it?" She watched the old man's mouth closely, so as not to miss a word.

The bishop's face grew pale in the fading afternoon light. "This," he said, lifting a gauntlet from the floor behind his table. The leather straps had been torn and the once-shiny metal was scuffed and dirty.

Max let out a small cry; Sölveig and Mihr Nûsh remained silent. It had belonged to Lutz.

Mihr Nûsh spoke first, in the best Norwegian she could: "No blood?"

The bishop shook his head. "Not where we found it. But, higher up the mountain – much had been spilled. The snow was dark with it."

Sölveig swallowed and hoped her voice would not crack. "But of the man? No remains?"

The Bishop looked down. "None. But that is not surprising. The tröllkónur left no trace of the sheep they stole, either. I am sure they will have ...used him horribly."

Sölveig's nostrils flared. "Was no attempt made to find him?"

The bishop's lips flecked with spit. "I led the search, supported by Almighty God, bringing with me the relics of St. Sunniva, to drive out the unclean monsters who had defiled our diocese! They did not dare to approach as we searched! And we came closer to their lair than I judge any others have before. But we could not scale the face of the entrance to their cave without great risk. We listened but heard only the base sounds of their ...of their feast."

Sölveig turned to Max, and turned him to face her. "Is that where you went looking, before?"

Max nodded.

Sölveig swallowed. Her mouth was suddenly as parched as a strip of dried fish. "We'll need some help," she said to the bishop.

"With what?"

"Disposing of the bodies, when we're through with them. But some support with the hunt would be appreciated."

The bishop was silent a moment before letting out a long breath. "You're sure you are able?"

Sölveig wanted to spit. "If the news from Hälsingøre hasn't reached you yet, it will soon." That was where Max had found them, following the news of a troll menacing the Danish town. He'd found them the night after they'd slain the monster, just as they were settling in to bed – and told them what Lutz had attempted, on his own, the great fool. Usually they worked together, to great success – and profit – but Lutz, it seemed, had had something to prove. Now here they all were.

The bishop's hands fidgeted with the lining of his robe. "I have heard of their troubles ...we can't promise to pay much."

Mihr Nûsh took a step forward, her boot thumping on the dark wooden floor. "How much were you going to pay Lutz?"

The bishop cleared his throat. "Of course, we will offer the same –"

Before he could finish, Max squeaked out the figure in silver. Mihr Nûsh smiled as the bishop blanched.

"That seems appropriate to me," said Sölveig. "Each."

"It's unheard of!" said the bishop.

"Yet I suspect you didn't bargain with Lutz."

"The man was a giant, whereas you are –"

"Don't," said Mihr Nûsh, "Or the price will triple."

The bishop sank heavily into his chair and pressed a hand to his left temple. "Very well. Make what arrangements you need; I will inform the authorities they are to support you in any way they can."

Sölveig bit back a longer reply and said only, "Thank you," and then left.

* * *

They were in position on the mountainside by mid-afternoon, because Sölveig counted on neither good light for the final ascent nor the discipline of the fifteen townspeople who had come along. The snowy slope had become so steep only a mountain goat would be able to scale it; no wonder Lutz had counted on drawing the tröllkónur out. There would be no way he could reach the cave in his plate armour. She wore her light helm, which didn't cover her ears, but her mail felt heavy enough, at this elevation. It brought back memories of her childhood, exploring up the mountainside with her friends, the thin air making them giddy. But now she forced herself to breathe slowly and deeply. She was conscious of every tiny noise their party made, the quiet scritch of pebbles scraping underfoot or the shifting hiss of snow cascading down. The people were too terrified to chatter, but even so Mihr Nûsh fixed them with a stern glare every now and then to keep them quiet.

The threat of being heard wasn't the only thing making Sölveig sweat. So far none of the townspeople had said anything to her, but she'd been conscious of them whispering to each other and looking her way – she couldn't hear anything they said; it was in exactly the middle range of pitch and volume inaudible to her – but they stopped talking as soon as she or Mihr Nûsh came near. Coming back to Bjørgvin and facing her old reputation was like trying to fit into old trews that were now too small and had been made for someone else in the first place. *She's the one who left her friends to die on the mountainside all those years ago*, she imagined them saying. *She looks different, but she's the one.*

She pushed her helm down and adjusted the strap again. After they got Lutz out – or what was left of him – and took care of these monsters, she'd collect their fee and leave, never to return. Perhaps go straight to Fiorenze and put this winter behind her.

The light was fading fast, even though they were high up the western face of the mountain, so Sölveig gave the signal to the leader of the volunteers, an innkeeper she hadn't known when she was younger. He nodded and motioned to the others, who quietly took their positions. Mihr Nûsh had already brought the ropes to just below the far side of the cave entrance; Sölveig took her place on the side opposite her. They gave each other a nod and began creeping up the icy, slippery rock, ropes dangling between them.

It would have been easier if they could have secured two lines to the mountainside; perhaps then they could have brought more people up to face the tröllkónur. But Mihr Nûsh didn't believe any of the people of Bjørgvin, even those brave enough to come with them, could be counted on in battle. And to make safe the lines, they would have had to hammer spikes into the rock face, which would have alerted the monsters. So now they climbed, slowly, carefully, until they reached the dark cave mouth.

Clouds had blown in from the sea and threatened to obscure what little light they had. Sölveig and Mihr Nûsh nodded and then climbed higher, just above the dark, rank opening. Once in position, each played out the rope until the elongated noose they shared surrounded it. The slip-knot would allow a quick tightening; Solveig prayed the rope's sinews would hold.

A moment; then Mihr Nûsh gave a tiny bleating, like a lamb in distress.

There was no sound from within the cave. Sölveig glanced up at the half-moon. Surely, at least one of the monsters would be awake by now?

Mihr Nûsh bleated again.

Then, a stirring, from the darkness; the scrape of something huge on gravel or stone. The warriors froze, barely breathing.

The towering tröllkona emerged from the cave, nostrils twitching on her great nose. Her head was as large as a barrel, her frightful hair a grey haystack in the moonlight, and her ragged teeth clear as she licked them hungrily.

Sölveig and Mihr Nûsh pulled on their ropes, hand over hand, barely making a whisper of sound. Before the tröllkóna knew it, the noose was about her neck and Mihr Nûsh had jumped onto her back while Sölveig kept the rope tight. The monster tried to cry out, her jagged teeth bare as she snarled, but the rope was already choking her. She cast about for the rope but Mihr Nûsh grabbed it as a handhold and pushed against the tröllkóna's neck and shoulders with her powerful legs. Sölveig released the rope, giving her comrade full control of the noose. The monster flailed, vicious fingernails glinting like spikes but unable reach behind her to grab Mihr Nûsh. Of course, plate armour might be better protection against a troll's falling-log-heavy swipes; but a scratch from their fetid nails could kill you, and mail was a fine defence against that. The trick was never to let a troll get its hands on you.

Sölveig leaped down, landing as softly as she could behind the troll; in a second she had her bastard sword out. The monster was wearing a huge rough-spun wool dress, but from her lower vantage Sölveig was still able to plunge her sword, two-handed, into the back of the tröllkóna's thigh.

With no breath to scream, the monster instead crumpled, right on the edge of the rock face. With a deft hop down the tröllkóna's back, Mihr Nûsh used her own weight to topple her over the edge, and with a grim smile, she went down with her. Sölveig heard the deep rumble and thump of the bodies hitting the snow on the slope below. If the townspeople were ready, the tröllkóna would be finished off quickly.

Sölveig did not spare a thought as to the identity of the monster she had helped dispatch. *You won't forget what you've seen?* that same tröllkóna had said to her, when she was just a girl chasing Peer and Elise up and down the slopes.

No. Unable to tear her eyes from Elise's bloody body in the tröllkóna's long, encircling fingers, nor from the memory of Peer's terrified eyes as the other troll-sister had carried him off up the mountain, still alive.

Good! with a snaggle-toothed grin. *For someone has to tell the tale.*

And as the tröllkóna had bounded away, Elise's arms flailing red and lifeless like a doll's, Sölveig had been unable to stop her.

Now the story would have a different ending.

Sölveig turned and crept into the twilight murk of the entrance, slowing her breath and listening. In the dead quiet following the tröllkona's tumble off the ledge, she'd be able to hear the soft noises of her sister moving, she hoped.

She knelt and laid the grip of her sword over her right knee as she carefully retrieved her flint from a belt pouch and a torch from a pocket in her cloak. A few strikes and she had light, flickering and fragile in the stench of the troll-sisters' cave. Replacing the flint, she held the torch in her left hand and rose with her sword in her right, and stepped carefully forward.

She expected to find bones strewn about the rough floor but it looked as though it had been swept clean. Her nostrils flared, straining to catch any movement of air or troll-sweat stink before a monster could loom out of the blackness at her. The yellow, wavering light she held glinted off her sword and made even the shadows of immutable stone wiggle and quiver.

Then, a glint of metal, against the wall to the left. She froze; when she saw no movement, eased forward. Piled neatly, as if on display, were pieces of Lutz's armour. The leather straps and other bindings had been ripped or cut; blood darkened the edges. His sword was nowhere to be seen.

Then she caught a familiar scent, mingled with the odours that permeated the cave. She knew it even as she had after sharing a bed with him, when his musk rubbed off on her. Lutz.

She held the torch higher, not daring to hope he was still alive.

There, in a clump of sheepskins, a glimpse of a pale arm.

She scanned all she could see in the wavering light, but there was no sign of anyone else. She took another step and tapped at the skins with her sword. Nothing. But now that she was closer, she could see a slight, regular movement. He was still breathing. She crept closer still. "Lutz!" she said, in the softest whisper she could. "It's me! Sölveig. Get up!"

A heartbeat, and then he stirred. His great blonde head rolled up and he squinted through the light at her. He gaped. He was naked but for the sheepskins, and when he sat up, his jaw moving soundlessly, she saw savage bruises all along his left arm.

His right arm, however, now ended at the elbow. The stump was already beginning to heal, but the cut looked ragged. She pulled the rest of his coverings off, and he curled up, shaking his head. Why didn't he speak? His left leg ended at the knee, and bruises in the shape of huge fingers striped his torso. The rest of him seemed undamaged.

She thought of the bishop's words, and of Peer's horror at being carried away by a tröllkóna. *They will have used him horribly.*

She threw a yellowed sheepskin over him and pulled under the armpit of his partly-severed arm. "Get up, you big idiot," she whispered. "Mihr Nûsh and I are here to get you out of this."

His eyes flashed and he shook his head, his mouth working soundlessly. She could see he still had his tongue. Her gut felt cold, beyond the mountain chill. She'd seen this sometimes, in terrorized peasants, survivors of the Great Plague, or even hardened soldiers after a siege. The horror that would not loose its hold. She remembered the faces of Peer and Elise's parents, mirroring the mute despair she'd felt as she told them what had happened. *If – when – I get out of here, I will go to them and show them the head of the monster. First, though, this idiot.*

"Come on," she said, supporting him with her shoulder. Almighty God, he was heavy, even half-starved! He went with her like a child. She was forced to sheath her sword and turn her back on the depths of the cave in order to keep hold of Lutz and her torch. Which is why she neither saw nor heard the second tröllkóna come at them from behind.

Lutz was suddenly ripped from her. He screamed. Sölveig spun, holding her torch out while she drew her sword. The trölkóna flung Lutz behind her, snaggled teeth bared in a snarl.

The monster's voice was a screech. "You don't dare!" she said. "This one is ours."

The potato-like nose and wild, dark hair were the same. "I know you," said Sölveig. "Eh?" said the tröllkóna.

Sölveig spoke clearly and raised her chin. "I remember. You and your sister took my friends, a boy and a girl, years ago. You let me live."

The tröllkóna chewed her lip, hesitating, squinting past the torchlight at Sölveig. Then she broke into a smile. "Yes …I do recall!" She licked her lips. "Well, when my sister returns with a few new lambs, we shall have a fine feast."

"Your sister is dead," said Sölveig. "Or did you think I came alone?"

The tröllkona grimaced. "Lies!"

Sölveig smiled grimly. "I'll be telling a different tale in Bjørgvin tomorrow morning."

The tröllkóna spat at her, a great gob of phlegm that hit the cave floor with a splat. The monster turned to reach above and behind her, drawing something out of a hole in the rock. Lutz's sword. "First, we shall have some sport."

Towering over Sölveig, the monster came at her holding the two-handed sword like a long dagger. Sölveig thrust her sword at the tröllkóna's face and turned so her profile was as narrow as possible. The monster swatted at her sword. Sölveig was used to dodging the long arms of a troll, but she misjudged the added reach of Lutz's sword. The tröllkóna clipped the tip of her bastard sword and it flew from her hand; the impact threw her off-balance. The tröllkóna swiped again as Sölveig stumbled, still clinging to the torch; this time the monster raked her torso and right arm with her vicious nails. Sölveig's mail prevented them from tearing her to shreds, but the blow felled her. She sprawled out of the cave mouth, her only weapon a dagger. Perhaps she could take the creature's eyes out before it dislocated her limbs and crushed her to death.

The tröllkóna stepped closer, nostrils twitching. "So, you did bring others …no matter. When they see what I will do to you, I think no more 'heroes' will come calling."

She raised the two-handed sword as if to pin Sölveig to the mountain. Then Sölveig had an idea. She and her comrades had tried something similar once, in Brouxelles, but she'd have to improvise.

As the troll-sister brought the sword-point down, Sölveig rolled, reaching for her flask of oil. She pulled the stopper out with her teeth and flung as much of its contents as she could at the tröllkóna, who was already leaning in to pluck her up. The oil spattered on the creature's dress, and for a split-second it left dark blotches on the wool in the moonlight. Then Sölveig plunged her torch into them.

"Now, Lutz!" she yelled, rolling again as close to the edge of the rockface as she dared.

The double distraction worked. The tröllkóna froze momentarily, looking over her shoulder and raising a long-fingered hand against an attack from behind, while her other hand dropped the sword and tried to douse the flames.

Sölveig didn't care whether Lutz was able or willing to help. She jumped up with the torch and set the tröllkóna's hair on fire. The monster swiped blindly at her and connected, knocking her against the side of the mountain. Sölveig's breath deserted her. She clawed for Lutz's huge sword as the tröllkona shrieked and tried to smother the flames on her head. They were near the precipice now. Sölveig realized the monster meant to climb down and roll in the snow. She grabbed the sword by grip and blade, cutting her glove and hand in the process. Stars swam in the darkness before her. *Relax, draw breath*, she told herself. Just as the tröllkona turned to scramble down, Sölveig grunted and drove the tip of Lutz's sword into her eye, pushing as though holding a battering ram. The tröllkóna howled and toppled over, the sword still embedded in her skull.

Sölveig dared a look over the edge. Mihr Nûsh was already darting forward, shadow dark on the silver snow. She drove her sword through the thrashing creature's heart. The townspeople swarmed the second troll-sister with a bloodthirsty, ragged cry. In the space of a few heartbeats, the second tröllkóna was dead. Mihr Nûsh signalled up to Sölveig, who gave the "all clear" sign. "We'll need ropes, and a litter!" she panted. Mihr Nûsh dispatched Max to get them.

Sölveig rolled over and caught her breath. Her ribs hurt. She didn't want to think how many had cracked, and the bruises she'd wear for weeks afterwards.

Why had Lutz gone alone?

She'd ask him that, when they were safe in Bjørgvin. Maybe by then he would be able to tell her. Before she cursed him out for being a fool, getting himself wounded and destroying any hope of a profitable year. Lutz had been the public face of their group, but now she doubted he'd be able to continue.

They'd collect their fee from the bishop, and make plans to depart. And these sisters, their bodies oozing dark, steaming blood on the bone-white snow ...their heads would bring silver, if not peace. Before leaving, perhaps, she could bear to visit her family, and that of Elise and Peer, and say, *it was too late, but I did what had to be done.*

Undine

Friedrich de la Motte Fouqué

To Undine

Undine! Thou fair and lovely sprite,
Since first from out an ancient lay
I saw gleam forth thy fitful light,
How hast thou sung my cares away!

How hast thou nestled next my heart,
And gently offered to impart
Thy sorrows to my listening ear,
Like a half-shy, half-trusting child,
The while my lute, in wood-notes wild,
Thine accents echoed far and near!

Then many a youth I won to muse
With love on thy mysterious ways,
With many a fair one to peruse
The legend of thy wondrous days.

And now both dame and youth would fain
List to my tale yet once again;
Nay, sweet Undine, be not afraid!
Enter their halls with footsteps light,
Greet courteously each noble knight,
But fondly every German maid.

And should they ask concerning me,
Oh, say, "He is a cavalier,
Who truly serves and valiantly,
In tourney and festivity,
With lute and sword, each lady fair!"

Chapter I

ON A BEAUTIFUL EVENING, many hundred years ago, a worthy old fisherman sat mending his nets. The spot where he dwelt was exceedingly picturesque. The green turf on which he had built his cottage ran far out into a great lake; and this slip of verdure appeared to stretch into it as much through love of its clear waters as the lake, moved by a like impulse, strove to fold the meadow, with its waving grass and flowers, and the cooling shade of the trees, in its embrace of love. They seemed to be drawn toward each other, and the one to be visiting the other as a guest.

With respect to human beings, indeed, in this pleasant spot, excepting the fisherman and his family, there were few, or rather none, to be met with. For as in the background of the scene, toward the west and north-west, lay a forest of extraordinary wildness, which, owing to its sunless gloom and almost impassable recesses, as well as to fear of the strange creatures and visionary illusions to be encountered in it, most people avoided entering, unless in cases of extreme necessity. The pious old fisherman, however, many times passed through it without harm, when he carried the fine fish which he caught by his beautiful strip of land to a great city lying only a short distance beyond the forest.

Now the reason he was able to go through this wood with so much ease may have been chiefly this, because he entertained scarcely any thoughts but such as were of a religious nature; and besides, every time he crossed the evil-reported shades, he used to sing some holy song with a clear voice and from a sincere heart.

Well, while he sat by his nets this evening, neither fearing nor devising evil, a sudden terror seized him, as he heard a rushing in the darkness of the wood, that resembled the tramping of a mounted steed, and the noise continued every instant drawing nearer and nearer to his little territory.

What he had fancied, when abroad in many a stormy night, respecting the mysteries of the forest, now flashed through his mind in a moment, especially the figure of a man of gigantic stature and snow-white appearance, who kept nodding his head in a portentous manner. And when he raised his eyes towards the wood, the form came before him in perfect distinctness, as he saw the nodding man burst forth from the mazy web-work of leaves and branches. But he immediately felt emboldened, when he reflected that nothing to give him alarm had ever befallen him even in the forest; and moreover, that on this open neck of land the evil spirit, it was likely, would be still less daring in the exercise of his power. At the same time he prayed aloud with the most earnest sincerity of devotion, repeating a passage of the Bible. This inspired him with fresh courage, and soon perceiving the illusion, and the strange mistake into which his imagination had betrayed him, he could with difficulty refrain from laughing. The white nodding figure he had seen became transformed, in the twinkling of an eye, to what in reality it was, a small brook, long and familiarly known to him, which ran foaming from the forest, and discharged itself into the lake.

But what had caused the startling sound was a knight arrayed in sumptuous apparel, who from under the shadows of the trees came riding toward the cottage. His doublet was violet embroidered with gold, and his scarlet cloak hung gracefully over it; on his cap of burnished gold waved red and violet-coloured plumes; and in his golden shoulder-belt flashed a sword, richly ornamented, and extremely beautiful. The white barb that bore the knight was more slenderly built than war-horses usually are, and he touched the turf with a step so light and elastic that the green and flowery carpet seemed hardly to receive the slightest injury from his tread. The old fisherman, notwithstanding, did not feel perfectly secure in his mind, although he was forced to believe that no evil could be feared from an appearance so pleasing, and therefore, as good manners dictated, he took off his hat on the knight's coming near, and quietly remained by the side of his nets.

When the stranger stopped, and asked whether he, with his horse, could have shelter and entertainment there for the night, the fisherman returned answer: "As to your horse, fair sir, I have no better stable for him than this shady meadow, and no better provender than the grass that is growing here. But with respect to yourself, you shall be welcome to our humble cottage, and to the best supper and lodging we are able to give you."

The knight was well contented with this reception; and alighting from his horse, which his host assisted him to relieve from saddle and bridle, he let him hasten away to the fresh pasture, and thus spoke: "Even had I found you less hospitable and kindly disposed, my worthy old friend, you would still, I suspect, hardly have got rid of me today; for here, I perceive, a broad lake lies before us, and as to riding back into that wood of wonders, with the shades of evening deepening around me, may Heaven in its grace preserve me from the thought."

"Pray, not a word of the wood, or of returning into it!" said the fisherman, and took his guest into the cottage.

There beside the hearth, from which a frugal fire was diffusing its light through the clean twilight room, sat the fisherman's aged wife in a great chair. At the entrance of their noble guest, she rose and gave him a courteous welcome, but sat down again in her seat of honour, not making the slightest offer of it to the stranger. Upon this the fisherman said with a smile:

"You must not be offended with her, young gentleman, because she has not given up to you the best chair in the house; it is a custom among poor people to look upon this as the privilege of the aged."

"Why, husband!" cried the old lady, with a quiet smile, "where can your wits be wandering? Our guest, to say the least of him, must belong to a Christian country; and how is it possible, then, that so well-bred a young man as he appears to be could dream of driving old people from their chairs? Take a seat, my young master," continued she, turning to the knight; "there is still quite a snug little chair on the other side of the room there, only be careful not to shove it about too roughly, for one of its legs, I fear, is none of the firmest."

The knight brought up the seat as carefully as she could desire, sat down upon it good-humouredly, and it seemed to him almost as if he must be somehow related to this little household, and have just returned home from abroad.

These three worthy people now began to converse in the most friendly and familiar manner. In relation to the forest, indeed, concerning which the knight occasionally made some inquiries, the old man chose to know and say but little; he was of opinion that slightly touching upon it at this hour of twilight was most suitable and safe; but of the cares and comforts of their home, and their business abroad, the aged couple spoke more freely, and listened also with eager curiosity as the knight recounted to them his travels, and how he had a castle near one of the sources of the Danube, and that his name was Sir Huldbrand of Ringstetten.

Already had the stranger, while they were in the midst of their talk, heard at times a splash against the little low window, as if some one were dashing water against it. The old man, every time he heard the noise, knit his brows with vexation; but at last, when the whole sweep of a shower came pouring like a torrent against the panes, and bubbling through the decayed frame into the room, he started up indignant, rushed to the window, and cried with a threatening voice:

"Undine! Will you never leave off these fooleries? – Not even today, when we have a stranger knight with us in the cottage?"

All without now became still, only a low laugh was just audible, and the fisherman said, as he came back to his seat, "You will have the goodness, my honoured guest, to pardon this freak, and it may be a multitude more; but she has no thought of evil or of any harm. This mischievous Undine, to confess the truth, is our adopted daughter, and she stoutly refuses to give over this frolicsome childishness of hers, although she has already entered her eighteenth year. But in spite of this, as I said before, she is at heart one of the very best children in the world."

"*You* may say so," broke in the old lady, shaking her head; "you can give a better account of her than I can. When you return home from fishing, or from selling your fish in the city, you may think her frolics very delightful, but to have her dancing about you the whole day long, and never from morning to night to hear her speak one word of sense; and then as she grows older, instead of having any help from her in the family, to find her a continual cause of anxiety, lest her wild humours should completely ruin us, that is quite another thing, and enough at last to weary out the patience even of a saint."

"Well, well," replied the master of the house with a smile, "you have your trials with Undine, and I have mine with the lake. The lake often beats down my dams, and breaks the meshes of my nets, but for all that I have a strong affection for it, and so have you, in spite of your mighty crosses and vexations, for our graceful little child. Is it not true?"

"One cannot be very angry with her," answered the old lady, as she gave her husband an approving smile.

That instant the door flew open, and a fair girl, of wondrous beauty, sprang laughing in, and said, "You have only been making a mock of me, father; for where now is the guest you mentioned?"

The same moment, however, she perceived the knight also, and continued standing before the young man in fixed astonishment. Huldbrand was charmed with her graceful figure, and viewed her lovely features with the more intense interest, as he imagined it was only her surprise that allowed him the opportunity, and that she would soon turn away from his gaze with increased bashfulness. But the event was the very reverse of what he expected; for, after looking at him for a long while, she became more confident, moved nearer, knelt down before him, and while she played with a gold medal which he wore attached to a rich chain on his breast, exclaimed:

"Why, you beautiful, you kind guest! How have you reached our poor cottage at last? Have you been obliged for years and years to wander about the world before you could catch one glimpse of our nook? Do you come out of that wild forest, my beautiful knight?"

The old woman was so prompt in her reproof as to allow him no time to answer. She commanded the maiden to rise, show better manners, and go to her work. But Undine, without making any reply, drew a little footstool near Huldbrand's chair, sat down upon it with her netting, and said in a gentle tone:

"I will work here."

The old man did as parents are apt to do with children to whom they have been over-indulgent. He affected to observe nothing of Undine's strange behaviour, and was beginning to talk about something else. But this the maiden did not permit him to do. She broke in upon him, "I have asked our kind guest from whence he has come among us, and he has not yet answered me."

"I come out of the forest, you lovely little vision," Huldbrand returned; and she spoke again:

"You must also tell me how you came to enter that forest, so feared and shunned, and the marvellous adventures you met with in it; for there is no escaping without something of this kind."

Huldbrand felt a slight shudder on remembering what he had witnessed, and looked involuntarily toward the window, for it seemed to him that one of the strange shapes which had come upon him in the forest must be there grinning in through the glass; but he discerned nothing except the deep darkness of night, which had now enveloped the whole prospect. Upon this he became more collected, and was just on the point of beginning his account, when the old man thus interrupted him:

"Not so, sir knight; this is by no means a fit hour for such relations."

But Undine, in a state of high excitement, sprang up from her little stool and cried, placing herself directly before the fisherman: "He shall *not* tell his story, father? He shall not? But it is my will: – he shall! – Stop him who may!"

Thus speaking, she stamped her little foot vehemently on the floor, but all with an air of such comic and good-humoured simplicity, that Huldbrand now found it quite as hard to withdraw his gaze from her wild emotion as he had before from her gentleness and beauty. The old man, on the contrary, burst out in unrestrained displeasure. He severely reproved Undine for her disobedience and her unbecoming carriage towards the stranger, and his good old wife joined him in harping on the same string.

By these rebukes Undine was only excited the more. "If you want to quarrel with me," she cried, "and will not let me hear what I so much desire, then sleep alone in your smoky old hut!" And swift as an arrow she shot from the door, and vanished amid the darkness of the night.

Huldbrand and the fisherman sprang from their seats, and were rushing to stop the angry girl; but before they could reach the cottage-door, she had disappeared in the stormy darkness without, and no sound, not so much even as that of her light footstep, betrayed the course she had taken. Huldbrand threw a glance of inquiry towards his host; it almost seemed to him as if the whole of the sweet apparition, which had so suddenly plunged again amid the night, were no other than a continuation of the wonderful forms that had just played their mad pranks with him in the forest. But the old man muttered between his teeth –

"This is not the first time she has treated us in this manner. Now must our hearts be filled with anxiety, and our eyes find no sleep for the whole night; for who can assure us, in spite of her past escapes, that she will not some time or other come to harm, if she thus continue out in the dark and alone until daylight?"

"Then pray, for God's sake, father, let us follow her," cried Huldbrand anxiously.

"Wherefore should we?" replied the old man. "It would be a sin were I to suffer you, all alone, to search after the foolish girl amid the lonesomeness of night; and my old limbs would fail to carry me to this wild rover, even if I knew to what place she has betaken herself."

"Still we ought at least to call after her, and beg her to return," said Huldbrand; and he began to call in tones of earnest entreaty, "Undine! Undine! Come back, come back!"

The old man shook his head, and said, "All your shouting, however loud and long, will be of no avail; you know not as yet, sir knight, how self-willed the little thing is." But still, even hoping against hope, he could not himself cease calling out every minute, amid the gloom of night, "Undine! Ah, dear Undine! I beseech you, pray come back – only this once."

It turned out, however, exactly as the fisherman had said. No Undine could they hear or see; and as the old man would on no account consent that Huldbrand should go in quest of the fugitive, they were both obliged at last to return into the cottage. There they found the fire on the hearth almost gone out, and the mistress of the house, who took Undine's flight and danger far less to heart than her husband, had already gone to rest. The old man blew up the coals, put on dry wood, and by the firelight hunted for a flask of wine, which he brought and set between himself and his guest.

"You, sir knight, as well as I," said he, "are anxious on the silly girl's account; and it would be better, I think, to spend part of the night in chatting and drinking, than keep turning and turning on our rush-mats, and trying in vain to sleep. What is your opinion?"

Huldbrand was well pleased with the plan; the fisherman pressed him to take the empty seat of honour, its late occupant having now left it for her couch; and they relished their beverage and enjoyed their chat as two such good men and true ever ought to do. To be sure, whenever the slightest thing moved before the windows, or at times when even nothing was moving, one of them would look up and exclaim, "Here she comes!" Then would they continue silent a few moments, and afterward, when nothing appeared, would shake their heads, breathe out a sigh, and go on with their talk.

But, as neither could think of anything but Undine, the best plan they could devise was, that the old fisherman should relate, and the knight should hear, in what manner Undine had come to the cottage. So the fisherman began as follows:

"It is now about fifteen years since I one day crossed the wild forest with fish for the city market. My wife had remained at home as she was wont to do; and at this time for a reason of more than common interest, for although we were beginning to feel the advances of age, God had bestowed upon us an infant of wonderful beauty. It was a little girl; and we already began to ask ourselves the question, whether we ought not, for the advantage of the new-comer, to quit our solitude, and, the better to bring up this precious gift of Heaven, to remove to some more inhabited place. Poor people, to be sure, cannot in these cases do all you may think they ought, sir knight; but we must all do what we can.

"Well, I went on my way, and this affair would keep running in my head. This slip of land was most dear to me, and I trembled when, amidst the bustle and broils of the city, I thought to myself, 'In a scene of tumult like this, or at least in one not much more quiet, I must soon take up my abode.' But I did not for this murmur against our good God; on the contrary, I praised Him in silence for the new-born babe. I should also speak an untruth, were I to say that anything befell me, either on my passage through the forest to the city, or on my returning homeward, that gave me more alarm than usual, as at that time I had never seen any appearance there which could terrify or annoy me. The Lord was ever with me in those awful shades."

Thus speaking he took his cap reverently from his bald head, and continued to sit for a considerable time in devout thought. He then covered himself again, and went on with his relation.

"On this side the forest, alas! It was on this side, that woe burst upon me. My wife came wildly to meet me, clad in mourning apparel, and her eyes streaming with tears. 'Gracious God!' I cried, 'Where's our child? Speak!'

" 'With Him on whom you have called, dear husband,' she answered, and we now entered the cottage together, weeping in silence. I looked for the little corpse, almost fearing to find what I was seeking; and then it was I first learnt how all had happened.

"My wife had taken the little one in her arms, and walked out to the shore of the lake. She there sat down by its very brink; and while she was playing with the infant, as free from all fear as she was full of delight, it bent forward on a sudden, as if seeing something very beautiful in the water. My wife saw her laugh, the dear angel, and try to catch the image in her tiny hands; but in a moment – with a motion swifter than sight – she sprang from her mother's arms, and sank in the lake, the watery glass into which she had been gazing. I searched for our lost darling again and again; but it was all in vain; I could nowhere find the least trace of her.

"The same evening we childless parents were sitting together by our cottage hearth. We had no desire to talk, even if our tears would have permitted us. As we thus sat in mournful stillness, gazing into the fire, all at once we heard something without, – a slight rustling at the door. The door flew open, and we saw a little girl, three or four years old, and more beautiful than I can say, standing on the threshold, richly dressed, and smiling upon us. We were struck dumb with astonishment, and I knew not for a time whether the tiny form were a real human being, or a mere mockery of enchantment. But I soon perceived water dripping from her golden hair and rich garments, and that the pretty child had been lying in the water, and stood in immediate need of our help.

" 'Wife,' said I, 'no one has been able to save our child for us; but let us do for others what would have made us so blessed could any one have done it for us.'

"We undressed the little thing, put her to bed, and gave her something to drink; at all this she spoke not a word, but only turned her eyes upon us – eyes blue and bright as sea or sky – and continued looking at us with a smile.

"Next morning we had no reason to fear that she had received any other harm than her wetting, and I now asked her about her parents, and how she could have come to us. But the account she gave was both confused and incredible. She must surely have been born far from here, not only because I have been unable for these fifteen years to learn anything of her birth, but because she then said, and at times continues to say, many things of so very singular a nature, that we neither of us know, after all, whether she may not have dropped among us from the moon; for her talk runs upon golden castles, crystal domes, and Heaven knows what extravagances beside. What, however, she related with most distinctness was this: that while she was once taking a sail with her mother on the great lake, she fell out of the boat into the water; and that when she first recovered her senses, she was here under our trees, where the gay scenes of the shore filled her with delight.

"We now had another care weighing upon our minds, and one that caused us no small perplexity and uneasiness. We of course very soon determined to keep and bring up the child we had found, in place of our own darling that had been drowned; but who could tell us whether she had been baptized or not? She herself could give us no light on the subject. When we asked her the question, she commonly made answer, that she well knew she was created for God's praise and glory, and that she was willing to let us do with her all that might promote His glory and praise.

"My wife and I reasoned in this way: 'If she has not been baptized, there can be no use in putting off the ceremony; and if she has been, it still is better to have too much of a good thing than too little.'

"Taking this view of our difficulty, we now endeavoured to hit upon a good name for the child, since, while she remained without one, we were often at a loss, in our familiar talk, to know what to call her. We at length agreed that Dorothea would be most suitable for her, as I had somewhere heard it said that this name signified a gift of God, and surely she had been sent to us by Providence as a gift, to comfort us in our misery. She, on the contrary, would not so much as hear Dorothea mentioned; she insisted, that as she had been named Undine by her parents, Undine she ought still to be called. It now occurred to me that this was a heathenish name, to be found in no calendar, and I resolved to ask the advice of a priest in the city. He would not listen to the name of Undine; and yielding to my urgent request, he came with me through the enchanted forest in order to perform the rite of baptism here in my cottage.

"The little maid stood before us so prettily adorned, and with such an air of gracefulness, that the heart of the priest softened at once in her presence; and she coaxed him so sweetly, and jested with him so merrily, that he at last remembered nothing of his many objections to the name of Undine.

"Thus, then, was she baptized Undine; and during the holy ceremony she behaved with great propriety and gentleness, wild and wayward as at other times she invariably was; for in this my wife was quite right, when she mentioned the anxiety the child has occasioned us. If I should relate to you –"

At this moment the knight interrupted the fisherman, to direct his attention to a deep sound as of a rushing flood, which had caught his ear during the talk of the old man. And now the waters came pouring on with redoubled fury before the cottage-windows. Both sprang to the door. There they saw, by the light of the now risen moon, the brook which issued from the wood rushing wildly over its banks, and whirling onward with it both stones and branches of trees in its rapid course. The storm, as if awakened by the uproar, burst forth from the clouds, whose immense masses of vapour coursed over the moon with the swiftness of thought; the lake roared beneath the wind that swept the foam from its waves; while the trees of this narrow peninsula groaned from root to topmost branch as they bowed and swung above the torrent.

"Undine! In God's name, Undine!" cried the two men in an agony. No answer was returned. And now, regardless of everything else, they hurried from the cottage, one in this direction, the other in that, searching and calling.

Chapter II

THE LONGER Huldbrand sought Undine beneath the shades of night, and failed to find her, the more anxious and confused he became. The impression that she was a mere phantom of the forest gained a new ascendency over him; indeed, amid the howling of the waves and the tempest, the crashing of the trees, and the entire change of the once so peaceful and beautiful scene, he was tempted to view the whole peninsula, together with the cottage and its inhabitants, as little more than some mockery of his senses. But still he heard afar off the fisherman's anxious and incessant shouting, "Undine!" and also his aged wife, who was praying and singing psalms.

At length, when he drew near to the brook, which had overflowed its banks, he perceived by the moonlight, that it had taken its wild course directly in front of the haunted forest, so as to change the peninsula into an island.

"Merciful God!" he breathed to himself, "If Undine has ventured a step within that fearful wood, what will become of her? Perhaps it was all owing to her sportive and wayward spirit, because I would give her no account of my adventures there. And now the stream is rolling between us, she may be weeping alone on the other side in the midst of spectral horrors!"

A shuddering groan escaped him; and clambering over some stones and trunks of overthrown pines, in order to step into the impetuous current, he resolved, either by wading or swimming, to seek the wanderer on the further shore. He felt, it is true, all the dread and shrinking awe creeping over him which he had already suffered by daylight among the now tossing and roaring branches of the forest. More than all, a tall man in white, whom he knew but too well, met his view, as he stood grinning and nodding on the grass beyond the water. But even monstrous forms like this only impelled him to cross over toward them, when the thought rushed upon him that Undine might be there alone and in the agony of death.

He had already grasped a strong branch of a pine, and stood supporting himself upon it in the whirling current, against which he could with difficulty keep himself erect; but he advanced deeper in with a courageous spirit. That instant a gentle voice of warning cried near him, "Do not venture, do not venture! – That *old man*, the *stream*, is too full of tricks to be trusted!" He knew the soft tones of the voice; and while he stood as it were entranced beneath the shadows which had now duskily veiled the moon, his head swam with the swelling and rolling of the waves as he saw them momentarily rising above his knee. Still he disdained the thought of giving up his purpose.

"If you are not really there, if you are merely gambolling round me like a mist, may I, too, bid farewell to life, and become a shadow like you, dear, dear Undine!" Thus calling aloud, he again moved deeper into the stream. "Look round you – ah, pray look round you, beautiful young stranger! Why rush on death so madly?" cried the voice a second time close by him; and looking on one side he perceived, by the light of the moon, again cloudless, a little island formed by the flood; and crouching upon its flowery turf, beneath the branches of embowering trees, he saw the smiling and lovely Undine.

O how much more gladly than before the young man now plied his sturdy staff! A few steps, and he had crossed the flood that was rushing between himself and the maiden; and he stood near her on the little spot of greensward in security, protected by the old trees. Undine half rose, and she threw her arms around his neck to draw him gently down upon the soft seat by her side.

"Here you shall tell me your story, my beautiful friend," she breathed in a low whisper; "here the cross old people cannot disturb us; and, besides, our roof of leaves here will make quite as good a shelter as their poor cottage."

"It is heaven itself," cried Huldbrand; and folding her in his arms, he kissed the lovely girl with fervour.

The old fisherman, meantime, had come to the margin of the stream, and he shouted across, "Why, how is this, sir knight! I received you with the welcome which one true-hearted man gives to another; and now you sit there caressing my foster-child in secret, while you suffer me in my anxiety to wander through the night in quest of her."

"Not till this moment did I find her myself, old father," cried the knight across the water.

"So much the better," said the fisherman, "but now make haste, and bring her over to me upon firm ground."

To this, however, Undine would by no means consent. She declared that she would rather enter the wild forest itself with the beautiful stranger, than return to the cottage where she was so thwarted in her wishes, and from which the knight would soon or late go away. Then, throwing her arms round Huldbrand, she sang the following verse with the warbling sweetness of a bird:

"A rill would leave its misty vale,
And fortunes wild explore,
Weary at length it reached the main,
And sought its vale no more."

The old fisherman wept bitterly at her song, but his emotion seemed to awaken little or no sympathy in her. She kissed and caressed her new friend, who at last said to her: "Undine, if the distress of the old man does not touch your heart, it cannot but move mine. We ought to return to him."

She opened her large blue eyes upon him in amazement, and spoke at last with a slow and doubtful accent, "If you think so, it is well, all is right to me which you think right. But the old man over there must first give me his promise that he will allow you, without objection, to relate what you saw in the wood, and – well, other things will settle themselves."

"Come – only come!" cried the fisherman to her, unable to utter another word. At the same time he stretched his arms wide over the current towards her, and to give her assurance that he would do what she required, nodded his head. This motion caused his white hair to fall strangely over his face, and Huldbrand could not but remember the nodding white man of the forest. Without allowing anything, however, to produce in him the least confusion, the young knight took the beautiful girl in his arms, and bore her across the narrow channel which the stream had torn away between her little island and the solid shore. The old man fell upon Undine's neck, and found it impossible either to express his joy or to kiss her enough; even the ancient dame came up and embraced the recovered girl most cordially. Every word of censure was carefully avoided; the more so, indeed, as even Undine, forgetting her waywardness, almost overwhelmed her foster-parents with caresses and the prattle of tenderness.

When at length the excess of their joy at recovering their child had subsided, morning had already dawned, shining upon the waters of the lake; the tempest had become hushed, the small birds sung merrily on the moist branches.

As Undine now insisted upon hearing the recital of the knight's promised adventures, the aged couple readily agreed to her wish. Breakfast was brought out beneath the trees which stood behind the cottage toward the lake on the north, and they sat down to it with contented hearts; Undine at the knight's feet on the grass. These arrangements being made, Huldbrand began his story in the following manner:

"It is now about eight days since I rode into the free imperial city which lies yonder on the farther side of the forest. Soon after my arrival a splendid tournament and running at the ring took place there, and I spared neither my horse nor my lance in the encounters.

"Once while I was pausing at the lists to rest from the brisk exercise, and was handing back my helmet to one of my attendants, a female figure of extraordinary beauty caught my attention, as, most magnificently attired, she stood looking on at one of the balconies. I learned, on making inquiry of a person near me, that the name of the young lady was Bertalda, and that she was a foster-daughter of one of the powerful dukes of this country. She too, I observed, was gazing at me, and the consequences were such as we young knights are wont to experience; whatever success in riding I might have had before, I was now favoured with still better fortune. That evening I was Bertalda's partner in the dance, and I enjoyed the same distinction during the remainder of the festival."

A sharp pain in his left hand, as it hung carelessly beside him, here interrupted Huldbrand's relation, and drew his eye to the part affected. Undine had fastened her pearly teeth, and not without some keenness too, upon one of his fingers, appearing at the same time very gloomy and displeased. On a sudden, however, she looked up in his eyes with an expression of tender melancholy, and whispered almost inaudibly:

"It is all your own fault."

She then covered her face; and the knight, strangely embarrassed and thoughtful, went on with his story.

"This lady, Bertalda, of whom I spoke, is of a proud and wayward spirit. The second day I saw her she pleased me by no means so much as she had the first, and the third day still less. But I continued about her because she showed me more favour than she did any other knight, and it so happened that I playfully asked her to give me one of her gloves. 'When you have entered the haunted forest all alone,' said she; 'when you have explored its wonders, and brought me a full account of them, the glove is yours.' As to getting her glove, it was of no importance to me whatever, but the word had been spoken, and no honourable knight would permit himself to be urged to such a proof of valour a second time."

"I thought," said Undine, interrupting him, "that she loved you."

"It did appear so," replied Huldbrand.

"Well!" exclaimed the maiden, laughing, "This is beyond belief; she must be very stupid. To drive from her one who was dear to her! And worse than all, into that ill-omened wood! The wood and its mysteries, for all I should have cared, might have waited long enough."

"Yesterday morning, then," pursued the knight, smiling kindly upon Undine, "I set out from the city, my enterprise before me. The early light lay rich upon the verdant turf. It shone so rosy on the slender boles of the trees, and there was so merry a whispering among the leaves, that in my heart I could not but laugh at people who feared meeting anything to terrify them in a spot so delicious. 'I shall soon pass through the forest, and as speedily return,' I said to myself, in the overflow of joyous feeling, and ere I was well aware, I had entered deep among the green shades, while of the plain that lay behind me I was no longer able to catch a glimpse.

"Then the conviction for the first time impressed me, that in a forest of so great extent I might very easily become bewildered, and that this, perhaps, might be the only danger which was likely to threaten those who explored its recesses. So I made a halt, and turned myself in the direction of the sun, which had meantime risen somewhat higher, and while I was looking up to observe it, I saw something black among the boughs of a lofty oak. My first thought was, 'It is a bear!' and I grasped my weapon. The object then accosted me from above in a human voice, but in a tone most harsh and hideous: 'If I, overhead here, do not gnaw off these dry branches, Sir Noodle, what shall we have to roast you with when midnight comes?' And with that it grinned, and made such a rattling with the branches that my courser became mad with affright, and rushed furiously forward with me before I had time to see distinctly what sort of a devil's beast it was."

"You must not speak so," said the old fisherman, crossing himself. His wife did the same, without saying a word, and Undine, while her eye sparkled with delight, looked at the knight and said, "The best of the story is, however, that as yet they have not roasted you! Go on, now, you beautiful knight."

The knight then went on with his adventures. "My horse was so wild, that he well-nigh rushed with me against limbs and trunks of trees. He was dripping with sweat through terror, heat, and the violent straining of his muscles. Still he refused to slacken his career. At last, altogether beyond my control, he took his course directly up a stony steep, when suddenly a tall white man flashed before me, and threw himself athwart the way my mad steed was taking. At this apparition he shuddered with new affright, and stopped trembling. I took this chance of recovering my command of him, and now for the first time perceived that my deliverer, so far from being a white man, was only a brook of silver brightness, foaming near me in its descent from the hill, while it crossed and arrested my horse's course with its rush of waters."

"Thanks, thanks, dear brook!" cried Undine, clapping her little hands. But the old man shook his head, and looked down in deep thought.

"Hardly had I well settled myself in my saddle, and got the reins in my grasp again," Huldbrand pursued, "when a wizard-like dwarf of a man was already standing at my side, diminutive and ugly beyond conception, his complexion of a brownish-yellow, and his nose scarcely smaller than the rest of him together. The fellow's mouth was slit almost from ear to ear, and he showed his teeth with a grinning smile of idiot courtesy, while he overwhelmed me with bows and scrapes innumerable. The farce now becoming excessively irksome, I thanked him in the fewest words I could well use, turned about my still trembling charger, and purposed either to seek another adventure, or, should I meet with none, to take my way back to the city; for the sun, during my wild chase, had passed the meridian, and was now hastening toward the west. But this villain of a dwarf sprang at the same instant, and, with a turn as rapid as lightning, stood before my horse again. 'Clear the way there!' I cried fiercely; 'the beast is wild, and will make nothing of running over you.'

" 'Ay, ay,' cried the imp with a snarl, and snorting out a laugh still more frightfully idiotic; 'pay me, first pay what you owe me. I stopped your fine little nag for you; without my help, both you and he would be now sprawling below there in that stony ravine. Hu! From what a horrible plunge I've saved you!'

" 'Well, don't make any more faces,' said I, 'but take your money and be off, though every word you say is false. It was the brook there, you miserable thing, and not you, that saved me,' and at the same time I dropped a piece of gold into his wizard cap, which he had taken from his head while he was begging before me.

"I then trotted off and left him, but he screamed after me; and on a sudden, with inconceivable quickness, he was close by my side. I started my horse into a gallop. He galloped on with me, though it seemed with great difficulty, and with a strange movement, half ludicrous and half horrible, forcing at the same time every limb and feature into distortion, he held up the gold piece and screamed at every leap, 'Counterfeit! False! False coin! Counterfeit!' and such was the strange sound that issued from his hollow breast, you would have supposed that at every scream he must have tumbled upon the ground dead. All this while his disgusting red tongue hung lolling from his mouth.

"I stopped bewildered, and asked, 'What do you mean by this screaming? Take another piece of gold, take two, but leave me.'

"He then began again his hideous salutations of courtesy, and snarled out as before, 'Not gold, it shall not be gold, my young gentleman. I have too much of that trash already, as I will show you in no time.'

"At that moment, and thought itself could not have been more instantaneous, I seemed to have acquired new powers of sight. I could see through the solid green plain, as if it were green glass, and the smooth surface of the earth were round as a globe, and within it I saw crowds of goblins, who were pursuing their pastime and making themselves merry with silver and gold. They were tumbling and rolling about, heads up and heads down; they pelted one another in sport with the precious metals, and with irritating malice blew gold-dust in one another's eyes. My odious companion ordered the others to reach him up a vast quantity of gold; this he showed to me with a laugh, and then flung it again ringing and chinking down the measureless abyss.

"After this contemptuous disregard of gold, he held up the piece I had given him, showing it to his brother goblins below, and they laughed immoderately at a coin so worthless, and hissed me. At last, raising their fingers all smutched with ore, they pointed them at me in scorn; and wilder and wilder, and thicker and thicker, and madder and madder, the crowd were clambering up to where I sat gazing at these wonders. Then terror seized me, as it had before seized my horse. I drove my spurs into his sides, and how far he rushed with me through the forest, during this second of my wild heats, it is impossible to say.

"At last, when I had now come to a dead halt again, the cool of evening was around me. I caught the gleam of a white footpath through the branches of the trees; and presuming it would lead me out of the forest toward the city, I was desirous of working my way into it. But a face, perfectly white and indistinct, with features ever changing, kept thrusting itself out and peering at me between the leaves. I tried to avoid it, but wherever I went, there too appeared the unearthly face. I was maddened with rage at this interruption, and determined to drive my steed at the appearance full tilt, when such a cloud of white foam came rushing upon me and my horse, that we were almost blinded and glad to turn about and escape. Thus from step to step it forced us on, and ever aside from the footpath, leaving us for the most part only one direction open. When we advanced in this, it kept following close behind us, yet did not occasion the smallest harm or inconvenience.

"When at times I looked about me at the form, I perceived that the white face, which had splashed upon us its shower of foam, was resting on a body equally white, and of more than gigantic size. Many a time, too, I received the impression that the whole appearance was nothing more than a wandering stream or torrent; but respecting this I could never attain to any certainty. We both of us, horse and rider, became weary as we shaped our course according to the movements of the white man, who continued nodding his head at us, as if he would say, 'Quite right!' And thus, at length, we came out here, at the edge of the wood, where I saw the fresh turf, the waters of the lake, and your little cottage, and where the tall white man disappeared."

"Well, Heaven be praised that he is gone!" cried the old fisherman; and he now began to talk of how his guest could most conveniently return to his friends in the city. Upon this, Undine began laughing to herself, but so very low that the sound was hardly perceivable. Huldbrand observing it, said, "I thought you were glad to see me here; why, then, do you now appear so happy when our talk turns upon my going away?"

"Because you cannot go away," answered Undine. "Pray make a single attempt; try with a boat, with your horse, or alone, as you please, to cross that forest stream which has burst its bounds; or rather, make no trial at all, for you would be dashed to pieces by the stones and trunks of trees which you see driven on with such violence. And as to the lake, I know that well; even my father dares not venture out with his boat far enough to help you."

Huldbrand rose, smiling, in order to look about and observe whether the state of things were such as Undine had represented it to be. The old man accompanied him, and the maiden went merrily dancing beside them. They found all, in fact, just as Undine had said, and that the knight, whether willing or not willing, must submit to remaining on the island, so lately a peninsula, until the flood should subside.

When the three were now returning to the cottage after their ramble, the knight whispered in the ear of the little maiden, "Well, dear Undine, are you angry at my remaining?"

"Ah," she pettishly replied, "do not speak to me! If I had not bitten you, who knows what fine things you would have put into your story about Bertalda?"

Chapter III

IT MAY HAVE happened to thee, my dear reader, after being much driven to and fro in the world, to reach at length a spot where all was well with thee. The love of home and of its peaceful joys, innate to all, again sprang up in thy heart; thou thoughtest that thy home was decked with all the flowers of childhood, and of that purest, deepest love which had grown upon the graves of thy beloved, and that here it was good to live and to build houses. Even if thou didst err, and hast had bitterly to mourn thy error, it is nothing to my purpose, and thou thyself wilt not like to dwell on the sad recollection. But recall those unspeakably sweet feelings, that angelic greeting of peace, and thou wilt be able to understand what was the happiness of the knight Huldbrand during his abode on that narrow slip of land.

He frequently observed, with heartfelt satisfaction, that the forest stream continued every day to swell and roll on with a more impetuous sweep; and this forced him to prolong his stay on the island. Part of the day he wandered about with an old cross-bow, which he found in a corner of the cottage, and had repaired in order to shoot the waterfowl that flew over; and all that he was lucky enough to hit he brought home for a good roast in the kitchen. When he came in with his booty, Undine seldom failed to greet him with a scolding, because he had cruelly deprived the happy joyous little creatures of life as they were sporting above in the blue ocean of the air; nay more, she often wept bitterly when she viewed the water-fowl dead in his hand. But at other times, when he returned without having shot any, she gave him a scolding equally serious, since, owing to his carelessness and want of skill, they must now put up with a dinner of fish. Her playful taunts ever touched his heart with delight; the more so, as she generally strove to make up for her pretended ill-humour with endearing caresses.

The old people saw with pleasure this familiarity of Undine and Huldbrand; they looked upon them as betrothed, or even as married, and living with them in their old age on their island, now torn off from the mainland. The loneliness of his situation strongly impressed also the young Huldbrand with the feeling that he was already Undine's bridegroom. It seemed to him as if, beyond those encompassing floods, there were no other world in existence, or at any rate as if he could never cross them, and again associate with the world of other men; and when at times his grazing steed raised his head and neighed to him, seemingly inquiring after his knightly achievements and reminding him of them, or when his coat-of-arms sternly shone upon him from the embroidery of his saddle and the caparisons of his horse, or when his sword happened to fall from the nail on which it was hanging in the cottage, and flashed on his eye as it slipped from the scabbard in its fall, he quieted the doubts of his mind by saying to himself, "Undine cannot be a fisherman's daughter. She is, in all probability, a native of some remote region, and a member of some illustrious family."

There was one thing, indeed, to which he had a strong aversion: this was to hear the old dame reproving Undine. The wild girl, it is true, commonly laughed at the reproof, making no attempt to conceal the extravagance of her mirth; but it appeared to him like touching his own honour; and still he found it impossible to blame the aged wife of the fisherman, since Undine always deserved at least ten times as many reproofs as she received; so he continued to feel in his heart an affectionate tenderness for the ancient mistress of the house, and his whole life flowed on in the calm stream of contentment.

There came, however, an interruption at last. The fisherman and the knight had been accustomed at dinner, and also in the evening when the wind roared without, as it rarely failed to do towards night, to enjoy together a flask of wine. But now their whole stock, which the fisherman had from time to time brought with him from the city, was at last exhausted, and they were both quite out of humour at the circumstance. That day Undine laughed at them excessively, but they were not disposed to join in her jests with the same gaiety as usual. Toward evening she went out of the cottage, to escape, as she said, the sight of two such long and tiresome faces.

While it was yet twilight, some appearances of a tempest seemed to be again mustering in the sky, and the waves already heaved and roared around them: the knight and the fisherman sprang to the door in terror, to bring home the maiden, remembering the anguish of that night when Huldbrand had first entered the cottage. But Undine met them at the same moment, clapping her little hands in high glee.

"What will you give me," she cried, "to provide you with wine? Or rather, you need not give me anything," she continued; "for I am already satisfied, if you look more cheerful, and are in better spirits, than throughout this last most wearisome day. Only come with me; the forest stream has driven ashore a cask; and I will be condemned to sleep through a whole week, if it is not a wine-cask."

The men followed her, and actually found, in a bushy cove of the shore, a cask, which inspired them with as much joy as if they were sure it contained the generous old wine for which they were thirsting. They first of all, and with as much expedition as possible, rolled it toward the cottage; for heavy clouds were again rising in the west, and they could discern the waves of the lake in the fading light lifting their white foaming heads, as if looking out for the rain, which threatened every instant to pour upon them. Undine helped the men as much as she was able; and as the shower, with a roar of wind, came suddenly sweeping on in rapid pursuit, she raised her finger with a merry menace toward the dark mass of clouds, and cried:

"You cloud, you cloud, have a care! Beware how you wet us; we are some way from shelter yet."

The old man reproved her for this sally, as a sinful presumption; but she laughed to herself softly, and no mischief came from her wild behaviour. Nay more, what was beyond their expectation, they reached their comfortable hearth unwet, with their prize secured; but the cask had hardly been broached, and proved to contain wine of a remarkably fine flavour, when the rain first poured down unrestrained from the black cloud, the tempest raved through the tops of the trees, and swept far over the billows of the deep.

Having immediately filled several bottles from the cask, which promised them a supply for a long time, they drew round the glowing hearth; and, comfortably secured from the tempest, they sat tasting the flavour of their wine and bandying jests.

But the old fisherman suddenly became extremely grave, and said: "Ah, great God! Here we sit, rejoicing over this rich gift, while he to whom it first belonged, and from whom it was wrested by the fury of the stream, must there also, it is more than probable, have lost his life."

"No such thing," said Undine, smiling, as she filled the knight's cup to the brim.

But he exclaimed: "By my unsullied honour, old father, if I knew where to find and rescue him, no fear of exposure to the night, nor any peril, should deter me from making the attempt. At least, I can promise you that if I again reach an inhabited country, I will find out the owner of this wine or his heirs, and make double and triple reimbursement."

The old man was gratified with this assurance; he gave the knight a nod of approbation, and now drained his cup with an easier conscience and more relish.

Undine, however, said to Huldbrand: "As to the repayment and your gold, you may do whatever you like. But what you said about your venturing out, and searching, and exposing yourself to danger, appears to me far from wise. I should cry my very eyes out, should you perish in such a wild attempt; and is it not true that you would prefer staying here with me and the good wine?"

"Most assuredly," answered Huldbrand, smiling.

"Then, you see," replied Undine, "you spoke unwisely. For charity begins at home; and why need we trouble ourselves about our neighbours?"

The mistress of the house turned away from her, sighing and shaking her head; while the fisherman forgot his wonted indulgence toward the graceful maiden, and thus rebuked her:

"That sounds exactly as if you had been brought up by heathens and Turks;" and he finished his reproof by adding, "May God forgive both me and you – unfeeling child!"

"Well, say what you will, that is what I think and feel," replied Undine, "whoever brought me up; and all your talking cannot help it."

"Silence!" exclaimed the fisherman, in a voice of stern rebuke; and she, who with all her wild spirit was extremely alive to fear, shrank from him, moved close up to Huldbrand, trembling, and said very softly:

"Are you also angry, dear friend?"

The knight pressed her soft hand, and tenderly stroked her locks. He was unable to utter a word, for his vexation, arising from the old man's severity towards Undine, closed his lips; and thus the two couples sat opposite to each other, at once heated with anger and in embarrassed silence.

In the midst of this stillness a low knocking at the door startled them all; for there are times when a slight circumstance, coming unexpectedly upon us, startles us like something supernatural. But there was the further source of alarm, that the enchanted forest lay so near them, and that their place of abode seemed at present inaccessible to any human being. While they were looking upon one another in doubt, the knocking was again heard, accompanied with a deep groan. The knight sprang to seize his sword. But the old man said, in a low whisper:

"If it be what I fear it is, no weapon of yours can protect us."

Undine in the meanwhile went to the door, and cried with the firm voice of fearless displeasure: "Spirits of the earth! if mischief be your aim, Kuhleborn shall teach you better manners."

The terror of the rest was increased by this wild speech; they looked fearfully upon the girl, and Huldbrand was just recovering presence of mind enough to ask what she meant, when a voice reached them from without:

"I am no spirit of the earth, though a spirit still in its earthly body. You that are within the cottage there, if you fear God and would afford me assistance, open your door to me."

By the time these words were spoken, Undine had already opened it; and the lamp throwing a strong light upon the stormy night, they perceived an aged priest without, who stepped back in terror, when his eye fell on the unexpected sight of a little damsel of such exquisite beauty. Well might he think there must be magic in the wind and witchcraft at work, when a form of such surpassing loveliness appeared at the door of so humble a dwelling. So he lifted up his voice in prayer:

"Let all good spirits praise the Lord God!"

"I am no spectre," said Undine, with a smile. "Do I look so very frightful? And you see that I do not shrink from holy words. I too have knowledge of God, and understand the duty of praising Him; every one, to be sure, has his own way of doing this, for so He has created us. Come in, father; you will find none but worthy people here."

The holy man came bowing in, and cast round a glance of scrutiny, wearing at the same time a very placid and venerable air. But water was dropping from every fold of his dark garments, from his long white beard and the white locks of his hair. The fisherman and the knight took him to another apartment, and furnished him with a change of raiment, while they gave his own clothes to the women to dry. The aged stranger thanked them in a manner the most humble and courteous; but on the knight's offering him his splendid cloak to wrap round him, he could not be persuaded to take it, but chose instead an old grey coat that belonged to the fisherman.

They then returned to the common apartment. The mistress of the house immediately offered her great chair to the priest, and continued urging it upon him till she saw him fairly in possession of it. "You are old and exhausted," said she, "and are, moreover, a man of God."

Undine shoved under the stranger's feet her little stool, on which at all other times she used to sit near to Huldbrand, and showed herself most gentle and amiable towards the old man. Huldbrand whispered some raillery in her ear, but she replied, gravely:

"He is a minister of that Being who created us all; and holy things are not to be treated with lightness."

The knight and the fisherman now refreshed the priest with food and wine; and when he had somewhat recovered his strength and spirits, he began to relate how he had the day before set out from his cloister, which was situated far off beyond the great lake, in order to visit the bishop, and acquaint him with the distress into which the cloister and its tributary villages had fallen, owing to the extraordinary floods. After a long and wearisome wandering, on account of the rise of the waters, he had been this day compelled toward evening to procure the aid of a couple of boatmen, and cross over an arm of the lake which had burst its usual boundary.

"But hardly," continued he, "had our small ferry-boat touched the waves, when that furious tempest burst forth which is still raging over our heads. It seemed as if the billows had been waiting our approach only to rush on us with a madness the more wild. The oars were wrested from the grasp of my men in an instant; and shivered by the resistless force, they drove farther and farther out before us upon the waves. Unable to direct our course, we yielded to the blind power of nature, and seemed to fly over the surges toward your distant shore, which we already saw looming through the mist and foam of the deep. Then it was at last that our boat turned short from its course, and rocked with a motion that became more wild and dizzy: I know not whether it was overset, or the violence of the motion threw me overboard. In my agony and struggle at the thought of a near and terrible death, the waves bore me onward, till I was cast ashore here beneath the trees of your island."

"Yes, an island!" cried the fisherman; "A short time ago it was only a point of land. But now, since the forest stream and lake have become all but mad, it appears to be entirely changed."

"I observed something of it," replied the priest, "as I stole along the shore in the obscurity; and hearing nothing around me but a sort of wild uproar, I perceived at last that the noise came from a point exactly where a beaten footpath disappeared. I now caught the light in your cottage, and ventured hither, where I cannot sufficiently thank my Heavenly Father that, after preserving me from the waters, He has also conducted me to such pious people as you are; and the more so, as it is difficult to say whether I shall ever behold any other persons in this world except you four."

"What mean you by those words?" asked the fisherman.

"Can you tell me, then, how long this commotion of the elements will last?" replied the priest. "I am old; the stream of my life may easily sink into the ground and vanish before the overflowing of that forest stream shall subside. And, indeed, it is not impossible that more and more of the foaming waters may rush in between you and yonder forest, until you are so far removed from the rest of the world, that your small fishing-canoe may be incapable of passing over, and the inhabitants of the continent entirely forget you in your old age amid the dissipation and diversions of life."

At this melancholy foreboding the old lady shrank back with a feeling of alarm, crossed herself, and cried, "God forbid!"

But the fisherman looked upon her with a smile and said, "What a strange being is man! Suppose the worst to happen; our state would not be different; at any rate, your own would not, dear wife, from what it is at present. For have you, these many years, been farther from home than the border of the forest? And have you seen a single human being beside Undine and myself? It is now only a short time since the coming of the knight and the priest. They will remain with us, even if we do become a forgotten island; so after all you will be a gainer."

"I know not," replied the ancient dame; "it is a dismal thought, when brought fairly home to the mind, that we are for ever separated from mankind, even though in fact we never do know nor see them."

"Then *you* will remain with us – then you will remain with us!" whispered Undine, in a voice scarcely audible and half singing, while she nestled closer to Huldbrand's side. But he was immersed in the deep and strange musings of his own mind. The region, on the farther side of the forest river, seemed, since the last words of the priest, to have been withdrawing farther and farther, in dim perspective, from his view; and the blooming island on which he lived grew green and smiled more freshly in his fancy. His bride glowed like the fairest rose, not of this obscure nook only, but even of the whole wide world; and the priest was now present.

Added to which, the mistress of the family was directing an angry glance at Undine, because, even in the presence of the priest, she leant so fondly on the knight; and it seemed as if she was on the point of breaking out in harsh reproof. Then burst forth from the mouth of Huldbrand, as he turned to the priest, "Father, you here see before you an affianced pair; and if this maiden and these good old people have no objection, you shall unite us this very evening."

The aged couple were both exceedingly surprised. They had often, it is true, thought of this, but as yet they had never mentioned it; and now, when the knight spoke, it came upon them like something wholly new and unexpected. Undine became suddenly grave, and looked down thoughtfully, while the priest made inquiries respecting the circumstances of their acquaintance, and asked the old people whether they gave their consent to the union. After a great number of questions and answers, the affair was arranged to the satisfaction of all; and the mistress of the house went to prepare the bridal apartment of the young couple, and also, with a view to grace the nuptial solemnity, to seek for two consecrated tapers, which she had for a long time kept by her, for this occasion.

The knight in the meanwhile busied himself about his golden chain, for the purpose of disengaging two of its links, that he might make an exchange of rings with his bride. But when she saw his object, she started from her trance of musing, and exclaimed:

"Not so! My parents by no means sent me into the world so perfectly destitute; on the contrary, they foresaw, even at that early period, that such a night as this would come."

Thus speaking she went out of the room, and a moment after returned with two costly rings, of which she gave one to her bridegroom, and kept the other for herself. The old fisherman was beyond measure astonished at this; and his wife, who was just re-entering the room, was even more surprised than he, that neither of them had ever seen these jewels in the child's possession.

"My parents," said Undine, "sewed these trinkets to that beautiful raiment which I wore the very day I came to you. They also charged me on no account whatever to mention them to any one before my wedding evening. At the time of my coming, therefore, I took them off in secret, and have kept them concealed to the present hour."

The priest now cut short all further questioning and wondering, while he lighted the consecrated tapers, placed them on a table, and ordered the bridal pair to stand opposite to him. He then pronounced the few solemn words of the ceremony, and made them one. The elder couple gave the younger their blessing; and the bride, gently trembling and thoughtful, leaned upon the knight.

The priest then spoke out: "You are strange people, after all; for why did you tell me that you were the only inhabitants of the island? So far is this from being true, I have seen, the whole time I was performing the ceremony, a tall, stately man, in a white mantle, standing opposite to me, looking in at the window. He must be still waiting before the door, if peradventure you would invite him to come in."

"God forbid!" cried the old lady, shrinking back; the fisherman shook his head, without opening his lips; and Huldbrand sprang to the window. It seemed to him that he could still discern a white streak, which soon disappeared in the gloom. He convinced the priest that he must have been mistaken in his impression; and they all sat down together round a bright and comfortable hearth.

Chapter IV

BEFORE THE nuptial ceremony, and during its performance, Undine had shown a modest gentleness and maidenly reserve; but it now seemed as if all the wayward freaks that effervesced within her burst forth with an extravagance only the more bold and unrestrained. She teased her bridegroom, her foster-parents, and even the priest, whom she had just now revered so highly, with all sorts of childish tricks; but when the ancient dame was about to reprove her too frolicsome spirit, the knight, in a few words, imposed silence upon her by speaking of Undine as his wife.

The knight was himself, indeed, just as little pleased with Undine's childish behaviour as the rest; but all his looks and half-reproachful words were to no purpose. It is true, whenever the bride observed the dissatisfaction of her husband – and this occasionally happened – she became more quiet, placed herself beside him, stroked his face with caressing fondness, whispered something smilingly in his ear, and in this manner smoothed the wrinkles that were gathering on his brow. But the moment after, some wild whim would make her resume her antic movements; and all went worse than before.

The priest then spoke in a kind although serious tone: "My fair young maiden, surely no one can look on you without pleasure; but remember betimes so to attune your soul that it may produce a harmony ever in accordance with the soul of your wedded bridegroom."

"*Soul!*" cried Undine with a laugh. "What you say has a remarkably pretty sound; and for most people, too, it may be a very instructive and profitable caution. But when a person has no soul at all, how, I pray you, can such attuning be then possible? And this, in truth, is just my condition."

The priest was much hurt, but continued silent in holy displeasure, and turned away his face from the maiden in sorrow. She, however, went up to him with the most winning sweetness, and said:

"Nay, I entreat you first listen to me, before you are angry with me; for your anger is painful to me, and you ought not to give pain to a creature that has not hurt you. Only have patience with me, and I will explain to you every word of what I meant."

It was evident that she had come to say something important; when she suddenly faltered as if seized with inward shuddering, and burst into a passion of tears. They were none of them able to understand the intenseness of her feelings; and, with mingled emotions of fear and anxiety, they gazed on her in silence. Then, wiping away her tears, and looking earnestly at the priest, she at last said:

"There must be something lovely, but at the same time something most awful, about a soul. In the name of God, holy man, were it not better that we never shared a gift so mysterious?"

Again she paused, and restrained her tears, as if waiting for an answer. All in the cottage had risen from their seats, and stepped back from her with horror. She, however, seemed to have eyes for no one but the holy man; an awful curiosity was painted on her features, which appeared terrible to the others.

"Heavily must the soul weigh down its possessor," she pursued, when no one returned her any answer – "very heavily! For already its approaching image overshadows me with anguish and mourning. And, alas, I have till now been so merry and light-hearted!" and she burst into another flood of tears, and covered her face with her veil.

The priest, going up to her with a solemn look, now addressed himself to her, and conjured her, by the name of God most holy, if any spirit of evil possessed her, to remove the light covering from her face. But she sank before him on her knees, and repeated after him every sacred expression he uttered, giving praise to God, and protesting "that she wished well to the whole world."

The priest then spoke to the knight: "Sir bridegroom, I leave you alone with her whom I have united to you in marriage. So far as I can discover, there is nothing of evil in her, but assuredly much that is wonderful. What I recommend to you is – prudence, love, and fidelity."

Thus speaking, he left the apartment; and the fisherman, with his wife, followed him, crossing themselves.

Undine had sunk upon her knees. She uncovered her face, and exclaimed, while she looked fearfully round upon Huldbrand, "Alas! You will now refuse to look upon me as your own; and still I have done nothing evil, poor unhappy child that I am!" She spoke these words with a look so infinitely sweet and touching, that her bridegroom forgot both the confession that had shocked, and the mystery that had perplexed him; and hastening to her, he raised her in his arms. She smiled through her tears; and that smile was like the morning light playing upon a small stream. "You cannot desert me!" she whispered confidingly, and stroked the knight's cheeks with her little soft hands. He turned away from the frightful thoughts that still lurked in the recesses of his soul, and were persuading him that he had been married to a fairy, or some spiteful and mischievous being of the spirit-world. Only the single question, and that almost unawares, escaped from his lips.

"Dearest Undine, tell me this one thing: what was it you meant by 'spirits of earth' and 'Kuhleborn,' when the priest stood knocking at the door?"

"Tales! Mere tales of children!" answered Undine, laughing, now quite restored to her wonted gaiety. "I first frightened you with them, and you frightened me. This is the end of the story, and of our nuptial evening."

"Nay, not so," replied the enamoured knight, extinguishing the tapers, and a thousand times kissing his beautiful and beloved bride; while, lighted by the moon that shone brightly through the windows, he bore her into their bridal apartment.

The fresh light of morning woke the young married pair: but Huldbrand lay lost in silent reflection. Whenever, during the night, he had fallen asleep, strange and horrible dreams of spectres had disturbed him; and these shapes, grinning at him by stealth, strove to disguise themselves as beautiful females; and from beautiful females they all at once assumed the appearance of dragons. And when he started up, aroused by the intrusion of these hideous forms, the moonlight shone pale and cold before the windows without. He looked affrighted at Undine, in whose arms he had fallen asleep: and she was reposing in unaltered beauty and sweetness beside him. Then pressing her rosy lips with a light kiss, he again fell into a slumber, only to be awakened by new terrors.

When fully awake, he had thought over this connection. He reproached himself for any doubt that could lead him into error in regard to his lovely wife. He also confessed to her his injustice; but she only gave him her fair hand, sighed deeply, and remained silent. Yet a glance of fervent tenderness, an expression of the soul beaming in her eyes, such as he had never witnessed there before, left him in undoubted assurance that Undine bore him no ill-will.

He then rose joyfully, and leaving her, went to the common apartment, where the inmates of the house had already met. The three were sitting round the hearth with an air of anxiety about them, as if they feared trusting themselves to raise their voice above a low, apprehensive undertone. The priest appeared to be praying in his inmost spirit, with a view to avert some fatal calamity. But when they observed the young husband come forth so cheerful, they dispelled the cloud that remained upon their brows: the old fisherman even began to laugh with the knight till his aged wife herself could not help smiling with great good-humour.

Undine had in the meantime got ready, and now entered the room; all rose to meet her, but remained fixed in perfect admiration – she was so changed, and yet the same. The priest, with paternal affection beaming from his countenance, first went up to her; and as he raised his hand to pronounce a blessing, the beautiful bride sank on her knees before him with religious awe; she begged his pardon in terms both respectful and submissive for any foolish things she might have uttered the evening before, and entreated him with emotion to pray for the welfare of her soul. She then rose, kissed her foster-parents, and, after thanking them for all the kindness they had shown her, said:

"Oh, I now feel in my inmost heart how much, how infinitely much, you have done for me, you dear, dear friends of my childhood!"

At first she was wholly unable to tear herself away from their affectionate caresses; but the moment she saw the good old mother busy in getting breakfast, she went to the hearth, applied herself to cooking the food and putting it on the table, and would not suffer her to take the least share in the work.

She continued in this frame of spirit the whole day: calm, kind attentive – half matronly, and half girlish. The three who had been longest acquainted with her expected every instant to see her capricious spirit break out in some whimsical change or sportive vagary. But their fears were quite unnecessary. Undine continued as mild and gentle as an angel. The priest found it all but impossible to remove his eyes from her; and he often said to the bridegroom:

"The bounty of Heaven, sir, through me its unworthy instrument, entrusted to you yesterday an invaluable treasure; cherish it as you ought, and it will promote your temporal and eternal welfare."

Toward evening Undine was hanging upon the knight's arm with lowly tenderness, while she drew him gently out before the door, where the setting sun shone richly over the fresh grass, and upon the high, slender boles of the trees. Her emotion was visible: the dew of sadness and love swam in her eyes, while a tender and fearful secret seemed to hover upon her lips, but was only made known by hardly-breathed sighs. She led her husband farther and farther onward without speaking. When he asked her questions, she replied only with looks, in which, it is true, there appeared to be no immediate answer to his inquiries, but a whole heaven of love and timid devotion. Thus they reached the margin of the swollen forest stream, and the knight was astonished to see it gliding away with so gentle a murmuring of its waves, that no vestige of its former swell and wildness was now discernible.

"By morning it will be wholly drained off," said the beautiful wife, almost weeping, "and you will then be able to travel, without anything to hinder you, whithersoever you will."

"Not without you, dear Undine," replied the knight, laughing; "think, only, were I disposed to leave you, both the Church and the spiritual powers, the Emperor and the laws of the realm, would require the fugitive to be seized and restored to you."

"All this depends on you – all depends on you," whispered his little companion, half weeping and half smiling. "But I still feel sure that you will not leave me; I love you too deeply to fear that misery. Now bear me over to that little island which lies before us. There shall the decision be made. I could easily, indeed, glide through that mere rippling of the water without your aid, but it is so sweet to lie in your arms; and should you determine to put me away, I shall have rested in them once more …for the last time."

Huldbrand was so full of strange anxiety and emotion, that he knew not what answer to make her. He took her in his arms and carried her over, now first realizing the fact that this was the same little island from which he had borne her back to the old fisherman, the first night of his arrival. On the farther side, he placed her upon the soft grass, and was throwing himself lovingly near his beautiful burden; but she said to him, "Not here, but opposite me. I shall read my doom in your eyes, even before your lips pronounce it: now listen attentively to what I shall relate to you." And she began:

"You must know, my own love, that there are beings in the elements which bear the strongest resemblance to the human race, and which, at the same time, but seldom become visible to you. The wonderful salamanders sparkle and sport amid the flames; deep in the earth the meagre and malicious gnomes pursue their revels; the forest-spirits belong to the air, and wander in the woods; while in the seas, rivers, and streams live the widespread race of water-spirits. These last, beneath resounding domes of crystal, through which the sky can shine with its sun and stars, inhabit a region of light and beauty; lofty coral-trees glow with blue and crimson fruits in their gardens; they walk over the pure sand of the sea, among exquisitely variegated shells, and amid whatever of beauty the old world possessed, such as the present is no more worthy to enjoy – creations which the floods covered with their secret veils of silver; and now these noble monuments sparkle below, stately and solemn, and bedewed by the water, which loves them, and calls forth from their crevices delicate moss-flowers and enwreathing tufts of sedge.

"Now the nation that dwell there are very fair and lovely to behold, for the most part more beautiful than human beings. Many a fisherman has been so fortunate as to catch a view of a delicate maiden of the waters, while she was floating and singing upon the deep. He would then spread far the fame of her beauty; and to such wonderful females men are wont to give the name of Undines. But what need of saying more? – You, my dear husband, now actually behold an Undine before you."

The knight would have persuaded himself that his lovely wife was under the influence of one of her odd whims, and that she was only amusing herself and him with her extravagant inventions. He wished it might be so. But with whatever emphasis he said this to himself, he still could not credit the hope for a moment: a strange shivering shot through his soul; unable to utter a word, he gazed upon the sweet speaker with a fixed eye. She shook her head in distress, sighed from her full heart, and then proceeded in the following manner: – "We should be far superior to you, who are another race of the human family, – for we also call ourselves human beings, as we resemble them in form and features – had we not one evil peculiar to ourselves. Both we and the beings I have mentioned as inhabiting the other elements vanish into air at death and go out of existence, spirit and body, so that no vestige of us remains; and when you hereafter awake to a purer state of being, we shall remain where sand, and sparks, and wind, and waves remain. Thus we have no souls; the element moves us, and, again, is obedient to our will, while we live, though it scatters us like dust when we die; and as we have nothing to trouble us, we are as merry as nightingales, little gold-fishes, and other pretty children of nature.

"But all beings aspire to rise in the scale of existence higher than they are. It was therefore the wish of my father, who is a powerful water-prince in the Mediterranean Sea, that his only daughter should become possessed of a soul, although she should have to endure many of the sufferings of those who share that gift.

"Now the race to which I belong have no other means of obtaining a soul than by forming with an individual of your own the most intimate union of love. I am now possessed of a soul, and my soul thanks you, my best beloved, and never shall cease to thank you, if you do not render my whole future life miserable. For what will become of me, if you avoid and reject me? Still, I would not keep you as my own by artifice. And should you decide to cast me off, then do it now, and return alone to the shore. I will plunge into this brook, where my uncle will receive me; my uncle, who here in the forest, far removed from his other friends, passes his strange and solitary existence. But he is powerful, as well as revered and beloved by many great rivers; and as he brought me hither to the fisherman a light-hearted and laughing child, he will take me home to my parents a woman, gifted with a soul, with power to love and to suffer."

She was about to add something more, when Huldbrand, with the most heartfelt tenderness and love, clasped her in his arms, and again bore her back to the shore. There, amid tears and kisses, he first swore never to forsake his affectionate wife, and esteemed himself even more happy than Pygmalion, for whom Venus gave life to his beautiful statue, and thus changed it into a beloved wife. Supported by his arm, and in the confidence of affection, Undine returned to the cottage; and now she first realized with her whole heart how little cause she had for regretting what she had left – the crystal palace of her mysterious father.

Chapter V

NEXT MORNING, when Huldbrand awoke from slumber, and perceived that his beautiful wife was not by his side, he began to give way again to his wild imaginations – that his marriage, and even the lovely Undine herself, were only shadows without substance – only mere illusions of enchantment. But she entered the door at the same moment, kissed him, seated herself on the bed by his side, and said:

"I have been out somewhat early this morning, to see whether my uncle keeps his word. He has already restored the waters of the flood to his own calm channel, and he now flows through the forest a rivulet as before, in a lonely and dreamlike current. His friends, too, both of the water and the air, have resumed their usual peaceful tenor; all will again proceed with order and tranquillity; and you can travel homeward, without fear of the flood, whenever you choose."

It seemed to the mind of Huldbrand that he must be in some waking dream, so little was he able to understand the nature of his wife's strange relative. Notwithstanding this he made no remark upon what she had told him, and her surpassing loveliness soon lulled every misgiving and discomfort to rest.

Some time afterwards, while he was standing with her before the door, and surveying the verdant point of land, with its boundary of bright waters, such a feeling of bliss came over him in this cradle of his love, that he exclaimed:

"Shall we, then, so early as today, begin our journey? Why should we? It is probable that abroad in the world we shall find no days more delightful than those we have spent in this green isle so secret and so secure. Let us yet see the sun go down here two or three times more."

"Just as my lord wills," replied Undine meekly. "Only we must remember, that my foster-parents will, at all events, see me depart with pain; and should they now, for the first time, discover the true soul in me, and how fervently I can now love and honour them, their feeble eyes would surely become blind with weeping. As yet they consider my present quietness and gentleness as of no better promise than they were formerly – like the calm of the lake just while the air remains tranquil – and they will learn soon to cherish a little tree or flower as they have cherished me. Let me not, then, make known to them this newly bestowed, this loving heart, at the very moment they must lose it for this world; and how could I conceal what I have gained, if we continued longer together?"

Huldbrand yielded to her representation, and went to the aged couple to confer with them respecting his journey, on which he proposed to set out that very hour. The priest offered himself as a companion to the young married pair; and, after taking a short farewell, he held the bridle, while the knight lifted his beautiful wife upon his horse; and with rapid steps they crossed the dry channel with her toward the forest. Undine wept in silent but intense emotion; the old people, as she moved away, were more clamorous in the expression of their grief. They appeared to feel, at the moment of separation, all that they were losing in their affectionate foster-daughter.

The three travellers had reached the thickest shades of the forest without interchanging a word. It must have been a fair sight, in that hall of leafy verdure, to see this lovely woman's form sitting on the noble and richly-ornamented steed, on her left hand the venerable priest in the white garb of his order, on her right the blooming young knight, clad in splendid raiment of scarlet, gold, and violet, girt with a sword that flashed in the sun, and attentively walking beside her. Huldbrand had no eyes but for his wife; Undine, who had dried her tears of tenderness, had no eyes but for him; and they soon entered into the still and voiceless converse of looks and gestures, from which, after some time, they were awakened by the low discourse which the priest was holding with a fourth traveller, who had meanwhile joined them unobserved.

He wore a white gown, resembling in form the dress of the priest's order, except that his hood hung very low over his face, and that the whole drapery floated in such wide folds around him as obliged him every moment to gather it up and throw it over his arm, or by some management of this sort to get it out of his way, and still it did not seem in the least to impede his movements. When the young couple became aware of his presence, he was saying:

"And so, venerable sir, many as have been the years I have dwelt here in this forest, I have never received the name of hermit in your sense of the word. For, as I said before, I know nothing of penance, and I think, too, that I have no particular need of it. Do you ask me why I am so attached to the forest? It is because its scenery is so peculiarly picturesque, and affords me so much pastime when, in my floating white garments, I pass through its world of leaves and dusky shadows; – and when a sweet sunbeam glances down upon me at times unexpectedly."

"You are a very singular man," replied the priest, "and I should like to have a more intimate acquaintance with you."

"And who, then, may you be yourself, to pass from one thing to another?" inquired the stranger.

"I am called Father Heilmann," answered the holy man; "and I am from the cloister of Our Lady of the Salutation, beyond the lake."

"Well, well," replied the stranger, "my name is Kuhleborn; and were I a stickler for the nice distinctions of rank, I might, with equal propriety, require you to give me the title of noble lord of Kuhleborn, or free lord of Kuhleborn; for I am as free as the birds in the forest, and, it may be, a trifle more so. For example, I now have something to tell that young lady there." And before they were aware of his purpose, he was on the other side of the priest, close to Undine, and stretching himself high into the air, in order to whisper something in her ear. But she shrank from him in terror, and exclaimed:

"I have nothing more to do with you."

"Ho, ho," cried the stranger with a laugh, "you have made a grand marriage indeed, since you no longer know your own relations! Have you no recollection, then, of your uncle Kuhleborn, who so faithfully bore you on his back to this region?"

"However that may be," replied Undine, "I entreat you never to appear in my presence again. I am now afraid of you; and will not my husband fear and forsake me, if he sees me associate with such strange company and kindred?"

"You must not forget, my little niece," said Kuhleborn, "that I am with you here as a guide; otherwise those madcap spirits of the earth, the gnomes that haunt this forest, would play you some of their mischievous pranks. Let me therefore still accompany you in peace. Even the old priest there had a better recollection of me than you have; for he just now assured me that I seemed to be very familiar to him, and that I must have been with him in the ferry-boat, out of which he tumbled into the waves. He certainly did see me there; for I was no other than the water-spout that tore him out of it, and kept him from sinking, while I safely wafted him ashore to your wedding."

Undine and the knight turned their eyes upon Father Heilmann; but he appeared to be moving forward, just as if he were dreaming or walking in his sleep, and no longer to be conscious of a word that was spoken. Undine then said to Kuhleborn: "I already see yonder the end of the forest. We have no further need of your assistance, and nothing now gives us alarm but yourself. I therefore beseech you, by our mutual love and good-will, to vanish, and allow us to proceed in peace."

Kuhleborn seemed to become angry at this: he darted a frightful look at Undine, and grinned fiercely upon her. She shrieked aloud, and called her husband to protect her. The knight sprang round the horse as quick as lightning, and, brandishing his sword, struck at Kuhleborn's head. But instead of severing it from his body, the sword merely flashed through a torrent, which rushed foaming near them from a lofty cliff; and with a splash, which much resembled in sound a burst of laughter, the stream all at once poured upon them and gave them a thorough wetting. The priest, as if suddenly awakening from a trance, coolly observed: "This is what I have been some time expecting, because the brook has descended from the steep so close beside us – though at first sight, indeed, it appeared to resemble a man, and to possess the power of speech."

As the waterfall came rushing from its crag, it distinctly uttered these words in Huldbrand's ear: "Rash knight! Valiant knight! I am not angry with you; I have no quarrel with you; only continue to defend your lovely little wife with the same spirit, you bold knight! You valiant champion!"

After advancing a few steps farther, the travellers came out upon open ground. The imperial city lay bright before them; and the evening sun, which gilded its towers with gold, kindly dried their garments that had been so completely drenched.

The sudden disappearance of the young knight, Huldbrand of Ringstetten, had occasioned much remark in the imperial city, and no small concern amongst those who, as well on account of his expertness in tourney and dance, as of his mild and amiable manners, had become attached to him. His attendants were unwilling to quit the place without their master, although not a soul of them had been courageous enough to follow him into the fearful recesses of the forest. They remained, therefore, at the hostelry, idly hoping, as men are wont to do, and keeping the fate of their lost lord fresh in remembrance by their lamentations.

Now when the violent storms and floods had been observed immediately after his departure, the destruction of the handsome stranger became all but certain; even Bertalda had openly discovered her sorrow, and detested herself for having been the cause of his taking that fatal excursion into the forest. Her foster-parents, the duke and duchess, had meanwhile come to take her away; but Bertalda persuaded them to remain with her until some certain news of Huldbrand should be obtained, whether he were living or dead. She endeavoured also to prevail upon several young knights, who were assiduous in courting her favour, to go in quest of the noble adventurer in the forest. But she refused to pledge her hand as the reward of the enterprise, because she still cherished, it might be, a hope of its being claimed by the returning knight; and no one would consent, for a glove, a riband, or even a kiss, to expose his life to bring back so very dangerous a rival.

When Huldbrand now made his sudden and unexpected appearance, his attendants, the inhabitants of the city, and almost every one rejoiced. This was not the case with Bertalda; for although it might be quite a welcome event to others that he brought with him a wife of such exquisite loveliness, and Father Heilmann as a witness of their marriage, Bertalda could not but view the affair with grief and vexation. She had, in truth, become attached to the young knight with her whole soul; and her mourning for his absence, or supposed death, had shown this more than she could now have wished.

But notwithstanding all this, she conducted herself like a wise maiden in circumstances of such delicacy, and lived on the most friendly terms with Undine, whom the whole city looked upon as a princess that Huldbrand had rescued in the forest from some evil enchantment. Whenever any one questioned either herself or her husband relative to surmises of this nature, they had wisdom enough to remain silent, or wit enough to evade the inquiries. The lips of Father Heilmann had been sealed in regard to idle gossip of every kind; and besides, on Huldbrand's arrival, he had immediately returned to his cloister: so that people were obliged to rest contented with their own wild conjectures; and even Bertalda herself ascertained nothing more of the truth than others.

For the rest, Undine daily felt more love for the fair maiden. "We must have been before acquainted with each other," she often used to say to her, "or else there must be some mysterious connection between us, for it is incredible that any one so perfectly without cause – I mean, without some deep and secret cause – should be so fondly attached to another as I have been to you from the first moment of our meeting."

And even Bertalda could not deny that she felt a confiding impulse, an attraction of tenderness toward Undine, much as she deemed this fortunate rival the cause of her bitterest disappointment. Under the influence of this mutual regard, they found means to persuade, the one her foster-parents, and the other her husband, to defer the day of separation to a period more and more remote; nay, more, they had already begun to talk of a plan for Bertalda's accompanying Undine to Castle Ringstetten, near one of the sources of the Danube.

Once on a fine evening they happened to be talking over their scheme just as they passed the high trees that bordered the public walk. The young married pair, though it was somewhat late, had called upon Bertalda to invite her to share their enjoyment; and all three proceeded familiarly up and down beneath the dark blue heaven, not seldom interrupted in their converse by the admiration which they could not but bestow upon the magnificent fountain in the middle of the square, and upon the wonderful rush and shooting upward of its waters. All was sweet and soothing to their minds. Among the shadows of the trees stole in glimmerings of light from the adjacent houses. A low murmur as of children at play, and of other persons who were enjoying their walk, floated around them – they were so alone, and yet sharing so much of social happiness in the bright and stirring world, that whatever had appeared rough by day now became smooth of its own accord. All the three friends could no longer see the slightest cause for hesitation in regard to Bertalda's taking the journey.

At that instant, while they were just fixing the day of their departure, a tall man approached them from the middle of the square, bowed respectfully to the company, and spoke something in the young bride's ear. Though displeased with the interruption and its cause, she walked aside a few steps with the stranger; and both began to whisper, as it seemed, in a foreign tongue. Huldbrand thought he recognized the strange man of the forest, and he gazed upon him so fixedly, that he neither heard nor answered the astonished inquiries of Bertalda. All at once Undine clapped her hands with delight, and turned back from the stranger, laughing: he, frequently shaking his head, retired with a hasty step and discontented air, and descended into the fountain. Huldbrand now felt perfectly certain that his conjecture was correct. But Bertalda asked:

"What, then, dear Undine, did the master of the fountain wish to say to you?"

Undine laughed within herself, and made answer: "The day after tomorrow, my dear child, when the anniversary of your name-day returns, you shall be informed." And this was all she could be prevailed upon to disclose. She merely asked Bertalda to dinner on the appointed day, and requested her to invite her foster-parents; and soon afterwards they separated.

"Kuhleborn?" said Huldbrand to his lovely wife, with an inward shudder when they had taken leave of Bertalda, and were now going home through the darkening streets.

"Yes, it was he," answered Undine; "and he would have wearied me with his foolish warnings. But, in the midst, quite contrary to his intentions, he delighted me with a most welcome piece of news. If you, my dear lord and husband, wish me to acquaint you with it now, you need only command me, and I will freely and from my heart tell you all without reserve. But would you confer upon your Undine a very, very great pleasure, wait till the day after tomorrow, and then you too shall have your share of the surprise."

The knight was quite willing to gratify his wife in what she had asked so sweetly. And even as she was falling asleep, she murmured to herself, with a smile: "How she will rejoice and be astonished at what her master of the fountain has told me! – Dear, dear Bertalda!"

Chapter VI

THE COMPANY were sitting at dinner. Bertalda, adorned with jewels and flowers without number, the presents of her foster-parents and friends, and looking like some goddess of spring, sat beside Undine and Huldbrand at the head of the table. When the sumptuous repast was ended, and the dessert was placed before them, permission was given that the doors should be left open: this was in accordance with the good old custom in Germany, that the common people might see and rejoice in the festivity of their superiors. Among these spectators the servants carried round cake and wine.

Huldbrand and Bertalda waited with secret impatience for the promised explanation, and hardly moved their eyes from Undine. But she still continued silent, and merely smiled to herself with secret and heartfelt satisfaction. All who were made acquainted with the promise she had given could perceive that she was every moment on the point of revealing a happy secret; and yet, as children sometimes delay tasting their choicest dainties, she still withheld the communication. Bertalda and Huldbrand shared the same delightful feeling, while in anxious hope they were expecting the unknown disclosure which they were to receive from the lips of their friend.

At this moment several of the company pressed Undine to sing. This she seemed pleased at; and ordering her lute to be brought, she sang the following words:

> *"Morning so bright,*
> *Wild-flowers so gay,*
> *Where high grass so dewy*
> *Crowns the wavy lake's border.*
>
> *On the meadow's verdant bosom*
> *What glimmers there so white?*
> *Have wreaths of snowy blossoms,*
> *Soft-floating, fallen from heaven?*
>
> *Ah, see! a tender infant! –*
> *It plays with flowers, unwittingly;*

It strives to grasp morn's golden beams.
O where, sweet stranger, where's your home?
Afar from unknown shores
The waves have wafted hither
This helpless little one.

Nay, clasp not, tender darling,
With tiny hand the flowers!
No hand returns the pressure,
The flowers are strange and mute.
They clothe themselves in beauty,
They breathe a rich perfume:

But cannot fold around you
A mother's loving arms; –
Far, far away that mother's fond embrace.

Life's early dawn just opening faint,
Your eye yet beaming heaven's own smile,
So soon your tenderest guardians gone;
Severe, poor child, your fate, –
All, all to you unknown.

A noble duke has crossed the mead,
And near you checked his steed's career:
Wonder and pity touch his heart;
With knowledge high, and manners pure,
He rears you, – makes his castle home your own.

How great, how infinite your gain!
Of all the land you bloom the loveliest;
Yet, ah! the priceless blessing,
The bliss of parents' fondness,
You left on strands unknown!"

Undine let fall her lute with a melancholy smile. The eyes of Bertalda's noble foster-parents were filled with tears.

"Ah yes, it was so – such was the morning on which I found you, poor orphan!" cried the duke, with deep emotion; "the beautiful singer is certainly right: still

'The priceless blessing,
The bliss of parents' fondness,'

it was beyond our power to give you."

"But we must hear, also, what happened to the poor parents," said Undine, as she struck the chords, and sung:

"Through her chambers roams the mother
Searching, searching everywhere;
Seeks, and knows not what, with yearning,
Childless house still finding there.

Childless house! – O sound of anguish!
She alone the anguish knows,
There by day who led her dear one,
There who rocked its night-repose.

Beechen buds again are swelling,
Sunshine warms again the shore;
Ah, fond mother, cease your searching!
Comes the loved and lost no more.

Then when airs of eve are fresh'ning,
Home the father wends his way,
While with smiles his woe he's veiling,
Gushing tears his heart betray.

Well he knows, within his dwelling,
Still as death he'll find the gloom,
Only hear the mother moaning, –
No sweet babe to smile him home."

"O, tell me, in the name of Heaven tell me, Undine, where are my parents?" cried the weeping Bertalda. "You certainly know; you must have discovered them, you wonderful being; for, otherwise you would never have thus torn my heart. Can they be already here? May I believe it possible?" Her eye glanced rapidly over the brilliant company, and rested upon a lady of high rank who was sitting next to her foster-father.

Then, bending her head, Undine beckoned toward the door, while her eyes overflowed with the sweetest emotion. "Where, then, are the poor parents waiting?" she asked; and the old fisherman, hesitating, advanced with his wife from the crowd of spectators. They looked inquiringly, now at Undine, and now at the beautiful lady who was said to be their daughter.

"It is she! It is she there before you!" exclaimed the restorer of their child, her voice half choked with rapture. And both the aged parents embraced their recovered daughter, weeping aloud and praising God.

But, terrified and indignant, Bertalda tore herself from their arms. Such a discovery was too much for her proud spirit to bear, especially at the moment when she had doubtless expected to see her former splendour increased, and when hope was picturing to her nothing less brilliant than a royal canopy and a crown. It seemed to her as if her rival had contrived all this on purpose to humble her before Huldbrand and the whole world. She reproached Undine; she reviled the old people; and even such offensive words as "deceiver, bribed and perjured impostors," burst from her lips.

The aged wife of the fisherman then said to herself, in a low voice: "Ah, my God, she has become wicked! And yet I feel in my heart that she is my child."

The old fisherman had meanwhile folded his hands, and offered up a silent prayer that she might *not* be his daughter.

Undine, faint and pale as death, turned from the parents to Bertalda, from Bertalda to the parents. She was suddenly cast dawn from all that heaven of happiness in which she had been dreaming, and plunged into an agony of terror and disappointment, which she had never known even in dreams.

"Have you, then, a soul? Have you indeed a soul, Bertalda?" she cried again and again to her angry friend, as if with vehement effort she would arouse her from a sudden delirium or some distracting dream of night, and restore her to recollection.

But when Bertalda became every moment only more and more enraged – when the disappointed parents began to weep aloud – and the company, with much warmth of dispute, were espousing opposite sides – she begged, with such earnestness and dignity, for the liberty of speaking in this her husband's hall, that all around her were in an instant hushed to silence. She then advanced to the upper end of the table, where, both humbled and haughty, Bertalda had seated herself, and, while every eye was fastened upon her, spoke in the following manner:

"My friends, you appear dissatisfied and disturbed; and you are interrupting, with your strife, a festivity I had hoped would bring joy to you and to me. Ah! I knew nothing of your heartless ways of thinking; and never shall understand them: I am not to blame for the mischief this disclosure has done. Believe me, little as you may imagine this to be the case, it is wholly owing to yourselves. One word more, therefore, is all I have to add; but this is one that must be spoken: – I have uttered nothing but truth. Of the certainty of the fact, I give you the strongest assurance. No other proof can I or will I produce, but this I will affirm in the presence of God. The person who gave me this information was the very same who decoyed the infant Bertalda into the water, and who, after thus taking her from her parents, placed her on the green grass of the meadow, where he knew the duke was to pass."

"She is an enchantress!" cried Bertalda; "a witch, that has intercourse with evil spirits. She acknowledges it herself."

"Never! I deny it!" replied Undine, while a whole heaven of innocence and truth beamed from her eyes. "I am no witch; look upon me, and say if I am."

"Then she utters both falsehood and folly," cried Bertalda; "and she is unable to prove that I am the child of these low people. My noble parents, I entreat you to take me from this company, and out of this city, where they do nothing but shame me."

But the aged duke, a man of honourable feeling, remained unmoved; and his wife remarked:

"We must thoroughly examine into this matter. God forbid that we should move a step from this hall before we do so."

Then the aged wife of the fisherman drew near, made a low obeisance to the duchess and said: "Noble and pious lady, you have opened my heart. Permit me to tell you, that if this evil-disposed maiden is my daughter, she has a mark like a violet between her shoulders, and another of the same kind on the instep of her left foot. If she will only consent to go out of the hall with me –"

"I will not consent to uncover myself before the peasant woman," interrupted Bertalda, haughtily turning her back upon her.

"But before me you certainly will," replied the duchess gravely. "You will follow me into that room, maiden; and the old woman shall go with us."

The three disappeared, and the rest continued where they were, in breathless expectation. In a few minutes the females returned – Bertalda pale as death; and the duchess said: "Justice must be done; I therefore declare that our lady hostess has spoken exact truth. Bertalda is the fisherman's daughter; no further proof is required; and this is all of which, on the present occasion, you need to be informed."

The princely pair went out with their adopted daughter; the fisherman, at a sign from the duke, followed them with his wife. The other guests retired in silence, or suppressing their murmurs; while Undine sank weeping into the arms of Huldbrand.

The lord of Ringstetten would certainly have been more gratified, had the events of this day been different; but even such as they now were, he could by no means look upon them as unwelcome, since his lovely wife had shown herself so full of goodness, sweetness, and kindliness.

"If I have given her a soul," he could not help saying to himself, "I have assuredly given her a better one than my own;" and now he only thought of soothing and comforting his weeping wife, and of removing her even so early as the morrow from a place which, after this cross accident, could not fail to be distasteful to her. Yet it is certain that the opinion of the public concerning her was not changed. As something extraordinary had long before been expected of her, the mysterious discovery of Bertalda's parentage had occasioned little or no surprise; and every one who became acquainted with Bertalda's story, and with the violence of her behaviour on that occasion, was only disgusted and set against her. Of this state of things, however, the knight and his lady were as yet ignorant; besides, whether the public condemned Bertalda or herself, the one view of the affair would have been as distressing to Undine as the other; and thus they came to the conclusion that the wisest course they could take, was to leave behind them the walls of the old city with all the speed in their power.

With the earliest beams of morning, a brilliant carriage for Undine drove up to the door of the inn; the horses of Huldbrand and his attendants stood near, stamping the pavement, impatient to proceed. The knight was leading his beautiful wife from the door, when a fisher-girl came up and met them in the way.

"We have no need of your fish," said Huldbrand, accosting her; "we are this moment setting out on a journey."

Upon this the fisher-girl began to weep bitterly; and then it was that the young couple first perceived it was Bertalda. They immediately returned with her to their apartment, when she informed them that, owing to her unfeeling and violent conduct of the preceding day, the duke and duchess had been so displeased with her, as entirely to withdraw from her their protection, though not before giving her a generous portion. The fisherman, too, had received a handsome gift, and had, the evening before, set out with his wife for his peninsula.

"I would have gone with them," she pursued, "but the old fisherman, who is said to be my father –"

"He is, in truth, your father, Bertalda," said Undine, interrupting her. "See, the stranger whom you took for the master of the water-works gave me all the particulars. He wished to dissuade me from taking you with me to Castle Ringstetten, and therefore disclosed to me the whole mystery."

"Well then," continued Bertalda, "my father – if it must needs be so – my father said: 'I will not take you with me until you are changed. If you will venture to come to us alone through the ill-omened forest, that shall be a proof of your having some regard for us. But come not to me as a lady; come merely as a fisher-girl.' I do as he bade me, for since I am abandoned by all the world, I will live and die in solitude, a poor fisher-girl, with parents equally poor. The forest, indeed, appears very terrible to me. Horrible spectres make it their haunt, and I am so fearful. But how can I help it? I have only come here at this early hour to beg the noble lady of Ringstetten to pardon my unbecoming behaviour of yesterday. Sweet lady, I have the fullest persuasion that you meant to do me a kindness, but you were not aware how severely you would wound me; and then, in my agony and surprise, so many rash and frantic expressions burst from my lips. Forgive me, ah, forgive me! I am in truth so unhappy, already. Only consider what I was but yesterday morning, what I was even at the beginning of your yesterday's festival, and what I am today!"

Her words now became inarticulate, lost in a passionate flow of tears, while Undine, bitterly weeping with her, fell upon her neck. So powerful was her emotion, that it was a long time before she could utter a word. At length she said:

"You shall still go with us to Ringstetten; all shall remain just as we lately arranged it; but say 'thou' to me again, and do not call me 'noble lady' any more. Consider, we were changed for each other when we were children; even then we were united by a like fate, and we will strengthen this union with such close affection as no human power shall dissolve. Only first of all you must go with us to Ringstetten. How we shall share all things as sisters, we can talk of after we arrive."

Bertalda looked up to Huldbrand with timid inquiry. He pitied her in her affliction, took her hand, and begged her tenderly to entrust herself to him and his wife.

"We will send a message to your parents," continued he, "giving them the reason why you have not come;" – and he would have added more about his worthy friends of the peninsula, when, perceiving that Bertalda shrank in distress at the mention of them, he refrained. He took her under the arm, lifted her first into the carriage, then Undine, and was soon riding blithely beside them; so persevering was he, too, in urging forward their driver, that in a short time they had left behind them the limits of the city, and a crowd of painful recollections; and now the ladies could take delight in the beautiful country which their progress was continually presenting.

After a journey of some days, they arrived, on a fine evening, at Castle Ringstetten. The young knight being much engaged with the overseers and menials of his establishment, Undine and Bertalda were left alone. They took a walk upon the high rampart of the fortress, and were charmed with the delightful landscape which the fertile Suabia spread around them. While they were viewing the scene, a tall man drew near, who greeted them with respectful civility, and who seemed to Bertalda much to resemble the director of the city fountain. Still less was the resemblance to be mistaken, when Undine, indignant at his intrusion, waved him off with an air of menace; while he, shaking his head, retreated with rapid strides, as he had formerly done, then glided among the trees of a neighbouring grove and disappeared.

"Do not be terrified, Bertalda," said Undine; "the hateful master of the fountain shall do you no harm this time." And then she related to her the particulars of her history, and who she was herself – how Bertalda had been taken away from the people of the peninsula, and Undine left in her place. This relation at first filled the young maiden with amazement and alarm; she imagined her friend must be seized with a sudden madness. But from the consistency of her story, she became more and more convinced that all was true, it so well agreed with former occurrences, and still more convinced from that inward feeling with which truth never fails to make itself known to us. She could not but view it as an extraordinary circumstance that she was herself now living, as it were, in the midst of one of those wild tales which she had formerly heard related. She gazed upon Undine with reverence, but could not keep from a shuddering feeling which seemed to come between her and her friend; and she could not but wonder when the knight, at their evening repast, showed himself so kind and full of love towards a being who appeared to her, after the discoveries just made, more to resemble a phantom of the spirit-world than one of the human race.

Chapter VII

THE WRITER of this tale, both because it moves his own heart and he wishes it to move that of others, asks a favour of you, dear reader. Forgive him if he passes over a considerable space of time in a few words, and only tells you generally what therein happened. He knows well that it might be unfolded skilfully, and step by step, how Huldbrand's heart began to turn from Undine and towards Bertalda – how Bertalda met the young knight with ardent love, and how they both looked upon the poor wife as a mysterious being, more to be dreaded than pitied – how Undine wept, and her tears stung the conscience of her husband, without recalling his former love; so that though at times he showed kindness to her, a cold shudder soon forced him to turn from her to his fellow-mortal Bertalda; – all this, the writer knows, might have been drawn out fully, and perhaps it ought to have been. But it would have made him too sad; for he has witnessed such things, and shrinks from recalling even their shadow. Thou knowest, probably, the like feeling, dear reader; for it is the lot of mortal man. Happy art thou if thou hast received the injury, not inflicted it; for in this case it is more blessed to receive than to give. Then only a soft sorrow at such a recollection passes through thy heart, and perhaps a quiet tear trickles down thy cheek over the faded flowers in which thou once so heartily rejoiced. This is enough: we will not pierce our hearts with a thousand separate stings, but only bear in mind that all happened as I just now said.

Poor Undine was greatly troubled; and the other two were very far from being happy. Bertalda in particular, whenever she was in the slightest degree opposed in her wishes, attributed the cause to the jealousy and oppression of the injured wife. She was therefore daily in the habit of showing a haughty and imperious demeanour, to which Undine yielded with a sad submission; and which was generally encouraged strongly by the now blinded Huldbrand.

What disturbed the inmates of the castle still more, was the endless variety of wonderful apparitions which assailed Huldbrand and Bertalda in the vaulted passages of the building, and of which nothing had ever been heard before within the memory of man. The tall white man, in whom Huldbrand but too plainly recognized Undine's uncle Kuhleborn, and Bertalda the spectral master of the waterworks, often passed before them with threatening aspect and gestures; more especially, however, before Bertalda, so that, through terror, she had several times already fallen sick, and had, in consequence, frequently thought of quitting the castle. Yet partly because Huldbrand was but too dear to her, and she trusted to her innocence, since no words of love had passed between them, and partly also because she knew not whither to direct her steps, she lingered where she was.

The old fisherman, on receiving the message from the lord of Ringstetten that Bertalda was his guest, returned answer in some lines almost too illegible to be deciphered, but still the best his advanced life and long disuse of writing permitted him to form.

"I have now become," he wrote, "a poor old widower, for my beloved and faithful wife is dead. But lonely as I now sit in my cottage, I prefer Bertalda's remaining where she is, to her living with me. Only let her do nothing to hurt my dear Undine, else she will have my curse."

The last words of this letter Bertalda flung to the winds; but the permission to remain from home, which her father had granted her, she remembered and clung to – just as we are all of us wont to do in similar circumstances.

One day, a few moments after Huldbrand had ridden out, Undine called together the domestics of the family, and ordered them to bring a large stone, and carefully to cover with it a magnificent fountain, that was situated in the middle of the castle court. The servants objected that it would oblige them to bring water from the valley below. Undine smiled sadly.

"I am sorry, my friends," replied she, "to increase your labour; I would rather bring up the water-vessels myself: but this fountain must indeed be closed. Believe me when I say that it must be done, and that only by doing it we can avoid a greater evil."

The domestics were all rejoiced to gratify their gentle mistress; and making no further inquiry, they seized the enormous stone. While they were raising it in their hands, and were now on the point of adjusting it over the fountain, Bertalda came running to the place, and cried, with an air of command, that they must stop; that the water she used, so improving to her complexion, was brought from this fountain, and that she would by no means allow it to be closed.

This time, however, Undine, while she showed her usual gentleness, showed more than her usual resolution: she said it belonged to her, as mistress of the house, to direct the household according to her best judgment; and that she was accountable in this to no one but her lord and husband.

"See, O pray see," exclaimed the dissatisfied and indignant Bertalda, "how the beautiful water is curling and curving, winding and waving there, as if disturbed at being shut out from the bright sunshine, and from the cheerful view of the human countenance, for whose mirror it was created."

In truth the water of the fountain was agitated, and foaming and hissing in a surprising manner; it seemed as if there were something within possessing life and will, that was struggling to free itself from confinement. But Undine only the more earnestly urged the accomplishment of her commands. This earnestness was scarcely required. The servants of the castle were as happy in obeying their gentle lady, as in opposing the haughty spirit of Bertalda; and however the latter might scold and threaten, still the stone was in a few minutes lying firm over the opening of the fountain. Undine leaned thoughtfully over it, and wrote with her beautiful fingers on the flat surface. She must, however, have had something very sharp and corrosive in her hand, for when she retired, and the domestics went up to examine the stone, they discovered various strange characters upon it, which none of them had seen there before.

When the knight returned home, toward evening, Bertalda received him with tears, and complaints of Undine's conduct. He cast a severe glance of reproach at his poor wife, and she looked down in distress; yet she said very calmly:

"My lord and husband, you never reprove even a bondslave before you hear his defence; how much less, then, your wedded wife!"

"Speak! what moved you to this singular conduct?" said the knight with a gloomy countenance.

"I could wish to tell you when we are entirely alone," said Undine, with a sigh.

"You can tell me equally well in the presence of Bertalda," he replied.

"Yes, if you command me," said Undine; "but do not command me – pray, pray do not!"

She looked so humble, affectionate, and obedient, that the heart of the knight was touched and softened, as if it felt the influence of a ray from better times. He kindly took her arm within his, and led her to his apartment, where she spoke as follows:

"You already know something, my beloved lord, of Kuhleborn, my evil-disposed uncle, and have often felt displeasure at meeting him in the passages of this castle. Several times has he terrified Bertalda even to swooning. He does this because he possesses no soul, being a mere elemental mirror of the outward world, while of the world within he can give no reflection. Then, too, he sometimes observes that you are displeased with me, that in my childish weakness I weep at this, and that Bertalda, it may be, laughs at the same moment. Hence it is that he imagines all is wrong with us, and in various ways mixes with our circle unbidden. What do I gain by reproving him, by showing displeasure, and sending him away? He does not believe a word I say. His poor nature has no idea that the joys and sorrows of love have so sweet a resemblance, and are so intimately connected that no power on earth is able to separate them. A smile shines in the midst of tears, and a smile calls forth tears from their dwelling-place."

She looked up at Huldbrand, smiling and weeping, and he again felt within his heart all the magic of his former love. She perceived it, and pressed him more tenderly to her, while with tears of joy she went on thus:

"When the disturber of our peace would not be dismissed with words, I was obliged to shut the door upon him; and the only entrance by which he has access to us is that fountain. His connection with the other water-spirits here in this region is cut off by the valleys that border upon us; and his kingdom first commences farther off on the Danube, in whose tributary streams some of his good friends have their abode. For this reason I caused the stone to be placed over the opening of the fountain, and inscribed characters upon it, which baffle all the efforts of my suspicious uncle; so that he now has no power of intruding either upon you or me, or Bertalda. Human beings, it is true, notwithstanding the characters I have inscribed there, are able to raise the stone without any extraordinary trouble; there is nothing to prevent them. If you choose, therefore, remove it, according to Bertalda's desire; but she assuredly knows not what she asks. The rude Kuhleborn looks with peculiar ill-will upon her; and should those things come to pass that he has predicted to me, and which may happen without your meaning any evil, ah! Dearest, even you yourself would be exposed to peril."

Huldbrand felt the generosity of his gentle wife in the depth of his heart, since she had been so active in confining her formidable defender, and even at the very moment she was reproached for it by Bertalda. He pressed her in his arms with the tenderest affection, and said with emotion:

"The stone shall remain unmoved; all remains, and ever shall remain, just as you choose to have it, my sweetest Undine!"

At these long-withheld expressions of tenderness, she returned his caresses with lowly delight, and at length said:

"My dearest husband, since you are so kind and indulgent today, may I venture to ask a favour of you? See now, it is with you as with summer. Even amid its highest splendour, summer puts on the flaming and thundering crown of glorious tempests, in which it strongly resembles a king and god on earth. You, too, are sometimes terrible in your rebukes; your eyes flash lightning, while thunder resounds in your voice; and although this may be quite becoming to you, I in my folly cannot but sometimes weep at it. But never, I entreat you, behave thus toward me on a river, or even when we are near any water. For if you should, my relations would acquire a right over me. They would inexorably tear me from you in their fury, because they would conceive that one of their race was injured; and I should be compelled, as long as I lived, to dwell below in the crystal palaces, and never dare to ascend to you again; or should *they send* me up to you! – O God! That would be far worse still. No, no, my beloved husband; let it not come to that, if your poor Undine is dear to you."

He solemnly promised to do as she desired, and, inexpressibly happy and full of affection, the married pair returned from the apartment. At this very moment Bertalda came with some work-people whom she had meanwhile ordered to attend her, and said with a fretful air, which she had assumed of late:

"Well, now the secret consultation is at an end, the stone may be removed. Go out, workmen, and see to it."

The knight, however, highly resenting her impertinence, said, in brief and very decisive terms: "The stone remains where it is!" He reproved Bertalda also for the vehemence that she had shown towards his wife. Whereupon the workmen, smiling with secret satisfaction, withdrew; while Bertalda, pale with rage, hurried away to her room.

When the hour of supper came, Bertalda was waited for in vain. They sent for her; but the domestic found her apartments empty, and brought back with him only a sealed letter, addressed to the knight. He opened it in alarm, and read:

"I feel with shame that I am only the daughter of a poor fisherman. That I for one moment forgot this, I will make expiation in the miserable hut of my parents. Farewell to you and your beautiful wife!"

Undine was troubled at heart. With eagerness she entreated Huldbrand to hasten after their friend, who had flown, and bring her back with him. Alas! She had no occasion to urge him. His passion for Bertalda again burst forth with vehemence. He hurried round the castle, inquiring whether any one had seen which way the fair fugitive had gone. He could gain no information; and was already in the court on his horse, determining to take at a venture the road by which he had conducted Bertalda to the castle, when there appeared a page, who assured him that he had met the lady on the path to the Black Valley. Swift as an arrow, the knight sprang through the gate in the direction pointed out, without hearing Undine's voice of agony, as she cried after him from the window:

"To the Black Valley? Oh, not there! Huldbrand, not there! Or if you will go, for Heaven's sake take me with you!"

But when she perceived that all her calling was of no avail, she ordered her white palfrey to be instantly saddled, and followed the knight, without permitting a single servant to accompany her.

The Black Valley lies secluded far among the mountains. What its present name may be I am unable to say. At the time of which I am speaking, the country-people gave it this appellation from the deep obscurity produced by the shadows of lofty trees, more especially by a crowded growth of firs that covered this region of moorland. Even the brook, which bubbled between the rocks, assumed the same dark hue, and showed nothing of that cheerful aspect which streams are wont to wear that have the blue sky immediately over them.

It was now the dusk of evening; and between the heights it had become extremely wild and gloomy. The knight, in great anxiety, skirted the border of the brook. He was at one time fearful that, by delay, he should allow the fugitive to advance too far before him; and then again, in his too eager rapidity, he was afraid he might somewhere overlook and pass by her, should she be desirous of concealing herself from his search. He had in the meantime penetrated pretty far into the valley, and might hope soon to overtake the maiden, provided he were pursuing the right track. The fear, indeed, that he might not as yet have gained it, made his heart beat with more and more of anxiety. In the stormy night which was now approaching, and which always fell more fearfully over this valley, where would the delicate Bertalda shelter herself, should he fail to find her? At last, while these thoughts were darting across his mind, he saw something white glimmer through the branches on the ascent of the mountain. He thought he recognized Bertalda's robe; and he directed his course towards it. But his horse refused to go forward; he reared with a fury so uncontrollable, and his master was so unwilling to lose a moment, that (especially as he saw the thickets were altogether impassable on horseback) he dismounted, and, having fastened his snorting steed to an elm, worked his way with caution through the matted underwood. The branches, moistened by the cold drops of the evening dew, struck against his forehead and cheeks; distant thunder muttered from the further side of the mountains; and everything put on so strange an appearance, that he began to feel a dread of the white figure, which now lay at a short distance from him upon the ground. Still, he could see distinctly that it was a female, either asleep or in a swoon, and dressed in long white garments such as Bertalda had worn the past day. Approaching quite near to her, he made a rustling with the branches and a ringing with his sword; but she did not move.

"Bertalda!" he cried, at first low, then louder and louder; yet she heard him not. At last, when he uttered the dear name with an energy yet more powerful, a hollow echo from the mountain-summits around the valley returned the deadened sound, "Bertalda!" Still the sleeper continued insensible. He stooped down; but the duskiness of the valley, and the obscurity of twilight would not allow him to distinguish her features. While, with painful uncertainty, he was bending over her, a flash of lightning suddenly shot across the valley. By this stream of light he saw a frightfully distorted visage close to his own, and a hoarse voice reached his ear:

"You enamoured swain, give me a kiss!" Huldbrand sprang upon his feet with a cry of horror, and the hideous figure rose with him.

"Go home!" it cried, with a deep murmur: "The fiends are abroad. Go home! Or I have you!" And it stretched towards him its long white arms.

"Malicious Kuhleborn!" exclaimed the knight, with restored energy; "If Kuhleborn you are, what business have you here? – What's your will, you goblin? There, take your kiss!" And in fury he struck his sword at the form. But it vanished like vapour; and a rush of water, which wetted him through and through, left him in no doubt with what foe he had been engaged.

"He wishes to frighten me back from my pursuit of Bertalda," said he to himself. "He imagines that I shall be terrified at his senseless tricks, and resign the poor distressed maiden to his power, so that he can wreak his vengeance upon her at will. But that he shall not, weak spirit of the flood! What the heart of man can do, when it exerts the full force of its will and of its noblest powers, the poor goblin cannot fathom."

He felt the truth of his words, and that they had inspired his heart with fresh courage. Fortune, too, appeared to favour him; for, before reaching his fastened steed, he distinctly heard the voice of Bertalda, weeping not far before him, amid the roar of the thunder and the tempest, which every moment increased. He flew swiftly towards the sound, and found the trembling maiden, just as she was attempting to climb the steep, hoping to escape from the dreadful darkness of this valley. He drew near her with expressions of love; and bold and proud as her resolution had so lately been, she now felt nothing but joy that the man whom she so passionately loved should rescue her from this frightful solitude, and thus call her back to the joyful life in the castle. She followed almost unresisting, but so spent with fatigue, that the knight was glad to bring her to his horse, which he now hastily unfastened from the elm, in order to lift the fair wanderer upon him, and then to lead him carefully by the reins through the uncertain shades of the valley.

But, owing to the wild apparition of Kuhleborn, the horse had become wholly unmanageable. Rearing and wildly snorting as he was, the knight must have used uncommon effort to mount the beast himself; to place the trembling Bertalda upon him was impossible. They were compelled, therefore, to return home on foot. While with one hand the knight drew the steed after him by the bridle, he supported the tottering Bertalda with the other. She exerted all the strengths in her power in order to escape speedily from this vale of terrors. But weariness weighed her down like lead; and all her limbs trembled, partly in consequence of what she had suffered from the extreme terror which Kuhleborn had already caused her, and partly from her present fear at the roar of the tempest and thunder amid the mountain forest.

At last she slid from the arm of the knight; and sinking upon the moss, she said: "Only let me lie here, my noble lord. I suffer the punishment due to my folly; and I must perish here through faintness and dismay."

"Never, gentle lady, will I leave you," cried Huldbrand, vainly trying to restrain the furious animal he was leading, for the horse was all in a foam, and began to chafe more ungovernably than before, till the knight was glad to keep him at such a distance from the exhausted maiden as to save her from a new alarm. But hardly had he withdrawn five steps with the frantic steed when she began to call after him in the most sorrowful accents, fearful that he would actually leave her in this horrible wilderness. He was at a loss what course to take. He would gladly have given the enraged beast his liberty; he would have let him rush away amid the night and exhaust his fury, had he not feared that in this narrow defile his iron-shod hoofs might come thundering over the very spot where Bertalda lay.

In this extreme peril and embarrassment he heard with delight the rumbling wheels of a waggon as it came slowly descending the stony way behind them. He called out for help; answer was returned in the deep voice of a man, bidding them have patience, but promising assistance; and two grey horses soon after shone through the bushes, and near them their driver in the white frock of a carter; and next appeared a great sheet of white linen, with which the goods he seemed to be conveying were covered. The greys, in obedience to a shout from their master, stood still. He came up to the knight, and aided him in checking the fury of the foaming charger.

"I know well enough," said he, "what is the matter with the brute. The first time I travelled this way my horses were just as wilful and headstrong as yours. The reason is, there is a water-spirit haunts this valley – and a wicked wight they say he is – who takes delight in mischief and witcheries of this sort. But I have learned a charm; and if you will let me whisper it in your horse's ear, he will stand just as quiet as my silver greys there."

"Try your luck, then, and help us as quickly as possible!" said the impatient knight.

Upon this the waggoner drew down the head of the rearing courser close to his own, and spoke some words in his ear. The animal instantly stood still and subdued; only his quick panting and smoking sweat showed his recent violence.

Huldbrand had little time to inquire by what means this had been effected. He agreed with the man that he should take Bertalda in his waggon, where, as he said, a quantity of soft cotton was stowed, and he might in this way convey her to Castle Ringstetten. The knight could accompany them on horseback. But the horse appeared to be too much exhausted to carry his master so far. Seeing this, the man advised him to mount the waggon with Bertalda. The horse could be attached to it behind.

"It is down-hill," said he, "and the load for my greys will therefore be light."

The knight accepted his offer, and entered the waggon with Bertalda. The horse followed patiently after, while the waggoner, sturdy and attentive, walked beside them.

Amid the silence and deepening obscurity of the night, the tempest sounding more and more remote, in the comfortable feeling of their security, a confidential conversation arose between Huldbrand and Bertalda. He reproached her in the most flattering words for her resentful flight. She excused herself with humility and feeling; and from every tone of her voice it shone out, like a lamp guiding to the beloved through night and darkness, that Huldbrand was still dear to her. The knight felt the sense of her words rather than heard the words themselves, and answered simply to this sense.

Then the waggoner suddenly shouted, with a startling voice: "Up, my greys, up with your feet! Hey, now together! – Show your spirit! – Remember who you are!"

The knight bent over the side of the waggon, and saw that the horses had stepped into the midst of a foaming stream, and were, indeed, almost swimming, while the wheels of the waggon were rushing round and flashing like mill-wheels; and the waggoner had got on before, to avoid the swell of the flood.

"What sort of a road is this? It leads into the middle of the stream!" cried Huldbrand to his guide.

"Not at all, sir," returned he, with a laugh; "it is just the contrary. The stream is running in the middle of our road. Only look about you, and see how all is overflowed!"

The whole valley, in fact, was in commotion, as the waters, suddenly raised and visibly rising, swept over it.

"It is Kuhleborn, that evil water-spirit, who wishes to drown us!" exclaimed the knight. "Have you no charm of protection against him, friend?"

"I have one," answered the waggoner; "but I cannot and must not make use of it before you know who I am."

"Is this a time for riddles?" cried the knight. "The flood is every moment rising higher; and what does it concern *me* to know who *you* are?"

"But mayhap it does concern you, though," said the guide; "for I am Kuhleborn."

Thus speaking he thrust his head into the waggon, and laughed with a distorted visage. But the waggon remained a waggon no longer; the grey horses were horses no longer; all was transformed to foam – all sank into the waters that rushed and hissed around them; while the waggoner himself, rising in the form of a gigantic wave, dragged the vainly-struggling courser under the waters, then rose again huge as a liquid tower, swept over the heads of the floating pair, and was on the point of burying them irrecoverably beneath it. Then the soft voice of Undine was heard through the uproar; the moon emerged from the clouds; and by its light Undine was seen on the heights above the valley. She rebuked, she threatened the floods below her. The menacing and tower-like billow vanished, muttering and murmuring; the waters gently flowed away under the beams of the moon; while Undine, like a hovering white dove, flew down from the hill, raised the knight and Bertalda, and bore them to a green spot, where, by her earnest efforts, she soon restored them and dispelled their terrors. She then assisted Bertalda to mount the white palfrey on which she had herself been borne to the valley; and thus all three returned homeward to Castle Ringstetten.

Chapter VIII

AFTER THIS last adventure they lived at the castle undisturbed and in peaceful enjoyment. The knight was more and more impressed with the heavenly goodness of his wife, which she had so nobly shown by her instant pursuit and by the rescue she had effected in the Black Valley, where the power of Kuhleborn again commenced. Undine herself enjoyed that peace and security which never fails the soul as long as it knows distinctly that it is on the right path; and besides, in the newly-awakened love and regard of her husband, a thousand gleams of hope and joy shone upon her.

Bertalda, on the other hand, showed herself grateful, humble, and timid, without taking to herself any merit for so doing. Whenever Huldbrand or Undine began to explain to her their reasons for covering the fountain, or their adventures in the Black Valley, she would earnestly entreat them to spare her the recital, for the recollection of the fountain occasioned her too much shame, and that of the Black Valley too much terror. She learnt nothing more about either of them; and what would she have gained from more knowledge? Peace and joy had visibly taken up their abode at Castle Ringstetten. They enjoyed their present blessings in perfect security, and now imagined that life could produce nothing but pleasant flowers and fruits.

In this happiness winter came and passed away; and spring, with its foliage of tender green, and its heaven of softest blue, succeeded to gladden the hearts of the three inmates of the castle. The season was in harmony with their minds, and their minds imparted their own hues to the season. What wonder, then, that its storks and swallows inspired them also with a disposition to travel? On a bright morning, while they were wandering down to one of the sources of the Danube, Huldbrand spoke of the magnificence of this noble stream, how it continued swelling as it flowed through countries enriched by its waters, with what splendour Vienna rose and sparkled on its banks, and how it grew lovelier and more imposing throughout its progress.

"It must be glorious to trace its course down to Vienna!" Bertalda exclaimed, with warmth; but immediately resuming the humble and modest demeanour she had recently shown, she paused and blushed in silence.

This much moved Undine; and with the liveliest wish to gratify her friend, she said, "What hinders our taking this little voyage?"

Bertalda leapt up with delight, and the two friends at the same moment began painting this enchanting voyage on the Danube in the most brilliant colours. Huldbrand, too, agreed to the project with pleasure; only he once whispered, with something of alarm, in Undine's ear:

"But at that distance Kuhleborn becomes possessed of his power again!"

"Let him come, let him come," she answered with a laugh; "I shall be there, and he dares do none of his mischief in my presence."

Thus was the last impediment removed. They prepared for the expedition, and soon set out upon it with lively spirits and the brightest hopes.

But be not surprised, O man, if events almost always happen very differently from what you expect. That malicious power which lies in ambush for our destruction delights to lull its chosen victim asleep with sweet songs and golden delusions; while, on the other hand, the messenger of heaven often strikes sharply at our door, to alarm and awaken us.

During the first days of their passage down the Danube they were unusually happy. The further they advanced upon the waters of this proud river, the views became more and more fair. But amid scenes otherwise most delicious, and from which they had promised themselves the purest delight, the stubborn Kuhleborn, dropping all disguise, began to show his power of annoying them. He had no other means of doing this, indeed, than by tricks – for Undine often rebuked the swelling waves or the contrary winds, and then the insolence of the enemy was instantly humbled and subdued; but his attacks were renewed, and Undine's reproofs again became necessary, so that the pleasure of the fellow-travellers was completely destroyed. The boatmen, too, were continually whispering to one another in dismay, and eying their three superiors with distrust, while even the servants began more and more to form dismal surmises, and to watch their master and mistress with looks of suspicion.

Huldbrand often said in his own mind, "This comes when like marries not like – when a man forms an unnatural union with a sea-maiden." Excusing himself, as we all love to do, he would add: "I did not, in fact, know that she was a maid of the sea. It is my misfortune that my steps are haunted and disturbed by the wild humours of her kindred, but it is not my crime."

By reflections like these, he felt himself in some measure strengthened; but, on the other hand, he felt the more ill-humour, almost dislike, towards Undine. He would look angrily at her, and the unhappy wife but too well understood his meaning. One day, grieved by this unkindness, as well as exhausted by her unremitted exertions to frustrate the artifices of Kuhleborn, she toward evening fell into a deep slumber, rocked and soothed by the gentle motion of the bark. But hardly had she closed her eyes, when every person in the boat, in whatever direction he might look, saw the head of a man, frightful beyond imagination: each head rose out of the waves, not like that of a person swimming, but quite perpendicular, as if firmly fastened to the watery mirror, and yet moving on with the bark. Every one wished to show to his companion what terrified himself, and each perceived the same expression of horror on the face of the other, only hands and eyes were directed to a different quarter, as if to a point where the monster, half laughing and half threatening, rose opposite to each.

When, however, they wished to make one another understand the site, and all cried out, "Look, there!" "No, there!" the frightful heads all became visible to each, and the whole river around the boat swarmed with the most horrible faces. All raised a scream of terror at the sight, and Undine started from sleep. As she opened her eyes, the deformed visages disappeared. But Huldbrand was made furious by so many hideous visions. He would have burst out in wild imprecations, had not Undine with the meekest looks and gentlest tone of voice said:

"For God's sake, my husband, do not express displeasure against me here – we are on the water."

The knight was silent, and sat down absorbed in deep thought. Undine whispered in his ear, "Would it not be better, my love, to give up this foolish voyage, and return to Castle Ringstetten in peace?"

But Huldbrand murmured wrathfully: "So I must become a prisoner in my own castle, and not be allowed to breathe a moment but while the fountain is covered? Would to Heaven that your cursed kindred –"

Then Undine pressed her fair hand on his lips caressingly. He said no more; but in silence pondered on all that Undine had before said.

Bertalda, meanwhile, had given herself up to a crowd of thronging thoughts. Of Undine's origin she knew a good deal, but not the whole; and the terrible Kuhleborn especially remained to her an awful, an impenetrable mystery – never, indeed, had she once heard his name. Musing upon these wondrous things, she unclasped, without being fully conscious of what she was doing, a golden necklace, which Huldbrand, on one of the preceding days of their passage, had bought for her of a travelling trader; and she was now letting it float in sport just over the surface of the stream, while in her dreamy mood she enjoyed the bright reflection it threw on the water, so clear beneath the glow of evening. That instant a huge hand flashed suddenly up from the Danube, seized the necklace in its grasp, and vanished with it beneath the flood. Bertalda shrieked aloud, and a scornful laugh came pealing up from the depth of the river.

The knight could now restrain his wrath no longer. He started up, poured forth a torrent of reproaches, heaped curses upon all who interfered with his friends and troubled his life, and dared them all, water-spirits or mermaids, to come within the sweep of his sword.

Bertalda, meantime, wept for the loss of the ornament so very dear to her heart, and her tears were to Huldbrand as oil poured upon the flame of his fury; while Undine held her hand over the side of the boat, dipping it in the waves, softly murmuring to herself, and only at times interrupting her strange mysterious whisper to entreat her husband:

"Do not reprove me here, beloved; blame all others as you will, but not me. You know why!" And in truth, though he was trembling with excess of passion, he kept himself from any word directly against her.

She then brought up in her wet hand, which she had been holding under the waves, a coral necklace, of such exquisite beauty, such sparkling brilliancy, as dazzled the eyes of all who beheld it. "Take this," said she, holding it out kindly to Bertalda, "I have ordered it to be brought to make some amends for your loss; so do not grieve any more, poor child."

But the knight rushed between then, and snatching the beautiful ornament out of Undine's hand, hurled it back into the flood; and, mad with rage, exclaimed: "So, then, you have still a connection with them! In the name of all witches go and remain among them with your presents, you sorceress, and leave us human beings in peace!"

With fixed but streaming eyes, poor Undine gazed on him, her hand still stretched out, just as when she had so lovingly offered her brilliant gift to Bertalda. She then began to weep more and more, as if her heart would break, like an innocent tender child, cruelly aggrieved. At last, wearied out, she said: "Farewell, dearest, farewell. They shall do you no harm; only remain true, that I may have power to keep them from you. But I must go hence! Go hence even in this early youth! Oh, woe, woe! What have you done! Oh, woe, woe!"

And she vanished over the side of the boat. Whether she plunged into the stream, or whether, like water melting into water, she flowed away with it, they knew not – her disappearance was like both and neither. But she was lost in the Danube, instantly and completely; only little waves were yet whispering and sobbing around the boat, and they could almost be heard to say, "Oh, woe, woe! Ah, remain true! Oh, woe!"

But Huldbrand, in a passion of burning tears, threw himself upon the deck of the bark; and a deep swoon soon wrapped the wretched man in a blessed forgetfulness of misery.

Shall we call it a good or an evil thing, that our mourning has no long duration? I mean that deep mourning which comes from the very well-springs of our being, which so becomes one with the lost objects of our love that we hardly realize their loss, while our grief devotes itself religiously to the honouring of their image until we reach that bourne which they have already reached!

Truly all good men observe in a degree this religious devotion; but yet it soon ceases to be that first deep grief. Other and new images throng in, until, to our sorrow, we experience the vanity of all earthly things. Therefore I must say: Alas, that our mourning should be of such short duration!

The lord of Ringstetten experienced this; but whether for his good, we shall discover in the sequel of this history. At first he could do nothing but weep – weep as bitterly as the poor gentle Undine had wept when he snatched out of her hand that brilliant ornament, with which she so kindly wished to make amends for Bertalda's loss. And then he stretched his hand out, as she had done, and wept again like her, with renewed violence. He cherished a secret hope, that even the springs of life would at last become exhausted by weeping. And has not the like thought passed through the minds of many of us with a painful pleasure in times of sore affliction? Bertalda wept with him; and they lived together a long while at the castle of Ringstetten in undisturbed quiet, honouring the memory of Undine, and having almost wholly forgotten their former attachment. And therefore the good Undine, about this time, often visited Huldbrand's dreams: she soothed him with soft and affectionate caresses, and then went away again, weeping in silence; so that when he awoke, he sometimes knew not how his cheeks came to be so wet – whether it was caused by her tears, or only by his own.

But as time advanced, these visions became less frequent, and the sorrow of the knight less keen; still he might never, perhaps, have entertained any other wish than thus quietly to think of Undine, and to speak of her, had not the old fisherman arrived unexpectedly at the castle, and earnestly insisted on Bertalda's returning with him as his child. He had received information of Undine's disappearance; and he was not willing to allow Bertalda to continue longer at the castle with the widowed knight. "For," said he, "whether my daughter loves me or not is at present what I care not to know; but her good name is at stake: and where that is the case, nothing else may be thought of."

This resolution of the old fisherman, and the fearful solitude that, on Bertalda's departure, threatened to oppress the knight in every hall and passage of the deserted castle, brought to light what had disappeared in his sorrow for Undine, – I mean, his attachment to the fair Bertalda; and this he made known to her father.

The fisherman had many objections to make to the proposed marriage. The old man had loved Undine with exceeding tenderness, and it was doubtful to his mind that the mere disappearance of his beloved child could be properly viewed as her death. But were it even granted that her corpse were lying stiff and cold at the bottom of the Danube, or swept away by the current to the ocean, still Bertalda had had some share in her death; and it was unfitting for her to step into the place of the poor injured wife. The fisherman, however, had felt a strong regard also for the knight: this and the entreaties of his daughter, who had become much more gentle and respectful, as well as her tears for Undine, all exerted their influence, and he must at last have been forced to give up his opposition, for he remained at the castle without objection, and a messenger was sent off express to Father Heilmann, who in former and happier days had united Undine and Huldbrand, requesting him to come and perform the ceremony at the knight's second marriage.

Hardly had the holy man read through the letter from the lord of Ringstetten, ere he set out upon the journey and made much greater dispatch on his way to the castle than the messenger from it had made in reaching him. Whenever his breath failed him in his rapid progress, or his old limbs ached with fatigue, he would say to himself:

"Perhaps I shall be able to prevent a sin; then sink not, withered body, before I arrive at the end of my journey!" And with renewed vigour he pressed forward, hurrying on without rest or repose, until, late one evening, he entered the shady court-yard of the castle of Ringstetten.

The betrothed were sitting side by side under the trees, and the aged fisherman in a thoughtful mood sat near them. The moment they saw Father Heilmann, they rose with a spring of joy, and pressed round him with eager welcome. But he, in a few words, asked the bridegroom to return with him into the castle; and when Huldbrand stood mute with surprise, and delayed complying with his earnest request, the pious preacher said to him:

"I do not know why I should want to speak to you in private; what I have to say as much concerns Bertalda and the fisherman as yourself; and what we must at some time hear, it is best to hear as soon as possible. Are you, then, so very certain, Knight Huldbrand, that your first wife is actually dead? I can hardly think it. I will say nothing, indeed, of the mysterious state in which she may be now existing; I know nothing of it with certainty. But that she was a most devoted and faithful wife is beyond all dispute. And for fourteen nights past, she has appeared to me in a dream, standing at my bedside wringing her tender hands in anguish, and sighing out, 'Ah, prevent him, dear father! I am still living! Ah, save his life! Ah, save his soul!'

"I did not understand what this vision of the night could mean, then came your messenger; and I have now hastened hither, not to unite, but, as I hope, to separate what ought not to be joined together. Leave her, Huldbrand! Leave him, Bertalda! He still belongs to another; and do you not see on his pale cheek his grief for his lost wife? That is not the look of a bridegroom; and the spirit says to me, that 'if you do not leave him you will never be happy!' "

The three felt in their inmost hearts that Father Heilmann spoke the truth; but they would not believe it. Even the old fisherman was so infatuated, that he thought it could not be otherwise than as they had latterly settled amongst themselves. They all, therefore, with a determined and gloomy eagerness, struggled against the representations and warnings of the priest, until, shaking his head and oppressed with sorrow, he finally quitted the castle, not choosing to accept their offered shelter even for a single night, or indeed so much as to taste a morsel of the refreshment they brought him. Huldbrand persuaded himself, however, that the priest was a mere visionary; and sent at daybreak to a monk of the nearest monastery, who, without scruple, promised to perform the ceremony in a few days.

Chapter IX

IT WAS BETWEEN night and dawn of day that Huldbrand was lying on his couch, half waking and half sleeping. Whenever he attempted to compose himself to sleep, a terror came upon him and scared him, as if his slumbers were haunted with spectres. But he made an effort to rouse himself fully. He felt fanned as by the wings of a swan, and lulled as by the murmuring of waters, till in sweet confusion of the senses he sank back into his state of half-consciousness.

At last, however, he must have fallen perfectly asleep; for he seemed to be lifted up by wings of the swans, and to be wafted far away over land and sea, while their music swelled on his ear most sweetly. "The music of the swan! The song of the swan!" he could not but repeat to himself every moment; "Is it not a sure foreboding of death?" Probably, however, it had yet another meaning. All at once he seemed to be hovering over the Mediterranean Sea. A swan sang melodiously in his ear, that this was the Mediterranean Sea. And while he was looking down upon the waves, they became transparent as crystal, so that he could see through them to the very bottom.

At this a thrill of delight shot through him, for he could see Undine where she was sitting beneath the clear crystal dome. It is true she was weeping very bitterly, and looked much sadder than in those happy days when they lived together at the castle of Ringstetten, both on their arrival and afterward, just before they set out upon their fatal passage down the Danube. The knight could not help thinking upon all this with deep emotion, but it did not appear that Undine was aware of his presence.

Kuhleborn had meanwhile approached her, and was about to reprove her for weeping, when she drew herself up, and looked upon him with an air so majestic and commanding, that he almost shrank back.

"Although I now dwell here beneath the waters," said she, "yet I have brought my soul with me. And therefore I may weep, little as you can know what such tears are. They are blessed, as everything is blessed to one gifted with a true soul."

He shook his head incredulously; and after some thought, replied, "And yet, niece, you are subject to our laws, as a being of the same nature with ourselves; and should *he* prove unfaithful to you and marry again, you are obliged to take away his life."

"He remains a widower to this very hour," replied Undine, "and I am still dear to his sorrowful heart."

"He is, however, betrothed," said Kuhleborn, with a laugh of scorn; "and let only a few days wear away, and then comes the priest with his nuptial blessing; and then you must go up to the death of the husband with two wives."

"I have not the power," returned Undine, with a smile. "I have sealed up the fountain securely against myself and all of my race."

"Still, should he leave his castle," said Kuhleborn, "or should he once allow the fountain to be uncovered, what then? for he thinks little enough of these things."

"For that very reason," said Undine, still smiling amid her tears, "for that very reason he is at this moment hovering in spirit over the Mediterranean Sea, and dreaming of the warning which our discourse gives him. I thoughtfully planned all this."

That instant, Kuhleborn, inflamed with rage, looked up at the knight, wrathfully threatened him, stamped on the ground, and then shot like an arrow beneath the waves. He seemed to swell in his fury to the size of a whale. Again the swans began to sing, to wave their wings and fly; the knight seemed to soar away over mountains and streams, and at last to alight at Castle Ringstetten, and to awake on his couch.

Upon his couch he actually did awake; and his attendant entering at the same moment, informed him that Father Heilmann was still lingering in the neighbourhood; that he had the evening before met with him in the forest, where he was sheltering himself under a hut, which he had formed by interweaving the branches of trees, and covering them with moss and fine brushwood; and that to the question "What he was doing there, since he would not give the marriage blessing?" his answer was:

"There are many other blessings than those given at marriages; and though I did not come to officiate at the wedding, I may still officiate at a very different solemnity. All things have their seasons; we must be ready for them all. Besides, marrying and mourning are by no means so very unlike; as every one not wilfully blinded must know full well."

The knight made many bewildered reflections on these words and on his dream. But it is very difficult to give up a thing which we have once looked upon as certain; so all continued as had been arranged previously.

Should I relate to you how passed the marriage-feast at Castle Ringstetten, it would be as if you saw a heap of bright and pleasant things, but all overspread with a black mourning crape, through whose darkening veil their brilliancy would appear but a mockery of the nothingness of all earthly joys.

It was not that any spectral delusion disturbed the scene of festivity; for the castle, as we well know, had been secured against the mischief of water-spirits. But the knight, the fisherman, and all the guests were unable to banish the feeling that the chief personage of the feast was still wanting, and that this chief personage could be no other than the gentle and beloved Undine.

Whenever a door was heard to open, all eyes were involuntarily turned in that direction; and if it was nothing but the steward with new dishes, or the cupbearer with a supply of wine of higher flavour than the last, they again looked down in sadness and disappointment, while the flashes of wit and merriment which had been passing at times from one to another, were extinguished by tears of mournful remembrance.

The bride was the least thoughtful of the company, and therefore the most happy; but even to her it sometimes seemed strange that she should be sitting at the head of the table, wearing a green wreath and gold-embroidered robe, while Undine was lying a corpse, stiff and cold, at the bottom of the Danube, or carried out by the current into the ocean. For ever since her father had suggested something of this sort, his words were continually sounding in her ear; and this day, in particular, they would neither fade from her memory, nor yield to other thoughts.

Evening had scarcely arrived, when the company returned to their homes; not dismissed by the impatience of the bridegroom, as wedding parties are sometimes broken up, but constrained solely by heavy sadness and forebodings of evil. Bertalda retired with her maidens, and the knight with his attendants, to undress, but there was no gay laughing company of bridesmaids and bridesmen at this mournful festival.

Bertalda wished to awaken more cheerful thoughts; she ordered her maidens to spread before her a brilliant set of jewels, a present from Huldbrand, together with rich apparel and veils, that she might select from among them the brightest and most beautiful for her dress in the morning. The attendants rejoiced at this opportunity of pouring forth good wishes and promises of happiness to their young mistress, and failed not to extol the beauty of the bride with the most glowing eloquence. This went on for a long time, until Bertalda at last, looking in a mirror, said with a sigh:

"Ah, but do you not see plainly how freckled I am growing? Look here on the side of my neck."

They looked at the place, and found the freckles, indeed, as their fair mistress had said; but they called them mere beauty spots, the faintest touches of the sun, such as would only heighten the whiteness of her delicate complexion. Bertalda shook her head, and still viewed them as a blemish. "And I could remove them," she said at last, sighing. "But the castle fountain is covered, from which I formerly used to have that precious water, so purifying to the skin. Oh, had I this evening only a single flask of it!"

"Is that all?" cried an alert waiting-maid, laughing as she glided out of the apartment.

"She will not be so foolish," said Bertalda, well-pleased and surprised, "as to cause the stone cover of the fountain to be taken off this very evening?" That instant they heard the tread of men passing along the court-yard, and could see from the window where the officious maiden was leading them directly up to the fountain, and that they carried levers and other instruments on their shoulders.

"It is certainly my will," said Bertalda with a smile, "if it does not take them too long." And pleased with the thought, that a word from her was now sufficient to accomplish what had formerly been refused with a painful reproof, she looked down upon their operations in the bright moonlit castle-court.

The men raised the enormous stone with an effort; some one of the number indeed would occasionally sigh, when he recollected they were destroying the work of their former beloved mistress. Their labour, however, was much lighter than they had expected. It seemed as if some power from within the fountain itself aided them in raising the stone.

"It appears," said the workmen to one another in astonishment, "as if the confined water had become a springing fountain." And the stone rose more and more, and, almost without the assistance of the work-people, rolled slowly down upon the pavement with a hollow sound. But an appearance from the opening of the fountain filled them with awe, as it rose like a white column of water; at first they imagined it really to be a fountain, until they perceived the rising form to be a pale female, veiled in white. She wept bitterly, raised her hands above her head, wringing them sadly as with slow and solemn step she moved toward the castle. The servants shrank back, and fled from the spring, while the bride, pale and motionless with horror, stood with her maidens at the window. When the figure had now come close beneath their room, it looked up to them sobbing, and Bertalda thought she recognized through the veil the pale features of Undine. But the mourning form passed on, sad, reluctant, and lingering, as if going to the place of execution. Bertalda screamed to her maids to call the knight; not one of them dared to stir from her place; and even the bride herself became again mute, as if trembling at the sound of her own voice.

While they continued standing at the window, motionless as statues, the mysterious wanderer had entered the castle, ascended the well-known stairs, and traversed the well-known halls in silent tears. Alas, how different had she once passed through these rooms!

The knight had in the meantime dismissed his attendants. Half-undressed and in deep dejection, he was standing before a large mirror, a wax taper burned dimly beside him. At this moment some one tapped at his door very, very softly. Undine had formerly tapped in this way, when she was playing some of her endearing wiles.

"It is all an illusion!" said he to himself. "I must to my nuptial bed."

"You must indeed, but to a cold one!" he heard a voice, choked with sobs, repeat from without; and then he saw in the mirror, that the door of his room was slowly, slowly opened, and the white figure entered, and gently closed it behind her.

"They have opened the spring," said she in a low tone; "and now I am here, and you must die."

He felt, in his failing breath, that this must indeed be; but covering his eyes with his hands, he cried: "Do not in my death-hour, do not make me mad with terror. If that veil conceals hideous features, do not lift it! Take my life, but let me not see you."

"Alas!" replied the pale figure, "Will you not then look upon me once more? I am as fair now as when you wooed me on the island!"

"Oh, if it indeed were so," sighed Huldbrand, "and that I might die by a kiss from you!"

"Most willingly, my own love," said she. She threw back her veil; heavenly fair shone forth her pure countenance. Trembling with love and the awe of approaching death, the knight leant towards her. She kissed him with a holy kiss; but she relaxed not her hold, pressing him more closely in her arms, and weeping as if she would weep away her soul. Tears rushed into the knight's eyes, while a thrill both of bliss and agony shot through his heart, until he at last expired, sinking softly back from her fair arms upon the pillow of his couch a corpse.

"I have wept him to death!" said she to some domestics, who met her in the ante-chamber; and passing through the terrified group, she went slowly out, and disappeared in the fountain.

Chapter X

FATHER HEILMANN had returned to the castle as soon as the death of the lord of Ringstetten was made known in the neighbourhood; and he arrived at the very hour when the monk who had married the unfortunate couple was hurrying from the door, overcome with dismay and horror.

When Father Heilmann was informed of this, he replied, "It is all well; and now come the duties of my office, in which I have no need of an assistant."

He then began to console the bride, now a widow though with little benefit to her worldly and thoughtless spirit.

The old fisherman, on the other hand, though severely afflicted, was far more resigned to the fate of his son-in-law and daughter; and while Bertalda could not refrain from accusing Undine as a murderess and sorceress, the old man calmly said, "After all, it could not happen otherwise. I see nothing in it but the judgment of God; and no one's heart was more pierced by the death of Huldbrand than she who was obliged to work it, the poor forsaken Undine!"

He then assisted in arranging the funeral solemnities as suited the rank of the deceased. The knight was to be interred in the village church-yard, in whose consecrated ground were the graves of his ancestors; a place which they, as well as himself, had endowed with rich privileges and gifts. His shield and helmet lay upon his coffin, ready to be lowered with it into the grave, for Lord Huldbrand of Ringstetten had died the last of his race. The mourners began their sorrowful march, chanting their melancholy songs beneath the calm unclouded heaven; Father Heilmann preceded the procession, bearing a high crucifix, while the inconsolable Bertalda followed, supported by her aged father.

Then they suddenly saw in the midst of the mourning females in the widow's train, a snow-white figure closely veiled, and wringing its hands in the wild vehemence of sorrow. Those next to whom it moved, seized with a secret dread, started back or on one side; and owing to their movements, the others, next to whom the white stranger now came, were terrified still more, so as to produce confusion in the funeral train. Some of the military escort ventured to address the figure, and attempt to remove it from the procession, but it seemed to vanish from under their hands, and yet was immediately seen advancing again, with slow and solemn step, among the followers of the body. At last, in consequence of the shrinking away of the attendants, it came close behind Bertalda. It now moved so slowly, that the widow was not aware of its presence, and it walked meekly and humbly behind her undisturbed.

This continued until they came to the church-yard, where the procession formed a circle round the open grave. Then it was that Bertalda perceived her unbidden companion, and, half in anger and half in terror, she commanded her to depart from the knight's place of final rest. But the veiled female, shaking her head with a gentle denial, raised her hands towards Bertalda in lowly supplication, by which she was greatly moved, and could not but remember with tears how Undine had shown such sweetness of spirit on the Danube when she held out to her the coral necklace.

Father Heilmann now motioned with his hand, and gave order for all to observe perfect stillness, that they might breathe a prayer of silent devotion over the body, upon which earth had already been thrown. Bertalda knelt without speaking; and all knelt, even the grave-diggers, who had now finished their work. But when they arose, the white stranger had disappeared. On the spot where she had knelt, a little spring, of silver brightness, was gushing out from the green turf, and it kept swelling and flowing onward with a low murmur, till it almost encircled the mound of the knight's grave; it then continued its course, and emptied itself into a calm lake, which lay by the side of the consecrated ground. Even to this day, the inhabitants of the village point out the spring; and hold fast the belief that it is the poor deserted Undine, who in this manner still fondly encircles her beloved in her arms.

The Raid of Le Vengeur

George Griffith

Chapter I
The Dream of Captain Flaubert

IT WAS the third morning after the naval manoeuvres at Cherbourg, and since their conclusion Captain Leon Flaubert, of the Marine Experimental Department of the French Navy, had not had three consecutive hours' sleep.

He was an enthusiast on the subject of submarine navigation. He firmly believed that the nation which could put to sea the first really effective fleet of submarine vessels would hold the fleets of rival nations at its mercy and acquire the whole ocean and its coasts as an exclusive territory. To anyone but an enthusiast it would have seemed a wild dream and yet only a few difficulties had still to be overcome, a few more discoveries made, and the realisation of the dream would be merely a matter of money and skilled labour.

Now the Cherbourg evolutions had proved three things. The submarines could sink and remain below the surface of the water. They could be steered vertically and laterally, but once ten feet or so below the water, they were as blind as bats in bright sunshine.

Moreover, when their electric head-lights were turned on, a luminous haze through which it was impossible to see more than a few metres, spread out in front of them and this was reflected on the surface of the water in the form of a semi-phosphorescent patch which infallibly betrayed the whereabouts of the submarine to scouting destroyers and prowling gun-boats. The sinking of a couple of pounds of dynamite with a time-fuse into this patch would have consequences unspeakable for the crew of the submarine since no human power could save them from a horrible death.

It was the fear of this discovery that had caused the rigid exclusion of all non-official spectators from the area of the experiments. Other trials conducted in daylight had further proved that the dim, hazy twilight of the lower waters was even worse than darkness. In short, the only chance of successful attack lay in coming to the surface, taking observations, probably under fire, and then sinking and discharging a torpedo at a venture. This, again, was an operation which could only be conducted with any chance of success in a smooth sea. In even moderately rough weather it would be absolutely impossible.

It was these difficulties which joined to a thousand exasperatingly stubborn technical details had kept Captain Flaubert awake for three nights. For him everything depended upon the solution of them. He was admittedly the best submarine engineer in France. The submarines had been proved to be practically non-effective. France looked to him to make them effective.

The troubles in the far East and, nearer home, in Morocco, had brought the Dual Alliance and the British Empire to the verge of war. At any moment something might happen which would shake a few sparks into the European powder magazine. Then the naval might of Britain would be let loose instantly. In a few hours her overwhelming fleets would be striking their swift and terrible blows at the nearest enemy – France – and yet, if he could only give the submarines eyes which could see through the water, France could send out an invisible squadron which would cripple the British fleets before they left port, destroy her mightiest battleships and her swiftest cruisers before they could fire a single shot, and so in a few days clear the Narrow Seas and make way for the invasion of England by the irresistible military might of France. Then the long spell would be broken, and the proudly boasted Isle Inviolate would be inviolate no longer.

It was a splendid dream – but, until the submarines could be made to see as well as steer, it was as far away as aerial navigation itself.

Day was just breaking on the third morning when a luminous ray of inspiration pierced the mists which hang over the border land of sleep and waking, of mingled dream and reality, amidst which Flaubert's soul was just then wandering.

He sat bolt upright in his little camp bed, clasped his hands across his close-cropped head, and, hardly knowing whether he was asleep or awake, heard himself say:

"*Nom de Dieu*, it is that! What foolishness not to have thought of that before. If we cannot see we must feel. Electric threads, balanced so as to be the same weight as water – ten, twenty, fifty, a hundred metres long, all round the boat, ahead and astern, to port and to starboard! Steel ships are magnetic, that is why they must swing to adjust their compasses."

"The end of each thread shall be a tiny electro-magnet. In-board they will connect with indicators, delicately swung magnetic needles, four of them, ahead, astern, and on each side; and, as *Le Vengeur* – yes, I will call her that, for we have no more forgotten Trafalgar than we have Fashoda – as she approaches the ships of the enemy, deep hidden under the waters, these threads, like the tentacles of the octopus, shall spread towards her prey!"

As she gets nearer and nearer they swing round and converge upon the ship that is nearest and biggest. As we dive under her they will point upwards. When they are perpendicular the overhead torpedo will be released. Its magnets will fasten it to the bottom of the doomed ship. *Le Vengeur* will sink deeper, obeying always the warning of the sounding indicator, and seek either a new victim or a safe place to rise in. In ten, fifteen, twenty minutes, as I please, the torpedo will explode, the battleship or the cruiser will break in two and go down, not knowing whose hand has struck her.

"Ah, Albion, my enemy, you are already conquered! You are only mistress of the seas until *Le Vengeur* begins her work. When that is done there will be no more English navy. The soldiers of France will avenge Waterloo on the soil of England, and Leon Flaubert will be the greatest name in the world. *Dieu Merci*, it is done! I have thought the thought which conquers a world – and now let me sleep."

His clasped hands fell away from his head; his eyelids drooped over his aching, staring eyes; his body swayed a little from side to side, and then fell backwards. As his head rested on the pillow a long deep sigh left his half-parted lips, and in a few moments a contented snore was reverberating through the little, plainly-furnished bedroom.

Chapter II
A Dinner at Albert Gate

CURIOUSLY ENOUGH, while Captain Leon Flaubert had been worrying himself to the verge of distraction over the problem of seeing under water, and had apparently solved it by substituting electric nerves of feeling for the sight-rays which had proved a failure, Mr. Wilfred Wallace Tyrrell had brought to a successful conclusion a long series of experiments bearing upon the self-same subject.

Mr. Tyrrell was the son of Sir Wilfred Tyrrell, one of the Junior Lords of the Admiralty. He was a year under thirty. He had taken a respectable degree at Cambridge, then he had gone to Heidelberg and taken a better one, after which he had come home entered at London, and made his bow to the world as the youngest D.Sc. that Burlington Gardens had ever turned out.

His Continental training had emancipated him from all the limitations under which his father, otherwise a man of very considerable intelligence, suffered. Like Captain Flaubert he was a firm believer in the possibility of submarine navigation, but, like his unknown French rival, he, too, had been confronted with that fatal problem of submarine blindness, and he had attacked it from a point of view so different to that of Captain Flaubert that the difference of method practically amounted to the difference between the genius of the two nations to which they belonged. Captain Flaubert had evaded the question and substituted electric feeling for sight. Wilfred Tyrrell had gone for sight and nothing less, and now he had every reason to believe that he had succeeded.

The night before Captain Flaubert had fallen asleep in his quarters at Cherbourg there was a little dinner-party at Sir Wilfred Tyrrell's house in Albert Gate. The most important of the guests from Wilfred's point of view was Lady Ethel Rivers, the only daughter of the Earl of Kirlew. She was a most temptingly pretty brunette with hopelessly dazzling financial prospects. He had been admiring her from a despairing distance for the last five years, in fact ever since she had crossed the line between girlhood and young womanhood.

Although it was quite within the bounds of possibility that she knew of his devotion, he had never yet ventured upon even the remotest approach to direct courtship. In every sense she seemed too far beyond him. Some day she would be a countess in her own right. Some day, too. she would inherit about half a million in London ground-rents, with much more to follow as the leases fell in, wherefore, as Wilfred Tyrrell reasoned, she would in due course marry a duke, or at least a European Prince.

Lady Ethel's opinions on the subject could only Ix gathered from the fact that she had already declined one Duke, two Viscounts, and a German Serene Highness, during her first season, and that she never seemed tired of listening when Wilfred Tyrrell was talking – which of itself was significant if his modesty had only permitted him to see it.

But while he was sitting beside her at dinner on this momentous night he felt that the distance between them had suddenly decreased. So far his career had been brilliant but unprofitable. Many other men had done as much as he had and ended in mediocrity. But now he had done something; he had made a discovery with which the whole world might be ringing in a few weeks' time. He had solved the problem of submarine navigation, and, as a preliminary method of defence, he had discovered a means of instantly detecting the presence of a submarine destroyer.

He was one of those secretive persons who possess that gift of silence, when critical matters are pending, which has served many generations of diplomats on occasions when the fates of empires were hanging in the balance.

Thus, having learnt to keep his love a secret for so many years, he knew how to mask that still greater secret, by the telling of which he could have astonished several of the distinguished guests round his father's dinner table into a paralysis of official incredulity. But he, being the son of an official, knew that such a premature disclosure might result, not only in blank scepticism, for which he did not care, but in semi-official revelations to the Press, for which he did care a great deal. So when the farewells were being said, he whispered to his mother:

"I want you and father and Lady Ethel and Lord Kirlew to come up to the laboratory after everyone has gone. I've got something to show you. You can manage that, can't you, mother?"

Lady Tyrrell nodded and managed it.

Wilfred Tyrrell's laboratory was away up at the top of the house in a long low attic, which had evidently been chosen for its seclusion.

As they were going up the stairs Wilfred, sure of his triumph, took a liberty which, under other circumstances, would have been almost unthinkable to him. He and Lady Ethel happened to be the last on the stairs, and he was a step or two behind her. He quickened his pace a little, and then laying his hand lightly on her arm he whispered:

"Lady Ethel."

"Oh, nonsense!" she whispered in reply, with a little tremble of her arm under his hand. "Lady Ethel, indeed! As if we hadn't known each other long enough. Well, never mind what you want to say. What are you going to show us?"

"Something that no human eyes except mine have ever seen before; something which I have even ventured to hope will make me worthy to ask you a question which a good many better men than I have asked –"

"I know what you mean," she replied in a whisper even lower than his own, and turning a pair of laughing eyes up to his. "You silly, couldn't you see before? I didn't want those Dukes and Serene Highnesses. Do something – so far I know you have only studied and dreamt, – and, much and all as I like you – Well, now?"

"Now," he answered, pulling her arm a little nearer to him, "I have done something. I quite see what you mean, and I believe it is something worthy even of winning your good opinion. Here we are; in a few minutes you will see for yourself."

III – The Water-Ray

THE LABORATORY was littered with the usual disorderly-order of similar apartments. In the middle of it on a big, bare, acid-stained deal table there stood a glass tank full of water, something like an aquarium tank, but the glass walls were made of the best white plate. The water with which it was filled had a faint greenish hue and looked like seawater. At one end of it there was a curious looking apparatus. A couple of boxes, like electric storage batteries, stood on either side of a combination of glass tubes mounted on a wooden stand so that they all converged into the opening of a much larger tube of pale blue glass. Fitted to the other end of this was a thick double concave lens also of pale blue glass. This was placed so that its axis pointed down towards the surface of the water in the tank at an angle of about thirty degrees.

"Well, Wallace," said Sir Wilfred as his son locked the door behind them, "what's this? Another of your wonderful inventions? Something else you want me to put before my lords of the Admiralty?"

"That's just it, father, and this time I really think that even the people at Whitehall will see that there's something in it. At any rate I'm perfectly satisfied that if I had a French or Russian Admiral in this room, and he saw what you're going to see, I could get a million sterling down for what there is on that table."

"But, of course you wouldn't think of doing that," said Lady Ethel, who was standing at the end of the table opposite the arrangement of glass tubes.

"That, I think, goes without saying, Ethel," said Lord Kirlew. "I am sure Mr. Tyrrell would be quite incapable of selling anything of service to his country to her possible enemies. At any rate, Tyrrell," he went on, turning to Sir Wilfred, "if I see anything in it, and your people won't take it up, I will. So now let us see what it is."

Tyrrell had meanwhile turned up a couple of gas-jets, one on either side of the room, and they saw that slender, twisted wires ran from the batteries to each of the tubes through the after end, which was sealed with glass. He came back to the table, and with a quick glance at Lady Ethel, he coughed slightly, after the fashion of a lecturer beginning to address an audience. Then he looked round at the inquiring faces, and said with a mock professional air:

"This, my Lord, ladies, and gentlemen, is an apparatus which I have every reason to believe removes the last and only difficulty in the way of the complete solution of the problem of submarine navigation."

"Dear me," said Lord Kirlew, adjusting his pince-nez and leaning over the arrangement of tubes, "I think I see now what you mean. You have found, if you will allow me to anticipate you, some sort of Roentgen Ray or other, which will enable you to see through water. Is that so?"

"That is just what it is," said Tyrrell. "Of course, you know that the great difficulty, in fact, the so far insuperable obstacle in the way of submarine navigation has been the fact that a submerged vessel is blind. She cannot see where she is going beyond a distance of a few yards at most."

"Now this apparatus will make it possible, not only for her to see where she is going up to a distance which is limited only by the power of her batteries, but it also makes it possible for those on a vessel on the surface of the water to sweep the bottom of the sea just as a search-light sweeps the surface, and therefore to find out anything underneath from a sunken mine to a submarine destroyer. I am going to show you, too, that it can be used either in daylight or in the dark, I'll try first with the gas up."

He turned a couple of switches on the boxes as he said this. The batteries began to hum gently. The tubes began to glow with a strange intense light which had two very curious properties. It was just as distinctly visible in the gaslight as if the room had been dark, and it was absolutely confined to the tubes. Not a glimmer of it extended beyond their outer surfaces.

Then the big blue tube began to glow, turning pale green the while. The next instant a blaze of greenish light shot in a direct ray from the lens down into the water. A moment later the astonished eyes of the spectators saw the water in the tank pierced by a spreading ray of intense and absolutely white light Some stones and sand and gravel that had been spread along the bottom of the tank stood out with magical distinctness wherever the ray touched them. The rest, lit up only by the gas, were dim and indistinct in comparison with them.

"You see that what I call the water-ray is quite distinct from gaslight," said Tyrrell in a tone which showed that the matter was now to him a commonplace. "It is just as distinct from daylight. Now we will try it in the dark. Lord Kirlew, would you mind turning out that light near you? Father, turn out the one on your side, will you?"

The lights were turned out in silence. People of good intelligence are as a rule silent in the presence of a new revelation. Every eye looked through the darkness at the tank. The tubes glowed with their strange light, but they stood out against the darkness of the room just like so many pencils of light, and that was all. The room was just as dark as though they had not been there. The intense ray from the lens was now only visible as a fan of light. Tank and water had vanished in the darkness. Nothing could be seen but the ray and the stones and sand which it fell on.

"You see," said Tyrrell, "that the ray does not diffuse itself. It is absolutely direct, and that is one of its most valuable qualities. The electric lights which they use on the French submarines throw a glow on the top of the water at night, and so it is pretty easy to locate them. The surface of the water there, you see, is perfectly dark. In fact the water has vanished altogether. Another advantage is that this ray is absolutely invisible in air. Look!"

As he said this he tilted the arrangement of tubes backwards so that the ray left the water, and that moment the room was in utter darkness. He turned it down towards the tank and again the brilliant fan of light became visible in the water.

"Now," he continued, "that's all. You can light the gas again, if you don't mind."

"Well, Wallace," said Lord Kirlew when they had got back to the library, "I think we can congratulate you upon having solved one of the greatest problems of the age, and if the Admiralty don't take your invention up, as I don't suppose they will, eh, Tyrrell? – You know them better than I do – I'll tell you what I'll do; I'll buy or build you a thirty-five knot destroyer which shall be fitted up to your orders, and until we get into a naval war with someone you can take a scientific cruise and use your water-ray to find out uncharted reefs and that sort of thing, and perhaps you might come across an old sunken treasure-ship. I believe there are still some millions at the bottom of Vigo Bay."

Before Lady Ethel left, Tyrrell found time and opportunity to ask her a very serious question, and her answer to it was:

"You clever goose! You might have asked that long ago. Yes, I'll marry you the day after you've blown up the first French submarine ship."

Chapter IV
In the Solent

FOR ONCE at least the British-Admiralty had shown an open mind. Sir Wilfred Tyrrell's official position, and Lord Kirlew's immense influence, may have had something to do with the stimulating of the official intellect, but, at any rate, within a month after the demonstration in the laboratory, a committee of experts had examined and wonderingly approved of the water-ray apparatus, and H.M. destroyer *Scorcher* had been placed at Tyrrell's disposal for a series of practical experiments.

Everything was, of course, kept absolutely secret, and the crew of the *Scorcher* were individually sworn to silence as to anything which they might see or hear during the experimental cruise. Moreover they were all picked men of proved devotion and integrity. Every one of them would have laid down his life at a moment's notice for the honour of the Navy, and so there was little fear of the momentous secret leaking out.

Meanwhile international events had been following each other with ominous rapidity, and those who were behind the scenes on both sides of the Channel knew that war was now merely a matter of weeks, perhaps only of days.

The *Scorcher* was lying in the South Dock, at Chatham, guarded by dock police who allowed no one to go within fifty yards of her without a permit direct from headquarters. She was fitted with four water-ray instalments, one ahead, one astern, and one amidships to port and starboard, and, in addition to her usual armament of torpedo-tubes and twelve and three-pounder quick-firers, she carried four torpedoes of the Brennan type which could be dropped into the water without making the slightest splash and steered along the path of the water-ray, towards any object which the ray had discovered.

The day before she made her trial trip Captain Flaubert had an important interview with the Minister of Marine. He had perfected his system of magnetic feelers, and *Le Vengeur* was lying in Cherbourg ready to go forth on her mission of destruction. Twenty other similar craft were being fitted with all speed at Cherbourg, Brest, and Toulon. *Le Vengeur* had answered every test demanded of her, and, at the French Marine, the days of the British Navy were already regarded as numbered.

"In a week you may do it, *mon Capitaine*," said the Minister, rising from his seat and holding out both his hands. "It must be war by then, or at least a few days later. Prove that you can do as you say, and France will know how to thank and reward you. Victory today will be to those who strike first, and it shall be yours to deliver the first blow at the common enemy."

At midnight a week after this conversation a terrible occurrence took place in the Solent. Her Majesty's first-class cruiser *Phyllis* was lying at anchor about two miles off Cowes Harbour, and the *Scorcher* was lying with steam up some quarter of a mile inside her. She was, in fact, ready to begin her first experimental voyage at 1 a.m. She had her full equipment on board just as though she were going to fight a fleet of submarines, for it had been decided to test, not only the working of the water-ray, but also the possibility of steering the diving torpedoes by directing them on to a sunken wreck which was lying in twenty fathoms off Portland Bill. The Fates, however, had decided that they were to be tried on much more interesting game than the barnacle-covered hull of a tramp steamer.

At fifteen minutes past twelve precisely, when Tyrrell and Lieutenant-Commander Farquar were taking a very limited promenade on the narrow, rubber-covered decks of the *Scorcher*, they felt the boat heave jerkily under their feet. The water was perfectly calm at the time.

"Good Heavens, what's that?" exclaimed Tyrrell, as they both stopped and stared out over the water. As it happened they were both facing towards the *Phyllis*, and they were just in time to see her rise on the top of a mountain of foaming water, break in two, and disappear.

"A mine or a submarine!" said Commander Farquar between his teeth; "Anyhow – war. Get your apparatus ready, Mr. Tyrrell. That's one of the French submarines we've been hearing so much about. If you can find him we mustn't let him out of here."

Inside twenty seconds the *Scorcher* had slipped her cable, her searchlight had flashed a quick succession of signals to Portsmouth and Southampton, her boilers were palpitating under a full head of steam, and her wonderful little engines were ready at a minute's notice to develop their ten thousand horse power and send her flying over the water at thirty-five knots an hour.

Meanwhile, too, four fan-shaped rays of intense white light pierced the dark waters of the Solent as a lightning flash pierces the blackness of night, and four torpedoes were swinging from the davits a foot above the water.

There was a tinkle in the engine-room, and she swung round towards the eddying area of water in which the Phyllis went down. Other craft, mostly torpedo boats and steam pinnaces from warships, were also hurrying towards the fatal spot. The head-ray from the *Scorcher* shot down to the bottom of the Solent, wavered hither and thither for a few moments, and then remained fixed. Those who looked down it saw a sight which no human words could describe.

The splendid warship which a couple of minutes before had been riding at anchor, perfectly equipped, ready to go anywhere and do anything, was lying on the weed-covered sand and rock, broken up into two huge fragments of twisted scrap-iron. Even some of her guns had been hurled out of their positions and flung yards away from her. Other light wreckage was strewn in all directions, and the mangled remains of what had so lately been British officers and sailors were floating about in the mid-depths of the still eddying waters.

"We can't do any good here, Mr. Tyrrell," said Commander Farquar. "That's the work of a submarine, and we've got to find him. He must have come in by Spithead. He'd never have dared the other way, and he'll probably go out as he came in. Keep your rays going and let's see if we can find him."

There was another tinkle in the engine-room. The *Scorcher* swung round to the eastward and began working in a zigzag course at quarter speed towards Spithead.

Captain Flaubert, however, had decided to do the unexpected and, thirty minutes after the destruction of the *Phyllis*, *Le Vengeur* was feeling her way back into the Channel past the Needles. She was steering, of course, by chart and compass, about twenty feet below the water. Her maximum speed was eight knots, but Captain Flaubert, in view of possible collisions with rocks or inequalities on the sea- floor, was content to creep along at two.

He had done his work. He had proved the possibility of stealing unseen and unsuspected into the most jealously guarded strip of water in the world, destroying a warship at anchor, and then, as he thought, going away unseen. After doing all that it would be a pity to meet with any accident. War would not be formally declared for three days at least, and he wanted to get back to Cherbourg and tell the Minister of Marine all about it.

The *Scorcher* zigzagged her way in and out between the forts, her four rays lighting up the water for a couple of hundred yards in every direction, for nearly an hour, but nothing was discovered.

"I believe he's tried the other way after all," said Commander Farquar after they had taken a wide, comprehensive sweep between Foreland and Southsea. "There's one thing quite certain, if he has got out this way into the Channel we might just as well look for a needle in a haystack. I think we'd better go back and look for him the other way."

The man at the wheel put the helm hard over, the bell tinkled full speed ahead in the engine-room. The throbbing screws flung columns of foam out from under the stern, and the little black craft swept round in a splendid curve, and went flying down the Solent towards Hurst Point at the speed of an express train. Off Ryde she slowed down to quarter speed, and the four rays began searching the sea bottom again in every direction.

Le Vengeur was just creeping out towards the Needles, feeling her way cautiously with the sounding indicator thirty feet below the surface, when Captain Flaubert, who was standing with his Navigating Lieutenant in the glass domed conning-tower, lit by one little electric bulb, experienced the most extraordinary sensation of his life. A shaft of light shot down through the water. It was as clean cut as a knife and bright as burnished silver. It wavered about hither and thither for a few moments, darting through the water like a lightning flash through thunderclouds, and then suddenly it dropped on to the conning-lower of *Le Vengeur* and illuminated it with an almost intolerable radiance. The Captain looked at his Lieutenant's face. It was almost snow white in the unearthly light Instinctively he knew that his own was the same.

"*Tonnere de Dieu!*" he whispered, with lips that trembled in spite of all his self-control, "what is this, Lieutenant? Is it possible that these accursed English have learnt to see under water? Or, worse still, suppose they have a submarine which can see?"

"In that case," replied the Lieutenant, also in a whisper, "though *Le Vengeur* has done her work, I fear she will not finish her trial trip. Look," he went on, pointing out towards the port side, "what is that?"

A dimly-shining, silvery body about five feet long, pointed at both ends, and driven by a rapidly whirling screw had plunged down the broad pathway of light and stopped about ten feet from *Le Vengeur*. Like a living thing it slowly headed this way and that, ever drawing nearer and nearer, inch by inch, and then began the most ghastly experience for the Captain and his Lieutenant that two human beings had ever endured.

They were both brave men well worthy the traditions of their country and their profession; but they were imprisoned in a fabric of steel thirty feet below the surface of the midnight sea, and this horrible thing was coming nearer and nearer. To rise to the surface meant not only capture but ignominious death to every man on board, for war was not declared yet, and the captain and crew of *Le Vengeur* were pirates and outlaws beyond the pale of civilisation. To remain where they were meant a death of unspeakable terror, a fate from which there was no possible escape.

"It is a torpedo," said the Lieutenant, muttering the words with white trembling lips, "a Brennan, too, for you see they can steer it. It has only to touch us and –"

A shrug of the shoulders more expressive than words said the rest.

"Yes," replied Captain Flaubert, "that is so, but how did we not know of it? These English must have learnt some wisdom lately. We will rise a little and see if we can get away from it."

He touched a couple of buttons on a signal board as he said this. *Le Vengeur* rose fifteen feet, her engines quickened, and she headed for the open sea at her best speed. She passed out of the field of the ray for a moment or two. Then three converging rays found her and flooded her with light. Another silvery shape descended, this time to the starboard side. Her engines were put to their utmost capacity. The other shape on the port side rose into view, and ran alongside the conning-tower at exactly equal speed.

Then *Le Vengeur* sank another thirty feet, doubled on her course, and headed back towards Spithead. The ray followed her, found her again, and presently there were the two ghostly attendants, one on each side, as before. She turned in zigzags and curves, wheeled round in circles, and made straight runs hither and thither, but it was no use. The four rays encircled her wherever she went, and the two torpedoes were ever alongside.

Presently another feature of this extraordinary chase began to develop itself. The torpedoes, with a horrible likeness to living things, began to shepherd *Le Vengeur* into a certain course. If she turned to starboard then the silvery shape on that side made a rush at her. If she did the same to port the other one ran up to within a yard or so of her and stopped as though it would say: "Another yard, and I'll blow you into scrap-iron."

The Lieutenant was a brave man, but he fainted after ten minutes of this. Captain Flaubert was a stronger spirit, and he stood to his work with one hand on the steering wheel and the fingers of the other on the signal-board. He knew that he was caught, and that he could expect nothing but hanging as a common criminal. He had failed the moment after success, and failure meant death. The Minister of Marine had given him very clearly to understand that France would not be responsible for the failure of *Le Vengeur*.

The line of his fate lay clear before him. The lives of his Lieutenant and five picked men who had dared everything for him might be saved. He had already grasped the meaning of the evolutions of the two torpedoes. He was being, as it were, steered into a harbour, probably into Portsmouth, where in time he would be compelled to rise to the surface and surrender. The alternative was being blown into eternity in little pieces, and, like the brave man that he was, he decided to accept the former alternative, and save his comrades by taking the blame on himself.

He touched two more of the buttons on the signal-board. The engines of *Le Vengeur* stopped, and presently Tyrrell and Commander Farquar saw from the deck of the *Scorcher* a long, shining, hale-backed object rise above the surface of the water.

At the forward end of it there was a little conning-tower covered by a dome of glass. The moment that it came in sight the *Scorcher* stopped, and then moved gently towards *Le Vengeur*. As she did so the glass dome slid back, and the head and shoulders of a man in the French naval uniform came into sight. His face looked like the face of a corpse as the rays of the searchlight flashed upon it. His hair, which an hour ago had been black, was iron-grey now, and his black eyes stared straight at the searchlight as though they were looking into eternity.

Then across the water there came the sound of a shrill, high-pitched voice which said in perfectly correct English:

"Gentlemen, I have succeeded and I have failed. I destroyed your cruiser yonder, I would have destroyed the whole British Navy if I could have done so, because I hate you and everything English. *Le Vengeur* surrenders to superior force for the sake of those on board her, but remember that I alone have planned and done this thing. The others have only done what I paid them to do, and France knows nothing of it. You will spare them, for they are innocent. For me it is finished."

As the *Scorcher*'s men looked down the rays of the searchlight they saw something glitter in his hand close to his head – a yellow flash shone in the midst of the white, there was a short flat bang, and the body of Captain Leon Flaubert dropped out of sight beside the still unconscious lieutenant.

Le Vengeur was taken into Portsmouth. Her crew were tried for piracy and murder, and sentenced to death. The facts of the chase and capture of *Le Vengeur* were laid before the French Government, which saw the advisability of paying an indemnity of ten million dollars as soon as *Le Vengeur*, fitted with Wilfred Tyrrell's water-ray apparatus, made her trial trip down Channel and blew up half-a-dozen sunken wrecks with perfect case and safety to herself.

A few weeks later, in recognition of his immense services, the Admiralty placed the third-class cruiser Venus at the disposal of Mr. Wilfred and Lady Ethel Tyrrell for their honeymoon trip down the Mediterranean.

The declaration of war of which the Minister had spoken to Captain Flaubert, remained a diplomatic secret, and the unfortunate incident which had resulted in the blowing up of a British cruiser in time of peace, was publicly admitted by the French Government to be an act of unauthorised piracy, the perpetrators of which had already paid the penalty of their crime. The reason for this was not very far to seek. As soon as Wilfred Tyrrell came back from his wedding trip *Le Vengeur* was dry-docked and taken literally to pieces and examined in every detail. Thus everything that the French engineers knew about submarine navigation was revealed.

A committee of the best engineers in the United Kingdom made a thorough inspection with a view to possible improvements, and the result was the building of a British submarine flotilla of thirty enlarged *Vengeurs*. And as a couple of these would be quite sufficient for the effective blockade of a port, the long-planned invasion of England was once more consigned to the limbo of things which may only be dreamt of.

The Man Without a Country

Edward Everett Hale

I **(footnote 1)** suppose that very few casual readers of the *New York Herald* of August 13, 1863, observed **(footnote 2)**, in an obscure corner, among the 'Deaths,' the announcement, –

"NOLAN. Died, on board U.S. Corvette 'Levant,' **(footnote 3)** *Lat. 2° 11' S., Long. 131° W., on the 11th of May, PHILIP NOLAN."*

I happened to observe it, because I was stranded at the old Mission House in Mackinaw, waiting for a Lake Superior steamer which did not choose to come, and I was devouring to the very stubble all the current literature I could get hold of, even down to the deaths and marriages in the *Herald*. My memory for names and people is good, and the reader will see, as he goes on, that I had reason enough to remember Philip Nolan. There are hundreds of readers who would have paused at that announcement, if the officer of the *Levant* who reported it had chosen to make it thus: "Died, May 11, *A Man Without a Country*." For it was as 'The Man without a Country' that poor Philip Nolan had generally been known by the officers who had him in charge during some fifty years, as, indeed, by all the men who sailed under them. I dare say there is many a man who has taken wine with him once a fortnight, in a three years' cruise, who never knew that his name was 'Nolan,' or whether the poor wretch had any name at all.

There can now be no possible harm in telling this poor creature's story. Reason enough there has been till now, ever since Madison's **(footnote 4)** administration went out in 1817, for very strict secrecy, the secrecy of honor itself, among the gentlemen of the navy who have had Nolan in successive charge. And certainly it speaks well for the *esprit de corps* of the profession, and the personal honor of its members, that to the press this man's story has been wholly unknown, – and, I think, to the country at large also. I have reason to think, from some investigations I made in the Naval Archives when I was attached to the Bureau of Construction, that every official report relating to him was burned when Ross burned the public buildings at Washington. One of the Tuckers, or possibly one of the Watsons, had Nolan in charge at the end of the war; and when, on returning from his cruise, he reported at Washington to one of the Crowninshields, – who was in the Navy Department when he came home, – he found that the Department ignored the whole business. Whether they really knew nothing about it, or whether it was a *'Non mi ricordo,'* determined on as a piece of policy, I do not know. But this I do know, that since 1817, and possibly before, no naval officer has mentioned Nolan in his report of a cruise.

But, as I say, there is no need for secrecy any longer. And now the poor creature is dead, it seems to me worth while to tell a little of his story, by way of showing young Americans of today what it is to be *A Man Without a Country*.

* * *

Philip Nolan was as fine a young officer as there was in the 'Legion of the West,' as the Western division of our army was then called. When Aaron Burr **(footnote 5)** made his first dashing expedition down to New Orleans in 1805, at Fort Massac, or somewhere above on the river, he met, as the Devil would have it, this gay, dashing, bright young fellow; at some dinner-party, I think. Burr marked him, talked to him, walked with him, took him a day or two's voyage in his flat-boat, and, in short, fascinated him. For the next year, barrack-life was very tame to poor Nolan. He occasionally availed himself of the permission the great man had given him to write to him. Long, high-worded, stilted letters the poor boy wrote and rewrote and copied. But never a line did he have in reply from the gay deceiver. The other boys in the garrison sneered at him, because he lost the fun which they found in shooting or rowing while he was working away on these grand letters to his grand friend. They could not understand why Nolan kept by himself while they were playing high-low jack. Poker was not yet invented. But before long the young fellow had his revenge. For this time His Excellency, Honorable Aaron Burr, appeared again under a very different aspect. There were rumors that he had an army behind him and everybody supposed that he had an empire before him. At that time the youngsters all envied him. Burr had not been talking twenty minutes with the commander before he asked him to send for Lieutenant Nolan. Then after a little talk he asked Nolan if he could show him something of the great river and the plans for the new post. He asked Nolan to take him out in his skiff to show him a canebrake or a cotton-wood tree, as he said, – really to seduce him; and by the time the sail was over, Nolan was enlisted body and soul. From that time, though he did not yet know it, he lived as *A Man Without a Country*.

What Burr meant to do I know no more than you, dear reader. It is none of our business just now. Only, when the grand catastrophe came, and Jefferson and the House of Virginia of that day undertook to break on the wheel all the possible Clarences of the then House of York, by the great treason trial at Richmond, some of the lesser fry in that distant Mississippi Valley, which was farther from us than Puget's Sound is today, introduced the like novelty on their provincial stage; and, to while away the monotony of the summer at Fort Adams, got up, for spectacles, a string of court-martials on the officers there. One and another of the colonels and majors were tried, and, to fill out the list, little Nolan, against whom, Heaven knows, there was evidence enough, – that he was sick of the service, had been willing to be false to it, and would have obeyed any order to march any-whither with any one who would follow him had the order been signed, "By command of His Exc. A. Burr." The courts dragged on. The big flies escaped, – rightly for all I know. Nolan was proved guilty enough, as I say; yet you and I would never have heard of him, reader, but that, when the president of the court asked him at the close whether he wished to say anything to show that he had always been faithful to the United States, he cried out, in a fit of frenzy, –

"Damn the United States! I wish I may never hear of the United States again!"

I suppose he did not know how the words shocked old Colonel Morgan, **(footnote 6)** who was holding the court. Half the officers who sat in it had served through the Revolution, and their lives, not to say their necks, had been risked for the very idea which he so cavalierly cursed in his madness. He, on his part, had grown up in the West of those days, in the midst of 'Spanish plot', 'Orleans plot', and all the rest. He had been educated on a plantation where the finest company was a Spanish officer or a French merchant from Orleans. His education, such as it was, had been perfected in commercial expeditions to Vera Cruz, and I think he told me his father once hired an Englishman to be a private tutor for a winter on the plantation. He had spent half his youth with an older brother, hunting horses in Texas; and, in a word, to him 'United States' was scarcely a reality. Yet he had been fed by 'United States' for all the years since he had been in the army. He had sworn on his faith as a Christian to be true to 'United States'. It was 'United States' which gave him the uniform he wore, and the sword by his side. Nay, my poor Nolan, it was only because 'United States' had picked you out first as one of her own confidential men of honor that 'A. Burr' cared for you a straw more than for the flat boat men who sailed his ark for him. I do not excuse Nolan; I only explain to the reader why he damned his country, and wished he might never hear her name again.

He never did hear her name but once again. From that moment, Sept. 23, 1807, till the day he died, May 11, 1863, he never heard her name again. For that half-century and more he was a man without a country.

Old Morgan, as I said, was terribly shocked. If Nolan had compared George Washington to Benedict Arnold, or had cried, "God save King George," Morgan would not have felt worse. He called the court into his private room, and returned in fifteen minutes, with a face like a sheet, to say, –

"Prisoner, hear the sentence of the Court! The Court decides, subject to the approval of the President, that you never hear the name of the United States again."

Nolan laughed. But nobody else laughed. Old Morgan was too solemn, and the whole room was hushed dead as night for a minute. Even Nolan lost his swagger in a moment. Then Morgan added, –

"Mr. Marshal, take the prisoner to Orleans in an armed boat, and deliver him to the naval commander there."

The marshal gave his orders and the prisoner was taken out of court.

"Mr. Marshal," continued old Morgan, "see that no one mentions the United States to the prisoner. Mr. Marshal, make my respects to Lieutenant Mitchell at Orleans, and request him to order that no one shall mention the United States to the prisoner while he is on board ship. You will receive your written orders from the officer on duty here this evening. The Court is adjourned without day."

I have always supposed that Colonel Morgan himself took the proceedings of the court to Washington city, and explained them to Mr. Jefferson. Certain it is that the President approved them, – certain, that is, if I may believe the men who say they have seen his signature. Before the *Nautilus* got round from New Orleans to the Northern Atlantic coast with the prisoner on board, the sentence had been approved, and he was a man without a country.

The plan then adopted was substantially the same which was necessarily followed ever after. Perhaps it was suggested by the necessity of sending him by water from Fort Adams and Orleans. The Secretary of the Navy – it must have been the first Crowninshield, though he is a man I do not remember – was requested to put Nolan on board a government vessel bound on a long cruise, and to direct that he should be only so far confined there as to make it certain that he never saw or heard of the country. We had few long cruises then, and the navy was very much out of favor; and as almost all of this story is traditional, as I have explained, I do not know certainly what his first cruise was. But the commander to whom he was intrusted, – perhaps it was Tingey or Shaw, though I think it was one of the younger men, – we are all old enough now, – regulated the etiquette and the precautions of the affair, and according to his scheme they were carried out, I suppose, till Nolan died.

When I was second officer of the *Intrepid*, some thirty years after, I saw the original paper of instructions. I have been sorry ever since that I did not copy the whole of it. It ran, however, much in this way: –

> "WASHINGTON (*with a date, which must have been late in 1807*).
>
> "Sir, – You will receive from Lieutenant Neale the person of Philip Nolan, late a lieutenant in the United States army.
>
> "This person on his trial by court-martial expressed, with an oath, the wish that he might 'never hear of the United States again.'
>
> "The Court sentenced him to have his wish fulfilled.
>
> "For the present, the execution of the order is intrusted by the President to this Department.
>
> "You will take the prisoner on board your ship, and keep him there with such precautions as shall prevent his escape.
>
> "You will provide him with such quarters, rations, and clothing as would be proper for an officer of his late rank, if he were a passenger on your vessel on the business of his Government.
>
> "The gentlemen on board will make any arrangements agreeable to themselves regarding his society. He is to be exposed to no indignity of any kind, nor is he ever unnecessarily to be reminded that he is a prisoner.
>
> "But under no circumstances is he ever to hear of his country or to see any information regarding it; and you will especially caution all the officers under your command to take care, that, in the various indulgences which may be granted, this rule, in which his punishment is involved, shall not be broken.
>
> "It is the intention of the Government that he shall never again see the country which he has disowned. Before the end of your cruise you will receive orders which will give effect to this intention.
>
> "Respectfully yours,
> "W. SOUTHARD, for the
> "Secretary of the Navy"

If I had only preserved the whole of this paper, there would be no break in the beginning of my sketch of this story. For Captain Shaw, if it were he, handed it to his successor in the charge, and he to his, and I suppose the commander of the *Levant* has it today as his authority for keeping this man in this mild custody.

The rule adopted on board the ships on which I have met 'the man without a country' was, I think, transmitted from the beginning. No mess liked to have him permanently, because his presence cut off all talk of home or of the prospect of return, of politics or letters, of peace or of war, – cut off more than half the talk men liked to have at sea. But it was always thought too hard that he should never meet the rest of us, except to touch hats, and we finally sank into one system. He was not permitted to talk with the men, unless an officer was by. With officers he had unrestrained intercourse, as far as they and he chose. But he grew shy, though he had favorites: I was one. Then the captain always asked him to dinner on Monday. Every mess in succession took up the invitation in its turn. According to the size of the ship, you had him at your mess more or less often at dinner. His breakfast he ate in his own state-room, – he always had a state-room – which was where a sentinel or somebody on the watch could see the door. And whatever else he ate or drank, he ate or drank alone. Sometimes, when the marines or sailors had any special jollification, they were permitted to invite 'Plain-Buttons', as they called him. Then Nolan was sent with some officer, and the men were forbidden to speak of home while he was there. I believe the theory was that the sight of his punishment did them good. They called him 'Plain-Buttons', because, while he always chose to wear a regulation army-uniform, he was not permitted to wear the army-button, for the reason that it bore either the initials or the insignia of the country he had disowned.

I remember, soon after I joined the navy, I was on shore with some of the older officers from our ship and from the *Brandywine*, which we had met at Alexandria. We had leave to make a party and go up to Cairo and the Pyramids. As we jogged along (you went on donkeys then), some of the gentlemen (we boys called them 'Dons', but the phrase was long since changed) fell to talking about Nolan, and some one told the system which was adopted from the first about his books and other reading. As he was almost never permitted to go on shore, even though the vessel lay in port for months, his time at the best hung heavy; and everybody was permitted to lend him books, if they were not published in America and made no allusion to it. These were common enough in the old days, when people in the other hemisphere talked of the United States as little as we do of Paraguay. He had almost all the foreign papers that came into the ship, sooner or later; only somebody must go over them first, and cut out any advertisement or stray paragraph that alluded to America. This was a little cruel sometimes, when the back of what was cut out might be as innocent as Hesiod. Right in the midst of one of Napoleon's battles, or one of Canning's speeches, poor Nolan would find a great hole, because on the back of the page of that paper there had been an advertisement of a packet for New York, or a scrap from the President's message. I say this was the first time I ever heard of this plan, which afterwards I had enough and more than enough to do with. I remember it, because poor Phillips, who was of the party, as soon as the allusion to reading was made, told a story of something which happened at the Cape of Good Hope on Nolan's first voyage; and it is the only thing I ever knew of that voyage. They had touched at the Cape, and had done the civil thing with the English Admiral and the fleet, and then, leaving for a long cruise up the Indian Ocean, Phillips had borrowed a lot of English books from an officer, which, in those days, as indeed in these, was quite a windfall. Among them, as the Devil would order, was the 'Lay of the Last Minstrel' **(footnote 7)**, which they had all of them heard of, but which most of them had never seen. I think it could not have been published long. Well, nobody thought there could be any risk of anything national in that, though Phillips swore old Shaw had cut out the *Tempest* from Shakespeare before he let Nolan have it, because he said "the Bermudas ought to be ours, and, by Jove, should be one day." So Nolan was permitted to join the circle one afternoon when a lot of them sat on deck smoking and reading aloud. People do not do such things so often now; but when I was young we got rid of a great deal of time so. Well, so it happened that in his turn Nolan took the book and read to the others; and he read very well, as I know. Nobody in the circle knew a line of the poem, only it was all magic and Border chivalry, and was ten thousand years ago. Poor Nolan read steadily through the fifth canto, stopped a minute and drank something, and then began, without a thought of what was coming, –

"Breathes there the man, with soul so dead,
Who never to himself hath said," –

It seems impossible to us that anybody ever heard this for the first time; but all these fellows did then, and poor Nolan himself went on, still unconsciously or mechanically, –

"This is my own, my native land!"

Then they all saw that something was to pay; but he expected to get through, I suppose, turned a little pale, but plunged on, –

"Whose heart hath ne'er within him burned,
As home his footsteps he hath turned
From wandering on a foreign strand? –
If such there breathe, go, mark him well," –

By this time the men were all beside themselves, wishing there was any way to make him turn over two pages; but he had not quite presence of mind for that; he gagged a little, colored crimson, and staggered on, –

"For him no minstrel raptures swell;
High though his titles, proud his name,
Boundless his wealth as wish can claim,
Despite these titles, power, and pelf,
The wretch, concentred all in self," –

and here the poor fellow choked, could not go on, but started up, swung the book into the sea, vanished into his state-room, "And by Jove," said Phillips, "we did not see him for two months again. And I had to make up some beggarly story to that English surgeon why I did not return his Walter Scott to him."

That story shows about the time when Nolan's braggadocio must have broken down. At first, they said, he took a very high tone, considered his imprisonment a mere farce, affected to enjoy the voyage, and all that; but Phillips said that after he came out of his state-room he never was the same man again. He never read aloud again, unless it was the Bible or Shakespeare, or something else he was sure of. But it was not that merely. He never entered in with the other young men exactly as a companion again. He was always shy afterwards, when I knew him, – very seldom spoke, unless he was spoken to, except to a very few friends. He lighted up occasionally, – I remember late in his life hearing him fairly eloquent on something which had been suggested to him by one of Fléchier's sermons, – but generally he had the nervous, tired look of a heart-wounded man.

When Captain Shaw was coming home, – if, as I say, it was Shaw, – rather to the surprise of everybody they made one of the Windward Islands, and lay off and on for nearly a week. The boys said the officers were sick of salt-junk, and meant to have turtle-soup before they came home. But after several days the *Warren* came to the same rendezvous; they exchanged signals; she sent to Phillips and these homeward-bound men letters and papers, and told them she was outward-bound, perhaps to the Mediterranean, and took poor Nolan and his traps on the boat back to try his second cruise. He looked very blank when he was told to get ready to join her. He had known enough of the signs of the sky to know that till that moment he was going 'home'. But this was a distinct evidence of something he had not thought of, perhaps, – that there was no going home for him, even to a prison. And this was the first of some twenty such transfers, which brought him sooner or later into half our best vessels, but which kept him all his life at least some hundred miles from the country he had hoped he might never hear of again.

It may have been on that second cruise, – it was once when he was up the Mediterranean, – that Mrs. Graff, the celebrated Southern beauty of those days, danced with him. They had been lying a long time in the Bay of Naples, and the officers were very intimate in the English fleet, and there had been great festivities, and our men thought they must give a great ball on board the ship. How they ever did it on board the *Warren* I am sure I do not know. Perhaps it was not the *Warren*, or perhaps ladies did not take up so much room as they do now. They wanted to use Nolan's state-room for something, and they hated to do it without asking him to the ball; so the captain said they might ask him, if they would be responsible that he did not talk with the wrong people, "who would give him intelligence." So the dance went on, the finest party that had ever been known, I dare say; for I never heard of a man-of-war ball that was not. For ladies, they had the family of the American consul, one or two travellers who had adventured so far, and a nice bevy of English girls and matrons, perhaps Lady Hamilton herself.

Well, different officers relieved each other in standing and talking with Nolan in a friendly way, so as to be sure that nobody else spoke to him. The dancing went on with spirit, and after a while even the fellows who took this honorary guard of Nolan ceased to fear any *contretemps*. Only when some English lady – Lady Hamilton, as I said, perhaps – called for a set of 'American dances,' an odd thing happened. Everybody then danced contra-dances. The black band, nothing loath, conferred as to what 'American dances' were, and started off with 'Virginia Reel', which they followed with 'Money-Musk', which, in its turn in those days, should have been followed by 'The Old Thirteen'. But just as Dick, the leader, tapped for his fiddles to begin, and bent forward, about to say, in true negro state, " 'The Old Thirteen,' gentlemen and ladies!" as he had said " 'Virginny Reel,' if you please!" and " 'Money-Musk,' if you please!" the captain's boy tapped him on the shoulder, whispered to him, and he did not announce the name of the dance; he merely bowed, began on the air, and they all fell to, – the officers teaching the English girls the figure, but not telling them why it had no name.

But that is not the story I started to tell. As the dancing went on, Nolan and our fellows all got at ease, as I said, – so much so, that it seemed quite natural for him to bow to that splendid Mrs. Graff, and say, –

"I hope you have not forgotten me, Miss Rutledge. Shall I have the honor of dancing?"

He did it so quickly, that Fellows, who was with him, could not hinder him. She laughed and said, –

"I am not Miss Rutledge any longer, Mr. Nolan; but I will dance all the same," just nodded to Fellows, as if to say he must leave Mr. Nolan to her, and led him off to the place where the dance was forming.

Nolan thought he had got his chance. He had known her at Philadelphia, and at other places had met her, and this was a Godsend. You could not talk in contra-dances, as you do in cotillions, or even in the pauses of waltzing; but there were chances for tongues and sounds, as well as for eyes and blushes. He began with her travels, and Europe, and Vesuvius, and the French; and then, when they had worked down, and had that long talking time at the bottom of the set, he said boldly, – a little pale, she said, as she told me the story years after, –

"And what do you hear from home, Mrs. Graff?"

And that splendid creature looked through him. Jove! How she must have looked through him!

"Home!! Mr. Nolan!!! I thought you were the man who never wanted to hear of home again!" – and she walked directly up the deck to her husband, and left poor Nolan alone, as he always was. – He did not dance again. I cannot give any history of him in order; nobody can now; and, indeed, I am not trying to.

These are the traditions, which I sort out, as I believe them, from the myths which have been told about this man for forty years. The lies that have been told about him are legion. The fellows used to say he was the 'Iron Mask'; and poor George Pons went to his grave in the belief that this was the author of *Junius*, who was being punished for his celebrated libel on Thomas Jefferson. Pons was not very strong in the historical line.

A happier story than either of these I have told is of the war. That came along soon after. I have heard this affair told in three or four ways, – and, indeed, it may have happened more than once. But which ship it was on I cannot tell. However, in one, at least, of the great frigate-duels with the English, in which the navy was really baptized **(footnote 8)**, it happened that a round-shot from the enemy entered one of our ports square, and took right down the officer of the gun himself, and almost every man of the gun's crew. Now you may say what you choose about courage, but that is not a nice thing to see. But, as the men who were not killed picked themselves up, and as they and the surgeon's people were carrying off the bodies, there appeared Nolan, in his shirt-sleeves, with the rammer in his hand, and, just as if he had been the officer, told them off with authority, – who should go to the cock-pit with the wounded men, who should stay with him, – perfectly cheery, and with that way which makes men feel sure all is right and is going to be right. And he finished loading the gun with his own hands, aimed it, and bade the men fire. And there he stayed, captain of that gun, keeping those fellows in spirits, till the enemy struck, – sitting on the carriage while the gun was cooling, though he was exposed all the time, – showing them easier ways to handle heavy shot, – making the raw hands laugh at their own blunders, – and when the gun cooled again, getting it loaded and fired twice as often as any other gun on the ship. The captain walked forward by way of encouraging the men, and Nolan touched his hat and said, –

"I am showing them how we do this in the artillery, sir."

And this is the part of the story where all the legends agree; the commodore said, –

"I see you do, and I thank you, sir; and I shall never forget this day, sir, and you never shall, sir."

And after the whole thing was over, and he had the Englishman's sword, in the midst of the state and ceremony of the quarter-deck, he said, –

"Where is Mr. Nolan? Ask Mr. Nolan to come here."

And when Nolan came, he said, –

"Mr. Nolan, we are all very grateful to you today; you are one of us today; you will be named in the despatches."

And then the old man took off his own sword of ceremony, and gave it to Nolan, and made him put it on. The man told me this who saw it. Nolan cried like a baby, and well he might. He had not worn a sword since that infernal day at Fort Adams. But always afterwards on occasions of ceremony, he wore that quaint old French sword of the commodore's.

The captain did mention him in the despatches. It was always said he asked that he might be pardoned. He wrote a special letter to the Secretary of War. But nothing ever came of it. As I said, that was about the time when they began to ignore the whole transaction at Washington, and when Nolan's imprisonment began to carry itself on because there was nobody to stop it without any new orders from home.

I have heard it said that he was with Porter when he took possession of the Nukahiwa Islands. Not this Porter, you know, but old Porter, his father, Essex Porter, – that is, the old Essex Porter, not this Essex **(footnote 9)**. As an artillery officer, who had seen service in the West, Nolan knew more about fortifications, embrasures, ravelins, stockades, and all that, than any of them did; and he worked with a right good-will in fixing that battery all right. I have always thought it was a pity Porter did not leave him in command there with Gamble. That would have settled all the question about his punishment. We should have kept the islands, and at this moment we should have one station in the Pacific Ocean. Our French friends, too, when they wanted this little watering-place, would have found it was preoccupied. But Madison and the Virginians, of course, flung all that away.

All that was near fifty years ago. If Nolan was thirty then, he must have been near eighty when he died. He looked sixty when he was forty. But he never seemed to me to change a hair afterwards. As I imagine his life, from what I have seen and heard of it, he must have been in every sea, and yet almost never on land. He must have known, in a formal way, more officers in our service than any man living knows. He told me once, with a grave smile, that no man in the world lived so methodical a life as he. "You know the boys say I am the Iron Mask, and you know how busy he was." He said it did not do for any one to try to read all the time, more than to do anything else all the time; and that he used to read just five hours a day. "Then," he said, "I keep up my notebooks, writing in them at such and such hours from what I have been reading; and I include in these my scrap-books." These were very curious indeed. He had six or eight, of different subjects. There was one of History, one of Natural Science, one which he called 'Odds and Ends.' But they were not merely books of extracts from newspapers. They had bits of plants and ribbons, shells tied on, and carved scraps of bone and wood, which he had taught the men to cut for him, and they were beautifully illustrated. He drew admirably. He had some of the funniest drawings there, and some of the most pathetic, that I have ever seen in my life. I wonder who will have Nolan's scrapbooks.

Well, he said his reading and his notes were his profession, and that they took five hours and two hours respectively of each day. "Then," said he, "every man should have a diversion as well as a profession. My Natural History is my diversion." That took two hours a day more. The men used to bring him birds and fish, but on a long cruise he had to satisfy himself with centipedes and cockroaches and such small game. He was the only naturalist I ever met who knew anything about the habits of the house-fly and the mosquito. All those people can tell you whether they are *Lepidoptera* or *Steptopotera*; but as for telling how you can get rid of them, or how they get away from you when you strike them, – why Linnaeus knew as little of that as John Foy the idiot did. These nine hours made Nolan's regular daily 'occupation.' The rest of the time he talked or walked. Till he grew very old, he went aloft a great deal. He always kept up his exercise; and I never heard that he was ill. If any other man was ill, he was the kindest nurse in the world; and he knew more than half the surgeons do. Then if anybody was sick or died, or if the captain wanted him to, on any other occasion, he was always ready to read prayers. I have said that he read beautifully.

My own acquaintance with Philip Nolan began six or eight years after the English war, on my first voyage after I was appointed a midshipman. It was in the first days after our Slave-Trade treaty, while the Reigning House, which was still the House of Virginia, had still a sort of sentimentalism about the suppression of the horrors of the Middle Passage, and something was sometimes done that way. We were in the South Atlantic on that business. From the time I joined, I believe I thought Nolan was a sort of lay chaplain, – a chaplain with a blue coat. I never asked about him. Everything in the ship was strange to me. I knew it was green to ask questions, and I suppose I thought there was a 'Plain-Buttons' on every ship. We had him to dine in our mess once a week, and the caution was given that on that day nothing was to be said about home. But if they had told us not to say anything about the planet Mars or the Book of Deuteronomy, I should not have asked why; there were a great many things which seemed to me to have as little reason. I first came to understand anything about "the man without a country" one day when we overhauled a dirty little schooner which had slaves on board. An officer was sent to take charge of her, and, after a few minutes, he sent back his boat to ask that some one might be sent him who could speak Portuguese. We were all looking over the rail when the message came, and we all wished we could interpret, when the captain asked who spoke Portuguese. But none of the officers did; and just as the captain was sending forward to ask if any of the people could, Nolan stepped out and said he should be glad to interpret, if the captain wished, as he understood the language. The captain thanked him, fitted out another boat with him, and in this boat it was my luck to go.

When we got there, it was such a scene as you seldom see, and never want to. Nastiness beyond account, and chaos run loose in the midst of the nastiness. There were not a great many of the negroes; but by way of making what there were understand that they were free, Vaughan had had their handcuffs and ankle-cuffs knocked off, and, for convenience' sake, was putting them upon the rascals of the schooner's crew. The negroes were, most of them, out of the hold, and swarming all round the dirty deck, with a central throng surrounding Vaughan and addressing him in every dialect, and patois of a dialect, from the Zulu click up to the Parisian of Beledeljereed **(footnote 10)**.

As we came on deck, Vaughan looked down from a hogshead, on which he had mounted in desperation, and said: –

"For God's love, is there anybody who can make these wretches understand something? The men gave them rum, and that did not quiet them. I knocked that big fellow down twice, and that did not soothe him. And then I talked Choctaw to all of them together; and I'll be hanged if they understood that as well as they understood the English."

Nolan said he could speak Portuguese, and one or two fine-looking Kroomen were dragged out, who, as it had been found already, had worked for the Portuguese on the coast at Fernando Po.

"Tell them they are free," said Vaughan; "and tell them that these rascals are to be hanged as soon as we can get rope enough."

Nolan "put that into Spanish," – that is, he explained it in such Portuguese as the Kroomen could understand, and they in turn to such of the negroes as could understand them. Then there was such a yell of delight, clinching of fists, leaping and dancing, kissing of Nolan's feet, and a general rush made to the hogshead by way of spontaneous worship of Vaughan, as the *deus ex machina* of the occasion.

"Tell them," said Vaughan, well pleased, "that I will take them all to Cape Palmas."

This did not answer so well. Cape Palmas was practically as far from the homes of most of them as New Orleans or Rio Janeiro was; that is, they would be eternally separated from home there. And their interpreters, as we could understand, instantly said, "*Ah, non Palmas*," and began to propose infinite other expedients in most voluble language. Vaughan was rather disappointed at this result of his liberality, and asked Nolan eagerly what they said. The drops stood on poor Nolan's white forehead, as he hushed the men down, and said: –

"He says, 'Not Palmas.' He says, 'Take us home, take us to our own country, take us to our own house, take us to our own pickaninnies and our own women.' He says he has an old father and mother who will die if they do not see him. And this one says he left his people all sick, and paddled down to Fernando to beg the white doctor to come and help them, and that these devils caught him in the bay just in sight of home, and that he has never seen anybody from home since then. And this one says," choked out Nolan, "that he has not heard a word from his home in six months, while he has been locked up in an infernal barracoon."

Vaughan always said he grew gray himself while Nolan struggled through this interpretation: I, who did not understand anything of the passion involved in it, saw that the very elements were melting with fervent heat, and that something was to pay somewhere. Even the negroes themselves stopped howling, as they saw Nolan's agony, and Vaughan's almost equal agony of sympathy. As quick as he could get words, he said: –

"Tell them yes, yes, yes; tell them they shall go to the Mountains of the Moon, if they will. If I sail the schooner through the Great White Desert, they shall go home!"

And after some fashion Nolan said so. And then they all fell to kissing him again, and wanted to rub his nose with theirs.

But he could not stand it long; and getting Vaughan to say he might go back, he beckoned me down into our boat. As we lay back in the stern-sheets and the men gave way, he said to me: "Youngster, let that show you what it is to be without a family, without a home, and without a country. And if you are ever tempted to say a word, or to do a thing that shall put a bar between you and your family, your home, and your country, pray God in His mercy to take you that instant home to His own heaven. Stick by your family, boy; forget you have a self, while you do everything for them. Think of your home, boy; write and send, and talk about it. Let it be nearer and nearer to your thought, the farther you have to travel from it; and rush back to it when you are free, as that poor black slave is doing now. And for your country, boy," and the words rattled in his throat, "– and for that flag," and he pointed to the ship, "never dream a dream but of serving her as she bids you, though the service carry you through a thousand hells. No matter what happens to you, no matter who flatters you or who abuses you, never look at another flag, never let a night pass but you pray God to bless that flag. Remember, boy, that behind all these men you have to do with, behind officers, and government, and people even, there is the Country Herself, your Country, and that you belong to Her as you belong to your own mother. Stand by Her, boy, as you would stand by your mother, if those devils there had got hold of her today!"

I was frightened to death by his calm, hard passion; but I blundered out that I would, by all that was holy, and that I had never thought of doing anything else. He hardly seemed to hear me; but he did, almost in a whisper, say: "O, if anybody had said so to me when I was of your age!"

I think it was this half-confidence of his, which I never abused, for I never told this story till now, which afterward made us great friends. He was very kind to me. Often he sat up, or even got up, at night, to walk the deck with me, when it was my watch. He explained to me a great deal of my mathematics, and I owe to him my taste for mathematics. He lent me books, and helped me about my reading. He never alluded so directly to his story again; but from one and another officer I have learned, in thirty years, what I am telling. When we parted from him in St. Thomas harbor, at the end of our cruise, I was more sorry than I can tell. I was very glad to meet him again in 1830; and later in life, when I thought I had some influence in Washington, I moved heaven and earth to have him discharged. But it was like getting a ghost out of prison. They pretended there was no such man, and never was such a man. They will say so at the Department now! Perhaps they do not know. It will not be the first thing in the service of which the Department appears to know nothing!

There is a story that Nolan met Burr once on one of our vessels, when a party of Americans came on board in the Mediterranean. But this I believe to be a lie; or, rather, it is a myth, *ben trovato*, involving a tremendous blowing-up with which he sunk Burr, – asking him how he liked to be 'without a country.' But it is clear from Burr's life, that nothing of the sort could have happened; and I mention this only as an illustration of the stories which get a-going where there is the least mystery at bottom.

Philip Nolan, poor fellow, repented of his folly, and then, like a man, submitted to the fate he had asked for. He never intentionally added to the difficulty or delicacy of the charge of those who had him in hold. Accidents would happen; but never from his fault. Lieutenant Truxton told me that, when Texas was annexed, there was a careful discussion among the officers, whether they should get hold of Nolan's handsome set of maps and cut Texas out of it, – from the map of the world and the map of Mexico. The United States had been cut out when the atlas was bought for him. But it was voted, rightly enough, that to do this would be virtually to reveal to him what had happened, or, as Harry Cole said, to make him think Old Burr had succeeded. So it was from no fault of Nolan's that a great botch happened at my own table, when, for a short time, I was in command of the George Washington corvette, on the South American station. We were lying in the La Plata, and some of the officers, who had been on shore and had just joined again, were entertaining us with accounts of their misadventures in riding the half-wild horses of Buenos Ayres. Nolan was at table, and was in an unusually bright and talkative mood. Some story of a tumble reminded him of an adventure of his own when he was catching wild horses in Texas with his adventurous cousin, at a time when he mast have been quite a boy. He told the story with a good deal of spirit, – so much so, that the silence which often follows a good story hung over the table for an instant, to be broken by Nolan himself. For he asked perfectly unconsciously. –

"Pray, what has become of Texas? After the Mexicans got their independence, I thought that province of Texas would come forward very fast. It is really one of the finest regions on earth; it is the Italy of this continent. But I have not seen or heard a word of Texas for near twenty years."

There were two Texan officers at the table. The reason he had never heard of Texas was that Texas and her affairs had been painfully cut out of his newspapers since Austin began his settlements; so that, while he read of Honduras and Tamaulipas, and, till quite lately, of California, – this virgin province, in which his brother had travelled so far, and, I believe, had died, had ceased to be to him. Waters and Williams, the two Texas men, looked grimly at each other and tried not to laugh. Edward Morris had his attention attracted by the third link in the chain of the captain's chandelier. Watrous was seized with a convulsion of sneezing. Nolan himself saw that something was to pay, he did not know what. And I, as master of the feast, had to say, –

"Texas is out of the map, Mr. Nolan. Have you seen Captain Back's curious account of Sir Thomas Roe's Welcome?"

After that cruise I never saw Nolan again. I wrote to him at least twice a year, for in that voyage we became even confidentially intimate; but he never wrote to me. The other men tell me that in those fifteen years he aged very fast, as well he might indeed, but that he was still the same gentle, uncomplaining, silent sufferer that he ever was, bearing as best he could his self-appointed punishment, – rather less social, perhaps, with new men whom he did not know, but more anxious, apparently, than ever to serve and befriend and teach the boys, some of whom fairly seemed to worship him. And now it seems the dear old fellow is dead. He has found a home at last, and a country.

* * *

Since writing this, and while considering whether or no I would print it, as a warning to the young Nolans and Vallandighams and Tatnalls of today of what it is to throw away a country, I have received from Danforth, who is on board the *Levant*, a letter which gives an account of Nolan's last hours. It removes all my doubts about telling this story. The reader will understand Danforth's letter, or the beginning of it, if he will remember that after ten years of Nolan's exile every one who had him in charge was in a very delicate position. The government had failed to renew the order of 1807 regarding him. What was a man to do? Should he let him go? What, then, if he were called to account by the Department for violating the order of 1807? Should he keep him? What, then, if Nolan should be liberated some day, and should bring an action for false imprisonment or kidnapping against every man who had had him in charge? I urged and pressed this upon Southard, and I have reason to think that other officers did the same thing. But the Secretary always said, as they so often do at Washington, that there were no special orders to give, and that we must act on our own judgment. That means, "If you succeed, you will be sustained; if you fail, you will be disavowed." Well, as Danforth says, all that is over now, though I do not know but I expose myself to a criminal prosecution on the evidence of the very revelation I am making.

Here is the letter: –

LEVANT, 2° 2' S. @ 131° W.

"*DEAR FRED: – I try to find heart and life to tell you that it is all over with dear old Nolan. I have been with him on this voyage more than I ever was, and I can understand wholly now the way in which you used to speak of the dear old fellow. I could see that he was not strong, but I had no idea the end was so near. The doctor has been watching him very carefully, and yesterday morning came to me and told me that Nolan was not so well, and had not left his state-room, – a thing I never remember before. He had let the doctor come and see him as he lay there, – the first time the doctor had been in the state-room, – and he said he should like to see me. Oh, dear! Do you remember the mysteries we boys used to invent about his room in the old 'Intrepid' days? Well, I went in, and there, to be sure, the poor fellow lay in his berth, smiling pleasantly as he gave me his hand, but looking very frail. I could not help a glance round, which showed me what a little shrine he had made of the box he was lying in. The stars and stripes were triced up above and around a picture of Washington, and he had painted a majestic eagle, with lightnings blazing from his beak and his foot just clasping the whole globe, which his wings overshadowed. The dear old boy saw my glance, and said, with a sad smile, 'Here, you see, I have a country!' And then he pointed to the foot of his bed, where I had not seen before a great map of the United States, as he had drawn it from memory, and which he had there to look upon as he lay. Quaint, queer old names were on it, in large letters: 'Indiana Territory,' 'Mississippi Territory,' and 'Louisiana Territory,' as I suppose our fathers learned such things: but the old fellow had patched in Texas, too; he had carried his western boundary all the way to the Pacific, but on that shore he had defined nothing.*

" 'O Captain,' he said, 'I know I am dying. I cannot get home. Surely you will tell me something now? – Stop! Stop! Do not speak till I say what I am sure you know, that there is not in this ship, that there is not in America, – God bless her! – A more loyal man than I. There cannot be a man who loves the old flag as I do, or prays for it as I do, or hopes for it as I do. There are thirty-four stars in it now, Danforth. I thank God for that, though I do not know what their names are. There has never been one taken away: I thank God for that. I know by that that there has never been any successful Burr, O Danforth, Danforth,' he sighed out, 'how like a wretched night's dream a boy's idea of personal fame or of separate sovereignty seems, when one looks back on it after such a life as mine! But tell me, – tell me something, – tell me everything, Danforth, before I die!'

"Ingham, I swear to you that I felt like a monster that I had not told him everything before. Danger or no danger, delicacy or no delicacy, who was I, that I should have been acting the tyrant all this time over this dear, sainted old man, who had years ago expiated, in his whole manhood's life, the madness of a boys treason? 'Mr. Nolan,' said I, 'I will tell you everything you ask about. Only, where shall I begin?'

"Oh, the blessed smile that crept over his white face! and he pressed my hand and said, 'God bless you!' 'Tell me their names,' he said, and he pointed to the stars on the flag. 'The last I know is Ohio. My father lived in Kentucky. But I have guessed Michigan and Indiana and Mississippi, – that was where Fort Adams is, – they make twenty. But where are your other fourteen? You have not cut up any of the old ones, I hope?'

"Well, that was not a bad text, and I told him the names in as good order as I could, and he bade me take down his beautiful map and draw them in as I best could with my pencil. He was wild with delight about Texas, told me how his cousin died there; he had marked a gold cross near where he supposed his grave was; and he had guessed at Texas. Then he was delighted as he saw California and Oregon; – that, he said, he had suspected partly, because he had never been permitted to land on that shore, though the ships were there so much. 'And the men,' said he, laughing, 'brought off a good deal besides furs.' Then he went back – heavens, how far! – to ask about the Chesapeake, and what was done to Barron for surrendering her to the Leopard, **(footnote 11)** *and whether Burr ever tried again, – and he ground his teeth with the only passion he showed. But in a moment that was over, and he said, 'God forgive me, for I am sure I forgive him.' Then he asked about the old war, – told me the true story of his serving the gun the day we took the Java, – asked about dear old David Porter, as he called him. Then he settled down more quietly, and very happily, to hear me tell in an hour the history of fifty years.*

"How I wished it had been somebody who knew something! But I did as well as I could. I told him of the English war. I told him about Fulton and the steamboat

beginning. I told him about old Scott, and Jackson; told him all I could think of about the Mississippi, and New Orleans, and Texas, and his own old Kentucky. And do you think, he asked who was in command of the 'Legion of the West.' I told him it was a very gallant officer named Grant and that, by our last news, he was about to establish his head-quarters at Vicksburg. Then, 'Where was Vicksburg?' I worked that out on the map; it was about a hundred miles, more or less, above his old Fort Adams; and I thought Fort Adams must be a ruin now. 'It must be at old Vick's plantation, at Walnut Hills,' said he: 'well, that is a change!'

"I tell you, Ingham, it was a hard thing to condense the history of half a century into that talk with a sick man. And I do not now know what I told him, – of emigration, and the means of it, – of steamboats, and railroads, and telegraphs, – of inventions, and books, and literature, – of the colleges, and West Point, and the Naval School, – but with the queerest interruptions that ever you heard. You see it was Robinson Crusoe asking all the accumulated questions of fifty-six years!

"I remember he asked, all of a sudden, who was President now; and when I told him, he asked if Old Abe was General Benjamin Lincoln's son. He said he met old General Lincoln, when he was quite a boy himself, at some Indian treaty. I said no, that Old Abe was a Kentuckian like himself, but I could not tell him of what family; he had worked up from the ranks. 'Good for him!' cried Nolan; 'I am glad of that. As I have brooded and wondered, I have thought our danger was in keeping up those regular successions in the first families.' Then I got talking about my visit to Washington. I told him of meeting the Oregon Congressman, Harding; I told him about the Smithsonian, and the Exploring Expedition; I told him about the Capitol, and the statues for the pediment, and Crawford's Liberty, and Greenough's Washington: Ingham, I told him everything I could think of that would show the grandeur of his country and its prosperity; but I could not make up my mouth to tell him a word about this infernal rebellion!

"And he drank it in and enjoyed it as I cannot tell you. He grew more and more silent, yet I never thought he was tired or faint. I gave him a glass of water, but he just wet his lips, and told me not to go away. Then he asked me to bring the Presbyterian 'Book of Public Prayer' which lay there, and said, with a smile, that it would open at the right place, – and so it did. There was his double red mark down the page; and I knelt down and read, and he repeated with me, 'For ourselves and our country, O gracious God, we thank These, that, notwithstanding our manifold transgressions of Thy holy laws, Thou hast continued to us Thy marvellous kindness,' – and so to the end of that thanksgiving. Then he turned to the end of the same book, and I read the words more familiar to me: 'Most heartily we beseech Thee with Thy favor to behold and bless Thy servant, the President of the United States, and all others in authority,' – and the rest of the Episcopal collect. 'Danforth,' said he, 'I have repeated those prayers night and morning, it is now fifty-five years.' And then he said he would go to sleep. He bent me down over him and kissed me; and he said, 'Look in my Bible, Captain, when I am gone.' And I went away.

"But I had no thought it was the end: I thought he was tired and would sleep. I knew he was happy, and I wanted him to be alone.

"But in an hour, when the doctor went in gently, he found Nolan had breathed his life away with a smile. He had something pressed close to his lips. It was his father's badge of the Order of the Cincinnati.

"We looked in his Bible, and there was a slip of paper at the place where he had marked the text. –

" 'They desire a country, even a heavenly: wherefore God is not ashamed to be called their God: for He hath prepared for them a city.'

"On this slip of paper he had written:

" 'Bury me in the sea; it has been my home, and I love it. But will not some one set up a stone for my memory **(footnote 12)** *at Fort Adams or at Orleans, that my disgrace may not be more than I ought to bear? Say on it:*

" 'In Memory of
" 'PHILIP NOLAN,
" 'Lieutenant in the Army of the United States.
" 'He loved his country as no other man has loved her;
but no man deserved less at her hands.' "

Footnote 1. Frederic Ingham, the 'I' of the narrative, is supposed to be a retired officer of the United States Navy.

Footnote 2. *Few readers ...observed.* In truth, no one observed it, because there was no such announcement there. The author has, however, met more than one person who assured him that they had seen this notice. So fallible is the human memory!

Footnote 3. The *Levant* was a corvette in the American navy, which sailed on her last voyage, with despatches for an American officer in Central America, from the port of Honolulu in 1860. She has never been heard of since, but one of her spars drifted ashore on one of the Hawaiian islands. I took her name intentionally, knowing that she was lost. As it happened, when this story was published, only two American editors recollected that the *Levant* no longer existed. We learn from the last despatch of Captain Hunt that he intended to take a northern course heading eastward toward the coast of California rather than southward toward the Equator. At the instance of Mr. James D. Hague, who was on board the *Levant* to bid Captain Hunt good bye on the day when she sailed from Hilo, a search has been made in the summer of 1904 for any reef or islands in that undiscovered region upon which she may have been wrecked. But no satisfactory results have been obtained.

Footnote 4. James Madison was President from March 4, 1809, to March 4, 1817. Personally he did not wish to make war with England, but the leaders of the younger men of the Democratic party – Mr. Clay, Mr. Calhoun, and others – pressed him against his will to declare war in 1812. The war was ended by the Treaty of Peace at Ghent in the year 1814. It is generally called 'The Short War'. There were many reasons for the war. The most exasperating was the impressment of American seamen to serve in the English navy. In the American State Department there were records of 6,257 such men, whose friends had protested to the American government. It is believed that more than twenty thousand Americans were held, at one time or another, in such service. For those who need to study this subject, I recommend Spears's *History of our Navy*, in four volumes. It is dedicated 'to those who would seek Peace and Pursue it.'

Footnote 5. Aaron Burr had been an officer in the American Revolution. He was Vice-President from 1801 to 1805, in the first term of Jefferson's administration. In July, 1804, in a duel, Burr killed Alexander Hamilton, a celebrated leader of the Federal party. From this duel may be dated the indignation which followed him through the next years of his life. In 1805, after his

Vice-Presidency, he made a voyage down the Ohio and Mississippi Rivers, to study the new acquisition of Louisiana. That name was then given to all the country west of the Mississippi as far as the Rocky Mountains. The next year he organized a military expedition, probably with the plan, vaguely conceived, of taking Texas from Spain. He was, however, betrayed and arrested by General Wilkinson, – then in command of the United States army, – with whom Burr had had intimate relations. He was tried for treason at Richmond but acquitted.

Footnote 6. Colonel Morgan is a fictitious character, like all the others in this book, except Aaron Burr.

Footnote 7. The 'Lay of the Last Minstrel' is one of the best poems of Walter Scott. It was first published in 1805. The whole passage referred to in the text is this: –

Breathes there the man, with soul so dead,
Who never to himself hath said,
This is my own, my native land!
Whose heart hath ne'er within him burn'd,
As home his footsteps he hath turn'd
From wandering on a foreign strand?
If such there breathe, go, mark him well!
For him no minstrel raptures swell;
High though his titles, proud his name,
Boundless his wealth as wish can claim,
Despite those titles, power, and pelf,
The wretch, concentred all in self,
Living, shall forfeit fair renown,
And, doubly dying, shall go down
To the vile dust, from whence he sprung,
Unwept, unhonour'd, and unsung.
O Caledonia! stern and wild,
Meet nurse for a poetic child!
Land of brown heath and shaggy wood;
Land of the mountain and the flood.

Footnote 8. ...*frigate-duels with the English, in which the navy was really baptized.* Several great sea fights in this short war gave to the Navy of the United States its reputation. Indeed, they charged the navies of all the world. The first of these great battles is the fight of the *Constitution* and *Guerrilére*, August 19, 1812.

Footnote 9. The frigate *Essex*, under Porter, took the Marquesas Islands, in the Pacific, in 1813. Captain Porter was father of the more celebrated Admiral Porter, who commanded the United States naval forces in the Gulf of Mexico in 1863, when this story was written.

Footnote 10. *Beledeljereed.* An Arab name. Beled el jerid means 'The Land of Dates'. As a name it has disappeared from the books of geography. But one hundred years ago it was given to the southern part of the Algeria of today, and somewhat vaguely to other parts of the ancient Numidia. It will be found spelled Biledelgerid. To use this word now is somewhat like speaking of the Liliput of Gulliver.

Footnote 11. The English cruisers on the American coast, in the great war between England and Napoleon, claimed the right to search American merchantmen and men of war, to find, if they could, deserters from the English navy. This was their way of showing their contempt for the United States. In 1807 the *Chesapeake*, a frigate of the United States, was met by the *Leopard*, an English frigate. She was not prepared for fighting, and Barron, her commander, struck his flag. This is the unfortunate vessel which surrendered to the *Shannon* on June 3, 1813.

Footnote 12. No one has erected this monument. Its proper place would be on the ruins of Fort Adams. That fort has been much worn away by the Mississippi River.

Advantage on the Kingdom of the Shore

Kelly A. Harmon

DIO!

The minute the silk slid off the weapon in the auction hall, Father Luciano knew what he was looking at. The ancient sword, *Vulsini*.

The sword appeared rusted, as he knew it would, but even still, he realized the enormity of the find. The corrosion on the blade belied its state. It might appear rusted on the surface, but that was only a part of its magic, hiding itself.

Luciano had had to stifle a gasp. It wouldn't do to reveal to the others what he suspected ...No, not suspected ...*knew*.

Silence reigned. Did the other bidders recognize the sword, or were they simply unwilling to start the bid?

"Five hundred lire," said Luciano. It was a reasonable sum for an above-average sword.

"Five-ten," said another, and so it went, until a throaty, feminine voice interrupted, "Two thousand lire."

All heads turned to the rear of the room.

"*Puttana*," he heard one whisper. *Whore.*

She wore pants, a cuffed shirt minus any ruff: her neck and throat were bare. He could see why they called her whore, but that was barely fair. She was decent, even if she wore trousers like a man. But he knew Signorita Marcelli's reputation. She was young. She took lovers. She lived alone.

She possessed another appellation, he knew: *Swordsmistress*, though he wondered about the accuracy of the title.

"Three-thousand lire," said Luciano.

The woman turned to him and raised an eyebrow. She walked from the back of the room toward him, the supple leather of her pants shushing against the velvet cushion as she sat in the chair next to his.

"Father," she said, darting a glance at the large crucifix hanging from his neck, "the church must pay you well if you can afford such an expensive item."

She leaned toward him as she spoke, and except for the brief touch of her eyes to his jeweled cross, she stared at the unveiled sword at the front of the room. She raised her left hand to increase the bid.

"Not only second sons find their way to the church, Mistress." He raised the bid again. "Where is the law that states only a poor man may be called by God to enter the church?"

"Then money is no object for you?"

Luciano raised his hand again and turned to her. "I didn't say that."

She nodded, appearing to consider his words, then tried a different tack.

"I didn't think collecting weapons would be an appropriate pursuit for a man teaching the word of God."

He chuckled. "You want to debate with me on the hobbies permitted to men of the cloth?"

"I want you to give up bidding on the weapon and allow me to have it."

"Impossible," he said.

She took a deep breath. "Then you must know what the sword can do."

"Only by rumor," he said. That was true. He only knew what he'd read and what little he'd gleaned from guarded conversations. Those who know of the sword, and its partner, are often reluctant to reveal their existence. So much of what he learned the swords could do was nothing more than hearsay and exaggeration. But he'd had sources the average rumor-monger did not. Access to the Vatican library is no small thing.

"Then you can see how Venice will benefit more from it if it were in my hands, rather than yours," Mistress Marcelli said.

"How so?" He failed to see how anyone but himself could benefit from the sword, by *any* sword.

"Vulsini is the *good* sword," she said. It belongs with a woman – one who knows its nature, knows how to employ its power for the good of the people."

"You think just because the sword is reputed to be the good sword it should belong to a woman?"

She nodded. "Women are inherently good."

"And men are inherently evil?" He raised his card again, shaking his head at her audacity. "You're mad," he said. "That kind of attitude in possession of the swords will cause nothing less than your own corruption. We can't even be sure *Vulsini* is the good sword."

"Of course it is," she said. "It's dark as night, corroded, limned with dirt: hiding its true nature from the world."

"That's woman's logic," he said, knowing at once he offended her by the stormy expression in her eyes. He wasn't certain himself, whether good or evil claimed Vulsini. No one he had talked with had known the answer, though he believed it to be evil. After all, he had held *Peccerillo* in his hands. Polished to a brilliant shine, its gemstone sparkling in the light, how could it not be claimed by goodness? The archangel Michael could name it for his own, such was its beauty.

He closed his eyes for a moment, feeling foolish for tumbling into the same logic trap Mistress Marcelli fell prey to. Composed, he opened his eyes.

Did she realize only the two of them continued to bid?

"This is ridiculous," he said, tiring of the conversation. "You won't win the sword. Do you continue to offer for it only to try to bankrupt me?" He raised his bid card again.

Her smile faded. "I can no longer keep up," she said, pouting. She leaned even closer to him, lowered her voice. "Perhaps we could come to an arrangement?" The corner of her mouth crept up, revealing a dimple.

Father Luciano felt himself smiling back. Still, he wouldn't rise to her bait. "Another time, Mistress," he said. "Now that I've won the sword, I find myself unwilling to bargain with it."

He stood and bowed to her, and turned to the front, intent on signing his cheque for the bid-price and making arrangements for the sword's delivery at the end of the auction.

"Do you plan to donate it to a museum?" she asked.

He turned back. "No. It will remain in my private collection." *But only long enough*, he thought, *until I can bury it so deep, no one will find it again.*

* * *

Merda!

He hadn't even gotten to hold *Vulsini*, to grip the pommel and assess the weight of it in his palm …to feel the sword, as if an extension of his own arm, before she had torn it from his possession.

Fiend!

Father Luciano changed clothes with a heavy heart. He should have known Mistress Marcelli was up to something when she asked about the sword's destination. He should have waited until the auction concluded and taken the sword home himself. Now, he had to steal – *steal!* – it back from her. Was it a sin to recover something which was originally stolen from you?

He was getting old, forgetting his former training, he thought, pulling the chasuble over his head and hanging it in the wardrobe. He untied the cincture at his waist even as he walked back to the dressing table, leaving the ends of his stole dangling as he walked.

No, he thought. *I'm becoming a better priest, assuming in the basic goodness of others. Doing unto others* …He dragged the stole from his neck, folding the narrow cloth twice over and kissing it, murmuring the prayer more by rote than reverence. Finally, he took off the alb and hung it in the wardrobe beside the chasuble. Only his dark pants and long-sleeved shirt remained.

Luciano bent and pulled a leather jerkin and boots from the floor of the cabinet. He donned the vest, and sitting on the edge of the bed, he bent and laced the boots. He eyed the weapons hanging on the wall, vying for space on both sides on an enormous crucifix, nearly as tall as himself. He tried to decide which blade would be best, then chose a rapier he'd fought with many times in his youth, coupling it with a long-bladed dagger he could use in his right hand.

Monsignor Alberto disliked his *collection*. But cells were private and allowed no visitors, and he knew the wall of various-sized blades was unlikely to collect comment. A weighty donation to the Monsignor eliminated further misgivings. And so he allowed Luciano his *hobby*, with one caveat: He could accumulate; but he could not use. Becoming a priest meant giving up the old ways, and until now, he'd been able to do so.

Luciano threw a cloak over his shoulders, concealing the sword at his hip and the dagger protruding from his boot, and made his way to the famed Signorita Marcelli's house, less than a mile down San Marco Canal.

His footsteps echoed through the narrow alleyways as darkness fell. The sword felt heavy on his hip. He couldn't remember the last time he'd actually carried one. It had been even longer since he had raised one in practice, let alone as a weapon of defense, or attack.

His ecclesiastical life provided him with vast amounts of the time to correspond with those who knew of the swords, and allowed him the use of the Vatican library to glean what knowledge he could …but it left him no time to practise, to retain the rhythms he'd learned in his youth. Monsignor Alberto could overlook sword collecting; sword practice he could not. He said, "What kind of priest speaks the words of peace yet prepares for armed combat?" He would not sanction the practice, even for exercise.

Copernicus was said to have held both swords in his hands, *Vulsini*, the dark sword, and *Peccerillo*, the blade with a pommel made of blue stone. It's said when he finally lifted them together, Copernicus threw them down in fear. *Destroy them*, he had said, *for mankind must never know their power.*

If this had actually happened …why hadn't the swords been destroyed?

Luciano considered the Copernicus tale a fable …but the fabric of most fables is woven to warn. Who knew what happened when both swords are joined together? He intended to find out …and then bury them so deep that no one would find them again.

He arrived at Mistress Marcelli's house, walked boldly to the front door and tried the knob. Locked.

Without hesitating, lest he appear to be the robber he meant to be, he entered the garden, looking for a window concealed by foliage.

"Now we have you," said a voice from the darkness. A light flared, the beam of a lantern unhooded in his direction. Three of the night watch, guarding this house as though it were the Doge's Palace. What a time to be caught naked of his robes. He looked like a common vagabond. He felt absurd.

"I'm sure there's been a mistake," he said. "I'm meeting Signorita Marcelli for a drink tonight." *God forgive me*, he thought. *Now I'm adding lying to my sins.*

"She said you would contrive a slanderous tale," the guard with the lantern said. "Can you produce the stiletto she says you stole from her?"

"*I* stole from her?"

The guard nodded. "She said you would come to rob her when she refused to part with the matched pair. You have the shorter blade, and now you're coming for the sword."

"I know nothing of a stiletto, but I have the receipt for the sale of the sword," Luciano said. "It is she who stole the sword from me."

"A likely tale," said the lantern-bearing guard, nodding.

An older soldier stepped forward. "Now drop your weapons, very slowly, please. I wouldn't want to gut you on Signorita Marcelli's doorstep."

"I can take you to the receipt," said Luciano, dropping his weapons, "if you will follow me home."

The guard looked as though he weighed the idea against the merits of taking Luciano to prison.

"What have you got to lose?" Luciano asked, eying their indecision.

"It *is* just the whore's word against his," the second guard said, retrieving Luciano's dagger and sword.

The old guard nodded, and Luciano led them back to the palazzo entrance of the church of San Giorgio Maggiore and walked to the door.

"Ho, there," said the sergeant, grabbing his wrist. "You'll not enter the church and claim sanctuary."

"I swear I won't," said Luciano. "Monsignor Alberto will vouch for me. He is in charge here and knows I collect weaponry." He motioned to the guard. "I will wait outside, if you wish, until you contact him."

A few moments later the guard returned along with Monsignor Alberto, who looked him up and down twice over.

"This is Father Luciano Spina," said Father Alberto. He spared a brief, disgusted glance with Luciano. "What he's told you is true." The Monsignor turned and went back into the church.

The old guard offered his apologies, motioned for the return of Luciano's weapons, and turned away into the night. Luciano entered the church and shut the door behind him.

"I told you that collection would get you into trouble," Monsignor Alberto said, stepping out of the darkness into Luciano's path. "Will you promise to get rid of it now?" he asked.

Luciano nodded, feeling sadness brim up. He had enjoyed it here, but it was time to move on. He would take the collection with him when he left to find a new post. But first, he had a job to do.

He returned to his cell and restored the rapier and dagger to their positions on the wall. Then, he reached for the large plaster crucifix hanging amid the weaponry and hefted it from its moorings. He lowered it to the ground, turning it backside-out, and leaned it against the wall. From a shallow niche he had carved himself from the plaster of the cross, Luciano retrieved a wrapped sword.

He pulled the canvas from *Peccerillo*, the silver blade shining even in the dim candlelight of his room. He slid it into a loop on his belt, then rehung the crucifix.

Once more, he left the church that evening.

* * *

"I was afraid it might come to this," Signorita Marcelli said from across the palazzo square. She pulled the sword from the scabbard at her hip and flexed her wrist, raising and lowering the tip of the blade.

Vulsini gleamed darker than the night. The tassels on Signorita Marcelli's red leather gloves looked like a splash of blood upon it. Street lamps in the palazzo offered limited light, their watery glow just enough to fight by. She had not cleaned the corrosion from the serrated edge of the sword.

Luciano jerked *Peccerillo* from the belt loop at his waist, the heavy, round blue jewel of its pommel feeling strange to a hand once accustomed to fighting with a lighter rapier. Still, it was well-balanced and fitted perfectly in his hand. He swung it a few times, keeping his eye on Mistress Marcelli, growing more comfortable with each stroke. *Peccerillo* glowed with its own light, a bronze nimbus emanating out from the hilt.

God, but his finest rapier never felt so good in his hand, he thought, sweeping the blade in front of him. How could a heavier sword feel so good? He could fight with this weapon for hours without tiring. Or, at least, he might once have been able to. It had been years since he'd fought, but besting a woman who lacked his height and breadth – no matter her training – should be a simple matter, no? He only wished he could do so without hurting her.

He watched her swing *Vulsini*, feeling strangely attracted to her lithe grace. There was something in the way she moved that drew his eyes toward her. Or did he feel drawn toward the blade, the sight of her a bonus?

She strode toward him, the heels of her booted feet clattering against the cobblestone and echoing throughout the deserted palazzo. As she neared him, she lifted the sword tip above her right shoulder and sliced down across the front of him.

Luciano blocked the thrust with *Peccerillo*, a shower of sparks erupting where the swords touched. The corrosion fell from *Vulsini* to the stones. Invisible lightening tickled up his arm, and he drew his sword back.

Mistress Marcelli laughed, her eyes dancing. "Did you feel that?"

He nodded, feeling his own lips curl into a smile. He was fighting again, putting his training to use. He felt a rightness within that he hadn't felt in years, even if he weren't on the offensive. It felt *right*, to be sparring. He felt more alive than he had in years.

He never felt this way when he lifted the swords of his collection from their places on the wall and swung them around in his cell. He thought, *is it the sword, or the fight, making me feel so alive?*

Signorita Marcelli swung again.

Luciano laughed, parrying the blow. Blue sparks rained down to the cobbles. Again he felt the tingling sensation in his arm. "You don't have the strength to beat me," he said.

"I don't need to," she said, swinging roundhouse in front of his chest. Luciano jumped back, swinging at her weapon and striking it, attempting to keep her off-balance and continue the rotation. The blades crossed at mid-length, then slid down the length of each to the end, sparks dancing along the metal wherever they touched. "The sword directs me," she said.

Luciano smiled. "You jest," he said, stepping forward and slicing against the dark sword as she recovered and attacked again. Perhaps he could force it out of her hand.

His swing went wide, nicking her arm just above the elbow. Had the sword *pulled* to the right? He stepped back, trying to move out of the fray, but with a tingling sensation, his legs instead moved him to the left, keeping him within striking distance. Mistress Marcelli advanced again.

His brow furrowed.

"I thought you knew their power?" she said, thrusting the sword toward him.

This time, he was able to jump back. She stepped forward and struck at him again. Again he tried to disarm her. Again the sword pulled right and drew blood.

"Mistress, I am loathe to fight you." he said. "And I beg pardon for cutting you."

She attacked and he parried, stepping back and drawing her around the side of the church, away from the palazzo and toward the canal. "Perhaps we can still come to an agreement you spoke of a day ago. An agreement in which I do not have to kill you."

"We are committed," she said, jumping forward. This time *Vulsini* slipped under his guard and sliced his thigh. Luciano felt the burn of the cut, the shock chilling him all over, even as the jagged serrated edge of the blade pulled back from the flesh of his leg. He could not suppress a groan, and he watched her eyes light as she heard it.

"I had no idea you found such pleasure in the pain of others," he said through gritted teeth, going on the offensive. He boldly marched two steps toward her, swung his blade, piercing her sword arm again – this time on purpose. He felt elation, then mortification, knowing the joy had been thrust upon him by the sword.

She cried out, and shuddered, and he knew he could have had her life. But unlike Mistress Marcelli, *he* was not committed.

He let her advance again, coming closer to the canal.

"It's the sword," she said. "It wishes to be joined with its partner, and ..." She raised *Vulsini* high.

" ...and become the most powerful sword in the universe," Luciano finished, feeling *Peccerillo* move even before he could urge his arm in another direction. The blade punctured her high on the rib cage, glancing off bone before hitting something vital. She crumbled.

Luciano released *Peccerillo*, catching Mistress Marcelli as she fell to the stone. He eased her down, kicked *Vulsini* from her hand, and held her until she drew her final breath.

* * *

A sword in each hand, he walked down the steps to the San Giorgio Maggiore Canal, grateful that now, at low tide, his task might be accomplished more quickly. He didn't feel the dread Copernicus was said to feel when he touched both swords simultaneously. But Copernicus had not been flush with anger from the senseless taking of a life. He felt no power; only disgust ...at first.

Then he felt the tingling in both arms, felt them drawn to push the blades together, flat to flat, hilt to hilt. He resisted.

Mate us.

He could almost hear the words aloud, so clear were they in his mind.

Mate us.

He paused at the water's edge, the urge to join the swords even greater. He tensed his wrists, lifting the points of each sword, pushing them almost near enough to touch.

What harm could it do, he thought, to touch the ends briefly? What would absolute power taste like, if for only an instant?

The tips moved closer.

What would absolute power taste like for an eternity?

Mate us.

Luciano felt himself grow cold all over, realizing the swords could make him do anything, think anything, and make him believe it were his own actions and his own thoughts.

What made him think he was a better man than Copernicus?

Luciano pulled the swords away from each other and thrust them away from himself, dropping them into the canal. Free of their sustaining influence, he sank to his knees and covered his face in his hands. He knelt there for a moment, feeling their power over him wane.

Once composed, he stood and dove in after the weapons, laying a hand on *Peccerillo, the bad sword*, he thought, when he touched the bottom. Peccerillo's jewel glowed, casting blue light in the water. By its light, he found *Vulsini* a few feet away, leaving it for the moment, to lay where it fell.

He felt his way to the foundation wall of San Giorgio Maggiore Church, and knelt.

He hurried, using the sword like a spade to dig a hole at the edge of the marble. The mud was soft, pliable, and he found that if he applied direct pressure to the weapon, it slid to the hilt beneath the stone wall of the church. He released the sword and the glow faded. Then, he grasped handfuls of the silky mud and heaped them atop the hilt, burying it.

One down, he thought, feeling around for *Vulsini*.

Luciano grasped the hilt and dragged it closer, pulling it into the palm of his hand as if he meant to fight, tilting the tip of the sword up, so that it would break free of the water before him.

Lungs burning, he pushed hard on the bottom of the canal, forcing himself to the surface. He shot up, coughing and gasping for air. He tossed the sword onto the cobblestone, and pulled himself over the edge of the canal to face the rear entrance of the Church of San Giorgio Maggiore.

He felt a momentary pang for what he planned to do with *Vulsini*. He could do so much with it. He could ...*No*, he could not. He smiled, realizing that perhaps *Peccerillo* hadn't been the bad sword after all.

Or, perhaps both were bad.

Luciano shook the water from his hair, stamped the water from his boots, and walked up the marble risers to the church entrance. The pink light of dawn colored the morning sky, and he could smell bread baking in one of the *trattorias* off the palazzo.

He had buried *Peccerillo*, and he would take *Vulsini* half a world away and bury it as well. In time, perhaps their names would be forgotten, and men would cease to search for the pair. Only time could bury them deeper than he could.

Now, he must take up his collection and leave.

The Artist of the Beautiful

Nathaniel Hawthorne

AN ELDERLY MAN, with his pretty daughter on his arm, was passing along the street, and emerged from the gloom of the cloudy evening into the light that fell across the pavement from the window of a small shop. It was a projecting window; and on the inside were suspended a variety of watches, pinchbeck, silver, and one or two of gold, all with their faces turned from the streets, as if churlishly disinclined to inform the wayfarers what o'clock it was. Seated within the shop, sidelong to the window with his pale face bent earnestly over some delicate piece of mechanism on which was thrown the concentrated lustre of a shade lamp, appeared a young man.

"What can Owen Warland be about?" muttered old Peter Hovenden, himself a retired watchmaker, and the former master of this same young man whose occupation he was now wondering at. "What can the fellow be about? These six months past I have never come by his shop without seeing him just as steadily at work as now. It would be a flight beyond his usual foolery to seek for the perpetual motion; and yet I know enough of my old business to be certain that what he is now so busy with is no part of the machinery of a watch."

"Perhaps, father," said Annie, without showing much interest in the question, "Owen is inventing a new kind of timekeeper. I am sure he has ingenuity enough."

"Poh, child! He has not the sort of ingenuity to invent anything better than a Dutch toy," answered her father, who had formerly been put to much vexation by Owen Warland's irregular genius. "A plague on such ingenuity! All the effect that ever I knew of it was to spoil the accuracy of some of the best watches in my shop. He would turn the sun out of its orbit and derange the whole course of time, if, as I said before, his ingenuity could grasp anything bigger than a child's toy!"

"Hush, father! He hears you!" whispered Annie, pressing the old man's arm. "His ears are as delicate as his feelings; and you know how easily disturbed they are. Do let us move on."

So Peter Hovenden and his daughter Annie plodded on without further conversation, until in a by-street of the town they found themselves passing the open door of a blacksmith's shop. Within was seen the forge, now blazing up and illuminating the high and dusky roof, and now confining its lustre to a narrow precinct of the coal-strewn floor, according as the breath of the bellows was puffed forth or again inhaled into its vast leathern lungs. In the intervals of brightness it was easy to distinguish objects in remote corners of the shop and the horseshoes that hung upon the wall; in the momentary gloom the fire seemed to be glimmering amidst the vagueness of unenclosed space. Moving about in this red glare and alternate dusk was the figure of the blacksmith, well worthy to be viewed in so picturesque an aspect of light and shade, where the bright blaze struggled with the black night, as if each would have snatched his comely strength from the other. Anon he drew a white-hot bar of iron from the coals, laid it on the anvil, uplifted his arm of might, and was soon enveloped in the myriads of sparks which the strokes of his hammer scattered into the surrounding gloom.

"Now, that is a pleasant sight," said the old watchmaker. "I know what it is to work in gold; but give me the worker in iron after all is said and done. He spends his labor upon a reality. What say you, daughter Annie?"

"Pray don't speak so loud, father," whispered Annie, "Robert Danforth will hear you."

"And what if he should hear me?" said Peter Hovenden. "I say again, it is a good and a wholesome thing to depend upon main strength and reality, and to earn one's bread with the bare and brawny arm of a blacksmith. A watchmaker gets his brain puzzled by his wheels within a wheel, or loses his health or the nicety of his eyesight, as was my case, and finds himself at middle age, or a little after, past labor at his own trade and fit for nothing else, yet too poor to live at his ease. So I say once again, give me main strength for my money. And then, how it takes the nonsense out of a man! Did you ever hear of a blacksmith being such a fool as Owen Warland yonder?"

"Well said, uncle Hovenden!" shouted Robert Danforth from the forge, in a full, deep, merry voice, that made the roof re-echo. "And what says Miss Annie to that doctrine? She, I suppose, will think it a genteeler business to tinker up a lady's watch than to forge a horseshoe or make a gridiron?"

Annie drew her father onward without giving him time for reply.

But we must return to Owen Warland's shop, and spend more meditation upon his history and character than either Peter Hovenden, or probably his daughter Annie, or Owen's old school-fellow, Robert Danforth, would have thought due to so slight a subject. From the time that his little fingers could grasp a penknife, Owen had been remarkable for a delicate ingenuity, which sometimes produced pretty shapes in wood, principally figures of flowers and birds, and sometimes seemed to aim at the hidden mysteries of mechanism. But it was always for purposes of grace, and never with any mockery of the useful. He did not, like the crowd of school-boy artisans, construct little windmills on the angle of a barn or watermills across the neighboring brook. Those who discovered such peculiarity in the boy as to think it worth their while to observe him closely, sometimes saw reason to suppose that he was attempting to imitate the beautiful movements of Nature as exemplified in the flight of birds or the activity of little animals. It seemed, in fact, a new development of the love of the beautiful, such as might have made him a poet, a painter, or a sculptor, and which was as completely refined from all utilitarian coarseness as it could have been in either of the fine arts. He looked with singular distaste at the stiff and regular processes of ordinary machinery. Being once carried to see a steam-engine, in the expectation that his intuitive comprehension of mechanical principles would be gratified, he turned pale and grew sick, as if something monstrous and unnatural had been presented to him. This horror was partly owing to the size and terrible energy of the iron laborer; for the character of Owen's mind was microscopic, and tended naturally to the minute, in accordance with his diminutive frame and the marvellous smallness and delicate power of his fingers. Not that his sense of beauty was thereby diminished into a sense of prettiness. The beautiful idea has no relation to size, and may be as perfectly developed in a space too minute for any but microscopic investigation as within the ample verge that is measured by the arc of the rainbow. But, at all events, this characteristic minuteness in his objects and accomplishments made the world even more incapable than it might otherwise have been of appreciating Owen Warland's genius. The boy's relatives saw nothing better to be done – as perhaps there was not – than to bind him apprentice to a watchmaker, hoping that his strange ingenuity might thus be regulated and put to utilitarian purposes.

Peter Hovenden's opinion of his apprentice has already been expressed. He could make nothing of the lad. Owen's apprehension of the professional mysteries, it is true, was inconceivably quick; but he altogether forgot or despised the grand object of a watchmaker's business, and cared no more for the measurement of time than if it had been merged into eternity. So long, however, as he remained under his old master's care, Owen's lack of sturdiness made it possible, by strict injunctions and sharp oversight, to restrain his creative eccentricity within bounds; but when his apprenticeship was served out, and he had taken the little shop which Peter Hovenden's failing eyesight compelled him to relinquish, then did people recognize how unfit a person was Owen Warland to lead old blind Father Time along his daily course. One of his most rational projects was to connect a musical operation with the machinery of his watches, so that all the harsh dissonances of life might be rendered tuneful, and each flitting moment fall into the abyss of the past in golden drops of harmony. If a family clock was intrusted to him for repair, – one of those tall, ancient clocks that have grown nearly allied to human nature by measuring out the lifetime of many generations, – he would take upon himself to arrange a dance or funeral procession of figures across its venerable face, representing twelve mirthful or melancholy hours. Several freaks of this kind quite destroyed the young watchmaker's credit with that steady and matter-of-fact class of people who hold the opinion that time is not to be trifled with, whether considered as the medium of advancement and prosperity in this world or preparation for the next. His custom rapidly diminished – a misfortune, however, that was probably reckoned among his better accidents by Owen Warland, who was becoming more and more absorbed in a secret occupation which drew all his science and manual dexterity into itself, and likewise gave full employment to the characteristic tendencies of his genius. This pursuit had already consumed many months.

After the old watchmaker and his pretty daughter had gazed at him out of the obscurity of the street, Owen Warland was seized with a fluttering of the nerves, which made his hand tremble too violently to proceed with such delicate labor as he was now engaged upon.

"It was Annie herself!" murmured he. "I should have known it, by this throbbing of my heart, before I heard her father's voice. Ah, how it throbs! I shall scarcely be able to work again on this exquisite mechanism tonight. Annie! Dearest Annie! Thou shouldst give firmness to my heart and hand, and not shake them thus; for if I strive to put the very spirit of beauty into form and give it motion, it is for thy sake alone. O throbbing heart, be quiet! If my labor be thus thwarted, there will come vague and unsatisfied dreams which will leave me spiritless tomorrow."

As he was endeavoring to settle himself again to his task, the shop door opened and gave admittance to no other than the stalwart figure which Peter Hovenden had paused to admire, as seen amid the light and shadow of the blacksmith's shop. Robert Danforth had brought a little anvil of his own manufacture, and peculiarly constructed, which the young artist had recently bespoken. Owen examined the article and pronounced it fashioned according to his wish.

"Why, yes," said Robert Danforth, his strong voice filling the shop as with the sound of a bass viol, "I consider myself equal to anything in the way of my own trade; though I should have made but a poor figure at yours with such a fist as this," added he, laughing, as he laid his vast hand beside the delicate one of Owen. "But what then? I put more main strength into one blow of my sledge hammer than all that you have expended since you were a 'prentice. Is not that the truth?"

"Very probably," answered the low and slender voice of Owen. "Strength is an earthly monster. I make no pretensions to it. My force, whatever there may be of it, is altogether spiritual."

"Well, but, Owen, what are you about?" asked his old school-fellow, still in such a hearty volume of tone that it made the artist shrink, especially as the question related to a subject so sacred as the absorbing dream of his imagination. "Folks do say that you are trying to discover the perpetual motion."

"The perpetual motion? Nonsense!" replied Owen Warland, with a movement of disgust; for he was full of little petulances. "It can never be discovered. It is a dream that may delude men whose brains are mystified with matter, but not me. Besides, if such a discovery were possible, it would not be worth my while to make it only to have the secret turned to such purposes as are now effected by steam and water power. I am not ambitious to be honored with the paternity of a new kind of cotton machine."

"That would be droll enough!" cried the blacksmith, breaking out into such an uproar of laughter that Owen himself and the bell glasses on his work-board quivered in unison. "No, no, Owen! No child of yours will have iron joints and sinews. Well, I won't hinder you any more. Good night, Owen, and success, and if you need any assistance, so far as a downright blow of hammer upon anvil will answer the purpose, I'm your man."

And with another laugh the man of main strength left the shop.

"How strange it is," whispered Owen Warland to himself, leaning his head upon his hand, "that all my musings, my purposes, my passion for the beautiful, my consciousness of power to create it, – a finer, more ethereal power, of which this earthly giant can have no conception, – all, all, look so vain and idle whenever my path is crossed by Robert Danforth! He would drive me mad were I to meet him often. His hard, brute force darkens and confuses the spiritual element within me; but I, too, will be strong in my own way. I will not yield to him."

He took from beneath a glass a piece of minute machinery, which he set in the condensed light of his lamp, and, looking intently at it through a magnifying glass, proceeded to operate with a delicate instrument of steel. In an instant, however, he fell back in his chair and clasped his hands, with a look of horror on his face that made its small features as impressive as those of a giant would have been.

"Heaven! What have I done?" exclaimed he. "The vapor, the influence of that brute force, – it has bewildered me and obscured my perception. I have made the very stroke – the fatal stroke – that I have dreaded from the first. It is all over – the toil of months, the object of my life. I am ruined!"

And there he sat, in strange despair, until his lamp flickered in the socket and left the Artist of the Beautiful in darkness.

Thus it is that ideas, which grow up within the imagination and appear so lovely to it and of a value beyond whatever men call valuable, are exposed to be shattered and annihilated by contact with the practical. It is requisite for the ideal artist to possess a force of character that seems hardly compatible with its delicacy; he must keep his faith in himself while the incredulous world assails him with its utter disbelief; he must stand up against mankind and be his own sole disciple, both as respects his genius and the objects to which it is directed.

For a time Owen Warland succumbed to this severe but inevitable test. He spent a few sluggish weeks with his head so continually resting in his hands that the towns-people had scarcely an opportunity to see his countenance. When at last it was again uplifted to the light of day, a cold, dull, nameless change was perceptible upon it. In the opinion of Peter Hovenden, however, and that order of sagacious understandings who think that life should be regulated, like clockwork, with leaden weights, the alteration was entirely for the better. Owen now, indeed, applied himself to business with dogged industry. It was marvellous to witness the obtuse gravity with which he would inspect the wheels of a great old silver watch thereby delighting the owner, in whose fob it had been worn till he deemed it a portion of his own life, and was accordingly jealous of its treatment. In consequence of the good report thus acquired, Owen Warland was invited by the proper authorities to regulate the clock in the church steeple. He succeeded so admirably in this matter of public interest that the merchants gruffly acknowledged his merits on 'Change; the nurse whispered his praises as she gave the potion in the sick-chamber; the lover blessed him at the hour of appointed interview; and the town in general thanked Owen for the punctuality of dinner time. In a word, the heavy weight upon his spirits kept everything in order, not merely within his own system, but wheresoever the iron accents of the church clock were audible. It was a circumstance, though minute, yet characteristic of his present state, that, when employed to engrave names or initials on silver spoons, he now wrote the requisite letters in the plainest possible style, omitting a variety of fanciful flourishes that had heretofore distinguished his work in this kind.

One day, during the era of this happy transformation, old Peter Hovenden came to visit his former apprentice.

"Well, Owen," said he, "I am glad to hear such good accounts of you from all quarters, and especially from the town clock yonder, which speaks in your commendation every hour of the twenty-four. Only get rid altogether of your nonsensical trash about the beautiful, which I nor nobody else, nor yourself to boot, could ever understand, – only free yourself of that, and your success in life is as sure as daylight. Why, if you go on in this way, I should even venture to let you doctor this precious old watch of mine; though, except my daughter Annie, I have nothing else so valuable in the world."

"I should hardly dare touch it, sir," replied Owen, in a depressed tone; for he was weighed down by his old master's presence.

"In time," said the latter, – "In time, you will be capable of it."

The old watchmaker, with the freedom naturally consequent on his former authority, went on inspecting the work which Owen had in hand at the moment, together with other matters that were in progress. The artist, meanwhile, could scarcely lift his head. There was nothing so antipodal to his nature as this man's cold, unimaginative sagacity, by contact with which everything was converted into a dream except the densest matter of the physical world. Owen groaned in spirit and prayed fervently to be delivered from him.

"But what is this?" cried Peter Hovenden abruptly, taking up a dusty bell glass, beneath which appeared a mechanical something, as delicate and minute as the system of a butterfly's anatomy. "What have we here? Owen! Owen! There is witchcraft in these little chains, and wheels, and paddles. See! With one pinch of my finger and thumb I am going to deliver you from all future peril."

"For Heaven's sake," screamed Owen Warland, springing up with wonderful energy, "as you would not drive me mad, do not touch it! The slightest pressure of your finger would ruin me forever."

"Aha, young man! And is it so?" said the old watchmaker, looking at him with just enough penetration to torture Owen's soul with the bitterness of worldly criticism. "Well, take your own course; but I warn you again that in this small piece of mechanism lives your evil spirit. Shall I exorcise him?"

"You are my evil spirit," answered Owen, much excited, – "you and the hard, coarse world! The leaden thoughts and the despondency that you fling upon me are my clogs, else I should long ago have achieved the task that I was created for."

Peter Hovenden shook his head, with the mixture of contempt and indignation which mankind, of whom he was partly a representative, deem themselves entitled to feel towards all simpletons who seek other prizes than the dusty one along the highway. He then took his leave, with an uplifted finger and a sneer upon his face that haunted the artist's dreams for many a night afterwards. At the time of his old master's visit, Owen was probably on the point of taking up the relinquished task; but, by this sinister event, he was thrown back into the state whence he had been slowly emerging.

But the innate tendency of his soul had only been accumulating fresh vigor during its apparent sluggishness. As the summer advanced he almost totally relinquished his business, and permitted Father Time, so far as the old gentleman was represented by the clocks and watches under his control, to stray at random through human life, making infinite confusion among the train of bewildered hours. He wasted the sunshine, as people said, in wandering through the woods and fields and along the banks of streams. There, like a child, he found amusement in chasing butterflies or watching the motions of water insects. There was something truly mysterious in the intentness with which he contemplated these living playthings as they sported on the breeze or examined the structure of an imperial insect whom he had imprisoned. The chase of butterflies was an apt emblem of the ideal pursuit in which he had spent so many golden hours; but would the beautiful idea ever be yielded to his hand like the butterfly that symbolized it? Sweet, doubtless, were these days, and congenial to the artist's soul. They were full of bright conceptions, which gleamed through his intellectual world as the butterflies gleamed through the outward atmosphere, and were real to him, for the instant, without the toil, and perplexity, and many disappointments of attempting to make them visible to the sensual eye. Alas that the artist, whether in poetry, or whatever other material, may not content himself with the inward enjoyment of the beautiful, but must chase the flitting mystery beyond the verge of his ethereal domain, and crush its frail being in seizing it with a material grasp. Owen Warland felt the impulse to give external reality to his ideas as irresistibly as any of the poets or painters who have arrayed the world in a dimmer and fainter beauty, imperfectly copied from the richness of their visions.

The night was now his time for the slow progress of re-creating the one idea to which all his intellectual activity referred itself. Always at the approach of dusk he stole into the town, locked himself within his shop, and wrought with patient delicacy of touch for many hours. Sometimes he was startled by the rap of the watchman, who, when all the world should be asleep, had caught the gleam of lamplight through the crevices of Owen Warland's shutters. Daylight, to the morbid sensibility of his mind, seemed to have an intrusiveness that interfered with his pursuits. On cloudy and inclement days, therefore, he sat with his head upon his hands, muffling, as it were, his sensitive brain in a mist of indefinite musings, for it was a relief to escape from the sharp distinctness with which he was compelled to shape out his thoughts during his nightly toil.

From one of these fits of torpor he was aroused by the entrance of Annie Hovenden, who came into the shop with the freedom of a customer, and also with something of the familiarity of a childish friend. She had worn a hole through her silver thimble, and wanted Owen to repair it.

"But I don't know whether you will condescend to such a task," said she, laughing, "now that you are so taken up with the notion of putting spirit into machinery."

"Where did you get that idea, Annie?" said Owen, starting in surprise.

"Oh, out of my own head," answered she, "and from something that I heard you say, long ago, when you were but a boy and I a little child. But come, will you mend this poor thimble of mine?"

"Anything for your sake, Annie," said Owen Warland, – "anything, even were it to work at Robert Danforth's forge."

"And that would be a pretty sight!" retorted Annie, glancing with imperceptible slightness at the artist's small and slender frame. "Well; here is the thimble."

"But that is a strange idea of yours," said Owen, "about the spiritualization of matter."

And then the thought stole into his mind that this young girl possessed the gift to comprehend him better than all the world besides. And what a help and strength would it be to him in his lonely toil if he could gain the sympathy of the only being whom he loved! To persons whose pursuits are insulated from the common business of life – who are either in advance of mankind or apart from it – there often comes a sensation of moral cold that makes the spirit shiver as if it had reached the frozen solitudes around the pole. What the prophet, the poet, the reformer, the criminal, or any other man with human yearnings, but separated from the multitude by a peculiar lot, might feel, poor Owen felt.

"Annie," cried he, growing pale as death at the thought, "how gladly would I tell you the secret of my pursuit! You, methinks, would estimate it rightly. You, I know, would hear it with a reverence that I must not expect from the harsh, material world."

"Would I not? To be sure I would!" replied Annie Hovenden, lightly laughing. "Come; explain to me quickly what is the meaning of this little whirligig, so delicately wrought that it might be a plaything for Queen Mab. See! I will put it in motion."

"Hold!" exclaimed Owen, "Hold!"

Annie had but given the slightest possible touch, with the point of a needle, to the same minute portion of complicated machinery which has been more than once mentioned, when the artist seized her by the wrist with a force that made her scream aloud. She was affrighted at the convulsion of intense rage and anguish that writhed across his features. The next instant he let his head sink upon his hands.

"Go, Annie," murmured he; "I have deceived myself, and must suffer for it. I yearned for sympathy, and thought, and fancied, and dreamed that you might give it me; but you lack the talisman, Annie, that should admit you into my secrets. That touch has undone the toil of months and the thought of a lifetime! It was not your fault, Annie; but you have ruined me!"

Poor Owen Warland! He had indeed erred, yet pardonably; for if any human spirit could have sufficiently reverenced the processes so sacred in his eyes, it must have been a woman's. Even Annie Hovenden, possibly might not have disappointed him had she been enlightened by the deep intelligence of love.

The artist spent the ensuing winter in a way that satisfied any persons who had hitherto retained a hopeful opinion of him that he was, in truth, irrevocably doomed to unutility as regarded the world, and to an evil destiny on his own part. The decease of a relative had put him in possession of a small inheritance. Thus freed from the necessity of toil, and having lost the steadfast influence of a great purpose, – great, at least, to him, – he abandoned himself to habits from which it might have been supposed the mere delicacy of his organization would have availed to secure him. But when the ethereal portion of a man of genius is obscured the earthly part assumes an influence the more uncontrollable, because the character is now thrown off the balance to which

Providence had so nicely adjusted it, and which, in coarser natures, is adjusted by some other method. Owen Warland made proof of whatever show of bliss may be found in riot. He looked at the world through the golden medium of wine, and contemplated the visions that bubble up so gayly around the brim of the glass, and that people the air with shapes of pleasant madness, which so soon grow ghostly and forlorn. Even when this dismal and inevitable change had taken place, the young man might still have continued to quaff the cup of enchantments, though its vapor did but shroud life in gloom and fill the gloom with spectres that mocked at him. There was a certain irksomeness of spirit, which, being real, and the deepest sensation of which the artist was now conscious, was more intolerable than any fantastic miseries and horrors that the abuse of wine could summon up. In the latter case he could remember, even out of the midst of his trouble, that all was but a delusion; in the former, the heavy anguish was his actual life.

From this perilous state he was redeemed by an incident which more than one person witnessed, but of which the shrewdest could not explain or conjecture the operation on Owen Warland's mind. It was very simple. On a warm afternoon of spring, as the artist sat among his riotous companions with a glass of wine before him, a splendid butterfly flew in at the open window and fluttered about his head.

"Ah," exclaimed Owen, who had drank freely, "are you alive again, child of the sun and playmate of the summer breeze, after your dismal winter's nap? Then it is time for me to be at work!"

And, leaving his unemptied glass upon the table, he departed and was never known to sip another drop of wine.

And now, again, he resumed his wanderings in the woods and fields. It might be fancied that the bright butterfly, which had come so spirit-like into the window as Owen sat with the rude revellers, was indeed a spirit commissioned to recall him to the pure, ideal life that had so etheralized him among men. It might be fancied that he went forth to seek this spirit in its sunny haunts; for still, as in the summer time gone by, he was seen to steal gently up wherever a butterfly had alighted, and lose himself in contemplation of it. When it took flight his eyes followed the winged vision, as if its airy track would show the path to heaven. But what could be the purpose of the unseasonable toil, which was again resumed, as the watchman knew by the lines of lamplight through the crevices of Owen Warland's shutters? The towns-people had one comprehensive explanation of all these singularities. Owen Warland had gone mad! How universally efficacious – how satisfactory, too, and soothing to the injured sensibility of narrowness and dulness – is this easy method of accounting for whatever lies beyond the world's most ordinary scope! From St. Paul's days down to our poor little Artist of the Beautiful, the same talisman had been applied to the elucidation of all mysteries in the words or deeds of men who spoke or acted too wisely or too well. In Owen Warland's case the judgment of his towns-people may have been correct. Perhaps he was mad. The lack of sympathy – that contrast between himself and his neighbors which took away the restraint of example – was enough to make him so. Or possibly he had caught just so much of ethereal radiance as served to bewilder him, in an earthly sense, by its intermixture with the common daylight.

One evening, when the artist had returned from a customary ramble and had just thrown the lustre of his lamp on the delicate piece of work so often interrupted, but still taken up again, as if his fate were embodied in its mechanism, he was surprised by the entrance of old Peter Hovenden. Owen never met this man without a shrinking of the heart. Of all the world he was most terrible, by reason of a keen understanding which saw so distinctly what it did see, and disbelieved so uncompromisingly in what it could not see. On this occasion the old watchmaker had merely a gracious word or two to say.

"Owen, my lad," said he, "we must see you at my house tomorrow night."

The artist began to mutter some excuse.

"Oh, but it must be so," quoth Peter Hovenden, "for the sake of the days when you were one of the household. What, my boy! don't you know that my daughter Annie is engaged to Robert Danforth? We are making an entertainment, in our humble way, to celebrate the event."

That little monosyllable was all he uttered; its tone seemed cold and unconcerned to an ear like Peter Hovenden's; and yet there was in it the stifled outcry of the poor artist's heart, which he compressed within him like a man holding down an evil spirit. One slight outbreak, however, imperceptible to the old watchmaker, he allowed himself. Raising the instrument with which he was about to begin his work, he let it fall upon the little system of machinery that had, anew, cost him months of thought and toil. It was shattered by the stroke!

Owen Warland's story would have been no tolerable representation of the troubled life of those who strive to create the beautiful, if, amid all other thwarting influences, love had not interposed to steal the cunning from his hand. Outwardly he had been no ardent or enterprising lover; the career of his passion had confined its tumults and vicissitudes so entirely within the artist's imagination that Annie herself had scarcely more than a woman's intuitive perception of it; but, in Owen's view, it covered the whole field of his life. Forgetful of the time when she had shown herself incapable of any deep response, he had persisted in connecting all his dreams of artistical success with Annie's image; she was the visible shape in which the spiritual power that he worshipped, and on whose altar he hoped to lay a not unworthy offering, was made manifest to him. Of course he had deceived himself; there were no such attributes in Annie Hovenden as his imagination had endowed her with. She, in the aspect which she wore to his inward vision, was as much a creature of his own as the mysterious piece of mechanism would be were it ever realized. Had he become convinced of his mistake through the medium of successful love, – had he won Annie to his bosom, and there beheld her fade from angel into ordinary woman, – the disappointment might have driven him back, with concentrated energy, upon his sole remaining object. On the other hand, had he found Annie what he fancied, his lot would have been so rich in beauty that out of its mere redundancy he might have wrought the beautiful into many a worthier type than he had toiled for; but the guise in which his sorrow came to him, the sense that the angel of his life had been snatched away and given to a rude man of earth and iron, who could neither need nor appreciate her ministrations, – this was the very perversity of fate that makes human existence appear too absurd and contradictory to be the scene of one other hope or one other fear. There was nothing left for Owen Warland but to sit down like a man that had been stunned.

He went through a fit of illness. After his recovery his small and slender frame assumed an obtuser garniture of flesh than it had ever before worn. His thin cheeks became round; his delicate little hand, so spiritually fashioned to achieve fairy task-work, grew plumper than the hand of a thriving infant. His aspect had a childishness such as might have induced a stranger to pat him on the head – pausing, however, in the act, to wonder what manner of child was here. It was as if the spirit had gone out of him, leaving the body to flourish in a sort of vegetable existence. Not that Owen Warland was idiotic. He could talk, and not irrationally. Somewhat of a babbler, indeed, did people begin to think him; for he was apt to discourse at wearisome length of marvels of mechanism that he had read about in books, but which he had learned to consider as absolutely fabulous. Among them he enumerated the Man of Brass, constructed by Albertus Magnus, and the Brazen Head of Friar Bacon; and, coming down to later times, the automata of a little coach and horses, which it was pretended had been manufactured for the Dauphin of France; together with an insect that buzzed about the ear like a living fly, and yet was but a contrivance of minute steel springs. There was a story, too, of a duck that waddled, and quacked, and ate; though, had any honest citizen purchased it for dinner, he would have found himself cheated with the mere mechanical apparition of a duck.

"But all these accounts," said Owen Warland, "I am now satisfied are mere impositions."

Then, in a mysterious way, he would confess that he once thought differently. In his idle and dreamy days he had considered it possible, in a certain sense, to spiritualize machinery, and to combine with the new species of life and motion thus produced a beauty that should attain to the ideal which Nature has proposed to herself in all her creatures, but has never taken pains to realize. He seemed, however, to retain no very distinct perception either of the process of achieving this object or of the design itself.

"I have thrown it all aside now," he would say. "It was a dream such as young men are always mystifying themselves with. Now that I have acquired a little common sense, it makes me laugh to think of it."

Poor, poor and fallen Owen Warland! These were the symptoms that he had ceased to be an inhabitant of the better sphere that lies unseen around us. He had lost his faith in the invisible, and now prided himself, as such unfortunates invariably do, in the wisdom which rejected much that even his eye could see, and trusted confidently in nothing but what his hand could touch. This is the calamity of men whose spiritual part dies out of them and leaves the grosser understanding to assimilate them more and more to the things of which alone it can take cognizance; but in Owen Warland the spirit was not dead nor passed away; it only slept.

How it awoke again is not recorded. Perhaps the torpid slumber was broken by a convulsive pain. Perhaps, as in a former instance, the butterfly came and hovered about his head and reinspired him, – as indeed this creature of the sunshine had always a mysterious mission for the artist, – reinspired him with the former purpose of his life. Whether it were pain or happiness that thrilled through his veins, his first impulse was to thank Heaven for rendering him again the being of thought, imagination, and keenest sensibility that he had long ceased to be.

"Now for my task," said he. "Never did I feel such strength for it as now."

Yet, strong as he felt himself, he was incited to toil the more diligently by an anxiety lest death should surprise him in the midst of his labors. This anxiety, perhaps, is common to all men who set their hearts upon anything so high, in their own view of it, that life becomes of importance only as conditional to its accomplishment. So long as we love life for itself, we seldom dread the losing it. When we desire life for the attainment of an object, we recognize the frailty of its texture. But, side by side with this sense of insecurity, there is a vital faith in our invulnerability to the shaft of death while engaged in any task that seems assigned by Providence as our proper thing to do, and which the world would have cause to mourn for should we leave it unaccomplished. Can the philosopher, big with the inspiration of an idea that is to reform mankind, believe that he is to be beckoned from this sensible existence at the very instant when he is mustering his breath to speak the word of light? Should he perish so, the weary ages may pass away – the world's, whose life sand may fall, drop by drop – before another intellect is prepared to develop the truth that might have been uttered then. But history affords many an example where the most precious spirit, at any particular epoch manifested in human shape, has gone hence untimely, without space allowed him, so far as mortal judgment could discern, to perform his mission on the earth. The prophet dies, and the man of torpid heart and sluggish brain lives on. The poet leaves his song half sung, or finishes it, beyond the scope of mortal ears, in a celestial choir. The painter – as Allston did – leaves half his conception on the canvas to sadden us with its imperfect beauty, and goes to picture forth the whole, if it be no irreverence to say so, in the hues of heaven. But rather such incomplete designs of this life will be perfected nowhere. This so frequent abortion of man's dearest projects must be taken as a proof that the deeds of earth, however etherealized by piety or genius, are without value, except as exercises and manifestations of the spirit. In heaven, all ordinary thought is higher and more melodious than Milton's song. Then, would he add another verse to any strain that he had left unfinished here?

But to return to Owen Warland. It was his fortune, good or ill, to achieve the purpose of his life. Pass we over a long space of intense thought, yearning effort, minute toil, and wasting anxiety, succeeded by an instant of solitary triumph: let all this be imagined; and then behold the artist, on a winter evening, seeking admittance to Robert Danforth's fireside circle. There he found the man of iron, with his massive substance thoroughly warmed and attempered by domestic influences. And there was Annie, too, now transformed into a matron, with much of her husband's plain and sturdy nature, but imbued, as Owen Warland still believed, with a finer grace, that might enable her to be the interpreter between strength and beauty. It happened, likewise, that old Peter Hovenden was a guest this evening at his daughter's fireside, and it was his well-remembered expression of keen, cold criticism that first encountered the artist's glance.

"My old friend Owen!" cried Robert Danforth, starting up, and compressing the artist's delicate fingers within a hand that was accustomed to gripe bars of iron. "This is kind and neighborly to come to us at last. I was afraid your perpetual motion had bewitched you out of the remembrance of old times."

"We are glad to see you," said Annie, while a blush reddened her matronly cheek. "It was not like a friend to stay from us so long."

"Well, Owen," inquired the old watchmaker, as his first greeting, "how comes on the beautiful? Have you created it at last?"

The artist did not immediately reply, being startled by the apparition of a young child of strength that was tumbling about on the carpet, – a little personage who had come mysteriously out of the infinite, but with something so sturdy and real in his composition that he seemed moulded out of the densest substance which earth could supply. This hopeful infant crawled towards the new-comer, and setting himself on end, as Robert Danforth expressed the posture, stared at Owen with a look of such sagacious observation that the mother could not help exchanging a proud glance with her husband. But the artist was disturbed by the child's look, as imagining a resemblance between it and Peter Hovenden's habitual expression. He could have fancied that the old watchmaker was compressed into this baby shape, and looking out of those baby eyes, and repeating, as he now did, the malicious question: "The beautiful, Owen! How comes on the beautiful? Have you succeeded in creating the beautiful?"

"I have succeeded," replied the artist, with a momentary light of triumph in his eyes and a smile of sunshine, yet steeped in such depth of thought that it was almost sadness. "Yes, my friends, it is the truth. I have succeeded."

"Indeed!" cried Annie, a look of maiden mirthfulness peeping out of her face again. "And is it lawful, now, to inquire what the secret is?"

"Surely; it is to disclose it that I have come," answered Owen Warland. "You shall know, and see, and touch, and possess the secret! For, Annie, – if by that name I may still address the friend of my boyish years, – Annie, it is for your bridal gift that I have wrought this spiritualized mechanism, this harmony of motion, this mystery of beauty. It comes late, indeed; but it is as we go onward in life, when objects begin to lose their freshness of hue and our souls their delicacy of perception, that the spirit of beauty is most needed. If, – forgive me, Annie, – if you know how – to value this gift, it can never come too late."

He produced, as he spoke, what seemed a jewel box. It was carved richly out of ebony by his own hand, and inlaid with a fanciful tracery of pearl, representing a boy in pursuit of a butterfly, which, elsewhere, had become a winged spirit, and was flying heavenward; while the boy, or youth, had found such efficacy in his strong desire that he ascended from earth to cloud, and from cloud to celestial atmosphere, to win the beautiful. This case of ebony the artist opened, and bade Annie place her fingers on its edge. She did so, but almost screamed as a butterfly fluttered forth, and, alighting on her finger's tip, sat waving the ample magnificence of its purple and gold-speckled wings, as if in prelude to a flight. It is impossible to express by words the glory, the splendor, the delicate gorgeousness which were softened into the beauty of this object. Nature's ideal butterfly was here realized in all its perfection; not in the pattern of such faded insects as flit among earthly flowers, but of those which hover across the meads of paradise for child-angels and the spirits of departed infants to disport themselves with. The rich down was visible upon its wings; the lustre of its eyes seemed instinct with spirit. The firelight glimmered around this wonder – the candles gleamed upon it; but it glistened apparently by its own radiance, and illuminated the finger and outstretched hand on which it rested with a white gleam like that of precious stones. In its perfect beauty, the consideration of size was entirely lost. Had its wings overreached the firmament, the mind could not have been more filled or satisfied.

"Beautiful! Beautiful!" exclaimed Annie. "Is it alive? Is it alive?"

"Alive? To be sure it is," answered her husband. "Do you suppose any mortal has skill enough to make a butterfly, or would put himself to the trouble of making one, when any child may catch a score of them in a summer's afternoon? Alive? Certainly! But this pretty box is undoubtedly of our friend Owen's manufacture; and really it does him credit."

At this moment the butterfly waved its wings anew, with a motion so absolutely lifelike that Annie was startled, and even awestricken; for, in spite of her husband's opinion, she could not satisfy herself whether it was indeed a living creature or a piece of wondrous mechanism.

"Is it alive?" she repeated, more earnestly than before.

"Judge for yourself," said Owen Warland, who stood gazing in her face with fixed attention.

The butterfly now flung itself upon the air, fluttered round Annie's head, and soared into a distant region of the parlor, still making itself perceptible to sight by the starry gleam in which the motion of its wings enveloped it. The infant on the floor followed its course with his sagacious little eyes. After flying about the room, it returned in a spiral curve and settled again on Annie's finger.

"But is it alive?" exclaimed she again; and the finger on which the gorgeous mystery had alighted was so tremulous that the butterfly was forced to balance himself with his wings. "Tell me if it be alive, or whether you created it."

"Wherefore ask who created it, so it be beautiful?" replied Owen Warland. "Alive? Yes, Annie; it may well be said to possess life, for it has absorbed my own being into itself; and in the secret of that butterfly, and in its beauty, – which is not merely outward, but deep as its whole system, – is represented the intellect, the imagination, the sensibility, the soul of an Artist of the Beautiful! Yes; I created it. But" – and here his countenance somewhat changed – "this butterfly is not now to me what it was when I beheld it afar off in the daydreams of my youth."

"Be it what it may, it is a pretty plaything," said the blacksmith, grinning with childlike delight. "I wonder whether it would condescend to alight on such a great clumsy finger as mine? Hold it hither, Annie."

By the artist's direction, Annie touched her finger's tip to that of her husband; and, after a momentary delay, the butterfly fluttered from one to the other. It preluded a second flight by a similar, yet not precisely the same, waving of wings as in the first experiment; then, ascending from the blacksmith's stalwart finger, it rose in a gradually enlarging curve to the ceiling, made one wide sweep around the room, and returned with an undulating movement to the point whence it had started.

"Well, that does beat all nature!" cried Robert Danforth, bestowing the heartiest praise that he could find expression for; and, indeed, had he paused there, a man of finer words and nicer perception could not easily have said more. "That goes beyond me, I confess. But what then? There is more real use in one downright blow of my sledge hammer than in the whole five years' labor that our friend Owen has wasted on this butterfly."

Here the child clapped his hands and made a great babble of indistinct utterance, apparently demanding that the butterfly should be given him for a plaything.

Owen Warland, meanwhile, glanced sidelong at Annie, to discover whether she sympathized in her husband's estimate of the comparative value of the beautiful and the practical. There was, amid all her kindness towards himself, amid all the wonder and admiration with which she contemplated the marvellous work of his hands and incarnation of his idea, a secret scorn – too secret, perhaps, for her own consciousness, and perceptible only to such intuitive discernment as that of the artist. But Owen, in the latter stages of his pursuit, had risen out of the region in which such a discovery might have been torture. He knew that the world, and Annie as the representative of the world, whatever praise might be bestowed, could never say the fitting word nor feel the fitting sentiment which should be the perfect recompense of an artist who, symbolizing a lofty moral by a material trifle, – converting what was earthly to spiritual gold, – had won the beautiful into his handiwork. Not at this latest moment was he to learn that the reward of all high performance must be sought within itself, or sought in vain. There was, however, a view of the matter which Annie and her husband, and even Peter Hovenden, might fully have understood, and which would have satisfied them that the toil of years had here been worthily bestowed. Owen Warland might have told them that this butterfly, this plaything, this bridal gift of a poor watchmaker to a blacksmith's wife, was, in truth, a gem of art that a monarch would have purchased with honors and abundant wealth, and have treasured it among the jewels of his kingdom as the most unique and wondrous of them all. But the artist smiled and kept the secret to himself.

"Father," said Annie, thinking that a word of praise from the old watchmaker might gratify his former apprentice, "do come and admire this pretty butterfly."

"Let us see," said Peter Hovenden, rising from his chair, with a sneer upon his face that always made people doubt, as he himself did, in everything but a material existence. "Here is my finger for it to alight upon. I shall understand it better when once I have touched it."

But, to the increased astonishment of Annie, when the tip of her father's finger was pressed against that of her husband, on which the butterfly still rested, the insect drooped its wings and seemed on the point of falling to the floor. Even the bright spots of gold upon its wings and body, unless her eyes deceived her, grew dim, and the glowing purple took a dusky hue, and the starry lustre that gleamed around the blacksmith's hand became faint and vanished.

"It is dying! It is dying!" cried Annie, in alarm.

"It has been delicately wrought," said the artist, calmly. "As I told you, it has imbibed a spiritual essence – call it magnetism, or what you will. In an atmosphere of doubt and mockery its exquisite susceptibility suffers torture, as does the soul of him who instilled his own life into it. It has already lost its beauty; in a few moments more its mechanism would be irreparably injured."

"Take away your hand, father!" entreated Annie, turning pale. "Here is my child; let it rest on his innocent hand. There, perhaps, its life will revive and its colors grow brighter than ever."

Her father, with an acrid smile, withdrew his finger. The butterfly then appeared to recover the power of voluntary motion, while its hues assumed much of their original lustre, and the gleam of starlight, which was its most ethereal attribute, again formed a halo round about it. At first, when transferred from Robert Danforth's hand to the small finger of the child, this radiance grew so powerful that it positively threw the little fellow's shadow back against the wall. He, meanwhile, extended his plump hand as he had seen his father and mother do, and watched the waving of the insect's wings with infantine delight. Nevertheless, there was a certain odd expression of sagacity that made Owen Warland feel as if here were old Pete Hovenden, partially, and but partially, redeemed from his hard scepticism into childish faith.

"How wise the little monkey looks!" whispered Robert Danforth to his wife.

"I never saw such a look on a child's face," answered Annie, admiring her own infant, and with good reason, far more than the artistic butterfly. "The darling knows more of the mystery than we do."

As if the butterfly, like the artist, were conscious of something not entirely congenial in the child's nature, it alternately sparkled and grew dim. At length it arose from the small hand of the infant with an airy motion that seemed to bear it upward without an effort, as if the ethereal instincts with which its master's spirit had endowed it impelled this fair vision involuntarily to a higher sphere. Had there been no obstruction, it might have soared into the sky and grown immortal. But its lustre gleamed upon the ceiling; the exquisite texture of its wings brushed against that earthly medium; and a sparkle or two, as of stardust, floated downward and lay glimmering on the carpet. Then the butterfly came fluttering down, and, instead of returning to the infant, was apparently attracted towards the artist's hand.

"Not so! Not so!" murmured Owen Warland, as if his handiwork could have understood him. "Thou has gone forth out of thy master's heart. There is no return for thee."

With a wavering movement, and emitting a tremulous radiance, the butterfly struggled, as it were, towards the infant, and was about to alight upon his finger; but while it still hovered in the air, the little child of strength, with his grandsire's sharp and shrewd expression in his face, made a snatch at the marvellous insect and compressed it in his hand. Annie screamed. Old Peter Hovenden burst into a cold and scornful laugh. The blacksmith, by main force, unclosed the infant's hand, and found within the palm a small heap of glittering fragments, whence the mystery of beauty had fled forever.

And as for Owen Warland, he looked placidly at what seemed the ruin of his life's labor, and which was yet no ruin. He had caught a far other butterfly than this. When the artist rose high enough to achieve the beautiful, the symbol by which he made it perceptible to mortal senses became of little value in his eyes while his spirit possessed itself in the enjoyment of the reality.

P.'s Correspondence

Nathaniel Hawthorne

MY UNFORTUNATE FRIEND P. has lost the thread of his life by the interposition of long intervals of partially disordered reason. The past and present are jumbled together in his mind in a manner often productive of curious results, and which will be better understood after the perusal of the following letter than from any description that I could give. The poor fellow, without once stirring from the little whitewashed, iron-grated room to which he alludes in his first paragraph, is nevertheless a great traveller, and meets in his wanderings a variety of personages who have long ceased to be visible to any eye save his own. In my opinion, all this is not so much a delusion as a partly wilful and partly involuntary sport of the imagination, to which his disease has imparted such morbid energy that he beholds these spectral scenes and characters with no less distinctness than a play upon the stage, and with somewhat more of illusive credence. Many of his letters are in my possession, some based upon the same vagary as the present one, and others upon hypotheses not a whit short of it in absurdity. The whole form a series of correspondence, which, should fate seasonably remove my poor friend from what is to him a world of moonshine, I promise myself a pious pleasure in editing for the public eye. P. had always a hankering after literary reputation, and has made more than one unsuccessful effort to achieve it. It would not be a little odd, if, after missing his object while seeking it by the light of reason, he should prove to have stumbled upon it in his misty excursions beyond the limits of sanity.

London, February 29, 1845

My Dear Friend: Old associations cling to the mind with astonishing tenacity. Daily custom grows up about us like a stone wall, and consolidates itself into almost as material an entity as mankind's strongest architecture. It is sometimes a serious question with me whether ideas be not really visible and tangible, and endowed with all the other qualities of matter. Sitting as I do at this moment in my hired apartment, writing beside the hearth, over which hangs a print of Queen Victoria, listening to the muffled roar of the world's metropolis, and with a window at but five paces distant, through which, whenever I please, I can gaze out on actual London, – with all this positive certainty as to my whereabouts, what kind of notion, do you think, is just now perplexing my brain? Why, – would you believe it? – that all this time I am still an inhabitant of that wearisome little chamber, – that whitewashed little chamber, – that little chamber with its one small window, across which, from some inscrutable reason of taste or convenience, my landlord had placed a row of iron bars, – that same little chamber, in short, whither your kindness has so often brought you to visit me! Will no length of time or breadth of space enfranchise me from that unlovely abode? I travel; but it seems to be like the snail, with my house upon my head. Ah, well! I am verging, I suppose, on that period of life when present scenes and events make but feeble impressions in comparison with those of yore; so that I must reconcile myself to be more and more the prisoner of Memory, who merely lets me hop about a little with her chain around my leg.

My letters of introduction have been of the utmost service, enabling me to make the acquaintance of several distinguished characters who, until now, have seemed as remote from the sphere of my personal intercourse as the wits of Queen Anne's time or Ben Jenson's compotators at the Mermaid. One of the first of which I availed myself was the letter to Lord Byron. I found his lordship looking much older than I had anticipated, although, considering his former irregularities of life and the various wear and tear of his constitution, not older than a man on the verge of sixty reasonably may look. But I had invested his earthly frame, in my imagination, with the poet's spiritual immortality. He wears a brown wig, very luxuriantly curled, and extending down over his forehead. The expression of his eyes is concealed by spectacles. His early tendency to obesity having increased, Lord Byron is now enormously fat, – so fat as to give the impression of a person quite overladen with his own flesh, and without sufficient vigor to diffuse his personal life through the great mass of corporeal substance which weighs upon him so cruelly. You gaze at the mortal heap; and, while it fills your eye with what purports to be Byron, you murmur within yourself, "For Heaven's sake, where is he?" Were I disposed to be caustic, I might consider this mass of earthly matter as the symbol, in a material shape, of those evil habits and carnal vices which unspiritualize man's nature and clog up his avenues of communication with the better life. But this would be too harsh; and, besides, Lord Byron's morals have been improving while his outward man has swollen to such unconscionable circumference. Would that he were leaner; for, though he did me the honor to present his hand, yet it was so puffed out with alien substance that I could not feel as if I had touched the hand that wrote Childe Harold.

On my entrance his lordship apologized for not rising to receive me, on the sufficient plea that the gout for several years past had taken up its constant residence in his right foot, which accordingly was swathed in many rolls of flannel and deposited upon a cushion. The other foot was hidden in the drapery of his chair. Do you recollect whether Byron's right or left foot was the deformed one.

The noble poet's reconciliation with Lady Byron is now, as you are aware, of ten years' standing; nor does it exhibit, I am assured, any symptom of breach or fracture. They are said to be, if not a happy, at least a contented, or at all events a quiet couple, descending the slope of life with that tolerable degree of mutual support which will enable them to come easily and comfortably to the bottom. It is pleasant to reflect how entirely the poet has redeemed his youthful errors in this particular. Her ladyship's influence, it rejoices me to add, has been productive of the happiest results upon Lord Byron in a religious point of view. He now combines the most rigid tenets of Methodism with the ultra doctrines of the Puseyites; the former being perhaps due to the convictions wrought upon his mind by his noble consort, while the latter are the embroidery and picturesque illumination demanded by his imaginative character. Much of whatever expenditure his increasing habits of thrift continue to allow him is bestowed in the reparation or beautifying of places of worship; and this nobleman, whose name was once considered a synonym of the foul fiend, is now all but canonized as a saint in many pulpits of the metropolis and elsewhere. In politics, Lord Byron is an uncompromising conservative, and loses no opportunity, whether in the House of Lords or in private circles, of denouncing and repudiating the mischievous and anarchical notions of his earlier day. Nor does he fail to visit similar sins in other people with the sincerest vengeance which his somewhat blunted pen is capable of inflicting. Southey and he are on the most intimate terms. You are aware that, some little time before the death of Moore, Byron caused that brilliant but reprehensible man to be evicted from his house. Moore took the insult so much to heart that, it is said to have been one great cause of the fit of illness which brought him to the grave. Others pretend that the lyrist died in a very happy state of mind, singing one of his own sacred melodies, and expressing his belief that it would be heard within the gate of paradise, and gain him instant and honorable admittance. I wish he may have found it so.

I failed not, as you may suppose, in the course of conversation with Lord Byron, to pay the weed of homage due to a mighty poet, by allusions to passages in Childe Harold, and Manfred, and Don Juan, which have made so large a portion of the music of my life. My words, whether apt or otherwise, were at least warm with the enthusiasm of one worthy to discourse of immortal poesy. It was evident, however, that they did not go precisely to the right spot. I could perceive that there was some mistake or other, and was not a little angry with myself, and ashamed of my abortive attempt to throw back, from my own heart to the gifted author's ear, the echo of those strains that have resounded throughout the world. But by and by the secret peeped quietly out. Byron, – I have the information from his own lips, so that you need not hesitate to repeat it in literary circles, – Byron is preparing a new edition of his complete works, carefully corrected, expurgated, and amended, in accordance with his present creed of taste, morals, politics, and religion. It so happened that the very passages of highest inspiration to which I had alluded were among the condemned and rejected rubbish which it is his purpose to cast into the gulf of oblivion. To whisper you the truth, it appears to me that his passions having burned out, the extinction of their vivid and riotous flame has deprived Lord Byron of the illumination by which he not merely wrote, but was enabled to feel and comprehend what he had written. Positively he no longer understands his own poetry.

This became very apparent on his favoring me so far as to read a few specimens of Don Juan in the moralized version. Whatever is licentious, whatever disrespectful to the sacred mysteries of our faith, whatever morbidly melancholic or splenetically sportive, whatever assails settled constitutions of government or systems of society, whatever could wound the sensibility of any mortal, except a pagan, a republican, or a dissenter, has been unrelentingly blotted out, and its place supplied by unexceptionable verses in his lordship's later style. You may judge how much of the poem remains as hitherto published. The result is not so good as might be wished; in plain terms, it is a very sad affair indeed; for, though the torches kindled in Tophet have been extinguished, they leave an abominably ill odor, and are succeeded by no glimpses of hallowed fire. It is to be hoped, nevertheless, that this attempt on Lord Byron's part to atone for his youthful errors will at length induce the Dean of Westminster, or whatever churchman is concerned, to allow Thorwaldsen's statue of the poet its due niche in the grand old Abbey. His bones, you know, when brought from Greece, were denied sepulture among those of his tuneful brethren there.

What a vile slip of the pen was that! How absurd in me to talk about burying the bones of Byron, who, I have just seen alive, and encased in a big, round bulk of flesh! But, to say the truth, a prodigiously fat man always impresses me as a kind of hobgoblin; in the very extravagance of his mortal system I find something akin to the immateriality of a ghost. And then that ridiculous old story darted into my mind, how that Byron died of fever at Missolonghi, above twenty years ago. More and more I recognize that we dwell in a world of shadows; and, for my part, I hold it hardly worth the trouble to attempt a distinction between shadows in the mind and shadows out of it. If there be any difference, the former are rather the more substantial.

Only think of my good fortune! The venerable Robert Burns – now, if I mistake not, in his eighty-seventh year – happens to be making a visit to London, as if on purpose to afford me an opportunity of grasping him by the hand. For upwards of twenty years past he has hardly left his quiet cottage in Ayrshire for a single night, and has only been drawn hither now by the irresistible persuasions of all the distinguished men in England. They wish to celebrate the patriarch's birthday by a festival. It will be the greatest literary triumph on record. Pray Heaven the little spirit of life within the aged bard's bosom may not be extinguished in the lustre of that hour! I have already had the honor of an introduction to him at the British Museum, where he was examining a collection of his own unpublished letters, interspersed with songs, which have escaped the notice of all his biographers.

Poh! Nonsense! What am I thinking of? How should Burns have been embalmed in biography when he is still a hearty old man?

The figure of the bard is tall and in the highest degree reverend, nor the less so that it is much bent by the burden of time. His white hair floats like a snowdrift around his face, in which are seen the furrows of intellect and passion, like the channels of headlong torrents that have foamed themselves away. The old gentleman is in excellent preservation, considering his time of life. He has that crickety sort of liveliness, – I mean the cricket's humor of chirping for any cause or none, – which is perhaps the most favorable mood that can befall extreme old age. Our pride forbids us to desire it for ourselves, although we perceive it to be a beneficence of nature in the case of others. I was surprised to find it in Burns. It seems as if his ardent heart and brilliant imagination had both burned down to the last embers, leaving only a little flickering flame in one corner, which keeps dancing upward and laughing all by itself. He is no longer capable of pathos. At the request of Allan Cunningham, he attempted to sing his own song to Mary in Heaven; but it was evident that the feeling of those verses, so profoundly true and so simply expressed, was entirely beyond the scope of his present sensibilities; and, when a touch of it did partially awaken him, the tears immediately gushed into his eyes and his voice broke into a tremulous cackle. And yet he but indistinctly knew wherefore he was weeping. Ah, he must not think again of Mary in Heaven until he shake off the dull impediment of time and ascend to meet her there.

Burns then began to repeat Tan O'Shanter; but was so tickled with its wit and humor – of which, however, I suspect he had but a traditionary sense – that he soon burst into a fit of chirruping laughter, succeeded by a cough, which brought this not very agreeable exhibition to a close. On the whole, I would rather not have witnessed it. It is a satisfactory idea, however, that the last forty years of the peasant poet's life have been passed in competence and perfect comfort. Having been cured of his bardic improvidence for many a day past, and grown as attentive to the main chance as a canny Scotsman should be, he is now considered to be quite well off as to pecuniary circumstances. This, I suppose, is worth having lived so long for.

I took occasion to inquire of some of the countrymen of Burns in regard to the health of Sir Walter Scott. His condition, I am sorry to say, remains the same as for ten years past; it is that of a hopeless paralytic, palsied not more in body than in those nobler attributes of which the body is the instrument. And thus he vegetates from day to day and from year to year at that splendid fantasy of Abbotsford, which grew out of his brain, and became a symbol of the great romancer's tastes, feelings, studies, prejudices, and modes of intellect. Whether in verse, prose, or architecture, he could achieve but one thing, although that one in infinite variety. There he reclines, on a couch in his library, and is said to spend whole hours of every day in dictating tales to an amanuensis, – to an imaginary amanuensis; for it is not deemed worth any one's trouble now to take down what flows from that once brilliant fancy, every image of which was formerly worth gold and capable of being coined. Yet Cunningham, who has lately seen him, assures me that there is now and then a touch of the genius, – a striking combination of incident, or a picturesque trait of character, such as no other man alive could have hit off, – a glimmer from that ruined mind, as if the sun had suddenly flashed on a half-rusted helmet in the gloom of an ancient hall. But the plots of these romances become inextricably confused; the characters melt into one another; and the tale loses itself like the course of a stream flowing through muddy and marshy ground.

For my part, I can hardly regret that Sir Walter Scott had lost his consciousness of outward things before his works went out of vogue. It was good that he should forget his fame rather than that fame should first have forgotten him. Were he still a writer, and as brilliant a one as ever, he could no longer maintain anything like the same position in literature. The world, nowadays, requires a more earnest purpose, a deeper moral, and a closer and homelier truth than he was qualified to supply it with. Yet who can be to the present generation even what Scott has been to the past? I had expectations from a young man, – one Dickens, – who published a few magazine articles, very rich in humor, and not without symptoms of genuine pathos; but the poor fellow died shortly after commencing an odd series of sketches, entitled, I think, the Pickwick Papers. Not impossibly the world has lost more than it dreams of by the untimely death of this Mr. Dickens.

Whom do you think I met in Pall Mall the other day? You would not hit it in ten guesses. Why, no less a man than Napoleon Bonaparte, or all that is now left of him, – that is to say, the skin, bones, and corporeal substance, little cocked hat, green coat, white breeches, and small sword, which are still known by his redoubtable name. He was attended only by two policemen, who walked quietly behind the phantasm of the old ex-emperor, appearing to have no duty in regard to him except to see that none of the light-fingered gentry should possess themselves of thee star of the Legion of Honor. Nobody save myself so much as turned to look after him; nor, it grieves me to confess, could even I contrive to muster up any tolerable interest, even by all that the warlike spirit, formerly manifested within that now decrepit shape, had wrought upon our globe. There is no surer method of annihilating the magic influence of a great renown than by exhibiting the possessor of it in the decline, the overthrow, the utter degradation of his powers, – buried beneath his own mortality, – and lacking even the qualities of sense that enable the most ordinary men to bear themselves decently in the eye of the world. This is the state to which disease, aggravated by long endurance of a tropical climate, and assisted by old age, – for he is now above seventy, – has reduced Bonaparte. The British government has acted shrewdly in re-transporting him from St. Helena to England. They should now restore him to Paris, and there let him once again review the relics of his armies. His eye is dull and rheumy; his nether lip hung down upon his chin. While I was observing him there chanced to be a little extra bustle in the street; and he, the brother of Caesar and Hannibal, – the great captain who had veiled the world in battle-smoke and tracked it round with bloody footsteps, – was seized with a nervous trembling, and claimed the protection of the two policemen by a cracked and dolorous cry. The fellows winked at one another, laughed aside, and, patting Napoleon on the back, took each an arm and led him away.

Death and fury! Ha, villain, how came you hither? Avaunt! or I fling my inkstand at your head. Tush, tush; it is all a mistake. Pray, my dear friend, pardon this little outbreak. The fact is, the mention of those two policemen, and their custody of Bonaparte, had called up the idea of that odious wretch – you remember him well – who was pleased to take such gratuitous and impertinent care of my person before I quitted New England. Forthwith up rose before my mind's eye that same little whitewashed room, with the iron-grated window, – strange that it should have been iron-grated! – where, in too easy compliance with the absurd wishes of my relatives, I have wasted several good years of my life. Positively it seemed to me that I was still sitting there, and that the keeper – not that he ever was my keeper neither, but only a kind of intrusive devil of a body-servant – had just peeped in at the door. The rascal! I owe him an old grudge, and will find a time to pay it yet. Fie! fie! The mere thought of him has exceedingly discomposed me. Even now that hateful chamber – the iron-grated window, which blasted the blessed sunshine as it fell through the dusty panes and made it poison to my soul-looks more distinct to my view than does this my comfortable apartment in the heart of London. The reality – that which I know to be such – hangs like remnants of tattered scenery over the intolerably prominent illusion. Let us think of it no more.

You will be anxious to hear of Shelley. I need not say, what is known to all the world, that this celebrated poet has for many years past been reconciled to the Church of England. In his more recent works he has applied his fine powers to the vindication of the Christian faith, with an especial view to that particular development. Latterly, as you may not have heard, he has taken orders, and been inducted to a small country living in the gift of the Lord Chancellor. Just now, luckily for me, he has come to the metropolis to superintend the publication of a volume of discourses treating of the poetico-philosophical proofs of Christianity on the basis of the Thirty-nine Articles. On my first introduction I felt no little embarrassment as to the manner of combining what I had to say to the author of 'Queen Mali', the 'Revolt of Islam', and 'Prometheus Unbound' with such acknowledgments as might be acceptable to a Christian minister and zealous upholder of the Established Church. But Shelley soon placed me at my ease. Standing where he now does, and reviewing all his successive productions from a higher point, he assures me that there is a harmony, an order, a regular procession, which enables him to lay his hand upon any one of the earlier poems and say, "This is my work," with precisely the same complacency of conscience wherewithal he contemplates the volume of discourses above mentioned. They are like the successive steps of a staircase, the lowest of which, in the depth of chaos, is as essential to the support of the whole as the highest and final one resting upon the threshold of the heavens. I felt half inclined to ask him what would have been his fate had he perished on the lower steps of his staircase, instead of building his way aloft into the celestial brightness.

How all this may be I neither pretend to understand nor greatly care, so long as Shelley has really climbed, as it seems he has, from a lower region to a loftier one. Without touching upon their religious merits, I consider the productions of his maturity superior, as poems, to those of his youth. They are warmer with human love, which has served as an interpreter between his mind and the multitude. The author has learned to dip his pen oftener into his heart, and has thereby avoided the faults into which a too exclusive use of fancy and intellect are wont to betray him. Formerly his page was often little other than a concrete arrangement of crystallizations, or even of icicles, as cold as they were brilliant. Now you take it to your heart, and are conscious of a heart-warmth responsive to your own. In his private character Shelley can hardly have grown more gentle, kind, and affectionate than his friends always represented him to be up to that disastrous night when he was drowned in the Mediterranean. Nonsense, again, – sheer nonsense! What, am I babbling about? I was thinking of that old figment of his being lost in the Bay of Spezzia, and washed ashore near Via Reggio, and burned to ashes on a funeral pyre, with wine, and spices, and frankincense; while Byron stood on the beach and beheld a flame of marvellous beauty rise heavenward from the dead poet's heart, and that his fire-purified relics were finally buried near his child in Roman earth. If all this happened three-and-twenty years ago, how could I have met the drowned and burned and buried man here in London only yesterday?

Before quitting the subject, I may mention that Dr. Reginald Heber, heretofore Bishop of Calcutta, but recently translated to a see in England, called on Shelley while I was with him. They appeared to be on terms of very cordial intimacy, and are said to have a joint poem in contemplation. What a strange, incongruous dream is the life of man!

Coleridge has at last finished his poem of Christabel. It will be issued entire by old John Murray in the course of the present publishing season. The poet, I hear, is visited with a troublesome affection of the tongue, which has put a period, or some lesser stop, to the life-long discourse that has hitherto been flowing from his lips. He will not survive it above a month, unless his accumulation of ideas be sluiced off in some other way. Wordsworth died only a week or two ago. Heaven rest his soul, and grant that he may not have completed 'The Excursion'! Methinks I am sick of everything he wrote, except his 'Laodamia'. It is very sad, this inconstancy of the mind to the poets whom it once worshipped. Southey is as hale as ever, and writes with his usual diligence. Old Gifford is still alive, in the extremity of age, and with most pitiable decay of what little sharp and narrow intellect the Devil had gifted him withal. One hates to allow such a man the privilege of growing old and infirm. It takes away our speculative license of kicking him.

Keats? No; I have not seen him except across a crowded street, with coaches, drays, horsemen, cabs, omnibuses, foot-passengers, and divers other sensual obstructions intervening betwixt his small and slender figure and my eager glance. I would fain have met him on the sea-shore, or beneath a natural arch of forest trees, or the Gothic arch of an old cathedral, or among Grecian ruins, or at a glimmering fireside on the verge of evening, or at the twilight entrance of a cave, into the dreamy depths of which he would have led me by the hand; anywhere, in short, save at Temple Bar, where his presence was blotted out by the porter-swollen bulks of these gross Englishmen. I stood and watched him fading away, fading away along the pavement, and could hardly tell whether he were an actual man or a thought that had slipped out of my mind and clothed itself in human form and habiliments merely to beguile me. At one moment he put his handkerchief to his lips, and withdrew it, I am almost certain, stained with blood. You never saw anything so fragile as his person. The truth is, Keats has all his life felt the effects of that terrible bleeding at the lungs caused by the article on his Endymion in the Quarterly Review, and which so nearly brought him to the grave. Ever since he has glided about the world like a ghost, sighing a melancholy tone in the ear of here and there a friend, but never sending forth his voice to greet the multitude. I can hardly think him a great poet. The burden of a mighty genius would never have been imposed upon shoulders so physically frail and a spirit so infirmly sensitive. Great poets should have iron sinews.

Yet Keats, though for so many years he has given nothing to the world, is understood to have devoted himself to the composition of an epic poem. Some passages of it have been communicated to the inner circle of his admirers, and impressed them as the loftiest strains that have been audible on earth since Milton's days. If I can obtain copies of these specimens, I will ask you to present them to James Russell Lowell, who seems to be one of the poet's most fervent and worthiest worshippers. The information took me by surprise. I had supposed that all Keats's poetic incense, without being embodied in human language, floated up to heaven and mingled with the songs of the immortal choristers, who perhaps were conscious of an unknown voice among them, and thought their melody the sweeter for it. But it is not so; he has positively written a poem on the subject of 'Paradise Regained', though in another sense than that which presented itself to the mind of Milton. In compliance, it may be imagined, with the dogma of those who pretend that all epic possibilities in the past history of the world are exhausted, Keats has thrown his poem forward into an indefinitely remote futurity. He pictures mankind amid the closing circumstances of the time-long warfare between good and evil. Our race is on the eve of its final triumph. Man is within the last stride of perfection; Woman, redeemed from the thraldom against which our sibyl uplifts so powerful and so sad a remonstrance, stands equal by his side or communes for herself with angels; the Earth, sympathizing with her children's happier state, has clothed herself in such luxuriant and loving beauty as no eye ever witnessed since our first parents saw the sun rise over dewy Eden. Nor then indeed; for this is the fulfilment of what was then but a golden promise. But the picture has its shadows. There remains to mankind another peril, – a last encounter with the evil principle. Should the battle go against us, we sink back into the slime and misery of ages. If we triumph – But it demands a poet's eye to contemplate the splendor of such a consummation and not to be dazzled.

To this great work Keats is said to have brought so deep and tender a spirit of humanity that the poem has all the sweet and warm interest of a village tale no less than the grandeur which befits so high a theme. Such, at least, is the perhaps partial representation of his friends; for I have not read or heard even a single line of the performance in question. Keats, I am told, withholds it from the press, under an idea that the age has not enough of spiritual insight to receive it worthily. I do not like this distrust; it makes me distrust the poet. The universe is waiting to respond to the highest word that the best child of time and immortality can utter. If it refuse to listen, it is because he mumbles and stammers, or discourses things unseasonable and foreign to the purpose.

I visited the House of Lords the other day to hear Canning, who, you know, is now a peer, with I forget what title. He disappointed me. Time blunts both point and edge, and does great mischief to men of his order of intellect. Then I stepped into the lower House and listened to a few words from Cobbett, who looked as earthy as a real clodhopper, or rather as if he had lain a dozen years beneath the clods. The men whom I meet nowadays often impress me thus; probably because my spirits are not very good, and lead me to think much about graves, with the long grass upon them, and weather-worn epitaphs, and dry bones of people who made noise enough in their day, but now can only clatter, clatter, clatter, when the sexton's spade disturbs them. Were it only possible to find out who are alive and who dead, it would contribute infinitely to my peace of mind. Every day of my life somebody comes and stares me in the face whom I had quietly blotted out of the tablet of living men, and trusted nevermore to be pestered with the sight or sound of him. For instance, going to Drury Lane Theatre a few evenings since, up rose before me, in the ghost of Hamlet's father, the bodily presence of the elder Kean, who did die, or ought to have died, in some drunken fit or other, so long ago that his fame is scarcely traditionary now. His powers are quite gone; he was rather the ghost of himself than the ghost of the Danish king.

In the stage-box sat several elderly and decrepit people, and among them a stately ruin of a woman on a very large scale, with a profile – for I did not see her front face – that stamped itself into my brain as a seal impresses hot wax. By the tragic gesture with which she took a pinch of snuff, I was sure it must be Mrs. Siddons. Her brother, John Kemble, sat behind, – a broken-down figure, but still with a kingly majesty about him. In lieu of all former achievements, Nature enables him to look the part of Lear far better than in the meridian of his genius. Charles Matthews was likewise there; but a paralytic affection has distorted his once mobile countenance into a most disagreeable one-sidedness, from which he could no more wrench it into proper form than he could rearrange the face of the great globe itself. It looks as if, for the joke's sake, the poor man had twisted his features into an expression at once the most ludicrous and horrible that he could contrive, and at that very moment, as a judgment for making himself so hideous, an avenging Providence had seen fit to petrify him. Since it is out of his own power, I would gladly assist him to change countenance, for his ugly visage haunts me both at noontide and night-time. Some other players of the past generation were present, but none that greatly interested me. It behooves actors, more than all other men of publicity, to vanish from the scene betimes. Being at best but painted shadows flickering on the wall and empty sounds that echo anther's thought, it is a sad disenchantment when the colors begin to fade and the voice to croak with age.

What is there new in the literary way on your side of the water? Nothing of the kind has come under any inspection, except a volume of poems published above a year ago by Dr. Channing. I did not before know that this eminent writer is a poet; nor does the volume alluded to exhibit any of the characteristics of the author's mind as displayed in his prose works; although some of the poems have a richness that is not merely of the surface, but glows still the brighter the deeper and more faithfully you look into then. They seem carelessly wrought, however, like those rings and ornaments of the very purest gold, but of rude, native manufacture, which are found among the gold-dust from Africa. I doubt whether the American public will accept them; it looks less to the assay of metal than to the neat and cunning manufacture. How slowly our literature grows up! Most of our writers of promise have come to untimely ends. There was that wild fellow, John Neal, who almost turned my boyish brain with his romances; he surely has long been dead, else he never could keep himself so quiet. Bryant has gone to his last sleep, with the 'Thanatopsis' gleaming over him like a sculptured marble sepulchre by moonlight. Halleck, who used to write queer verses in the newspapers and published a Don Juanic poem called 'Fanny', is defunct as a poet, though averred to be exemplifying the metempsychosis as a man of business. Somewhat later there was Whittier, a fiery Quaker youth, to whom the muse had perversely assigned a battle-trumpet, and who got himself lynched, ten years agone, in South Carolina. I remember, too, a lad just from college, Longfellow by name, who scattered some delicate verses to the winds, and went to Germany, and perished, I think, of intense application, at the University of Gottingen. Willis – what a pity! – was lost, if I recollect rightly, in 1833, on his voyage to Europe, whither he was going to give us sketches of the world's sunny face. If these had lived, they might, one or all of them, have grown to be famous men.

And yet there is no telling: it may be as well that they have died. I was myself a young man of promise. O shattered brain, O broken spirit, where is the fulfilment of that promise? The sad truth is, that, when fate would gently disappoint the world, it takes away the hopefulest mortals in their youth; when it would laugh the world's hopes to scorn, it lets them live. Let me die upon this apothegm, for I shall never make a truer one.

What a strange substance is the human brain! Or rather, – for there is no need of generalizing the remark, – what an odd brain is mine! Would you believe it? Daily and nightly there come scraps of poetry humming in my intellectual ear – some as airy as bird notes, and some as delicately neat as parlor-music, and a few as grand as organ-peals – that seem just such verses as those departed poets would have written had not an inexorable destiny snatched them from their inkstands. They visit me in spirit, perhaps desiring to engage my services as the amanuensis of their posthumous productions, and thus secure the endless renown that they have forfeited by going hence too early. But I have my own business to attend to; and besides, a medical gentleman, who interests himself in some little ailments of mine, advises me not to make too free use of pen and ink. There are clerks enough out of employment who would be glad of such a job.

Goodbye! Are you alive or dead? And what are you about? Still scribbling for the Democratic? And do those infernal compositors and proof-readers misprint your unfortunate productions as vilely as ever? It is too bad. Let every man manufacture his own nonsense, say I. Expect me home soon, and – to whisper you a secret – in company with the poet Campbell, who purposes to visit Wyoming and enjoy the shadow of the laurels that he planted there. Campbell is now an old man. He calls himself well, better than ever in his life, but looks strangely pale, and so shadow-like that one might almost poke a finger through his densest material. I tell him, by way of joke, that he is as dim and forlorn as Memory, though as unsubstantial as Hope.

Your true friend, P.
P. S. – Pray present my most respectful regards to our venerable and revered friend Mr. Brockden Brown.

It gratifies me to learn that a complete edition of his works, in a double-columned octavo volume, is shortly to issue from the press at Philadelphia. Tell him that no American writer enjoys a more classic reputation on this side of the water. Is old Joel Barlow yet alive? Unconscionable man! Why, he must have nearly fulfilled his century. And does he meditate an epic on the war between Mexico and Texas with machinery contrived on the principle of the steam-engine, as being the nearest to celestial agency that our epoch can boast? How can he expect ever to rise again, if, while just sinking into his grave, he persists in burdening himself with such a ponderosity of leaden verses?

The Sandman

E.T.A. Hoffmann

Nathaniel to Lothaire

CERTAINLY YOU MUST all be uneasy that I have not written for so long – so very long. My mother, I'm sure, is angry, and Clara will believe that I am passing my time in dissipation, entirely forgetful of her fair, angelic image that is so deeply imprinted on my heart. Such, however, is not the case. Daily and hourly I think of you all; and the dear form of my lovely Clara passes before me in my dreams, smiling upon me with her bright eyes as she did when I was among you. But how can I write to you in the distracted mood which has been disturbing my every thought! A horrible thing has crossed my path. Dark forebodings of a cruel, threatening fate tower over me like dark clouds, which no friendly sunbeam can penetrate. I will now tell you what has occurred. I must do so – that I plainly see – the mere thought of it sets me laughing like a madman. Ah, my dear Lothaire, how shall I begin? How shall I make you in any way realize that what happened to me a few days ago can really have had such a fatal effect on my life? If you were here you could see for yourself; but, as it is, you will certainly take me for a crazy fellow who sees ghosts. To be brief, this horrible occurrence, the painful impression of which I am in vain endeavouring to throw off, is nothing more than this – that some days ago, namely on the 30th of October at twelve o'clock noon, a barometer dealer came into my room and offered me his wares. I bought nothing, and threatened to throw him downstairs, upon which he took himself off of his own accord.

Only circumstances of the most peculiar kind, you will suspect, and exerting the greatest influence over my life, can have given any import to this occurrence. Moreover, the person of that unlucky dealer must have had an evil effect upon me. So it was, indeed. I must use every endeavour to collect myself, and patiently and quietly tell you so much of my early youth as will bring the picture plainly and clearly before your eyes. As I am about to begin, I fancy that I hear you laughing, and Clara exclaiming, "Childish stories indeed!" Laugh at me, I beg of you, laugh with all your heart. But, oh God! My hair stands on end, and it is in mad despair that I seem to be inviting your laughter, as Franz Moor did Daniel's in Schiller's play. But to my story.

Excepting at dinner-time I and my brothers and sisters used to see my father very little during the day. He was, perhaps, busily engaged at his ordinary profession. After supper, which was served according to the old custom at seven o'clock, we all went with my mother into my father's study, and seated ourselves at the round table, where he would smoke and drink his large glass of beer. Often he told us wonderful stories, and grew so warm over them that his pipe continually went out. Whereupon I had to light it again with a burning spill, which I thought great sport. Often, too, he would give us picture-books, and sit in his arm-chair, silent and thoughtful, puffing out such thick clouds of smoke that we all seemed to be swimming in the clouds. On such evenings as these my mother was very melancholy, and immediately the clock struck nine she would say: "Now, children, to bed – to bed! The Sandman's coming, I can see." And indeed on each occasion I used to hear something with a heavy, slow step come thudding up the stairs. That I thought must be the Sandman.

Once when the dull noise of footsteps was particularly terrifying I asked my mother as she bore us away: "Mamma, who is this naughty Sandman, who always drives us away from Papa? What does he look like?"

"There is no Sandman, dear child," replied my mother. "When I say the Sandman's coming, I only mean that you're sleepy and can't keep your eyes open – just as if sand had been sprinkled into them."

This answer of my mother's did not satisfy me – nay, the thought soon ripened in my childish mind that she only denied the Sandman's existence to prevent our being terrified of him. Certainly I always heard him coming up the stairs. Most curious to know more of this Sandman and his particular connection with children, I at last asked the old woman who looked after my youngest sister what sort of man he was.

"Eh, Natty," said she, "don't you know that yet? He is a wicked man, who comes to children when they won't go to bed, and throws a handful of sand into their eyes, so that they start out bleeding from their heads. He puts their eyes in a bag and carries them to the crescent moon to feed his own children, who sit in the nest up there. They have crooked beaks like owls so that they can pick up the eyes of naughty human children."

A most frightful picture of the cruel Sandman became impressed upon my mind; so that when in the evening I heard the noise on the stairs I trembled with agony and alarm, and my mother could get nothing out of me but the cry, "The Sandman, the Sandman!" stuttered forth through my tears. I then ran into the bedroom, where the frightful apparition of the Sandman terrified me during the whole night.

I had already grown old enough to realize that the nurse's tale about him and the nest of children in the crescent moon could not be quite true, but nevertheless this Sandman remained a fearful spectre, and I was seized with the utmost horror when I heard him once, not only come up the stairs, but violently force my father's door open and go in. Sometimes he stayed away for a long period, but after that his visits came in close succession. This lasted for years, but I could not accustom myself to the terrible goblin; the image of the dreadful Sandman did not become any fainter. His intercourse with my father began more and more to occupy my fancy. Yet an unconquerable fear prevented me from asking my father about it. But if I, myself, could penetrate the mystery and behold the wondrous Sandman – that was the wish which grew upon me with the years. The Sandman had introduced me to thoughts of the marvels and wonders which so readily gain a hold on a child's mind. I enjoyed nothing better than reading or hearing horrible stories of goblins, witches, pigmies, etc.; but most horrible of all was the Sandman, whom I was always drawing with chalk or charcoal on the tables, cupboards and walls, in the oddest and most frightful shapes.

When I was ten years old my mother removed me from the night nursery into a little chamber situated in a corridor near my father's room. Still, as before, we were obliged to make a speedy departure on the stroke of nine, as soon as the unknown step sounded on the stair. From my little chamber I could hear how he entered my father's room, and then it was that I seemed to detect a thin vapour with a singular odour spreading through the house. Stronger and stronger, with my curiosity, grew my resolution somehow to make the Sandman's acquaintance. Often I sneaked from my room to the corridor when my mother had passed, but never could I discover anything; for the Sandman had always gone in at the door when I reached the place where I might have seen him. At last, driven by an irresistible impulse, I resolved to hide myself in my father's room and await his appearance there.

From my father's silence and my mother's melancholy face I perceived one evening that the Sandman was coming. I, therefore, feigned great weariness, left the room before nine o'clock, and hid myself in a corner close to the door. The house-door groaned and the heavy, slow, creaking step came up the passage and towards the stairs. My mother passed me with the rest of the children. Softly, very softly, I opened the door of my father's room. He was sitting, as usual, stiff end silent, with his back to the door. He did not perceive me, and I swiftly darted into the room and behind the curtain which covered an open cupboard close to the door, in which my father's clothes were hanging. The steps sounded nearer and nearer – there was a strange coughing and scraping and murmuring without. My heart trembled with anxious expectation. A sharp step close, very close, to the door – the quick snap of the latch, and the door opened with a rattling noise. Screwing up my courage to the uttermost, I cautiously peeped out. The Sandman was standing before my father in the middle of the room, the light of the candles shone full upon his face. The Sandman, the fearful Sandman, was the old advocate Coppelius, who had often dined with us.

But the most hideous form could not have inspired me with deeper horror than this very Coppelius. Imagine a large broad-shouldered man, with a head disproportionately big, a face the colour of yellow ochre, a pair of bushy grey eyebrows, from beneath which a pair of green cat's eyes sparkled with the most penetrating lustre, and with a large nose curved over his upper lip. His wry mouth was often twisted into a malicious laugh, when a couple of dark red spots appeared upon his cheeks, and a strange hissing sound was heard through his gritted teeth. Coppelius always appeared in an ashen-grey coat, cut in old-fashioned style, with waistcoat and breeches of the same colour, while his stockings were black, and his shoes adorned with agate buckles.

His little peruke scarcely reached farther than the crown of his head, his curls stood high above his large red ears, and a broad hair-bag projected stiffly from his neck, so that the silver clasp which fastened his folded cravat might be plainly seen. His whole figure was hideous and repulsive, but most disgusting to us children were his coarse brown hairy fists. Indeed we did not like to eat anything he had touched with them. This he had noticed, and it was his delight, under some pretext or other, to touch a piece of cake or some nice fruit, that our kind mother might quietly have put on our plates, just for the pleasure of seeing us turn away with tears in our eyes, in disgust and abhorrence, no longer able to enjoy the treat intended for us. He acted in the same manner on holidays, when my father gave us a little glass of sweet wine. Then would he swiftly put his hand over it, or perhaps even raise the glass to his blue lips, laughing most devilishly, and we could only express our indignation by silent sobs. He always called us the little beasts; we dared not utter a sound when he was present, end we heartily cursed the ugly, unkind man who deliberately marred our slightest pleasures. My mother seemed to hate the repulsive Coppelius as much as we did, since as soon as he showed himself her liveliness, her open and cheerful nature, were changed for a gloomy solemnity. My father behaved towards him as though he were a superior being, whose bad manners were to be tolerated and who was to be kept in good humour at any cost. He need only give the slightest hint, and favourite dishes were cooked, the choicest wines served.

When I now saw this Coppelius, the frightful and terrific thought took possession of my soul, that indeed no one but he could be the Sandman. But the Sandman was no longer the bogy of a nurse's tale, who provided the owl's nest in the crescent moon with children's eyes. No, he was a hideous, spectral monster, who brought with him grief, misery and destruction – temporal and eternal – wherever he appeared.

I was riveted to the spot, as if enchanted. At the risk of being discovered and, as I plainly foresaw, of being severely punished, I remained with my head peeping through the curtain. My father received Coppelius with solemnity.

"Now to our work!" cried the latter in a harsh, grating voice, as he flung off his coat.

My father silently and gloomily drew off his dressing gown, and both attired themselves in long black frocks. Whence they took these I did not see. My father opened the door of what I had always thought to be a cupboard. But I now saw that it was no cupboard, but rather a black cavity in which there was a little fireplace. Coppelius went to it, and a blue flame began to crackle up on the hearth. All sorts of strange utensils lay around. Heavens! As my old father stooped down to the fire, he looked quite another man. Some convulsive pain seemed to have distorted his mild features into a repulsive, diabolical countenance. He looked like Coppelius, whom I saw brandishing red-hot tongs, which he used to take glowing masses out of the thick smoke; which objects he afterwards hammered. I seemed to catch a glimpse of human faces lying around without any eyes – but with deep holes instead.

"Eyes here, eyes!" roared Coppelius tonelessly. Overcome by the wildest terror, I shrieked out and fell from my hiding place upon the floor. Coppelius seized me and, baring his teeth, bleated out, "Ah – little wretch – little wretch!" Then he dragged me up and flung me on the hearth, where the fire began to singe my hair. "Now we have eyes enough – a pretty pair of child's eyes," he whispered, and, taking some red-hot grains out of the flames with his bare hands, he was about to sprinkle them in my eyes.

My father upon this raised his hands in supplication, crying: "Master, master, leave my Nathaniel his eyes!"

Whereupon Coppelius answered with a shrill laugh: "Well, let the lad have his eyes and do his share of the world's crying, but we will examine the mechanism of his hands and feet."

And then he seized me so roughly that my joints cracked, and screwed off my hands and feet, afterwards putting them back again, one after the other. "There's something wrong here," he mumbled. "But now it's as good as ever. The old man has caught the idea!" hissed and lisped Coppelius. But all around me became black, a sudden cramp darted through my bones and nerves – and I lost consciousness. A gentle warm breath passed over my face; I woke as from the sleep of death. My mother had been stooping over me.

"Is the Sandman still there?" I stammered.

"No, no, my dear child, he has gone away long ago – he won't hurt you!" said my mother, kissing her darling, as he regained his senses.

Why should I weary you, my dear Lothaire, with diffuse details, when I have so much more to tell? Suffice it to say that I had been discovered eavesdropping and ill-used by Coppelius. Agony and terror had brought on delirium and fever, from which I lay sick for several weeks.

"Is the Sandman still there?" That was my first sensible word and the sign of my amendment – my recovery. I have only to tell you now of this most frightful moment in all my youth, and you will be convinced that it is no fault of my eyes that everything seems colourless to me. You will, indeed, know that a dark fatality has hung over my life a gloomy veil of clouds, which I shall perhaps only tear away in death.

Coppelius was no more to be seen; it was said he had left the town.

About a year might have elapsed, and we were sitting, as of old, at the round table. My father was very cheerful, and was entertaining us with stories about his travels in his youth; when, as the clock struck nine, we heard the house-door groan on its hinges, and slow steps, heavy as lead, creaked through the passage and up the stairs.

"That is Coppelius," said my mother, turning pale.

"Yes! – that is Coppelius," repeated my father in a faint, broken voice. The tears started to my mother's eyes.

"But father – father!" she cried, "must it be so?"

"He is coming for the last time, I promise you," was the answer. "Only go now, go with the children – go – go to bed. Good night!"

I felt as if I were turned to cold, heavy stone – my breath stopped. My mother caught me by the arm as I stood immovable. "Come, come, Nathaniel!" I allowed myself to be led, and entered my chamber! "Be quiet – be quiet – go to bed – go to sleep!" cried my mother after me; but tormented by restlessness and an inward anguish perfectly indescribable, I could not close my eyes.

The hateful, abominable Coppelius stood before me with fiery eyes, and laughed maliciously at me. It was in vain that I endeavoured to get rid of his image. About midnight there was a frightful noise, like the firing of a gun. The whole house resounded. There was a rattling and rustling by my door, and the house door was closed with a violent bang.

"That is Coppelius!" I cried, springing out of bed in terror.

Then there was a shriek, as of acute, inconsolable grief. I darted into my father's room; the door was open, a suffocating smoke rolled towards me, and the servant girl cried: "Ah, my master, my master!" On the floor of the smoking hearth lay my father dead, with his face burned, blackened and hideously distorted – my sisters were shrieking and moaning around him – and my mother had fainted.

"Coppelius! – cursed devil! You have slain my father!" I cried, and lost my senses.

When, two days afterwards, my father was laid in his coffin, his features were again as mild and gentle as they had been in his life. My soul was comforted by the thought that his compact with the satanic Coppelius could not have plunged him into eternal perdition.

The explosion had awakened the neighbours, the occurrence had become common talk, and had reached the ears of the magistracy, who wished to make Coppelius answerable. He had, however, vanished from the spot, without leaving a trace.

If I tell you, my dear friend, that the barometer dealer was the accursed Coppelius himself, you will not blame me for regarding so unpropitious a phenomenon as the omen of some dire calamity. He was dressed differently, but the figure and features of Coppelius are too deeply imprinted in my mind for an error in this respect to be possible. Besides, Coppelius has not even altered his name. He describes himself, I am told, as a Piedmontese optician, and calls himself Giuseppe Coppola.

I am determined to deal with him, and to avenge my father's death, be the issue what it may.

Tell my mother nothing of the hideous monster's appearance. Remember me to my dear sweet Clara, to whom I will write in a calmer mood. Farewell.

* * *

Clara to Nathaniel

It is true that you have not written to me for a long time; but, nevertheless, I believe that I am still in your mind and thoughts. For assuredly you were thinking of me most intently when, designing to send your last letter to my brother Lothaire, you directed it to me instead of to him. I joyfully opened the letter, and did not perceive my error till I came to the words: "Ah, my dear Lothaire."

No, by rights I should have read no farther, but should have handed over the letter to my brother. Although you have often, in your childish teasing mood, charged me with having such a quiet, womanish, steady disposition, that, even if the house were about to fall in, I should smooth down a wrong fold in the window curtain in a most ladylike manner before I ran away, I can hardly tell you how your letter shocked me. I could scarcely breathe – the light danced before my eyes.

Ah, my dear Nathaniel, how could such a horrible thing have crossed your path? To be parted from you, never to see you again – the thought darted through my breast like a burning dagger. I read on and on. Your description of the repulsive Coppelius is terrifying. I learned for the first time the violent manner of your good old father's death. My brother Lothaire, to whom I surrendered the letter, sought to calm me, but in vain. The fatal barometer dealer, Giuseppe Coppola, followed me at every step; and I am almost ashamed to confess that he disturbed my healthy and usually peaceful sleep with all sorts of horrible visions. Yet soon even the next day – I was quite changed again. Do not be offended, dearest one, if Lothaire tells you that in spite of your strange fears that Coppelius will in some manner injure you, I am in the same cheerful and unworried mood as ever.

I must honestly confess that, in my opinion, all the terrible things of which you speak occurred merely in your own mind, and had little to do with the actual external world. Old Coppelius may have been repulsive enough, but his hatred of children was what really caused the abhorrence you children felt towards him.

In your childish mind the frightful Sandman in the nurse's tale was naturally associated with old Coppelius. Why, even if you had not believed in the Sandman, Coppelius would still have seemed to you a monster, especially dangerous to children. The awful business which he carried on at night with your father was no more than this: that they were making alchemical experiments in secret, which much distressed your mother since, besides a great deal of money being wasted, your father's mind was filled with a fallacious desire after higher wisdom, and so alienated from his family – as they say is always the case with such experimentalists. Your father, no doubt, occasioned his own death, by some act of carelessness of which Coppelius was completely guiltless. Let me tell you that I yesterday asked our neighbour, the apothecary, whether such a sudden and fatal explosion was possible in these chemical experiments?

"Certainly," he replied and, after his fashion, told me at great length and very circumstantially how such an event might take place, uttering a number of strange-sounding names which I am unable to recollect. Now, I know you will be angry with your Clara; you will say that her cold nature is impervious to any ray of the mysterious, which often embraces man with invisible arms; that she only sees the variegated surface of the world, and is as delighted as a silly child at some glittering golden fruit, which contains within it a deadly poison.

Ah! My dear Nathaniel! Can you not then believe that even in open, cheerful, careless minds may dwell the suspicion of some dread power which endeavours to destroy us in our own selves? Forgive me, if I, a silly girl, presume in any manner to present to you my thoughts on such an internal struggle. I shall not find the right words, of course, and you will laugh at me, not because my thoughts are foolish, but because I express them so clumsily.

If there is a dark and hostile power, laying its treacherous toils within us, by which it holds us fast and draws us along the path of peril and destruction, which we should not otherwise have trod; if, I say there is such a power, it must form itself inside us and out of ourselves, indeed; it must become identical with ourselves. For it is only in this condition that we can believe in it, and grant it the room which it requires to accomplish its secret work. Now, if we have a mind which is sufficiently firm, sufficiently strengthened by the joy of life, always to recognize this strange enemy as such, and calmly to follow the path of our own inclination and calling, then the dark power will fail in its attempt to gain a form that shall be a reflection of ourselves. Lothaire adds that if we have willingly yielded ourselves up to the dark powers, they are known often to impress upon our minds any strange, unfamiliar shape which the external world has thrown in our way; so that we ourselves kindle the spirit, which we in our strange delusion believe to be speaking to us. It is the phantom of our own selves, the close relationship with which, and its deep operation on our mind, casts us into hell or transports us into heaven.

You see, dear Nathaniel, how freely Lothaire and I are giving our opinion on the subject of the dark powers; which subject, to judge by my difficulties in writing down its most important features, appears to be a complicated one. Lothaire's last words I do not quite comprehend. I can only suspect what he means, and yet I feel as if it were all very true. Get the gruesome advocate Coppelius, and the barometer dealer, Giuseppe Coppola, quite out of your head, I beg of you. Be convinced that these strange fears have no power over you, and that it is only a belief in their hostile influence that can make them hostile in reality. If the great disturbance in your mind did not speak from every line of your letter, if your situation did not give me the deepest pain, I could joke about the Sandman-Advocate and the barometer dealer Coppelius. Cheer up, I have determined to play the part of your guardian spirit. If the ugly Coppelius takes it into his head to annoy you in your dreams, I'll scare him away with loud peals of laughter. I am not a bit afraid of him nor of his disgusting hands; he shall neither spoil my sweetmeats as an Advocate, nor my eyes as a Sandman. Ever yours, my dear Nathaniel.

* * *

Nathaniel to Lothaire

I am very sorry that in consequence of the error occasioned by my distracted state of mind, Clara broke open the letter intended for you, and read it. She has written me a very profound philosophical epistle, in which she proves, at great length, that Coppelius and Coppola only exist in my own mind, and are phantoms of myself, which will be dissipated directly I recognize them as such. Indeed, it is quite incredible that the mind which so often peers out of those bright, smiling, childish eyes with all the charm of a dream, could make such intelligent professorial definitions. She cites you – you, it seems have been talking about me. I suppose you read her logical lectures, so that she may learn to separate and sift all matters acutely. No more of that, please. Besides, it is quite certain that the barometer dealer, Giuseppe Coppola, is not the advocate Coppelius. I attend the lectures of the professor of physics, who has lately arrived. His name is the same as that of the famous natural philosopher Spalanzani, and he is of Italian origin. He has known Coppola for years and, moreover, it is clear from his accent that he is really a Piedmontese. Coppelius was a German, but I think no honest one. Calmed I am not, and though you and Clara may consider me a gloomy visionary, I cannot get rid of the impression which the accursed face of Coppelius makes upon me. I am glad that Coppola has left the town – so Spalanzani says.

This professor is a strange fellow – a little round man with high cheek-bones, a sharp nose, pouting lips and little, piercing eyes. Yet you will get a better notion of him than from this description, if you look at the portrait of Cagliostro, drawn by Chodowiecki in one of the Berlin annuals; Spalanzani looks like that exactly. I lately went up his stairs, and perceived that the curtain, which was generally drawn completely over a glass door, left a little opening on one side. I know not what curiosity impelled me to look through. A very tall and slender lady, extremely well-proportioned and most splendidly attired, sat in the room by a little table on which she had laid her arms, her hands being folded together. She sat opposite the door, so that I could see the whole of her angelic countenance. She did not appear to see me, and indeed there was something fixed about her eyes as if, I might almost say, she had no power of sight. It seemed to me that she was sleeping with her eyes open. I felt very uncomfortable, and therefore I slunk away into the lecture room close at hand.

Afterwards I learned that the form I had seen was that of Spalanzani's daughter Olympia, whom he keeps confined in a very strange and barbarous manner, so that no one can approach her. After all, there may be something the matter with her; she is half-witted perhaps, or something of the kind. But why should I write you all this? I could have conveyed it better and more circumstantially by word of mouth. For I shall see you in a fortnight. I must again behold my dear, sweet angelic Clara. My evil mood will then be dispersed, though I must confess that it has been struggling for mastery over me ever since her sensible but vexing letter. Therefore I do not write to her today. A thousand greetings, etc.

* * *

Nothing more strange and chimerical can be imagined than the fate of my poor friend, the young student Nathaniel, which I, gracious reader, have undertaken to tell you. Have you ever known something that has completely filled your heart, thoughts and senses, to the exclusion of every other object? There was a burning fermentation within you; your blood seethed like a molten glow through your veins, sending a higher colour to your cheeks. Your glance was strange, as if you were seeking in empty space forms invisible to all other eyes, and your speech flowed away into dark sighs. Then your friends asked you: "What is it, my dear sir?" "What is the matter?" And you wanted to draw the picture in your mind in all its glowing tints, in all its light and shade, and laboured hard to find words only to begin. You thought that you should crowd together in the very first sentence all those wonderful, exalted, horrible, comical, frightful events, so as to strike every hearer at once as with an electric shock. But every word, every thing that takes the form of speech, appeared to you colourless, cold and dead. You hunt and hunt, and stutter and stammer, and your friends' sober questions blow like icy wind upon your internal fire until it is almost out. Whereas if, like a bold painter, you had first drawn an outline of the internal picture with a few daring strokes, you might with small trouble have laid on the colours brighter and brighter, and the living throng of varied shapes would have borne your friends away with it. Then they would have seen themselves, like you, in the picture that your mind had bodied forth. Now I must confess to you, kind reader, that no one has really asked me for the history of the young Nathaniel, but you know well enough that I belong to the queer race of authors who, if they have anything in their minds such as I have just described, feel as if everyone who comes near them, and the whole world besides, is insistently demanding: "What is it then – tell it, my dear friend?"

Thus was I forcibly compelled to tell you of the momentous life of Nathaniel. The marvellous singularity of the story filled my entire soul, but for that very reason and because, my dear reader, I had to make you equally inclined to accept the uncanny, which is no small matter, I was puzzled how to begin Nathaniel's story in a manner as inspiring, original and striking as possible. "Once upon a time," the beautiful beginning of every tale, was too tame. "In the little provincial town of S– lived" – was somewhat better, as it at least prepared for the climax. Or should I dart at once, *medias in res*, with " 'Go to the devil,' cried the student Nathaniel with rage and horror in his wild looks, when the barometer dealer, Giuseppe Coppola …?" – I had indeed already written this down, when I fancied that I could detect something ludicrous in the wild looks of the student Nathaniel, whereas the story is not comical at all. No form of language suggested itself to my mind which seemed to reflect ever in the slightest degree the colouring of the internal picture. I resolved that I would not begin it at all.

So take, gentle reader, the three letters which friend Lothaire was good enough to give me, as the sketch of the picture which I shall endeavour to colour more and more brightly as I proceed with my narrative. Perhaps, like a good portrait painter, I may succeed in catching the outline in this way, so that you will realize it is a likeness even without knowing the original, and feel as if you had often seen the person with your own corporeal eyes. Perhaps, dear reader, you will then believe that nothing is stranger and madder than actual life; which the poet can only catch in the form of a dull reflection in a dimly polished mirror.

To give you all the information that you will require for a start, we must supplement these letters with the news that shortly after the death of Nathaniel's father, Clara and Lothaire, the children of a distant relative, who had likewise died and left them orphans, were taken by Nathaniel's mother into her own home. Clara and Nathaniel formed a strong attachment for each other; and no one in the world having any objection to make, they were betrothed when Nathaniel left the place to pursue his studies in G–. And there he is, according to his last letter, attending the lectures of the celebrated professor of physics, Spalanzani.

Now, I could proceed in my story with confidence, but at this moment Clara's picture stands so plainly before me that I cannot turn away; as indeed was always the case when she gazed at me with one of her lovely smiles. Clara could not by any means be reckoned beautiful, that was the opinion of all who are by their calling competent judges of beauty. Architects, nevertheless, praised the exact symmetry of her frame, and painters considered her neck, shoulders and bosom almost too chastely formed; but then they all fell in love with her wondrous hair and colouring, comparing her to the Magdalen in Battoni's picture at Dresden. One of them, a most fantastical and singular fellow, compared Clara's eyes to a lake by Ruysdael, in which the pure azure of a cloudless sky, the wood and flowery field, the whole cheerful life of the rich landscape are reflected.

Poets and composers went still further. "What is a lake what is a mirror!" said they. "Can we look upon the girl without wondrous, heavenly music flowing towards us from her glances, to penetrate our inmost soul so that all there is awakened and stirred? If we don't sing well then, there is not much in us, as we shall learn from the delicate smile which plays on Clara's lips, when we presume to pipe up before her with something intended to pass for a song, although it is only a confused jumble of notes."

So it was. Clara had the vivid fancy of a cheerful, unembarrassed child; a deep, tender, feminine disposition; an acute, clever understanding. Misty dreamers had not a chance with her; since, though she did not talk – talking would have been altogether repugnant to her silent nature – her bright glance and her firm ironical smile would say to them: "Good friends, how can you imagine that I shall take your fleeting shadowy images for real shapes imbued with life and motion?" On this account Clara was censured by many as cold, unfeeling and prosaic; while others, who understood life to its clear depths, greatly loved the feeling, acute, childlike girl; but none so much as Nathaniel, whose perception in art and science was clear and strong. Clara was attached to her lover with all her heart, and when he parted from her the first cloud passed over her life. With what delight, therefore, did she rush into his arms when, as he had promised in his last letter to Lothaire, he actually returned to his native town and entered his mother's room! Nathaniel's expectations were completely fulfilled; for directly he saw Clara he thought neither of the Advocate Coppelius nor of her 'sensible' letter. All gloomy forebodings had gone.

However, Nathaniel was quite right, when he wrote to his friend Lothaire that the form of the repulsive barometer dealer, Coppola, had had a most evil effect on his life. All felt, even in the first days, that Nathaniel had undergone a complete change in his whole being. He sank into a gloomy reverie, and behaved in a strange manner that had never been known in him before. Everything, his whole life, had become to him a dream and a foreboding, and he was always saying that man, although he might think himself free, only served for the cruel sport of dark powers. These he said it was vain to resist; man must patiently resign himself to his fate. He even went so far as to say that it is foolish to think that we do anything in art and science according to our own independent will; for the inspiration which alone enables us to produce anything does not proceed from within ourselves, but is the effect of a higher principle without.

To the clear-headed Clara this mysticism was in the highest degree repugnant, but contradiction appeared to be useless. Only when Nathaniel proved that Coppelius was the evil principle, which had seized him at the moment when he was listening behind the curtain, and that this repugnant principle would in some horrible manner disturb the happiness of their life, Clara grew very serious, and said: "Yes, Nathaniel, you are right. Coppelius is an evil, hostile principle; he can produce terrible effects, like a diabolical power that has come visibly into life; but only if you will not banish him from your mind and thoughts. So long as you believe in him, he really exists and exerts his influence; his power lies only in your belief."

Quite indignant that Clara did not admit the demon's existence outside his own mind, Nathaniel would then come out with all the mystical doctrine of devils and powers of evil. But Clara would break off peevishly by introducing some indifferent matter, to the no small annoyance of Nathaniel. He thought that such deep secrets were closed to cold, unreceptive minds, without being clearly aware that he was counting

Clara among these subordinate natures; and therefore he constantly endeavoured to initiate her into the mysteries. In the morning, when Clara was getting breakfast ready, he stood by her, reading out of all sorts of mystical books till she cried: "But dear Nathaniel, suppose I blame you as the evil principle that has a hostile effect upon my coffee? For if, to please you, I drop everything and look in your eyes while you read, my coffee will overflow into the fire, and none of you will get any breakfast."

Nathaniel closed the book at once and hurried indignantly to his chamber. Once he had a remarkable forte for graceful, lively tales, which he wrote down, and to which Clara listened with the greatest delight; now his creations were gloomy, incomprehensible and formless, so that although, out of compassion, Clara did not say so, he plainly felt how little she was interested. Nothing was more unbearable to Clara than tediousness; her looks and words expressed mental drowsiness which she could not overcome. Nathaniel's productions were, indeed, very tedious. His indignation at Clara's cold, prosaic disposition constantly increased; and Clara could not overcome her dislike of Nathaniel's dark, gloomy, boring mysticism, so that they became mentally more and more estranged without either of them perceiving it. The shape of the ugly Coppelius, as Nathaniel himself was forced to confess, was growing dimmer in his fancy, and it often cost him some pains to draw him with sufficient colour in his stories, where he figured as the dread bogy of ill omen.

It occurred to him, however, in the end to make his gloomy foreboding, that Coppelius would destroy his happiness, the subject of a poem. He represented himself and Clara as united by true love, but occasionally threatened by a black hand, which appeared to dart into their lives, to snatch away some new joy just as it was born. Finally, as they were standing at the altar, the hideous Coppelius appeared and touched Clara's lovely eyes. They flashed into Nathaniel's heart, like bleeding sparks, scorching and burning, as Coppelius caught him, and flung him into a flaming, fiery circle, which flew round with the swiftness of a storm, carrying him along with it, amid its roaring. The roar is like that of the hurricane, when it fiercely lashes the foaming waves, which rise up, like black giants with white heads, for the furious combat. But through the wild tumult he hears Clara's voice: "Can't you see me then? Coppelius has deceived you. Those, indeed, were not my eyes which so burned in your breast – they were glowing drops of your own heart's blood. I have my eyes still – only look at them!" Nathaniel reflects: "That is Clara, and I am hers for ever!" Then it seems to him as though this thought has forcibly entered the fiery circle, which stands still, while the noise dully ceases in the dark abyss. Nathaniel looks into Clara's eyes, but it is death that looks kindly upon him from her eyes.

While Nathaniel composed this poem, he was very calm and collected; he polished and improved every line, and having subjected himself to the fetters of metre, he did not rest till all was correct and melodious. When at last he had finished and read the poem aloud to himself, a wild horror seized him. "Whose horrible voice is that?" he cried out. Soon, however, the whole appeared to him a very successful work, and he felt that it must rouse Clara's cold temperament, although he did not clearly consider why Clara was to be excited, nor what purpose it would serve to torment her with frightful pictures threatening a horrible fate, destructive to their love. Both of them – that is to say, Nathaniel and Clara – were sitting in his mother's little garden, Clara very cheerful, because Nathaniel had not teased her with his dreams and his forebodings during the three days in which he had been writing his poem.

He was even talking cheerfully, as in the old days, about pleasant matters, which caused Clara to remark: "Now for the first time I have you again! Don't you see that we have driven the ugly Coppelius away?"

Not till then did it strike Nathaniel that he had in his pocket the poem, which he had intended to read. He at once drew the sheets out and began, while Clara, expecting something tedious as usual, resigned herself and began quietly to knit. But as the dark cloud rose ever blacker and blacker, she let the stocking fall and looked him full in the face. He was carried irresistibly along by his poem, an internal fire deeply reddened his cheeks, tears flowed from his eyes.

At last, when he had concluded, he groaned in a state of utter exhaustion and, catching Clara's hand, sighed forth, as if melted into the most inconsolable grief: "Oh Clara! – Clara!" Clara pressed him gently to her bosom, and said softly, but very solemnly and sincerely: "Nathaniel, dearest Nathaniel, do throw that mad, senseless, insane stuff into the fire!"

Upon this Nathaniel sprang up enraged and, thrusting Clara from him, cried: "Oh, inanimate, accursed automaton!"

With which he ran off; Clara, deeply offended, shed bitter tears, and sobbed aloud: "Ah, he has never loved me, for he does not understand me."

Lothaire entered the arbour; Clara was obliged to tell him all that had occurred. He loved his sister with all his soul, and every word of her complaint fell like a spark of fire into his heart, so that the indignation which he had long harboured against the visionary Nathaniel now broke out into the wildest rage. He ran to Nathaniel and reproached him for his senseless conduct towards his beloved sister in hard words, to which the infuriated Nathaniel retorted in the same style. The appellation of 'fantastical, mad fool,' was answered by that of 'miserable commonplace fellow.' A duel was inevitable. They agreed on the following morning, according to the local student custom, to fight with sharp rapiers on the far side of the garden. Silently and gloomily they slunk about. Clara had overheard the violent dispute and, seeing the fencing master bring the rapiers at dawn, guessed what was to occur.

Having reached the place of combat, Lothaire and Nathaniel had in gloomy silence flung off their coats, and with the lust of battle in their flaming eyes were about to fall upon one another, when Clara rushed through the garden door, crying aloud between her sobs: "You wild cruel men! Strike me down before you attack each other. For how can I live on if my lover murders my brother, or my brother murders my lover?"

Lothaire lowered his weapon, and looked in silence on the ground; but in Nathaniel's heart, amid the most poignant sorrow, there revived all his love for the beautiful Clara, which he had felt in the prime of his happy youth. The weapon fell from his hand, he threw himself at Clara's feet. "Can you ever forgive me, my only – my beloved Clara? Can you forgive me, my dear brother, Lothaire?"

Lothaire was touched by the deep contrition of his friend; all three embraced in reconciliation amid a thousand tears, and vowed eternal love and fidelity.

Nathaniel felt as though a heavy and oppressive burden had been rolled away, as though by resisting the dark power that held him fast he had saved his whole being, which had been threatened with annihilation. Three happy days he passed with his dear friends, and then went to G–, where he intended to stay a year, and then to return to his native town for ever.

All that referred to Coppelius was kept a secret from his mother. For it was well known that she could not think of him without terror since she, as well as Nathaniel, held him guilty of causing her husband's death.

* * *

How surprised was Nathaniel when, proceeding to his lodging, he saw that the whole house was burned down, and that only the bare walls stood up amid the ashes. However, although fire had broken out in the laboratory of the apothecary who lived on the ground floor, and had therefore consumed the house from top to bottom, some bold active friends had succeeded in entering Nathaniel's room in the upper story in time to save his books, manuscripts and instruments. They carried all safe and sound into another house, where they took a room, to which Nathaniel moved at once. He did not think it at all remarkable that he now lodged opposite to Professor Spalanzani; neither did it appear singular when he perceived that his window looked straight into the room where Olympia often sat alone, so that he could plainly recognize her figure, although the features of her face were indistinct and confused. At last it struck him that Olympia often remained for hours in that attitude in which he had once seen her through the glass door, sitting at a little table without any occupation, and that she was plainly enough looking over at him with an unvarying gaze. He was forced to confess that he had never seen a more lovely form but, with Clara in his heart, the stiff Olympia was perfectly indifferent to him. Occasionally, to be sure, he gave a transient look over his textbook at the beautiful statue, but that was all.

He was just writing to Clara, when he heard a light tap at the door; it stopped as he answered, and the repulsive face of Coppola peeped in. Nathaniel's heart trembled within him, but remembering what Spalanzani had told him about his compatriot Coppola, and also the firm promise he had made to Clara with respect to the Sandman Coppelius, he felt ashamed of his childish fear and, collecting himself with all his might, said as softly and civilly as possible: "I do not want a barometer, my good friend; pray go."

Upon this, Coppola advanced a good way into the room, his wide mouth distorted into a hideous laugh, and his little eyes darting fire from beneath their long grey lashes: "Eh, eh – no barometer – no barometer?" he said in a hoarse voice, "I have pretty eyes too – pretty eyes!"

"Madman!" cried Nathaniel in horror. "How can you have eyes? Eyes?"

But Coppola had already put his barometer aside and plunged his hand into his wide coat pocket, whence he drew lorgnettes and spectacles, which he placed upon the table.

"There – there – spectacles on the nose, those are my eyes – pretty eyes!" he gabbled, drawing out more and more spectacles, until the whole table began to glisten and sparkle in the most extraordinary manner.

A thousand eyes stared and quivered, their gaze fixed upon Nathaniel; yet he could not look away from the table, where Coppola kept laying down still more and more spectacles, and all those flaming eyes leapt in wilder and wilder confusion, shooting their blood red light into Nathaniel's heart.

At last, overwhelmed with horror, he shrieked out: "Stop, stop, you terrify me!" and seized Coppola by the arm, as he searched his pockets to bring out still more spectacles, although the whole table was already covered.

Coppola gently extricated himself with a hoarse repulsive laugh; and with the words: "Ah, nothing for you – but here are pretty glasses!" collected all the spectacles, packed them away, and from the breast pocket of his coat drew forth a number of telescopes large and small. As soon as the spectacles were removed Nathaniel felt quite easy and, thinking of Clara, perceived that the hideous phantom was but the creature of his own mind, that this Coppola was an honest optician and could not possibly be the accursed double of Coppelius. Moreover, in all the glasses which Coppola now placed on the table, there was nothing remarkable, or at least nothing so uncanny as in the spectacles; and to set matters right Nathaniel resolved· to make a purchase. He took up a little, very neatly constructed pocket telescope, and looked through the window to try it. Never in his life had he met a glass which brought objects so clearly and sharply before his eyes. Involuntarily he looked into Spalanzani's room; Olympia was sitting as usual before the little table, with her arms laid upon it, and her hands folded.

For the first time he could see the wondrous beauty in the shape of her face; only her eyes seemed to him singularly still and dead. Nevertheless, as he looked more keenly through the glass, it seemed to him as if moist moonbeams were rising in Olympia's eyes. It was as if the power of seeing were being kindled for the first time; her glances flashed with constantly increasing life. As if spellbound, Nathaniel reclined against the window, meditating on the charming Olympia. A humming and scraping aroused him as if from a dream.

Coppola was standing behind him: "Tre zecchini – three ducats!" He had quite forgotten the optician, and quickly paid him what he asked. "Is it not so? A pretty glass – a pretty glass?" asked Coppola, in his hoarse, repulsive voice, and with his malicious smile.

"Yes – yes," replied Nathaniel peevishly; "Good-bye, friend."

Coppola left the room, but not without casting many strange glances at Nathaniel. He heard him laugh loudly on the stairs.

"Ah," thought Nathaniel, "he is laughing at me because, no doubt, I have paid him too much for this little glass."

While he softly uttered these words, it seemed as if a deep and lugubrious sigh were sounding fearfully through the room; and his breath was stopped by inward anguish. He perceived, however, that it was himself that had sighed.

"Clara is right," he said to himself, "in taking me for a senseless dreamer, but it is pure madness – nay, more than madness, that the stupid thought of having paid Coppola too much for the glass still pains me so strangely. I cannot see the cause."

He now sat down to finish his letter to Clara; but a glance through the window assured him that Olympia was still sitting there, and he instantly sprang up, as if impelled by an irresistible power, seized Coppola's glass, and could not tear himself away from the seductive sight of Olympia till his friend and brother Sigismund called him to go to Professor Spalanzani's lecture. The curtain was drawn close before the fatal room, and he could see Olympia no longer, nor could he upon the next day or the next, although he scarcely ever left his window and constantly looked through Coppola's glass. On the third day the windows were completely covered. In utter despair, filled with a longing and a burning desire, he ran out of the town gate. Olympia's form floated before him in the air, stepped forth from the bushes, and peeped at him with large beaming eyes from the clear brook. Clara's image had completely vanished from his mind; he thought of nothing but Olympia, and complained aloud in a murmuring voice: "Ah, noble, sublime star of my love, have you only risen upon me to vanish immediately, and leave me in dark hopeless night?"

As he returned to his lodging, however, he perceived a great bustle in Spalanzani's house. The doors were wide open, all sorts of utensils were being carried in, the windows of the first floor were being taken out, maid-servants were going about sweeping and dusting with great hairbrooms, and carpenters and upholsterers were knocking and hammering within. Nathaniel remained standing in the street in a state of perfect wonder, when Sigismund came up to him laughing, and said: "Now, what do you say to our old Spalanzani?"

Nathaniel assured him that he could say nothing because he knew nothing about the professor, but on the contrary perceived with astonishment the mad proceedings in a house otherwise so quiet and gloomy. He then learnt from Sigismund that Spalanzani intended to give a grand party on the following day – a concert and ball – and that half the university was invited. It was generally reported that Spalanzani, who had so long kept his daughter most scrupulously from every human eye, would now let her appear for the first time.

Nathaniel found a card of invitation, and with heart beating high went at the appointed hour to the professor's, where the coaches were already arriving and the lights shining in the decorated rooms. The company was numerous and brilliant. Olympia appeared dressed with great richness and taste. Her beautifully shaped face and her figure roused general admiration. The somewhat strange arch of her back and the wasp-like thinness of her waist seemed to be produced by too tight lacing. In her step and deportment there was something measured and stiff, which struck many as unpleasant, but it was ascribed to the constraint produced by the company. The concert began. Olympia played the harpsichord with great dexterity, and sang a virtuoso piece, with a voice like the sound of a glass bell, clear and almost piercing. Nathaniel was quite enraptured; he stood in the back row, and could not perfectly recognize Olympia's features in the dazzling light. Therefore, quite unnoticed, he took out Coppola's glass and looked towards the fair creature. Ah! then he saw with what a longing glance she gazed towards him, and how every note of her song plainly sprang from that loving glance, whose fire penetrated his inmost soul. Her accomplished roulades seemed to Nathaniel the exultation of a mind transfigured by love, and when at last, after the cadence, the long trill sounded shrilly through the room, he felt as if clutched by burning arms. He could restrain himself no longer, but with mingled pain and rapture shouted out, "Olympia!"

Everyone looked at him, and many laughed. The organist of the cathedral made a gloomier face than usual, and simply said: "Well, well."

The concert had finished, the ball began. "To dance with her – with her!" That was the aim of all Nathaniel's desire, of all his efforts; but how to gain courage to ask her, the queen of the ball? Nevertheless – he himself did not know how it happened – no sooner had the dancing begun than he was standing close to Olympia, who had not yet been asked to dance. Scarcely able to stammer out a few words, he had seized her hand. Olympia's hand was as cold as ice; he felt a horrible deathly chill thrilling through him. He looked into her eyes, which beamed back full of love and desire, and at the same time it seemed as though her pulse began to beat and her life's blood to flow into her cold hand. And in the soul of Nathaniel the joy of love rose still higher; he clasped the beautiful Olympia, and with her flew through the dance. He thought that his dancing was usually correct as to time, but the peculiarly steady rhythm with which Olympia moved, and which often put him completely out, soon showed him that his time was most defective. However, he would dance with no other lady, and would have murdered anyone who approached Olympia for the purpose of asking her. But this only happened twice, and to his astonishment Olympia remained seated until the next dance, when he lost no time in making her rise again.

Had he been able to see any other object besides the fair Olympia, all sorts of unfortunate quarrels would have been inevitable. For the quiet, scarcely suppressed laughter which arose among the young people in every corner was manifestly directed towards Olympia, whom they followed with very curious glances – one could not tell why. Heated by the dance and by the wine, of which he had freely partaken, Nathaniel had laid aside all his ordinary reserve. He sat by Olympia with her hand in his and, in a high state of inspiration, told her his passion, in words which neither he nor Olympia understood.

Yet perhaps she did; for she looked steadfastly into his face and sighed several times, "Ah, ah!" Upon this, Nathaniel said, "Oh splendid, heavenly lady! Ray from the promised land of love – deep soul in whom all my being is reflected !" with much more stuff of the like kind. But Olympia merely went on sighing, "Ah – ah!"

Professor Spalanzani occasionally passed the happy pair, and smiled on them with a look of singular satisfaction. To Nathaniel, although he felt in quite another world, it seemed suddenly as though Professor Spalanzani's face was growing considerably darker, and when he looked around he perceived, to his no small horror, that the last two candles in the empty room had burned down to their sockets, and were just going out. The music and dancing had ceased long ago.

"Parting – parting!" he cried in wild despair; he kissed Olympia's hand, he bent towards her mouth, when his glowing lips were met by lips cold as ice! Just as when he had touched her cold hand, he felt himself overcome by horror; the legend of the dead bride darted suddenly through his mind, but Olympia pressed him fast, and her lips seemed to spring to life at his kiss. Professor Spalanzani strode through the empty hall, his steps caused a hollow echo, and his figure, round which a flickering shadow played, had a fearful, spectral appearance.

"Do you love me, do you love me, Olympia? Only one word! Do you love me?" whispered Nathaniel; but as she rose Olympia only sighed, "Ah – ah!"

"Yes, my gracious, my beautiful star of love," said Nathaniel, "you have risen upon me, and you will shine, for ever lighting my inmost soul."

"Ah – ah!" replied Olympia, as she departed. Nathaniel followed her; they both stood before the professor.

"You have had a very animated conversation with my daughter," said he, smiling; "So, dear Herr Nathaniel, if you have any pleasure in talking with a silly girl, your visits shall be welcome."

Nathaniel departed with a whole heaven beaming in his heart. The next day Spalanzani's party was the general subject of conversation. Notwithstanding that the professor had made every effort to appear splendid, the wags had all sorts of incongruities and oddities to talk about. They were particularly hard upon the dumb, stiff Olympia whom, in spite of her beautiful exterior, they considered to be completely stupid, and they were delighted to find in her stupidity the reason why Spalanzani had kept her so long concealed. Nathaniel did not hear this without secret anger. Nevertheless he held his peace. "For," thought he, "is it worth while convincing these fellows that it is their own stupidity that prevents their recognizing Olympia's deep, noble mind?"

One day Sigismund said to him: "Be kind enough, brother, to tell me how a sensible fellow like you could possibly lose your head over that wax face, over that wooden doll up there?"

Nathaniel was about to fly out in a passion, but he quickly recollected himself and retorted: "Tell me, Sigismund, how it is that Olympia's heavenly charms could escape your active and intelligent eyes, which generally perceive things so clearly? But, for that very reason, Heaven be thanked, I have not you for my rival; otherwise, one of us must have fallen a bleeding corpse!"

Sigismund plainly perceived his friend's condition. So he skillfully gave the conversation a turn and, after observing that in love affairs there was no disputing about the object, added: "Nevertheless, it is strange that many of us think much the same about Olympia. To us – pray do not take it ill, brother she appears singularly stiff and soulless. Her shape is well proportioned – so is her face – that is true! She might pass for beautiful if her glance were not so utterly without a ray of life – without the power of vision. Her pace is strangely regular, every movement seems to depend on some wound-up clockwork. Her playing and her singing keep the same unpleasantly correct and spiritless time as a musical box, and the same may be said of her dancing. We find your Olympia quite uncanny, and prefer to have nothing to do with her. She seems to act like a living being, and yet has some strange peculiarity of her own."

Nathaniel did not completely yield to the bitter feeling which these words of Sigismund's roused in him, but mastered his indignation, and merely said with great earnestness, "Olympia may appear uncanny to you, cold, prosaic man. Only the poetical mind is sensitive to its like in others. To me alone was the love in her glances revealed, and it has pierced my mind and all my thought; only in the love of Olympia do I discover my real self. It may not suit you that she does not indulge in idle chit-chat like other shallow minds. She utters few words, it is true, but these few words appear as genuine hieroglyphics of the inner world, full of love and deep knowledge of the spiritual life, and contemplation of the eternal beyond. But you have no sense for all this, and my words are wasted on you."

"God preserve you, brother," said Sigismund very mildly, almost sorrowfully. "But you seem to me to be in an evil way. You may depend upon me, if all – no, no, I will not say anything further."

All of a sudden it struck Nathaniel that the cold, prosaic Sigismund meant very well towards him; he therefore shook his proffered hand very heartily.

Nathaniel had totally forgotten the very existence of Clara, whom he had once loved; his mother, Lothaire – all had vanished from his memory; he lived only for Olympia, with whom he sat for hours every day, uttering strange fantastical stuff about his love, about the sympathy that glowed to life, about the affinity of souls, to all of which Olympia listened with great devotion. From the very bottom of his desk he drew out all that he had ever written. Poems, fantasies, visions, romances, tales – this stock was daily increased by all sorts of extravagant sonnets, stanzas and canzoni, and he read them all tirelessly to Olympia for hours on end. Never had he known such an admirable listener. She neither embroidered nor knitted, she never looked out of the window, she fed no favourite bird, she played neither with lapdog nor pet cat, she did not twist a slip of paper or anything else in her hand, she was not obliged to suppress a yawn by a gentle forced cough. In short, she sat for hours, looking straight into her lover's eyes, without stirring, and her glance became more and more lively and animated. Only when Nathaniel rose at last, and kissed her hand and her lips did she say, "Ah, ah!" to which she added: "Good night, dearest."

"Oh deep, noble mind!" cried Nathaniel in his own room, "you, you alone, dear one, fully understand me."

He trembled with inward rapture, when he considered the wonderful harmony that was revealed more and more every day between his own mind and that of Olympia. For it seemed to him as if Olympia had spoken concerning him and his poetical talent out of the depths of his own mind; as if her voice had actually sounded from within himself. That must indeed have been the case, for Olympia never uttered any words whatever beyond those which have already been recorded. Even when Nathaniel, in clear and sober moments, as for instance upon waking in the morning, remembered Olympia's utter passivity and her painful lack of words, he merely said: "Words words! The glance of her heavenly eye speaks more than any language here below. Can a child of heaven adapt herself to the narrow confines drawn by a miserable mundane necessity?"

Professor Spalanzani appeared highly delighted at the intimacy between his daughter and Nathaniel. To the latter he gave the most unequivocal signs of approbation; and when Nathaniel ventured at last to hint at a union with Olympia, his whole face smiled as he observed that he would leave his daughter a free choice in the matter. Encouraged by these words and with burning passion in his heart, Nathaniel resolved to implore Olympia on the very next day to say directly and in plain words what her kind glance had told him long ago; namely, that she loved him. He sought the ring which his mother had given him at parting, to give it to Olympia as a symbol of his devotion, of his life which budded forth and bloomed with her alone. Clara's letters and Lothaire's came to his hands during the search; but he flung them aside indifferently, found the ring, pocketed it and hastened over to Olympia. Already on the steps, in the hall, he heard a strange noise, which seemed to proceed from Spalanzani's room. There was a stamping, a clattering, a pushing, a banging against the door, intermingled with curses and imprecations.

Let go – let go! Rascal! – Scoundrel! – Body and soul I've risked upon it! – Ha, ha, ha! – That's not what we agreed to! – I, I made the eyes! – I made the clockwork! – Stupid blockhead with your clockwork! – Accursed dog of a bungling watch-maker! – or with you! – Devil ! – Stop! – Pipe-maker! – Infernal beast! – Stop! – Get out! – Let go!"

These words were uttered by the voices of Spalanzani and the hideous Coppelius, who were raging and wrangling together. Nathaniel rushed in, overcome by the most inexpressible anguish.

The professor was holding a female figure fast by the shoulders, the Italian Coppola grasped it by the feet, and there they were tugging and pulling, this way and that, contending for the possession of it with the utmost fury. Nathaniel started back with horror when in the figure he recognized Olympia. Boiling with the wildest indignation, he was about to rescue his beloved from these infuriated men. But at that moment Coppola, whirling round with the strength of a giant, wrenched the figure from the professor's hand, and then dealt him a tremendous blow with the object itself, which sent him reeling and tumbling backwards over the table, upon which stood vials, retorts, bottles and glass cylinders. All these were dashed to a thousand shivers. Now Coppola flung the figure across his shoulders, and with a frightful burst of shrill laughter dashed down the stairs, so fast that the feet of the figure, which dangled in the most hideous manner, rattled with a wooden sound on every step.

Nathaniel stood paralyzed; he had seen but too plainly that Olympia's waxen, deathly-pale countenance had no eyes, but black holes instead – she was, indeed, a lifeless doll. Spalanzani was writhing on the floor; the pieces of glass had cut his head, his breast and his arms, and the blood was spurting up as from so many fountains. But he soon collected all his strength.

"After him – after him – what are you waiting for? Coppelius, Coppelius – has robbed me of my best automaton – a work of twenty years – body and soul risked upon it – the clockwork – the speech – the walk, mine; the eyes stolen from you. The infernal rascal – after him; fetch Olympia – there you see the eyes!"

And now Nathaniel saw that a pair of eyes lay upon the ground, staring at him; these Spalanzani caught up, with his unwounded hand, and flung into his bosom. Then madness seized Nathaniel in its burning claws, and clutched his very soul, destroying his every sense and thought.

"Ho – ho – ho – a circle of fire! Of fire! Spin round, circle! Merrily, merrily! Ho, wooden doll – spin round, pretty doll!" he cried, flying at the professor, and clutching at his throat.

He would have strangled him had not the noise attracted a crowd, who rushed in and forced Nathaniel to let go, thus saving the professor, whose wounds were immediately dressed. Sigismund, strong as he was, was not able to master the mad Nathaniel, who kept crying out in a frightening voice: "Spin round, wooden doll!" and laid about him with clenched fists. At last the combined force of many succeeded in overcoming him, in flinging him to the ground and binding him. His words were merged into one hideous roar like that of a brute, and in this insane condition he was taken raging to the mad house.

Before I proceed to tell you, gentle reader, what more befell the unfortunate Nathaniel, should you by chance take an interest in that skilful optician and automaton maker Spalanzani, I can inform you that he was completely healed of his wounds. He was, however, obliged to leave the university, because Nathaniel's story had created a sensation, and it was universally considered a quite unpardonable trick to smuggle a wooden doll into respectable tea parties in place of a living person – for Olympia had been quite a success at tea parties. The lawyers called it a most subtle deception, and the more culpable, inasmuch as he had planned it so artfully against the public that not a single soul – a few cunning students excepted – had detected it, although all now wished to play the wiseacre, and referred to various facts which had appeared to them suspicious. Nothing very clever was revealed in this way. Would it strike anyone as so very suspicious, for instance, that, according to the expression of an elegant tea-ite, Olympia had, contrary to all usage, sneezed oftener than she had yawned? "The former," remarked this fashionable person, "was the sound of the concealed clockwork winding itself up. Moreover, it had creaked audibly." And so on.

The professor of poetry and eloquence took a pinch of snuff, clapped the lid of his box to, cleared his throat, and said solemnly: "Ladies and gentlemen, do you not perceive where the trick lies? It is all an allegory – a sustained metaphor – you understand me – *sapienti sat.*"

But many were not satisfied with this; the story of the automaton had struck deep root into their souls and, in fact, a pernicious mistrust of human figures in general had begun to creep in. Many lovers, to be quite convinced that they were not enamoured of wooden dolls, would request their mistresses to sing and dance a little out of time, to embroider and knit, and play with their lapdogs, while listening to reading, etc., and, above all, not merely to listen, but also sometimes to talk, in such a manner as presupposed actual thought and feeling. With many the bond of love became firmer and more entrancing, though others, on the contrary, slipped gently out of the noose. "One cannot really answer for this," said some. At tea parties yawning prevailed to an incredible extent, and there was no sneezing at all, that all suspicion might be avoided. Spalanzani, as already stated, was obliged to decamp, to escape a criminal prosecution for fraudulently introducing an automaton into human society. Coppola had vanished also.

Nathaniel awakened as from a heavy, frightful dream; as he opened his eyes, he felt an indescribable sensation of pleasure glowing through him with heavenly warmth. He was in bed in his own room, in his father's house, Clara was stooping over him, and Lothaire and his mother were standing near.

"At last, at last, beloved Nathaniel, you have recovered from your serious illness – now you are mine again!" said Clara, from the very depth of her soul, and clasped Nathaniel in her arms.

It was with mingled sorrow and delight that the bright tears fell from his eyes, as he answered with a deep sigh: "My own – my own Clara!"

Sigismund, who had faithfully remained with his friend in his hour of trouble, now entered. Nathaniel stretched out his hand to him. "And you, faithful brother, have you not deserted me?"

Every trace of Nathaniel's madness had vanished, and he soon gained strength under the care of his mother, his beloved and his friends. Good fortune also had visited the house, for a miserly old uncle of whom nothing had been expected had died, leaving their mother, besides considerable property, an estate in a pleasant spot near the town. Thither Nathaniel decided to go, with his Clara, whom he now intended to marry, his mother and Lothaire. He had grown milder and more docile than ever he had been before, and now, for the first time, he understood the heavenly purity and the greatness of Clara's mind. No one, by the slightest hint, reminded him of the past.

Only, when Sigismund took leave of him, Nathaniel said: "Heavens, brother, I was in an evil way, but a good angel led me betimes on to the path of light! Ah, that was Clara!"

Sigismund did not let him carry the discourse further for fear that grievous recollections might burst forth in all their lurid brightness.

At about this time the four lucky persons thought of going to the estate. It was noon and they were walking in the streets of the city, where they had made several purchases. The high steeple of the town hall was already casting its gigantic shadow over the market place.

"Oh," said Clara, "let us climb it once more and look out at the distant mountains!"

No sooner said than done. Nathaniel and Clara both ascended the steps, the mother returned home with the servant, and Lothaire, who was not inclined to clamber up so many stairs, chose to remain below. The two lovers stood arm-in-arm on the highest gallery of the tower, and looked down upon the misty forests, behind which the blue mountains rose like a gigantic city.

"Look there at that curious little grey bush," said Clara. "It actually looks as if it were striding towards us."

Nathaniel mechanically put his hand into his breast pocket – he found Coppola's telescope, and pointed it to one side. Clara was in the way of the glass. His pulse and veins leapt convulsively. Pale as death, he stared at Clara, soon streams of fire flashed and glared from his rolling eyes, he roared frightfully, like a hunted beast. Then he sprang high into the air and, punctuating his words with horrible laughter, he shrieked out in a piercing tone, "Spin round, wooden doll! – spin round!" Then seizing Clara with immense force, he tried to hurl her down, but with the desperate strength of one battling against death she clutched the railings.

Lothaire heard the raging of the madman – he heard Clara's shriek of agony – fearful forebodings darted through his mind, he ran up, the door to the second flight was fastened, Clara's shrieks became louder and still louder. Frantic with rage and anxiety, he threw himself against the door, which finally burst open. Clara's voice was becoming weaker and weaker. "Help – help save me!" With these words the voice seemed to die on the air.

"She is gone – murdered by that madman!" cried Lothaire.

The door of the gallery was also closed, but despair gave him a giant's strength, and he burst it from the hinges. Heavens! Grasped by the mad Nathaniel, Clara was hanging in the air over the gallery – with one hand only she still held one of the iron railings. Quick as lightning, Lothaire caught his sister and drew her in, at the same moment striking the madman in the face with his clenched fist to such effect that he reeled and let go his prey.

Lothaire ran down with his fainting sister in his arms. She was saved. Nathaniel went raging about the gallery, leaping high in the air and crying, "Circle of fire, spin round! Spin round!"

The people collected at the sound of his wild shrieks and among them, prominent for his gigantic stature, was the advocate Coppelius, who had just come to the town, and was proceeding straight to the market place. Some wished to climb up and secure the madman, but Coppelius only laughed, saying, "Ha, ha – just wait – he will soon come down of his own accord," and looked up like the rest. Nathaniel suddenly stood still as if petrified.

Then, perceiving Coppelius, he stooped down, and yelled out, "Ah, pretty eyes – pretty eyes!" with which he sprang over the railing.

When Nathaniel lay on the stone pavement with his head shattered, Coppelius had disappeared in the crowd.

Many years afterwards it is said that Clara was seen in a remote spot, sitting hand in hand with a kind-looking man before the door of a country house, while two lively boys played before her. From this it may be inferred that she at last found a quiet domestic happiness suitable to her serene and cheerful nature, a happiness which the morbid Nathaniel would never have given her.

Spectrum

Liam Hogan

NEHA RUBBED THE SCAR that ran down her cheek. It went further, as well; split and twisted, both inside and out, a permanent, painful, crippling reminder of their disastrous arrival twenty-five years ago: the *Accra* plummeting through the magnetic storms in Icaria's turbulent, alien atmosphere; navigation, guidance, and even life-support systems glitching out before their inevitable crash.

Then: the desperate fight of the survivors to awaken the sleeping cargo before the cryo-pods failed as well. The horror of that day; the futile efforts, the terrible losses.

Instead of a colony of a thousand, with the best tools and technology their mother planet had to offer, they had been reduced to a mere fifty, reduced also to improvised and temperamental steam engines, every electronic component more complicated than a resistor snuffed out in the eddies and whorls of that unforeseen electromagnetic maelstrom.

Almost unforeseen: of those awake for the landing, only Neha had seen the purple clouds spitting and snapping below, had not understood why no-one else on the bridge seemed concerned.

It was a talent she'd long had, even though she'd never actually known it for what it was. Her uncanny ability to identify dead circuitry was part of it; a talent that had paved her way through University, that had earned her Second Engineer status for this prestigious African Federation mission. A skill that spoke to her superiors louder than her youth, her sex, or indeed, her mixed parentage; Indian mother, Ghanaian father: neither native nor foreign, an outsider wherever she went.

A skill that, this day at least, was turned to new purpose.

They were up on the high plateau a half mile from the crater the *Accra* had dug and where, in the aftermath, the settlers had carved their homes in the shattered rock. Neha had been hauled up by two of those born to this planet, young men who lifted her and her wheelchair over the boulders and crevasses. She had spent more time being carried than pushed; an undignified and arduous journey, but necessary.

She'd consulted and advised on the plans for the flyer, *The Daedalus*; worked on the manual controls for rudder and aileron. But it was still so much more fragile than she'd expected; a chimera of pot-bellied stove and the glistening wings of a dragonfly, hi-tech material from a scavenged solar-sail stretched taut over a rude wooden frame.

She marvelled at the bravery of the young pilot destined to sit in the cramped space behind the boiler. The young *female* pilot; it had to be a woman and a slim one at that, to attain the height they hoped to achieve.

But her bravery would be for naught unless Neha could identify a window of opportunity for her ascent.

She watched the electrical bands form and reform, tangled sheets dancing across the sky, sometimes threatening to dip to ground but never quite able to, torn to wisps still high above the plateau.

"How long will it take you to get to altitude?" she asked the pilot.

"Twenty to twenty-five minutes," Ama replied, after a look that travelled the length of Neha's broken body. Neha returned the appraisal, the comparison was not in her favour. Ama was brimming with vitality and youth, every ounce of fat expunged by the necessities of this mission, even her hair cropped short in a fashion that made Neha strangely wistful.

She shook her head, conscious of the weight of her own hair that she'd grown out to hide where the old wound began.

"Too long."

Abeni, nearby, overheard and strode up, his left arm stiff and withered. Their Captain had been lucky; he showed the scars of the crash less than most. Age and the harsh conditions of Icaria had not been so kind, he was an old man before his time, thin and stooped, the bristles of his moustache pure white.

"What's that? Is there a problem?"

"No problem, Sir –" the pilot began.

"– It won't work." Neha interrupted.

Abeni turned rheumy eyes on her. "Why not?"

"The fields are too volatile. Even if we spot the perfect window, it won't last twenty-five minutes."

"Twenty …" muttered Ama.

Abeni gazed up at the grey clouds above, as if for a moment he too could see the roiling streams of electromagnetic flux.

The Captain's voice was quiet, but firm. "The *Niamey* is due. We have to try."

"We only get one shot," Neha pointed out. "If the electronics on the transmitter get fried then it's game over. There are no spares."

Abeni spat into the thin dust. "Fifteen years we've been gearing up to this! Fifteen years of effort to reach this point. And now – and only now – you tell us it won't work?"

Neha shrugged. "This is my first time at the launch site. My first chance to observe the conditions."

The Captain's one good hand clenched and unclenched. "Another day, perhaps?"

"Perhaps," Neha rubbed her scar again before dragging her fingers down to her lap, embarrassed by the nervous habit. "Though there are no guarantees this doesn't count as a calm day. Or …or I could fly it."

"You!" spluttered Ama, Abeni's cold gaze cutting off the rest of her retort.

"You can fly?" Abeni asked.

"Yes."

"With no legs?" Ama cruelly added.

"What use are they once you're in the air? And I dare say my upper body strength is equal to yours, for about the same weight."

There was a snort. "But still, you've not trained –"

"I have my wings," Neha said. "Trained as a shuttle pilot. Which means I'm trained to fly anything. Flown more hours than Ama here. Trained by Obafemi himself."

That quietened them down. As well it should; it was Obafemi Mbadiwe who had managed to land the *Accra* blind, with no instruments and damned little in the way of control. Without him, there would be no conversation taking place.

She didn't bother pointing out that she'd never *actually* flown anything, that even gravity had been faked in the on-board simulators. She'd never really expected to; it had been something to pass the time, her training taking place in the six months between the awakening of the landing crew out on the outskirts of the solar system and the *Accra* digging its final resting place on the planet's craggy surface.

"What's going on?"

Their conference had been joined by *The Daedalus*'s engineer; Sam Clintock, the Scot who had, for a hobby, built and repaired steam engines in museums back on Earth. Skills that had turned out to be a lot more useful than Genetic Engineering, or Nano-Fabrication.

So much had depended on modern electronics. Not just the tools, either: the scanning microscopes and the field manipulators. Advanced electronics were at the core of what should have been their knowledge base, their libraries. Only a scant few physical books, a thousand years worth of technology crammed onto tiny nickel plates, put on board for this worst of worse-case scenarios, had survived.

But even they were useless without a certain level of prior knowledge, a familiarity with terms and concepts. Without Earth-trained engineers and without hobbyists like Sam. The steam-age on Icaria might only last another ten years, might fizzle out with the deaths of the original colonists, with the failure of the few devices that they had managed to construct. Such as the fragile flyer, *The Daedalus*.

"Change of pilot." Abeni said, simply.

Sam looked between the sour-faced Ama and the wheelchair bound Neha. "For real?"

"I should be the one," Ama muttered, "She's completely unprepared."

"This is the maiden flight, right?" Neha insisted, "No one's prepared. No one's flown *The Daedalus* yet. Not me, not Ama. No one."

"No, she hasn't," Clintock agreed, "But she's flown – and crashed – the prototypes, and that counts for something."

"So she knows how to crash! If a crash is involved, we've already failed." Neha smiled, as if realising something for the first time. "Only I can navigate what only I can see. So unless you've got a steam engine capable of lifting *two* people above the clouds, I was always going to have to be your pilot."

"You knew that? All along?" Ama looked horrified, and Neha quickly shook her head.

"No. And believe me, it's not something I *want* to do. But it's obvious, isn't it? It has to be me."

It took five minutes for the doubtful Ama to teach Neha the simple controls, while Clintock carefully primed the compact steam engine.

"You'll take off fully loaded," he said, "but you'll only achieve maximum height when the last of the fuel is burnt, when the last of the water is exhausted, and as long as you keep remembering to dump the ash."

He grinned, a hard grin behind his mask of soot. "Not a task for the faint of heart, Neha. You'll have no power at all for the return, you'll be gliding in."

"I've done plenty of that," Neha said.

"In the last twenty-five years?"

"In the last twenty-five years, no." She laughed.

"Ah well. It's a fool's errand anyway. I, for one, would rather you crashed and burned than this young lassy."

He winked at Ama, who pursed her lips and turned away.

Neha shook her head. "Thanks for the vote of confidence, Clintock."

Samuel Clintock was one of the few Europeans aboard the *Accra*, and the only one still alive after the crash and twenty-five years of hard subsistence living. His thinning red hair would live on, though, as long as the colony didn't die out; he'd already sired three children, all daughters, all the Pilot's age; dark skinned, flame haired.

An odd mix, but no odder than Neha's: her muddy olive skin, hair somewhere between straight and tightly curled. Growing up, being teased mercilessly at school, her father had shown her photos of mixed-race afro-asian children, one a former Miss South Africa. The message was clear: she too could end up just as beautiful.

She hadn't. She'd ended up short, with bushy eyebrows and plain features, easily overlooked by the boys.

As one University 'friend' had put it, "Ah, poor Neha. The worst of both worlds."

Fortunately, by then she'd moved on to other interests. Dedicated herself to diodes and transistors, to complex circuitry that didn't judge her in return.

All those early dreams had done was to leave her with a strange attraction to leggy, exotic beauties. Such as Clintock's daughters. Tall and undeniably beautiful, though even in this small, struggling settlement, considered vain. And, of course, completely uninterested in crippled, old, solitary Neha.

It was something she had not been able, nor, truth be told, wanted, to do: to add to the next generation. If this mission failed, if the *Niamey* crashed as they had, then perhaps that was for the best.

"Show me again how to adjust the air-flow," she demanded.

"The lever, here," Clintock said, "It'll start half closed, but you'll need to open it up as the oxygen level begins to drop at altitude, otherwise your steam pressure will fall."

Neha's hands trembled as she pulled on a pair of thick gloves, a guard both against the cold wind and the hot boiler. A test flight would have been nice. Except this particular craft was too precious for such luxuries; an attempted landing was the second most dangerous thing it could do.

The first being its difficult take-off, fully laden, into turbulent, uncertain skies.

It could turn out to be the shortest mission ever.

"Here," Ama said, after watching for a while. "You'll need these." She handed over her pair of goggles, turned away before Neha could thank her, striding off to some vantage point nearby.

It was all on the thinnest of margins; blind science with a fat finger stuck in the air. At what elevation would the electronic interference drop to the point where she could uncover the heavily shielded electronics without them being fried? At what elevation would they be able to transmit their desperately short message to one of the three satellites that were hopefully still in orbit, still capable of relaying that message to the colony ships on their way here?

There had been some doubts that the message was even necessary. Would not their quarter-century of silence speak just as eloquently?

And yet, it could not be left to chance. Not for the second ship to arrive, nor the stranded remnants of the first. Their colony was unsustainable despite the best efforts of the survivors. Only the safe arrival of the *Niamey* would assure their long term survival.

Assuming it had ever set off. Assuming it was still on course. Assuming it had not already arrived and suffered a similar, or worse fate, than the *Accra*, its cargo of people and equipment strewn across this barely habitable planet.

Gloomy thoughts, to match the raging storms above.

Abeni was the last to shake her hand, his skin dry as parchment and feeling just as fragile. "Kwenda Nzuri," he said, as he backed away with a bow.

She raised her thumb, smiled a smile she didn't feel. The small group waved as she began her taxi: Clintock, Abeni, the pair who had carried her wheelchair and lifted her into the aircraft, and a half-dozen besides. There was no sign of Ama.

She pulled back on the throttle and the propeller glinted in the hazy light, turning faster and faster until it became a solid blur. That component, at least, was as high-tech as it got; the *Accra* had held a dozen such propellers of different sizes, all light weight and perfectly balanced. Most of them had survived.

The boiler belched a thick cloud of black smoke and she coughed and spluttered in reply, glad of Ama's goggles as she craned to the side to peer ahead.

The edge of the plateau, the escarpment that fell a hundred feet towards the wreck of the *Accra*, was coming up fast. Much *too* fast. *The Daedalus* felt leaden, as earthbound as she was.

Oh god; her muscles screamed as she pulled hard at the controls, as if somehow adding her meagre strength could force the craft into the air.

She wasn't sure if the wheels left the ground before the ground left the wheels. She felt her stomach *lurch* as she and flyer went over the side, dipped into the valley below, and then pulled up, pulled back level, and very slowly began to climb.

Looking down, she saw she had an audience larger than the group up on the plateau. Around the shattered *Accra*, two dozen ant-like figures waved arms and sheets and whatever else they had to hand. She couldn't hear them, of course, and she doubted she was much more to them than a solitary bird high in the sky, but she waved back anyway as she steered the flyer in an ascending loop back towards the plateau. She didn't want to get too far away from her only landing site.

She turned her attention to the turbulent skies, hoping for a gap.

She needed to avoid the worst of the electromagnetic storm, the deep purple and blues that only she could see. The shielded electronics would still fall prey to the full force of their power; she wouldn't be able to shed the cover and transmit the recording until she was above and clear.

A cross wind tugged at the flyer and she fought for control, before lining up against the gusts and flying into them, quickly gaining another hundred feet.

One of the simulations she'd done to get her wings was in the Wright Flyer; a craft that only flew on mankind's maiden flight because of a stiff headwind. She wondered if Ama had managed to learn that particular lesson in *The Daedalus*'s predecessors.

She was closer now to the full fury of the EM storm, closer than she'd been since crashing through it in the fatally wounded *Accra*. The threads twisted and snaked, too dense and active to predict. She spied better conditions ahead, except, when she got there, they weren't better, if anything they were worse. Looping the flyer back she flew once again over a now distant plateau and, beyond it, the skeletal bulk of the great spaceship diminished to that of decaying bug, being slowly stripped bare, the long scar of its impact revealing its death throes.

Frustrated, she circled again, and again, maintaining height as she sought for an opening, watching as the water level in the boiler sank below the first mark.

"After the second mark," Clintock had warned, "you'd better be through and climbing, or you won't get high enough to transmit."

Each time she started an approach the tendrils of purple, the threads of electromagnetic flux, seemed to close the gap, to feel their way towards her delicate craft and its precious cargo.

It was if they were reaching for her.

For a moment, she forgot to breath.

It was *exactly* like they were reaching for her.

What if it could sense the electronic payload hidden beneath the heavy metal shielding? Was it sniffing it out, like some tasty morsel?

Or ...or maybe it wasn't the transmitter. Maybe it was *her*?

Maybe it had been her, all along.

She'd known she was special; the only one able to see the violent storms that raged above, somehow tuned to a spectrum that no-one else could perceive. But what if that meant the electromagnetic flux could, in return, see her?

She should land; abort the mission, let Ama take the craft up. Or land and try again without the electronic payload. To scientifically check what the purple threads were attracted to.

But there was a reason all their eggs were in one basket. It wasn't just the transmitter that was irreplaceable, the scant few robust or simply lucky components that had survived the lightening storm of their descent and the *Accra's* impact. *The Daedalus* was no less precious, the labour of many months, of years.

To risk a landing without first completing her mission, would be to risk failure.

She swore to the shining ones, to the Hindu Deities her mother had told her about, to Vayu, the Lord of the winds, to Surya, the God of the sky. Gods she didn't believe in, except as characters in bedtime stories. Even that had been enough to single her out in the devoutly Christian Missionary school she'd first attended.

Whether it was her or the electronic box where her feet should be, this mission was doomed.

And yet ...if it was *her* that the tendrils were seeking out, then might that be what had also doomed the *Accra*? Uncomfortable though that thought was, might the *Niamey* be safe as a result? After all, those early autonomous surveys had shown nothing more than the usual aurora caused by solar winds, the welcoming signs of a protecting magnetic field. Nothing like what had torn through the *Accra*.

Be rational, she told herself. *Think it through. How do I test this theory?*

Not by landing, that was for sure.

Perhaps by letting the storm claim its prize?

The Daedalus needed no electronics to function, nor did she. The transmitter was the only thing at risk, and precious though that was, knowing the truth was more important.

Steeling herself, she eased back the controls, flying straight up into the waiting clouds.

Purple enveloped her and pain exploded across every nerve ending, even ones she knew she no longer had. It was that sensation: needles stabbed into knees and legs and feet, that prevented her from jerking the controls into a rapid and most probably unrecoverable descent; the awareness that somehow this wasn't real.

It didn't stop it hurting like hell.

Slowly, it eased, leaving a raw, tingling sensation, her nerves strumming. Blue lightning danced along the edges of the solar-sail wings, sparks crackled over the blackened belly of the boiler.

"*Neha*," a voice whispered.

A shape loomed out of the bruised clouds before her. A head sculpted from delicate purple strands. Her head, complete with a livid scar. She twisted the control stick, felt the flyer shudder under her harsh treatment. The head evaporated, only to reform on her new setting, the eyes blinking open, a thin smile on its – her – lips.

"You return," it said.

Neha shook her head. This wasn't happening. Was she hallucinating? How high up was she; what was the oxygen level?

A faint descending whine caught her attention – the boiler! Whether she was seeing things or not, the air *was* thinner here and the flames that gave rise to steam were dying out. She pushed the lever that regulated the air flow wide open.

"Such wonder!" the head spoke, though the lips didn't move and there was no way she should have heard it over the rush of air, the clanking of the steam engine, *"To find another sentience, someone from so very far away ...And in such an unusual form; intelligent life contained within the substrate of an organic body. Truly the Universe is a marvellous place! We reached out to you, but then you were gone.*

"We thought you lost, Neha," the apparition added, the smile fading, an air of sadness in the impossible voice, *"lost when you fell so swiftly from the sky. Why did you fall?"*

Behind the goggles, Neha's eyes filled with tears.

"You – your emanations. They clashed with our instruments, our controls."

"Ahh ...sorrow! We ...did not know."

Then, as an afterthought: *"There were others with you?"*

"Yes," Neha sobbed. "Yes. There were. There are. I do not think they can sense you, though. And ...there are more coming."

"That is good. Companionship is good. Now we look for them, we can sense them, they do not burn as brightly as you. We are glad. We are many; we feared you were alone."

"No, I'm not alone." She almost laughed; at that moment, the blood of the *Accra* on her hands, she felt as alone as she'd ever been. "But, please, when they come, don't reach out to them?"

"As you wish. But now, we sense your craft is failing. Your time among us is short. Hurry down safely, Neha. Find a way to return to us, when you can?"

* * *

The undercarriage was too rigid and too fragile, weight saved at the expense of strength. She'd tried as best she could to line up her approach with the prepared dirt runway, the thin strip cleared of bush and loose stone, but at the last a gust slewed her sideways. Had she had legs, they would have been crushed as the lightweight craft stumbled and rolled, as the thin frame crumpled up against the heavy boiler in front.

Ama got there first; the rest were with her seconds later, cutting Neha loose, dragging her clear, though the flames of the furnace had long since died out and the cloud of steam that rose up from the pipes of the superheater quickly dissipated. She'd been running on empty for a while.

Clintock pointed at the metal shield still around the transmitter, the shield that would have had to be shed to send the signal. "You ...you failed?" he asked, his voice tremulous and trailing off.

"Not quite," she smiled. She could still feel a tingle at her fingertips. "The *Niamey* will be safe."

"How can you know that?" Abeni asked.

"Long story," she looked back at the twisted flyer, one wing torn in two. "Sorry about *The Daedalus*."

Clintock shrugged. "I've seen worse landings."

And then Ama wrapped her arms around her, hugging her tight, until Clintock coughed in embarrassment.

Neha looked up at the young pilot in surprise, a question on her lips, a question that was answered as it was stifled by Ama's kiss.

No, she wasn't alone.

The heavens roared in amusement and delight and Ama's eyes lit up in wonder as sparks danced from Neha's hands to hers. "Do you hear laughter?" she asked, in astonishment.

Neha smiled and nodded.

Never alone.

Never again.

Skulls in the Stars

Robert E. Howard

*He told how murders walk the earth
Beneath the curse of Cain,
With crimson clouds before their eyes
And flames about their brain:
For blood has left upon their souls
Its everlasting stain.*
Hood

Chapter I

THERE ARE two roads to Torkertown. One, the shorter and more direct route, leads across a barren upland moor, and the other, which is much longer, winds its tortuous way in and out among the hummocks and quagmires of the swamps, skirting the low hills to the east. It was a dangerous and tedious trail; so Solomon Kane halted in amazement when a breathless youth from the village he had just left overtook him and implored him for God's sake to take the swamp road.

"The swamp road!" Kane stared at the boy. He was a tall, gaunt man, Solomon Kane, his darkly pallid face and deep brooding eyes made more sombre by the drab Puritanical garb he affected.

"Yes, sir, 'tis far safer," the youngster answered to his surprised exclamation.

"Then the moor road must be haunted by Satan himself, for your townsmen warned me against traversing the other."

"Because of the quagmires, sir, that you might not see in the dark. You had better return to the village and continue your journey in the morning, sir."

"Taking the swamp road?"

"Yes, sir."

Kane shrugged his shoulders and shook his head.

"The moon rises almost as soon as twilight dies. By its light I can reach Torkertown in a few hours, across the moor."

"Sir, you had better not. No one ever goes that way. There are no houses at all upon the moor, while in the swamp there is the house of old Ezra who lives there all alone since his maniac cousin, Gideon, wandered off and died in the swamp and was never found – and old Ezra though a miser would not refuse you lodging should you decide to stop until morning. Since you must go, you had better go the swamp road."

Kane eyed the boy piercingly. The lad squirmed and shuffled his feet.

"Since this moor road is so dour to wayfarers," said the Puritan, "why did not the villagers tell me the whole tale, instead of vague mouthings?"

"Men like not to talk of it, sir. We hoped that you would take the swamp road after the men advised you to, but when we watched and saw that you turned not at the forks, they sent me to run after you and beg you to reconsider."

"Name of the Devil!" exclaimed Kane sharply, the unaccustomed oath showing his irritation; "the swamp road and the moor road – what is it that threatens me and why should I go miles out of my way and risk the bogs and mires?"

"Sir," said the boy, dropping his voice and drawing closer, "we be simple villagers who like not to talk of such things lest foul fortune befall us, but the moor road is a way accurst and hath not been traversed by any of the countryside for a year or more. It is death to walk those moors by night, as hath been found by some score of unfortunates. Some foul horror haunts the way and claims men for his victims."

"So? And what is this thing like?"

"No man knows. None has ever seen, it and lived, but late-farers have heard terrible laughter far out on the fen and men have heard the horrid shrieks of its victims. Sir, in God's name return to the village, there pass the night, and tomorrow take the swamp trail to Torkertown."

Far back in Kane's gloomy eyes a scintillant light had begun to glimmer, like a witch's torch glinting under fathoms of cold grey ice. His blood quickened. Adventure! The lure of life-risk and drama! Not that Kane recognized his sensations as such. He sincerely considered that he voiced his real feelings when he said: "These things be deeds of some power of evil. The lords of darkness have laid a curse upon the country. A strong man is needed to combat Satan and his might. Therefore I go, who have defied him many a time."

"Sir," the boy began, then closed his mouth as he saw the futility of argument. He only added, "The corpses of the victims are bruised and torn, sir."

He stood there at the crossroads, sighing regretfully as he watched the tall, rangy figure swinging up the road that led toward the moors.

The sun was setting as Kane came over the brow of the low hill which debouched into the upland fen. Huge and blood-red it sank down behind the sullen horizon of the moors, seeming to touch the rank grass with fire; so for a moment the watcher seemed to be gazing out across a sea of blood. Then the dark shadows came gliding from the east, the western blaze faded, and Solomon Kane struck out, boldly in the gathering darkness.

The road was dim from disuse but was clearly defined. Kane went swiftly but warily, sword and pistols at hand. Stars blinked out and night winds whispered among the grass like weeping spectres. The moon began to rise, lean and haggard, like a skull among the stars.

Then suddenly Kane stopped short. From somewhere in front of him sounded a strange and eery echo – or something like an echo. Again, this time louder. Kane started forward again. Were his senses deceiving him? No!

Far out, there pealed a whisper of frightful slaughter. And again, closer this time. No human being ever laughed like that – there was no mirth in it, only hatred and horror and soul-destroying terror. Kane halted. He was not afraid, but for the second he was almost unnerved. Then, stabbing through that awesome laughter, came the sound of a scream that was undoubtedly human. Kane started forward, increasing his gait. He cursed the illusive lights and flickering shadows which veiled the moor in the rising moon and made accurate sight impossible. The laughter continued, growing louder, as did the screams.

Then sounded faintly the drum of frantic human feet. Kane broke into a run. Some human was being hunted to death out there on the fen, and by what manner of horror God only knew. The sound of the flying feet halted abruptly and the screaming rose unbearably, mingled with other sounds unnameable and hideous. Evidently the man had been overtaken, and Kane, his flesh crawling, visualized some ghastly fiend of the darkness crouching on the back of its victim crouching and tearing. Then the noise of a terrible and short struggle came clearly through the abysmal silence of the night and the footfalls began again, but stumbling and uneven. The screaming continued, but with a gasping gurgle. The sweat stood cold on Kane's forehead and body. This was heaping horror on horror in an intolerable manner. God, for a moment's clear light! The frightful drama was being enacted within a very short distance of him, to judge by the ease with which the sounds reached him. But this hellish half-light veiled all in shifting shadows, so that the moors appeared a haze of blurred illusions, and stunted trees, and bushes seemed like giants.

Kane shouted, striving to increase the speed of his advance. The shrieks of the unknown broke into a hideous shrill squealing; again there was the sound of a struggle, and then from the shadows of the tall grass a thing came reeling – a thing that had once been a man – a gore-covered, frightful thing that fell at Kane's feet and writhed and grovelled and raised its terrible face to the rising moon, and gibbered and yammered, and fell down again and died in its own blood.

The moon was up now and the light was better. Kane bent above the body, which lay stark in its unnameable mutilation, and he shuddered; a rare thing for him, who had seen the deeds of the Spanish Inquisition and the witch-finders.

Some wayfarer, he supposed. Then like a hand of ice on his spine he was aware that he was not alone. He looked up, his cold eyes piercing the shadows whence the dead man had staggered. He saw nothing, but he knew – he felt – that other eyes gave back his stare, terrible eyes not of this earth. He straightened and drew a pistol, waiting. The moonlight spread like a lake of pale blood over the moor, and trees and grasses took on their proper sizes. The shadows melted, and Kane saw! At first he thought it only a shadow of mist, a wisp of moor fog that swayed in the tall grass before him. He gazed. More illusion, he thought. Then the thing began to take on shape, vague and indistinct. Two hideous eyes flamed at him – eyes which held all the stark horror which has been the heritage of man since the fearful dawn ages – eyes frightful and insane, with an insanity transcending earthly insanity. The form of the thing was misty and vague, a brain-shattering travesty on the human form, like, yet horribly unlike. The grass and bushes beyond showed clearly through it.

Kane felt the blood pound in his temples, yet he was as cold as ice. How such an unstable being as that which wavered before him could harm a man in a physical way was more than he could understand, yet the red horror at his feet gave mute testimony that the fiend could act with terrible material effect.

Of one thing Kane was sure; there would be no hunting of him across the dreary moors, no screaming and fleeing to be dragged down again and again. If he must die he would die in his tracks, his wounds in front.

Now a vague and grisly mouth gaped wide and the demoniac laughter again shrieked but, soul-shaking in its nearness. And in the midst of feat threat of doom, Kane deliberately levelled his long pistol and fired. A maniacal yell of rage and mockery answered the report, and the thing came at him like a flying sheet of smoke, long shadowy arms stretched to drag him down.

Kane, moving with the dynamic speed of a famished wolf, fired the second pistol with as little effect, snatched his long rapier from its sheath and thrust into the centre of the misty attacker. The blade sang as it passed clear through, encountering no solid resistance, and Kane felt icy fingers grip his limbs, bestial talons tear his garments and the skin beneath.

He dropped the useless sword and sought to grapple with his foe. It was like fighting a floating mist, a flying shadow armed with dagger-like claws. His savage blows met empty air, his leanly mighty arms, in whose grasp strong men had died, swept nothingness and clutched emptiness. Naught was solid or real save the flaying, apelike fingers with their crooked talons, and the crazy eyes which burned into the shuddering depths of his soul.

Kane realized that he was in a desperate plight indeed. Already his garments hung in tatters and he bled from a score of deep wounds. But he never flinched, and the thought of flight never entered his mind. He had never fled from a single foe, and had the thought occurred to him he would have flushed with shame.

He saw no help for it now, but that his form should lie there beside the fragments of the other victim, but the thought held no terrors for him. His only wish was to give as good an account of himself as possible before the end came, and if he could, to inflict some damage on his unearthly foe. There above the dead man's torn body, man fought with demon under the pale light of the rising moon, with all the advantages with the demon, save one. And that one was enough to overcome the others. For if abstract hate may bring into material substance a ghostly thing, may not courage, equally abstract, form a concrete weapon to combat that ghost? Kane fought with his arms and his feet and his hands, and he was aware at last that the ghost began to give back before him, and the fearful slaughter changed to screams of baffled fury. For man's only weapon is courage that flinches not from the gates of Hell itself, and against such not even the legions of Hell can stand. Of this Kane knew nothing; he only knew that the talons which tore and rended him seemed to grow weaker and wavering, that a wild light grew and grew in the horrible eyes. And reeling and gasping, he rushed in, grappled the thing at last and threw it, and as they tumbled about on the moor and it writhed and lapped his limbs like a serpent of smoke, his flesh crawled and his hair stood on end, for he began to understand its gibbering. He did not hear and comprehend as a man hears and comprehends the speech of a man, but the frightful secrets it imparted in whisperings and yammerings and screaming silences sank fingers of ice into his soul, and he knew.

Chapter II

THE HUT of old Ezra the miser stood by the road in the midst of the swamp, half screened by the sullen trees which grew about it. The walls were rotting, the roof crumbling, and great pallid and green fungus-monsters clung to it and writhed about the doors and windows, as if seeking to peer within. The trees leaned above it and their grey branches intertwined so that it crouched in semi-darkness like a monstrous dwarf over whose shoulder ogres leer.

The road, which wound down into the swamp among rotting stumps and rank hummocks and scummy, snake-haunted pools and bogs, crawled past the hut. Many people passed that way these days, but few saw old Ezra, save a glimpse of a yellow face, peering through the fungus-screened windows, itself like an ugly fungus.

Old Ezra the miser partook much of the quality of the swamp, for he was gnarled and bent and sullen; his fingers were like clutching parasitic plants and his locks hung like drab moss above eyes trained to the murk of the swamplands. His eyes were like a dead man's, yet hinted of depths abysmal and loathsome as the dead lakes of the swamplands.

These eyes gleamed now at the man who stood in front of his hut. This man was tall and gaunt and dark, his face was haggard and claw-marked, and he was bandaged of arm and leg. Somewhat behind this man stood a number of villagers.

"You are Ezra of the swamp road?"

"Aye, and what want ye of me?"

"Where is your cousin Gideon, the maniac youth who abode with you?"

"Gideon?"

"Aye."

"He wandered away into the swamp and never came back. No doubt he lost his way and was set upon by wolves or died in a quagmire or was struck by an adder."

"How long ago?"

"Over a year."

"Aye. Hark ye, Ezra the miser. Soon after your cousin's disappearance, a countryman, coming home across the moors, was set upon by some unknown fiend and torn to pieces, and thereafter it became death to cross those moors. First men of the countryside, then strangers who wandered over the fen, fell to the clutches of the thing. Many men have died, since the first one.

"Last night I crossed the moors, and heard the flight and pursuing of another victim, a stranger who knew not the evil of the moors. Ezra the miser, it was a fearful thing, for the wretch twice broke from the fiend, terribly wounded, and each time the demon caught and dragged him down again. And at last he fell dead at my very, feet, done to death in a manner that would freeze the statue of a saint."

The villagers moved restlessly and murmured fearfully to each other, and old Ezra's eyes shifted furtively. Yet the sombre expression of Solomon Kane never altered, and his condor-like stare seemed to transfix the miser.

"Aye, aye!" muttered old Ezra hurriedly; "a bad thing, a bad thing! Yet why do you tell this thing to me?"

"Aye, a sad thing. Harken further, Ezra. The fiend came out of the shadows and I fought with it over the body of its victim. Aye, how I overcame it, I know not, for the battle was hard and long but the powers of good and light were on my side, which are mightier than the powers of Hell."

"At the last I was stronger, and it broke from me and fled, and I followed to no avail. Yet before it fled it whispered to me a monstrous truth."

Old Ezra started, stared wildly, seemed to shrink into himself.

"Nay, why tell me this?" he muttered.

"I returned to the village and told my tale, said Kane, 'for I knew that now I had the power to rid the moors of its curse forever.' Ezra, come with us!"

"Where?" gasped the miser.

"To the rotting oak on the moors." Ezra reeled as though struck; he screamed incoherently and turned to flee.

On the instant, at Kane's sharp order, two brawny villagers sprang forward and seized the miser. They twisted the dagger from his withered hand, and pinioned his arms, shuddering as their fingers encountered his clammy flesh.

Kane motioned them to follow, and turning strode up the trail, followed by the villagers, who found their strength taxed to the utmost in their task of bearing their prisoner along.

Through the swamp they went and out, taking a little-used trail which led up over the low hills and out on the moors.

The sun was sliding down the horizon and old Ezra stared at it with bulging eyes – stared as if he could not gaze enough. Far out on the moors geared up the great oak tree, like a gibbet, now only a decaying shell. There Solomon Kane halted.

Old Ezra writhed in his captor's grasp and made inarticulate noises.

"Over a year ago," said Solomon Kane, "you, fearing that your insane cousin Gideon would tell men of your cruelties to him, brought him away from the swamp by the very trail by which we came, and murdered him here in the night."

Ezra cringed and snarled.

"You can not prove this lie!"

Kane spoke a few words to an agile villager. The youth clambered up the rotting bole of the tree and from a crevice, high up, dragged something that fell with a clatter at the feet of the miser. Ezra went limp with a terrible shriek.

The object was a man's skeleton, the skull cleft.

"You – how knew you this? You are Satan!" gibbered old Ezra.

Kane folded his arms.

"The thing I, fought last night told me this thing as we reeled in battle, and I followed it to this tree. For the fiend is Gideon's ghost."

Ezra shrieked again and fought savagely.

"You knew," said Kane sombrely, "you knew what things did these deeds. You feared the ghost the maniac, and that is why you chose to leave his body on the fen instead of concealing it in the swamp. For you knew the ghost would haunt the place of his death. He was insane in life, and in death he did not know where to find his slayer; else he had come to you in your hut. He hates man but you, but his mazed spirit can not tell one man from another, and he slays all, lest he let his killer escape. Yet he will know you and rest in peace, forever after. Hate hath made of his ghost, solid thing that can rend and slay, and though he feared you terribly in life, in death he fears you not at all."

Kane halted. He glanced at the sun.

"All this I had from Gideon's ghost, in his yammerings and his whisperings and his shrieking silences. Naught but your death will lay that ghost."

Ezra listened in breathless silence and Kane pronounced the words of his doom.

"A hard thing it is," said Kane sombrely, "to sentence a man to death in cold blood and in such a manner as I have in mind, but you must die that others may live – and God knoweth you deserve death.

"You shall not die by noose, bullet or sword, but at the talons of him you slew – for naught else will satiate him."

At these words Ezra's brain shattered, his knees gave way and he fell grovelling and screaming for death, begging them to burn him at the stake, to flay him alive. Kane's face was set like death, and the villagers, the fear rousing their cruelty, bound the screeching wretch to the oak tree, and one of them bade him make his peace with God. But Ezra made no answer, shrieking in a high shrill voice with unbearable monotony. Then the villager would have struck the miser across the face, but Kane stayed him.

"Let him make his peace with Satan, whom he is more like to meet," said the Puritan grimly. "The sun is about to set. Loose his cords so that he may work loose by dark, since it is better to meet death free and unshackled than bound like a sacrifice."

As they turned to leave him, old Ezra yammered and gibbered unhuman sounds and then fell silent, staring at the sun with terrible intensity.

They walked away across the fen, and Kane flung a last look at the grotesque form bound to the tree, seeming in the uncertain light like a great fungus growing to the bole. And suddenly the miser screamed hideously: "Death! Death! There are skulls in the Stars!"

"Life was good to him, though he was gnarled and churlish and evil," Kane sighed. "Mayhap God has a place for such souls where fire and sacrifice may cleanse them of their dross as fire cleans the forest of fungus things. Yet my heart is heavy within me."

"Nay, sir," one of the villagers spoke, "you have done but the will of God, and good alone shall come of this night's deed."

"Nay," answered Kane heavily. "I know not – I know not."

The sun had gone down and night spread with amazing swiftness, as if great shadows came rushing down from unknown voids to cloak the world with hurrying darkness. Through the thick night came a weird echo, and the men halted and looked back the way they had come.

Nothing could be seen. The moor was an ocean of shadows and the tall grass about them bent in long waves before the, faint wind, breaking the deathly stillness with breathless murmurings.

Then far away the red disk of the moon rose over the fen, and for an instant a grim silhouette was etched blackly against it. A shape came flying across the face of the moon – a bent, grotesque thing whose feet seemed scarcely to touch the earth; and close behind came a thing like a flying shadow – a nameless, shapeless horror.

A moment the racing twain stood out boldly against the moon; then they merged into one unnameable, formless mass, and vanished in the shadows.

Far across the fen sounded a single shriek of terrible laughter.

Rip Van Winkle

Washington Irving

Chapter I

WHOEVER HAS MADE a voyage up the Hudson must remember the Catskill Mountains. They are a branch of the great Appalachian family, and are seen away to the west of the river, swelling up to a noble height, and lording it over the surrounding country. Every change of season, every change of weather, indeed, every hour of the day, produces some change in the magical hues and shapes of these mountains, and they are regarded by all the goodwives, far and near, as perfect barometers.

At the foot of these fairy mountains the traveler may have seen the light smoke curling up from a village, whose shingle roofs gleam among the trees, just where the blue tints of the upland melt away into the fresh green of the nearer landscape. It is a little village of great age, having been founded by some of the Dutch colonists in the early times of the province, just about the beginning of the government of the good Peter Stuyvesant (may he rest in peace!), and there were some of the houses of the original settlers standing within a few years, built of small yellow bricks brought from Holland, having latticed windows and gable fronts, surmounted with weathercocks.

In that same village, and in one of these very houses, there lived, many years since, while the country was yet a province of Great Britain, a simple, good-natured fellow, of the name of Rip Van Winkle. He was a descendant of the Van Winkles who figured so gallantly in the chivalrous days of Peter Stuyvesant, and accompanied him to the siege of Fort Christina. He inherited, however, but little of the martial character of his ancestors. I have observed that he was a simple, good-natured man; he was, moreover, a kind neighbor and an obedient, henpecked husband.

Certain it is that he was a great favorite among all the goodwives of the village, who took his part in all family squabbles; and never failed, whenever they talked those matters over in their evening gossipings, to lay all the blame on Dame Van Winkle. The children of the village, too, would shout with joy whenever he approached. He assisted at their sports, made their playthings, taught them to fly kites and shoot marbles, and told them long stories of ghosts, witches, and Indians. Whenever he went dodging about the village, he was surrounded by a troop of them, hanging on his skirts, clambering on his back, and playing a thousand tricks on him; and not a dog would bark at him throughout the neighborhood.

The great error in Rip's composition was a strong dislike of all kinds of profitable labor. It could not be from the want of perseverance; for he would sit on a wet rock, with a rod as long and heavy as a lance, and fish all day without a murmur, even though he should not be encouraged by a single nibble. He would carry a fowling piece on his shoulder for hours together, trudging through woods and swamps, and up hill and down dale, to shoot a few squirrels or wild pigeons. He would never refuse to assist a neighbor even in the roughest toil, and was a foremost man at all country frolics for husking Indian corn, or building stone fences; the women of the village, too, used to employ him to run their errands, and to do such little odd jobs as their less obliging husbands would not do for them. In a word, Rip was ready to attend to anybody's business but his own; but as to doing family duty, and keeping his farm in order, he found it impossible.

His children, too, were as ragged and wild as if they belonged to nobody. His son Rip promised to inherit the habits, with the old clothes, of his father. He was generally seen trooping like a colt at his mother's heels, equipped in a pair of his father's cast-off breeches, which he had much ado to hold up with one hand, as a fine lady does her train in bad weather.

Rip Van Winkle, however, was one of those happy mortals, of foolish, well-oiled dispositions, who take the world easy, eat white bread or brown, whichever can be got with least thought or trouble, and would rather starve on a penny than work for a pound. If left to himself, he would have whistled life away in perfect contentment; but his wife kept continually dinning in his ear about his idleness, his carelessness, and the ruin he was bringing on his family. Morning, noon, and night, her tongue was incessantly going, and everything he said or did was sure to produce a torrent of household eloquence. Rip had but one way of replying to all lectures of the kind, and that, by frequent use, had grown into a habit. He shrugged his shoulders, shook his head, cast up his eyes, but said nothing. This, however, always provoked a fresh volley from his wife; so that he was fain to draw off his forces, and take to the outside of the house – the only side which, in truth, belongs to a henpecked husband.

Rip's sole domestic adherent was his dog Wolf, who was as much henpecked as his master; for Dame Van Winkle regarded them as companions in idleness, and even looked upon Wolf with an evil eye, as the cause of his master's going so often astray. True it is, in all points of spirit befitting an honorable dog, he was as courageous an animal as ever scoured the woods; but what courage can withstand the ever-enduring and all-besetting terrors of a woman's tongue? The moment Wolf entered the house his crest fell, his tail drooped to the ground or curled between his legs, he sneaked about with a gallows air, casting many a sidelong glance at Dame Van Winkle, and at the least flourish of a broomstick or ladle he would fly to the door with yelping precipitation.

Times grew worse and worse with Rip Van Winkle as years of matrimony rolled on. A tart temper never mellows with age, and a sharp tongue is the only edged tool that grows keener with constant use. For a long while he used to console himself, when driven from home, by frequenting a kind of perpetual club of sages, philosophers, and other idle personages of the village, which held its sessions on a bench before a small inn, designated by a rubicund portrait of His Majesty George III. Here they used to sit in the shade of a long, lazy summer's day, talking listlessly over village gossip, or telling endless sleepy stories about nothing. But it would have been worth any statesman's money to have heard the profound discussions which sometimes took place, when by chance an old newspaper fell into their hands from some passing traveler. How solemnly they would listen to the contents, as drawled out by Derrick Van Bummel, the schoolmaster, – a dapper, learned little man, who was not to be daunted by the mostgigantic word in the dictionary! And how sagely they would deliberate upon public events some months after they had taken place!

The opinions of this junto were completely controlled by Nicholas Vedder, a patriarch of the village, and landlord of the inn, at the door of which he took his seat from morning till night, just moving sufficiently to avoid the sun, and keep in the shade of a large tree; so that the neighbors could tell the hour by his movements as accurately as by a sun-dial. It is true, he was rarely heard to speak, but smoked his pipe incessantly. His adherents, however (for every great man has his adherents), perfectly understood him, and knew how to gather his opinions. When anything that was read or related displeased him, he was observed to smoke his pipe vehemently, and to send forth short, frequent, and angry puffs; but, when pleased, he would inhale the smoke slowly and tranquilly, and emit it in light and placid clouds, and sometimes, taking the pipe from his mouth, and letting the fragrant vapor curl about his nose, would nod his head in approbation.

From even this stronghold the unlucky Rip was at length routed by his termagant wife, who would suddenly break in upon the tranquility of the assemblage, and call the members all to naught; nor was that august personage, Nicholas Vedder himself, sacred from the daring tongue of this terrible virago, who charged him with encouraging her husband in habits of idleness.

Poor Rip was at last reduced almost to despair; and his only alternative, to escape from the labor of the farm and clamor of his wife, was to take gun in hand and stroll away into the woods. Here he would sometimes seat himself at the foot of a tree, and share the contents of his wallet with Wolf, with whom he sympathized as a fellow-sufferer in persecution. "Poor Wolf," he would say, "thy mistress leads thee a dog's life of it; but never mind, my lad, whilst I live thou shalt never want a friend to stand by thee." Wolf would wag his tail, look wistfully in his master's face; and if dogs can feel pity, I verily believe he reciprocated the sentiment with all his heart.

In a long ramble of the kind on a fine autumnal day, Rip had unconsciously scrambled to one of the highest parts of the Catskill Mountains. He was after his favorite sport of squirrel-shooting, and the still solitudes had echoed and re-echoed with the reports of his gun. Panting and fatigued, he threw himself, late in the afternoon, on a green knoll, covered with mountain herbage, that crowned the brow of a precipice. From an opening between the trees he could overlook all the lower country for many a mile of rich woodland. He saw at a distance the lordly Hudson, far, far below him, moving on its silent but majestic course, with the reflection of a purple cloud, or the sail of a lagging bark, here and there sleeping on its glassy bosom, and at last losing itself in the blue highlands.

On the other side he looked down into a deep mountain glen, wild and lonely, the bottom filled with fragments from the overhanging cliffs, and scarcely lighted by the reflected rays of the setting sun. For some time Rip lay musing on this scene; evening was gradually advancing; the mountains began to throw their long blue shadows over the valleys; he saw that it would be dark long before he could reach the village, and he heaved a heavy sigh when he thought of encountering the terrors of Dame Van Winkle.

As he was about to descend, he heard a voice from a distance, hallooing, "Rip Van Winkle! Rip Van Winkle!" He looked round, but could see nothing but a crow winging its solitary flight across the mountain. He thought his fancy must have deceived him, and turned again to descend, when he heard the same cry ring through the still evening air: "Rip Van Winkle! Rip Van Winkle!" – at the same time Wolf bristled up his back, and giving a low growl, skulked to his master's side, looking fearfully down into the glen. Rip now felt a vague apprehension stealing over him; he looked anxiously in the same direction, and perceived a strange figure slowly toiling up the rocks, and bending under the weight of something he carried on his back. He was surprised to see any human being in this lonely and unfrequented place; but supposing it to be some one of the neighborhood in need of his assistance, he hastened down to yield it.

On nearer approach he was still more surprised at the singularity of the stranger's appearance. He was a short, square-built old fellow, with thick bushy hair, and a grizzled beard. His dress was of the antique Dutch fashion, – a cloth jerkin strapped round the waist, and several pair of breeches, the outer one of ample volume, decorated with rows of buttons down the sides. He bore on his shoulder a stout keg that seemed full of liquor, and made signs for Rip to approach and assist him with the load. Though rather shy and distrustful of this new acquaintance, Rip complied with his usual alacrity, and relieving one another, they clambered up a narrow gully, apparently the dry bed of a mountain torrent.

As they ascended, Rip every now and then heard long, rolling peals, like distant thunder, that seemed to issue out of a deep ravine, or rather cleft, between lofty rocks, toward which their rugged path conducted. He paused for an instant, but supposing it to be the muttering of one of those transient thundershowers which often take place in mountain heights, he proceeded. Passing through the ravine, they came to a hollow, like a small amphitheater, surrounded by perpendicular precipices, over the brinks of which trees shot their branches, so that you only caught glimpses of the azure sky and the bright evening cloud. During the whole time Rip and his companion had labored on in silence; for though the former marveled greatly, what could be the object of carrying a keg of liquor up this wild mountain, yet there was something strange and incomprehensible about the unknown that inspired awe and checked familiarity.

On entering the amphitheater new objects of wonder presented themselves. On a level spot in the center was a company of odd-looking personages playing at ninepins. They were dressed in a quaint, outlandish fashion; some wore short doublets, others jerkins, with long knives in their belts, and most of them had enormous breeches, of similar style with that of the guide's. Their visages, too, were peculiar: one had a large head, broad face, and small, piggish eyes; the face of another seemed to consist entirely of nose, and was surmounted by a white sugar-loaf hat, set off with a little red cock's tail. They all had beards, of various shapes and colors. There was one who seemed to be the commander. He was a stout old gentleman, with a weather-beaten countenance; he wore a laced doublet, broad belt and hanger, high-crowned hat and feather, red stockings, and high-heeled shoes, with roses in them. The whole group reminded Rip of the figures in an old Flemish painting, in the parlor of Dominie Van Shaick, the village parson, which had been brought over from Holland at the time of the settlement.

What seemed particularly odd to Rip was that, though these folks were evidently amusing themselves, yet they maintained the gravest faces, the most mysterious silence, and were, withal, the most melancholy party of pleasure he had ever witnessed. Nothing interrupted the stillness of the scene but the noise of the balls, which, whenever they were rolled, echoed along the mountains like rumbling peals of thunder.

As Rip and his companion approached them, they suddenly desisted from their play, and stared at him with such fixed, statue-like gaze, and such strange, uncouth countenances, that his heart turned within him, and his knees smote together. His companion now emptied the contents of the keg into large flagons, and made signs to him to wait upon the company. He obeyed with fear and trembling; they quaffed the liquor in profound silence, and then returned to their game.

By degrees Rip's awe and apprehension subsided. He even ventured, when no eye was fixed upon him, to taste the beverage, which he found had much of the flavor of excellent Hollands. He was naturally a thirsty soul, and was soon tempted to repeat the draught. One taste provoked another; and he repeated his visits to the flagon so often that at length his senses were overpowered, his eyes swam in his head, his head gradually declined, and he fell into a deep sleep.

Chapter II

ON WAKING he found himself on the green knoll whence he had first seen the old man of the glen. He rubbed his eyes – it was a bright, sunny morning. The birds were hopping and twittering among the bushes, and the eagle was wheeling aloft, and breasting the pure mountain breeze. "Surely," thought Rip, "I have not slept here all night." He recalled the occurrences before he fell asleep. The strange man with a keg of liquor – the mountain ravine – the wild retreat among the rocks – the woe-begone party at ninepins – the flagon – "Oh! That flagon! That wicked flagon!" thought Rip; "what excuse shall I make to Dame Van Winkle?"

He looked round for his gun, but in place of the clean, well-oiled fowling piece, he found an old firelock lying by him, the barrel incrusted with rust, the lock falling off, and the stock worm-eaten. He now suspected that the grave revelers of the mountain had put a trick upon him and, having dosed him with liquor, had robbed him of his gun. Wolf, too, had disappeared, but he might have strayed away after a squirrel or partridge. He whistled after him, and shouted his name, but all in vain; the echoes repeated his whistle and shout, but no dog was to be seen.

He determined to revisit the scene of the last evening's gambol, and if he met with any of the party, to demand his dog and gun. As he rose to walk, he found himself stiff in the joints, and wanting in his usual activity. "These mountain beds do not agree with me," thought Rip, "and if this frolic should lay me up with a fit of the rheumatism, I shall have a blessed time with Dame Van Winkle." With some difficulty he got down into the glen; he found the gully up which he and his companion had ascended the preceding evening; but to his astonishment a mountain stream was now foaming down it, leaping from rock to rock, and filling the glen with babbling murmurs. He, however, made shift to scramble up its sides, working his toilsome way through thickets of birch, sassafras, and witch-hazel, and sometimes tripped up or entangled by the wild grapevines that twisted their coils from tree to tree, and spread a kind of network in his path.

At length he reached to where the ravine had opened through the cliffs to the amphitheater; but no traces of such opening remained. The rocks presented a high, impenetrable wall, over which the torrent came tumbling in a sheet of feathery foam, and fell into a broad, deep basin, black from the shadows of the surrounding forest. Here, then, poor Rip was brought to a stand. He again called and whistled after his dog; he was only answered by the cawing of a flock of idle crows sporting high in air about a dry tree that overhung a sunny precipice; and who, secure in their elevation, seemed to look down and scoff at the poor man's perplexities. What was to be done? – the morning was passing away, and Rip felt famished for want of his breakfast. He grieved to give up his dog and gun; he dreaded to meet his wife; but it would not do to starve among the mountains. He shook his head, shouldered the rusty firelock, and, with a heart full of trouble and anxiety, turned his steps homeward.

As he approached the village he met a number of people, but none whom he knew, which somewhat surprised him, for he had thought himself acquainted with every one in the country round. Their dress, too, was of a different fashion from that to which he was accustomed. They all stared at him with equal marks of surprise, and whenever they cast their eyes upon him, invariably stroked their chins. The constant recurrence of this gesture induced Rip, involuntarily, to do the same, when, to his astonishment, he found his beard had grown a foot long!

He had now entered the skirts of the village. A troop of strange children ran at his heels, hooting after him, and pointing at his gray beard. The dogs, too, not one of which he recognized for an old acquaintance, barked at him as he passed. The very village was altered; it was larger and more populous. There were rows of houses which he had never seen before, and those which had been his familiar haunts had disappeared. Strange names were over the doors – strange faces at the windows – everything was strange. His mind now misgave him; he began to doubt whether both he and the world around him were not bewitched. Surely this was his native village, which he had left but the day before. There stood the Catskill Mountains – there ran the silver Hudson at a distance – there was every hill and dale precisely as it had always been. Rip was sorely perplexed. "That flagon last night," thought he, "has addled my poor head sadly!"

It was with some difficulty that he found the way to his own house, which he approached with silent awe, expecting every moment to hear the shrill voice of Dame Van Winkle. He found the house gone to decay – the roof fallen in, the windows shattered, and the doors off the hinges. A half-starved dog that looked like Wolf was skulking about it. Rip called him by name, but the cur snarled, showed his teeth, and passed on. This was an unkind cut indeed. "My very dog," sighed Rip, "has forgotten me!"

He entered the house, which, to tell the truth, Dame Van Winkle had always kept in neat order. It was empty, forlorn, and apparently abandoned. He called loudly for his wife and children – the lonely chambers rang for a moment with his voice, and then all again was silence.

Chapter III

HE NOW HURRIED forth, and hastened to his old resort, the village inn – but it, too, was gone. A large, rickety wooden building stood in its place, with great gaping windows, some of them broken and mended with old hats and petticoats, and over the door was painted, "The Union Hotel, by Jonathan Doolittle." Instead of the great tree that used to shelter the quiet little Dutch inn of yore, there now was reared a tall, naked pole, with something on the top that looked like a red nightcap, and from it was fluttering a flag, on which was a singular assemblage of stars and stripes; all this was strange and incomprehensible. He recognized on the sign, however, the ruby face of King George, under which he had smoked so many a peaceful pipe; but even this was singularly changed. The red coat was changed for one of blue and buff, a sword was held in the hand instead of a scepter, the head was decorated with a cocked hat, and underneath was painted in large characters, General Washington.

There was, as usual, a crowd of folk about the door, but none that Rip recollected. The very character of the people seemed changed. There was a busy, bustling tone about it, instead of the accustomed drowsy tranquility. He looked in vain for the sage Nicholas Vedder, with his broad face, double chin, and long pipe, uttering clouds of tobacco smoke instead of idle speeches; or Van Bummel, the schoolmaster, doling forth the contents of an ancient newspaper. In place of these, a lean fellow, with his pockets full of handbills, was haranguing vehemently about rights of citizens – elections – members of congress – Bunker's Hill – heroes of seventy-six – and other words, which were a perfect jargon to the bewildered Van Winkle.

The appearance of Rip, with his long, grizzled beard, his rusty fowling piece, his uncouth dress, and an army of women and children at his heels, soon attracted the attention of the tavern politicians. They crowded round him, eyeing him from head to foot with great curiosity. The orator bustled up to him, and, drawing him partly aside, inquired "On which side he voted?" Rip stared in vacant stupidity. Another short but busy little fellow pulled him by the arm, and, rising on tiptoe, inquired in his ear, "Whether he was Federal or Democrat?" Rip was equally at a loss to comprehend the question; when a knowing, self-important old gentleman, in a sharp cocked hat, made his way through the crowd, putting them to the right and left with his elbows as he passed, and planting himself before Van Winkle, with one arm akimbo, the other resting on his cane, his keen eyes and sharp hat penetrating, as it were, into his very soul, demanded, in an austere tone, "What brought him to the election with a gun on his shoulder, and a mob at his heels; and whether he meant to breed a riot in the village?" – "Alas! Gentlemen," cried Rip, somewhat dismayed, "I am a poor, quiet man, a native of the place, and a loyal subject of the king, God bless him!"

Here a general shout burst from the bystanders–"A tory! A tory! A spy! A refugee! Hustle him! Away with him!" It was with great difficulty that the self-important man in the cocked hat restored order; and having assumed a tenfold austerity of brow, demanded again of the unknown culprit, what he came there for, and whom he was seeking! The poor man humbly assured him that he meant no harm, but merely came there in search of some of his neighbors.

"Well – who are they? Name them."

Rip bethought himself a moment, and inquired, "Where's Nicholas Vedder?"

There was a silence for a little while, when an old man replied, in a thin, piping voice, "Nicholas Vedder! Why, he is dead and gone these eighteen years! There was a wooden tombstone in the churchyard that used to tell all about him, but that's rotten and gone, too."

"Where's Brom Dutcher?"

"Oh, he went off to the army in the beginning of the war; some say he was killed at the storming of Stony Point; others say he was drowned in a squall at the foot of Anthony's Nose. I don't know; he never came back again."

"Where's Van Brummel, the schoolmaster?"

"He went off to the wars, too, was a great militia general, and is now in congress."

Rip's heart died away at hearing of these sad changes in his home and friends and finding himself thus alone in the world. Every answer puzzled him, too, by treating of such enormous lapses of time, and of matters which he could not understand: war – congress – Stony Point. He had no courage to ask after any more friends, but cried out in despair, "Does nobody here know Rip Van Winkle?"

"Oh, Rip Van Winkle!" exclaimed two or three, "Oh, to be sure! That's Rip Van Winkle yonder, leaning against the tree."

Rip looked, and beheld a precise counterpart of himself, as he went up the mountain – apparently as lazy and certainly as ragged. The poor fellow was now completely confounded. He doubted his own identity, and whether he was himself or another man. In the midst of his bewilderment, the man in the cocked hat demanded who he was, and what was his name.

"God knows," exclaimed he, at his wits' end; "I'm not myself – I'm somebody else – that's me yonder – no – that's somebody else got into my shoes – I was myself last night, but I fell asleep on the mountain, and they've changed my gun, and everything's changed, and I'm changed, and I can't tell what's my name, or who I am!"

The bystanders began now to look at each other, nod, wink significantly, and tap their fingers against their foreheads. There was a whisper, also, about securing the gun, and keeping the old fellow from doing mischief, at the very suggestion of which the self-important man in the cocked hat retired with some precipitation. At this critical moment a fresh, comely woman pressed through the throng to get a peep at the gray-bearded man. She had a chubby child in her arms, which, frightened at his looks, began to cry. "Hush, Rip," cried she, "hush, you little fool; the old man won't hurt you." The name of the child, the air of the mother, the tone of her voice, all awakened a train of recollections in his mind. "What is your name, my good woman?" asked he.

"Judith Gardenier."

"And your father's name?"

"Ah, poor man, Rip Van Winkle was his name, but it's twenty years since he went away from home with his gun, and never has been heard of since – his dog came home without him; but whether he shot himself, or was carried away by the Indians, nobody can tell. I was then but a little girl."

Rip had but one question more to ask; but he put it with a faltering voice:

"Where's your mother?"

"Oh, she, too, had died but a short time since; she broke a blood-vessel in a fit of passion at a New England peddler."

There was a drop of comfort, at least, in this intelligence. The honest man could contain himself no longer. He caught his daughter and her child in his arms. "I am your father!" cried he – "Young Rip Van Winkle once – Old Rip Van Winkle now! Does nobody know poor Rip Van Winkle?"

All stood amazed until an old woman, tottering out from among the crowd, put her hand to her brow, and peering under it in his face for a moment, exclaimed, "Sure enough! It is Rip Van Winkle – it is himself! Welcome home again, old neighbor. Why, where have you been these twenty long years?"

Rip's story was soon told, for the whole twenty years had been to him but as one night. The neighbors stared when they heard it; some were seen to wink at each other, and put their tongues in their cheeks: and the self-important man in the cocked hat, who when the alarm was over had returned to the field, screwed down the corners of his mouth, and shook his head–upon which there was a general shaking of the head throughout the assemblage.

It was determined, however, to take the opinion of old Peter Vanderdonk, who was seen slowly advancing up the road. He was a descendant of the historian of that name, who wrote one of the earliest accounts of the province. Peter was the most ancient inhabitant of the village, and well versed in all the wonderful events and traditions of the neighborhood. He recollected Rip at once, and corroborated his story in the most satisfactory manner. He assured the company that it was a fact, handed down from his ancestor the historian, that the Catskill Mountains had always been haunted by strange beings. It was affirmed that the great Hendrick Hudson, the first discoverer of the river and country, kept a kind of vigil there every twenty years, with his crew of the *Half-moon*; being permitted in this way to revisit the scenes of his enterprise, and keep a guardian eye upon the river and the great city called by his name. His father had once seen them in their old Dutch dresses playing at ninepins in a hollow of the mountain; and he himself had heard, one summer afternoon, the sound of their balls, like distant peals of thunder.

To make a long story short, the company broke up and returned to the more important concerns of the election. Rip's daughter took him home to live with her; she had a snug, well-furnished house, and a stout, cheery farmer for a husband, whom Rip recollected for one of the urchins that used to climb upon his back. As to Rip's son and heir, who was the ditto of himself, seen leaning against the tree, he was employed to work on the farm; but showed an hereditary disposition to attend to anything else but his business.

The Aerial Burglar

Percival Leigh

WE LATELY submitted ourselves to the process of being Mesmerised; and during the magnetic state, which was that of the highest degree of clairvoyance, were favoured with a peep into futurity. We recollect nothing, whatever, of all that we saw; but we are told that we wrote part of it down at the time, our eyes then being fast closed, and we sitting in a Windsor-chair upon the points of twelve tenpenny nails, which, for our own accommodation, and for the satisfaction of the company present, that we were in a slate of physical insensibility, had been driven up through the bottom of it.

The ensuing narrative is compiled from the account, which, as we are informed, we indited upon that occasion.

We found ourselves, all at once (where many Mesmerists, as well as their patients – also sundry metaphysicians, theologians, and moralists – very often lose themselves), in the clouds.

Over the broad fields of air were spread innumerable islands of immense magnitude, of a circular form, and flattened above and below, so – to compare great things with small – as to resemble Cheshire cheeses. These we at first thought were planets, but we presently came to find that they were structures of human invention, composed as follows: over a case, forming an enormous air-cushion, was disposed a sort of wood-pavement, made of cork, which had been subjected to a process securing it from decomposition. Upon this was placed an artificial soil of earth, where grew herbage and trees of various kinds; and on which, dwelling-places, made of light yet warm materials, had been erected. The interiors of these artificial islands were filled with the Mesmeric fluid itself, – a gas many millions of times lighter than the most rarefied hydrogen; enabling them, notwithstanding the weight of their solid parts, to remain suspended in the air. Each of them was furnished with a stop-cock, whereby the gas might be let out at pleasure, and upon them all there was kept a large number of cats, from which creatures it had been discovered that the Mesmerogen, as the gas was termed, was procurable. These islands were tenanted by men, women, children, cattle, and other animals. When the aerial islanders wanted to descend, they let a quantity of the fluid out; when they wished to rise, they forced some of it in; displacing, of course, by so doing, the atmospheric air. This was Dean Swift's idea of a flying island realised, without the aid of magic!

The epoch in which we were existing, was the year 2000, – to such a pitch had science by that time attained! But, alas! Morality had not made a corresponding advancement; and it was with pain that we contemplated an aerial police, patrolling on flying machines, which were like huge turbots with wings, between the isles in mid-air. There was no mistaking them; the dark blue of their attire was relieved upon the lighter azure, their collars were lettered and numbered, and they wore list around their cuffs, which shewed that they were upon duty.

Yes; crime, without leaving the earth, had soared into the sky; and theft and robbery contaminated the air.

Dodging among the clouds, and evidently desirous of avoiding observation, we remarked an individual on a machine that seemed like a flying narwhal, or unicorn fish, the snout being furnished with a long and formidable spike resembling that creature's horn. As he threaded his way through the darker masses of vapours, he threw around him into every nook and corner the rays of a dark lantern, which lighted up their gloomy recesses and kindled their lurid promontories with a red glare. As night came on these appearances were the more observable, and the policemen, now indistinguishable in the darkness, save by the lanterns which they also carried, seemed like portentous meteors flashing athwart the sky.

Our consciousness, now, for a moment, became suspended. When it returned, we found ourselves in a bedchamber of a small cottage, which stood upon the verge of one of these islands. It was still night. The moon was shining through the open casement, in whose front, overshadowing the right angle, hung a graceful cluster of ivy, through which the night-breeze was sighing at intervals. Lights, now rendered less conspicuous by the moonshine, were still gliding about at a distance, and leisurely emerging from, and then disappearing amidst the clouds.

Whilst we were enjoying this singular and wonderful spectacle, a light footstep approached; the chamber door opened, and a young and lovely girl, whose age might have been about twenty, entered with a rushlight in her hand. She was attired with a mixture of elegance and simplicity, in virgin-white muslin, with a black ribbon round the waist; a dress which became a cheek fair, but slightly pale, sparkling grey eyes, raven tresses, and a snowy brow, exceedingly. In a comer, on a chair, hung a richer garment of similar hue, but of satin, with appropriate accompaniments; ready to all appearance for the morrow, and being, unequivocally, a wedding costume. Placing her candle on the toilette-table, whereupon were arranged a variety of articles of feminine elegance, she approached the window, and pensively reclined with her cheek upon her hand, and her elbow on the sill.

Presently a voice was heard below, singing to the accompaniment of an ophicleide.

> *"Louisa, sleep till morning's sun*
> *Shall gild thy cloud-built home;*
> *And rise to see us two made one,*
> *In yonder sacred dome.*
> *La, la, la, lira la!*
> *Until the holy rite be done,*
> *Ah! whither shall I roam?*
> *Lira la!"*

" 'Tis Edward!" exclaimed the maiden. "Oh, Edward, go to bed; thou wilt catch cold in the night air."

"Not a bit of it," answered the lover, with the accents of youth. "I can't go to bed. I am all impatience for the happy hour that shall unite me for ever with thee. Meanwhile I shall be unable to close these eyes. But I will not disturb thy slumbers, Louisa. First let me charm thee, with the magic power of melody, to repose; and then, whirled about on my trusty Pegasus, I go to wander till mom in the moonlit air."

At these words the maiden threw herself listlessly on her couch; and the lover commenced a slow and soothing lullaby on his deep-toned instrument. In a few moments she slept, and the musician, striking into a lively air, which seemed very much like 'The girls we leave behind us,' mounted his machine, and, the tune dying away as he ascended, was soon out of sight.

Louisa still slept, and the chamber, save with her musical breathing, was hushed. The rushlight was burning low, and the room consequently darkened, when suddenly a flash of light illuminated its interior, as some aerial navigator glided by. Presently this phenomenon was repeated; the person, whoever he was, having again crossed the window, and, during his course, having evidently taken a glance at the apartment.

In a few moments there was a noise outside, as of somebody alighting; and suddenly the apparition of a man presented itself at the window, leaning with folded arms upon the sill, and gazing full into the room. The countenance was singularly forbidding; the eyes were deeply set in the head, the nose snubbed, the lips thick, and the whole expression sullen and scowling. There was a short pipe in the mouth, and a thick bludgeon, crossing the chest diagonally, rose over the left shoulder. The individual wore a white hat, much battered, with a piece of black crape round it, and by this circumstance we identified him with the person we had seen lurking among the clouds.

After standing in this position for a second or two, he looked cautiously around, first on the right and then on the left, as if to see whether any one was watching him. He then noiselessly lifted one leg up through the casement into the room, displaying the lower part of a nether garment of soiled drab, a not very clean white stocking, and a boot, laced in front, which came a little above the ankle. He then introduced the other leg; and next resting himself on the palm of either hand, let himself down into the room. He looked a tall powerful man, and was dressed in a velveteen shooting jacket, and a waistcoat of faded black. A figured cotton neckcloth, twisted like a rope, was tied around his throat in a knot, and from the pocket of his coat there stuck out the stock of a pistol. It was plain that he was a burglar.

He now, with the pace of one who is treading upon eggs, a precaution which his hob-nailed boots rendered very necessary, approached the fair sleeper. He bent over her, and threw the light of his lantern full in her face. She moved not – with a gesture expressive of satisfaction he put his finger to the side of his nose; and then, after fumbling a little in his pocket, drew forth a large clasp knife. Raising the implement of destruction, he was about to plunge it in her breast, when a sudden cry of "Past twelve o'clock," outside the window, arrested his uplifted arm, and baulked his sanguinary purpose; he slunk hastily behind the bed. The whizzing sound of the watchman's flying machine died away in the distance; the coast was now clear again, and the housebreaker, emerging from his place of concealment, proceeded to make the most of his time, by transferring to his pockets as many moveables as he could find. A brooch, a vinaigrette, a gold clasp, a tortoiseshell-comb, a white cambric handkerchief, and the miniature of a young gentleman, had been thus feloniously appropriated, when the ruffian proceeded to lay his profane hands on the satin wedding-dress, which, as before stated, was hanging on a chair in a corner. The rustling of the material awoke the sleeper, who instantly started up from the bed, and, perceiving a man in the room, gave utterance to a loud scream.

The robber for a moment stood aghast; during which interval the courageous girl, with an unavailing instinct of self-defence, discharged one of her tiny slippers at the villain's head. Ducking, he avoided the harmless missile; and his next act was to rush upon the shrieking victim; and, while with one hand he stopped her mouth, fumbled in his waistcoat pocket for his knife with the other. She, in the meanwhile, perceiving the pistol projecting from beneath the lappet of his coat, with wonderful presence of mind snatched it out, and discharged it full in his face. The ball infringed upon the skull; but instead of penetrating the brain, and thus terminating at once his career of guilt, it glanced, as often happens, and making the circuit of the head beneath the scalp, came out by the hole by which it went in; to the imminent peril of the young lady, one of whose curls it grazed in its backward passage, and then lodged in the bed-post.

Half stunned, the housebreaker staggered back for an instant; and then collecting himself, and brandishing his knife, prepared, with clenched teeth and flashing eyes, to spring, tiger-like, on his prey, when a violent hammering at the door convinced him that the family was alarmed. He rushed, therefore, to the window, but as he was getting out the undaunted Louisa clung to the skirts of his coat. Not a moment was to be lost! Suddenly seizing her in his arms, he disappeared through the casement; and, quick as thought, mounting his aerostatic vehicle, flew off like a sparrow-hawk with a chicken.

At this moment the unhappy Edward arrived from his midnight ramble, just in time to behold all that he held dear upon earth, apparently on her way to the moon. Sounding a fearful blast of alarm upon his ophicleide, he instantly touched a spring in his own conveyance, which let on the steam that it was moved by, and started after the villain in full chase; the whole aerial police, whom the summons had called to his aid, joining in the hue and cry.

It was a grand sight to behold myriads of oxy-hydrogen lights, far and wide over the islets, blazing with an instantaneous splendour, and darting their noon-day radiance deep into the bosom of night. It appeared that every dwelling in the regions of air was furnished with these precautionary appliances, which were capable of being put in action at a moment's notice.

The chase, of which a complete view was thus afforded was animated beyond description. The burglar kept for some time considerably in advance of his pursuers, who however, at last, rapidly gained upon him. He then sought to baffle them by turning and winding, after the manner of a fox, in and out of the clouds. Now he plunged, with Edward, closely followed by the police, each on his several machine directly upon his track, into a dense body of vapour; now he appeared rounding the illuminated outline of one of its bold capes; the hunters instantly succeeding him. Then he dived with incredible velocity beneath an island, and anon soared aloft again, till both he and they looked like small specks among the stars.

The different flying machines of the police force, also, formed a singular display. Some were in the form of birds or of fishes, others resembled dragons, griffins, and other fabulous animals; and the noise which they made in their progress, with the steam by which they were moved, was terrific.

At length the housebreaker was seen descending, with the officers of justice hard upon him. He now made a desperate effort and stood at bay, darting, with infuriated despair into the midst of the throng, and running, with the spike with which his car was armed, full tilt against his foes, whose dexterity in avoiding him was admirable. At last, one of the policemen knocked off that dangerous weapon with his truncheon.

The miscreant, upon this, perceived that his only safety lay in flight; and, with a cruelty and cowardice that must be considered unparalleled, by a sudden jerk disengaged himself from the burden of his prey. Horrible sight for a lover! Louisa fell screaming, with a velocity increasing with the square of the distance, earthward; but the wings of love are fleeter than the force of gravitation, and, ere she had fallen half a mile, Edward, descending with the rapidity of a sunbeam, had caught her in his arms. He conveyed her instantly to her parental home. She had fainted, and was apparently dead; but a dose of *elixir vitae* having been promptly administered to her, she speedily returned to life and love. Lovers only can understand the transports which were then the lot of herself and her Edward.

In the meantime the burglar, surrounded by his pursuers, used every effort to escape. At last, finding all other resources fail him, he drew his remaining pistol; and balancing his car, stood in act to fire. His aim was known to be unerring, and it was clear that he could only be taken alive at the expense of the life of some one of those around him.

Accordingly C. 24, drawing an electrical blunderbuss from a case which hung at his girdle, discharged a flash of lightning at his guilty head. The blow was sure and fatal. His hat, singed and blazing, flew to the winds, and his blackened and shattered form fell, with innumerable gyrations to earth; nor rested till it stuck upon some area railings.

The next morning Edward and Louisa were married, with every prospect of a life of perpetual bliss, enhanced by a recollection of the peril which attended its commencement.

The Crime of a Windcatcher

B.C. Matthews

THE SHARP CRACK of the cat o' nine against Jackson's bare flesh made Midshipman Bourne stifle a wince, his eyes watering against the tears that threatened to spill. But no one aboard the frigate H.M.S. *Novelty* would dare to look away, not with their Captain's bloodshot eyes constantly searching the crowd of faces for any hint of sympathy.

Jackson moaned, bare to the waist, his thick ropy muscles taught as he strained against the cables binding him to the mainmast. The whip lashes stood out on his back as if some ragged-edged claw had raked its vicious talons through his flesh. Shuddering, Bourne watched as the ropes pulled away blood and flesh. Once the knotted ropes were blooded, it became heavier, more vicious, and the sharp crack became a meaty *thwap*.

Captain Ramsay's rough voice matched his wind-tanned craggy face, as he read from the Articles of War, "If any shall strike of his superior officers, every such person being convicted of any such offense shall suffer death." Those wild bloodshot eyes scanned the crew and settled on Bourne for just a moment, and the young midshipman fought not to readjust his stance beneath the weight. "Traitorous dogs shall suffer the pain of Hell, and I shall bring it to them like the right-hand of the Almighty Himself."

Bourne's fellow midshipmen, all younger than him by several years, shuddered and stared at the deck.

But Bourne could feel it. The pull, the tension and crackle that threaded just beneath the surface of his skin, like the sensation of a storm brewing. Others on deck fidgeted.

The mains'ls above flapped wildly in the calm of the natural wind. But this was no natural wind.

The cat o' nine struck Jackson again and the tops'ls shuddered in the opposite direction of the true wind buffeting across the full sails.

"Even if that person be," said the Captain, teeth clenched, "a Master Windcatcher." The strange source of wind made eddies against their feet, hot and dry, though the sky churned cold and grey. "If that treacherous wretch so much as moves my hair a finger's width with his Devil's gift, by God, I'll have him flogged to the bottom of the sea."

The twelfth strike landed between the Windcatcher's shoulder blades and Jackson let out a throat-shredding scream. Blood stained the deck, and the large master's mate who held the whip flicked the blood from his hands, his eyes haunted.

On Sunday, they would begin again. Another dozen lashes. And again. And again.

Bourne quivered, squeezing his hat so hard beneath his arm that he crushed it.

It had been almost three months of this.

"Mr. Bourne," called the Captain, his eyes glinting. "And Mr. Westerly, take the scum below and look to his wounds."

The ship's surgeon was a thin wisp of a man with overly large brown eyes behind dirty spectacles, and an overall weak pallor, which did not improve as he hefted the Windcatcher on his shoulder. Bourne moved quickly to support the wounded man. Jackson's heavily muscled frame almost felled them both, but Bourne's hair stood on end as a pulse of wind held up the man from collapsing.

How the Windcatcher had enough strength to use his innate gift, Bourne didn't know. But he did know how dangerous it was for him to use it in the Captain's presence.

"Don't," Bourne whispered desperately.

The unnatural force holding the man partially aloft died as the Windcatcher's eyes rolled into the back of his head.

* * *

"It used to be a Windcatcher brought luck," said Jackson with a wan version of his accustomed wry smile. "Looks like my luck has turned, eh?"

Bourne had heard the stories of Windcatchers bravely snapping the enemy's mainmasts in twain by calling on the winds until their bodies expired, but the midshipman kept his hands busy dabbing at the man's ragged back, while Westerly poured their dwindling supply of salt into the wounds. The Captain had threatened that if suppuration managed to kill him, that Westerly would answer for it in Hell, and so every time the salt was rubbed into fresh wounds.

"But he's always hated me," Jackson whispered, teeth clenched as the salt burned. "Thinks my gift is from the Devil. But what true ship o' our good King goes without a Windcatcher?" Tears formed in the man's eyes, and the robust fellow tried vainly to keep them at bay. His hand shot out and grasped at Bourne's hand, clenching with astonishing strength. "I didn't try to kill Cap'n Ramsay, I swear to you, sir. I would *never* use my God-given gift to try to strangle a' man with the force o' wind. God, you *must* believe me."

Tears spilled down the Windcatcher's face, but Bourne's tongue sat limply in his mouth. "You mustn't speak, Jackson. Save your strength."

"For what?" Jackson's grip dug harder into the bones of Bourne's wrist. "To wait for Sunday only to be cast in Hell again?"

Bourne tried not to tremble. "I – I can't halt the flogging, Jackson."

But he could with one simple sentence. Bourne's stomach turned at his cowardice.

Ramsay's bony fingers were holding him under the water, drowning him. And Bourne fought back, desperate to breathe, able to see only the Captain's vile smile through his watery grave. "I knew you had the Devil in you, boy," the Captain growled. "You tried to hide it, but tainted souls show through 'n' through."

The nightmare from three months past still struck at him in his waking hours. The one to which the winds had reacted, even in sleep, coming to his aid as they had always done. The one which had stranded him in this guilty Hell.

"Captains are lords o' their ships," said the surgeon, and Westerly peered around them. "Our souls are theirs. Your fate is in Ramsay's hands, son."

Even if Captain Ramsay was a vicious madman.

Jackson's hands clenched at Bourne's wrist until Bourne could no longer feel his fingertips. The Windcatcher's glassy eyes were dark, no more than obsidian pits. "No true Windcatcher would kill a man with his gift, Mr. Bourne, for the wind exacts its own price for murder. There's no man I hate enough to suffer the torture when the wind decides to turn on you for your crime."

That heavy weight that had been crushing his chest into painful embers only increased. It felt like a pulse of pressure was forcing him to nod. Only it wasn't from Jackson.

The knowledge that that man's fate was still firmly in his hands crushed until Bourne couldn't take breath.

* * *

No one on deck dared to peer in the Captain's direction as the storm began brewing. They needed to treble reef the mains'ls but Ramsay's wild glare kept even the first lieutenant from daring to order such a simple and necessary act. Bourne could feel the storm brewing along his skin, beneath his fingertips, sitting behind his eyes. His head pounded as the sea spray soaked him even beneath his oilcoat; one deckhand fell as a wave nearly took the man over the side in a spray of icy foam.

Madness.

A Windcatcher could keep the storm from tearing them apart.

Captain Ramsay's eye rested on him, a bitterly smug half-smile on his craggy face. "Mr. Bourne!"

"*Sir?*" Bourne bellowed over the stinging wind, quickly leaping up to the quarterdeck.

"You know that today is Sunday?" Water sluiced steadily off of the sides of the Captain's athwartships-style hat.

"Aye, sir," Bourne said. When in doubt the safest utterance on any ship was 'aye sir.'

"Gather the traitor and let's run that bastard through the gauntlet," the Captain growled, his craggy cheeks flush, his eyes fever bright.

Bourne attempted not to gape at such an order, and he stuttered nonsensically before he blurted, "But sir, with the storm …the men cannot leave their posts to …to …"

To attend to the gauntlet: instead of the master's mate flogging Jackson, a line of men forty deep would lash him as the Windcatcher walked through the middle.

The Captain raised a fuzzy grey brow. "Is that sympathy for the bedeviled wretch I hear, Mr. Bourne?"

He could hear the sound of one of the sails ripping, and several men shouted, pointing. Several scurried up the rigging quick as rats, but paused halfway up. Uncertain. Their Captain had made it clear no action was to be made without his explicit instruction. The tension within him mounted. Why wasn't the Captain ordering the sails reefed? Good bleeding God, would Ramsay willingly sink them?

"No, sir. Of course not, sir," Bourne said. "It's only that we need to treble reef –"

"Are you telling me how to run my own ship, Mr. Bourne? Do you think you're so clever, boy? You do, don't you." The Captain's cheeks grew flushed even in the icy wind. "You know nothing. These storm winds were made by a Windcatcher. To test me. Even though he clapped his hellish invisible fingers around my throat to kill me in the dead of night, does he think he can so easily frighten me with a mere windstorm?"

Bourne was certain the Captain expected no response. "Sir, if you please, Westerly and I will bring the prisoner, but certainly some of the men must still attend to the storm."

"No," the Captain growled.

"But, sir –"

Those vicious eyes narrowed. "Your protestations stink of disobedience to your lawful superior."

Bourne lowered his chin, casting his eye to his boots. But within his blood boiled in hatred, and the tingling sensation in his fingers increased like lightning darting beneath his skin. His hair began to stand on end as if charged. The feeling of wanting to *push* against that invisible barrier swelled within him, his mind focusing on saving the largest sails first, *needing* to redirect the wild winds –

And he bit down on his tongue so hard that it drew blood, daring to lift his eye to regard his Captain.

Ramsay's bloodshot eyes were boring into him, mouth twisted in expectation.

"Aye, aye, sir," Bourne said stiffly. "I will bring Jackson promptly."

The midshipman spun on heel and fled across the storm-tossed deck, feeling sick to his stomach, but not in seasickness. As he darted down below, he could hear the banshee whistling through the planks, could hear the pumps going full in the bilge, desperate to keep the *Novelty* from taking on too much water. But he heard another sound as he approached where Jackson was being kept.

The singing voice was fair, but rough in pain:

> *Farewell and adieu to you, Spanish ladies*
> *Farewell and adieu to you, ladies of Spain*
> *For we're under orders*
> *For to sail to old England,*
> *And we may ne'er see you fair ladies again.*

Jackson had frequently crowed such an anthem while on deck, and when off duty the jovial man had sung it playfully with his fiddle as accompaniment, teaching Bourne all of the hearty words to 'Spanish Ladies'.

But this had the sound of one desperately trying to focus on something other than the howling winds, or his own constant pain. The lyrics continued, spoken now rather than sung, more like a chant. Slowly, Westerly's frog-like croak added to the verses, belting out louder than was normal for the pinch-face fellow.

When Bourne came within sight, both men trailed off on: *with the wind at the sou'west.*

Westerly's mouth was agape, his pupils mere pinpricks behind his spectacles. "Dear God, not now certainly?"

"O' course, now," muttered Jackson, sweat at his brow. "He wants to see me fight the *need*." And then the Windcatcher hoarsely sang another song, one Bourne had only heard his father sing when coming back with the day's catch, *"For the winds they will tell, and the blood it'll boil. We soar on wings of reverent joy, and the wind it'll dance to our tune –"*

"No," Bourne said sharply, even though no one would hear. "No Windcatcher songs."

That had been the last song his father had sung before he lost his mind and soul to the winds, no more than an empty flesh vessel unable to do more than breathe. His father's last words had been: *Don't touch the winds, boy. Don't ever use your talent, for it'll one day take you.*

Jackson clenched his teeth as Westerly fought to help the man to his feet. "You don't understand the desire, boy, to lose yourself in the wind itself. Not to fight it or be its master. But to join it and never know anything else. I'm close to losing myself …Will it be like Heaven?"

When Bourne clasped Jackson's upper arm the flesh was too warm, and he peered at the man's back, seeing one of the many runnels in the rent flesh filled with yellowing pus.

That's why Westerly was singing so loudly. The surgeon was drunk.

How far would the suppuration spread until it took the Windcatcher's life? Bourne's stomach churned, his grip on the man unsteady as he hauled the Windcatcher above deck; as the winds howled, hot tears traveled down Bourne's cheeks. "I'm so sorry, Jackson. Please forgive me."

"Not your fault, sir." The Windcatcher gave a fair approximation of his old smile.

He had to reveal the truth, to vent his guilt and receive forgiveness, however small, from the man he had unknowingly condemned. "Jackson, I –"

Now above deck, the Captain shouted, "To the gauntlet!"

The men were already aligned, holding spare bits of rope; not a one met Jackson's eye.

"Mr. Bourne!" barked the Captain. "Lead him forward! You get to offer the final blows."

Bourne swallowed, throat tight. He could speak now, could save Jackson from a crime he didn't commit. But the words were dammed behind his teeth, and only a half-sob came out. He stood in front of Jackson, facing the man – staring into his face while each sailor struck a blow upon his bare back. He could hear the mizzenmast creaking as if it would tear itself from the ship itself to fly free. Bourne fought to keep his mind from the hands of wind roaring against the sails, but the tingling beneath his skin became a roaring fire; as Jackson peered around him as one struck dumb, the man stumbled and Bourne had to catch him.

Bourne could stand it no longer. He would halt the wind. He would proclaim who the true traitor was who had unwittingly used his gift to steal the very breath from his Captain's lungs.

"Don't," the Windcatcher said in Bourne's ear.

Bourne held up the sagging fellow, but Jackson clasped his arms around him, holding him close. "Don't touch the storm, or it'll take you. Don't say a word, not a whisper. Now, put me back on my feet."

Bourne hefted the man, shaking his head in denial. He had to speak or the crushing weight would consume him until there was nothing left. Someone placed the cat o' nine into his trembling fingers, and like one dazed, he stared down at the wicked device, at the dried blood on its ends turning to liquid once more as the rain spilled over it.

"Strike now!" the Captain's monstrous voice crowed.

He didn't have the strength to lift the cat o' nine even a fraction. It slipped from his fingertips and fell to the deck.

Jackson lifted his arms as if in benediction.

The Captain pointed, looming from the quarterdeck, lord of his domain. "Strike him, Mr. Bourne, or I'll consider it a dereliction of your duty!"

The powerful force seemed to burst from Jackson's mouth in a scream, halting the spray of the sea in midair as the *Novelty* plunged into the next trough. Several men around him fell from the percussive punch of air, but the winds around the billowing sails ceased. Jackson's primal roar strengthened, and for a moment the black-grey skies parted. Blood streamed from the Windcatcher's nose, from the corners of his enraptured eyes.

When the storm winds around the ship failed to pound against the overtaxed masts, the *Novelty* seemed to sigh in relief.

The midshipman held the Windcatcher up, but Bourne knew the man's mind was gone. Wind-lost.

Ramsay descended from on high, standing amongst the silent crew, his expression as stormy as the black clouds above. "A man who tried to murder his superior cannot flee judgment so easily." Still staring into Bourne's eyes, never turning, he said, "Mr. Westerly."

The surgeon was wobbling on his feet, trying hard to appear remorseless. But the quivering fellow failed. "S-Sir?"

Ramsay's bony, gnarled finger pointed to the cat o' nine stranded on deck. "Since everyone here is so tired of flogging the bastard, I want you to install the tails o' the cat upon the man's very head. Sew them in good and tight. Then when necessary on Sunday, the cretin can flog himself."

Such a fierce surge turned Bourne's blood into molten liquid, that he had to reign in everything in order not to murder his Captain then and there.

"Aye, aye, sir," Westerly croaked.

And the surgeon lifted the blood soaked tails, while Ramsay's thin lips lifted in a tight-lipped smile.

* * *

Jackson stumbled on deck as one already dead. His flesh was pale as a cadaver, his eyes sunken into hollow sockets, bruised and blood encrusted. Where once a thick mane of curls had sat beneath a jaunty hat, his shaved pate showed where the cat o' nine's ropes had been sewn into the flesh of his scalp. The ropes trailed from him like long, knotted strands of hair, almost down to his back. Gangrenous pus leaked from the seams, and a trail of blackened, necrotic flesh surrounded each sewn hole where the ropes protruded.

Bourne was ordered to be his keeper now, but he could do nothing other than to make sure the man didn't jump into the churning seas to end it.

At every third bell, Bourne was required to nudge the tormented soul without rest until Jackson expired. Exhausted, Bourne stumbled from lack of sleep and placed his hand on the Windcatcher's bare shoulder. Those feverish eyes glazed over as Jackson looked at him, and the man smiled that vacant smile. With a half-sob, the doomed Windcatcher threw his head violently back, and the ropes embedded in his scalp whipped around to strike his ragged back. His voice cracked as he crowed out, "*Farewell and adieu to you, Spanish Ladies! Farewell and adieu to you, ladies of Spain!*"

He whipped his neck back and forth and the whistle of the cat's ropes sang through the salty air. Blood welled up from the new ragged gouges in his back. Bourne had been so sick upon the deck that his body trembled with the weakness of not eating.

"I'm so sorry, Jackson," Bourne whispered for the hundredth time. "I can never truly ask for your forgiveness now ..."

The Windcatcher grinned and continued 'Spanish Ladies'. Bourne sang alongside the doomed man until they reached the very end of the song, voices harsh with, "*We'll drink and be jolly and drown melancholy, and here's to the health of each true-hearted soul!*"

* * *

Bourne had not slept for thirty-six hours, and the sobs and cries of his fellow man rent his soul in twain. The moon shone watery above them, and finally Jackson's whisper-singing of "drown melancholy" made something within the young midshipman snap.

Jackson could no longer stand, but Bourne helped the dying man to his feet with a rush of air to assist. The heat of the man's skin blazed iron-hot, as if it were cannon shot heated in a furnace. With a weak smile, Jackson began to croak out the beginning of 'Spanish Ladies'.

It would mean his death, Bourne knew. Even if he did live to see a court martial. Moving with his comrade in arms, Bourne nodded to the Windcatcher as they approached the gunwale.

They both stared into the dark ocean.

Up on the quarterdeck, the Captain paced, hands calmly behind his back. But he stopped to watch them, those dark eyes no more than cruel pits.

With a gentle shove of wind, Bourne lifted the dying man from the ship and out into the sea. Jackson didn't even flail, but was consumed by the waters as if folded back into their embrace with that same vacant grin.

An eerie calm descended over him, the crushing guilt dissipating as he touched the fickle winds with a secret Windcatcher's joy.

Captain Ramsay smiled at him smugly, the corners of his mouth stretching into its malicious formation.

The man had known. He'd *known*. And still he'd watched as Bourne remained silent and Jackson had paid the ultimate price. As a test. To flush out his quarry, to make Bourne reveal his secret sin.

A dark and frozen wrath consumed him, and the wispy clouds above grew heavy and grey, the breeze hammering inside of his veins, ready to pour forth. It pulsed inside of him, calling with eager joy at such destruction.

Ramsay pointed his bony finger, just like in Bourne's nightmare. "There. Now we see the true Devil revealed."

Bourne lips twisted in revulsion. "Aye, sir, we do."

Without gesture or movement, Bourne directed the full force of wind to gather the Captain from his throne upon the quarterdeck, and lifted the man into the air – hovering like a spectre. Ramsay's eyes bulged as the air was sucked from his lungs; the man clasped at his throat, his fingernails scratching furrows into his neck in desperation. Bourne lifted him higher, almost to the top of the mainmast, and the roar of ecstasy burrowed deep under his skin; the Captain's face grew taught and pale, the muscles of his neck standing out like ropes.

The gale force moved the condemned man out over the sea, hovering over the place where Jackson had gone under. And with a gleeful cry, Bourne held the man underwater, just as Ramsay had done in Bourne's nightmare. The waves battered over the craggy visage struggling against the water entering his mouth. He was laughing now, breathless, as the Captain's body went rigid, then sank beneath the waters to attend to his eternal grave.

Bourne's triumph lasted for but a moment, before the wind beneath his skin, traveling through his veins, turned to pain. It lashed at him, until his chest felt struck a blow from a hard fist. The soaring sensation became fire, burning him from the inside. It flayed him, the percussive force rending his flesh – he could see lash marks rising over his hands, realizing blearily that his veins were rupturing.

The wind lifted him of its own accord. Higher. The wind blasted his cheeks raw; he blinked blood, but saw that the sea awaited him below. And in desperation he tried to wrestle with the invisible force, but was only met with more agony.

He felt the lurch as the wind released him. And he fell.

The sea smashed his body into pulp, and he sank downward. Down toward the seabed where Ramsay and Jackson awaited.

And all he thought before his air abandoned him completely was: *Farewell and adieu.*

War Mage

Angus McIntyre

THE FIGHTING HULL was three times the height of a man, a flattened steel egg perched on the front of an armored chassis that bristled with firing slits and stubby smoke-vents. In its glossy black paint, it reminded Getan of the big black ants that were everywhere on his uncle's farm in the Brintels.

The paint had lost some of its gloss now, scarred and stained by a month at the front. Infantrymen with buckets of water had washed off much of the mud, but they could do little about the bright dings left by rifle rounds or the scorch marks that covered most of the right side. A near-miss from an enemy projector had bubbled and blistered the paint, giving it a scabrous look.

"Tough old girl," observed Otring. Getan grunted. He felt no inclination to romanticize the hull. It was an ugly implement of destruction, the latest murderous fad in a pointless war. More particularly, it was his personal place of imprisonment. He had spent the last six weeks squeezed inside that steel egg with seven other war mages, sweating in his leather harness, dope-dazed and deafened by the thunder of the pistons at his back. He hated it intimately, hated the fear and discomfort, hated being part of the war machine. Unlike Otring, he had not learned to submerge his resentment in facile patriotism.

He took two cigarettes from the pocket of his uniform blouse and murmured a fire spell to light them both. He stuck one in his mouth and passed the other to Otring.

They sat smoking in silence, enjoying the calm of the meadow. The trees here were in full leaf, spreading their shade over soil that had not been churned to mud or burned to sand by thaumaturgic fire. The breeze did not smell of smoke or rotting bodies, and there were no piled sandbags or trenches choked with human remains. Eight miles from the front-line, it was possible to imagine that the whole world was at peace. The only sour note was the looming monstrosity of the hull, a malignant presence squatting in the middle of the green field.

They were on their third cigarette when the asthmatic wheeze of a steam car broke the quiet. Getan turned his head to watch the vehicle lumber down the cart track towards them.

"Here comes the war again," he said. Otring sighed.

There were three men in the car, two soldiers in khaki and a thin figure in mage's gray. As the vehicle slowed to a halt, the mage jumped down and stood for a moment looking up at the hull as if unsure what to do next.

"Over here," Otring called. The gray-clad figure turned, caught sight of the two men under the tree, and hurried over.

"War Mage Fourth Class Myrell, reporting for duty, sir." The newcomer was fresh-faced and almost eerily clean. Getan thought he looked too young to be in uniform.

"You don't have to salute us," said Otring. "War Mage Fourth Otring. And the Norlander lout next to me is called Absyne. What are you, Absyne? Sixth Class? Seventh?"

"Third Class, brevetted," said Getan. "Which makes me your superior. A little respect, please."

The boy looked back and forth between them.

"Please, sir," he said. "Where are the others?"

Otring waved a hand toward the line of tents farther down the field. "Four are sleeping out the hot part of the day over there. And poor Roshan is sleeping rather more permanently under about four feet of earth on the far side of that hedge. Brain aneurysm during the last push."

The boy glanced toward the hedge, then looked back at Otring.

"That's right," said Otring. "You're his replacement."

* * *

The hull lurched and came down with a tooth-rattling thump, tracks clattering and shrieking. Getan groaned as he was flung against his harness, his head smacking against the inadequate padding of the headrest. His nostrils were full of the stink of sweat and leather.

"One hundred yards. Prepare to engage." The voice of the fire director was barely audible over the clamor of the pistons behind him.

He let himself submerge into the gestalt again, becoming one with the other seven mages. Their auras blended with his, their collective energy building up like a thunderstorm around him. Sparks of mage-fire crawled over the inside of the steel shell, shedding a bluish light that turned the faces of the men inside into hollow-eyed skulls.

The hull jolted again and Getan's boot thumped into the shoulder of the man seated in front of him. The mages were seated in two banked rows, jammed shoulder to shoulder with hardly room to breathe, let alone move. There was some science to the exact proportions of the hull, the engineers insisting that it had to be kept as small as possible in order to focus the combined energies to optimal effect. All Getan knew was that riding the hull was as close to Hell as anything he expected to experience in this lifetime.

The energy was building still, but the shape of the field was wrong. Getan could feel Myrell shrinking away from the gestalt, beginning to drain his power out of the field. He remembered his own first battle, how close he had come to panicking and collapsing the thaumaturgic bubble completely. Only an effort of will had kept him from cowering down in his seat and wrapping all the power he had protectively around himself.

He pushed more of his own energy into the field, feeling out the threads of Myrell's energy and buttressing them, guiding the lines of force outwards to meld into the whole again. Myrell relaxed fractionally, his panic receding. The bubble swelled again, full and perfect.

"Target in range." The guide vanes re-aligned with a metallic scrape. The bubble of magical energy pulsed, sustained now by the combined will of all eight mages.

"Discharge." Getan's skin crawled as the accumulated energy was released. The steel egg of the hull vomited a bolus of thaumaturgic power toward the target. There was a distant boom of thunder, followed by the patter of rock and rubble cascading back to earth. Getan had no idea what they had just fired at: an enemy hull, a line of infantry, a fortification. There was no way to see out of the egg, but sometimes you could feel men dying, tiny sparks of life that flickered and faded. Getan was relieved that this time there was none of that.

"Prepare to recharge." The vehicle snorted steam, the tracks ground into reverse, and the hull lurched backwards. Getan braced himself and started feeding energy into the field again.

* * *

"Is it always like that?" Myrell asked. His upper lip was crusted with dried blood and his face was deathly pale.

"That was an easy one," said Otring hoarsely.

Getan leaned back against a pile of sandbags. They were still close enough to the front that he could hear the distant crack of rifle fire and the occasional hollow boom of thaumaturgic artillery. There were death spells being used somewhere too, probably Keldite mages probing the Shulan forward trenches. He could feel them at a distance, pinpoints of dark magic picking at the fabric of reality.

He felt sick and shaky, with a slow ache in his bones that was more than just the result of spending too much energy in too short a time. The alchemists had changed the formula of the dope again. The new stuff was more potent, rich with magical ingredients and stimulants, but the come-down was a killer. He peered at the injection site in his arm. It looked swollen and angry and he wondered if it was infected. He would have to watch that; hygiene was next to impossible at the front.

"Go get some sleep," Otring told the boy. "We may be back in action in a few hours."

They watched the younger mage stumble off toward the rear of the inn, where the stables had been turned into an improvised bunkroom.

"Not going to make it," Otring said when Myrell was out of sight.

"He'll be fine," said Getan, not really believing it. "The first time is tough for everyone."

"He's weak," Otring insisted. "You felt it."

Getan closed his eyes. Not weak, he thought, but strong. Strong enough not to give in. Strong enough to try to be himself.

Otring was right, though. Myrell was not going to make it.

* * *

The inn that served as their usual forward staging post was almost a mile behind the front line. It must once have been an elegant establishment, with graceful roofs in the Shulan style shading broad porches at front and back. Now the wide windows were boarded up and the eaves were hung with ugly protective charms. An infantry regiment was camped in the adjacent field. The stench of the field latrines overpowered the smell of the roses in the inn's walled garden.

The crews of three hulls occupied the top floor and the stables. The ground floor was filled with nurses from the nearby field hospital. The women worked even longer hours than the mages. Getan saw them only in passing, staggering home exhausted in twos and threes to snatch a few hours of sleep before they were called back to work.

So it was a surprise when he opened the wooden door to the garden and saw one of the nurses sitting by the dried-up fishpond. He started to close the door again, but the woman saw him, and signaled him to come in.

"I'm not disturbing you, am I?" he said.

She shook her head. "The garden's big enough for two, I think," she said, with a slight smile.

"Yes, ma'am."

She raised her eyebrows. "Ma'am?" she said. "The war must have aged me more than I thought."

Getan flushed. It was not like him to be awkward around girls. He remembered his manners, and bowed, bringing his heels smartly together.

"War mage Absyne, at your service ...nurse."

"War mage. So you crew one of those horrid things outside?"

"Yes, m–"

She smiled again. "My name is Hana. You can use it if you'll promise to stop ma'am'ing me. Do you have a first name?"

"Getan."

"That's a Norland name, yes?"

"My father was a Norlander."

She nodded. "Honored to meet you, Getan." She waved one slender hand. "Please, sit down. You make me nervous, towering over me."

"Yes, ma'am."

* * *

After that first meeting, Getan started to make a point of looking in on the garden whenever he was off duty. Most of the time he went away disappointed, but on a few occasions he was rewarded by the sight of Hana sitting on one of the benches, her nose usually deep in a book. He had a sense that she too was finding pretexts to be there. On their third meeting, he got up the courage to ask her whether she would go for a walk with him.

He took her to a place he had found where an avenue of trees flanked an overgrown cart track: not the most romantic destination, but one of the least touched by war. Only a stretch of stone wall pockmarked by rifle fire and the twisted ribs of a dirigible that had foundered in an adjoining field hinted at the conflict.

"Did you always want to be a soldier?" she asked as he helped her over a stile.

He shook his head. "Never."

"But you volunteered –"

"No." He waited, thinking she did not understand. "The Conscription Act requires anyone who possesses certain ...abilities ...to serve."

"And you can't just leave? Disappear?"

"They call that desertion. The penalties are severe." Not death, he thought. A mage was too valuable. But death might be kinder. "There are special units of mages," he explained. "They call them Ravens. Their job is to prevent any desertions."

She leaned against the fence. "But if you could get away, would you?"

A sudden suspicion seized him. Was she an agent provocateur, sent to test his loyalty?

"I'm a patriot," he said. "My place is here. Until our victory."

Her face was unreadable. "Of course," she said.

* * *

Officially, the war was going well. Privately, Getan suspected that it was stalemate. Hunkered down in their trenches, the infantry sniped unenthusiastically at each other. At dusk, the hulls lumbered out to throw a few futile fireballs at the enemy fortifications, then clanked home again at dawn, the mages in their steel shells shaking and spent, drained by the energies that had flowed through them. One of Getan's crew was invalided home, flash-burned by a fireball from an enemy battery that almost overwhelmed their collective defenses. A mage even younger than Myrell took his place.

Getan slept, ate, fought, then slept again. When he could, he spent time with Hana, but her own routine was as punishing as his. The flow of sick and wounded from the front had not slowed.

One morning, when the hull returned at dawn from a sortie, she was waiting for him by the inn door. Bleary-eyed, he would have walked right past her if Otring had not nudged him.

"There's your girl," Otring said. "Better not keep her waiting. You know how women are when they want it."

Behind him, Myrell grinned. His face was blotched with dried blood – another nosebleed – and the effect was ghastly.

Getan waited until the other mages had stumbled off to their beds and then let Hana lead him to the garden. He was happy to let the others think it was a simple assignation, but he guessed that she had something more serious in mind.

"I asked you once if you wanted to get away," she said, as soon as they were alone. "I'll ask you one more time."

He studied her face in the weak dawn light. Not a trap, he decided. Or if it was, she was an extraordinary actress.

"How?" he asked.

It was her turn to look at him distrustfully.

"Listen," said Getan. "I need to know if you're serious. Which means I need to know how your scheme works."

Hana was silent for a long time. At last, she sighed. "We dress you in khaki. Send you back on a hospital train."

"I thought it was something like that." He shook his head. "Won't work. The Ravens check every transport leaving the front. They –"

"We know about the Ravens. We can suppress your magic so they won't sense you."

"That's not possible. Not unless –"

"We use chokeberry," Hana said. "It's a natural antagonist to magic. Just as redfoil and mallow enhance magic, chokeberry suppresses it."

"Chokeberry is toxic. And the quantity you'd need to use –"

"I didn't say it was pleasant. But there's an antidote for that too."

"Fine," Getan said. "Let's say you can do it. Why me?"

She gave him a look of exasperation.

He flushed. "I mean, why not one of those poor bastards over there?" He waved a hand at the infantry lines across the road.

"Because you're a mage. You can change things. With enough mages, we could end this war."

A price, he thought. There is always a price.

"So if you get me home, I have to work for you," he said. "Is that it?"

Just say 'yes', the voice in his head told him. Anything is better than staying here and dying.

Hana looked at him coldly. "You do what you think best," she said. "We get you away from the front. What you do after that is up to you."

He sat in silence, thinking. It was a gamble. He would be trusting his life to a woman who was almost a stranger, trusting not only that she was not trying to trap him, but also that she and whoever she was working with knew what they were doing. It was madness.

It was his only chance.

"Yes," he heard himself say. Then, "When?"

"The next train leaves in two days time, eleven in the morning. Meet me here at six. Just you. No one else."

She turned then and left, walking away quickly as if anxious to leave before he changed his mind.

* * *

The next morning, the Ravens came.

There were three of them, a captain with the silver sigil of a mage-inquisitor on the sleeve of his tunic, and two sergeants. In their broad-brimmed hats and heavy black capes, the resemblance to their namesakes was eerie.

When Getan saw them, his first thought was that Hana had betrayed him after all, that he had condemned himself and perhaps others as well to torture and exile. He felt a sudden vertigo, as if the ground had dropped out from underneath him.

"Beg pardon, mages." The landlord of the inn appeared from behind the Ravens, like a fat little rabbit pulled from a hat. He rubbed his pudgy hands together nervously. "I have to ask you to move out of your room."

Getan blinked at him, bewildered.

"I can make you comfortable," the landlord babbled. "In the stables. I'll send the girl over with clean blankets."

Very slowly it began to dawn on Getan that he was not being arrested. He nodded, trying not to let the relief show in his face.

"That's fine," he said.

The two Raven sergeants waited outside the door while Getan and Otring packed up their kit. One of the inn maids fumbled her way around the room, flapping ineffectually at the furniture with a duster, trying vainly to displace the accumulated grime of months of neglect. Evidently, the panic had become general.

"Gods, but I hate those bastards," muttered Otring to Getan as they laid out their bedrolls in the stables later. Getan glanced over at the adjacent cots where Myrell and the other junior mage were sleeping.

"Guilty conscience?" he said.

Otring flushed. "You know me," he said. "But even so …" He shook his head.

"Mmm."

"I just don't like having them around. Make me feel like I've done something wrong even when I haven't."

"I know what you mean," said Getan.

Later, as he walked across the yard, he saw Hana emerge from the inn with two other nurses, on their way to the field hospital. She did not meet his eye.

* * *

Getan was woken by a long whistle that ended with a muffled thud, like a door slamming. He lay awake, trying to make sense of the sounds.

The mages had lain down to sleep early, in anticipation of another night sortie. The luminous hands of the watch hanging by his cot showed it to be just after nine. He had been asleep no more than two hours.

There was another whistle and another thump, much louder this time. The dangling watch trembled.

Getan was suddenly wide awake. He leapt up from his cot.

"Get up!" he shouted, shaking Otring. "Artillery!"

Otring sat up, rubbing his eyes. "Can't use artillery –" he said.

"The mage screen is down! They –" His words were cut off by a fresh shriek from overhead and a tremendous crash.

Outside, everything was chaos. There were screams from the meadow where the infantry regiment was encamped, half-drowned by the howl of escaping steam. Normally, both sides protected their front lines against artillery with screen mages trained to intercept incoming shells and fling them back at their source. The mages lived in secure bunkers well back from the forward lines; if the Shulan screen was down, then either the Keldites had infiltrated a suicide squad or the entire front was collapsing.

Again, he heard the rising howl of an incoming shell. This time, the thunderclap of the explosion was deafeningly close, accompanied by a brilliant blue-orange flash. A hot wind filled with fragments of stone and metal battered at the shield that Getan flung up. Part of the inn vomited flame and collapsed.

By the light of the burning building at his back he could see that two of the parked hulls were unsalvageable, riddled with splinters, bleeding fuel and water. The third had steam up, its crew of stokers and soldiers already aboard.

"We should wait for the others –" Otring panted as they ran for the hull.

"You saw where the shell hit," Getan said. He jumped onto the vehicle and heaved open the hatch on the back of the steel egg. Looking back over his shoulder, he saw that Myrell and another mage he did not recognize had followed them out of the inferno. Four was enough to make a gestalt. It would have to be.

Another shell screamed overhead and detonated somewhere behind them. The enemy gunners were changing their point of aim with each round, walking the shots toward the rear lines, toward the hospital and the railhead beyond.

The vehicle commander's head and shoulders appeared in the hatch as Getan strapped himself in. "Orders, war mage?"

Getan felt in the pocket beside his seat for his injector, hoping that someone had remembered to refill it. "The enemy guns can't be far from their front line," he said. "We're going to have to punch through. Take out the guns or the mages directing the fire."

The commander nodded. He ducked back, slamming the hatch shut. With a long hoarse whistle from the steam siren, the vehicle lurched into motion.

* * *

Getan stumbled blindly through the pale light of dawn, beyond fatigue, beyond awareness of anything except the need to keep putting one foot after another. Fighting was still going on somewhere to the east, the snap of rifle rounds mingled with the hiss of mage-fire. No more shells whistled overhead.

"Can stop now ..." said Otring, his voice thick with exhaustion. "... safe here." He slumped down on a firestep, his back against the muddy trench wall. A group of soldiers in Shulan uniforms stared at them curiously.

Getan kept walking, his eyes fixed on the humped shape of the ruined inn silhouetted against the dawn sky. He leaned to one side as he walked, unbalanced by the weight of Myrell's body over his shoulder.

Something moved in the gloom and for a moment Getan thought he was hallucinating again. Then the black bird-shape resolved into the figure of a man in a black uniform, a silver sigil on his sleeve glinting in the dawn light.

"Where are you going, mage?" the Raven asked.

"Hospital," Getan said.

"And the guns?"

"Destroyed."

The Raven stepped back. "Good work," he said. "You'll probably get a commendation for that."

Getan walked on without answering. It was hard to speak or think now. He felt a trickle of blood run down his chin.

By the inn fence, he eased Myrell gently off his shoulder and set him down on his feet. "You have to walk now," he told the young mage. "I can't carry you any more."

"Can't we just stop here?" Myrell's face was chalk-white, the front of his uniform soaked in blood. His voice was scarcely more than a whisper.

"Not yet," Getan said. "Soon." He slipped his shoulder under Myrell's arm, forcing him to stand upright.

Hana was waiting for them by the walled garden, accompanied by two orderlies. Her eyes widened at the sight of them.

"I can't take both of you," she said. "I only have papers for one."

"I know," said Getan.

The orderlies took Myrell from him and laid the young mage gently down on a stretcher.

"What will you do now?" Hana asked.

"I'll think of something," Getan said.

He kissed her then. Afterwards, he held her for a long moment, breathing in the smell of her hair, feeling her warm breath on his neck. Then he turned away from her and went back to the war.

Three Lines Of Old French

A. Merritt

"BUT RICH AS WAS the war for surgical science," ended Hawtry, "opening up through mutilation and torture unexplored regions which the genius of man was quick to enter, and, entering, found ways to checkmate suffering and death – for always, my friend, the distillate from the blood of sacrifice is progress – great as all this was, the world tragedy has opened up still another region wherein even greater knowledge will be found. It was the clinic unsurpassed for the psychologist even more than for the surgeon."

Latour, the great little French doctor, drew himself out of the depths of the big chair; the light from the fireplace fell ruddily upon his keen face.

"That is true," he said. "Yes, that is true. There in the furnace the mind of man opened like a flower beneath a too glowing sun. Beaten about in that colossal tempest of primitive forces, caught in the chaos of energies both physical and psychical – which, although man himself was its creator, made of their maker a moth in a whirlwind – all those obscure, those mysterious factors of mind which men, for lack of knowledge, have named the soul, were stripped of their inhibitions and given power to appear.

"How could it have been otherwise – when men and women, gripped by one shattering sorrow or joy, will manifest the hidden depths of spirit – how could it have been otherwise in that steadily maintained crescendo of emotion?" McAndrews spoke.

"Just which psychological region do you mean, Hawtry?" he asked.

There were four of us in front of the fireplace of the Science Club – Hawtry, who rules the chair of psychology in one of our greatest colleges, and whose name is an honored one throughout the world; Latour, an immortal of France; McAndrews, the famous American surgeon whose work during the war has written a new page in the shining book of science; and myself. These are not the names of the three, but they are as I have described them; and I am pledged to identify them no further.

"I mean the field of suggestion," replied the psychologist.

"The mental reactions which reveal themselves as visions – an accidental formation in the clouds that becomes to the overwrought imaginations of the beholders the so-eagerly-prayed-for hosts of Joan of Arc marching out from heaven; moonlight in the cloud rift that becomes to the besieged a fiery cross held by the hands of archangels; the despair and hope that are transformed into such a legend as the bowmen of Mons, ghostly archers who with their phantom shafts overwhelm the conquering enemy; wisps of cloud over No Man's Land that are translated by the tired eyes of those who peer out into the shape of the Son of Man himself walking sorrowfully among the dead. Signs, portents, and miracles, the hosts of premonitions, of apparitions of loved ones – all dwellers in this land of suggestion; all born of the tearing loose of the veils of the subconscious. Here, when even a thousandth part is gathered, will be work for the psychological analyst for twenty years."

"And the boundaries of this region?" asked McAndrews.

"Boundaries?" Hawtry plainly was perplexed.

McAndrews for a moment was silent. Then he drew from his pocket a yellow slip of paper, a cablegram.

"Young Peter Laveller died today," he said, apparently irrelevantly. "Died where he had set forth to pass – in the remnants of the trenches that cut through the ancient domain of the Seigneurs of Tocquelain, up near Bethune."

"Died there!" Hawtry's astonishment was profound. "But I read that he had been brought home; that, indeed, he was one of your triumphs, McAndrews!"

"I said he went there to die," repeated the surgeon slowly.

So that explained the curious reticence of the Lavellers as to what had become of their soldier son – a secrecy which had puzzled the press for weeks. For young Peter Laveller was one of the nation's heroes. The only boy of old Peter Laveller – and neither is that the real name of the family, for, like the others, I may not reveal it – he was the heir to the grim old coal king's millions, and the secret, best loved pulse of his heart.

Early in the war he had enlisted with the French. His father's influence might have abrogated the law of the French army that every man must start from the bottom up – I do not know – but young Peter would have none of it. Steady of purpose, burning with the white fire of the first Crusaders, he took his place in the ranks.

Clean-cut, blue-eyed, standing six feet in his stocking feet, just twenty-five, a bit of a dreamer, perhaps, he was one to strike the imagination of the *poilus*, and they loved him. Twice was he wounded in the perilous days, and when America came into the war he was transferred to our expeditionary forces. It was at the siege of Mount Kemmel that he received the wounds that brought him back to his father and sister. McAndrews had accompanied him overseas, I knew, and had patched him together – or so all thought.

What had happened then – and why had Laveller gone back to France, to die, as McAndrews put it?

He thrust the cablegram back into his pocket.

"There is a boundary, John," he said to Hawtry. "Laveller's was a borderland case. I'm going to tell it to you." He hesitated. "I ought not to, maybe; and yet I have an idea that Peter would like it told; after all, he believed himself a discoverer." Again he paused; then definitely made up his mind, and turned to me.

"Merritt, you may make use of this if you think it interesting enough. But if you do so decide, then change the names, and be sure to check description short of any possibility of ready identification. After all, it is what happened that is important – and those to whom it happened do not matter."

I promised, and I have observed my pledge. I tell the story as he whom I call McAndrews reconstructed it for us there in the shadowed room, while we sat silent until he had ended.

Laveller stood behind the parapet of a first-line trench. It was night – an early April night in northern France – and when that is said, all is said to those who have been there.

Beside him was a trench periscope. His gun lay touching it. The periscope is practically useless at night; so through a slit in the sandbags he peered out over the three-hundred-foot-wide stretch of No Man's Land.

Opposite him he knew that other eyes lay close to similar slits in the German parapet, watchful as his were for the least movement.

There were grotesque heaps scattered about No Man's Land, and when the star-shells burst and flooded it with their glare these heaps seemed to stir to move – some to raise themselves, some to gesticulate, to protest. And this was very horrible, for those who moved under the lights were the dead – French and English, Prussian and Bavarian – dregs of a score of carryings to the red wine-press of war set up in this sector.

There were two Jocks on the entanglements; kilted Scots, one colandered by machine-gun hail just as he was breaking through. The shock of the swift, manifold death had hurled his left arm about the neck of the comrade close beside him; and this man had been stricken within the same second. There they leaned, embracing – and as the star-shells flared and died, flared and died, they seemed to rock, to try to break from the wire, to dash forward, to return.

Laveller was weary, weary beyond all understanding. The sector was a bad one and nervous. For almost seventy-two hours he had been without sleep – for the few minutes now and then of dead stupor broken by constant alarms was worse than sleep.

The shelling had been well-nigh continuous, and the food scarce and perilous to get; three miles back through the fire they had been forced to go for it; no nearer than that could the ration dumps be brought.

And constantly the parapets had to be rebuilt and the wires repaired – and when this was done the shells destroyed again, and once more the dreary routine had to be gone through; for the orders were to hold this sector at all costs.

All that was left of Laveller's consciousness was concentrated in his eyes; only his seeing faculty lived. And sight, obeying the rigid, inexorable will commanding every reserve of vitality to concentrate on the duty at hand, was blind to everything except the strip before it that Laveller must watch until relieved. His body was numb; he could not feel the ground with his feet, and sometimes he seemed to be floating in air like – like the two Scots upon the wire!

Why couldn't they be still? What right had men whose blood had drained away into a black stain beneath them to dance and pirouette to the rhythm of the flares? Damn them – why couldn't a shell drop down and bury them?

There was a chateau half a mile up there to the right – at least it had been a chateau. Under it were deep cellars into which one could creep and sleep. He knew that, because ages ago, when first he had come into this part of the line, he had slept a night there.

It would be like reentering paradise to crawl again into those cellars, out of the pitiless rain; sleep once more with a roof over his head.

"I will sleep and sleep and sleep – and sleep and sleep and sleep," he told himself; then stiffened as at the slumber-compelling repetition of the word darkness began to gather before him.

The star-shells flared and died, flared and died; the staccato of a machine gun reached him. He thought that it was his teeth chattering until his groping consciousness made him realize what it really was – some nervous German riddling the interminable movement of the dead.

There was a squidging of feet through the chalky mud. No need to look; they were friends, or they could not have passed the sentries at the angle of the traverse. Nevertheless, involuntarily, his eyes swept toward the sounds, took note of three cloaked figures regarding him.

There were half a dozen of the lights floating overhead now, and by the gleams they cast into the trench he recognized the party.

One of them was that famous surgeon who had come over from the base hospital at Bethune to see made the wounds he healed; the others were his major and his captain

– all of them bound for those cellars, no doubt. Well, some had all the luck! Back went his eyes to the slit.

"What's wrong?" It was the voice of the major addressing the visitor.

"What's wrong – what's wrong – what's wrong?" The words repeated themselves swiftly, insistently, within his brain, over and over again, striving to waken it.

Well, what was wrong? Nothing was wrong! Wasn't he, Laveller, there and watching? The tormented brain writhed angrily. Nothing was wrong – why didn't they go away and let him watch in peace?

"Nothing." It was the surgeon – and again the words kept babbling in Laveller's ears, small, whispering, rapidly repeating themselves over and over; "Nothing – nothing – nothing – nothing."

But what was this the surgeon was saying? Fragmentarily, only half understood, the phrases registered:

"Perfect case of what I've been telling you. This lad here – utterly worn, weary – all his consciousness centered upon just one thing – watchfulness ...consciousness worn to finest point ...behind it all his subconsciousness crowding to escape ...consciousness will respond to only one stimulus – movement from without ...but the subconsciousness, so close to the surface, held so lightly in leash ...what will it do if that little thread is loosed ...a perfect case."

What were they talking about? Now they were whispering.

"Then, if I have your permission –" It was the surgeon speaking again. Permission for what? Why didn't they go away and not bother him? Wasn't it hard enough just to watch without having to hear? Some thing passed before his eyes. He looked at it blindly, unrecognizing. His sight must be clouded.

He raised a hand and brushed at his lids. Yes, it must have been his eyes – for it had gone.

A little circle of light glowed against the parapet near his face. It was cast by a small flash. What were they looking for? A hand appeared in the circle, a hand with long, flexible fingers which held a piece of paper on which there was writing. Did they want him to read, too? Not only watch and hear – but read! He gathered himself together to protest.

Before he could force his stiffened lips to move he felt the upper button of his greatcoat undone, a hand slipped through the opening and thrust something into his tunic pocket just above the heart.

Someone whispered "Lucie de Tocquelain." What did it mean? That was not the password. There was a great singing in his head – as though he were sinking through water. What was that light that dazzled him even through his closed lids? Painfully he opened his eyes.

Laveller looked straight into the disk of a golden sun slowly setting over a row of noble oaks. Blinded, he dropped his gaze. He was standing ankle-deep in soft, green grass, starred with small clumps of blue flowerets. Bees buzzed about in their chalices. Little yellow-winged butterflies hovered over them. A gentle breeze blew, warm and fragrant.

Oddly he felt no sense of strangeness – then – this was a normal home world – a world as it ought to be. But he remembered that he had once been in another world, far, far unlike this; a place of misery and pain, of blood-stained mud and filth, of cold and wet; a world of cruelty, whose nights were tortured hells of glaring lights and fiery, slaying sounds, and tormented men who sought for rest and sleep and found none, and dead who danced. Where was it? Had there ever really been such a world? He was not sleepy now.

He raised his hands and looked at them. They were grimed and cut and stained. He was wearing a greatcoat, wet, mud-bespattered, filthy. High boots were on his legs. Beside one dirt-incrusted foot lay a cluster of the blue flowerets, half-crushed. He groaned in pity, and bent, striving to raise the broken blossoms.

"Too many dead now – too many dead," he whispered; then paused. He had come from that nightmare world! How else in this happy, clean one could he be so unclean?

Of course he had – but where was it? How had he made his way from it here? Ah, there had been a password – what had it been?

He had it: "Lucie de Tocquelain!"

Laveller cried it aloud – still kneeling.

A soft little hand touched his cheek. A low, sweet-toned voice caressed his ears.

"I am Lucie de Tocquelain," it said. "And the flowers will grow again – yet it is dear of you to sorrow for them."

He sprang to his feet. Beside him stood a girl, a slender maid of eighteen, whose hair was a dusky cloud upon her proud little head and in whose great, brown eyes, resting upon his, tenderness and a half-amused pity dwelt.

Peter stood silent, drinking her in – the low, broad, white forehead; the curved, red lips; the rounded, white shoulders, shining through the silken web of her scarf; the whole lithe sweet body of her in the clinging, quaintly fashioned gown, with its high, clasping girdle.

She was fair enough; but to Peter's starved eyes she was more than that – she was a spring gushing from the arid desert, the first cool breeze of twilight over a heat-drenched isle, the first glimpse of paradise to a soul fresh risen from centuries of hell. And under the burning worship of his eyes her own dropped; a faint rose stained the white throat, crept to her dark hair.

"I – I am the Demoiselle de Tocquelain, messire," she murmured. "And you –"

He recovered his courtesy with a shock. "Laveller – Peter Laveller – is my name, mademoiselle," he stammered. "Pardon my rudeness – but how I came here I know not – nor from whence, save that it was – it was a place unlike this. And you – you are so beautiful, mademoiselle!"

The clear eyes raised themselves for a moment, a touch of roguishness in their depths, then dropped demurely once more – but the blush deepened.

He watched her, all his awakening heart in his eyes; then perplexity awoke, touched him insistently.

"Will you tell me what place this is, mademoiselle," he faltered, "and how I came here, if you –" He stopped. From far, far away, from league upon league of space, a vast weariness was sweeping down upon him. He sensed it coming – closer, closer; it touched him; it lapped about him; he was sinking under it; being lost – falling – falling –

Two soft, warm hands gripped his. His tired head dropped upon them. Through the little palms that clasped so tightly pulsed rest and strength. The weariness gathered itself, began to withdraw slowly, so slowly – and was gone!

In its wake followed an ineffable, an uncontrollable desire to weep – to weep in relief that the weariness had passed, that the devil world whose shadows still lingered in his mind was behind him, and that he was here with this maid. And his tears fell, bathing the little hands.

Did he feel her head bent to his, her lips touch his hair? Peace came to him. He rose shamefacedly.

"I do not know why I wept, mademoiselle –" he began; and then saw that her white fingers were clasped now in his blackened ones. He released them in sudden panic.

"I am sorry," he stammered. "I ought not touch you –"

She reached out swiftly, took his hands again in hers, patted them half savagely. Her eyes flashed.

"I do not see them as you do, Messire Pierre," she answered. "And if I did, are not their stains to me as the stains from hearts of her brave sons on the gonfalons of France? Think no more of your stains save as decorations, messire."

France – France? Why, that was the name of the world he had left behind; the world where men sought vainly for sleep, and the dead danced.

The dead danced – what did that mean? He turned wistful eyes to her.

And with a little cry of pity she clung to him for a moment.

"You are so tired – and you are so hungry," she mourned. "And think no more, nor try to remember, messire, till you have eaten and drunk with us and rested for a space."

They had turned. And now Laveller saw not far away a chateau. It was pinnacled and stately, serene in its gray stone and lordly with its spires and slender turrets thrust skyward from its crest like plumes flung high from some proud prince's helm. Hand in hand like children the Demoiselle de Tocquelain and Peter Laveller approached it over the greensward.

"It is my home, messire," the girl said. "And there among the roses my mother awaits us. My father is away, and he will be sorrowful that he met you not, but you shall meet him when you return."

He was to return, then? That meant he was not to stay. But where was he to go – whence was he to return? His mind groped blindly; cleared again. He was walking among roses; there were roses everywhere, great, fragrant, opened blooms of scarlets and of saffrons, of shell pinks and white; clusters and banks of them, climbing up the terraces, masking the base of the chateau with perfumed tide.

And as he and the maid, still hand in hand, passed between them, they came to a table dressed with snowy napery and pale porcelains beneath a bower.

A woman sat there. She was a little past the prime of life, Peter thought. Her hair, he saw, was powdered white, her cheeks as pink and white as a child's, her eyes the sparkling brown of those of the demoiselle – and gracious – gracious, Peter thought, as some *grande dame* of old France.

The demoiselle dropped her a low curtsy.

"*Ma mère*," she said, "I bring you the Sieur Pierre la Vallière, a very brave and gallant gentleman who has come to visit us for a little while."

The clear eyes of the older woman scanned him, searched him. Then the stately white head bowed, and over the table a delicate hand was stretched toward him.

It was meant for him to kiss, he knew – but he hesitated awkwardly, miserably, looking at his begrimed own.

"The Sieur Pierre will not see himself as we do," the girl said in half merry reproof; then she laughed, a caressing, golden chiming, "*Ma mère*, shall he see his hands as we do?"

The white-haired woman smiled and nodded, her eyes kindly and, Laveller noted, with that same pity in them as had been in those of the demoiselle when first he had turned and beheld her.

The girl touched Peter's eyes lightly, held his palms up before him – they were white and fine and clean and in some unfamiliar way beautiful!

Again the indefinable amaze stifled him, but his breeding told. He conquered the sense of strangeness, bowed from the hips, took the dainty fingers of the stately lady in his, and raised them to his lips.

She struck a silver bell. Through the roses came two tall men in livery, who took from Laveller his greatcoat. They were followed by four small black boys in gay scarlet slashed with gold. They bore silver platters on which were meat and fine white bread and cakes, fruit, and wine in tall crystal flagons.

And Laveller remembered how hungry he was. But of that feast he remembered little – up to a certain point. He knows that he sat there filled with a happiness and content that surpassed the sum of happiness of all his twenty-five years.

The mother spoke little, but the Demoiselle Lucie and Peter Laveller chattered and laughed like children – when they were not silent and drinking each the other in.

And ever in Laveller's heart an adoration for this maid, met so perplexingly, grew – grew until it seemed that his heart could not hold his joy. Ever the maid's eyes as they rested on his were softer, more tender, filled with promise; and the proud face beneath the snowy hair became, as it watched them, the essence of that infinitely gentle sweetness that is the soul of the madonnas.

At last the Demoiselle de Tocquelain, glancing up and meeting that gaze, blushed, cast down her long lashes, and hung her head; then raised her eyes bravely.

"Are you content, my mother?" she asked gravely.

"My daughter, I am well content," came the smiling answer.

Swiftly followed the incredible, the terrible – in that scene of beauty and peace it was, said Laveller, like the flashing forth of a gorilla's paw upon a virgin's breast, a wail from deepest hell lancing through the song of angels.

At his right, among the roses, a light began to gleam – a fitful, flaring light that glared and died, glared and died. In it were two shapes. One had an arm clasped about the neck of the other; they leaned embracing in the light, and as it waxed and waned they seemed to pirouette, to try to break from it, to dash forward, to return – to dance!

The dead who danced!

A world where men sought rest and sleep, and could find neither, and where even the dead could find no rest, but must dance to the rhythm of the star-shells!

He groaned; sprang to his feet; watched, quivering in every nerve. Girl and woman followed his rigid gaze; turned to him again with tear-filled, pitiful eyes.

"It is nothing!" said the maid. "It is nothing! See – there is nothing there!"

Once more she touched his lids; and the light and the swaying forms were gone. But now Laveller knew. Back into his consciousness rushed the full tide of memory – memory of the mud and the filth, the stenches, and the fiery, slaying sounds, the cruelty, the misery and the hatreds; memory of torn men and tormented dead; memory of whence he had come, the trenches.

The trenches! He had fallen asleep, and all this was but a dream! He was sleeping at his post, while his comrades were trusting him to watch over them. And those two ghastly shapes among the roses – they were the two Scots on the wires summoning him back to his duty; beckoning, beckoning him to return. He must waken! He must waken!

Desperately he strove to drive himself from his garden of illusion; to force himself back to that devil world which during this hour of enchantment had been to his mind only as a fog bank on a far horizon. And as he struggled, the brown-eyed maid and the snowy-tressed woman watched – with ineffable pity, tears falling.

"The trenches!" gasped Laveller. "O God, wake me up! I must get back! O God, make me wake."

"Am I only a dream, then, *ma mie*?"

It was the Demoiselle Lucie's voice – a bit piteous, the golden tones shaken.

"I must get back," he groaned – although at her question his heart seemed to die within him. "Let me wake!"

"Am I a dream?" Now the voice was angry; the demoiselle drew close. "Am I not real?"

A little foot stamped furiously on his, a little hand darted out, pinched him viciously close above his elbow. He felt the sting of the pain and rubbed it, gazing at her stupidly.

"Am I a dream, think you?" she murmured, and, raising her palms, set them on his temples, bringing down his head until his eyes looked straight into hers.

Laveller gazed – gazed down, down deep into their depths, lost himself in them, felt his heart rise like the spring from what he saw there. Her warm, sweet breath fanned his cheek; whatever this was, wherever he was – she was no dream!

"But I must return – get back to my trench!" The soldier in him clung to the necessity.

"My son" – it was the mother speaking now – "my son, you are in your trench."

Laveller gazed at her, bewildered. His eyes swept the lovely scene about him. When he turned to her again it was with the look of a sorely perplexed child. She smiled.

"Have no fear," she said. "Everything is well. You are in your trench – but your trench centuries ago; yes, twice a hundred years ago, counting time as you do – and as once we did."

A chill ran through him. Were they mad? Was he mad? His arm slipped down over a soft shoulder; the touch steadied him.

"And you?" he forced himself to ask. He caught a swift glance between the two, and in answer to some unspoken question the mother nodded. The Demoiselle Lucie pressed soft hands against Peter's face, looked again into his eyes.

"Ma mie," she said gently, "we have been" – she hesitated – "what you call – dead – to your world these two hundred years!"

But before she had spoken the words Laveller, I think, had sensed what was coming. And if for a fleeting instant he had felt a touch of ice in every vein, it vanished beneath the exaltation that raced through him, vanished as frost beneath a mist-scattering sun. For if this were true – why, then there was no such thing as death! And it was true!

It was true! He knew it with a shining certainty that had upon it not the shadow of a shadow – but how much his desire to believe entered into this certainty who can tell?

He looked at the chateau. Of course! It was that whose ruins loomed out of the darkness when the flares split the night – in whose cellars he had longed to sleep. Death – oh, the foolish, fearful hearts of men! – this death? This glorious place of peace and beauty? And this wondrous girl whose brown eyes were the keys of heart's desire! Death – he laughed and laughed again.

Another thought struck him, swept through him like a torrent. He must get back, must get back to the trenches and tell them this great truth he had found. Why, he was like a traveler from a dying world who unwittingly stumbles upon a secret to turn that world dead to hope into a living heaven!

There was no longer need for men to fear the splintering shell, the fire that seared them, the bullets, or the shining steel. What did they matter when this – this – was the truth? He must get back and tell them. Even those two Scots would lie still on the wires when he whispered this to them.

But he forgot – they knew now. But they could not return to tell – as he could. He was wild with joy, exultant, lifted up to the skies, a demigod – the bearer of a truth that would free the devil-ridden world from its demons; a new Prometheus who bore back to mankind a more precious flame than had the old.

"I must go!" he cried. "I must tell them! Show me how to return – swiftly!"

A doubt assailed him; he pondered it.

"But they may not believe me," he whispered. "No. I must show them proof. I must carry something back to prove this to them."

The Lady of Tocquelain smiled. She lifted a little knife from the table and, reaching over to a rose-tree, cut from it a cluster of buds; thrust it toward his eager hand.

Before he could grasp it the maid had taken it.

"Wait!" she murmured. "I will give you another message."

There was a quill and ink upon the table, and Peter wondered how they had come; he had not seen them before – but with so many wonders, what was this small one? There was a slip of paper in the Demoiselle Lucie's hand, too. She bent her little, dusky head and wrote; blew upon the paper, waved it in the air to dry; sighed, smiled at Peter, and wrapped it about the stem of the rosebud cluster; placed it on the table, and waved back Peter's questing hand.

"Your coat," she said. "You'll need it – for now you must go back."

She thrust his arms into the garment. She was laughing – but there were tears in the great, brown eyes; the red mouth was very wistful.

Now the older woman arose, stretched out her hand again; Laveller bent over it, kissed it.

"We shall be here waiting for you, my son," she said softly. "When it is time for you to – come back."

He reached for the roses with the paper wrapped about their stem. The maid darted a hand over his, lifted them before he could touch them.

"You must not read it until you have gone," she said – and again the rose flame burned throat and cheeks.

Hand in hand, like children, they sped over the greensward to where Peter had first met her. There they stopped, regarding each other gravely – and then that other miracle which had happened to Laveller and that he had forgotten in the shock of his wider realization called for utterance.

"I love you!" whispered Peter Laveller to this living, long-dead Demoiselle de Tocquelain. She sighed, and was in his arms.

"Oh, I know you do!" she cried. "I know you do, dear one – but I was so afraid you would go without telling me so."

She raised her sweet lips, pressed them long to his, drew back.

"I loved you from the moment I saw you standing here," she told him, "and I will be here waiting for you when you return. And now you must go, dear love of mine; but wait –"

He felt a hand steal into the pocket of his tunic, press something over his heart.

"The messages," she said. "Take them. And remember – I will wait. I promise. I, Lucie de Tocquelain –"

There was a singing in his head. He opened his eyes. He was back in his trench, and in his ears still rang the name of the demoiselle, and over his heart he felt still the pressure of her hand. His head was half turned toward three men who were regarding him.

One of them had a watch in his hand; it was the surgeon. Why was he looking at his watch? Had he been gone long? he wondered.

Well, what did it matter, when he was the bearer of such a message? His weariness had gone; he was transformed, jubilant; his soul was shouting paeans. Forgetting discipline, he sprang toward the three.

"There is no such thing as death!" he cried. "We must send this message along the lines – at once! At once, do you understand! Tell it to the world – I have proof –"

He stammered and choked in his eagerness. The three glanced at each other. His major lifted his electric flash, clicked it in Peter's face, started oddly – then quietly walked over and stood between the lad and his rifle.

"Just get your breath a moment, my boy, and then tell us all about it," he said.

They were devilishly unconcerned, were they not? Well, wait till they had heard what he had to tell them!

And tell them Peter did, leaving out only what had passed between him and the demoiselle – for, after all, wasn't that their own personal affair? And gravely and silently they listened to him. But always the trouble deepened in his major's eyes as Laveller poured forth the story.

"And then – I came back, came back as quickly as I could, to help us all; to lift us out of all this" – his hands swept out in a wide gesture of disgust – "for none of it matters! When we die – we live!" he ended.

Upon the face of the man of science rested profound satisfaction.

"A perfect demonstration; better than I could ever have hoped!" he spoke over Laveller's head to the major. "Great, how great is the imagination of man!"

There was a tinge of awe in his voice.

Imagination? Peter was cut to the sensitive, vibrant soul of him.

They didn't believe him! He would show them!

"But I have the proof!" he cried.

He threw open his greatcoat, ran his hand into his tunic-pocket; his fingers closed over a bit of paper wrapped around a stem. Ah – now he would show them!

He drew it out, thrust it toward them.

"Look!" His voice was like a triumphal trumpet-call.

What was the matter with them? Could they not see? Why did their eyes search his face instead of realizing what he was offering them? He looked at what he held – then, incredulous, brought it close to his own eyes, gazed and gazed, with a sound in his ears as though the universe were slipping away around him, with a heart that seemed to have forgotten to beat. For in his hand, stem wrapped in paper, was no fresh and fragrant rosebud cluster his brown-eyed demoiselle's mother had clipped for him in the garden.

No – there was but a sprig of artificial buds, worn and torn and stained, faded and old!

A great numbness crept over Peter.

Dumbly he looked at the surgeon, at his captain, at the major whose face was now troubled indeed and somewhat stern.

"What does it mean?" he muttered.

Had it all been a dream? Was there no radiant Lucie – save in his own mind – no brown-eyed maid who loved him and whom he loved?

The scientist stepped forward, took the worn little sprig from the relaxed grip. The bit of paper slipped off, remained in Peter's fingers.

"You certainly deserve to know just what you've been through, my boy," the urbane, capable voice beat upon his dulled hearing, "after such a reaction as you have provided to our little experiment." He laughed pleasantly.

Experiment? Experiment? A dull rage began to grow in Peter – vicious, slowly rising.

"Monsieur!" called the major appealingly, somewhat warningly, it seemed, to his distinguished visitor.

"Oh, by your leave, major," went on the great man, "here is a lad of high intelligence – of education, you could know that by the way he expressed himself – he will understand."

The major was not a scientist – he was a Frenchman, human, and with an imagination of his own. He shrugged; but he moved a little closer to the resting rifle.

"We had been discussing, your officers and I," the capable voice went on, "dreams that are the half-awakened mind's effort to explain some touch, some unfamiliar sound, or what not that has aroused it from its sleep. One is slumbering, say, and a window nearby is broken. The sleeper hears, the consciousness endeavors to learn – but it has given over its control to the subconscious. And this rises accommodatingly to its mate's assistance. But it is irresponsible, and it can express itself only in pictures.

"It takes the sound and – well, weaves a little romance around it. It does its best to explain – alas! Its best is only a more or less fantastic lie – recognized as such by the consciousness the moment it becomes awake.

"And the movement of the subconsciousness in this picture production is inconceivably rapid. It can depict in the fraction of a second a series of incidents that if actually lived would take hours – yes, days – of time. You follow me, do you not? Perhaps you recognize the experience I outline?"

Laveller nodded. The bitter, consuming rage was mounting within him steadily. But he was outwardly calm, all alert. He would hear what this self-satisfied devil had done to him, and then –

"Your officers disagreed with some of my conclusions. I saw you here, weary, concentrated upon the duty at hand, half in hypnosis from the strain and the steady flaring and dying of the lights. You offered a perfect clinical subject, a laboratory test unexcelled –"

Could he keep his hands from his throat until he had finished? Laveller wondered. Lucie, his Lucie, a fantastic lie –

"Steady, *mon vieux*" – it was his major whispering. Ah, when he struck, he must do it quickly – his officer was too close, too close. Still – he must keep his watch for him through the slit. He would be peering there, perhaps, when he, Peter, leaped.

"And so" – the surgeon's tones were in his best student-clinic manner – "and so I took a little sprig of artificial flowers that I had found pressed between the leaves of an old missal I had picked up in the ruins of the chateau yonder. On a slip of paper I wrote a line of French – for then I thought you a French soldier. It was a simple line from the ballad of 'Aucassin and Nicolette' –"

And there she waits to greet him
When all his days are run.

"Also, there was a name written on the title-page of the missal, the name, no doubt, of its long-dead owner – 'Lucie de Tocquelain' –"

Lucie! Peter's rage and hatred were beaten back by a great surge of longing – rushed back stronger than ever.

"So I passed the sprig of flowers before your unseeing eyes; consciously unseeing, I mean, for it was certain your subconsciousness would take note of them. I showed you the line of writing – your subconsciousness absorbed this, too, with its suggestion of a love troth, a separation, an awaiting. I wrapped it about the stem of the sprig, I thrust them both into your pocket, and called the name of Lucie de Tocquelain into your ear.

"The problem was what your other self would make of those four things – the ancient cluster, the suggestion in the line of writing, the touch, and the name – a fascinating problem, indeed!

"And hardly had I withdrawn my hand, almost before my lips closed on the word I had whispered – you had turned to us shouting that there was no such thing as death, and pouring out, like one inspired, that remarkable story of yours – all, all built by your imagination from –"

But he got no further. The searing rage in Laveller had burst all bounds, had flared forth murderously and hurled him silently at the surgeon's throat. There were flashes of flame before his eyes – red, sparkling sheets of flame. He would die for it, but he would kill this cold-blooded fiend who could take a man out of hell, open up to him heaven, and then thrust him back into hell grown now a hundred times more cruel, with all hope dead in him for eternity.

Before he could strike strong hands gripped him, held him fast. The scarlet, curtained flares before his eyes faded away. He thought he heard a tender, golden voice whispering to him:

"It is nothing! It is nothing! See as I do!"

He was standing between his officers, who held him fast on each side. They were silent, looking at the now white-faced surgeon with more than somewhat of cold, unfriendly sternness in their eyes.

"My boy, my boy" – that scientist's poise was gone; his voice trembling, agitated. "I did not understand – I am sorry – I never thought you would take it so seriously."

Laveller spoke to his officers – quietly. "It is over, sirs. You need not hold me."

They looked at him, released him, patted him on the shoulder, fixed again their visitor with that same utter contempt.

Laveller turned stumblingly to the parapet. His eyes were full of tears. Brain and heart and soul were nothing but a blind desolation, a waste utterly barren of hope or of even the ghost of the wish to hope. That message of his, the sacred truth that was to set the feet of a tormented world on the path to paradise – a dream.

His Lucie, his brown-eyed demoiselle who had murmured her love for him – a thing compounded of a word, a touch, a writing, and an artificial flower!

He could not, would not believe it. Why, he could feel still the touch of her soft lips on his, her warm body quivering in his arms. And she had said he would come back – and promised to wait for him.

What was that in his hand? It was the paper that had wrapped the rosebuds – the cursed paper with which that cold devil had experimented with him.

Laveller crumpled it savagely – raised it to hurl it at his feet.

Someone seemed to stay his hand.

Slowly he opened it.

The three men watching him saw a glory steal over his face, a radiance like that of a soul redeemed from endless torture. All its sorrow, its agony, was wiped out, leaving it a boy's once more.

He stood wide-eyed, dreaming.

The major stepped forward, gently drew the paper from Laveller.

There were many star-shells floating on high now, the trench was filled with their glare, and in their light he scanned the fragment.

On his face when he raised it there was a great awe – and as they took it from him and read this same awe dropped down upon the others like a veil.

For over the line the surgeon had written were now three other lines – in old French: –

"Nor grieve, dear heart, nor fear the seeming –
Here is waking after dreaming.
– She who loves you, Lucie."

That was McAndrews's story, and it was Hawtry who finally broke the silence that followed his telling of it.

"The lines had been on the paper, of course," he said; "they were probably faint, and your surgeon had not noticed them. It was drizzling, and the dampness brought them out."

"No," answered McAndrews; "they had not been there."

"But how can you be so sure?" remonstrated the Psychologist.

"Because I was the surgeon," said McAndrews quietly. "The paper was a page torn from my note book. When I wrapped it about the sprig it was blank – except for the line I myself had written there.

"But there was one more bit of – well, shall we call it evidence, John? – the hand in which Laveller's message was penned was the hand in the missal in which I had found the flowers – and the signature 'Lucie' was that same signature, curve for curve and quaint, old-fashioned angle for angle."

A longer silence fell, broken once more by Hawtry, abruptly.

"What became of the paper?" he asked. "Was the ink analyzed? Was –"

"As we stood there wondering," interrupted McAndrews, "a squall swept down upon the trench. It tore the paper from my hand; carried it away. Laveller watched it go; made no effort to get it."

" 'It does not matter. I know now,' he said – and smiled at me, the forgiving, happy smile of a joyous boy. 'I apologize to you, doctor. You're the best friend I ever had. I thought at first you had done to me what no other man would do to another – I see now that you have done for me what no other man could.'

"And that is all. He went through the war neither seeking death nor avoiding it. I loved him like a son. He would have died after that Mount Kemmel affair had it not been for me. He wanted to live long enough to bid his father and sister goodbye, and I – patched him up. He did it, and then set forth for the trench beneath the shadow of the ruined old chateau where his brown-eyed demoiselle had found him."

"Why?" asked Hawtry.

"Because he thought that from there he could – go back – to her more quickly."

"To me an absolutely unwarranted conclusion," said the psychologist, wholly irritated, half angry. "There is some simple, natural explanation of it all."

"Of course, John," answered McAndrews soothingly – "of course there is. Tell us it, can't you?"

But Hawtry, it seemed, could not offer any particulars.

Pen Dragons

Dan Micklethwaite

A BOY of about nine years old tracks through the grass and the moss and the reeds of the swamp. These are the Marches. Rough country, unless you get used to it quickly. Grow up within it, rather than staying apart. His mother would have preferred him to remain in the keep, by the fire, with the old women watching over. His father pushed him out of the door as soon as he could walk.

"You'll have to be strong, boy, if you want to follow me."

His feet pass from slippery log to slippery grass without wavering. He can do, and has done, such things with eyes shut. A helpful talent, not least when the mist from the marsh lake is thickest, is clogging the channels in between trees.

He has his eyes open tonight though, as he treads the shore of that lake. He sees the sky through the elms glow all hearth-fire and lilac. Tongues of flame belch intermittently from the silt up ahead.

Through their glare, their gaseous haze, he checks for the figure in the distance, making sure that he hasn't lost track.

The white robes the man wears are a beacon. They draw the boy onwards, deeper into the woodland: birthplace and home of all rumour and myth.

The boy pulls closer; his nimble feet, booted in calfskin, outdoing the old man's stumbling gait. The man's white linen is spattered with mud, patterned with moss on the sleeves where he brushes too close to the centurion oaks. Dead leaves catch and then crumble from grey hair and grey beard. The man's long, gnarly staff plunges into and out of the marsh-dirt with a sound like toads in their mating.

The boy has watched these toads, lit by stars, lit by will o' the wisps, with his father beside him. One of the rare times that his father didn't just shoo him away. It was quite dull – really dull – when it happened, but glows now like a blade in remembering. His father so often at war of late, keeping other chieftains at bay. His mother so often by the fireside, weeping, unsure if he'll ever return.

It is this worry, in part, which has brought the boy here.

The old man turns his head and the boy flattens his frame to the trunk of a sycamore, not daring to breathe even a little, in case the old man, even from this distance, can hear him or detect a slight change in the air.

He has come because there are murmurs the old man is a druid. That he keeps communion with the old gods, with the spirits. That he can work spells.

And a man like that must be helpful in war, good to have on your side.

Surely.

The boy grows a tad doubtful, however, when they reach the man's hovel. The walls are crooked. The thatch is damp and grey-green and thin. Mushrooms gathering and overlapping like slates at one edge. The door, such as it is, doesn't sit quite right on its frame.

If he himself could do magic, he wouldn't live in a dung-heap like this.

Still, all stories have to start for a reason. Usually a good one, he thinks, keeping some kind of faith.

Squatting in the long grass on the edge of the clearing, he soon sees weird, vivid lights, a whole range of colours, begin to flicker through cracks in the oaken shutter, which stoppers what should be a window but is more simply a haphazard hole in the wall.

Mothlike, adept, the boy floats over towards it. Presses an eye to a suitable gap.

* * *

The old man leans over a dark, heavy table. In this light, his white robes show far more shades than simply mud-brown and moss-green; they're dappled, almost, with a rainbow's blood. Beside his thin blue hands are a range of small earthenware bowls, roughly the same size, striped with more colours still.

He adds seeds, berries, even what appear to be flakes of stone to the mixture. Works them together with a bleached animal bone.

Candles burn nearby. Occasionally, dust will be churned up by the motion, and hit a flame, flare out, glitter then die. The old man adds what might be swamp water, might be beer. The harshness of grinding becomes a river-like slosh.

At the window, the boy sees the birthing of magic. His eyes at the wood are unblinking, don't want to miss how these potions are made.

The old man sees only work. Once satisfied that each mixture is right, he sets the bowls on a wooden plank and then lifts it with a delicate, trembling grace. He carries it over to another table, just beneath and beside the window. There is only a single candle there, resting on the yellowed skull of a ram; wax forming frozen waterfalls across the sockets of the eyes, the nose, the gaping, deathly jester's mouth. The light it throws across the small pools of liquid makes the colours, each distinct, pop out and glimmer. Cats' eyes, owls' eyes, in the focus of some nocturnal hunt.

The boy meets their stare, only faintly afraid.

He watches as the druid picks up a slender, sharpened stick – which, from the rumours, from the fireside myths, he believes must be a wand – and holds it precarious over one of the potions. The red one. A blood-moon in a bowl.

But, rather than muttering an incantation – as, again, he's been led to think that druids do – the old man dips the wand into the potion. Scratches it across the lightened surface of this wood.

Patterns happen. Runes. Other shades besides red are added. An island begins to take shape. Beasts, humped and spitting out steam from their backs, move in blue swirls that he takes to be some kind of river. Fishing boats appear all around them. Small men holding spears …

Then, the scratching stops. And the druid turns towards the shutter. And rises. And the eyehole goes black.

* * *

The boy sits on the floor in the corner, drinking beer from a cup made from hollowed-out horn.

At the other side of the room, the druid is still working. The stick scratches again at the surface of the table. The candle still dances on top of the skull.

After a while, the boy stops sniffing and sipping and screwing his face up at the strange taste of the brew. He starts to ask questions. All of which go unanswered. So many of which go unanswered that he starts to worry the druid doesn't understand the common tongue.

He asks him this straight out, to be sure.

And is corrected and rewarded with a string of raw curses, told to be quiet and to drink up and sit still.

He stays in the corner and focuses on figuring out what kind of beer this is; on keeping it down and not adding further to the wreckage of the old man's floor. Bugs like walking shields, like the Roman phalanx formation, scuttle and slither among food-scraps and rags.

He shivers, kicks out at them. He tries to stay quiet, but the effort doesn't last long.

Soon, he is up and peering over the druid's shoulder, watching as the stick speeds across what he can tell now isn't the moon-pale surface of the table, but rather a length of vellum, stretched taut and flat.

Glancing around, it's clear that at least some of the rubbish in the room is other pieces of this, bundled and bound up into scrolls. Amassed in great quantity; stored without any real planning or care. The bugs seem to use them as tunnels, as thoroughfares.

"Is this what druids do, then?" he asks.

And: "What's that bit mean?"

And: "How about this?"

"And this man with a sword?"

He is transfixed. He's never seen pictures of this type or quality before in his life.

From his wanderings in town, he knows the etchings on doorposts outside taverns – shapes that he gathers mean wicked things (according to his mother and his nurses) but he can't make out exactly what.

These ones here, though, he can make out right away. The warriors. The ships. The forest.

The waters. The deer. The peasants. The bandits. The keep.

It is only the small dark markings dotted in and amongst all of these pictures that give him pause, that confuse him. A question loiters on his tongue, but, as if able to sense it, the druid swivels round and stops it with a look.

The boy glances again at the walls of the room, at the various shabby sheets he now recognises as further scrolls, for any clues, anything that might aid understanding. But there are none.

Vaguely disheartened, he heads back to the corner, treading on bugs as he goes.

* * *

Even now, years later, the boy has never learnt to read. The young man. Not for want of trying to teach him, on the druid's part, but rather due to a lack of focus in his pupil. A tendency to become distracted by the figures beside the text. To be swept off into dreaming. A tendency that only increases as the situation in the region worsens.

His mother, once so pitiful and endearing in her worries for his father, becomes almost placid in his absence now. The longer his father has survived, despite all of the injuries suffered, the more she's exhausted her stockpile of care. No matter what her husband, who dares now to openly call himself King, does, there is no peace in the Marches, no easing of the panic and the darkness that has set about the land. So, she has said to her son, pleaded of him, what is the use of it all?

"He encourages the bastards," she says. "He taunts them."

The village is no longer safe from attack, either by the men of other chieftains or by wandering rogues. Old women and old men, and children, suffer worst in these raids. Horrors his mother will no longer speak of. Findings that turn his father's face stony, even in the middle of a hearty feast. Where there was once ribaldry, challenge, greasy ribs tossed with a laugh to the wolfhounds, now there is only a drear wait for the end.

"May I be excused?"

If he were still so young, he would not be allowed out of the keep. He would never learn to navigate the swamps so well that he could do it even in thick fog, even eyes-closed.

Certainly, his younger brother never will.

Several times this past year he has been grateful for his knowledge, for the mud and the moss and the lake that baptised him, taught him where not to fall. Brought him close to his drowning.

With the ways being so fearful, and in exchange for his continued free stay at the hovel, and for being taught how to make what the druid calls 'ink', he now gathers the ingredients for this from the woodland himself. In so doing, crouching amidst squelching earth and cracking twigs, he is sometimes caught off-guard by bandits. Each time, however, he manages to escape, to lose them in the woods.

Or, if they are too many, and block his ways, then he draws his dagger, his broadsword, and stabs out at them, slashes. Though his training is not yet complete, he sometimes gets lucky – he clove a man through the ribs once, the bones springing out like the bloodied jaws of a wolf – but mainly his hope is to drive them into the water. With the weight of their stolen gold, and the tangle of grasses and weeds in even the shallower parts, they don't stand much chance of escaping alive.

Whatever scratches he incurs in return for his efforts, the druid always tends.

Whatever scratches he incurs, he feels that they're worth it.

Not long after he first started coming here, the druid gave in to his questions and began to explain to him some of the scrolls. Over time, these explanations turned into fully-fledged histories, overstuffed myths.

He comes now, he mixes the inks, smashing the seeds and the berries in all proper quantities; carries them to the second table, which the druid now rarely leaves, and waits to see which song comes next.

Whilst the old man works at the vellum, he retreats to his corner, padded now with hay – when he can steal some from his father's stables – and drinks beer from the cup made of hollowed-out horn.

When he's ready, the druid turns to face the young prince, the ram's skull leering snow-blindly over his shoulder, and he sings about empires and fiefdoms undreamed of, about madness and freedom on the far side of the world.

* * *

One day, in an effort to filch more hay from the stables, he is caught by his father. He is forced into armour. He is placed in a saddle. He is told that the war is getting worse. That the chieftain on the next hill is pushing for victory; that all of this, the castle and the village, is on the verge of being lost.

The prince doesn't have so much time to go and listen to the old man's stories after that. His days are spent in open combat in muddy fields.

The rainbow of the druid's palette fades.

There are now three colours only: iron, blood and earth.

His nights are spent in deep sleep without allowance for dreaming.

His mother worries again, for his sake, but is prone now to rages at his father. Accuses her husband of trying to murder their son, so that he cannot challenge for the throne. Claims he is under thrall of witchcraft. That he has made a deal with some demon, some succubus, so that their firstborn will not rule.

She becomes increasingly distant. Goes missing for days at a time.

During those wanderings, his father looks almost half-cheerful again. Relaxed. Carries the day's new battle-scars lightly.

Until, at last, he doesn't.

* * *

When the prince barges in through the door of the hovel, the old man turns around calmly, amidst flickering candles and fluttering scrolls, as though he already knows what his visitor will say.

"You are a druid, are you not? All this time you have beguiled me with songs and with pictures, when I came out here at first to learn of your spells. To seek your help against our enemies."

The old man is silent.

"Well? Where are they? Do I not deserve them, after all that I have done for you?"

Still the old man doesn't speak.

"My father lies slain in a field and they have taken his flag. I will have my revenge. And I will have your help."

"Why don't you sit down, boy?" the druid says. "I have a story that might be of use."

"No. I do not need stories. I need spells. I need to take my enemy's blood."

Silence.

"Will you help me or not?" the youth says, with his hand on the hilt of his sword.

"What is it that you want most to gain from this war?" the old man says. "What end would satisfy you, if it were indeed within my power to give?"

The youth thinks.

He glares.

He clenches and unclenches his fist on the sword-hilt.

"I would be true Lord and King of this land, having bested all enemies. I would be known as the bringer of unity. The bringer of peace."

The druid pauses, then nods: "I can do this for you. But it will take time. And you, for once, must be patient. And you must leave me alone to this task for a while."

* * *

Barely three days after his father is buried, his mother leaves the castle to live with the man whose army took the old king's life.

There are other defections.

He takes a wife, but suspects her constantly of being unfaithful. Whenever he's wounded in battle, he raises his hand to her face, makes her share the hurt. Reminds her: "We are in this together. Win or lose."

Though he says the latter word, he doesn't believe it to be a possibility. He doesn't want to. He wants to keep faith in the powers of his old friend. He tells himself – even tells his wife, in his quieter, gentler, rarer moods – that the druid's spell will work out. That he will be unchallenged King, and she will be unchallenged Queen.

But this faith is tested, daily. As he rides back, usually muddied, frequently bloodied, and looks up at the ramshackle husk of the keep, stamped against the lilac and hearth-fire of dusk. As he imagines the walls, the foundations beneath them simply giving up and sliding down the hill and disappearing into a river, into what the druid had said was an ocean, of blood.

And it is tested most sorely and sharply when the axe of an enemy cleaves through his collarbone, before he can push the man back and end his life with a thrust.

It is strained for weeks, whilst his wife sits by his bedside, keeps the hearth-fire burning, keeps the wound clean. Weeps onto his fevered brow. Wails into his sweat-and-piss-and-shit-drenched sheets.

Looks at that brow in a rare moment of stillness, of coolness, and wonders if it will ever, now, bear the weight of a crown.

* * *

Recovered, though tender, he resolves to ride out to the forest. He has been patient enough, he reasons. It has been half a year, perhaps longer, and he can afford to wait no more. Not with the village at breaking point.

His shoulder still pained – the skin there a pink welt like a length of rope or a snake underneath it – he cannot carry the weight of armour, and nor can he swing a sword or do much else with his left hand. This leaves him, though vulnerable, at least light on his feet, and despite it being a decade since he first mastered the path to the druid's hut, and the vegetation being subject to its usual rhythm of summer-growths and frost-culls, the lake's border changing, he finds his way easily.

But what he sees doesn't please him, doesn't offer him hope. He hangs back, crouched in the long grass, pressed close to a willow. Through its swaying fronds, he sees the roofing thatch gone sparser, more ragged than ever. The shutter hangs off its hinges. The door buckles inwards where it didn't before.

Through the hole in the wall, even before he enters, he can tell the place is deserted. It has been cleared out or raided, that much is plain.

He pushes through the door with his left shoulder. Normally, the wind that accompanied his entrance would ruffle vellum, tremble flames. But now it finds emptiness, its passage untroubled, except by the thick dark wedge of the table. On that table, the mixing-place, there are only shards and fragments of the small earthenware bowls.

On the other, there is only the ram's skull, caved in.

And a lone scroll beside it.

As he approaches, he looks for others on the walls and on the floor, but there are none. In fact, the floor has never been so clean. Even the bugs have deserted, their legions decamped. All that mars it are a few drops of dark red, which he scuffs with his boot to see how they flake. They might be ink. They might be blood. He doesn't quite want to get down on his knees and taste.

He opens the scroll. At the start and down the sides, for a part of its length, there are pictures. There is a warrior in a crown, with hair of a colour that could be taken for his.

There is a woman who, though he never introduced her to the druid, looks very much like his wife. Even down to the cobalt blue of her eyes. There are his enemies before him, wasted and slain. And there is the red dragon of his father's flag, crawling up along one side. And the spiralling turrets of a massive castle ascending the other. A stone castle. Much more impressive than the current wooden fort.

But the rest is dark scratches. The ones the old man did try to explain but which he never quite grasped. The ones he realises now must be the lines of an incantation, a spell.

He doesn't even recognise his own name in the tangle. Arturus.

Perhaps if he'd learnt all this when he was young, he thinks, he could have defeated his enemies without anyone's help.

But he didn't.

And he won't.

This scroll, spell or not, is no good without a druid to read it. And his druid is gone. The best he can hope for now is to get back to his wife and take her to safety, before his enemies charge the hill and breach the keep wall.

He rushes outside, feet plunging into and out of the mud with the noise of toads in their mating.

He thinks of his father, his legacy ending.

He thinks of his wife again, how she's with-child.

A son of his own? A prince?

He can't give up on that. The crown. Not so quickly. Not after all this. The druid must have come through, kept his promise, put the magic in action before whatever befell. He just has to stay patient. Have faith. Get somewhere safe.

He thinks of the magnificent castle he'd seen on the scroll.

Of a flag flying, winged and red, at the top of high towers.

He runs on, unarmed and alone, through the dusk of the swamp.

Between the trees, through the gathering mist, he catches sight of the sky, all hearth-fire and lilac.

It is beautiful. Homely.

For a moment, as he watches, as he runs, as he dreams, he forgets the changed line of the shore of the lake.

The Clock that Went Backward

Edward Page Mitchell

I

A ROW of Lombardy poplars stood in front of my great-aunt Gertrude's house, on the bank of the Sheepscot River. In personal appearance my aunt was surprisingly like one of those trees. She had the look of hopeless anemia that distinguishes them from fuller blooded sorts. She was tall, severe in outline, and extremely thin. Her habiliments clung to her. I am sure that had the gods found occasion to impose upon her the fate of Daphne she would have taken her place easily and naturally in the dismal row, as melancholy a poplar as the rest.

Some of my earliest recollections are of this venerable relative. Alive and dead she bore an important part in the events I am about to recount: events which I believe to be without parallel in the experience of mankind.

During our periodical visits of duty to Aunt Gertrude in Maine, my cousin Harry and myself were accustomed to speculate much on her age. Was she sixty, or was she six score? We had no precise information; she might have been either. The old lady was surrounded by old-fashioned things. She seemed to live altogether in the past. In her short half-hours of communicativeness, over her second cup of tea, or on the piazza where the poplars sent slim shadows directly toward the east, she used to tell us stories of her alleged ancestors. I say alleged, because we never fully believed that she had ancestors.

A genealogy is a stupid thing. Here is Aunt Gertrude's, reduced to its simplest forms:

Her great-great-grandmother (1599–1642) was a woman of Holland who married a Puritan refugee, and sailed from Leyden to Plymouth in the ship Ann in the year of our Lord 1632. This Pilgrim mother had a daughter, Aunt Gertrude's great-grandmother (1640–1718). She came to the Eastern District of Massachusetts in the early part of the last century, and was carried off by the Indians in the Penobscot wars. Her daughter (1680–1776) lived to see these colonies free and independent, and contributed to the population of the coming republic not less than nineteen stalwart sons and comely daughters. One of the latter (1735–1802) married a Wiscasset skipper engaged in the West India trade, with whom she sailed. She was twice wrecked at sea – once on what is now Seguin Island and once on San Salvador. It was on San Salvador that Aunt Gertrude was born.

We got to be very tired of hearing this family history. Perhaps it was the constant repetition and the merciless persistency with which the above dates were driven into our young ears that made us skeptics. As I have said, we took little stock in Aunt Gertrude's ancestors. They seemed highly improbable. In our private opinion the great-grandmothers and grandmothers and so forth were pure myths, and Aunt Gertrude herself was the principal in all the adventures attributed to them, having lasted from century to century while generations of contemporaries went the way of all flesh.

On the first landing of the square stairway of the mansion loomed a tall Dutch clock. The case was more than eight feet high, of a dark red wood, not mahogany, and it was curiously inlaid with silver. No common piece of furniture was this. About a hundred years ago there flourished in the town of Brunswick a horologist named Cary, an industrious and accomplished workman. Few well-to-do houses on that part of the coast lacked a Cary timepiece. But Aunt Gertrude's clock had marked the hours and minutes of two full centuries before the Brunswick artisan was born. It was running when William the Taciturn pierced the dikes to relieve Leyden. The name of the maker, Jan Lipperdam, and the date, 1572, were still legible in broad black letters and figures reaching quite across the dial. Cary's masterpieces were plebeian and recent beside this ancient aristocrat. The jolly Dutch moon, made to exhibit the phases over a landscape of windmills and polders, was cunningly painted. A skilled hand had carved the grim ornament at the top, a death's head transfixed by a two-edged sword. Like all timepieces of the sixteenth century, it had no pendulum. A simple Van Wyck escapement governed the descent of the weights to the bottom of the tall case.

But these weights never moved. Year after year, when Harry and I returned to Maine, we found the hands of the old clock pointing to the quarter past three, as they had pointed when we first saw them. The fat moon hung perpetually in the third quarter, as motionless as the death's head above. There was a mystery about the silenced movement and the paralyzed hands. Aunt Gertrude told us that the works had never performed their functions since a bolt of lightning entered the clock; and she showed us a black hole in the side of the case near the top, with a yawning rift that extended downward for several feet. This explanation failed to satisfy us. It did not account for the sharpness of her refusal when we proposed to bring over the watchmaker from the village, or for her singular agitation once when she found Harry on a stepladder, with a borrowed key in his hand, about to test for himself the clock's suspended vitality.

One August night, after we had grown out of boyhood, I was awakened by a noise in the hallway. I shook my cousin. "Somebody's in the house," I whispered.

We crept out of our room and on to the stairs. A dim light came from below. We held breath and noiselessly descended to the second landing. Harry clutched my arm. He pointed down over the banisters, at the same time drawing me back into the shadow.

We saw a strange thing.

Aunt Gertrude stood on a chair in front of the old clock, as spectral in her white nightgown and white nightcap as one of the poplars when covered with snow. It chanced that the floor creaked slightly under our feet. She turned with a sudden movement, peering intently into the darkness, and holding a candle high toward us, so that the light was full upon her pale face. She looked many years older than when I bade her good night. For a few minutes she was motionless, except in the trembling arm that held aloft the candle. Then, evidently reassured, she placed the light upon a shelf and turned again to the clock.

We now saw the old lady take a key from behind the face and proceed to wind up the weights. We could hear her breath, quick and short. She rested a band on either side of the case and held her face close to the dial, as if subjecting it to anxious scrutiny. In this attitude she remained for a long time. We heard her utter a sigh of relief, and she half turned toward us for a moment. I shall never forget the expression of wild joy that transfigured her features then.

The hands of the clock were moving; they were moving backward.

Aunt Gertrude put both arms around the clock and pressed her withered cheek against it. She kissed it repeatedly. She caressed it in a hundred ways, as if it had been a living and beloved thing. She fondled it and talked to it, using words which we could hear but could not understand. The hands continued to move backward.

Then she started back with a sudden cry. The clock had stopped. We saw her tall body swaying for an instant on the chair. She stretched out her arms in a convulsive gesture of terror and despair, wrenched the minute hand to its old place at a quarter past three, and fell heavily to the floor.

II

AUNT GERTRUDE'S WILL left me her bank and gas stocks, real estate, railroad bonds, and city sevens, and gave Harry the clock. We thought at the time that this was a very unequal division, the more surprising because my cousin had always seemed to be the favorite. Half in seriousness we made a thorough examination of the ancient timepiece, sounding its wooden case for secret drawers, and even probing the not complicated works with a knitting needle to ascertain if our whimsical relative had bestowed there some codicil or other document changing the aspect of affairs. We discovered nothing.

There was testamentary provision for our education at the University of Leyden. We left the military school in which we had learned a little of the theory of war, and a good deal of the art of standing with our noses over our heels, and took ship without delay. The clock went with us. Before many months it was established in a corner of a room in the Breede Straat.

The fabric of Jan Lipperdam's ingenuity, thus restored to its native air, continued to tell the hour of quarter past three with its old fidelity. The author of the clock had been under the sod for nearly three hundred years. The combined skill of his successors in the craft at Leyden could make it go neither forward nor backward.

We readily picked up enough Dutch to make ourselves understood by the townspeople, the professors, and such of our eight hundred and odd fellow students as came into intercourse. This language, which looks so hard at first, is only a sort of polarized English. Puzzle over it a little while and it jumps into your comprehension like one of those simple cryptograms made by running together all the words of a sentence and then dividing in the wrong places.

The language acquired and the newness of our surroundings worn off, we settled into tolerably regular pursuits. Harry devoted himself with some assiduity to the study of sociology, with especial reference to the round-faced and not unkind maidens of Leyden. I went in for the higher metaphysics.

Outside of our respective studies, we had a common ground of unfailing interest. To our astonishment, we found that not one in twenty of the faculty or students knew or cared a sliver about the glorious history of the town, or even about the circumstances under which the university itself was founded by the Prince of Orange. In marked contrast with the general indifference was the enthusiasm of Professor Van Stopp, my chosen guide through the cloudiness of speculative philosophy.

This distinguished Hegelian was a tobacco-dried little old man, with a skullcap over features that reminded me strangely of Aunt Gertrude's. Had he been her own brother the facial resemblance could not have been closer. I told him so once, when we were together in the Stadthuis looking at the portrait of the hero of the siege, the Burgomaster Van der Werf. The professor laughed. "I will show you what is even a more extraordinary coincidence," said he; and, leading the way across the hall to the great picture of the siege, by Warmers, he pointed out the figure of a burgher participating in the defense. It was true. Van Stopp might have been the burgher's son; the burgher might have been Aunt Gertrude's father.

The professor seemed to be fond of us. We often went to his rooms in an old house in the Rapenburg Straat, one of the few houses remaining that antedate 1574. He would walk with us through the beautiful suburbs of the city, over straight roads lined with poplars that carried us back to the bank of the Sheepscot in our minds. He took us to the top of the ruined Roman tower in the center of the town, and from the same battlements from which anxious eyes three centuries ago had watched the slow approach of Admiral Boisot's fleet over the submerged polders, he pointed out the great dike of the Landscheiding, which was cut that the oceans might bring Boisot's Zealanders to raise the leaguer and feed the starving. He showed us the headquarters of the Spaniard Valdez at Leyderdorp, and told us how heaven sent a violent northwest wind on the night of the first of October, piling up the water deep where it had been shallow and sweeping the fleet on between Zoeterwoude and Zwieten up to the very walls of the fort at Lammen, the last stronghold of the besiegers and the last obstacle in the way of succor to the famishing inhabitants. Then he showed us where, on the very night before the retreat of the besieging army, a huge breach was made in the wall of Leyden, near the Cow Gate, by the Walloons from Lammen.

"Why!" cried Harry, catching fire from the eloquence of the professor's narrative, "that was the decisive moment of the siege."

The professor said nothing. He stood with his arms folded, looking intently into my cousin's eyes.

"For," continued Harry, "had that point not been watched, or had defense failed and the breach been carried by the night assault from Lammen, the town would have been burned and the people massacred under the eyes of Admiral Boisot and the fleet of relief. Who defended the breach?"

Van Stopp replied very slowly, as if weighing every word:

"History records the explosion of the mine under the city wall on the last night of the siege; it does not tell the story of the defense or give the defender's name. Yet no man that ever lived had a more tremendous charge than fate entrusted to this unknown hero. Was it chance that sent him to meet that unexpected danger? Consider some of the consequences had he failed. The fall of Leyden would have destroyed the last hope of the Prince of Orange and of the free states. The tyranny of Philip would have been reestablished. The birth of religious liberty and of self-government by the people would have been postponed, who knows for how many centuries? Who knows that there would or could have been a republic of the United States of America had there been no United Netherlands? Our University, which has given to the world Grotius, Scaliger, Arminius, and Descartes, was founded upon this hero's successful defense of the breach. We owe to him our presence here today. Nay, you owe to him your very existence. Your ancestors were of Leyden; between their lives and the butchers outside the walls he stood that night."

The little professor towered before us, a giant of enthusiasm and patriotism. Harry's eyes glistened and his cheeks reddened.

"Go home, boys," said Van Stopp, "and thank God that while the burghers of Leyden were straining their gaze toward Zoeterwoude and the fleet, there was one pair of vigilant eyes and one stout heart at the town wall just beyond the Cow Gate!"

III

THE RAIN was splashing against the windows one evening in the autumn of our third year at Leyden, when Professor Van Stopp honored us with a visit in the Breede Straat. Never had I seen the old gentleman in such spirits. He talked incessantly. The gossip of the town, the news of Europe, science, poetry, philosophy, were in turn touched upon and treated with the same high and good humor. I sought to draw him out on Hegel, with whose chapter on the complexity and interdependency of things I was just then struggling.

"You do not grasp the return of the Itself into Itself through its Otherself?" he said smiling. "Well, you will, sometime."

Harry was silent and preoccupied. His taciturnity gradually affected even the professor. The conversation flagged, and we sat a long while without a word. Now and then there was a flash of lightning succeeded by distant thunder.

"Your clock does not go," suddenly remarked the professor. "Does it ever go?"

"Never since we can remember," I replied. "That is, only once, and then it went backward. It was when Aunt Gertrude –"

Here I caught a warning glance from Harry. I laughed and stammered, "The clock is old and useless. It cannot be made to go."

"Only backward?" said the professor, calmly, and not appearing to notice my embarrassment. "Well, and why should not a clock go backward? Why should not Time itself turn and retrace its course?"

He seemed to be waiting for an answer. I had none to give.

"I thought you Hegelian enough," he continued, "to admit that every condition includes its own contradiction. Time is a condition, not an essential. Viewed from the Absolute, the sequence by which future follows present and present follows past is purely arbitrary. Yesterday, today, tomorrow; there is no reason in the nature of things why the order should not be tomorrow, today, yesterday."

A sharper peal of thunder interrupted the professor's speculations.

"The day is made by the planet's revolution on its axis from west to east. I fancy you can conceive conditions under which it might turn from east to west, unwinding, as it were, the revolutions of past ages. Is it so much more difficult to imagine Time unwinding itself; Time on the ebb, instead of on the flow; the past unfolding as the future recedes; the centuries countermarching; the course of events proceeding toward the Beginning and not, as now, toward the End?"

"But," I interposed, "we know that as far as we are concerned the –"

"We know!" exclaimed Van Stopp, with growing scorn. "Your intelligence has no wings. You follow in the trail of Compte and his slimy brood of creepers and crawlers. You speak with amazing assurance of your position in the universe. You seem to think that your wretched little individuality has a firm foothold in the Absolute. Yet you go to bed tonight and dream into existence men, women, children, beasts of the past or of the future. How do you know that at this moment you yourself, with all your conceit of nineteenth-century thought, are anything more than a creature of a dream of the future, dreamed, let us say, by some philosopher of the sixteenth century? How do you know that you are anything more than a creature of a dream of the past, dreamed by some Hegelian of the twenty-sixth century? How do you know, boy, that you will not vanish into the sixteenth century or 2060 the moment the dreamer awakes?"

There was no replying to this, for it was sound metaphysics. Harry yawned. I got up and went to the window. Professor Van Stopp approached the clock.

"Ah, my children," said he, "there is no fixed progress of human events. Past, present, and future are woven together in one inextricable mesh. Who shall say that this old clock is not right to go backward?"

A crash of thunder shook the house. The storm was over our heads.

When the blinding glare had passed away, Professor Van Stopp was standing upon a chair before the tall timepiece. His face looked more than ever like Aunt Gertrude's. He stood as she had stood in that last quarter of an hour when we saw her wind the clock.

The same thought struck Harry and myself.

"Hold!" we cried, as he began to wind the works. "It may be death if you –"

The professor's sallow features shone with the strange enthusiasm that had transformed Aunt Gertrude's.

"True," he said, "it may be death; but it may be the awakening. Past, present, future; all woven together! The shuttle goes to and fro, forward and back –"

He had wound the clock. The hands were whirling around the dial from right to left with inconceivable rapidity. In this whirl we ourselves seemed to be borne along. Eternities seemed to contract into minutes while lifetimes were thrown off at every tick. Van Stopp, both arms outstretched, was reeling in his chair. The house shook again under a tremendous peal of thunder. At the same instant a ball of fire, leaving a wake of sulphurous vapor and filling the room with dazzling light, passed over our heads and smote the clock. Van Stopp was prostrated. The hands ceased to revolve.

IV

THE ROAR of the thunder sounded like heavy cannonading. The lightning's blaze appeared as the steady light of a conflagration. With our hands over our eyes, Harry and I rushed out into the night.

Under a red sky people were hurrying toward the Stadthuis. Flames in the direction of the Roman tower told us that the heart of the town was afire. The faces of those we saw were haggard and emaciated. From every side we caught disjointed phrases of complaint or despair. "Horseflesh at ten schillings the pound," said one, "and bread at sixteen schillings." "Bread indeed!" an old woman retorted: "It's eight weeks gone since I have seen a crumb." "My little grandchild, the lame one, went last night." "Do you know what Gekke Betje, the washerwoman, did? She was starving. Her babe died, and she and her man –"

A louder cannon burst cut short this revelation. We made our way on toward the citadel of the town, passing a few soldiers here and there and many burghers with grim faces under their broad-brimmed felt hats.

"There is bread plenty yonder where the gunpowder is, and full pardon, too. Valdez shot another amnesty over the walls this morning."

An excited crowd immediately surrounded the speaker. "But the fleet!" they cried.

"The fleet is grounded fast on the Greenway polder. Boisot may turn his one eye seaward for a wind till famine and pestilence have carried off every mother's son of ye, and his ark will not be a rope's length nearer. Death by plague, death by starvation, death by fire and musketry – that is what the burgomaster offers us in return for glory for himself and kingdom for Orange."

"He asks us," said a sturdy citizen, "to hold out only twenty-four hours longer, and to pray meanwhile for an ocean wind."

"Ah, yes!" sneered the first speaker. "Pray on. There is bread enough locked in Pieter Adriaanszoon van der Werf's cellar. I warrant you that is what gives him so wonderful a stomach for resisting the Most Catholic King."

A young girl, with braided yellow hair, pressed through the crowd and confronted the malcontent. "Good people," said the maiden, "do not listen to him. He is a traitor with a Spanish heart. I am Pieter's daughter. We have no bread. We ate malt cakes and rapeseed like the rest of you till that was gone. Then we stripped the green leaves from the lime trees and willows in our garden and ate them. We have eaten even the thistles and weeds that grew between the stones by the canal. The coward lies."

Nevertheless, the insinuation had its effect. The throng, now become a mob, surged off in the direction of the burgomaster's house. One ruffian raised his hand to strike the girl out of the way. In a wink the cur was under the feet of his fellows, and Harry, panting and glowing, stood at the maiden's side, shouting defiance in good English at the backs of the rapidly retreating crowd.

With the utmost frankness she put both her arms around Harry's neck and kissed him.

"Thank you," she said. "You are a hearty lad. My name is Gertruyd van der Wert."

Harry was fumbling in his vocabulary for the proper Dutch phrases, but the girl would not stay for compliments. "They mean mischief to my father"; and she hurried us through several exceedingly narrow streets into a three-cornered market place dominated by a church with two spires. "There he is," she exclaimed, "on the steps of St. Pancras."

There was a tumult in the market place. The conflagration raging beyond the church and the voices of the Spanish and Walloon cannon outside of the walls were less angry than the roar of this multitude of desperate men clamoring for the bread that a single word from their leader's lips would bring them. "Surrender to the King!" they cried, "or we will send your dead body to Lammen as Leyden's token of submission."

One tall man, taller by half a head than any of the burghers confronting him, and so dark of complexion that we wondered how he could be the father of Gertruyd, heard the threat in silence. When the burgomaster spoke, the mob listened in spite of themselves.

"What is it you ask, my friends? That we break our vow and surrender Leyden to the Spaniards? That is to devote ourselves to a fate far more horrible than starvation. I have to keep the oath! Kill me, if you will have it so. I can die only once, whether by your hands, by the enemy's, or by the hand of God. Let us starve, if we must, welcoming starvation because it comes before dishonor. Your menaces do not move me; my life is at your disposal. Here, take my sword, thrust it into my breast, and divide my flesh among you to appease your hunger. So long as I remain alive expect no surrender."

There was silence again while the mob wavered. Then there were mutterings around us. Above these rang out the clear voice of the girl whose hand Harry still held-unnecessarily, it seemed to me.

"Do you not feel the sea wind? It has come at last. To the tower! And the first man there will see by moonlight the full white sails of the prince's ships."

For several hours I scoured the streets of the town, seeking in vain my cousin and his companion; the sudden movement of the crowd toward the Roman tower had separated us. On every side I saw evidences of the terrible chastisement that had brought this stout-hearted people to the verge of despair. A man with hungry eyes chased a lean rat along the bank of the canal. A young mother, with two dead babes in her arms, sat in a doorway to which they bore the bodies of her husband and father, just killed at the walls. In the middle of a deserted street I passed unburied corpses in a pile twice as high as my head. The pestilence had been there-kinder than the Spaniard, because it held out no treacherous promises while it dealt its blows.

Toward morning the wind increased to a gale. There was no sleep in Leyden, no more talk of surrender, no longer any thought or care about defense. These words were on the lips of everybody I met: "Daylight will bring the fleet!"

Did daylight bring the fleet? History says so, but I was not a witness. I know only that before dawn the gale culminated in a violent thunderstorm, and that at the same time a muffled explosion, heavier than the thunder, shook the town. I was in the crowd that watched from the Roman Mound for the first signs of the approaching relief. The concussion shook hope out of every face. "Their mine has reached the wall!" But where? I pressed forward until I found the burgomaster, who was standing among the rest. "Quick!" I whispered. "It is beyond the Cow Gate, and this side of the Tower of Burgundy." He gave me a searching glance, and then strode away, without making any attempt to quiet the general panic. I followed close at his heels.

It was a tight run of nearly half a mile to the rampart in question. When we reached the Cow Gate this is what we saw:

A great gap, where the wall had been, opening to the swampy fields beyond: in the moat, outside and below, a confusion of upturned faces, belonging to men who struggled like demons to achieve the breach, and who now gained a few feet and now were forced back; on the shattered rampart a handful of soldiers and burghers forming a living wall where masonry had failed; perhaps a double handful of women and girls, serving stones to the defenders and boiling water in buckets, besides pitch and oil and unslaked lime, and some of them quoiting tarred and burning hoops over the necks of the Spaniards in the moat; my cousin Harry leading and directing the men; the burgomaster's daughter Gertruyd encouraging and inspiring the women.

But what attracted my attention more than anything else was the frantic activity of a little figure in black, who, with a huge ladle, was showering molten lead on the heads of the assailing party. As he turned to the bonfire and kettle which supplied him with ammunition, his features came into the full light. I gave a cry of surprise: the ladler of molten lead was Professor Van Stopp.

The burgomaster Van der Werf turned at my sudden exclamation. "Who is that?" I said. "The man at the kettle?"

"That," replied Van der Werf, "is the brother of my wife, the clockmaker Jan Lipperdam."

The affair at the breach was over almost before we had had time to grasp the situation. The Spaniards, who had overthrown the wall of brick and stone, found the living wall impregnable. They could not even maintain their position in the moat; they were driven off into the darkness. Now I felt a sharp pain in my left arm. Some stray missile must have hit me while we watched the fight.

"Who has done this thing?" demanded the burgomaster. "Who is it that has kept watch on today while the rest of us were straining fools' eyes toward tomorrow?"

Gertruyd van der Werf came forward proudly, leading my cousin. "My father," said the girl, "he has saved my life."

"That is much to me," said the burgomaster, "but it is not all. He has saved Leyden and he has saved Holland."

I was becoming dizzy. The faces around me seemed unreal. Why were we here with these people? Why did the thunder and lightning forever continue? Why did the clockmaker, Jan Lipperdam, turn always toward me the face of Professor Van Stopp? "Harry!" I said, "Come back to our rooms."

But though he grasped my hand warmly his other hand still held that of the girl, and he did not move. Then nausea overcame me. My head swam, and the breach and its defenders faded from sight.

V

THREE DAYS LATER I sat with one arm bandaged in my accustomed seat in Van Stopp's lecture room. The place beside me was vacant.

"We hear much," said the Hegelian professor, reading from a notebook in his usual dry, hurried tone, "of the influence of the sixteenth century upon the nineteenth. No philosopher, as far as I am aware, has studied the influence of the nineteenth century upon the sixteenth. If cause produces effect, does effect never induce cause? Does the law of heredity, unlike all other laws of this universe of mind and matter, operate in one direction only? Does the descendant owe everything to the ancestor, and the ancestor nothing to the descendant? Does destiny, which may seize upon our existence, and for its own purposes bear us far into the future, never carry us back into the past?"

I went back to my rooms in the Breede Straat, where my only companion was the silent clock.

The Unparalleled Adventure of One Hans Pfaall

Edgar Allan Poe

> *With a heart of furious fancies,*
> *Whereof I am commander,*
> *With a burning spear and a horse of air,*
> *To the wilderness I wander.*
> **Tom O'Bedlam's Song**

BY LATE ACCOUNTS from Rotterdam, that city seems to be in a high state of philosophical excitement. Indeed, phenomena have there occurred of a nature so completely unexpected – so entirely novel – so utterly at variance with preconceived opinions – as to leave no doubt on my mind that long ere this all Europe is in an uproar, all physics in a ferment, all reason and astronomy together by the ears.

It appears that on the – day of – , (I am not positive about the date) a vast crowd of people, for purposes not specifically mentioned, were assembled in the great square of the Exchange in the well-conditioned city of Rotterdam. The day was warm – unusually so for the season – there was hardly a breath of air stirring; and the multitude were in no bad humor at being now and then besprinkled with friendly showers of momentary duration, that fell from large white masses of cloud profusely distributed about the blue vault of the firmament. Nevertheless, about noon, a slight but remarkable agitation became apparent in the assembly; the clattering of ten thousand tongues succeeded; and, in an instant afterwards, ten thousand faces were upturned towards the heavens, ten thousand pipes descended simultaneously from the corners of ten thousand mouths, and a shout, which could be compared to nothing but the roaring of Niagara, resounded long, loudly and furiously, through all the city and through all the environs of Rotterdam.

The origin of this hubbub soon became sufficiently evident. From behind the huge bulk of one of those sharply defined masses of cloud already mentioned, was seen slowly to emerge into an open area of blue space, a queer, heterogeneous, but apparently solid substance, so oddly shaped, so whimsically put together, as not to be in any manner comprehended, and never to be sufficiently admired, by the host of sturdy burghers who stood open-mouthed below. What could it be? In the name of all the devils in Rotterdam, what could it possibly portend? No one knew; no one could imagine; no one – not even the burgomaster Mynheer Superbus Von Underduk – had the slightest clew by which to unravel the mystery; so, as nothing more reasonable could be done, every one to a man replaced his pipe carefully in the corner of his mouth, and maintaining an eye steadily upon the phenomenon, puffed, paused, waddled about, and grunted significantly – then waddled back, grunted, paused, and finally – puffed again.

In the meantime, however, lower and still lower towards the goodly city, came the object of so much curiosity, and the cause of so much smoke. In a very few minutes it arrived near enough to be accurately discerned. It appeared to be – yes! It *was* undoubtedly a species of balloon; but surely no *such* balloon had ever been seen in Rotterdam before. For who, let me ask, ever heard of a balloon manufactured entirely of dirty newspapers? No man in Holland certainly; yet here, under the very noses of the people, or rather at some distance *above* their noses, was the identical thing in question, and composed, I have it on the best authority, of the precise material which no one had ever before known to be used for a similar purpose. It was an egregious insult to the good sense of the burghers of Rotterdam. As to the shape of the phenomenon, it was even still more reprehensible. Being little or nothing better than a huge fool's-cap turned upside down. And this similitude was regarded as by no means lessened, when upon nearer inspection, the crowd saw a large tassel depending from its apex, and, around the upper rim or base of the cone, a circle of little instruments, resembling sheep-bells, which kept up a continual tinkling to the tune of Betty Martin. But still worse. – Suspended by blue ribbons to the end of this fantastic machine, there hung, by way of car, an enormous drab beaver hat, with a brim superlatively broad, and a hemispherical crown with a black band and a silver buckle. It is, however, somewhat remarkable that many citizens of Rotterdam swore to having seen the same hat repeatedly before; and indeed the whole assembly seemed to regard it with eyes of familiarity; while the vrow Grettel Pfaall, upon sight of it, uttered an exclamation of joyful surprise, and declared it to be the identical hat of her good man himself. Now this was a circumstance the more to be observed, as Pfaall, with three companions, had actually disappeared from Rotterdam about five years before, in a very sudden and unaccountable manner, and up to the date of this narrative all attempts at obtaining intelligence concerning them had failed. To be sure, some bones which were thought to be human, mixed up with a quantity of odd-looking rubbish, had been lately discovered in a retired situation to the east of the city; and some people went so far as to imagine that in this spot a foul murder had been committed, and that the sufferers were in all probability Hans Pfaall and his associates. – But to return.

The balloon (for such no doubt it was) had now descended to within a hundred feet of the earth, allowing the crowd below a sufficiently distinct view of the person of its occupant. This was in truth a very singular somebody. He could not have been more than two feet in height; but this altitude, little as it was, would have been sufficient to destroy his *equilibrium*, and tilt him over the edge of his tiny car, but for the intervention of a circular rim reaching as high as the breast, and rigged on to the cords of the balloon. The body of the little man was more than proportionally broad, giving to his entire figure a rotundity highly absurd. His feet, of course, could not be seen at all. His hands were enormously large. His hair was gray, and collected into a *queue* behind. His nose was prodigiously long, crooked and inflammatory; his eyes full, brilliant, and acute; his chin and cheeks, although wrinkled with age, were broad, puffy, and double: but of ears of any kind there was not semblance to be discovered upon any portion of his head. This odd little gentleman was dressed in a loose surtout of sky-blue satin, with tight breeches to match, fastened with silver buckles at the knees. His vest was of some bright yellow material; a white taffety cap was set jauntily on one side of his head; and, to complete his equipment, a blood-red silk handkerchief enveloped his throat, and fell down, in a dainty manner, upon his bosom, in a fantastic bow-knot of super-eminent dimensions.

Having descended, as I said before, to about one hundred feet from the surface of the earth, the little old gentleman was suddenly seized with a fit of trepidation, and appeared disinclined to make any nearer approach to *terra firma*. Throwing out therefore, a quantity of sand from a canvass bag, which he lifted with great difficulty, he became stationary in an instant. He then proceeded in a hurried and agitated manner, to extract from a side-pocket in his surtout a large morocco pocket-book. This he poised suspiciously in his hand; then eyed it with an air of extreme surprise, and was evidently astonished at its weight. He at length opened it, and, drawing therefrom a huge letter sealed with red sealing-wax and tied carefully with red tape, let it fall precisely at the feet of the burgomaster Superbus Von Underduk. His Excellency stooped to take it up. But the æronaut, still greatly discomposed, and having apparently no further business to detain him in Rotterdam, began at this moment to make busy preparations for departure; and, it being necessary to discharge a portion of ballast to enable him to reascend, the half dozen bags which he threw out, one after another, without taking the trouble to empty their contents, tumbled, every one of them, most unfortunately, upon the back of the burgomaster, and rolled him over and over no less than half a dozen times, in the face of every individual in Rotterdam. It is not to be supposed, however, that the great Underduk suffered this impertinence on the part of the little old man to pass off with impunity. It is said, on the contrary, that during each of his half dozen circumvolutions, he emitted no less than half a dozen distinct and furious whiffs from his pipe, to which he held fast the whole time with all his might, and to which he intends holding fast (God willing), until the day of his decease.

In the meantime the balloon arose like a lark, and, soaring far away above the city, at length drifted quietly behind a cloud similar to that from which it had so oddly emerged, and was thus lost forever to the wondering eyes of the good citizens of Rotterdam. All attention was now directed to the letter, the descent of which, and the consequences attending thereupon, had proved so fatally subversive of both person and personal dignity to his Excellency, Von Underduk. That functionary, however, had not failed, during his circumgyratory movements, to bestow a thought upon the important object of securing the epistle, which was seen, upon inspection, to have fallen into the most proper hands, being actually addressed to himself and Professor Rubadub, in their official capacities of President and Vice-President of the Rotterdam College of Astronomy. It was accordingly opened by those dignitaries upon the spot, and found to contain the following extraordinary, and indeed very serious, communication: –

To their Excellencies Von Underduk and Rubadub, President and Vice-President of the States' College of Astronomers, in the city of Rotterdam.

Your Excellencies may perhaps be able to remember an humble artizan, by name Hans Pfaall, and by occupation a mender of bellows, who, with three others, disappeared from Rotterdam, about five years ago, in a manner which must have been considered unaccountable. If, however, it so please your Excellencies, I, the writer of this communication, am the identical Hans Pfaall himself. It is well known to most of my fellow-citizens, that for the period of forty years I continued to occupy the little square brick building, at the head of the alley called Sauerkraut, in which I resided at the time of my disappearance. My ancestors have also resided therein time out of mind – they, as well as myself, steadily following the respectable and indeed lucrative profession of mending of bellows:

for, to speak the truth, until of late years, that the heads of all the people have been set agog with politics, no better business than my own could an honest citizen of Rotterdam either desire or deserve. Credit was good, employment was never wanting, and there was no lack of either money or good will. But, as I was saying, we soon began to feel the effects of liberty, and long speeches, and radicalism, and all that sort of thing. People who were formerly the very best customers in the world, had now not a moment of time to think of us at all. They had as much as they could do to read about the revolutions, and keep up with the march of intellect and the spirit of the age. If a fire wanted fanning, it could readily be fanned with a newspaper; and as the government grew weaker, I have no doubt that leather and iron acquired durability in proportion – for, in a very short time, there was not a pair of bellows in all Rotterdam that ever stood in need of a stitch or required the assistance of a hammer. This was a state of things not to be endured. I soon grew as poor as a rat, and, having a wife and children to provide for, my burdens at length became intolerable, and I spent hour after hour in reflecting upon the most convenient method of putting an end to my life. Duns, in the meantime, left me little leisure for contemplation. My house was literally besieged from morning till night. There were three fellows in particular, who worried me beyond endurance, keeping watch continually about my door, and threatening me with the law. Upon these three I vowed the bitterest revenge, if ever I should be so happy as to get them within my clutches; and I believe nothing in the world but the pleasure of this anticipation prevented me from putting my plan of suicide into immediate execution, by blowing my brains out with a blunderbuss. I thought it best, however, to dissemble my wrath, and to treat them with promise and fair words, until, by some good turn of fate, an opportunity of vengeance should be afforded me.

One day, having given them the slip, and feeling more than usually dejected, I continued for a long time to wander about the most obscure streets without object, until at length I chanced to stumble against the corner of a bookseller's stall. Seeing a chair close at hand, for the use of customers, I threw myself doggedly into it, and, hardly knowing why, opened the pages of the first volume which came within my reach. It proved to be a small pamphlet treatise on Speculative Astronomy, written either by Professor Encke of Berlin, or by a Frenchman of somewhat similar name. I had some little tincture of information on matters of this nature, and soon became more and more absorbed in the contents of the book – reading it actually through twice before I awoke to a recollection of what was passing around me. By this time it began to grow dark, and I directed my steps toward home. But the treatise (in conjunction with a discovery in pneumatics, lately communicated to me as an important secret by a cousin from Nantz) had made an indelible impression on my mind, and, as I sauntered along the dusky streets, I revolved carefully over in my memory the wild and sometimes unintelligible reasonings of the writer. There are some particular passages which affected my imagination in an extraordinary manner. The longer I meditated upon these, the more intense grew the interest which had been excited within me. The limited nature of my education in general, and more especially my ignorance on subjects connected with natural philosophy, so far from rendering me diffident of my own ability to comprehend what I had read, or inducing me to mistrust the many vague notions which had arisen in consequence, merely served as a farther stimulus to imagination; and I was vain enough, or perhaps reasonable enough, to doubt whether those crude ideas which, arising in ill-regulated minds, have all the appearance, may not often in effect possess all the force, the reality, and other inherent properties of instinct or intuition.

It was late when I reached home, and I went immediately to bed. My mind, however, was too much occupied to sleep, and I lay the whole night buried in meditation. Arising early in the morning, I repaired eagerly to the bookseller's stall, and laid out what little ready money I possessed, in the purchase of some volumes of Mechanics and Practical Astronomy. Having arrived at home safely with these, I devoted every spare moment to their perusal, and soon made such proficiency in studies of this nature as I thought sufficient for the execution of a certain design with which either the devil or my better genius had inspired me. In the intervals of this period, I made every endeavor to conciliate the three creditors who had given me so much annoyance. In this I finally succeeded – partly by selling enough of my household furniture to satisfy a moiety of their claim, and partly by a promise of paying the balance upon completion of a little project which I told them I had in view, and for assistance in which I solicited their services. By these means (for they were ignorant men) I found little difficulty in gaining them over to my purpose.

Matters being thus arranged, I contrived, by the aid of my wife, and with the greatest secrecy and caution, to dispose of what property I had remaining, and to borrow, in small sums, under various pretences, and without giving any attention (I am ashamed to say) to my future means of repayment, no inconsiderable quantity of ready money. With the means thus accruing I proceeded to procure at intervals, cambric muslin, very fine, in pieces of twelve yards each; twine; a lot of the varnish of caoutchouc; a large and deep basket of wicker-work, made to order; and several other articles necessary in the construction and equipment of a balloon of extraordinary dimensions. This I directed my wife to make up as soon as possible, and gave her all requisite information as to the particular method of proceeding. In the meantime I worked up the twine into net-work of sufficient dimensions; rigged it with a hoop and the necessary cords; and made purchase of numerous instruments and materials for experiment in the upper regions of the upper atmosphere. I then took opportunities of conveying by night, to a retired situation east of Rotterdam, five iron-bound casks, to contain about fifty gallons each, and one of a larger size; six tin tubes, three inches in diameter, properly shaped, and ten feet in length; a quantity of a *particular metallic substance, or semi-metal* which I shall not name, and a dozen demijohns of a *very common acid*. The gas to be formed from these latter materials is a gas never yet generated by any other person than myself or at least never applied to any similar purpose. I can only venture to say here, that it is a *constituent of azote*, so long considered irreducible, and that its density is about 37.4 times *less than that of hydrogen*. It is tasteless, but not odorless; burns, when pure, with a greenish flame, and is instantaneously fatal to animal life. Its full secret I would make no difficulty in disclosing, but that it of right belongs (as I have before hinted) to a citizen of Nantz, in France, by whom it was conditionally communicated to myself. The same individual submitted to me, without being at all aware of my intentions, a method of constructing balloons from the membrane of a certain animal, through which substance any escape of gas was nearly an impossibility. I found it, however, altogether too expensive, and was not sure, upon the whole, whether cambric muslin with a coating of gum caoutchouc, was not equally as good. I mention this circumstance, because I think it probable that hereafter the individual in question may attempt a balloon ascension with the novel gas and material I have spoken of, and I do not wish to deprive him of the honor of a very singular invention.

On the spot which I intended each of the smaller casks to occupy respectively during the inflation of the balloon, I privately dug a small hole; the holes forming in this manner a circle twenty-five feet in diameter. In the centre of this circle, being the station designed for the large cask, I also dug a hole of greater depth. In each of the five smaller holes, I deposited a canister containing fifty pounds, and in the larger one a keg holding one hundred and fifty pounds of cannon powder. These – the keg and the canisters – I connected in a proper manner with covered trains; and having let into one of the canisters the end of about four feet of slow-match, I covered up the hole, and placed the cask over it, leaving the other end of the match protruding about an inch, and barely visible beyond the cask. I then filled up the remaining hole, and placed the barrels over them in their destined situation!

Besides the articles above enumerated, I conveyed to the *dêpot*, and there secreted, one of M. Grimm's improvements upon the apparatus for condensation of the atmospheric air. I found this machine, however, to require considerable alteration before it could be adapted to the purposes to which I intended making it applicable. But, with severe labor and unremitting perseverance, I at length met with entire success in all my preparations. My balloon was soon completed. It would contain more than forty thousand cubic feet of gas; would take me up easily, I calculated, with all my implements, and, if I managed rightly, with one hundred and seventy-five pounds of ballast into the bargain. It had received three coats of varnish, and I found the cambric muslin to answer all the purposes of silk itself, being quite as strong and a good deal less expensive.

Everything being now ready, I exacted from my wife an oath of secrecy in relation to all my actions from the day of my first visit to the bookseller's stall; and promising, on my part, to return as soon as circumstance would permit, I gave her what little money I had left, and bade her farewell. Indeed I had no fear on her account. She was what people call a notable woman, and could manage matters in the world without my assistance. I believe, to tell the truth, she always looked upon me as an idle body – a mere make-weight – good for nothing but building castles in the air – and was rather glad to get rid of me. It was a dark night when I bade her good bye, and taking with me, as *aides-de-camp*, the three creditors who had given me so much trouble, we carried the balloon, with the car and accoutrements, by a roundabout way, to the station where the other articles were deposited. We there found them all unmolested, and I proceeded immediately to business.

It was the first of April. The night, as I said before, was dark; there was not a star to be seen; and a drizzling rain, falling at intervals, rendered us very uncomfortable. But my chief anxiety was concerning the balloon, which, in spite of the varnish with which it was defended, began to grow rather heavy with the moisture; the powder also was liable to damage. I therefore kept my three duns working with great diligence, pounding down ice around the central cask, and stirring the acid in the others. They did not cease, however, importuning me with questions as to what I intended to do with all this apparatus, and expressed much dissatisfaction at the terrible labor I made them undergo. They could not perceive (so they said) what good was likely to result from their getting wet to the skin, merely to take a part in such horrible incantations. I began to get uneasy, and worked away with all my might; for I verily believe the idiots supposed that I had entered into a compact with the devil, and that, in short, what I was now doing was nothing better than it should be. I was, therefore, in great fear of their leaving me altogether. I contrived, however, to pacify them by promises of payment of all scores in full, as soon as I could bring the present business to a termination. To these speeches they gave of course their own interpretation; fancying, no doubt, that at all events I should come into possession of vast quantities of ready money; and provided I paid them all I owed, and a trifle more, in consideration of their services, I dare say they cared very little what became of either my soul or my carcass.

In about four hours and a half I found the balloon sufficiently inflated. I attached the car, therefore, and put all my implements in it – a telescope; a barometer, with some important modifications; a thermometer; an electrometer; a compass; a magnetic needle; a seconds watch; a bell; a speaking trumpet, etc., etc. – also a globe of glass, exhausted of air, and carefully closed with a stopper – not forgetting the condensing apparatus, some unslacked lime, a stick of sealing wax, a copious supply of water, and a large quantity of provisions, such as pemmican, in which much nutriment is contained in comparatively little bulk. I also secured in the car a pair of pigeons and a cat.

It was now nearly daybreak, and I thought it high time to take my departure. Dropping a lighted cigar on the ground, as if by accident, I took the opportunity, in stooping to pick it up, of igniting privately the piece of slow match, the end of which, as I said before, protruded a little beyond the lower rim of one of the smaller casks. This manœuvre was totally unperceived on the part of the three duns; and, jumping into the car, I immediately cut the single cord which held me to the earth, and was pleased to find that I shot upwards with inconceivable rapidity, carrying with all ease one hundred and seventy-five pounds of leaden ballast, and able to have carried up as many more. As I left the earth, the barometer stood at thirty inches, and the centigrade thermometer at 19°.

Scarcely, however, had I attained the height of fifty yards, when, roaring and rumbling up after me in the most tumultuous and terrible manner, came so dense a hurricane of fire, and gravel, and burning wood, and blazing metal, and mangled limbs, that my very heart sunk within me, and I fell down in the bottom of the car, trembling with terror. Indeed, I now perceived that I had entirely overdone the business, and that the main consequences of the shock were yet to be experienced. Accordingly, in less than a second, I felt all the blood in my body rushing to my temples, and, immediately thereupon, a concussion, which I shall never forget, burst abruptly through the night and seemed to rip the very firmament asunder. When I afterwards had time for reflection, I did not fail to attribute the extreme violence of the explosion, as regarded myself, to its proper cause – my situation directly above it, and in the line of its greatest power. But at the time, I thought only of preserving my life. The balloon at first collapsed, then furiously expanded, then whirled round and round with sickening velocity, and finally, reeling and staggering like a drunken man, hurled me over the rim of the car, and left me dangling, at a terrific height, with my head downward, and my face outward, by a piece of slender cord about three feet in length, which hung accidentally through a crevice near the bottom of the wicker-work, and in which, as I fell, my left foot became most providentially entangled. It is impossible – utterly impossible – to form any adequate idea of the horror of my situation. I gasped convulsively for breath – a shudder resembling a fit of the ague agitated every nerve and muscle in my frame – I felt my eyes starting from their sockets – a horrible nausea overwhelmed me – and at length I lost all consciousness in a swoon.

How long I remained in this state it is impossible to say. It must, however, have been no inconsiderable time, for when I partially recovered the sense of existence, I found the day breaking, the balloon at a prodigious height over a wilderness of ocean, and not a trace of land to be discovered far and wide within the limits of the vast horizon. My sensations, however, upon thus recovering, were by no means so replete with agony as might have been anticipated. Indeed, there was much of madness in the calm survey which I began to take of my situation. I drew up to my eyes each of my hands, one after the other, and wondered what occurrence could have given rise to the swelling of the veins, and the horrible blackness of the finger nails. I afterwards carefully examined my head, shaking it repeatedly, and feeling it with minute attention, until I succeeded in satisfying myself that it was not, as I had more than half suspected, larger than my balloon. Then, in a knowing manner, I felt in both my breeches pockets, and, missing therefrom a set of tablets and a tooth-pick case, endeavored to account for their disappearance, and, not being able to do so, felt inexpressibly chained. It now occurred to me that I suffered great uneasiness in the joint of my left ankle, and a dim consciousness of my situation began to glimmer through my mind. But, strange to say! I was neither astonished nor horror-stricken. If I felt any emotion at all, it was a kind of chuckling satisfaction at the cleverness I was about to display in extricating myself from this dilemma; and never, for a moment, did I look upon my ultimate safety as a question susceptible of doubt. For a few minutes I remained wrapped in the profoundest meditation. I have a distinct recollection of frequently compressing my lips, putting my fore-finger to the side of my nose, and making use of other gesticulations and grimaces common to men who, at ease in their arm-chairs, meditate upon matters of intricacy or importance. Having, as I thought, sufficiently collected my ideas, I now, with great caution and deliberation, put my hands behind my back, and unfastened the large iron buckle which belonged to the waistband of my pantaloons. This buckle had three teeth, which, being somewhat rusty, turned with great difficulty on their axis. I brought them, however, after some trouble, at right angles to the body of the buckle, and was glad to find them remain firm in that position. Holding within my teeth the instrument thus obtained, I now proceeded to untie the knot of my cravat. I had to rest several times before I could accomplish this manœuvre; but it was at length accomplished. To one end of the cravat I then made fast the buckle, and the other end I tied, for greater security, tightly around my wrist. Drawing now my body upwards, with a prodigious exertion of muscular force, I succeeded, at the very first trial, in throwing the buckle over the car, and entangling it, as I had anticipated, in the circular rim of the wicker-work.

My body was now inclined towards the side of the car, at aft angle of about forty-five degrees; but it must not be understood that I was therefore only forty-five degrees below the perpendicular. So far from it, I still lay nearly level with the plane of the horizon; for the change of situation which I had acquired, had forced the bottom of the car considerably outward from my position, which was accordingly one of the most imminent peril. It should be remembered, however, that when I fell, in the first instance, from the car, if I had fallen with my face turned toward the balloon, instead of turned outwardly from it as it actually was – or if, in the second place, the cord by which I was suspended had chanced to hang over the upper edge, instead of through a crevice near the bottom of the car – I say it may readily be conceived that, in either of these supposed cases, I should have been unable to accomplish even as much as I had now accomplished, and the disclosures now made would have been utterly lost to posterity. I had therefore every reason to be grateful; although, in point of fact, I was still too stupid to be any thing at all, and hung for, perhaps, a quarter of an hour, in that extraordinary manner, without making the slightest farther exertion, and in a singularly tranquil state of idiotic enjoyment. But this feeling did not fail to die rapidly away, and thereunto succeeded horror, and dismay, and a sense of utter helplessness and ruin. In fact, the blood so long accumulating in the vessels of my head and throat, and which had hitherto buoyed up my spirits with delirium, had now begun to retire within their proper channels, and the distinctness which was thus added to my perception of the danger, merely served to deprive me of the self-possession and courage to encounter it. But this weakness was, luckily for me, of no very long duration. In good time came to my rescue the spirit of despair, and, with frantic cries and struggles, I jerked my way bodily upwards, till, at length, clutching with a vice-like grip the long-desired rim, I writhed my person over it, and fell headlong and shuddering within the car.

It was not until some time afterward that I recovered myself sufficiently to attend to the ordinary cares of the balloon. I then, however, examined it with attention, and found it, to my great relief, uninjured. My implements were all safe, and, fortunately, I had lost neither ballast nor provisions. Indeed, I had so well secured them in their places, that such an accident was entirely out of the question. Looking at my watch, I found it six o'clock. I was still rapidly ascending, and the barometer gave a present altitude of three and three-quarter miles. Immediately beneath me in the ocean, lay a small black object, slightly oblong in shape, seemingly about the size of a domino, and in every respect bearing a great resemblance to one of those toys. Bringing my telescope to bear upon it, I plainly discerned it to be a British ninety-four-gun ship, close-hauled, and pitching heavily in the sea with her head to the W. S. W. Besides this ship, I saw nothing but the ocean and the sky, and the sun, which had long arisen.

It is now high time that I should explain to your Excellencies the object of my voyage. Your Excellencies will bear in mind that distressed circumstances in Rotterdam had at length driven me to the resolution of committing suicide. It was not, however, that to life itself I had any positive disgust, but that I was harassed beyond endurance by the adventitious miseries attending my situation. In this state of mind, wishing to live, yet wearied with life, the treatise at the stall of the bookseller, backed by the opportune discovery of my cousin of Nantz, opened a resource to my imagination. I then finally made up my mind. I determined to depart, yet live – to leave the world, yet continue to exist – in short, to drop enigmas, I resolved, let what would ensue, to force a passage, if I could, *to the moon*. Now, lest I should be supposed more of a madman than I actually am, I will detail, as well as I am able, the considerations which led me to believe that an achievement of this nature, although without doubt difficult, and full of danger, was not absolutely, to a bold spirit, beyond the confines of the possible.

The moon's actual distance from the earth was the first thing to be attended to. Now, the mean or average interval between the *centres* of the two planets is 59.9643 of the earth's equatorial *radii*, or only about 237,000 miles. I say the mean or average interval; but it must be borne in mind that the form of the moon's orbit being an ellipse of eccentricity amounting to no less than 0.05484 of the major semi-axis of the ellipse itself, and the earth's centre being situated in its focus, if I could, in any manner, contrive to meet the moon in its perigee, the above-mentioned distance would be materially diminished. But to say nothing, at present, of this possibility, it was very certain that, at all events, from the 237,000 miles I would have to deduct the *radius* of the earth, say 4000, and the radius of the moon, say 1080, in all 5080, leaving an actual interval to be traversed, under average circumstances, of 231,920 miles. Now this, I reflected, was no very extraordinary distance. Travelling on the land has been repeatedly accomplished at the rate of sixty miles per hour; and indeed a much greater speed may be anticipated. But even at this velocity, it would take me no more than 161 days to reach the surface of the moon. There were, however, many particulars inducing me to believe that my average rate of travelling might possibly very much exceed that of sixty miles per hour, and, as these considerations did not fail to make a deep impression upon my mind, I will mention them more fully hereafter.

The next point to be regarded was one of far greater importance. From indications afforded by the barometer, we find that, in ascensions from the surface of the earth we have, at the height of a 1000 feet, left below us about one-thirtieth of the entire mass of atmospheric air; that at 10,600, we have ascended through nearly one-third; and that at 18,000, which is not far from the elevation of Cotopaxi, we have surmounted one-half the material, or, at all events, one-half the *ponderable* body of air incumbent upon our globe. It is also calculated, that at an altitude not exceeding the hundredth part of the earth's diameter – that is, not exceeding eighty miles – the rarefaction would be so excessive that animal life could in no manner be sustained, and, moreover, that the most delicate means we possess of ascertaining the presence of the atmosphere, would be inadequate to assure us of its existence. But I did not fail to perceive that these latter calculations are founded altogether on our experimental knowledge of the properties of air, and the mechanical laws regulating its dilation and compression, in what may be called, comparatively speaking, *the immediate vicinity* of the earth itself; and, at the same time, it is taken for granted that animal life is and must be essentially *incapable of modification* at any given unattainable distance from the surface. Now, all such reasoning and from such *data*, must of course be simply analogical. The greatest height ever reached by man was that of 25,000 feet, attained in the æronautic expedition of Messieurs Gay-Lussac and Biot. This is a moderate altitude, even when compared with the eighty miles in question; and I could not help thinking that the subject admitted room for doubt, and great latitude for speculation.

But, in point of fact, an ascension being made to any given altitude, the ponderable quantity of air surmounted in any *farther* ascension, is by no means in proportion to the additional height ascended (as may be plainly seen from what has been stated before), but in a *ratio* constantly decreasing. It is therefore evident that, ascend as high as we may, we cannot, literally speaking, arrive at a limit beyond which *no* atmosphere is to be found. It *must exist*, I argued; although it *may* exist in a state of infinite rarefaction.

On the other hand, I was aware that arguments have not been wanting to prove the existence of a real and definite limit to the atmosphere, beyond which there is absolutely no air whatsoever. But a circumstance which has been left out of view by those who contend for such a limit, seemed to me, although no positive refutation of their creed, still a point worthy very serious investigation. On comparing the intervals between the successive arrivals of Encke's comet at its perihelion, after giving credit, in the most exact manner, for all the disturbances due to the attractions of the planets, it appears that the periods are gradually diminishing; that is to say, the major axis of the comet's ellipse is growing shorter, in a low but perfectly regular decrease. Now, this is precisely what ought to be the case, if we suppose a resistance experienced from the comet from an extremely *rare ethereal medium* pervading the regions of its orbit. For it is evident that such a medium must, in retarding the comet's velocity, increase its centripetal, by weakening its centrifugal force. In other words, the sun's attraction would be constantly attaining greater power, and the comet would be drawn nearer at every revolution. Indeed, there is no other way of accounting for the variation in question. But again: – The real diameter of the same comet's nebulosity, is observed to contract rapidly as it approaches the sun, and dilate with equal rapidity in its departure toward its aphelion. Was I not justifiable in supposing, with M. Valz, that this apparent condensation of volume has its origin in the compression of the same ethereal medium I have spoken of before, and which is dense in proportion to its vicinity to the sun? The lenticular-shaped phenomenon, also, called the zodiacal light, was a matter worthy of attention. This radiance, so apparent in the tropics, and which cannot be mistaken for any meteoric lustre, extends from the horizon obliquely upwards, and follows generally the direction of the sun's equator. It appeared to me evidently in the nature of a rare atmosphere extending from the sun outwards, beyond the orbit of Venus at least, and I believed indefinitely farther. Indeed, this medium I could not suppose confined to the path of the comet's ellipse, or to the immediate neighborhood of the sun. It was easy, on the contrary, to imagine it pervading the entire regions of our planetary system, condensed into what we call atmosphere at the planets themselves, and perhaps at some of them modified by considerations purely geological; that is to say, modified, or varied in its proportions (or absolute nature) by matters volatilized from the respective orbs.

Having adopted this view of the subject, I had little farther hesitation. Granting that on my passage I should meet with atmosphere *essentially* the same as at the surface of the earth, conceived that, by means of the very ingenious apparatus of M. Grimm, I should readily be enabled to condense it in sufficient quantity for the purposes of respiration. This would remove the chief obstacle in a journey to the moon. I had indeed spent some money and great labor in adapting the apparatus to the object intended, and confidently looked forward to its successful application, if I could manage to complete the voyage within any reasonable period. This brings me back to the *rate* at which it would be possible to travel.

It is true that balloons, in the first stage of their ascensions from the earth, are known to rise with a velocity comparatively moderate. Now, the power of elevation lies altogether in the superior gravity of the atmospheric air compared with the gas in the balloon; and, at first sight, it does not appear probable that, as the balloon acquires altitude, and consequently arrives successively in atmospheric *strata* of densities rapidly diminishing – I say, it does not appear at all reasonable that, in this its progress upward, the original velocity should be accelerated. On the other hand, I was not aware that, in any recorded ascension, a *diminution* had been proved to be apparent in the absolute rate of ascent; although such should have been the case, if on account of nothing else, on account of the escape of gas through balloons ill-constructed, and varnished with no better material than the ordinary varnish. It seemed, therefore, that the effect of such escape was only sufficient to counterbalance the effect of the acceleration attained in the diminishing of the balloon's distance from the gravitating centre. I now considered that, provided in my passage I found the medium I had imagined, and provided it should prove to be essentially what we denominate atmospheric air, it could make comparatively little difference at what extreme state of rarefaction I should discover it – that is to say, in regard to my power of ascending – for the gas in the balloon would not only be itself subject to similar rarefaction (in proportion to the occurrence of which, I could suffer an escape of so much as would be requisite to prevent explosion), but, *being what it was*, would, at all events, continue specifically lighter than any compound whatever of mere nitrogen and oxygen. Thus there was a chance – in fact, there was a strong probability – that, *at no epoch of my ascent, I should reach a point where the united weights of my immense balloon, the inconceivably rare gas within it, the car, and its contents, should equal the weight of the mass of the surrounding atmosphere displaced;* and this will be readily understood as the sole condition upon which my upward flight would be arrested. But, if this point were even attained, I could dispense with ballast and other weight to the amount of nearly 300 pounds. In the meantime, the force of gravitation would be constantly diminishing, in proportion to the squares of the distances, and so, with a velocity prodigiously accelerating, I should at length arrive in those distant regions where the force of the earth's attraction would be superseded by that of the moon.

There was another difficulty however, which occasioned me some little disquietude. It has been observed, that, in balloon ascensions to any considerable height, besides the pain attending respiration, great uneasiness is experienced about the head and body, often accompanied with bleeding at the nose, and other symptoms of an alarming kind, and growing more and more inconvenient in proportion to the altitude attained. This was a reflection of a nature somewhat startling. Was it not probable that these symptoms would increase until terminated by death itself. I finally thought not. Their origin was to be looked for in the progressive removal of the *customary* atmospheric pressure upon the surface of the body, and consequent distention of the superficial blood vessels – not in any positive disorganization of the animal system, as in the case of difficulty in breathing, where the atmospheric density is *chemically insufficient* for the due renovation of blood in a ventricle of the heart. Unless for default of this renovation, I could see no reason, therefore, why life could not be sustained even in a vacuum; for the expansion and compression of chest, commonly called breathing, is action purely muscular, and the *cause*, not the *effect*, of respiration. In a word, I conceived that, as the body should become habituated to the want of atmospheric pressure, these sensations of pain would gradually diminish – and to endure them while they continued, I relied with confidence upon the iron hardihood of my constitution.

Thus, may it please your Excellencies, I have detailed some, though by no means all, the considerations which led me to form the project of a lunar voyage. I shall now proceed to lay before you the result of an attempt so apparently audacious in conception, and, at all events, so utterly unparalleled in the annals of mankind.

Having attained the altitude before mentioned – that is to say, three miles and three quarters – I threw out from the car a quantity of feathers, and found that I still ascended with sufficient rapidity; there was, therefore, no necessity for discharging any ballast. I was glad of this, for I wished to retain with me as much weight as I could carry, for the obvious reason that I could not be *positive* either about the gravitation or the atmospheric density of the moon. I as yet suffered no bodily inconvenience, breathing with great freedom, and feeling no pain whatever in the head. The cat was lying very demurely upon my coat, which I had taken off, and eyeing the pigeons with an air of *nonchalance*. These latter being tied by the leg, to prevent their escape, were busily employed in picking up some grains of rice scattered for them in the bottom of the car.

At twenty minutes past six o'clock, the barometer showed an elevation of 26,400 feet, or five miles to a fraction. The prospect seemed unbounded. Indeed, it is very easily calculated by means of spherical geometry, how great an extent of the earth's area I beheld. The convex surface of any segment of a sphere is, to the entire surface of the sphere itself, as the versed sine of the segment to the diameter of the sphere. Now, in my case, the versed sine – that is to say, the *thickness* of the segment beneath me – was about equal to my elevation, or the elevation of the point of eight above the surface. 'As five miles, then, to eight thousand,' would express the proportion of the earth's area seen by me. In other words, I beheld as much sixteen-hundredth part of the whole surface of the globe. The sea appeared unruffled as a mirror, although, by means of the telescope, I could perceive it to be in a state of violent agitation. The ship was no longer visible, having drifted away, apparently, to the eastward. I now began to experience, at intervals, severe pain in the head, especially about the ears – still, however, breathing with tolerable freedom. The cat and pigeons seemed to suffer no inconvenience whatsoever.

At twenty minutes before seven, the balloon entered a long series of dense cloud, which put me to great trouble, by damaging my condensing apparatus, and wetting me to the skin. This was, to be sure, a singular *rencontre*, for I had not believed it possible that a cloud of this nature could be sustained at so great an elevation. I thought it best, however, to throw out two five-pound pieces of ballast, reserving still a weight of one hundred and sixty-five pounds. Upon so doing, I soon rose above the difficulty and perceived immediately, that I had obtained a great increase in my rate of ascent. In a few seconds after my leaving the cloud, a flash of vivid lightning shot from one end of it to the other, and caused it to kindle up, throughout its vast extent, like a mass of ignited charcoal. This, it must be remembered, was in the broad light of day. No fancy may picture the sublimity which might have been exhibited by a similar phenomenon taking place amid the darkness of the night. Hell itself might then have found a fitting image. Even as it was, my hair stood on end, while I gazed afar down within the yawning abysses, letting imagination descend, and stalk about in the strange vaulted halls, and ruddy gulfs, and red ghastly chasm: of the hideous and unfathomable fire. I had indeed made a narrow escape. Had the balloon remained a very short while longer within the cloud – that is to say, had not the inconvenience of getting wet, determined me to discharge the ballast – my destruction might, and probably would, have been the consequence. Such perils, although little considered, are perhaps the greatest which must be encountered in balloons. I had by this time, however, attained too great an elevation to be any longer uneasy on this head.

I was now rising rapidly, and by seven o'clock the barometer indicated an altitude of no less than nine miles and a half. I began to find great difficulty in drawing my breath. My head, too, was excessively painful; and, having felt for some time a moisture about my cheeks, I at length discovered it to be blood, which was oozing quite fast from the drums of my ears. My eyes, also, gave me great uneasiness. Upon passing the hand over them they seemed to have protruded from their sockets in no inconsiderable degree; and all objects in the car, and even the balloon itself appeared distorted to my vision. These symptoms were more than I had expected, and occasioned me some alarm. At this juncture, very imprudently, and without consideration, I threw out from the car three five-pound pieces of ballast. The accelerated rate of ascent thus obtained, carried me too rapidly, and without sufficient gradation, into a highly rarefied *stratum* of the atmosphere, and the result had nearly proved fatal to my expedition and to myself. I was suddenly seized with a spasm which lasted for more than five minutes, and even when this, in a measure, ceased, I could catch my breath only at long intervals, and in a gasping manner, – bleeding all the while copiously at the nose and ears, and even slightly at the eyes. The pigeons appeared distressed in the extreme, and struggled to escape; while the cat mewed piteously, and, with her tongue hanging out of her mouth, staggered to and fro in the car as if under the influence of poison. I now too late discovered the great rashness of which I had been guilty in discharging the ballast, and my agitation was excessive. I anticipated nothing less than death, and death in a few minutes. The physical suffering I underwent contributed also to render me nearly incapable of making any exertion for the preservation of my life. I had, indeed, little power of reflection left, and the violence of the pain in my head seemed to be greatly on the increase. Thus I found that my senses would shortly give way altogether, and I had already clutched one of the valve ropes with the view of attempting a descent, when the recollection of the trick I had played the three creditors, and the possible consequences to myself, should I return, operated to deter me for the moment. I lay down in the bottom of the car, and endeavored to collect my faculties. In this I so far succeeded as to determine upon the experiment of losing blood. Having no lancet, however, I was constrained to perform the operation in the best manner I was able, and finally succeeded in opening a vein in my left arm, with the blade of my penknife. The blood had hardly commenced flowing when I experienced a sensible relief, and by the time I had lost about half a moderate basin-full, most of the worst symptoms had abandoned me entirely. I nevertheless did not think it expedient to attempt getting on my feet immediately; but, having tied up my arm as well as I could, I lay still for about a quarter of an hour. At the end of this time I arose, and found myself freer from absolute *pain* of any kind than I had been during the last hour and a quarter of my ascension. The difficulty of breathing, however, was diminished in a very slight degree, and I found that it would soon be positively necessary to make use of my condenser. In the meantime, looking towards the cat, who was again snugly stowed away upon my coat, I discovered, to my infinite surprise, that she had taken the opportunity of my indisposition to bring into light a litter of three little kittens. This was an addition to the number of passengers on my part altogether unexpected; but I was pleased at the occurrence. It would afford me a chance of bringing to a kind of test the truth of a surmise, which, more than any thing else, had influenced me in attempting this ascension. I had imagined that the *habitual* endurance of the atmospheric pressure at the surface of the earth was the cause, or nearly so, of the pain attending animal existence at a distance above the surface. Should the kittens be found to suffer uneasiness *in an equal degree with their mother*, I must consider my theory in fault, but a failure to do so I should look upon as a strong confirmation of my idea.

By eight o'clock I had actually attained an elevation of seventeen miles above the surface of the earth. Thus it seemed to me evident that my rate of ascent was not only on the increase, but that the progression would have been apparent in a slight degree even had I not discharged the ballast which I did. The pains in my head and ears returned, at intervals, with violence, and I still continued to bleed occasionally at the nose: but, upon the whole, I suffered much less than might have been expected. I breathed, however, at every moment, with more and more difficulty, and each inhalation was attended with a troublesome spasmodic action of the chest. I now unpacked the condensing apparatus, and got it ready for immediate use.

The view of the earth, at this period of my ascension, was beautiful indeed. To the westward, the northward, and the southward, as far as I could see, lay a boundless sheet of apparently unruffled ocean, which every moment gained a deeper and deeper tint of blue. At a vast distance to the eastward, although perfectly discernible, extended the islands of Great Britain, the entire Atlantic coasts of France and Spain, with a small portion of the northern part of the continent of Africa. Of individual edifices not a trace could be discovered, and the proudest cities of mankind had utterly faded away from the face of the earth.

What mainly astonished me, in the appearance of things below, was the seeming concavity of the surface of the globe. I had, thoughtlessly enough, expected to see its real *convexity* become evident as I ascended; but a very little reflection sufficed to explain the discrepancy. A line, dropped from my position perpendicularly to the earth, would have formed the perpendicular of a right-angled triangle, of which the base would have extended from the right angle to the horizon, and the hypothenuse from the horizon to my position. But my height was little or nothing in comparison with my prospect. In other words, the base and hypothenuse of the supposed triangle would, in my case, have been so long, when compared to the perpendicular, that the two former might have been regarded as nearly parallel. In this manner the horizon of the æronaut appears always to be *upon a level* with the car. But as the point immediately beneath him seems, and is, at a great distance below him, it seems, of course, also at a great distance below the horizon. Hence the impression of concavity; and this impression must remain, until the elevation shall bear so great a proportion to the prospect, that the apparent parallelism of the base and hypothenuse disappears.

The pigeons about this time seeming to undergo much suffering, I determined upon giving them their liberty. I first untied one of them, a beautiful gray-mottled pigeon, and placed him upon the rim of the wicker-work. He appeared extremely uneasy, looking anxiously around him, fluttering his wings, and making a loud cooing noise, but could not be persuaded to trust himself from the car. I took him up at last, and threw him to about half-a-dozen yards from the balloon. He made, however, no attempt to descend as I had expected, but struggled with great vehemence to get back, uttering at the same time very shrill and piercing cries. He at length succeeded in regaining his former station on the rim, but had hardly done so when his head dropped upon his breast, and he fell dead within the car. The other one did not prove so unfortunate. To prevent his following the example of his companion, and accomplishing a return, I threw him downwards with all my force, and was pleased to find him continue his descent, with great velocity, making use of his wings with ease, and in a perfectly natural manner. In a very short time he was out of sight, and I have no doubt he reached home in safety. Puss, who seemed in a great measure recovered from her illness, now made a hearty meal of the dead bird, and then went to sleep with much apparent satisfaction. Her kittens were quite lively, and so far evinced not the slightest sign of any uneasiness.

At a quarter-past eight, being able no longer to draw breath without the most intolerable pain, I proceeded, forthwith, to adjust around the car the apparatus belonging to the condenser. This apparatus will require some little explanation, and your Excellencies will please to bear in mind that my object, in the first place, was to surround myself and car entirely with a barricade against the highly rarefied atmosphere in which I was existing, with the intention of introducing within this barricade, by means of my condenser, a quantity of this same atmosphere sufficiently condensed for the purposes of respiration. With this object in view I had prepared a very strong, perfectly air-tight, but flexible gum-elastic bag. In this bag, which was of sufficient dimensions, the entire car was in a manner placed. That is to say, it (the bag) was drawn over the whole bottom of the car, up its sides, and so on, along the outside of the ropes, to the upper rim or hoop where the net-work is attached. Having pulled the bag up in this way, and formed a complete enclosure on all sides, and at bottom, it was now necessary to fasten up its top or mouth, by passing its material over the hoop of the net-work, – in other words, between the net-work and the hoop. But if the net-work were separated from the hoop to admit this passage, what was to sustain the car in the meantime? Now the net-work was not permanently fastened to the hoop, but attached by a series of running loops or nooses. I therefore undid only a few of these loops at one time, leaving the car suspended by the remainder. Having thus inserted a portion of the cloth forming the upper part of the bag, I refastened the loops – not to the hoop, for that would have been impossible, since the cloth now intervened, – but to a series of large buttons, affixed to the cloth itself, about three feet below the mouth of the bag; the intervals between the buttons having been made to correspond to the intervals between the loops. This done, a few more of the loops were unfastened from the rim, a farther portion of the cloth introduced, and the disengaged loops then connected with their proper buttons. In this way it was possible to insert the whole upper part of the bag between the net-work and the hoop. It is evident that the hoop would now drop down within the car, while the whole weight of the car itself, with all its contents, would be held up merely by the strength of the buttons. This, at first sight, would seem an inadequate dependence; but it was by no means so, for the buttons were not only very strong in themselves, but so close together that a very slight portion of the whole weight was supported by any one of them. Indeed, had the car and contents been three times heavier than they were, I should not have been at all uneasy. I now raised up the hoop again within the covering of gum-elastic, and propped it at nearly its former height by means of three light poles prepared for the occasion. This was done, of course, to keep the bag distended at the top, and to preserve the lower part of the net-work in its proper situation. All that now remained was to fasten up the mouth of the enclosure; and this was readily accomplished by gathering the folds of the material together, and twisting them up very tightly on the inside by means of a kind of stationary *tourniquet*.

In the sides of the covering thus adjusted round the car, had been inserted three circular panes of thick but clear glass, through which I could see without difficulty around me in every horizontal direction. In that portion of the cloth forming the bottom, was likewise a fourth window, of the same kind, and corresponding with a small aperture in the floor of the car itself. This enabled me to see perpendicularly down, but having found it impossible to place any similar contrivance overhead, on account of the peculiar manner of closing up the opening there, and the consequent wrinkles in the cloth, I could expect to see no objects situated directly in my zenith. This, of course, was a matter of little consequence; for, had I even been able to place a window at top, the balloon itself would have prevented my making any use of it.

About a foot below one of the side windows was a circular opening, three inches in diameter, and fitted with a brass rim adapted in its inner edge to the winding of a screw. In this rim was screwed the large tube of the condenser, the body of the machine being, of course, within the chamber of gum-elastic. Through this tube a quantity of the rare atmosphere circumjacent being drawn by means of a *vacuum* created in the body of the machine, was thence discharged, in a state of condensation, to mingle with the thin air already in the chamber. This operation, being repeated several times, at length filled the chamber with atmosphere proper for all the purposes of respiration. But in so confined a space it would, in a short time, necessarily become foul, and unfit for use from frequent contact with the lungs. It was then ejected by a small valve at the bottom of the car; – the dense air readily sinking into the thinner atmosphere below. To avoid the inconvenience of making a total *vacuum* at any moment within the chamber, this purification was never accomplished all at one, but in a gradual manner, – the valve being opened only for a few seconds, then closed again, until one or two strokes from the pump of the condenser had supplied the place of the atmosphere ejected. For the sake of experiment I had put the cat and kittens in a small basket, and suspended it outside the car to a button at the bottom, close by the valve, through which I could feed them at any moment when necessary. I did this at some little risk, and before closing the mouth of the chamber, by reaching under the car with one of the poles before mentioned to which a hook had been attached. As soon as dense air was admitted in the chamber, the hoop and poles became unnecessary; the expansion of the enclosed atmosphere powerfully distending the gum-elastic.

By the time I had fully completed these arrangements and filled the chamber as explained, it wanted only ten minutes of nine o'clock. During the whole period of my being thus employed, I endured the most terrible distress from difficulty of respiration; and bitterly did I repent the negligence, or rather fool-hardiness, of which I had been guilty, of putting off to the last moment a matter of so much importance. But having at length accomplished it, I soon began to reap the benefit of my invention. Once again I breathed with perfect freedom and ease – and indeed why should I not? I was also agreeably surprised to find myself, in a great measure, relieved from the violent pains which had hitherto tormented me. A slight headache, accompanied with a sensation of fulness or distention about the wrists, the ankles, and the throat, was nearly all of which I had now to complain. Thus it seemed evident that a greater part of the uneasiness attending the removal of atmospheric pressure had actually *worn off*, as I had expected, and that much of the pain endured for the last two hours should have been attributed altogether to the effects of a deficient respiration.

At twenty minutes before nine o'clock – that is to say, a short time prior to my closing up the mouth of the chamber, the mercury attained its limit, or ran down, in the barometer, which, as I mentioned before, was one of an extended construction. It then indicated an altitude on my part of 132,000 feet, or five-and-twenty miles, and I consequently surveyed at that time an extent of the earth's area amounting to no less than the three-hundred-and-twentieth part of its entire superficies. At nine o'clock I had again lost sight of land to the eastward, but not before I became aware that the balloon was drifting rapidly to the N. N. W. The ocean beneath me still retained its apparent concavity, although my view was often interrupted by the masses of cloud which floated to and fro.

At half past nine I tried the experiment of throwing out a handful of feathers through the valve. They did not float as I had expected; but dropped down perpendicularly, like a bullet, *en massse*, and with the greatest velocity, – being out of sight in a very few seconds. I did not at first know what to make of this extraordinary phenomenon; not being able to believe that my rate of ascent had, of a sudden, met with so prodigious an acceleration. But it soon occurred to me that the atmosphere was now far too rare to sustain even the feathers; that they actually fell, as they appeared to do, with great rapidity; and that I had been surprised by the united velocities of their descent and my own elevation.

By ten o'clock I found that I had very little to occupy my immediate attention. Affairs went on swimmingly, and I believed the balloon to be going upwards with a speed increasing momently, although I had no longer any means of ascertaining the progression of the increase. I suffered no pain or uneasiness of any kind, and enjoyed better spirits than I had at any period since my departure from Rotterdam; busying myself now in examining the state of my various apparatus, and now in regenerating the atmosphere within the chamber. This latter point I determined to attend to at regular interval of forty minutes, more on account of the preservation of my health, than from so frequent a renovation being absolutely necessary. In the meanwhile I could not help making anticipations. Fancy revelled in the wild and dreamy regions of the moon. Imagination, feeling herself for once unshackled, roamed at will among the ever-changing wonders of a shadowy and unstable land. Now there were hoary and time-honored forests, and craggy precipices, and waterfalls tumbling with a loud noise into abysses without a bottom. Then I came suddenly into still noonday solitudes, where no wind of heaven ever intruded, and where vast meadows of poppies, and slender, lily-looking flowers spread themselves out a weary distance, all silent and motionless for ever. Then again I journeyed far down away into another country where it was all one dim and vague lake, with a boundary-line of clouds. But fancies such as these were not the sole possessors of my brain. Horrors of a nature most stern and most appalling would too frequently obtrude themselves upon my mind, and shake the innermost depths of my soul with the bare supposition of their possibility. Yet I would not suffer my thoughts for any length of time to dwell upon these latter speculations, rightly judging the real and palpable dangers of the voyage sufficient for my undivided attention.

At five o'clock, p.m., being engaged in regenerating the atmosphere within the chamber, I took that opportunity of observing the cat and kittens through the valve. The cat herself appeared to suffer again very much, and I had no hesitation in attributing her uneasiness chiefly to a difficulty in breathing; but my experiment with the kittens had resulted very strangely. I had expected, of course, to see them betray a sense of pain, although in a less degree than their mother; and this would have been sufficient to confirm my opinion concerning the habitual endurance of atmospheric pressure. But I was not prepared to find them, upon close examination, evidently enjoying a high degree of health, breathing with the greatest ease and perfect regularity, and evincing not the slightest sign of any uneasiness. I could only account for all this by extending my theory, and supposing that the highly rarefied atmosphere around, might perhaps not be, as I had taken for granted, chemically insufficient for the purposes of life, and that a person born in such a *medium* might, possibly, be unaware of any inconvenience attending its inhalation, while, upon removal to the denser *strata* near the earth, he might endure tortures of a similar nature to those I had so lately experienced. It has since been to me a matter of deep regret that an awkward accident, at this time, occasioned me the loss of my little family of cats, and deprived me of the insight into this matter which a continued experiment might have afforded. In passing my hand through the valve, with a cup of water for the old puss, the sleeve of my shirt became entangled in the loop which sustained the basket, and thus, in a moment, loosened it from the button. Had the whole actually vanished into air, it could not have shot from my sight in a more abrupt and instantaneous manner. Positively, there could not have intervened the tenth part of a second between the disengagement of the basket and its absolute disappearance with all that it contained. My good wishes followed it to the earth, but, of course, I had no hope that either cat or kittens would ever live to tell the tale of their misfortune.

At six o'clock, I perceived a great portion of the earth's visible area to the eastward involved in thick shadow, which continued to advance with great rapidity, until, at five minutes before seven, the whole surface in view was enveloped in the darkness of night. It was not, however, until long after this time that the rays of the setting sun ceased to illumine the balloon; and this circumstance, although of course fully anticipated, did not fail to give me an infinite deal of pleasure. It was evident that, in the morning, I should behold the rising luminary many hours at least before the citizens of Rotterdam, in spite of their situation so much farther to the eastward, and thus; day after day, in proportion to the height ascended, would I enjoy the light of the sun for a longer and a longer period. I now determined to keep a journal of my passage, reckoning the days from one to twenty-four hours continuously, without taking into consideration the intervals of darkness.

At ten o'clock, feeling sleepy, I determined to lie down for the rest of the night but here a difficulty presented itself, which, obvious as it may appear, had escaped my attention up to the very moment of which I am now speaking. If I went to sleep as I proposed, how could the atmosphere in the chamber be regenerated in the *interim?* To breathe it for more than an hour, at the farthest, would be a matter of impossibility; or, if even this term could be extended to an hour and a quarter, the most ruinous consequences might ensue. The consideration of this dilemma gave me no little disquietude; and it will hardly be believed, that, after the dangers I had undergone, I should look upon this business in so serious a light, as to give up all hope of accomplishing my ultimate design, and finally make up my mind to the necessity of a descent. But this hesitation was only momentary. I reflected that man is the veriest slave of custom, and that many points in the routine of his existence are deemed *essentially* important, which are only so *at all* by his having rendered them habitual. It was very certain that I could not do without sleep; but I might easily bring myself to feel no inconvenience from being awakened at intervals of an hour during the whole period of my repose. It would require but five minutes at most, to regenerate the atmosphere in the fullest manner – and the only real difficulty was, to contrive a method of arousing myself at the proper moment for so doing. But this was a question which, I am willing to confess, occasioned me no little trouble in its solution. To be sure, I had heard of the student who, to prevent his falling asleep over his books, held in one hand a ball of copper, the din of whose descent into a basin of the same metal on the floor beside his chair, served effectually to startle him up, if, at any moment, he should be overcome with drowsiness. My own case, however, was very different indeed, and left me no room for any similar idea; for I did not wish to keep awake, but to be aroused from slumber at regular intervals of time. I at length hit upon the following expedient, which, simple as it may seem, was hailed by me, at the moment of discovery, as an invention fully equal to that of the telescope, the steam-engine, or the art of printing itself.

It is necessary to premise, that the balloon, at the elevation now attained, continued its course upwards with an even and undeviating ascent, and the car consequently followed with a steadiness so perfect that it would have been impossible to detect in it the slightest vacillation. This circumstance favored me greatly in the project I now determined to adopt. My supply of water had been put on board in kegs containing five gallons each, and ranged very securely around the interior of the car. I unfastened one of these, and taking two ropes, tied them tightly across the rim of the wicker-work from one side to the other; placing them about a foot apart and parallel, so as to form a kind of shelf, upon which I placed the keg, and steadied it in a horizontal position. About eight inches immediately below these ropes, and four feet from the bottom of the car, I fastened another shelf – but made of thin plank, being the only similar piece of wood I had. Upon this latter shelf, and exactly beneath one of the rims of the keg, a small earthen pitcher was deposited. I now bored a hole in the end of the keg over the pitcher, and fitted in a plug of soft wood, cut in a tapering or conical shape. This plug I pushed in or pulled out, as might happen, until, after a few experiments, It arrived at that exact degree of tightness, at which the water, oozing from the hole, and falling into the pitcher below, would fill the latter to the brim in the period of sixty minutes. This, of course, was a matter briefly and easily ascertained, by noticing the proportion of the pitcher filled in any given time. Having arranged all this, the rest of the plan is obvious. My bed was so contrived upon the floor of the car, as to bring my head, in lying down, immediately below the mouth of the pitcher. It was evident, that, at the expiration of an hour, the pitcher, getting full, would be forced to run over, and to run over at the mouth which was somewhat lower than the rim. It was also evident, that the water, thus falling from a height of more than four feet, could not do otherwise than fall upon my face, and that the sure consequence would be, to waken me up instantaneously, even from the soundest slumber in the world.

It was fully eleven by the time I had completed these arrangements, and I immediately betook myself to bed, with full confidence in the efficiency of my invention. Nor in this matter was I disappointed. Punctually every sixty minutes was I aroused by my trusty chronometer, when, having emptied the pitcher into the bung-hole of the keg, and performed the duties of the condenser, I retired again to bed. These regular interruptions to my slumber caused me even less discomfort than I had anticipated; and when I finally arose for the day, it was seven o'clock, and the sun had attained many degrees above the line of my horizon.

April 3rd. I found the balloon at an immense height indeed, and the earth's convexity had now become strikingly manifest. Below me in the ocean lay a cluster of black specks, which undoubtedly were islands. Overhead, the sky was of a jetty black, and the stars were brilliantly visible; indeed they had been so constantly since the first day of ascent. Far away to the northward I perceived a thin, white, and exceedingly brilliant line, or streak, on the edge of the horizon, and I had no hesitation in supposing it to be the southern disc of the ices of the Polar sea. My curiosity was greatly excited, for I had hopes of passing on much farther to the north, and might possibly, at some period, find myself placed directly above the Pole itself. I now lamented that my great elevation would, in this case, prevent my taking as accurate a survey as I could wish. Much, however, might be ascertained.

Nothing else of an extraordinary nature occurred during the day. My apparatus all continued in good order, and the balloon still ascended without any perceptible vacillation. The cold was intense, and obliged me to wrap up closely in an overcoat. When darkness came over the earth, I betook myself to bed, although it was for many hours afterwards broad daylight all around my immediate situation. The water-clock was punctual in its duty, and I slept until next morning soundly, with the exception of the periodical interruption.

April 4th. Arose in good health and spirits, and was astonished at the singular change which had taken place in the appearance of the sea. It had lost, in a great measure, the deep tint of blue it had hitherto worn, being now of a grayish-white, and of a lustre dazzling to the eye. The convexity of the ocean had become so evident, that the entire mass of the distant water seemed to be tumbling headlong over the abyss of the horizon, and I found myself listening on tiptoe for the echoes of the mighty cataract. The islands were no longer visible; whether they had passed down the horizon to the southeast, or whether my increasing elevation had left them out of sight, it is impossible to say. I was inclined, however, to the latter opinion. The rim of ice to the northward was growing more and more apparent. Cold by no means so intense. Nothing of importance occurred, and I passed the day in reading, having taken care to supply myself with books.

April 5th. Beheld the singular phenomenon of the sun rising while nearly the whole visible surface of the earth continued to be involved in darkness. In time, however, the light spread itself over all, and I again saw the line of ice to the northward. It was now very distinct, and appeared of a much darker hue than the waters of the ocean. I was evidently approaching it, and with great rapidity. Fancied I could again distinguish a strip of land to the eastward, and one also to the westward, but could not be certain. Weather moderate. Nothing of any consequence happened during the day. Went early to bed.

April 6th. Was surprised at finding the rim of ice at a very moderate distance, and an immense field of the same material stretching away off to the horizon in the north. It was evident that if the balloon held its present course, it would soon arrive above the Frozen Ocean, and I had now little doubt of ultimately seeing the Pole. During the whole of the day I continued to near the ice. Towards night the limits of my horizon very suddenly and materially increased, owing undoubtedly to the earth's form being that of an oblate spheroid, and my arriving above the flattened regions in the vicinity of the Arctic circle. When darkness at length overtook me, I went to bed in great anxiety, fearing to pass over the object of so much curiosity when I should have no opportunity of observing it.

April 7th. Arose early, and, to my great joy, at length beheld what there could be no hesitation in supposing the northern Pole itself. It was there, beyond a doubt, and immediately beneath my feet; but, alas! I had now ascended to so vast a distance, that nothing could with accuracy be discerned. Indeed, to judge from the progression of the numbers indicating my various altitudes, respectively, at different periods, between six, a.m., on the second of April, and twenty minutes before nine, a.m., of the same day (at which time the barometer ran down), it might be fairly inferred that the balloon had now, at four o'clock in the morning of April the seventh, reached a height of *not less*, certainly, than 7254 miles above the surface of the sea. This elevation may appear immense, but the estimate upon which it is calculated gave a result in probability far inferior to the truth. At all events I undoubtedly beheld the whole of the earth's major diameter; the entire northern hemisphere lay beneath me like a chart orthographically projected; and the great circle of the equator itself formed the boundary line of my horizon. Your Excellencies may, however, readily imagine that the confined regions hitherto unexplored within the limits of the Arctic circle, although situated directly beneath me, and therefore seen without any appearance of being foreshortened, were still, in themselves, comparatively too diminutive, and at too great a distance from the point of sight, to admit of any very accurate examination. Nevertheless, what could be seen was of a nature singular and exciting. Northwardly from that huge rim before mentioned, and which, with slight qualification, may be called the limit of human discovery in these regions, one unbroken, or nearly unbroken sheet of ice continues to extend. In the first few degrees of this progress, its surface is very sensibly flattened, farther on depressed into a plane, and finally, becoming *not a little concave*, it terminates, at the Pole itself, in a circular centre, sharply defined, whose apparent diameter subtended at the balloon an angle of about sixty-five seconds, and whose dusky hue, varying in intensity, was, at all times, darker than any other spot upon the visible hemisphere, and occasionally deepened into the most absolute blackness. Farther than this, little could be ascertained. By twelve o'clock the circular centre had materially decreased in circumference, and by seven, p.m., I lost sight of it entirely; the balloon passing over the western limb of the ice, and floating away rapidly in the direction of the equator.

April 8th. Found a sensible diminution in the earth's apparent diameter, besides a material alteration in its general color and appearance. The whole visible area partook in different degrees of a tint of pale yellow, and in some portions had acquired a brilliancy even painful to the eye. My view downwards was also considerably impeded by the dense atmosphere in the vicinity of the surface being loaded with clouds, between whose masses I could only now and then obtain a glimpse of the earth itself. This difficulty of direct vision had troubled me more or less for the last forty-eight hours; but my present enormous elevation brought closer together, as it were, the floating bodies of vapor, and the inconvenience became, of course, more and more palpable in proportion to my ascent. Nevertheless, I could easily perceive that the balloon now hovered above the range of great lakes in the continent of North America, and was holding a course, due south, which would soon bring me to the tropics. This circumstance did not fail to give me the most heartfelt satisfaction, and I hailed it as a happy omen of ultimate success. Indeed, the direction I had hitherto taken, had filled me with uneasiness; for it was evident that, had I continued it much longer, there would have been no possibility of my arriving at the moon at all, whose orbit is inclined to the ecliptic at only the small angle of 5° 8' 48". Strange as it may seem, it was only at this late period that I began to understand the great error I had committed, in not taking my departure from earth at some point *in the plane of the lunar ellipse*.

April 9th. Today the earth's diameter was greatly diminished, and the color of the surface assumed hourly a deeper tint of yellow. The balloon kept steadily on her course to the southward, and arrived, at nine, p.m.., over the northern edge of the Mexican Gulf.

April 10th. I was suddenly aroused from slumber, about five o'clock this morning, by a loud, crackling, and terrific sound, for which I could in no manner account. It was of very brief duration, but, while it lasted, resembled nothing in the world of which I had any previous experience. It is needless to say that I became excessively alarmed, having, in the first instance, attributed the noise to the bursting of the balloon. I examined all my apparatus, however, with great attention, and could discover nothing out of order. Spent a great part of the day in meditating upon an occurrence so extraordinary, but could find no means whatever of accounting for it. Went to bed dissatisfied, and in a state of great anxiety and agitation.

April 11th. Found a startling diminution in the apparent diameter of the earth, and a considerable increase, now observable for the first time, in that of the moon itself, which wanted only a few days of being full. It now required long and excessive labor to condense within the chamber sufficient atmospheric air for the sustenance of life.

April 12th. A singular alteration took place in regard to the direction of the balloon, and although fully anticipated, afforded me the most unequivocal delight. Having reached, in its former course, about the twentieth parallel of southern latitude, it turned off suddenly, at an acute angle, to the eastward, and thus proceeded throughout the day, keeping nearly, if not altogether, *in the exact plane of the lunar ellipse*. What was worthy of remark, a very perceptible vacillation in the car was a consequence of this change of route, – a vacillation which prevailed, in a more or less degree, for a period of many hours.

April 13th. Was again very much alarmed by a repetition of the loud crackling noise which terrified me on the tenth. Thought long upon the subject, but was unable to form any satisfactory conclusion. Great decrease in the earth's apparent diameter, which now subtended from the balloon an angle of very little more than twenty-five degrees. The moon could not be seen at all, being nearly in my zenith. I still continued in the plane of the ellipse, but made little progress to the eastward.

April 14th. Extremely rapid decrease in the diameter of the earth. Today I became strongly impressed with the idea, that the balloon was now actually running up the line of apsides to the point of perigee, – in other words, holding the direct course which would bring it immediately to the moon in that part of its orbit the nearest to the earth. The moon itself was directly overhead, and consequently hidden from my view. Great and long continued labor necessary for the condensation of the atmosphere.

April 15th. Not even the outlines of continents and seas could now be traced upon the earth with distinctness. About twelve o'clock I became aware, for the third time, of that appalling sound which had so astonished me before. It now, however, continued for some moments, and gathered intensity as it continued. At length, while, stupified and terror-stricken, I stood in expectation of I knew not what hideous destruction, the car vibrated with excessive violence, and a gigantic and flaming mass of some material which I could not distinguish, came with a voice of a thousand thunders, roaring and booming by the balloon. When my fears and astonishment had in some degree subsided, I had little difficulty in supposing it to be some mighty volcanic fragment ejected from that world to which I was so rapidly approaching, and, in all probability, one of that singular class of substances occasionally picked up on the earth, and termed meteoric stones for want of a better appellation.

April 16th. Today, looking upwards as well as I could, through each of the side windows alternately, I beheld, to my great delight, a very small portion of the moon's disk protruding, as it were, on all sides beyond the huge circumference of the balloon. My agitation was extreme; for I had now little doubt of soon reaching the end of my perilous voyage. Indeed, the labor now required by the condenser, had increased to a most oppressive degree, and allowed me scarcely any respite from exertion. Sleep was a matter nearly out of the question. I became quite ill, and my frame trembled with exhaustion. It was impossible that human nature could endure this state of intense suffering much longer. During the now brief interval of darkness a meteoric stone again passed in my vicinity, and the frequency of these phenomena began to occasion me much apprehension.

April 17th. This morning proved an epoch in my voyage. It will be remembered, that, on the thirteenth, the earth subtended an angular breadth of twenty-five degrees. On the fourteenth, this had greatly diminished; on the fifteenth, a still more rapid decrease was observable; and, on retiring for the night of the sixteenth, I had noticed an angle of no more than about seven degrees and fifteen minutes. What, therefore, must have been my amazement, on awakening from a brief and disturbed slumber, on the morning of this day, the seventeenth, at finding the surface beneath me so suddenly and wonderfully *augmented* in volume, as to subtend no less than thirty-nine degrees in apparent angular diameter! I was thunderstruck! No words can give any adequate idea of the extreme, the absolute horror and astonishment, with which I was seized, possessed, and altogether overwhelmed. My knees tottered beneath me – my teeth chattered – my hair started up on end. "The balloon, then, had actually burst!" These were the first tumultuous ideas which hurried through my mind: "The balloon had positively burst! – I was falling – falling with the most impetuous, the most unparalleled velocity! To judge from the immense distance already so quickly passed over, it could not be more than ten minutes, at the farthest, before I should meet the surface of the earth, and be hurled into annihilation!" But at length reflection came to my relief. I paused; I considered; and I began to doubt. The matter was impossible. I could not in any reason have so rapidly come down. Besides, although I was evidently approaching the surface below me, it was with a speed by no means commensurate with the velocity I had at first conceived. This consideration served to calm the perturbation of my mind, and I finally succeeded in regarding the phenomenon in its proper point of view. In fact, amazement must have fairly deprived me of my senses, when I could not see the vast difference, in appearance, between the surface below me, and the surface of my mother earth. The latter was indeed over my head, and completely hidden by the balloon, while the moon – the moon itself in all its glory – lay beneath me, and at my feet.

The stupor and surprise produced in my mind by this extraordinary change in the posture of affairs, was perhaps, after all, that part of the adventure least susceptible of explanation. For the *bouleversement* in itself was not only natural and inevitable, but had been long actually anticipated, as a circumstance to be expected whenever I should arrive at that exact point of my voyage where the attraction of the planet should be superseded by the attraction of the satellite – or, more precisely, where the gravitation of the balloon towards the earth should be less powerful than its gravitation towards the moon. To be sure I arose from a sound slumber, with all my senses in confusion, to the contemplation of a very startling phenomenon, and one which, although expected, was not expected at the moment. The revolution itself must, of course, have taken place in an easy and gradual manner, and it is by no means clear that, had I even been awake at the time of the occurrence, I should have been made aware of it by any *internal* evidence of an inversion – that is to say, by any inconvenience or disarrangement, either about my person or about my apparatus.

It is almost needless to say, that, upon coming to a due sense of my situation, and emerging from the terror which had absorbed every faculty of my soul, my attention was, in the first place, wholly directed to the contemplation of the general physical appearance of the moon. It lay beneath me like a chart – and although I judged it to be still at no inconsiderable distance, the indentures of its surface were defined to my vision with a most striking and altogether unaccountable distinctness. The entire absence of ocean or sea, and indeed of any lake or river, or body of water whatsoever, struck me, at the first glance, as the most extraordinary feature in its geological condition. Yet, strange to say, I beheld vast level regions of a character decidedly alluvial, although by far the greater portion of the hemisphere in sight was covered with innumerable volcanic mountains, conical in shape, and having more the appearance of artificial than of natural protuberances. The highest among them does not exceed three and three-quarter miles in perpendicular elevation; but a map of the volcanic districts of the Campi Phlegræi would afford to your Excellencies a better idea of their general surface than any unworthy description I might think proper to attempt. The greater part of them were in a state of evident eruption, and gave me fearfully to understand their fury and their power, by the repeated thunders of the miscalled meteoric stones, which now rushed upwards by the balloon with a frequency more and more appalling.

April 18th. Today I found an enormous increase in the moon's apparent bulk – and the evidently accelerated velocity of my descent, began to fill me with alarm. It will be remembered, that, in the earliest stage of my speculations upon the possibility of a passage to the moon, the existence, in its vicinity, of an atmosphere dense in proportion to the bulk of the planet, had entered largely into my calculations; this too in spite of many theories to the contrary, and, it may added, in spite of a general disbelief in the existence of any lunar atmosphere at all. But, in addition to what I have already urged in regard to Encke's comet and the zodiacal light, I had been strengthened in my opinion by certain observations of Mr. Schroeter, of Lilienthal. He observed the moon, when two days and a half old, in the evening soon after sunset, before the dark part was visible, and continued to watch it until it became visible. The two cusps appeared tapering in a very sharp faint prolongation, each exhibiting its farthest extremity faintly illuminated by the solar rays, before any part of the dark hemisphere was visible. Soon afterwards, the whole dark limb became illuminated. This prolongation of the cusps beyond the semicircle, I thought, must have arisen from the refraction of the sun's rays by the moon's atmosphere. I computed, also, the height of the atmosphere (which could refract light enough into its dark hemisphere, to produce a twilight more luminous than the light reflected from the earth when the moon is about 32° from the new) to be 1356 Paris feet; in this view, I supposed the greatest height capable of refracting the solar ray, to be 5376 feet. My ideas upon this topic had also received confirmation by a passage in the eighty-second volume of the Philosophical Transactions, in which it is stated, that, at an occultation of Jupiter's satellites, the third disappeared after having been about 1" or 2" of time indistinct, and the fourth became indiscernible near the limb. Upon the resistance, or more properly, upon the support of an atmosphere, existing in the state of density imagined, I had, of course, entirely depended for the safety of my ultimate descent. Should I then, after all, prove to have been mistaken, I had in consequence nothing better to expect, as a *finale* to my adventure, than being dashed into atoms against the rugged surface of the satellite. And, indeed, I had now every reason to be terrified. My distance from the moon was comparatively trifling, while the labor required by the condenser was diminished not at all, and I could discover no indication whatever of a decreasing rarity in the air.

April 19th. This morning, to my great joy, about nine o'clock, the surface of the moon being frightfully near, and my apprehensions excited to the utmost, the pump of my condenser at length gave evident tokens of an alteration in the atmosphere. By ten, I had reason to believe its density considerably increased. By eleven, very little labor was necessary at the apparatus; and at twelve o'clock, with some hesitation, I ventured to unscrew the tourniquet, when, finding no inconvenience from having done so, I finally threw open the gum-elastic chamber, and unrigged it from around the car. As might have been expected, spasms and violent headache were the immediate consequences of an experiment so precipitate and full of danger. But these and other difficulties attending respiration, as they were by no means so great as to put me in peril of my life, I determined to endure as I best could, in consideration of my leaving them behind me momently in my approach to the denser *strata* near the moon. This approach, however, was still impetuous in the extreme; and it soon became alarmingly certain that, although I had probably not been deceived in the expectation of an atmosphere dense in proportion to the mas of the satellite, still I had been wrong in supposing this density, even at the surface, at all adequate to the support of the great weight contained in the car of my balloon. Yet this *should* have been the case, and in an equal degree as at the surface of the earth, the actual gravity of bodies at either planet supposed in the ratio of the atmospheric condensation. That it *was not* the case, however, my precipitous downfall gave testimony enough; *why* it was not so, can only be explained by a reference to those possible geological disturbances to which I have formerly alluded. At all events I was now close upon the planet, and coming down with the most terrible impetuosity. I lost not a moment, accordingly, in throwing overboard first my ballast, then my water-kegs, then my condensing apparatus and gum-elastic chamber, and finally every article within the car. But it was all to no purpose. I still fell with horrible rapidity, and was now not more than half a mile from the surface. As a last resource, therefore, having got rid of my coat, hat, and boots, I cut loose from the balloon *the car itself*, which was of no inconsiderable weight, and thus, clinging with both hands to the net-work, I had barely time to observe that the whole country, as far as the eye could reach, was thickly interspersed with diminutive habitations, ere I tumbled headlong into the very heart of a fantastical-looking city, and into the middle of a vast crowd of ugly little people, who none of them uttered a single syllable, or gave themselves the least trouble to render me assistance, but stood, like a parcel of idiots, grinning in a ludicrous manner, and eyeing me and my balloon askant, with their arms set a-kimbo. I turned from them in contempt, and, gazing upwards at the earth so lately left, and left perhaps for ever, beheld it like a huge, dull, copper shield, about two degrees in diameter, fixed immovably in the heavens overhead, and tipped on one of its edges with a crescent border of the most brilliant gold. No traces of land or water could be discovered, and the whole was clouded with variable spots, and belted with tropical and equatorial zones.

Thus, may it please your Excellencies, after a series of great anxieties, unheard-of dangers, and unparalleled escapes, I had, at length, on the nineteenth day of my departure from Rotterdam, arrived in safety at the conclusion of a voyage undoubtedly the most extraordinary, and the most momentous, ever accomplished, undertaken, or conceived by any denizen of earth. But my adventures yet remain to be related. And indeed your Excellencies may well imagine that, after a residence of five years upon a planet not only deeply interesting in its own peculiar character, but rendered doubly so by its intimate connection, in capacity of satellite, with the world inhabited by man, I may have intelligence for the private ear of the States' College of Astronomers of far more importance than the details, however wonderful, of the mere *voyage* which so happily concluded. This is, in fact, the case. I have much – very much which it would give me the greatest pleasure to communicate. I have much to say of the climate of the planet; of its wonderful alternations of heat and cold; of unmitigated and burning sunshine for one fortnight, and more than polar frigidity for the next; of a constant transfer of moisture, by distillation like that in *vacuo*, from the point beneath the sun to the point the farthest from it; of a variable zone of running water; of the people themselves; of their manners, customs, and political institutions; of their peculiar physical construction; of their ugliness; of their want of ears, those useless appendages in an atmosphere so peculiarly modified; of their consequent ignorance of the use and properties of speech; of their substitute for speech in a singular method of inter-communication; of the incomprehensible connection between each particular individual in the moon, with some particular individual on the earth – a connection analogous with, and depending upon that of the orbs of the planet and the satellite, and by means of which the lives and destines of the inhabitants of the one are interwoven with the lives and destinies of the inhabitants of the other; and above all, if it so please your Excellencies – above all of those dark and hideous mysteries which lie in the outer regions of the moon, – regions which, owing to the almost miraculous accordance of the satellite's rotation on its own axis with its sidereal revolution about the earth, have never yet been turned, and, by God's mercy, never shall be turned, to the scrutiny of the telescopes of man. All this, and more – much more – would I most willingly detail. But, to be brief, I must have my reward. I am pining for a return to my family and to my home: and as the price of any farther communications on my part – in consideration of the light which I have it in my power to throw upon many very important branches of physical and metaphysical science – I must solicit, through the influence of your honorable body, a pardon for the crime of which I have been guilty in the death of the creditors upon my departure from Rotterdam. This, then, is the object the present paper. Its bearer, an inhabitant of the moon, whom I have prevailed upon, and properly instructed, to be my messenger to the earth, will await your Excellencies' pleasure, and return to me with the pardon in question, if it can, in any manner, be obtained.

I have the honor to be, etc., your Excellencies' very humble servant,
Hans Pfall.

Upon finishing the perusal of this very extraordinary document, Professor Rubadub, it is said, dropped his pipe upon the ground in the extremity of his surprise, and Mynheer Superbus Von Underduk having taken off his spectacles, wiped them, and deposited them in his pocket, so far forgot both himself and his dignity, as to turn round three times upon his heel in the quintessence of astonishment and admiration. There was no doubt about the matter – the pardon should be obtained. So at least swore, with a round oath, Professor Rubadub, and so finally thought the illustrious Von Underduk, as he took the arm of his brother in science, and without saying a word, began to make the best of his way home to deliberate upon the measures to be adopted. Having reached the door, however, of the burgomaster's dwelling, the professor ventured to suggest that as the messenger had thought proper to disappear – no doubt frightened to death by the savage appearance of the burghers of Rotterdam – the pardon would be of little use, as no one but a man of the moon would undertake a voyage to so vast a distance. To the truth of this observation the burgomaster assented, and the matter was therefore at an end. Not so, however, rumors and speculations. The letter, having been published, gave rise to a variety of gossip and opinion. Some of the over-wise even made themselves ridiculous by decrying the whole business as nothing better than a hoax. But hoax, with these sort of people, is, I believe, a general term for all matters above their comprehension. For my part, I cannot conceive upon what data they have founded such an accusation. Let us see what they say:

Imprimis. That certain wags in Rotterdam have certain especial antipathies to certain burgomasters and astronomers.

Secondly. That an odd little dwarf and bottle conjurer, both of whose ears, for some misdemeanor, have been cut off close to his head, has been missing for several days from the neighboring city of Bruges.

Thirdly. That the newspapers which were stuck all over the little balloon were newspapers of Holland, and therefore could not have been made in the moon. They were dirty papers – very dirty – and Gluck, the printer, would take his bible oath to their having been printed in Rotterdam.

Fourthly. That Hans Pfall himself, the drunken villain, and the three very idle gentlemen styled his creditors, were all seen, no longer than two or three days ago, in a tippling house in the suburbs, having just returned, with money in their pockets, from a trip beyond the sea.

Lastly. That it is an opinion very generally received, or which ought to be generally received, that the College of Astronomers in the city of Rotterdam, as well as all other colleges in all other parts of the world, – not to mention colleges and astronomers in general, – are, to say the least of the matter, not a whit better, nor greater, nor wiser than they ought to be.

The Winning of a Sword
from Part II of The Story of King Arthur and his Knights

Howard Pyle

Here beginneth the story of certain adventures of Arthur after that he had become King, wherein it is told how, with great knightly courage and prowess, he fought a very fierce and bloody battle with a certain Sable Knight. Likewise, it is told how he achieved, in consequence of that battle, a certain Sword so famous and glorious that its renown shall last as long as our speech shall be spoken. For the like of that sword was never seen in all the world before that time, and it hath never been beheld since then; and its name was Excalibur.

So, if it please you to read this story, I believe it will afford you excellent entertainment, and will, without doubt, greatly exalt your spirit because of the remarkable courage which those two famous and worthy knights displayed when they fought together that famous battle. Likewise you shall find great cheer in reading therein of the wonderful marvellousness of a certain land of Faerie into which King Arthur wandered, and where he found a Lake of Enchantment and held converse with a mild and beautiful lady of that land who directed him how to obtain that renowned sword aforementioned.

For it hath given me such pleasure to write these things that my heart would, at times, be diluted as with a pure joy, wherefore, I entertain great hopes that you also may find much pleasure in them as I have already done. So I pray you to listen unto what follows.

Chapter I

How There Came a Certain Wounded Knight Unto the Court of King Arthur, How a Young Kinght of the King's Court Sought To Avenge Him and Failed and How the King Thereupon Took That Assay Upon Himself.

NOW IT FELL UPON a certain pleasant time in the Springtide season that King Arthur and his Court were making a royal progression through that part of Britain which lieth close to the Forests of the Usk. At that time the weather was exceedingly warm, and so the King and Court made pause within the forest under the trees in the cool and pleasant shade that the place afforded, and there the King rested for a while upon a couch of rushes spread with scarlet cloth.

And the knights then present at that Court were, Sir Gawaine, and Sir Ewaine, and Sir Kay, and Sir Pellias, and Sir Bedevere, and Sir Caradoc, and Sir Geraint, and Sir Bodwin of Britain and Sir Constantine of Cornwall, and Sir Brandiles and Sir Mador de la Porte, and there was not to be found anywhere in the world a company of such noble and exalted knights as these.

Now as the King lay drowsing and as these worthies sat holding cheerful converse together at that place, there came, of a sudden, a considerable bustle and stir upon the outskirts of the Court, and presently there appeared a very sad and woful sight. For there came thitherward a knight, sore wounded, and upheld upon his horse by a golden-haired page, clad in an apparel of white and azure. And, likewise, the knight's apparel and the trappings of his horse were of white and azure, and upon his shield he bore the emblazonment of a single lily flower of silver upon a ground of pure azure.

But the knight was in a very woful plight. For his face was as pale as wax and hung down upon his breast. And his eyes were glazed and saw naught that passed around him, and his fair apparel of white and blue was all red with the blood of life that ran from a great wound in his side. And, as they came upon their way, the young page lamented in such wise that it wrung the heart for to hear him.

Now, as these approached, King Arthur aroused cried out, "Alas! What doleful spectacle is that which I behold? Now hasten, ye my lords, and bring succor to yonder knight; and do thou, Sir Kay, go quickly and bring that fair young page hither that we may presently hear from his lips what mishap hath befallen his lord."

So certain of those knights hastened at the King's bidding and gave all succor to the wounded knight, and conveyed him to King Arthur's own pavilion, which had been pitched at a little distance. And when he had come there the King's chirurgeon presently attended upon him – albeit his wounds were of such a sort he might not hope to live for a very long while.

Meantime, Sir Kay brought that fair young page before the King, where he sat, and the King thought that he had hardly ever seen a more beautiful countenance. And the King said, "I prithee tell me, Sir Page, who is thy master, and how came he in such a sad and pitiable condition as that which we have just now beheld."

"That will I so, Lord," said the youth. "Know that my master is entitled Sir Myles of the White Fountain, and that he cometh from the country north of where we are and at a considerable distance from this. In that country he is the Lord of seven castles and several noble estates, wherefore, as thou mayst see, he is of considerable consequence. A fortnight ago (being doubtless moved thereunto by the lustiness of the Springtime), he set forth with only me for his esquire, for he had a mind to seek adventure in such manner as beseemed a good knight who would be errant. And we had several adventures, and in all of them my lord was entirely successful; for he overcame six knights at various places and sent them all to his castle for to attest his valor unto his lady.

"At last, this morning, coming to a certain place situated at a considerable distance from this, we came upon a fair castle of the forest, which stood in a valley surrounded by open spaces of level lawn, bedight with many flowers of divers sorts. There we beheld three fair damsels who tossed a golden ball from one to another, and the damsels were clad all in flame-colored satin, and their hair was of the color of gold. And as we drew nigh to them they stinted their play, and she who was the chief of those damsel called out to my lord, demanding of him whither he went and what was his errand.

"To her my lord made answer that he was errant and in search of adventure, and upon this, the three damsels laughed, and she who had first spoken said, 'An thou art in search of adventure, Sir Knight, happily I may be able to help thee to one that shall satisfy thee to thy heart's content.'

"Unto this my master made reply 'I prithee, fair damsel, tell me what that adventure may be so that I may presently assay it.'

"Thereupon this lady bade my master to take a certain path, and to follow the same for the distance of a league or a little more, and that he would then come to a bridge of stone that crossed a violent stream, and she assured him that there he might find adventure enough for to satisfy any man.

So my master and I wended thitherward as that damoiselle had directed, and, by and by, we came unto the bridge whereof she had spoken. And, lo! Beyond the bridge was a lonesome castle with a tall straight tower, and before the castle was a wide and level lawn of well-trimmed grass. And immediately beyond the bridge was an apple tree hung over with a multitude of shields. And midway upon the bridge was a single shield, entirely of black; and beside it hung a hammer of brass; and beneath the shield was written these words in letters of red:

Whoso Smiteth This Shield Doeth So At His Peril.

"Now, my master, Sir Myles, when he read those words went straightway to that shield and, seizing the hammer that hung beside it, he smote upon it a blow so that it rang like thunder.

"Thereupon, as in answer, the portcullis of the castle was let fall, and there immediately came forth a knight, clad all from head to foot in sable armor. And his apparel and the trappings of his horse and all the appointments thereof were likewise entirely of sable.

"Now when that Sable Knight perceived my master he came riding swiftly across the meadow and so to the other end of the bridge. And when he had come there he drew rein and saluted my master and cried out, 'Sir Knight, I demand of thee why thou didst smite that shield. Now let me tell thee, because of thy boldness, I shall take away from thee thine own shield, and shall hang it upon yonder apple tree, where thou beholdest all those other shields to be hanging.' Unto this my master made reply. 'That thou shalt not do unless thou mayst overcome me, as knight to knight.' And thereupon, immediately, he dressed his shield and put himself into array for an assault at arms.

"So my master and this Sable Knight, having made themselves ready for that encounter, presently drave together with might and main. And they met in the middle of the course, where my master's spear burst into splinters. But the spear of the Sable knight held and it pierced through Sir Myles, his shield, and it penetrated his side, so that both he and his horse were overthrown violently into the dust; he being wounded so grievously that he could not arise again from the ground whereon he lay.

"Then the Sable Knight took my master's shield and hung it up in the branches of the apple tree where the other shields were hanging, and, thereupon, without paying further heed to my master, or inquiring as to his hurt, he rode away into his castle again, whereof the portcullis was immediately closed behind him.

"So, after that he had gone, I got my master to his horse with great labor, and straightway took him thence, not knowing where I might find harborage for him, until I came to this place. And that, my lord King, is the true story of how my master came by that mortal hurt which he hath suffered."

"Ha! By the glory of Paradise!" cried King Arthur, "I do consider it a great shame that in my Kingdom and so near to my Court strangers should be so discourteously treated as Sir Myles hath been served. For it is certainly a discourtesy for to leave a fallen knight upon the ground, without tarrying to inquire as to his hurt how grievous it may be. And still more discourteous is it for to take away the shield of a fallen knight who hath done good battle."

And so did all the knights of the King's Court exclaim against the discourtesy of that Sable Knight.

Then there came forth a certain esquire attendant upon the King's person, by name Griflet, who was much beloved by his Royal Master, and he kneeled before the King and cried out in a loud voice: "I crave a boon of thee, my lord King! and do beseech thee that thou wilt grant it unto me!"

Then King Arthur uplifted his countenance upon the youth as he knelt before him and he said, "Ask, Griflet, and thy boon shall be granted unto thee."

Thereupon Griflet said, "It is this that I would ask – I crave that thou wilt make me straightway knight, and that thou wilt let me go forth and endeavor to punish this unkindly knight, by overthrowing him, and so redeeming those shields which he hath hung upon that apple tree."

Then was King Arthur much troubled in his spirit, for Griflet was as yet only an esquire and altogether untried in arms. So he said, "Behold, thou art yet too young to have to do with so potent a knight as this sable champion must be, who has thus overthrown so many knights without himself suffering any mishap. I prithee, dear Griflet, consider and ask some other boon." But young Griflet only cried the more, "A boon! A boon! And thou hast granted it unto me."

Thereupon King Arthur said, "Thou shalt have thy boon, though my heart much misgiveth me that thou wilt suffer great ill and misfortune from this adventure."

So that night Griflet kept watch upon his armor in a chapel of the forest, and, in the morning, having received the Sacrament, he was created a knight by the hand of King Arthur – and it was not possible for any knight to have greater honor than that. Then King Arthur fastened the golden spurs to Sir Griflet's heels with his own hand.

So Griflet was made a knight, and having mounted his charger, he rode straightway upon his adventure, much rejoicing and singing for pure pleasure.

And it was at this time that Sir Myles died of his hurt, for it is often so that death and misfortune befall some, whiles others laugh and sing for hope and joy, as though such grievous things as sorrow and death could never happen in the world wherein they live.

Now that afternoon King Arthur sat waiting with great anxiety for word of that young knight, but there was no word until toward evening, when there came hurrying to him certain of his attendants, proclaiming that Sir Griflet was returning, but without his shield, and in such guise that it seemed as though a great misfortune had befallen him. And straightway thereafter came Sir Griflet himself, sustained upon his horse on the one hand by Sir Constantine and upon the other by Sir Brandiles. And, lo! Sir Griflet's head hung down upon his breast, and his fair new armor was all broken and stained with blood and dust. And so woful was he of appearance that King Arthur's heart was contracted with sorrow to behold that young knight in so pitiable a condition.

So, at King Arthur's bidding, they conducted Sir Griflet to the Royal Pavilion, and there they laid him down upon a soft couch. Then the King's chirurgeon searched his wounds and found that the head of a spear and a part of the shaft thereof were still piercing Sir Griflet's side, so that he was in most woful and grievous pain.

And when King Arthur beheld in what a parlous state Sir Griflet lay he cried out, "Alas! My dear young knight, what hath happened thee to bring thee unto such a woful condition as this which I behold?"

Then Sir Griflet, speaking in a very weak voice, told King Arthur how he had fared. And he said that he had proceeded through the forest, until he had discovered the three beautiful damsels whereof the page of Sir Myles had spoken. And he said that these damsels had directed him as to the manner in which he should pursue his adventure. And he said that he had found the bridge whereon hung the shield and the brazen mall, and that he had there beheld the apple tree hung full of shields; and he said that he smote the shield of the Sable Knight with the brazen mall, and that the Sable Knight had thereupon come riding out against him. And he said that this knight did not appear of a mind to fight with him; instead, he cried out to him with a great deal of nobleness that he was too young and too untried in arms to have to do with a seasoned knight; wherefore he advised Sir Griflet to withdraw him from that adventure ere it was too late. But, notwithstanding this advice, Sir Griflet would not withdraw but declared that he would certainly have to do with that other knight in sable. Now at the very first onset Sir Griflet's spear had burst into pieces, but the spear of the Sable Knight had held and had pierced through Sir Griflet's shield and into his side, causing him this grievous wound whereof he suffered. And Sir Griflet said that the Sable Knight had then, most courteously, uplifted him upon his horse again (albeit he had kept Sir Griflet's shield and had hung it upon the tree with those others that hung there) and then directed him upon his way, so that he had made shift to ride thither, though with great pain and dole.

Then was King Arthur very wode and greatly disturbed in his mind, for indeed he loved Sir Griflet exceedingly well. Wherefore he declared that he himself would now go forth for to punish that Sable Knight, and for to humble him with his own hand. And, though the knights of his Court strove to dissuade him from that adventure, yet he declared that he with his own hand would accomplish that proud knight's humiliation, and that he would undertake the adventure, with God His Grace, upon the very next day.

And so disturbed was he that he could scarce eat his food that evening for vexation, nor would he go to his couch to sleep, but, having inquired very narrowly of Sir Griflet where he might find that valley of flowers and those three damsels, he spent the night in walking up and down his pavilion, awaiting for the dawning of the day.

Now, as soon as the birds first began to chirp and the east to brighten with the coming of the daylight, King Arthur summoned his two esquires, and, having with their aid donned his armor and mounted a milk-white war-horse, he presently took his departure upon that adventure which he had determined upon.

And, indeed it is a very pleasant thing for to ride forth in the dawning of a Springtime day. For then the little birds do sing their sweetest song, all joining in one joyous medley, whereof one may scarce tell one note from another, so multitudinous is that pretty roundelay; then do the growing things of the earth – the fair flowers, the shrubs, and the blossoms upon the trees; then doth the dew bespangle all the sward as with an incredible multitude of jewels of various colors; then is all the world sweet and clean and new, as though it had been fresh created for him who came to roam abroad so early in the morning.

So King Arthur's heart expanded with great joy, and he chanted a quaint song as he rode through the forest upon the quest of that knightly adventure.

So, about noon-tide, he came to that part of the forest lands whereof he had heard those several times before. For of a sudden, he discovered before him a wide and gently sloping valley, a-down which ran a stream as bright as silver. And, lo! The valley was strewn all over with an infinite multitude of fair and fragrant flowers of divers sorts. And in the midst of the valley there stood a comely castle, with tall red roofs and many bright windows, so that it seemed to King Arthur that it was a very fine castle indeed. And upon a smooth green lawn he perceived those three damoiselles clad in flame-colored satin of whom the page of Sir Myles and Sir Griflet had spoken. And they played at ball with a golden ball, and the hair of each was of the hue of gold, and it seemed to King Arthur, as he drew nigh, that they were the most beautiful damoiselles that he had ever beheld in all of his life.

Now as King Arthur came unto them the three ceased tossing the ball, and she who was the fairest of all damoiselles demanded of him whither he went and upon what errand he was bound.

Then King Arthur made reply: "Ha! Fair lady! Whither should a belted knight ride upon such a day as this, and upon what business, other than the search of adventure such as beseemeth a knight of a proper strength of heart and frame who would be errant?"

Then the three damoiselles smiled upon the King, for he was exceedingly comely of face and they liked him very well. "Alas, Sir Knight!" said she who had before spoken, "I prithee be in no such haste to undertake a dangerous adventure, but rather tarry with us for a day or two or three, for to feast and make merry with us. For surely good cheer doth greatly enlarge the heart, and we enjoy the company of so gallant a knight as thou appearest to be. Yonder castle is ours and all this gay valley is ours, and those who have visited it are pleased, because of its joyousness, to call it the Valley of Delight. So tarry with us for a little and be not in such haste to go forward."

"Nay," said King Arthur, "I may not tarry with ye, fair ladies, for I am bent upon an adventure of which ye may wot right well, when I tell ye that I seek that Sable Knight, who hath overcome so many other knights and hath taken away their shields. So I do pray ye of your grace for to tell me where I may find him."

"Grace of Heaven!" cried she who spake for the others, "This is certainly a sorry adventure which ye seek, Sir Knight! For already, in these two days, have two knights assayed with that knight, and both have fallen into great pain and disregard. Ne'theless, an thou wilt undertake this peril, yet shalt thou not go until thou hast eaten and refreshed thyself." So saying, she lifted a little ivory whistle that hung from her neck by a chain of gold, and blew upon it very shrilly.

In answer to this summons there came forth from the castle three fair young pages, clad all in flame-colored raiment, bearing among them a silver table covered with a white napkin. And after them came five other pages of the same appearance, bearing flagons of white wine and red, dried fruits and comfits and manchets of white fair bread.

Then King Arthur descended from his war-horse with great gladness, for he was both hungry and athirst, and, seating himself at the table with the damsels beside him, he ate with great enjoyment, discoursing pleasantly the while with those fair ladies, who listened to him with great cheerfulness of spirit. Yet he told them not who he was, though they greatly marvelled who might be the noble warrior who had come thus into that place.

So, having satisfied his hunger and his thirst, King Arthur mounted his steed again, and the three damsels conducted him across the valley a little way – he riding upon his horse and they walking beside him. So, by and by, he perceived where was a dark pathway that led into the farther side of the forest land; and when he had come thither the lady who had addressed him before said to him, "Yonder is the way that thou must take an thou wouldst enter upon this adventure. So fare thee well, and may good hap go with thee, for, certes, thou art the Knight most pleasant of address who hath come hitherward for this long time."

Thereupon King Arthur, having saluted those ladies right courteously, rode away with very great joy of that pleasant adventure through which he had thus passed.

Now when King Arthur had gone some ways he came, by and by, to a certain place where charcoal burners plied their trade. For here were many mounds of earth, all a-smoke with the smouldering logs within, whilst all the air was filled with the smell of the dampened fires.

As the King approached this spot, he presently beheld that something was toward that was sadly amiss. For, in the open clearing, he beheld three sooty fellows with long knives in their hands, who pursued one old man, whose beard was as white as snow. And he beheld that the reverend old man, who was clad richly in black, and whose horse stood at a little distance, was running hither and thither, as though to escape from those wicked men, and he appeared to be very hard pressed and in great danger of his life.

"Pardee!" quoth the young King to himself, "here, certes, is one in sore need of succor." Whereupon he cried out in a great voice, "Hold, villains! What would you be at!" and therewith set spurs to his horse and dropped his spear into rest and drove down upon them with a noise like to thunder for loudness.

But when the three wicked fellows beheld the armed Knight thus thundering down upon them, they straightway dropped their knives and, with loud outcries of fear, ran away hither and thither until they had escaped into the thickets of the forest, where one upon a horse might not hope to pursue them.

Whereupon, having driven away those wicked fellows, King Arthur rode up to him whom he had succored, thinking to offer him condolence. And behold! when he had come nigh to him, he perceived that the old man was the Enchanter Merlin. Yet whence he had so suddenly come, who had only a little while before been at the King's Court at Carleon, and what he did in that place, the King could in no wise understand. Wherefore he bespoke the Enchanter in this wise, "Ha! Merlin, it seemeth to me that I have saved thy life. For, surely, thou hadst not escaped from the hands of those wicked men had I not happened to come hitherward at this time."

"Dost thou think so, Lord?" said Merlin. "Now let me tell thee that I did maybe appear to be in danger, yet I might have saved myself very easily had I been of a mind to do so. But, as thou sawst me in this seeming peril, so may thou know that a real peril, far greater than this, lieth before thee, and there will be no errant knight to succor thee from it. Wherefore, I pray thee, Lord, for to take me with thee upon this adventure that thou art set upon, for I do tell thee that thou shalt certainly suffer great dole and pain therein."

"Merlin," said King Arthur, "even an I were to face my death, yet would I not turn back from this adventure. But touching the advice thou givest me, meseems it will be very well to take thee with me if such peril lieth before me as thou sayest." And Merlin said, "Yea, it would be very well for thee to do so."

So Merlin mounted upon his palfrey, and King Arthur and he betook their way from that place in pursuit of that adventure which the King had undertaken to perform.

Chapter II

How King Arthur Fought With the Sable Knight and How He Was Sorely Wounded. Likewise How Merlin Brought Him Safe Away From the Field of Battle.

SO KING ARTHUR and Merlin rode together through the forest for a considerable while, until they perceived that they must be approaching nigh to the place where dwelt the Sable Knight whom the King sought so diligently. For the forest, which had till then been altogether a wilderness, very deep and mossy, began to show an aspect more thin and open, as though a dwelling-place of mankind was close at hand.

And, after a little, they beheld before them a violent stream of water, that rushed through a dark and dismal glen. And, likewise, they perceived that across this stream of water there was a bridge of stone, and that upon the other side of the bridge there was a smooth and level lawn of green grass, whereon Knights-contestants might joust very well. And beyond this lawn they beheld a tall and forbidding castle, with smooth walls and a straight tower; and this castle was built upon the rocks so that it appeared to be altogether a part of the stone. So they wist that this must be the castle whereof the page and Sir Griflet had spoken.

For, midway upon the bridge, they beheld that there hung a sable shield and a brass mall exactly as the page and Sir Griflet had said; and that upon the farther side of the stream was an apple tree, amid the leaves of which hung a very great many shields of various devices, exactly as those two had reported: and they beheld that some of those shields were clean and fair, and that some were foul and stained with blood, and that some were smooth and unbroken, and that some were cleft as though by battle of knight with knight. And all those shields were the shields of different knights whom the Sable Knight, who dwelt within the castle, had overthrown in combat with his own hand.

"Splendor of Paradise!" quoth King Arthur, "that must, indeed, be a right valiant knight who, with his own single strength, hath overthrown and cast down so many other knights. For, indeed, Merlin, there must be an hundred shields hanging in yonder tree!"

Unto this Merlin made reply, "And thou, Lord, mayst be very happy an thy shield, too, hangeth not there ere the sun goeth down this eventide."

"That," said King Arthur, with a very steadfast countenance, "shall be as God willeth. For, certes, I have a greater mind than ever for to try my power against yonder knight. For, consider, what especial honor would fall to me should I overcome so valiant a warrior as this same Sable Champion appeareth to be, seeing that he hath been victorious over so many other good knights."

Thereupon, having so spoken his mind, King Arthur immediately pushed forward his horse and so, coming upon the bridge, he clearly read that challenge writ in letters of red beneath the shield:

Whoso Smiteth This Shield Doeth So At His Peril.

Upon reading these words, the King seized the brazen mall, and smote that shield so violent a blow that the sound thereof echoed back from the smooth walls of the castle, and from the rocks whereon it stood, and from the skirts of the forest around about, as though twelve other shields had been struck in those several places.

And in answer to that sound, the portcullis of the castle was immediately let fall, and there issued forth a knight, very huge of frame, and clad all in sable armor. And, likewise, all of his apparel and all the trappings of his horse were entirely of sable, so that he presented a most grim and forbidding aspect. And this Sable Knight came across that level meadow of smooth grass with a very stately and honorable gait; for neither did he ride in haste, nor did he ride slowly, but with great pride and haughtiness of mien, as became a champion who, haply, had never yet been overcome in battle. So, reaching the bridgehead, he drew rein and saluted King Arthur with great dignity, and also right haughtily. "Ha! Sir Knight!" quoth he, "Why didst thou, having read those words yonder inscribed, smite upon my shield? Now I do tell thee that, for thy discourtesy, I shall presently take thy shield away from thee, and shall hang it up upon yonder apple tree where thou beholdest all those other shields to be hanging. Wherefore, either deliver thou thy shield unto me without more ado or else prepare for to defend it with thy person – in the which event thou shalt certainly suffer great pain and discomfort to thy body."

"Gramercy for the choice thou grantest me," said King Arthur. "But as for taking away my shield – I do believe that that shall be as Heaven willeth, and not as thou willest. Know, thou unkind knight, that I have come hither for no other purpose than to do battle with thee and so to endeavor for to redeem with my person all those shields that hang yonder upon that apple tree. So make thou ready straightway that I may have to do with thee, maybe to thy great disadvantage."

"That will I so," replied the Sable Knight. And thereupon he turned his horse's head and, riding back a certain distance across the level lawn, he took stand in such place as appeared to him to be convenient. And so did King Arthur ride forth also upon that lawn, and take his station as seemed to him to be convenient.

Then each knight dressed his spear and his shield for the encounter, and, having thus made ready for the assault, each shouted to his war-horse and drave his spurs deep into its flank.

Then those two noble steeds rushed forth like lightning, coursing across the ground with such violent speed that the earth trembled and shook beneath them, an it were by cause of an earthquake. So those two knights met fairly in the midst of the centre of the field, crashing together like a thunderbolt. And so violently did they smite the one against the other that the spears burst into splinters, even unto the guard and the truncheon thereof, and the horses of the riders staggered back from the onset, so that only because of the extraordinary address of the knights-rider did they recover from falling before that shock of meeting.

But, with great spirit, these two knights uplifted each his horse with his own spirit, and so completed his course in safety.

And indeed King Arthur was very much amazed that he had not overthrown his opponent, for, at that time, as aforesaid, he was considered to be the very best knight and the one best approved in deeds of arms that lived in all of Britain. Wherefore he marvelled at the power and the address of that knight against whom he had driven, that he had not been overthrown by the greatness of the blow that had been delivered against his defences. So, when they met again in the midst of the field, King Arthur gave that knight greeting, and bespoke him with great courtesy, addressing him in this wise: 'Sir Knight, I know not who thou art, but I do pledge my knightly word that thou art the most potent knight that ever I have met in all of my life. Now I do bid thee get down straightway from thy horse, and let us two fight this battle with sword and upon foot, for it were pity to let it end in this way."

"Not so," quoth the Sable Knight – "not so, nor until one of us twain be overthrown will I so contest this battle upon foot." And upon this he shouted, "Ho! Ho!" in a very loud voice, and straightway thereupon the gateway of the castle opened and there came running forth two tall esquires clad all in black, pied with crimson. And each of these esquires bare in his hand a great spear of ash-wood, new and well-seasoned, and never yet strained in battle.

So King Arthur chose one of these spears and the Sable Knight took the other, and thereupon each returned to that station wherefrom he had before essayed the encounter.

Then once again each knight rushed his steed to the assault, and once again did each smite so fairly in the midst of the defence of the other that the spears were splintered, so that only the guard and the truncheon thereof remained in the grasp of the knight who held it.

Then, as before, King Arthur would have fought the battle out with swords and upon foot, but again the Sable Knight would not have it so, but called aloud upon those within the castle, whereupon there immediately came forth two other esquires with fresh, new spears of ash-wood. So each knight again took him a spear, armed himself therewith, chose each his station upon that fair, level lawn of grass.

And now, for the third time, having thus prepared themselves thereof assault, those two excellent knights hurled themselves together in furious assault. And now, as twice before, did King Arthur strike the Sable Knight so fairly in the centre of his defence that the spear which he held was burst into splinters. But this time, the spear of the Sable Knight did not so break in that manner, but held; and so violent was the blow that he delivered upon King Arthur's shield that he pierced through the centre of it. Then the girths of the King's saddle burst apart by that great, powerful blow, and both he and his steed were cast violently backward. So King Arthur might have been overcast, had he not voided his saddle with extraordinary skill and knightly address, wherefore, though his horse was overthrown, he himself still held his footing and did not fall into the dust. Ne'theless, so violent was the blow that he received that, for a little space, he was altogether bereft of his senses so that everything whirled around before his eyes.

But when his sight returned to him he was filled with an anger so vehement that it appeared to him as though all the blood in his heart rushed into his brains so that he saw naught but red, as of blood, before his eyes. And when this also had passed he perceived the Sable Knight that he sat his horse at no great distance. Then immediately King Arthur ran to him and catching the bridle-rein of his horse, he cried out aloud unto that Sable Knight with great violence: "Come down, thou black knight! And fight me upon foot and with thy sword."

"That will I not do," said the Sable Knight, "for, lo! I have overthrown thee. Wherefore deliver thou to me thy shield, that I may hang it upon yonder apple tree, and go thy way as others have done before thee."

"That will I not!" cried King Arthur, with exceeding passion, "Neither will I yield myself nor go hence until either thou or I have altogether conquered the other." Thereupon he thrust the horse of the Sable Knight backward by the bridle-rein so vehemently, that the other was constrained to void his saddle to save himself from being overthrown upon the ground.

And now each knight was as entirely furious as the other, wherefore, each drew his sword and dressed his shield, and thereupon rushed together like two wild bulls in battle. They foined, they smote, they traced, they parried, they struck again and again, and the sound of their blows, crashing and clashing the one upon the other, filled the entire surrounding space with an extraordinary uproar. Nor may any man altogether conceive of the entire fury of that encounter, for, because of the violence of the blows which the one delivered upon the other, whole cantels of armor were hewn from their bodies and many deep and grievous wounds were given and received, so that the armor of each was altogether stained with red because of the blood that flowed down upon it.

At last King Arthur, waxing, as it were, entirely mad, struck so fierce a blow that no armor could have withstood that stroke had it fallen fairly upon it. But it befell with that stroke that his sword broke at the hilt and the blade thereof flew into three several pieces into the air. Yet was the stroke so wonderfully fierce that the Sable Knight groaned, and staggered, and ran about in a circle as though he had gone blind and knew not whither to direct his steps.

But presently he recovered himself again, and perceiving King Arthur standing near by, and not knowing that his enemy had now no sword for to defend himself withal, he cast aside his shield and took his own sword into both hands, and therewith smote so dolorous a stroke that he clave through King Arthur's shield and through his helmet and even to the bone of his brain-pan.

Then King Arthur thought that he had received his death-wound, for his brains swam like water, his thighs trembled exceedingly, and he sank down to his knees, whilst the blood and sweat, commingled together in the darkness of his helmet, flowed down into his eyes in a lather and blinded him. Thereupon, seeing him thus grievously hurt, the Sable Knight called upon him with great vehemence for to yield himself and to surrender his shield, because he was now too sorely wounded for to fight any more.

But King Arthur would not yield himself, but catching the other by the sword-belt, he lifted himself to his feet. Then, being in a manner recovered from his amazement, he embraced the other with both arms, and placing his knee behind the thigh of the Sable Knight, he cast him backward down upon the ground so violently that the sound of the fall was astounding to hear. And with that fall the Sable Knight was, awhile, entirely bereft of consciousness. Then King Arthur straightway unlaced the helm of the Sable Knight and so beheld his face, and he knew him in spite of the blood that still ran down his own countenance in great quantities, and he knew that knight was King Pellinore, aforenamed in this history, who had twice warred against King Arthur. (It hath already been said how King Arthur had driven that other king from the habitations of men and into the forests, so that now he dwelt in this poor gloomy castle whence he waged war against all the knights who came unto that place.)

Now when King Arthur beheld whom it was against whom he had done battle, he cried out aloud, "Ha! Pellinore, is it then thou? Now yield thee to me, for thou art entirely at my mercy." And upon this he drew his misericordia and set the point thereof at King Pellinore's throat.

But by now King Pellinore had greatly recovered from his fall, and perceiving that the blood was flowing down in great measure from out his enemy's helmet, he wist that that other must have been very sorely wounded by the blow which he had just now received. Wherefore he catched King Arthur's wrist in his hand and directed the point of the dagger away from his own throat so that no great danger threatened therefrom.

And, indeed, what with his sore wound and with the loss of blood, King Arthur was now fallen exceedingly sick and faint, so that it appeared to him that he was nigh to death. Accordingly, it was with no very great ado that King Pellinore suddenly heaved himself up from the ground and so overthrew his enemy that King Arthur was now underneath his knees.

And by this King Pellinore was exceedingly mad with the fury of the sore battle he had fought. For he was so enraged that his eyes were all beshot with blood like those of a wild boar, and a froth, like the champings of a wild boar, stood in the beard about his lips. Wherefore he wrenched the dagger out of his enemy's hand, and immediately began to unlace his helm, with intent to slay him where he lay. But at this moment Merlin came in great haste, crying out, "Stay! Stay! Sir Pellinore; what would you be at? Stay your sacrilegious hand! For he who lieth beneath you is none other than Arthur, King of all this realm!"

At this King Pellinore was astonished beyond measure. And for a little he was silent, and then after awhile he cried out in a very loud voice, "Say you so, old man? Then verily your words have doomed this man unto death. For no one in all this world hath ever suffered such ill and such wrongs as I have suffered at his hands. For, lo! He hath taken from me power, and kingship, and honors, and estates, and hath left me only this gloomy, dismal castle of the forest as an abiding-place. Wherefore, seeing that he is thus in my power, he shall now presently die; if for no other reason than because if I now let him go free, he will certainly revenge himself when he shall have recovered from all the ill he hath suffered at my hands."

Then Merlin said, "Not so! He shall not die at thy hands, for I, myself, shall save him." Whereupon he uplifted his staff and smote King Pellinore across the shoulders. Then immediately King Pellinore fell down and lay upon the ground on his face like one who had suddenly gone dead.

Upon this, King Arthur uplifted himself upon his elbow and beheld his enemy lying there as though dead, and he cried out, "Ha! Merlin! what is this that thou hast done? I am very sorry, for I do perceive that thou, by thy arts of magic, hath slain one of the best knights in all the world."

"Not so, my lord King!" said Merlin; "For, in sooth, I tell thee that thou art far nigher to thy death than he. For he is but in sleep and will soon awaken; but thou art in such a case that it would take only a very little for to cause thee to die."

And indeed King Arthur was exceeding sick, even to the heart, with the sore wound he had received, so that it was only with much ado that Merlin could help him up upon his horse. Having done the which and having hung the King's shield upon the horn of his saddle, Merlin straightway conveyed the wounded man thence across the bridge, and, leading the horse by the bridle, so took him away into the forest.

Now I must tell you that there was in that part of the forest a certain hermit so holy that the wild birds of the woodland would come and rest upon his hand whiles he read his breviary; and so sanctified was he in gentleness that the wild does would come even to the door of his hermitage, and there stand whilst he milked them for his refreshment. And this hermit dwelt in that part of the forest so remote from the habitations of man that when he ran the bell for matins or for vespers, there was hardly ever anyone to hear the sound thereof excepting the wild creatures that dwelt thereabout. Yet, ne'theless, to this remote and lonely place royal folk and others of high degree would sometimes come, as though on a pilgrimage, because of the hermit's exceeding saintliness.

So Merlin conveyed King Arthur unto this sanctuary, and, having reached that place, he and the hermit lifted the wounded man down from his saddle – the hermit giving many words of pity and sorrow – and together they conveyed him into the holy man's cell. There they laid him upon a couch of moss and unlaced his armor and searched his wounds and bathed them with pure water and dressed his hurts, for that hermit was a very skilful leech. So for all that day and part of the next, King Arthur lay upon the hermit's pallet like one about to die; for he beheld all things about him as though through thin water, and the breath hung upon his lips and fluttered, and he could not even lift his head from the pallet because of the weakness that lay upon him.

Now upon the afternoon of the second day there fell a great noise and tumult in that part of the forest. For it happened that the Lady Guinevere of Cameliard, together with her Court, both of ladies and of knights, had come upon a pilgrimage to that holy man, the fame of whose saintliness had reached even unto the place where she dwelt. For that lady had a favorite page who was very sick of a fever, and she trusted that the holy man might give her some charm or amulet by the virtue of which he might haply be cured. Wherefore she had come to that place with her entire Court so that all that part of the forest was made gay with fine raiment and the silence thereof was made merry with the sound of talk and laughter and the singing of songs and the chattering of many voices and the neighing of horses. And the Lady Guinevere rode in the midst of her damsels and her Court, and her beauty outshone the beauty of her damsels as the splendor of the morning star outshines that of all the lesser stars that surround it. For then and afterward she was held by all the Courts of Chivalry to be the most beautiful lady in the world.

Now when the Lady Guinevere had come to that place, she perceived the milk-white war-horse of King Arthur where it stood cropping the green grass of the open glade nigh to the hermitage. And likewise she perceived Merlin, where he stood beside the door of the cell. So of him she demanded whose was that noble war-horse that stood browsing upon the grass at that lonely place, and who was it that lay within that cell. And unto her Merlin made answer, "Lady, he who lieth within is a knight, very sorely wounded, so that he is sick nigh unto death!"

"Pity of Heaven!" cried the Lady Guinevere. "What a sad thing is this that thou tellest me! Now I do beseech thee to lead me presently unto that knight that I may behold him. For I have in my Court a very skilful leech, who is well used to the cure of hurts such as knights receive in battle."

So Merlin brought the lady into the cell, and there she beheld King Arthur where he lay stretched upon the pallet. And she wist not who he was. Yet it appeared to her that in all her life she had not beheld so noble appearing a knight as he who lay sorely wounded in that lonely place. And King Arthur cast his looks upward to where she stood beside his bed of pain, surrounded by her maidens, and in the great weakness that lay upon him he wist not whether she whom he beheld was a mortal lady or whether she was not rather some tall straight angel who had descended from one of the Lordly Courts of Paradise for to visit him in his pain and distresses. And the Lady Guinevere was filled with a great pity at beholding King Arthur's sorrowful estate. Wherefore she called to her that skilful leech who was with her Court. And she bade him bring a certain alabaster box of exceedingly precious balsam. And she commanded him for to search that knight's wounds and to anoint them with the balsam, so that he might be healed of his hurts with all despatch.

So that wise and skilful leech did according to the Lady Guinevere's commands, and immediately King Arthur felt entire ease of all his aches and great content of spirit. And when the Lady and her Court had departed, he found himself much uplifted in heart, and three days thereafter he was entirely healed and was as well and strong and lusty as ever he had been in all of his life.

And this was the first time that King Arthur ever beheld that beautiful lady, the Lady Guinevere of Cameliard, and from that time forth he never forgot her, but she was almost always present in his thoughts. Wherefore, when he was recovered he said thus to himself: "I will forget that I am a king and I will cherish the thought of this lady and will serve her faithfully as a good knight may serve his chosen dame."

Chapter III

How King Arthur Found a Noble Sword in a Very Wonderful Manner. And How He Again Fought With It and Won That Battle.

NOW, as soon as King Arthur had, by means of that extraordinary balsam, been thus healed of those grievous wounds which he had received in his battle with King Pellinore, he found himself to be moved by a most-vehement desire to meet his enemy again for to try issue of battle with him once more, and so recover the credit which he had lost in that combat. Now, upon the morning of the fourth day, being entirely cured, and having broken his fast, he walked for refreshment beside the skirts of the forest, listening the while to the cheerful sound of the wood-birds singing their matins, all with might and main. And Merlin walked beside him, and King Arthur spake his mind to Merlin concerning his intent to engage once more in knightly contest with King Pellinore. And he said, "Merlin, it doth vex me very sorely for to have come off so ill in my late encounter with king Pellinore. Certes, he is the very best knight in all the world whom I have ever yet encountered. Ne'theless, it might have fared differently with me had I not broken my sword, and so left myself altogether defenceless in that respect. Howsoever that may be, I am of a mind for to assay this adventure once more, and so will I do as immediately as may be."

Thereunto Merlin made reply, "Thou art, assuredly, a very brave man to have so much appetite for battle, seeing how nigh thou camest unto thy death not even four days ago. Yet how mayst thou hope to undertake this adventure without due preparation? For, lo! Thou hast no sword, nor hast thou a spear, nor hast thou even thy misericordia for to do battle withal. How then mayst thou hope for to assay this adventure?"

And King Arthur said, "That I know not, nevertheless I will presently seek for some weapon as soon as may be. For, even an I have no better weapon than an oaken cudgel, yet would I assay this battle again with so poor a tool as that."

"Ha! Lord," said Merlin, "I do perceive that thou art altogether fixed in thy purpose for to renew this quarrel. Wherefore, I will not seek to stay thee therefrom, but will do all that in me lies for to aid thee in thy desires. Now to this end I must tell thee that in one part of this forest (which is, indeed, a very strange place) there is a certain woodland sometimes called Arroy, and other times called the Forest of Adventure. For no knight ever entereth therein but some adventure befalleth him. And close to Arroy is a land of enchantment which has several times been seen. And that is a very wonderful land, for there is in it a wide and considerable lake, which is also of enchantment. And in the centre of that lake there hath for some time been seen the appearance as of a woman's arm – exceedingly beautiful and clad in white samite, and the hand of this arm holdeth a sword of such exceeding excellence and beauty that no Merlin telleth eye hath ever beheld its like. And the name of this sword is Excalibur – it being so named by those who have beheld it because of its marvellous brightness and beauty. For it hath come to pass that several knights have already seen that sword and have endeavored to obtain it for their own, but, heretofore, no one hath been able to touch it, and many have lost their lives in that adventure. For when any man draweth near unto it, either he sinks into the lake, or else the arm disappeareth entirely, or else it is withdrawn beneath the lake; wherefore no man hath ever been able to obtain the possession of that sword. Now I am able to conduct thee unto that Lake of Enchantment, and there thou mayst see Excalibur with thine own eyes. Then when thou hist seen him thou mayst, haply, have the desire to obtain him; which, an thou art able to do, thou wilt have a sword very fitted for to do battle with."

"Merlin," quoth the King, "this is a very strange thing which thou tellest me. Now I am desirous beyond measure for to attempt to obtain this sword for mine own, wherefore I do beseech thee to lead me with all despatch to this enchanted lake whereof thou tellest me." And Merlin said, "I will do so."

So that morning King Arthur and Merlin took leave of that holy hermit (the King having kneeled in the grass to receive his benediction), and so, departing from that place, they entered the deeper forest once more, betaking their way to that part which was known as Arroy.

And after awhile they came to Arroy, and it was about noon-tide. And when they had entered into those woodlands they came to a certain little open place, and in that place they beheld a white doe with a golden collar about its neck. And King Arthur said, "Look, Merlin, yonder is a wonderful soft." And Merlin said, "Let us follow that doe." And upon this the doe turned and they followed it. And by and by in following it they came to an opening in the trees where was a little lawn of sweet soft grass. Here they beheld a bower and before the bower was a table spread with a fair snow-white cloth, and set with refreshments of white bread, wine, and meats of several sorts. And at the door of this bower there stood a page, clad all in green, and his hair was as black as ebony, and his eyes as black as jet and exceeding bright. And when this page beheld King Arthur and Merlin, he gave them greeting, and welcomed the King very pleasantly saying, "Ha! King Arthur, thou art welcome to this place. Now I prithee dismount and refresh thyself before going farther."

Then was King Arthur a-doubt as to whether there might not be some enchantment in this for to work him an ill, for he was astonished that that page in the deep forest should know him so well. But Merlin bade him have good cheer, and he said, "Indeed, Lord, thou mayst freely partake of that refreshment which, I may tell thee, was prepared especially for thee. Moreover in this thou mayst foretell a very happy issue unto this adventure."

So King Arthur sat down to the table with great comfort of heart (for he was an hungered) and that page and another like unto him ministered unto his needs, serving him all the food upon silver plates, and all the wine in golden goblets, as he was used to being served in his own court – only that those things were much more cunningly wrought and fashioned, and were more beautiful than the table furniture of the King's court.

Then, after he had eaten his fill and had washed his hands – from a silver basin which the first page offered to him, and had wiped his hands upon a fine linen napkin which the other page brought unto him, and after Merlin had also refreshed himself, they went their way, greatly rejoicing at this pleasant adventure, which, seemed to the King, could not but betoken a very good issue to his undertaking.

Now about the middle of the afternoon King Arthur and Merlin came, of a sudden, out from the forest and upon a fair and level plain, bedight all over with such a number of flowers that no man could conceive of their quantity nor of the beauty thereof.

And this was a very wonderful land, for, lo! All the air appeared as it were to be as of gold – so bright was it and so singularly radiant. And here and there upon that plain were sundry trees all in blossom; and the fragrance of the blossoms was so sweet that the King had never smelt any fragrance like to it. And in the branches of those trees were a multitude of birds of many colors, and the melody of their singing ravished the heart of the hearer. And midway in the plain was a lake of water as bright as silver, and all around the borders of the lake were incredible numbers of lilies and of daffodils. Yet, although this place was so exceedingly fair, there was, nevertheless, nowhere about it a single sign of human life of any sort, but it appeared altogether as lonely as the hollow sky upon a day of summer. So, because of all the marvellous beauty of this place, and because of its strangeness and its entire solitude, King Arthur perceived that he must have come into a land of powerful enchantment where, happily, dwelt a fairy of very exalted quality; wherefore his spirit was enwrapped in a manner of fear, as he pushed his great milk-white war-horse through that long fair grass, all bedight with flowers, and he wist not what strange things were about to befall him.

So when he had come unto the margin of the lake he beheld there the miracle that Merlin had told him of aforetime. For, lo! In the midst of the expanse of water there was the appearance of a fair and beautiful arm, as of a woman, clad all in white samite. And the arm was encircled with several bracelets of wrought gold; and the hand held a sword of marvellous workmanship aloft in the air above the surface of the water; and neither the arm nor the sword moved so much as a hairsbreadth, but were motionless like to a carven image upon the surface of the lake. And, behold! the sun of that strange land shone down upon the hilt of the sword, and it was of pure gold beset with jewels of several sorts, so that the hilt of the sword and the bracelets that encircled the arm glistered in the midst of the lake like to some singular star of exceeding splendor. And King Arthur sat upon his war-horse and gazed from a distance at the arm and the sword, and he greatly marvelled thereat; yet he wist not how he might come at that sword, for the lake was wonderfully wide and deep, wherefore he knew not how he might come thereunto for to make it his own. And as he sat pondering this thing within himself, he was suddenly aware of a strange lady, who approached him through those tall flowers that bloomed along the margin of the lake. And when he perceived her coming toward him he quickly dismounted from his war-horse and he went forward for to meet her with the bridle-rein over his arm. And when he had come nigh to her, he perceived that she was extraordinarily beautiful, and that her face was like wax for clearness, and that her eyes were perfectly black, and that they were as bright and glistening as though they were two jewels set in ivory. And he perceived that her hair was like silk and as black as it was possible to be, and so long that it reached unto the ground as she walked. And the lady was clad all in green – only that a fine cord of crimson and gold was interwoven into the plaits of her hair. And around her neck there hung a very beautiful necklace of several strands of opal stones and emeralds, set in cunningly wrought gold; and around her wrists were bracelets of the like sort – of opal stones and emeralds set into gold. So when King Arthur beheld her wonderful appearance, that it was like to an ivory statue of exceeding beauty clad all in green, he immediately kneeled before her in the midst of all those flowers as he said, "I do certainly perceive that thou art no mortal damoiselle, but that thou art Fay. Also that this place, because of its extraordinary beauty, can be no other than some land of Faerie into which I have entered."

And the Lady replied, "King Arthur, thou sayest soothly, for I am indeed Faerie. Moreover, I may tell thee that my name is Nymue, and that I am the chiefest of those Ladies of the Lake of whom thou mayst have heard people speak. Also thou art to know that what thou beholdest yonder as a wide lake is, in truth, a plain like unto this, all bedight with flowers. And likewise thou art to know that in the midst of that plain there standeth a castle of white marble and of ultramarine illuminated with gold. But, lest mortal eyes should behold our dwelling-place, my sisters and I have caused it to be that this appearance as of a lake should extend all over that castle so that it is entirely hidden from sight. Nor may any mortal man cross that lake, saving in one way – otherwise he shall certainly perish therein."

"Lady," said King Arthur, "that which thou tellest me causes me to wonder a very great deal. And, indeed, I am afraid that in coming hitherward I have been doing amiss for to intrude upon the solitude of your dwelling-place."

"Nay, not so, King Arthur," said the Lady of the Lake, "for, in truth, thou art very welcome hereunto. Moreover, I may tell thee that I have a greater friendliness for thee and those noble knights of thy court than thou canst easily wot of. But I do beseech thee of thy courtesy for to tell me what it is that brings thee to our land?"

"Lady," quoth the King, "I will tell thee the entire truth. I fought of late a battle with a certain sable knight, in the which I was sorely and grievously wounded, and wherein I burst my spear and snapped my sword and lost even my misericordia, so that I had not a single thing left me by way of a weapon. In this extremity Merlin, here, told me of Excalibur, and of how he is continually upheld by an arm in the midst of this magical lake. So I came hither and, behold, I find it even as he hath said. Now, Lady, an it be possible, I would fain achieve that excellent sword, that, by means of it I might fight my battle to its entire end."

"Ha! My lord King," said the Lady of the Lake, "that sword is no easy thing for to achieve, and, moreover, I may tell thee that several knights have lost their lives by attempting that which thou hast a mind to do. For, in sooth, no man may win yonder sword unless he be without fear and without reproach."

"Alas, Lady!" quoth King Arthur, "that is indeed a sad saying for me. For, though I may not lack in knightly courage, yet, in truth, there be many things wherewith I do reproach myself withal. Ne'theless, I would fain attempt this thing, even an it be to my great endangerment. Wherefore' I prithee tell me how I may best undertake this adventure."

"King Arthur," said the Lady of the Lake, "I will do what I say to aid thee in thy wishes in this matter." Whereupon she lifted a single emerald that hung by a small chain of gold at her girdle and, lo! The emerald was cunningly carved into the form of a whistle. And she set the whistle to her lips and blew upon it very shrilly. Then straightway there appeared upon the water, a great way off, a certain thing that shone very brightly. And this drew near with great speed, and as it came nigh, behold! it was a boat all of carven brass. And the prow of the boat was carved into the form of a head of a beautiful woman, and upon either side were wings like the wings of a swan. And the boat moved upon the water like a swan – very swiftly – so that long lines, like to silver threads, stretched far away behind, across the face of the water, which otherwise was like unto glass for smoothness. And when the brazen boat had reached the bank it rested there and moved no more.

Then the Lady of the Lake bade King Arthur to enter the boat, and so he entered it. And immediately he had done so, the boat moved away from the bank as swiftly as it had come thither. And Merlin and the Lady of the Lake stood upon the margin of the water, and gazed after King Arthur and the brazen boat.

And King Arthur beheld that the boat floated swiftly across the lake to where was the arm uplifting the sword, and that the arm and the sword moved not but remained where they were.

Then King Arthur reached forth and took the sword in his hand, and immediately the arm disappeared beneath the water, and King Arthur held the sword and the scabbard thereof and the belt thereof in his hand and, lo! They were his own.

Then verily his heart swelled with joy an it would burst within his bosom, for Excalibur was an hundred times more beautiful than he had thought possible. Wherefore his heart was nigh breaking for pure joy at having obtained that magic sword.

Then the brazen boat bore him very quickly back to the land again and he stepped ashore where stood the Lady of the Lake and Merlin. And when he stood upon the shore, he gave the Lady great thanks beyond measure for all that she had done for to aid him in his great undertaking; and she gave him cheerful and pleasing words in reply.

Then King Arthur saluted the lady, as became him, and, having mounted his war-horse, and Merlin having mounted his palfrey, they rode away thence upon their business – the King's heart still greatly expanded with pure delight at having for his own that beautiful sword – the most beautiful and the most famous sword in all the world.

That night King Arthur and Merlin abided with the holy hermit at the forest sanctuary, and when the next morning had come (the King having bathed himself in the ice-cold forest fountain, and being exceedingly refreshed thereby) they took their departure, offering thanks to that saintly man for the harborage he had given them.

Anon, about noon-tide, they reached the valley of the Sable Knight, and there were all things appointed exactly as when King Arthur had been there before: to wit, that gloomy castle, the lawn of smooth grass, the apple tree covered over with shields, and the bridge whereon hung that single shield of sable.

"Now, Merlin," quoth King Arthur, "I do this time most strictly forbid thee for to interfere in this quarrel. Nor shalt thou, under pain of my displeasure, exert any of thy arts of magic in my behalf. So hearken thou to what I say, and heed it with all possible diligence."

Thereupon, straightway, the King rode forth upon the bridge and, seizing the brazen mall, he smote upon the sable shield with all his might and main. Immediately the portcullis of the castle was let fall as afore told and, in the same manner as that other time, the Sable Knight rode forth therefrom, already bedight and equipped for the encounter. So he came to the bridgehead and there King Arthur spake to him in this wise: "Sir Pellinore, we do now know one another entirely well, and each doth judge that he hath cause of quarrel with the other: thou, that I, for mine own reasons as seemed to me to be fit, have taken away from thee thy kingly estate, and have driven thee into this forest solitude: I, that thou has set thyself up here for to do injury and affront to knights and lords and other people of this kingdom of mine. Wherefore, seeing that I am here as an errant Knight, I do challenge thee for to fight with me, man to man, until either thou or I have conquered the other."

Unto this speech King Pellinore bowed his head in obedience, and thereupon he wheeled his horse, and, riding to some little distance, took his place where he had afore stood. And King Arthur also rode to some little distance, and took his station where he had afore stood. At the same time there came forth from the castle one of those tall pages clad all in sable, pied with crimson, and gave to King Arthur a good, stout spear of ash-wood, well seasoned and untried in battle; and when the two Knights were duly prepared, they shouted and drave their horses together, the one smiting the other so fairly in the midst of his defences that the spears shivered in the hand of each, bursting all into small splinters as they had aforetime done.

Then each of these two knights immediately voided his horse with great skill and address, and drew each his sword. And thereupon they fell to at a combat, so furious and so violent, that two wild bulls upon the mountains could not have engaged in a more desperate encounter.

But now, having Excalibur for to aid him in his battle, King Arthur soon overcame his enemy. For he gave him several wounds and yet received none himself, nor did he shed a single drop of blood in all that fight, though his enemy's armor was in a little while all stained with crimson. And at last King Arthur delivered so vehement a stroke that King Pellinore was entirely benumbed thereby, wherefore his sword and his shield fell down from their defence, his thighs trembled beneath him and he sank unto his knees upon the ground, Then he called upon King Arthur to have mercy, saying, "Spare my life and I will yield myself unto thee."

And King Arthur said, "I will spare thee and I will do more than that. For now that thou hast yielded thyself unto me, lo! I will restore unto thee thy power and estate. For I bear no ill-will toward thee, Pellinore, ne'theless, I can brook no rebels against my power in this realm. For, as God judges me, I do declare that I hold singly in my sight the good of the people of my kingdom. Wherefore, he who is against me is also against them, and he who is against them is also against me. But now that thou hast acknowledged me I will take thee into my favor. Only as a pledge of thy good faith toward me in the future, I shall require it of thee that thou shalt send me as hostage of thy good-will, thy two eldest sons, to wit: Sir Aglaval and Sir Lamorack. Thy young son, Dornar, thou mayest keep with thee for thy comfort."

So those two young knights above mentioned came to the Court of King Arthur, and they became very famous knights, and by and by were made fellows in great honor of the Round Table.

And King Arthur and King Pellinore went together into the castle of King Pellinore, and there King Pellinore's wounds were dressed and he was made comfortable. That night King Arthur abode in the castle of King Pellinore, and when the next morning had come, he and Merlin returned unto the Court of the King, where it awaited him in the forest at that place where he had established it.

Now King Arthur took very great pleasure unto himself as he and Merlin rode together in return through that forest; for it was the leafiest time of all the year, what time the woodlands decked themselves in their best apparel of clear, bright green. Each bosky dell and dingle was full of the perfume of the thickets, and in every tangled depth the small bird sang with all his might and main, and as though he would burst his little throat with the melody of his singing. And the ground beneath the horses' feet was so soft with fragrant moss that the ear could not hear any sound of hoof-beats upon the earth. And the bright yellow sunlight came down through the leaves so that all the ground was scattered over with a great multitude of trembling circles as of pure yellow gold. And, anon, that sunlight would fall down upon the armed knight as he rode, so that every little while his armor appeared to catch fire with a great glory, shining like a sudden bright star amid the dark shadows of the woodland.

So it was that King Arthur took great joy in that forest land, for he was without ache or pain of any sort and his heart was very greatly elated with the wonderfulness of the success of that adventure into which he had entered. For in that adventure he had not only won a very bitter enemy into a friend who should be of great usefulness and satisfaction to him, but likewise, he had obtained for himself a sword, the like of which the world had never before beheld. And whenever he would think of that singularly splendid sword which now hung by his side, and whenever he remembered that land of Faerie into which he had wandered, and of that which had befallen him therein, his heart would become so greatly elated with pure joyousness that he hardly knew how to contain himself because of the great delight that filled his entire bosom.

And, indeed, I know of no greater good that I could wish for you in all of your life than to have you enjoy such happiness as cometh to one when he hath done his best endeavor and hath succeeded with great entirety in his undertaking. For then all the world appears to be filled as with a bright shining light, and the body seemeth to become so elated that the feet are uplifted from heaviness and touch the earth very lightly because of the lightness of the spirit within. Wherefore, it is, that if I could have it in my power to give you the very best that the world hath to give, I would wish that you might win your battle as King Arthur won his battle at that time, and that you might ride homeward in such triumph and joyousness as filled him that day, and that the sunlight might shine around you as it shone around him, and that the breezes might blow and that all the little birds might sing with might and main as they sang for him, and that your heart also might sing its song of rejoicing in the pleasantness of the world in which you live.

Now as they rode thus through the forest together, Merlin said to the King: "Lord, which wouldst thou rather have, Excalibur, or the sheath that holds him?" To which King Arthur replied, "Ten thousand times would I rather have Excalibur than his sheath." "In that thou art wrong, my Lord," said Merlin, "for let me tell thee, that though Excalibur is of so great a temper that he may cut in twain either a feather or a bar of iron, yet is his sheath of such a sort that he who wears it can suffer no wound in battle, neither may he lose a single drop of blood. In witness whereof, thou mayst remember that, in thy late battle with King Pellinore, thou didst suffer no wound, neither didst thou lose any blood."

Then King Arthur directed a countenance of great displeasure upon his companion and he said, "Now, Merlin, I do declare that thou hast taken from me the entire glory of that battle which I have lately fought. For what credit may there be to any knight who fights his enemy by means of enchantment such as thou tellest me of? And, indeed, I am minded to take this glorious sword back to that magic lake and to cast it therein where it belongeth; for I believe that a knight should fight by means of his own strength, and not by means of magic."

"My Lord," said Merlin, "assuredly thou art entirely right in what thou holdest. But thou must bear in mind that thou art not as an ordinary errant knight, but that thou art a King, and that thy life belongeth not unto thee, but unto thy people. Accordingly thou hast no right to imperil it, but shouldst do all that lieth in thy power for to preserve it. Wherefore thou shouldst keep that sword so that it may safeguard thy life."

Then King Arthur meditated that saying for a long while in silence; and when he spake it was in this wise: "Merlin, thou art right in what thou sayest, and, for the sake of my people, I will keep both Excalibur for to fight for them, and likewise his sheath for to preserve my life for their sake. Ne'theless, I will never use him again saving in serious battle." And King Arthur held to that saying, so that thereafter he did no battle in sport excepting with lance and a-horseback.

King Arthur kept Excalibur as the chiefest treasure of all his possessions. For he said to himself, "Such a sword as this is fit for a king above other kings and a lord above other lords. Now, as God hath seen fit for to intrust that sword into my keeping in so marvellous a manner as fell about, so must He mean that I am to be His servant for to do unusual things. Wherefore I will treasure this noble weapon not more for its excellent worth than because it shall be unto me as a sign of those great things that God, in His mercy, hath evidently ordained for me to perform for to do Him service."

So King Arthur had made for Excalibur a strong chest or coffer, bound around with many bands of wrought iron, studded all over with great nails of iron, and locked with three great padlocks. In this strong-box he kept Excalibur lying upon a cushion of crimson silk and wrapped in swathings of fine linen, and very few people ever beheld the sword in its glory excepting when it shone like a sudden flame in the uproar of battle.

For when the time came for King Arthur to defend his realm or his subjects from their enemies, then he would take out the sword, and fasten it upon the side of his body; and when he did so he was like unto a hero of God girt with a blade of shining lightning. Yea; at such times Excalibur shone with so terrible a brightness that the very sight thereof would shake the spirits of every wrong-doer with such great fear that he would, in a manner, suffer the pangs of death ere ever the edge of the blade had touched his flesh.

So King Arthur treasured Excalibur and the sword remained with him for all of his life, wherefore the name of Arthur and of Excalibur are one. So, I believe that that sword is the most famous of any that ever was seen or heard tell of in all the Courts of Chivalry.

As for the sheath of the blade, King Arthur lost that through the treachery of one who should, by rights, have been his dearest friend (as you shall hear of anon), and in the end the loss of that miraculous sheath brought it about that he suffered a very great deal of pain and sorrow.

All that also you shall read of, God willing, in due season.

So endeth the story of the winning of Excalibur, and may God give unto you in your life, that you may have His truth to aid you, like a shining sword, for to overcome your enemies; and may He give you Faith (for Faith containeth Truth as a scabbard containeth its sword), and may that Faith heal all your wounds of sorrow as the sheath of Excalibur healed all the wounds of him who wore that excellent weapon. For with Truth and Faith girded upon you, you shall be as well able to fight all your battles as did that noble hero of old, whom men called King Arthur.

Taking Care of Business

Victoria Sandbrook

STEAM-POWERED gates hissed open, inviting the silent ticket holders up to the mansion's dark facade. Anna's indecision held her feet fast to the wet pavement as the others shuffled forward around her. They were outside one of Tom Norman's store fronts to gape at freaks; in that there would have been no shame. This one-act curiosity show had every mama and vicar in London throwing fits. And Anna had already been. Twice.

But the show's *artiste* was claiming more and more of Anna's thoughts, and staying away the past week had only made the wanting worse. He was worth the risk of sure ruin if an acquaintance saw her in the crowd. So little stood between them now that she'd even paid the steam-hack to wait around the corner.

Anna squared her shoulders and shuffled down the path with the others. The men wore their woolen jacket collars high beneath their top hats, and the women pulled their coats and scarves tightly over evening silks. Any of them might have been more or less respectable than she, an MP's eldest daughter, but they had all arrived as nondescript as they could manage. In such anonymity they could stare and gawk and ogle all they wanted. But none of them understood him like Anna did.

At the front door, Anna smiled and placed her blank ticket in the maid's extended mech hand. The iron-jawed bio-mech didn't smile back. Anna didn't care; at least she'd tried to be polite. A custom-wired plate in the mechanical palm heated the thick stub until brown stains formed on the ticket: a lightning bolt and the letters T, C, and B. The bio-mech woman waved Anna further inside with a creak of cheaply oiled joints. There was no mech to take her coat; after all, the show wasn't long. A forbidden thrill coursed through Anna. Leaving now would only draw attention.

The line of attendees trickled into the sprawling salon. The richly papered walls recessed into the shadows. A gas-lit chandelier hung in the middle, throwing off a dim, mellow light. Fifty-some chairs formed tight crescent rows around a tall figure on a pedestal.

Black silk, draping to the floor, obscured the form's finer details. Anna knew better than anyone the shape of his head, the line of his shoulder, the angle of his elbow, covered or no. Her fingers itched to pull the silk away, so much that she almost allowed her feet to carry her towards him, but she distracted herself from her fluttering heart by looking for a good seat.

There weren't many options – she'd wanted something with a good view, but near an end. She sank into a chair in the third row and looked up to see the plume of a hat obscuring the pedestal. Anna clenched her teeth. After a quick glance around, she shifted her chair into the aisle slightly. Someone behind her coughed. Anna went cold with fear.

She moved the chair back without turning around. If she craned her neck just so, she could pretend nothing was amiss. It would have to do.

The doctor entered the room from a door behind the figure. He walked with his arms folded across his chest, his dark eyebrows drawn together. He stopped near the figure and looked out to the crowd.

"Ladies and gentlemen," he said, "tonight I present to you an extraordinary show. Some of you may have seen curiosities rolled out as acts at the theater. Some of you may have seen the novelties of my good colleague Mr. Norman. But unless you have been here before – and I know some of you have …" Anna's heart skipped a beat, but he continued without looking at her. "– unless you have been here before you have never seen anything quite so …" He paused and smiled. "…electrifying as the curiosity I have for you this evening.

"This marvel defies everything you know about our modern capabilities. He is not some humble chimera like the bio-mechs that sweep your streets and polish your shoes, but an Adonis. In his own time, even Aphrodite would not be able to resurrect him, but our noble science pulled him back across the temporal river and breathed life into him."

Anna licked her lips and held her breath.

The doctor's fingers closed on the fabric. An age could have passed in her mind before he continued.

"I give you the one, the only …The King!" And he pulled the silk off the figure with a single sweep of his arm.

And there he was: the one who kept her heart beating fast in daylight and darkness. The gaslight echoed off of the jewels on the breast and collar of his pure white suit. His bio-mechanical right arm was bare, a knotted mass of gears and pistons extending to a hinged elbow, a pivoted wrist, and stiff, jointed digits. Thin rubber hoses connected various parts, pulsing and pumping with some unknown fluid, all running back under the cloth at his shoulder. Through the material of the left leg of his trousers, a light blinked every so often, belying the machinery beneath. And on his feet: a pair of suede shoes in the most remarkable shade of sapphire.

How much of him was man and how much was mech, Anna had yet to discover. Her insides twisted and shivered at the prospect of seeing more of him. She took as big a breath as her corset would allow and let it out slowly. She shouldn't enjoy this – it was unseemly, unnatural, unholy – but she could never turn away.

The bio-mech's blue eyes glowed beneath lowered lids, not focusing on anything in particular as the mechanical bits of his torso and limbs whirred and hissed to life. His skin was pale, but a muscle in his firm jaw twitched; he swallowed and blinked. His head, at least, was human. His right side jerked and repositioned itself slightly. He ran his still-human left hand through his thick black hair and bit his lower lip. Anna bit her own lip and sat on the edge of her chair. A strand of hair fell onto his brow as he lifted the strangely-shaped guitar slung over his shoulder. She saw his chest rise and fall once – a steadying breath – was he as nervous as she? – and then he placed his fingers on the frets and breathed in.

The music was otherworldly: four simple strummed notes that skipped and rolled and hiccupped and pulsed. Everything about it was motion, building, cycling, and building again. Was all music like this where or when he was from? How anyone could think straight if it was? And just as Anna thought her heart was catching up, the bio-mech added his voice to the mix.

She still couldn't breathe when she heard his smooth, deep baritone. His mouth formed words in a syncopated murmur that gripped the bottom of her ribcage and lured her forward. His head swung with the beat, keeping time until his shoulders joined in, loose and languid. Then he looked up into the audience, straight into the eyes of some fortunate woman as he crooned, "Don't be cruel ...."

Anna's hands gripped the seat of her chair until her fingers hurt, her mouth shaping the now-familiar lyrics in silence. He couldn't see her. If he had seen her, he would be singing to her. She needed him to see her.

The song's second verse ended and the bio-mech moved his weight onto his toes and twisted his heels once, a sharp precursor to what was to come. Anna couldn't keep herself from smiling as the chords changed and the music mirrored the rocking of his hips. He leaned forward for a few words then stood up straight on the phrase's last beat. He leaned forward again for the next line, and Anna leaned toward him. And as he straightened, his eyes found her.

She gasped, dizzy with glee as she looked into his eyes. He smiled a bit more, as she'd always hoped someone would smile at her. Not the way normal men leered at normal women. The King was of that elusive breed of gentlemen that frequented the pages of novels but not the streets of London. He was the type to bring her flowers and enjoy cigars with Father and kiss her hand goodnight. She could tell from his smile.

He had to look elsewhere then; Anna knew he had to please the crowd. But he'd conveyed volumes in that brief moment. He'd been thinking of her, too.

The song drove on, the heads in front of her dipped and rocked to the beat. Someone in the crowd started clapping in time. The pulse, muted by gloves and propriety, spread through the room, infectious and undeniable. The music crested and the song ended, accompanied by polite applause and a few indiscreet whoops.

"Thank you," the bio-mech said, modestly. "Thank you, ladies and gentleman." He stepped back into a neutral position, took a breath and looked up.

"This next song ..." He cleared his throat and leaned to the right, his mechanical knee whirring as it bent. "See, you gotta stand like this to sing this song because if you stand up straight you'll strip your gears, man." He looked at the floor, his shoulders tensing in an inaudible chuckle at his own words. His hair fell further over his brow; Anna fought the urge to stand and brush it away.

The bio-mech's face tightened into a sly smile that pulled his mouth to one side and collected in the wrinkles around his eyes. She liked this side of him: impish, playful. His hands were at the ready. And before his strumming even joined in, he unleashed his voice upon the crowd.

Anna hadn't heard this one about the 'hound dog' before. She bit her lip and smiled up at him. This ...this was the song he chose to sing after seeing her again! She needed to know what it meant. But until then she could watch him move. She could watch him move forever.

All motion flowed from the lower half of his body. His hips rocked his weight onto his toes, then his heels. They led and the rest of him followed, a duet in a single body, thrusting the guitar out toward the audience on the downbeats. His knees worked in concert, bending and straightening, then teasing toward each other for a moment as if drawn by a magnet before flying outward again.

Anna's heart was in her throat. She pressed her legs together; she would come apart at the seams otherwise. How could she say goodbye to him after this? How could she live, only seeing him in these brief, forbidden moments?

The crowd burst into another round of clapping, then everyone was on their feet. Anna couldn't see over the shoulders in front of her, so she walked in front of them all, staying closer to the seats than to the pedestal. They'd never been this close. For the first time, there was no one standing between them. She smiled until her ears hurt.

He kept time with his right heel, leaning deeply into his enhanced knee, the left swinging freely to match. And then he looked down at her and winked.

She clasped her hands to her heart and screamed. All of the unbridled excitement inside her projected into that shrill affirmation of his power over her. He couldn't possibly doubt her adoration.

But as Anna's breath ran short, the others joined in. Lace fans worked furiously to cool flushed skin as women's giggles and shrieks mingled with gruff coughs and grumbles of clapping men. The King's smile grew in the glow of their obvious esteem. Anna's stomach lurched. Surely he didn't love them more than her. She was sure of it.

After the second verse, he stopped singing and channeled everything he had into the music and the dance. Forward went the hips; sideways, backwards, rolling forward again. His human and mechanical joints both circled smoothly over strong legs, always bent. His hips gyrated in ways Anna would not have thought possible. She wanted to match that movement, to be the guitar he so lovingly strummed. Her bosoms pressed against her bodice and her mouth was dry.

Three other women – now five, no six – were shouldering Anna out of the way, screaming, swooning until she could barely hear the music at all. One chit threw her handkerchief at him; Anna had to fist her hands to keep from tearing the trollop's cap from her head. He picked it up without missing a beat. There was no time to waste, it seemed.

Anna pushed her way back to the front, not caring who she jostled or how hard. The women to either side of her squealed in protest, but it was no matter: Anna was so close to him she could smell his machine oil. When he bent his knees, his metal hand grazing the strings was level with her face. His heels tapped and his hips rocked until Anna couldn't help herself.

Anna reached out, grabbed his mechanical hand, and pulled herself up onto the pedestal. The bio-mech stopped singing abruptly, jaw slack and eyes wide when he looked at her. She slipped her hand behind his neck and pulled him down for a kiss. Her fingers discovered knobs and wires along the back of his neck, but his lips were soft, entirely human. Not at all demanding or overpowering. The doctor was right: he was the King. He was *her* King.

Hands knotted in Anna's coat and skirts to pull her backward. She clung to him with her arms and teeth. He was hers. Hers to save from the rabid crowds. Hers to bring home to her parents.

Her assailants' burly mech arms were winning out over her devotion. Her hand found the King's lapel, warm from the bio-mech components and his exertion. A hose threaded through a small hole, connecting the mech to the man. This couldn't be the last time she touched him. They would be happy together. He would dance and sing for her every night. It would just take time and patience. Or something bolder than she'd ever dared …

Her finger looped around the hose and tore.

The bio-mech servants severed her grip with brute force. Dark, warm viscous liquid splattered Anna from hem to hair. She licked a drop off her lip and gasped as her love toppled backward into the frenzied mob behind the pedestal. Everyone else in the audience was screaming, fighting for the chance to touch the King. Anna flailed, unable to do more than kick her own skirts about as she howled after him.

His mechanical hand grappled for the edge of the pedestal. He pulled himself upright again, his human limb cradling the guitar. He placed the instrument on the platform. His eyes, now as wide and round as they were bright and blue, met Anna's. A sharp pain ate at her stomach when she saw his misery.

More mechs with batons streamed into the room. A servant's metal-clad arm looped around Anna's waist and hauled her away.

Anna wiggled and writhed, but his arm was too strong and when they were free of the crowd, she was over the man's shoulder. From this perch, she could see the King. Black oil pulsed onto his white jacket, which was ripped down his torso exposing metal and wire and gears. She wanted to tell him that all would be well, that she'd fix everything, reconnect the hoses, mend his suit by the fireside while he read the evening news. She could almost feel the metal beneath her hands.

Two bouncers looped the King's arms around their shoulders and carried him away. He looked back for a brief moment and Anna's heart fluttered. He wanted to make sure she was alright!

But his eyes went to the guitar, still untouched and forgotten atop the pedestal. The tension in his face eased, and his head hung forward as they hauled him out of the room.

With every step, the servant carried Anna further and further away from the mob. Her heart pounded in her ears. It was done; they'd never let her see him again. She looked down at the hose clenched in her fist. How would she go on without him?

"So vulgar!" a woman in front of Anna said. "Just shameful for a man to move like that."

"No gentleman would," the woman's companion agreed, his mustache twitching. "Only a machine or savage could be so indecent in a public place."

A hundred harsh words welled up in Anna's throat. If they couldn't see the warmth and purpose behind all that metal, they were blind. He was just as invisible as she was, and it made her ache to her core.

She tugged on the back of the guard's coat. Maybe because he was a bio-mech, too …

"How can you listen to that?" she asked him over the din of the receding crowd.

"Can't get angry at the patrons, love," he said. She tried again to pull free, and he smacked her backside like it was nothing. "Settle down, pet. He worked finer fillies than you into a lather tonight."

Anna seethed. This one was just like the rest of them: base like the men and directionless like the mechs. And if he couldn't see, he wouldn't help her.

She pushed herself upwards until she could reach the back of his head.

He kept talking as if she were listening. "You poppets are too precious –"

Anna pulled a handful of tubes and wires out of his neck. He ground to a halt and stopped speaking. The last of the exiting crowd paid them no heed. The room was empty; the other servants must have been busy with patrons. This servant was gasping for air, his human parts revolting against the loss of the mech. He couldn't do more than mumble through his inoperable lips. If no one stumbled on the quickly fading hulk of crude engineering and morality in time to repair him, it would be no great loss.

Anna pried herself out of his grip. Oil dribbled down his back and pooled on the floor. She avoided the puddle as she climbed down, shed her soaked coat, and rearranged her wool skirts.

She was glad she'd thought to wear such nondescript attire. No one would pay a girl so plain any mind if she kept her head down. So very little stood between Anna and her love: what were dark hallways, a couple doors, a few mech servants easily dispatched? She licked her lips. She would find him, console him, reassure him that someone saw beneath his skin and mech. Fix him body and soul. She smiled as she stepped into the shadows at the edge of the room.

A trail of his oil led down a gas-lit corridor, past dark doors and silent rooms. Ahead, a servant bustled through swinging double doors into the hallway and hurried away. Anna darted ahead on silent feet, easing the swinging door closed behind her.

The bare-chested King was prone on a wheeled exam table. The doctor stood before him, hands and lab coat covered in oil, tools of his trade strewn about side tables and the floor. Anna froze, but the man didn't acknowledge her.

The King's mech was still; his skin pale. His blue eyes were dark and blank. His lips hung loose above his perfect, white teeth. She wanted to kiss them until he awoke.

But the doctor was between them. He was a man, not a mech. An unexpected hurdle. But it could not be harder to dispatch mortal life than it had been to end a mechanical one. Anna picked up a wrench with a head as big as her fist. She stepped forward. Then the doctor spoke.

"Hand me that plumber's wrench, Sophia."

He reached backwards and snapped twice. Anna's throat went dry. When she didn't move, the doctor turned.

"Where the devil is Sophia?"

Anna swallowed. "Kitchen?"

He snatched the tool out of her hand, and fit it over a huge nut above where the King's heart should be. After two turns, the doctor threw a switch in the middle of the mech's metal chest.

Lights blinked furtively. Gears whirred, stuttered, whirred again.

"Blast! Have you no will to live?" The doctor slammed his fist on the mech so hard, even the King's feet twitched. "I didn't bring you here to die again, damn it!"

The doctor's hand went back to the switch as an alarm cry met their ears. Anna's blood ran cold: they'd found the bio-mech servant in the salon. Feet ran past the door, and the doctor cursed again. He stood and wiped his hands on his coat.

"Shut him down," he said and brushed past her without waiting for a reply.

The doors rocked closed. The sounds of alarm retreated. There was only the pounding of Anna's heart and the weak hiccupping of the King's mech.

Alone! She flew to his side and brought her face close to his, running her hands across skin and mech. A gasp escaped her lips. His eyes flickered; he'd recognized her. She kissed his lips until they shuddered. She laughed, choking back tears of relief and joy.

"I'm here, my love," she whispered.

His lips twitched again and his lungs ground out an attempt at a sound. She watched carefully, stroking his face as he tried again and again to speak.

"He...lp." His eyes rolled toward the door and his fingers twitched toward the edge of the table. She took his hand. His voice got stronger. "Help."

"Yes," Anna assured him. "Yes, I'm here to help." She released the breaks on the table and turned it toward the doors.

She sped through hallways toward the back of the house where the steam-hack would be waiting.

The loading dock was deserted except for her driver. His eyebrows shot up when he saw the King.

"I ain't no hired thief, miss," he protested. "My hack's mech, but I ain't sunk that low yet."

"Get him in the back and keep to your own business," she told him, more calm and sure than she'd ever been. "He's mine."

My Aunt Margaret's Mirror

Walter Scott

Introduction

THE SPECIES of publication which has come to be generally known by the title of *Annual*, being a miscellany of prose and verse, equipped with numerous engravings, and put forth every year about Christmas, had flourished for a long while in Germany before it was imitated in this country by an enterprising bookseller, a German by birth, Mr. Ackermann. The rapid success of his work, as is the custom of the time, gave birth to a host of rivals, and, among others, to an Annual styled *The Keepsake*, the first volume of which appeared in 1828, and attracted much notice, chiefly in consequence of the very uncommon splendour of its illustrative accompaniments. The expenditure which the spirited proprietors lavished on this magnificent volume is understood to have been not less than from ten to twelve thousand pounds sterling!

Various gentlemen of such literary reputation that any one might think it an honour to be associated with them had been announced as contributors to this Annual, before application was made to me to assist in it; and I accordingly placed with much pleasure at the Editor's disposal a few fragments, originally designed to have been worked into the Chronicles of the Canongate, besides a manuscript drama, the long-neglected performance of my youthful days – 'The House of Aspen.'

The Keepsake for 1828 included, however, only three of these little prose tales, of which the first in order was that entitled 'My Aunt Margaret's Mirror.' By way of *Introduction* to this, when now included in a general collection of my lucubrations, I have only to say that it is a mere transcript, or at least with very little embellishment, of a story that I remembered being struck with in my childhood, when told at the fireside by a lady of eminent virtues and no inconsiderable share of talent, one of the ancient and honourable house of Swinton. She was a kind of relation of my own, and met her death in a manner so shocking – being killed, in a fit of insanity, by a female attendant who had been attached to her person for half a lifetime – that I cannot now recall her memory, child as I was when the catastrophe occurred, without a painful reawakening of perhaps the first images of horror that the scenes of real life stamped on my mind.

This good spinster had in her composition a strong vein of the superstitious, and was pleased, among other fancies, to read alone in her chamber by a taper fixed in a candlestick which she had had formed out of a human skull. One night this strange piece of furniture acquired suddenly the power of locomotion, and, after performing some odd circles on her chimney-piece, fairly leaped on the floor, and continued to roll about the apartment. Mrs. Swinton calmly proceeded to the adjoining room for another light, and had the satisfaction to penetrate the mystery on the spot. Rats abounded in the ancient building she inhabited, and one of these had managed to ensconce itself within her favourite *Memento Mori*. Though thus endowed with a more than feminine share of nerve, she entertained largely that belief in supernaturals which in those times was not considered as sitting ungracefully on the grave and aged of her condition; and the story of the Magic Mirror was one for which she vouched with particular confidence, alleging indeed that one of her own family had been an eye-witness of the incidents recorded in it.

"I tell the tale as it was told to me."

Stories now of much the same cast will present themselves to the recollection of such of my readers as have ever dabbled in a species of lore to which I certainly gave more hours, at one period of my life, than I should gain any credit by confessing.

August 1831.

Aunt Margaret's Mirror

*"There are times
When Fancy plays her gambols, in despite
Even of our watchful senses – when in sooth
Substance seems shadow, shadow substance seems –
When the broad, palpable, and mark'd partition
'Twixt that which is and is not seems dissolved,
As if the mental eye gain'd power to gaze
Beyond the limits of the existing world.
Such hours of shadowy dreams I better love
Than all the gross realities of life."*
Anonymous

MY AUNT MARGARET was one of that respected sisterhood upon whom devolve all the trouble and solicitude incidental to the possession of children, excepting only that which attends their entrance into the world. We were a large family, of very different dispositions and constitutions. Some were dull and peevish – they were sent to Aunt Margaret to be amused; some were rude, romping, and boisterous – they were sent to Aunt Margaret to be kept quiet, or rather that their noise might be removed out of hearing; those who were indisposed were sent with the prospect of being nursed; those who were stubborn, with the hope of their being subdued by the kindness of Aunt Margaret's discipline; in short, she had all the various duties of a mother, without the credit and dignity of the maternal character. The busy scene of her various cares is now over. Of the invalids and the robust, the kind and the rough, the peevish and pleased children, who thronged her little parlour from morning to night, not one now remains alive but myself, who, afflicted by early infirmity, was one of the most delicate of her nurslings, yet, nevertheless, have outlived them all.

It is still my custom, and shall be so while I have the use of my limbs, to visit my respected relation at least three times a week. Her abode is about half a mile from the suburbs of the town in which I reside, and is accessible, not only by the highroad, from which it stands at some distance, but by means of a greensward footpath leading through some pretty meadows.

I have so little left to torment me in life, that it is one of my greatest vexations to know that several of these sequestered fields have been devoted as sites for building. In that which is nearest the town, wheelbarrows have been at work for several weeks in such numbers, that, I verily believe, its whole surface, to the depth of at least eighteen inches, was mounted in these monotrochs at the same moment, and in the act of being transported from one place to another. Huge triangular piles of planks are also reared in different parts of the devoted message; and a little group of trees that still grace the eastern end, which rises in a gentle ascent, have just received warning to quit, expressed by a daub of white paint, and are to give place to a curious grove of chimneys.

It would, perhaps, hurt others in my situation to reflect that this little range of pasturage once belonged to my father (whose family was of some consideration in the world), and was sold by patches to remedy distresses in which he involved himself in an attempt by commercial adventure to redeem his diminished fortune. While the building scheme was in full operation, this circumstance was often pointed out to me by the class of friends who are anxious that no part of your misfortunes should escape your observation. "Such pasture-ground! – lying at the very town's end – in turnips and potatoes, the parks would bring L20 per acre; and if leased for building – oh, it was a gold mine! And all sold for an old song out of the ancient possessor's hands!" My comforters cannot bring me to repine much on this subject. If I could be allowed to look back on the past without interruption, I could willingly give up the enjoyment of present income and the hope of future profit to those who have purchased what my father sold. I regret the alteration of the ground only because it destroys associations, and I would more willingly (I think) see the Earl's Closes in the hands of strangers, retaining their silvan appearance, than know them for my own, if torn up by agriculture, or covered with buildings. Mine are the sensations of poor Logan:

> "The horrid plough has rased the green
> Where yet a child I strayed;
> The axe has fell'd the hawthorn screen,
> The schoolboy's summer shade."

I hope, however, the threatened devastation will not be consummated in my day. Although the adventurous spirit of times short while since passed gave rise to the undertaking, I have been encouraged to think that the subsequent changes have so far damped the spirit of speculation that the rest of the woodland footpath leading to Aunt Margaret's retreat will be left undisturbed for her time and mine. I am interested in this, for every step of the way, after I have passed through the green already mentioned, has for me something of early remembrance: – There is the stile at which I can recollect a cross child's-maid upbraiding me with my infirmity as she lifted me coarsely and carelessly over the flinty steps, which my brothers traversed with shout and bound. I remember the suppressed bitterness of the moment, and, conscious of my own inferiority, the feeling of envy with which I regarded the easy movements and elastic steps of my more happily formed brethren. Alas! These goodly barks have all perished on life's wide ocean, and only that which seemed so little seaworthy, as the naval phrase goes, has reached the port when the tempest is over. Then there is the pool, where, manoeuvring our little navy, constructed out of the broad water-flags, my elder brother fell in, and was scarce saved from the watery element to die under Nelson's banner. There is the hazel copse also, in which my brother Henry used to gather nuts, thinking little that he was to die in an Indian jungle in quest of rupees.

There is so much more of remembrance about the little walk, that – as I stop, rest on my crutch-headed cane, and look round with that species of comparison between the thing I was and that which I now am – it almost induces me to doubt my own identity; until I find myself in face of the honeysuckle porch of Aunt Margaret's dwelling, with its irregularity of front, and its odd, projecting latticed windows, where the workmen seem to have made it a study that no one of them should resemble another in form, size, or in the old-fashioned stone entablature and labels which adorn them. This tenement, once the manor house of the Earl's Closes, we still retain a slight hold upon; for, in some family arrangements, it had been settled upon Aunt Margaret during the term of her life. Upon this frail tenure depends, in a great measure, the last shadow of the family of Bothwell of Earl's Closes, and their last slight connection with their paternal inheritance. The only representative will then be an infirm old man, moving not unwillingly to the grave, which has devoured all that were dear to his affections.

When I have indulged such thoughts for a minute or two, I enter the mansion, which is said to have been the gate-house only of the original building, and find one being on whom time seems to have made little impression; for the Aunt Margaret of today bears the same proportional age to the Aunt Margaret of my early youth that the boy of ten years old does to the man of (by'r Lady!) some fifty-six years. The old lady's invariable costume has doubtless some share in confirming one in the opinion that time has stood still with Aunt Margaret.

The brown or chocolate-coloured silk gown, with ruffles of the same stuff at the elbow, within which are others of Mechlin lace; the black silk gloves, or mitts; the white hair combed back upon a roll; and the cap of spotless cambric, which closes around the venerable countenance – as they were not the costume of 1780, so neither were they that of 1826; they are altogether a style peculiar to the individual Aunt Margaret. There she still sits, as she sat thirty years since, with her wheel or the stocking, which she works by the fire in winter and by the window in summer; or, perhaps, venturing as far as the porch in an unusually fine summer evening. Her frame, like some well-constructed piece of mechanics, still performs the operations for which it had seemed destined – going its round with an activity which is gradually diminished, yet indicating no probability that it will soon come to a period.

The solicitude and affection which had made Aunt Margaret the willing slave to the inflictions of a whole nursery, have now for their object the health and comfort of one old and infirm man – the last remaining relative of her family, and the only one who can still find interest in the traditional stores which she hoards, as some miser hides the gold which he desires that no one should enjoy after his death.

My conversation with Aunt Margaret generally relates little either to the present or to the future. For the passing day we possess as much as we require, and we neither of us wish for more; and for that which is to follow, we have, on this side of the grave, neither hopes, nor fears, nor anxiety. We therefore naturally look back to the past, and forget the present fallen fortunes and declined importance of our family in recalling the hours when it was wealthy and prosperous.

With this slight introduction, the reader will know as much of Aunt Margaret and her nephew as is necessary to comprehend the following conversation and narrative.

Last week, when, late in a summer evening, I went to call on the old lady to whom my reader is now introduced, I was received by her with all her usual affection and benignity, while, at the same time, she seemed abstracted and disposed to silence. I asked her the reason.

"They have been clearing out the old chapel," she said; "John Clayhudgeons having, it seems, discovered that the stuff within – being, I suppose, the remains of our ancestors – was excellent for top-dressing the meadows."

Here I started up with more alacrity than I have displayed for some years; but sat down while my aunt added, laying her hand upon my sleeve, "The chapel has been long considered as common ground, my dear, and used for a pinfold, and what objection can we have to the man for employing what is his own to his own profit? Besides, I did speak to him, and he very readily and civilly promised that if he found bones or monuments, they should be carefully respected and reinstated; and what more could I ask? So, the first stone they found bore the name of Margaret Bothwell, 1585, and I have caused it to be laid carefully aside, as I think it betokens death, and having served my namesake two hundred years, it has just been cast up in time to do me the same good turn. My house has been long put in order, as far as the small earthly concerns require it; but who shall say that their account with, Heaven is sufficiently revised?"

"After what you have said, aunt," I replied, "perhaps I ought to take my hat and go away; and so I should, but that there is on this occasion a little alloy mingled with your devotion. To think of death at all times is a duty – to suppose it nearer from the finding an old gravestone is superstition; and you, with your strong, useful common sense, which was so long the prop of a fallen family, are the last person whom I should have suspected of such weakness."

"Neither would I deserve your suspicions, kinsman," answered Aunt Margaret, "if we were speaking of any incident occurring in the actual business of human life. But for all this, I have a sense of superstition about me, which I do not wish to part with. It is a feeling which separates me from this age, and links me with that to which I am hastening; and even when it seems, as now, to lead me to the brink of the grave, and bid me gaze on it, I do not love that it should be dispelled. It soothes my imagination, without influencing my reason or conduct."

"I profess, my good lady," replied I, "that had any one but you made such a declaration, I should have thought it as capricious as that of the clergyman, who, without vindicating his false reading, preferred, from habit's sake, his old Mumpsimus to the modern Sumpsimus."

"Well," answered my aunt, "I must explain my inconsistency in this particular by comparing it to another. I am, as you know, a piece of that old-fashioned thing called a Jacobite; but I am so in sentiment and feeling only, for a more loyal subject never joined in prayers for the health and wealth of George the Fourth, whom God long preserve! But I dare say that kind-hearted sovereign would not deem that an old woman did him much injury if she leaned back in her arm-chair, just in such a twilight as this, and thought of the high-mettled men whose sense of duty called them to arms against his grandfather; and how, in a cause which they deemed that of their rightful prince and country,

> "They fought till their hand to the broadsword was glued,
> They fought against fortune with hearts unsubdued."

Do not come at such a moment, when my head is full of plaids, pibrochs, and claymores, and ask my reason to admit what, I am afraid, it cannot deny – I mean, that the public advantage peremptorily demanded that these things should cease to exist. I cannot, indeed, refuse to allow the justice of your reasoning; but yet, being convinced against my will, you will gain little by your motion. You might as well read to an infatuated lover the catalogue of his mistress's imperfections; for when he has been compelled to listen to the summary, you will only get for answer that 'he lo'es her a' the better.' "

I was not sorry to have changed the gloomy train of Aunt Margaret's thoughts, and replied in the same tone, "Well, I can't help being persuaded that our good King is the more sure of Mrs. Bothwell's loyal affection, that he has the Stewart right of birth as well as the Act of Succession in his favour."

"Perhaps my attachment, were its source of consequence, might be found warmer for the union of the rights you mention," said Aunt Margaret; "but, upon my word, it would be as sincere if the King's right were founded only on the will of the nation, as declared at the Revolution. I am none of your *Jure Divino* folks."

"And a Jacobite notwithstanding."

"And a Jacobite notwithstanding – or rather, I will give you leave to call me one of the party which, in Queen Anne's time, were called, *Whimsicals*, because they were sometimes operated upon by feelings, sometimes by principle. After all, it is very hard that you will not allow an old woman to be as inconsistent in her political sentiments as mankind in general show themselves in all the various courses of life; since you cannot point out one of them in which the passions and prejudices of those who pursue it are not perpetually carrying us away from the path which our reason points out."

"True, aunt; but you are a wilful wanderer, who should be forced back into the right path."

"Spare me, I entreat you," replied Aunt Margaret. "You remember the Gaelic song, though I dare say I mispronounce the words –

> 'Hatil mohatil, na dowski mi.'
> 'I am asleep, do not waken me.'

I tell you, kinsman, that the sort of waking dreams which my imagination spins out, in what your favourite Wordsworth calls 'moods of my own mind,' are worth all the rest of my more active days. Then, instead of looking forwards, as I did in youth, and forming for myself fairy palaces, upon the verge of the grave I turn my eyes backward upon the days and manners of my better time; and the sad, yet soothing recollections come so close and interesting, that I almost think it sacrilege to be wiser or more rational or less prejudiced than those to whom I looked up in my younger years."

"I think I now understand what you mean," I answered, "and can comprehend why you should occasionally prefer the twilight of illusion to the steady light of reason."

"Where there is no task," she rejoined, "to be performed, we may sit in the dark if we like it; if we go to work, we must ring for candles."

"And amidst such shadowy and doubtful light," continued I, "imagination frames her enchanted and enchanting visions, and sometimes passes them upon the senses for reality."

"Yes," said Aunt Margaret, who is a well-read woman, "to those who resemble the translator of Tasso, –

> 'Prevailing poet, whose undoubting mind
> Believed the magic wonders which he sung.'

It is not required for this purpose that you should be sensible of the painful horrors which an actual belief in such prodigies inflicts. Such a belief nowadays belongs only to fools and children.

It is not necessary that your ears should tingle and your complexion change, like that of Theodore at the approach of the spectral huntsman. All that is indispensable for the enjoyment of the milder feeling of supernatural awe is, that you should be susceptible of the slight shuddering which creeps over you when you hear a tale of terror – that well-vouched tale which the narrator, having first expressed his general disbelief of all such legendary lore, selects and produces, as having something in it which he has been always obliged to give up as inexplicable. Another symptom is a momentary hesitation to look round you, when the interest of the narrative is at the highest; and the third, a desire to avoid looking into a mirror when you are alone in your chamber for the evening. I mean such are signs which indicate the crisis, when a female imagination is in due temperature to enjoy a ghost story. I do not pretend to describe those which express the same disposition in a gentleman."

"That last symptom, dear aunt, of shunning the mirror seems likely to be a rare occurrence amongst the fair sex."

"You are a novice in toilet fashions, my dear cousin. All women consult the looking-glass with anxiety before they go into company; but when they return home, the mirror has not the same charm. The die has been cast – the party has been successful or unsuccessful in the impression which she desired to make. But, without going deeper into the mysteries of the dressing-table, I will tell you that I myself, like many other honest folks, do not like to see the blank, black front of a large mirror in a room dimly lighted, and where the reflection of the candle seems rather to lose itself in the deep obscurity of the glass than to be reflected back again into the apartment, That space of inky darkness seems to be a field for Fancy to play her revels in. She may call up other features to meet us, instead of the reflection of our own; or, as in the spells of Hallowe'en, which we learned in childhood, some unknown form may be seen peeping over our shoulder. In short, when I am in a ghost-seeing humour, I make my handmaiden draw the green curtains over the mirror before I go into the room, so that she may have the first shock of the apparition, if there be any to be seen, But, to tell you the truth, this dislike to look into a mirror in particular times and places has, I believe, its original foundation in a story which came to me by tradition from my grandmother, who was a party concerned in the scene of which I will now tell you."

The Mirror
Chapter I

YOU ARE FOND (said my aunt) of sketches of the society which has passed away. I wish I could describe to you Sir Philip Forester, the 'chartered libertine' of Scottish good company, about the end of the last century. I never saw him indeed; but my mother's traditions were full of his wit, gallantry, and dissipation. This gay knight flourished about the end of the seventeenth and beginning of the eighteenth century. He was the Sir Charles Easy and the Lovelace of his day and country – renowned for the number of duels he had fought, and the successful intrigues which he had carried on. The supremacy which he had attained in the fashionable world was absolute; and when we combine it with one or two anecdotes, for which, "if laws were made for every degree," he ought certainly to have been hanged, the popularity of such a person really serves to show, either that the present times are much more decent, if not more virtuous, than they formerly were, or that high-breeding then was of more difficult attainment than that which is now so called, and consequently entitled the successful professor to a proportional degree of plenary indulgences and privileges. No beau of this day could have borne out so ugly a story as that of Pretty Peggy Grindstone, the miller's daughter at Sillermills – it had well-nigh made work for the Lord Advocate. But it hurt Sir Philip Forester no more than the hail hurts the hearthstone. He was as well received in society as ever, and dined with the Duke of A– the day the poor girl was buried. She died of heartbreak. But that has nothing to do with my story.

Now, you must listen to a single word upon kith, kin, and ally; I promise you I will not be prolix. But it is necessary to the authenticity of my legend that you should know that Sir Philip Forester, with his handsome person, elegant accomplishments, and fashionable manners, married the younger Miss Falconer of King's Copland. The elder sister of this lady had previously become the wife of my grandfather, Sir Geoffrey Bothwell, and brought into our family a good fortune. Miss Jemima, or Miss Jemmie Falconer, as she was usually called, had also about ten thousand pounds sterling – then thought a very handsome portion indeed.

The two sisters were extremely different, though each had their admirers while they remained single. Lady Bothwell had some touch of the old King's Copland blood about her. She was bold, though not to the degree of audacity, ambitious, and desirous to raise her house and family; and was, as has been said, a considerable spur to my grandfather, who was otherwise an indolent man, but whom, unless he has been slandered, his lady's influence involved in some political matters which had been more wisely let alone. She was a woman of high principle, however, and masculine good sense, as some of her letters testify, which are still in my wainscot cabinet.

Jemmie Falconer was the reverse of her sister in every respect. Her understanding did not reach above the ordinary pitch, if, indeed, she could be said to have attained it. Her beauty, while it lasted, consisted, in a great measure, of delicacy of complexion and regularity of features, without any peculiar force of expression. Even these charms faded under the sufferings attendant on an ill-assorted match. She was passionately attached to her husband, by whom she was treated with a callous yet polite indifference, which, to one whose heart was as tender as her judgment was weak, was more painful perhaps than absolute ill-usage. Sir Philip was a voluptuary – that is, a completely selfish egotist – whose disposition and character resembled the rapier he wore, polished, keen, and brilliant, but inflexible and unpitying. As he observed carefully all the usual forms towards his lady, he had the art to deprive her even of the compassion of the world; and useless and unavailing as that may be while actually possessed by the sufferer, it is, to a mind like Lady Forester's, most painful to know she has it not.

The tattle of society did its best to place the peccant husband above the suffering wife. Some called her a poor, spiritless thing, and declared that, with a little of her sister's spirit, she might have brought to reason any Sir Philip whatsoever, were it the termagant Falconbridge himself. But the greater part of their acquaintance affected candour, and saw faults on both sides – though, in fact, there only existed the oppressor and the oppressed. The tone of such critics was, "To be sure, no one will justify Sir Philip Forester, but then we all know Sir Philip, and Jemmie Falconer might have known what she had to expect from the beginning. What made her set her cap at Sir Philip? He would never have looked at her if she had not thrown herself at his head, with her poor ten thousand pounds. I am sure, if it is money he wanted, she spoiled his market. I know where Sir Philip could have done much better. And then, if she *would* have the man, could not she try to make him more comfortable at home, and have his friends oftener, and not plague him with the squalling children, and take care all was handsome and in good style about the house? I declare I think Sir Philip would have made a very domestic man, with a woman who knew how to manage him."

Now these fair critics, in raising their profound edifice of domestic felicity, did not recollect that the corner-stone was wanting, and that to receive good company with good cheer, the means of the banquet ought to have been furnished by Sir Philip, whose income (dilapidated as it was) was not equal to the display of the hospitality required, and at the same time to the supply of the good knight's *Menus Plaisirs*. So, in spite of all that was so sagely suggested by female friends, Sir Philip carried his good-humour everywhere abroad, and left at home a solitary mansion and a pining spouse.

At length, inconvenienced in his money affairs, and tired even of the short time which he spent in his own dull house, Sir Philip Forester determined to take a trip to the Continent, in the capacity of a volunteer. It was then common for men of fashion to do so; and our knight perhaps was of opinion that a touch of the military character, just enough to exalt, but not render pedantic, his qualities as a *beau garcon*, was necessary to maintain possession of the elevated situation which he held in the ranks of fashion.

Sir Philip's resolution threw his wife into agonies of terror; by which the worthy baronet was so much annoyed, that, contrary to his wont, he took some trouble to soothe her apprehensions, and once more brought her to shed tears, in which sorrow was not altogether unmingled with pleasure. Lady Bothwell asked, as a favour, Sir Philip's permission to receive her sister and her family into her own house during his absence on the Continent. Sir Philip readily assented to a proposition which saved expense, silenced the foolish people who might have talked of a deserted wife and family, and gratified Lady Bothwell, for whom he felt some respect, as for one who often spoke to him, always with freedom and sometimes with severity, without being deterred either by his raillery or the *prestige* of his reputation.

A day or two before Sir Philip's departure, Lady Bothwell took the liberty of asking him, in her sister's presence, the direct question, which his timid wife had often desired, but never ventured, to put to him: –

"Pray, Sir Philip, what route do you take when you reach the Continent?"

"I go from Leith to Helvoet by a packet with advices."

"That I comprehend perfectly," said Lady Bothwell dryly; "but you do not mean to remain long at Helvoet, I presume, and I should like to know what is your next object."

"You ask me, my dear lady," answered Sir Philip, "a question which I have not dared to ask myself. The answer depends on the fate of war. I shall, of course, go to headquarters, wherever they may happen to be for the time; deliver my letters of introduction; learn as much of the noble art of war as may suffice a poor interloping amateur; and then take a glance at the sort of thing of which we read so much in the *Gazette*."

"And I trust, Sir Philip," said Lady Bothwell, "that you will remember that you are a husband and a father; and that, though you think fit to indulge this military fancy, you will not let it hurry you into dangers which it is certainly unnecessary for any save professional persons to encounter."

"Lady Bothwell does me too much honour," replied the adventurous knight, "in regarding such a circumstance with the slightest interest. But to soothe your flattering anxiety, I trust your ladyship will recollect that I cannot expose to hazard the venerable and paternal character which you so obligingly recommend to my protection, without putting in some peril an honest fellow, called Philip Forester, with whom I have kept company for thirty years, and with whom, though some folks consider him a coxcomb, I have not the least desire to part."

"Well, Sir Philip, you are the best judge of your own affairs. I have little right to interfere – you are not my husband."

"God forbid!" said Sir Philip hastily; instantly adding, however, "God forbid that I should deprive my friend Sir Geoffrey of so inestimable a treasure."

"But you are my sister's husband," replied the lady; "and I suppose you are aware of her present distress of mind –"

"If hearing of nothing else from morning to night can make me aware of it," said Sir Philip, "I should know something of the matter."

"I do not pretend to reply to your wit, Sir Philip," answered Lady Bothwell; "but you must be sensible that all this distress is on account of apprehensions for your personal safety."

"In that case, I am surprised that Lady Bothwell, at least, should give herself so much trouble upon so insignificant a subject."

"My sister's interest may account for my being anxious to learn something of Sir Philip Forester's motions; about which, otherwise, I know he would not wish me to concern myself. I have a brother's safety too to be anxious for."

"You mean Major Falconer, your brother by the mother's side? What can he possibly have to do with our present agreeable conversation?"

"You have had words together, Sir Philip," said Lady Bothwell.

"Naturally; we are connections," replied Sir Philip, "and as such have always had the usual intercourse."

"That is an evasion of the subject," answered the lady. "By words, I mean angry words, on the subject of your usage of your wife."

"If," replied Sir Philip Forester, "you suppose Major Falconer simple enough to intrude his advice upon me, Lady Bothwell, in my domestic matters, you are indeed warranted in believing that I might possibly be so far displeased with the interference as to request him to reserve his advice till it was asked."

"And being on these terms, you are going to join the very army in which my brother Falconer is now serving?"

"No man knows the path of honour better than Major Falconer," said Sir Philip. "An aspirant after fame, like me, cannot choose a better guide than his footsteps."

Lady Bothwell rose and went to the window, the tears gushing from her eyes.

"And this heartless raillery," she said, "is all the consideration that is to be given to our apprehensions of a quarrel which may bring on the most terrible consequences? Good God! of what can men's hearts be made, who can thus dally with the agony of others?"

Sir Philip Forester was moved; he laid aside the mocking tone in which he had hitherto spoken.

"Dear Lady Bothwell," he said, taking her reluctant hand, "we are both wrong. You are too deeply serious; I, perhaps, too little so. The dispute I had with Major Falconer was of no earthly consequence. Had anything occurred betwixt us that ought to have been settled *par voie du fait*, as we say in France, neither of us are persons that are likely to postpone such a meeting.

Permit me to say, that were it generally known that you or my Lady Forester are apprehensive of such a catastrophe, it might be the very means of bringing about what would not otherwise be likely to happen. I know your good sense, Lady Bothwell, and that you will understand me when I say that really my affairs require my absence for some months. This Jemima cannot understand. It is a perpetual recurrence of questions, why can you not do this, or that, or the third thing? and, when you have proved to her that her expedients are totally ineffectual, you have just to begin the whole round again. Now, do you tell her, dear Lady Bothwell, that *you* are satisfied. She is, you must confess, one of those persons with whom authority goes farther than reasoning. Do but repose a little confidence in me, and you shall see how amply I will repay it."

Lady Bothwell shook her head, as one but half satisfied. "How difficult it is to extend confidence, when the basis on which it ought to rest has been so much shaken! But I will do my best to make Jemima easy; and further, I can only say that for keeping your present purpose I hold you responsible both to God and man."

"Do not fear that I will deceive you," said Sir Philip. "The safest conveyance to me will be through the general post-office, Helvoetsluys, where I will take care to leave orders for forwarding my letters. As for Falconer, our only encounter will be over a bottle of Burgundy; so make yourself perfectly easy on his score."

Lady Bothwell could *not* make herself easy; yet she was sensible that her sister hurt her own cause by *taking on*, as the maidservants call it, too vehemently, and by showing before every stranger, by manner, and sometimes by words also, a dissatisfaction with her husband's journey that was sure to come to his ears, and equally certain to displease him. But there was no help for this domestic dissension, which ended only with the day of separation.

I am sorry I cannot tell, with precision, the year in which Sir Philip Forester went over to Flanders; but it was one of those in which the campaign opened with extraordinary fury, and many bloody, though indecisive, skirmishes were fought between the French on the one side and the Allies on the other. In all our modern improvements, there are none, perhaps, greater than in the accuracy and speed with which intelligence is transmitted from any scene of action to those in this country whom it may concern. During Marlborough's campaigns, the sufferings of the many who had relations in, or along with, the army were greatly augmented by the suspense in which they were detained for weeks after they had heard of bloody battles, in which, in all probability, those for whom their bosoms throbbed with anxiety had been personally engaged. Amongst those who were most agonized by this state of uncertainty was the – I had almost said deserted – wife of the gay Sir Philip Forester. A single letter had informed her of his arrival on the Continent; no others were received. One notice occurred in the newspapers, in which Volunteer Sir Philip Forester was mentioned as having been entrusted with a dangerous reconnaissance, which he had executed with the greatest courage, dexterity, and intelligence, and received the thanks of the commanding officer. The sense of his having acquired distinction brought a momentary glow into the lady's pale cheek; but it was instantly lost in ashen whiteness at the recollection of his danger. After this, they had no news whatever, neither from Sir Philip, nor even from their brother Falconer. The case of Lady Forester was not indeed different from that of hundreds in the same situation; but a feeble mind is necessarily an irritable one, and the suspense which some bear with constitutional indifference or philosophical resignation, and some with a disposition to believe and hope the best, was intolerable to Lady Forester, at once solitary and sensitive, low-spirited, and devoid of strength of mind, whether natural or acquired.

The Mirror
Chapter II

AS SHE received no further news of Sir Philip, whether directly or indirectly, his unfortunate lady began now to feel a sort of consolation even in those careless habits which had so often given her pain. "He is so thoughtless," she repeated a hundred times a day to her sister, "he never writes when things are going on smoothly. It is his way. Had anything happened, he would have informed us."

Lady Bothwell listened to her sister without attempting to console her. Probably she might be of opinion that even the worst intelligence which could be received from Flanders might not be without some touch of consolation; and that the Dowager Lady Forester, if so she was doomed to be called, might have a source of happiness unknown to the wife of the gayest and finest gentleman in Scotland. This conviction became stronger as they learned from inquiries made at headquarters that Sir Philip was no longer with the army – though whether he had been taken or slain in some of those skirmishes which were perpetually occurring, and in which he loved to distinguish himself, or whether he had, for some unknown reason or capricious change of mind, voluntarily left the service, none of his countrymen in the camp of the Allies could form even a conjecture. Meantime his creditors at home became clamorous, entered into possession of his property, and threatened his person, should he be rash enough to return to Scotland. These additional disadvantages aggravated Lady Bothwell's displeasure against the fugitive husband; while her sister saw nothing in any of them, save what tended to increase her grief for the absence of him whom her imagination now represented – as it had before marriage – gallant, gay, and affectionate.

About this period there appeared in Edinburgh a man of singular appearance and pretensions. He was commonly called the Paduan Doctor, from having received his education at that famous university. He was supposed to possess some rare receipts in medicine, with which, it was affirmed, he had wrought remarkable cures. But though, on the one hand, the physicians of Edinburgh termed him an empiric, there were many persons, and among them some of the clergy, who, while they admitted the truth of the cures and the force of his remedies, alleged that Doctor Baptista Damiotti made use of charms and unlawful arts in order to obtain success in his practice. The resorting to him was even solemnly preached against, as a seeking of health from idols, and a trusting to the help which was to come from Egypt. But the protection which the Paduan Doctor received from some friends of interest and consequence enabled him to set these imputations at defiance, and to assume, even in the city of Edinburgh, famed as it was for abhorrence of witches and necromancers, the dangerous character of an expounder of futurity. It was at length rumoured that, for a certain gratification, which of course was not an inconsiderable one, Doctor Baptista Damiotti could tell the fate of the absent, and even show his visitors the personal form of their absent friends, and the action in which they were engaged at the moment. This rumour came to the ears of Lady Forester, who had reached that pitch of mental agony in which the sufferer will do anything, or endure anything, that suspense may be converted into certainty.

Gentle and timid in most cases, her state of mind made her equally obstinate and reckless, and it was with no small surprise and alarm that her sister, Lady Bothwell, heard her express a resolution to visit this man of art, and learn from him the fate of her husband.

Lady Bothwell remonstrated on the improbability that such pretensions as those of this foreigner could be founded in anything but imposture.

"I care not," said the deserted wife, "what degree of ridicule I may incur; if there be any one chance out of a hundred that I may obtain some certainty of my husband's fate, I would not miss that chance for whatever else the world can offer me."

Lady Bothwell next urged the unlawfulness of resorting to such sources of forbidden knowledge.

"Sister," replied the sufferer, "he who is dying of thirst cannot refrain from drinking even poisoned water. She who suffers under suspense must seek information, even were the powers which offer it unhallowed and infernal. I go to learn my fate alone, and this very evening will I know it; the sun that rises tomorrow shall find me, if not more happy, at least more resigned."

"Sister," said Lady Bothwell, "if you are determined upon this wild step, you shall not go alone. If this man be an impostor, you may be too much agitated by your feelings to detect his villainy. If, which I cannot believe, there be any truth in what he pretends, you shall not be exposed alone to a communication of so extraordinary a nature. I will go with you, if indeed you determine to go. But yet reconsider your project, and renounce inquiries which cannot be prosecuted without guilt, and perhaps without danger."

Lady Forester threw herself into her sister's arms, and, clasping her to her bosom, thanked her a hundred times for the offer of her company, while she declined with a melancholy gesture the friendly advice with which it was accompanied.

When the hour of twilight arrived – which was the period when the Paduan Doctor was understood to receive the visits of those who came to consult with him – the two ladies left their apartments in the Canongate of Edinburgh, having their dress arranged like that of women of an inferior description, and their plaids disposed around their faces as they were worn by the same class; for in those days of aristocracy the quality of the wearer was generally indicated by the manner in which her plaid was disposed, as well as by the fineness of its texture. It was Lady Bothwell who had suggested this species of disguise, partly to avoid observation as they should go to the conjurer's house, and partly in order to make trial of his penetration, by appearing before him in a feigned character. Lady Forester's servant, of tried fidelity, had been employed by her to propitiate the Doctor by a suitable fee, and a story intimating that a soldier's wife desired to know the fate of her husband – a subject upon which, in all probability, the sage was very frequently consulted.

To the last moment, when the palace clock struck eight, Lady Bothwell earnestly watched her sister, in hopes that she might retreat from her rash undertaking; but as mildness, and even timidity, is capable at times of vehement and fixed purposes, she found Lady Forester resolutely unmoved and determined when the moment of departure arrived. Ill satisfied with the expedition, but determined not to leave her sister at such a crisis, Lady Bothwell accompanied Lady Forester through more than one obscure street and lane, the servant walking before, and acting as their guide. At length he suddenly turned into a narrow court, and knocked at an arched door which seemed to belong to a building of some antiquity. It opened, though no one appeared to act as porter; and the servant, stepping aside from the entrance, motioned the ladies to enter. They had no sooner done so than it shut, and excluded their guide. The two ladies found themselves in a small vestibule, illuminated by a dim lamp, and having, when the door was closed, no communication with the external light or air. The door of an inner apartment, partly open, was at the farther side of the vestibule.

"We must not hesitate now, Jemima," said Lady Bothwell, and walked forwards into the inner room, where, surrounded by books, maps, philosophical utensils, and other implements of peculiar shape and appearance, they found the man of art.

There was nothing very peculiar in the Italian's appearance. He had the dark complexion and marked features of his country, seemed about fifty years old, and was handsomely but plainly dressed in a full suit of black clothes, which was then the universal costume of the medical profession. Large wax-lights, in silver sconces, illuminated the apartment, which was reasonably furnished. He rose as the ladies entered, and, notwithstanding the inferiority of their dress, received them with the marked respect due to their quality, and which foreigners are usually punctilious in rendering to those to whom such honours are due.

Lady Bothwell endeavoured to maintain her proposed incognito, and, as the Doctor ushered them to the upper end of the room, made a motion declining his courtesy, as unfitted for their condition. "We are poor people, sir," she said; "only my sister's distress has brought us to consult your worship whether –"

He smiled as he interrupted her – "I am aware, madam, of your sister's distress, and its cause; I am aware, also, that I am honoured with a visit from two ladies of the highest consideration – Lady Bothwell and Lady Forester. If I could not distinguish them from the class of society which their present dress would indicate, there would be small possibility of my being able to gratify them by giving the information which they come to seek."

"I can easily understand –" said Lady Bothwell.

"Pardon my boldness to interrupt you, milady," cried the Italian; "your ladyship was about to say that you could easily understand that I had got possession of your names by means of your domestic. But in thinking so, you do injustice to the fidelity of your servant, and, I may add, to the skill of one who is also not less your humble servant – Baptista Damiotti."

"I have no intention to do either, sir," said Lady Bothwell, maintaining a tone of composure, though somewhat surprised; "but the situation is something new to me. If you know who we are, you also know, sir, what brought us here."

"Curiosity to know the fate of a Scottish gentleman of rank, now, or lately, upon the Continent," answered the seer. "His name is Il Cavaliero Philippo Forester, a gentleman who has the honour to be husband to this lady, and, with your ladyship's permission for using plain language, the misfortune not to value as it deserves that inestimable advantage."

Lady Forester sighed deeply, and Lady Bothwell replied, –

"Since you know our object without our telling it, the only question that remains is, whether you have the power to relieve my sister's anxiety?"

"I have, madam," answered the Paduan scholar; "but there is still a previous inquiry. Have you the courage to behold with your own eyes what the Cavaliero Philippo Forester is now doing? or will you take it on my report?"

"That question my sister must answer for herself," said Lady Bothwell.

"With my own eyes will I endure to see whatever you have power to show me," said Lady Forester, with the same determined spirit which had stimulated her since her resolution was taken upon this subject.

"There may be danger in it."

"If gold can compensate the risk," said Lady Forester, taking out her purse.

"I do not such things for the purpose of gain," answered the foreigner; "I dare not turn my art to such a purpose. If I take the gold of the wealthy, it is but to bestow it on the poor;

nor do I ever accept more than the sum I have already received from your servant. Put up your purse, madam; an adept needs not your gold."

Lady Bothwell, considering this rejection of her sister's offer as a mere trick of an empiric, to induce her to press a larger sum upon him, and willing that the scene should be commenced and ended, offered some gold in turn, observing that it was only to enlarge the sphere of his charity.

"Let Lady Bothwell enlarge the sphere of her own charity," said the Paduan, "not merely in giving of alms, in which I know she is not deficient, but in judging the character of others; and let her oblige Baptista Damiotti by believing him honest, till she shall discover him to be a knave. Do not be surprised, madam, if I speak in answer to your thoughts rather than your expressions; and tell me once more whether you have courage to look on what I am prepared to show?"

"I own, sir," said Lady Bothwell, "that your words strike me with some sense of fear; but whatever my sister desires to witness, I will not shrink from witnessing along with her."

"Nay, the danger only consists in the risk of your resolution failing you. The sight can only last for the space of seven minutes; and should you interrupt the vision by speaking a single word, not only would the charm be broken, but some danger might result to the spectators. But if you can remain steadily silent for the seven minutes, your curiosity will be gratified without the slightest risk; and for this I will engage my honour."

Internally Lady Bothwell thought the security was but an indifferent one; but she suppressed the suspicion, as if she had believed that the adept, whose dark features wore a half-formed smile, could in reality read even her most secret reflections. A solemn pause then ensued, until Lady Forester gathered courage enough to reply to the physician, as he termed himself, that she would abide with firmness and silence the sight which he had promised to exhibit to them. Upon this, he made them a low obeisance, and saying he went to prepare matters to meet their wish, left the apartment. The two sisters, hand in hand, as if seeking by that close union to divert any danger which might threaten them, sat down on two seats in immediate contact with each other – Jemima seeking support in the manly and habitual courage of Lady Bothwell; and she, on the other hand, more agitated than she had expected, endeavouring to fortify herself by the desperate resolution which circumstances had forced her sister to assume. The one perhaps said to herself that her sister never feared anything; and the other might reflect that what so feeble-minded a woman as Jemima did not fear, could not properly be a subject of apprehension to a person of firmness and resolution like her own.

In a few moments the thoughts of both were diverted from their own situation by a strain of music so singularly sweet and solemn that, while it seemed calculated to avert or dispel any feeling unconnected with its harmony, increased, at the same time, the solemn excitation which the preceding interview was calculated to produce. The music was that of some instrument with which they were unacquainted; but circumstances afterwards led my ancestress to believe that it was that of the harmonica, which she heard at a much later period in life.

When these heaven-born sounds had ceased, a door opened in the upper end of the apartment, and they saw Damiotti, standing at the head of two or three steps, sign to them to advance. His dress was so different from that which he had worn a few minutes before, that they could hardly recognize him; and the deadly paleness of his countenance, and a certain stern rigidity of muscles, like that of one whose mind is made up to some strange and daring action, had totally changed the somewhat sarcastic expression with which he had previously regarded them both, and particularly Lady Bothwell. He was barefooted, excepting a species of sandals in the antique fashion; his legs were naked beneath the knees; above them he wore hose, and a doublet of dark crimson silk close to his body; and over that a flowing loose robe, something resembling a surplice, of snow-white linen. His throat and neck were uncovered, and his long, straight, black hair was carefully combed down at full length.

As the ladies approached at his bidding, he showed no gesture of that ceremonious courtesy of which he had been formerly lavish. On the contrary, he made the signal of advance with an air of command; and when, arm in arm, and with insecure steps, the sisters approached the spot where he stood, it was with a warning frown that he pressed his finger to his lips, as if reiterating his condition of absolute silence, while, stalking before them, he led the way into the next apartment.

This was a large room, hung with black, as if for a funeral. At the upper end was a table, or rather a species of altar, covered with the same lugubrious colour, on which lay divers objects resembling the usual implements of sorcery. These objects were not indeed visible as they advanced into the apartment; for the light which displayed them, being only that of two expiring lamps, was extremely faint. The master – to use the Italian phrase for persons of this description – approached the upper end of the room, with a genuflection like that of a Catholic to the crucifix, and at the same time crossed himself. The ladies followed in silence, and arm in arm. Two or three low broad steps led to a platform in front of the altar, or what resembled such. Here the sage took his stand, and placed the ladies beside him, once more earnestly repeating by signs his injunctions of silence. The Italian then, extending his bare arm from under his linen vestment, pointed with his forefinger to five large flambeaux, or torches, placed on each side of the altar. They took fire successively at the approach of his hand, or rather of his finger, and spread a strong light through the room. By this the visitors could discern that, on the seeming altar, were disposed two naked swords laid crosswise; a large open book, which they conceived to be a copy of the Holy Scriptures, but in a language to them unknown; and beside this mysterious volume was placed a human skull. But what struck the sisters most was a very tall and broad mirror, which occupied all the space behind the altar, and, illumined by the lighted torches, reflected the mysterious articles which were laid upon it.

The master then placed himself between the two ladies, and, pointing to the mirror, took each by the hand, but without speaking a syllable. They gazed intently on the polished and sable space to which he had directed their attention. Suddenly the surface assumed a new and singular appearance. It no longer simply reflected the objects placed before it, but, as if it had self-contained scenery of its own, objects began to appear within it, at first in a disorderly, indistinct, and miscellaneous manner, like form arranging itself out of chaos; at length, in distinct and defined shape and symmetry. It was thus that, after some shifting of light and darkness over the face of the wonderful glass, a long perspective of arches and columns began to arrange itself on its sides, and a vaulted roof on the upper part of it, till, after many oscillations, the whole vision gained a fixed and stationary appearance, representing the interior of a foreign church. The pillars were stately, and hung with scutcheons; the arches were lofty and magnificent; the floor was lettered with funeral inscriptions. But there were no separate shrines, no images, no display of chalice or crucifix on the altar. It was, therefore, a Protestant church upon the Continent. A clergyman dressed in the Geneva gown and band stood by the communion table, and, with the Bible opened before him, and his clerk awaiting in the background, seemed prepared to perform some service of the church to which he belonged.

At length, there entered the middle aisle of the building a numerous party, which appeared to be a bridal one, as a lady and gentleman walked first, hand in hand, followed by a large concourse of persons of both sexes, gaily, nay richly, attired. The bride, whose features they could distinctly see, seemed not more than sixteen years old, and extremely beautiful. The bridegroom, for some seconds, moved rather with his shoulder towards them, and his face averted; but his elegance of form and step struck the sisters at once with the same apprehension. As he turned his face suddenly, it was frightfully realized, and they saw, in the gay bridegroom before them, Sir Philip Forester. His wife uttered an imperfect exclamation, at the sound of which the whole scene stirred and seemed to separate.

"I could compare it to nothing," said Lady Bothwell, while recounting the wonderful tale, "but to the dispersion of the reflection offered by a deep and calm pool, when a stone is suddenly cast into it, and the shadows become dissipated and broken." The master pressed both the ladies' hands severely, as if to remind them of their promise, and of the danger which they incurred. The exclamation died away on Lady Forester's tongue, without attaining perfect utterance, and the scene in the glass, after the fluctuation of a minute, again resumed to the eye its former appearance of a real scene, existing within the mirror, as if represented in a picture, save that the figures were movable instead of being stationary.

The representation of Sir Philip Forester, now distinctly visible in form and feature, was seen to lead on towards the clergyman that beautiful girl, who advanced at once with diffidence and with a species of affectionate pride. In the meantime, and just as the clergyman had arranged the bridal company before him, and seemed about to commence the service, another group of persons, of whom two or three were officers, entered the church. They moved, at first, forward, as though they came to witness the bridal ceremony; but suddenly one of the officers, whose back was towards the spectators, detached himself from his companions, and rushed hastily towards the marriage party, when the whole of them turned towards him, as if attracted by some exclamation which had accompanied his advance. Suddenly the intruder drew his sword; the bridegroom unsheathed his own, and made towards him; swords were also drawn by other individuals, both of the marriage party and of those who had last entered. They fell into a sort of confusion, the clergyman, and some elder and graver persons, labouring apparently to keep the peace, while the hotter spirits on both sides brandished their weapons. But now, the period of the brief space during which the soothsayer, as he pretended, was permitted to exhibit his art, was arrived. The fumes again mixed together, and dissolved gradually from observation; the vaults and columns of the church rolled asunder, and disappeared; and the front of the mirror reflected nothing save the blazing torches and the melancholy apparatus placed on the altar or table before it.

The doctor led the ladies, who greatly required his support, into the apartment from whence they came, where wine, essences, and other means of restoring suspended animation, had been provided during his absence. He motioned them to chairs, which they occupied in silence – Lady Forester, in particular, wringing her hands, and casting her eyes up to heaven, but without speaking a word, as if the spell had been still before her eyes.

"And what we have seen is even now acting?" said Lady Bothwell, collecting herself with difficulty.

"That," answered Baptista Damiotti, "I cannot justly, or with certainty, say. But it is either now acting, or has been acted during a short space before this. It is the last remarkable transaction in which the Cavalier Forester has been engaged."

Lady Bothwell then expressed anxiety concerning her sister, whose altered countenance and apparent unconsciousness of what passed around her excited her apprehensions how it might be possible to convey her home.

"I have prepared for that," answered the adept. "I have directed the servant to bring your equipage as near to this place as the narrowness of the street will permit. Fear not for your sister, but give her, when you return home, this composing draught, and she will be better tomorrow morning. Few," he added in a melancholy tone, "leave this house as well in health as they entered it. Such being the consequence of seeking knowledge by mysterious means, I leave you to judge the condition of those who have the power of gratifying such irregular curiosity. Farewell, and forget not the potion."

"I will give her nothing that comes from you," said Lady Bothwell; "I have seen enough of your art already. Perhaps you would poison us both to conceal your own necromancy. But we are persons who want neither the means of making our wrongs known, nor the assistance of friends to right them."

"You have had no wrongs from me, madam," said the adept. "You sought one who is little grateful for such honour. He seeks no one, and only gives responses to those who invite and call upon him. After all, you have but learned a little sooner the evil which you must still be doomed to endure. I hear your servant's step at the door, and will detain your ladyship and Lady Forester no longer. The next packet from the Continent will explain what you have already partly witnessed. Let it not, if I may advise, pass too suddenly into your sister's hands."

So saying, he bid Lady Bothwell good-night. She went, lighted by the adept, to the vestibule, where he hastily threw a black cloak over his singular dress, and opening the door, entrusted his visitors to the care of the servant. It was with difficulty that Lady Bothwell sustained her sister to the carriage, though it was only twenty steps distant. When they arrived at home, Lady Forester required medical assistance. The physician of the family attended, and shook his head on feeling her pulse.

"Here has been," he said, "a violent and sudden shock on the nerves. I must know how it has happened."

Lady Bothwell admitted they had visited the conjurer, and that Lady Forester had received some bad news respecting her husband, Sir Philip.

"That rascally quack would make my fortune, were he to stay in Edinburgh," said the graduate; "this is the seventh nervous case I have heard of his making for me, and all by effect of terror." He next examined the composing draught which Lady Bothwell had unconsciously brought in her hand, tasted it, and pronounced it very germain to the matter, and what would save an application to the apothecary. He then paused, and looking at Lady Bothwell very significantly, at length added, "I suppose I must not ask your ladyship anything about this Italian warlock's proceedings?"

"Indeed, doctor," answered Lady Bothwell, "I consider what passed as confidential; and though the man may be a rogue, yet, as we were fools enough to consult him, we should, I think, be honest enough to keep his counsel."

"*May* be a knave! Come," said the doctor, "I am glad to hear your ladyship allows such a possibility in anything that comes from Italy."

"What comes from Italy may be as good as what comes from Hanover, doctor. But you and I will remain good friends; and that it may be so, we will say nothing of Whig and Tory."

"Not I," said the doctor, receiving his fee, and taking his hat; "a Carolus serves my purpose as well as a Willielmus. But I should like to know why old Lady Saint Ringan, and all that set, go about wasting their decayed lungs in puffing this foreign fellow."

"Ay – you had best set him down a Jesuit, as Scrub says." On these terms they parted.

The poor patient – whose nerves, from an extraordinary state of tension, had at length become relaxed in as extraordinary a degree – continued to struggle with a sort of imbecility, the growth of superstitious terror, when the shocking tidings were brought from Holland which fulfilled even her worst expectations.

They were sent by the celebrated Earl of Stair, and contained the melancholy event of a duel betwixt Sir Philip Forester and his wife's half-brother, Captain Falconer, of the Scotch-Dutch, as they were then called, in which the latter had been killed. The cause of quarrel rendered the incident still more shocking. It seemed that Sir Philip had left the army suddenly, in consequence of being unable to pay a very considerable sum which he had lost to another volunteer at play. He had changed his name, and taken up his residence at Rotterdam, where he had insinuated himself into the good graces of an ancient and rich burgomaster, and, by his handsome person and graceful manners, captivated the affections of his only child, a very young person, of great beauty, and the heiress of much wealth. Delighted with the specious attractions of his proposed son-in-law, the wealthy merchant – whose idea of the British character was too high to admit of his taking any precaution to acquire evidence of his condition and circumstances – gave his consent to the marriage. It was about to be celebrated in the principal church of the city, when it was interrupted by a singular occurrence.

Captain Falconer having been detached to Rotterdam to bring up a part of the brigade of Scottish auxiliaries, who were in quarters there, a person of consideration in the town, to whom he had been formerly known, proposed to him for amusement to go to the high church to see a countryman of his own married to the daughter of a wealthy burgomaster. Captain Falconer went accordingly, accompanied by his Dutch acquaintance, with a party of his friends, and two or three officers of the Scotch brigade. His astonishment may be conceived when he saw his own brother-in-law, a married man, on the point of leading to the altar the innocent and beautiful creature upon whom he was about to practise a base and unmanly deceit. He proclaimed his villainy on the spot, and the marriage was interrupted, of course. But against the opinion of more thinking men, who considered Sir Philip Forester as having thrown himself out of the rank of men of honour, Captain Falconer admitted him to the privilege of such, accepted a challenge from him, and in the rencounter received a mortal wound. Such are the ways of Heaven, mysterious in our eyes. Lady Forester never recovered the shock of this dismal intelligence.

"And did this tragedy," said I, "take place exactly at the time when the scene in the mirror was exhibited?"

"It is hard to be obliged to maim one's story," answered my aunt, "but to speak the truth, it happened some days sooner than the apparition was exhibited."

"And so there remained a possibility," said I, "that by some secret and speedy communication the artist might have received early intelligence of that incident."

"The incredulous pretended so," replied my aunt.

"What became of the adept?" demanded I.

"Why, a warrant came down shortly afterwards to arrest him for high treason, as an agent of the Chevalier St. George; and Lady Bothwell, recollecting the hints which had escaped the doctor, an ardent friend of the Protestant succession, did then call to remembrance that this man was chiefly *prone* among the ancient matrons of her own political persuasion. It certainly seemed probable that intelligence from the Continent, which could easily have been transmitted by an active and powerful agent, might have enabled him to prepare such a scene of phantasmagoria as she had herself witnessed. Yet there were so many difficulties in assigning a natural explanation, that, to the day of her death, she remained in great doubt on the subject, and much disposed to cut the Gordian knot by admitting the existence of supernatural agency."

"But, my dear aunt," said I, "what became of the man of skill?"

"Oh, he was too good a fortune-teller not to be able to foresee that his own destiny would be tragical if he waited the arrival of the man with the silver greyhound upon his sleeve. He made, as we say, a moonlight flitting, and was nowhere to be seen or heard of. Some noise there was about papers or letters found in the house; but it died away, and Doctor Baptista Damiotti was soon as little talked of as Galen or Hippocrates."

"And Sir Philip Forester," said I, "did he too vanish for ever from the public scene?"

"No," replied my kind informer. "He was heard of once more, and it was upon a remarkable occasion. It is said that we Scots, when there was such a nation in existence, have, among our full peck of virtues, one or two little barley-corns of vice. In particular, it is alleged that we rarely forgive, and never forget, any injuries received – that we make an idol of our resentment, as poor Lady Constance did of her grief, and are addicted, as Burns says, to 'nursing our wrath to keep it warm.' Lady Bothwell was not without this feeling; and, I believe, nothing whatever, scarce the restoration of the Stewart line, could have happened so delicious to her feelings as an opportunity of being revenged on Sir Philip Forester for the deep and double injury which had deprived her of a sister and of a brother. But nothing of him was heard or known till many a year had passed away.

"At length – it was on a Fastern's E'en (Shrovetide) assembly, at which the whole fashion of Edinburgh attended, full and frequent, and when Lady Bothwell had a seat amongst the lady patronesses, that one of the attendants on the company whispered into her ear that a gentleman wished to speak with her in private.

" 'In private? and in an assembly room? – he must be mad. Tell him to call upon me tomorrow morning.'

" 'I said so, my lady,' answered the man, 'but he desired me to give you this paper.'

"She undid the billet, which was curiously folded and sealed. It only bore the words, '*On Business of Life and Death*,' written in a hand which she had never seen before. Suddenly it occurred to her that it might concern the safety of some of her political friends. She therefore followed the messenger to a small apartment where the refreshments were prepared, and from which the general company was excluded. She found an old man, who, at her approach, rose up and bowed profoundly. His appearance indicated a broken constitution, and his dress, though sedulously rendered conforming to the etiquette of a ballroom, was worn and tarnished, and hung in folds about his emaciated person. Lady Bothwell was about to feel for her purse, expecting to get rid of the supplicant at the expense of a little money, but some fear of a mistake arrested her purpose. She therefore gave the man leisure to explain himself.

" 'I have the honour to speak with the Lady Bothwell?'

" 'I am Lady Bothwell; allow me to say that this is no time or place for long explanations. What are your commands with me?'

" 'Your ladyship,' said the old man, 'had once a sister.'

" 'True; whom I loved as my own soul.'

" 'And a brother.'

" 'The bravest, the kindest, the most affectionate!' said Lady Bothwell.

" 'Both these beloved relatives you lost by the fault of an unfortunate man,' continued the stranger.

" 'By the crime of an unnatural, bloody-minded murderer,' said the lady.

" 'I am answered,' replied the old man, bowing, as if to withdraw.

" 'Stop, sir, I command you,' said Lady Bothwell. 'Who are you that, at such a place and time, come to recall these horrible recollections? I insist upon knowing.'

" 'I am one who intends Lady Bothwell no injury, but, on the contrary, to offer her the means of doing a deed of Christian charity, which the world would wonder at, and which Heaven would reward; but I find her in no temper for such a sacrifice as I was prepared to ask.'

" 'Speak out, sir; what is your meaning?' said Lady Bothwell.

" 'The wretch that has wronged you so deeply,' rejoined the stranger, 'is now on his death-bed. His days have been days of misery, his nights have been sleepless hours of anguish – yet he cannot die without your forgiveness. His life has been an unremitting penance – yet he dares not part from his burden while your curses load his soul.'

" 'Tell him,' said Lady Bothwell sternly, 'to ask pardon of that Being whom he has so greatly offended, not of an erring mortal like himself. What could my forgiveness avail him?'

" 'Much,' answered the old man. 'It will be an earnest of that which he may then venture to ask from his Creator, lady, and from yours. Remember, Lady Bothwell, you too have a death-bed to look forward to; Your soul may – all human souls must – feel the awe of facing the judgment-seat, with the wounds of an untented conscience, raw, and rankling – what thought would it be then that should whisper, "I have given no mercy, how then shall I ask it?"'

" 'Man, whosoever thou mayest be,' replied Lady Bothwell, 'urge me not so cruelly. It would be but blasphemous hypocrisy to utter with my lips the words which every throb of my heart protests against. They would open the earth and give to light the wasted form of my sister, the bloody form of my murdered brother. Forgive him? – Never, never!'

" 'Great God!' cried the old man, holding up his hands, 'is it thus the worms which Thou hast called out of dust obey the commands of their Maker? Farewell, proud and unforgiving woman. Exult that thou hast added to a death in want and pain the agonies of religious despair; but never again mock Heaven by petitioning for the pardon which thou hast refused to grant.'

"He was turning from her.

" 'Stop,' she exclaimed; 'I will try – yes, I will try to pardon him.'

" 'Gracious lady,' said the old man, 'you will relieve the over-burdened soul which dare not sever itself from its sinful companion of earth without being at peace with you. What do I know – your forgiveness may perhaps preserve for penitence the dregs of a wretched life.'

" 'Ha!' said the lady, as a sudden light broke on her, 'it is the villain himself!' And grasping Sir Philip Forester – for it was he, and no other – by the collar, she raised a cry of 'Murder, murder! Seize the murderer!'

"At an exclamation so singular, in such a place, the company thronged into the apartment; but Sir Philip Forester was no longer there. He had forcibly extricated himself from Lady Bothwell's hold, and had run out of the apartment, which opened on the landing-place of the stair. There seemed no escape in that direction, for there were several persons coming up the steps, and others descending. But the unfortunate man was desperate. He threw himself over the balustrade, and alighted safely in the lobby, though a leap of fifteen feet at least, then dashed into the street, and was lost in darkness.

Some of the Bothwell family made pursuit, and had they come up with the fugitive they might perhaps have slain him; for in those days men's blood ran warm in their veins. But the police did not interfere, the matter most criminal having happened long since, and in a foreign land. Indeed it was always thought that this extraordinary scene originated in a hypocritical experiment, by which Sir Philip desired to ascertain whether he might return to his native country in safety from the resentment of a family which he had injured so deeply. As the result fell out so contrary to his wishes, he is believed to have returned to the Continent, and there died in exile."

So closed the tale of the *Mysterious Mirror.*

Death of the Laird's Jock

Walter Scott

*[The manner in which this trifle was introduced at the time to Mr. F.M.
Reynolds, editor of 'The Keepsake of 1828', leaves no occasion for a preface.]*
August, 1831.

To the Editor of the Keepsake

You have asked me, sir, to point out a subject for the pencil, and I feel the difficulty of
complying with your request; although I am not certainly unaccustomed to literary
composition, or a total stranger to the stores of history and tradition, which afford the best
copies for the painter's art. But although *sicut pictura poesis* is an ancient and undisputed
axiom – although poetry and painting both address themselves to the same object of
exciting the human imagination, by presenting to it pleasing or sublime images of ideal
scenes; yet the one conveying itself through the ears to the understanding, and the other
applying itself only to the eyes, the subjects which are best suited to the bard or tale-
teller are often totally unfit for painting, where the artist must present in a single glance all
that his art has power to tell us. The artist can neither recapitulate the past nor intimate
the future. The single *now* is all which he can present; and hence, unquestionably, many
subjects which delight us in poetry or in narrative, whether real or fictitious, cannot with
advantage be transferred to the canvass.

Being in some degree aware of these difficulties, though doubtless unacquainted both
with their extent, and the means by which they may be modified or surmounted, I have,
nevertheless, ventured to draw up the following traditional narrative as a story in which,
when the general details are known, the interest is so much concentrated in one strong
moment of agonizing passion, that it can be understood, and sympathized with, at a
single glance. I therefore presume that it may be acceptable as a hint to some one among
the numerous artists, who have of late years distinguished themselves as rearing up and
supporting the British school.

Enough has been said and sung about

> *The well contested ground,*
> *The warlike border-land –*

to render the habits of the tribes who inhabited them before the union of England
and Scotland familiar to most of your readers. The rougher and sterner features of their
character were softened by their attachment to the fine arts, from which has arisen the
saying that, on the frontiers, every dale had its battle, and every river its song. A rude species

of chivalry was in constant use, and single combats were practised as the amusement of the few intervals of truce which suspended the exercise of war. The inveteracy of this custom may be inferred from the following incident.

Bernard Gilpin, the apostle of the north, the first who undertook to preach the Protestant doctrines to the Border dalesmen, was surprised, on entering one of their churches, to see a gauntlet or mail-glove hanging above the altar. Upon enquiring the meaning of a symbol so indecorous being displayed in that sacred place, he was informed by the clerk that the glove was that of a famous swordsman, who hung it there as an emblem of a general challenge and gage of battle, to any who should dare to take the fatal token down. "Reach it to me," said the reverend churchman.

The clerk and sexton equally declined the perilous office, and the good Bernard Gilpin was obliged to remove the glove with his own hands, desiring those who were present to inform the champion that he, and no other, had possessed himself of the gage of defiance. But the champion was as much ashamed to face Bernard Gilpin as the officials of the church had been to displace his pledge of combat.

The date of the following story is about the latter years of Queen Elizabeth's reign; and the events took place in Liddesdale, a hilly and pastoral district of Roxburghshire, which, on a part of its boundary, is divided from England only by a small river.

During the good old times of *rugging and riving*, (that is, tugging and tearing,) under which term the disorderly doings of the warlike age are affectionately remembered, this valley was principally cultivated by the sept or clan of the Armstrongs. The chief of this warlike race was the Laird of Mangerton. At the period of which I speak, the estate of Mangerton, with the power and dignity of chief, was possessed by John Armstrong, a man of great size, strength, and courage. While his father was alive, he was distinguished from others of his clan who bore the same name, by the epithet of the Laird's Jock, that is to say, the Laird's son Jock, or Jack. This name he distinguished by so many bold and desperate achievements, that he retained it even after his father's death, and is mentioned under it both in authentic records and in tradition. Some of his feats are recorded in the *Minstrelsy of the Scottish Border*, and others mentioned in contemporary chronicles.

At the species of singular combat which we have described, the Laird's Jock was unrivalled, and no champion of Cumberland, Westmoreland, or Northumberland, could endure the sway of the huge two-handed sword which he wielded, and which few others could even lift. This 'awful sword,' as the common people term it, was as dear to him as Durindana or Fushberta to their respective masters, and was nearly as formidable to his enemies as those renowned falchions proved to the foes of Christendom. The weapon had been bequeathed to him by a celebrated English outlaw named Hobbie Noble, who, having committed some deed for which he was in danger from justice fled to Liddesdale, and became a follower, or rather a brother-in-arms, to the renowned Laird's Jock; till, venturing into England with a small escort, a faithless guide, and with a light single-handed sword instead of his ponderous brand, Hobbie Noble, attacked by superior numbers, was made prisoner and executed.

With this weapon, and by means of his own strength and address, the Laird's Jock maintained the reputation of the best swordsman on the border side, and defeated or slew many who ventured to dispute with him the formidable title.

But years pass on with the strong and the brave as with the feeble and the timid. In process of, time, the Laird's Jock grew incapable of wielding his weapons, and finally of all active exertion, even of the most ordinary kind. The disabled champion became at length totally bed-ridden, and entirely dependent for his comfort on the pious duties of an only daughter, his perpetual attendant and companion.

Besides this dutiful child, the Laird's Jock had an only son, upon whom devolved the perilous task of leading the clan to battle, and maintaining the warlike renown of his native country, which was now disputed by the English upon many occasions. The young Armstrong was active, brave, and strong, and brought home from dangerous adventures many tokens of decided success. Still the ancient chief conceived, as it would seem, that his son was scarce yet entitled by age and experience to be entrusted with the two-handed sword, by the use of which he had himself been so dreadfully distinguished.

At length, an English champion, one of the name of Foster, (if I rightly recollect,) had the audacity to send a challenge to the best swordsman in Liddesdale; and young Armstrong, burning for chivalrous distinction, accepted the challenge.

The heart of the disabled old man swelled with joy, when he heard that the challenge was passed and accepted, and the meeting fixed at a neutral spot, used as the place of rencontre upon such occasions, and which he himself had distinguished by numerous victories. He exulted so much in the conquest which he anticipated, that, to nerve his son to still bolder exertions, he conferred upon him, as champion of his clan and province, the celebrated weapon which he had hitherto retained in his own custody.

This was not all. When the day of combat arrived, the Laird's Jock, in spite of his daughter's affectionate remonstrances, determined, though he had not left his bed for two years to be a personal witness of the duel. His will was still a law to his people, who bore him on their shoulders, wrapt in plaids and blankets, to the spot where the combat was to take place, and seated him on a fragment of rock, which is still called the Laird's Jock's stone. There he remained with eyes fixed on the lists or barrier, within which the champions were about to meet. His daughter, having done all she could for his accommodation, stood motionless beside him, divided between anxiety for his health, and for the event of the combat to her beloved brother. Ere yet the fight began, the old men gazed on their chief, now seen for the first time after several years, and sadly compared his altered features and wasted frame, with the paragon of strength and manly beauty which they once remembered. The young men gazed on his large form and powerful make, as upon some antediluvian giant who had survived the destruction of the Flood.

But the sound of the trumpets on both sides recalled the attention of every one to the lists, surrounded as they were by numbers of both nations eager to witness the event of the day. The combatants met in the lists. It is needless to describe the struggle: the Scottish champion fell. Foster, placing his foot on his antagonist, seized on the redoubted sword, so precious in the eyes of its aged owner, and brandished it over his head as a trophy of his conquest. The English shouted in triumph. But the despairing cry of the aged champion, who saw his country dishonoured, and his sword, long the terror of their race, in possession of an Englishman, was heard high above the acclamations of victory. He seemed, for an instant, animated by all his wonted power; for he started from the rock on which he sat, and while the garments with which he had been invested fell from his wasted frame, and showed the ruins of his strength, he tossed his arms wildly to heaven, and uttered a cry of indignation, horror, and despair, which, tradition says, was heard to a preternatural distance and resembled the cry of a dying lion more than a human sound.

His friends received him in their arms as he sank utterly exhausted by the effort, and bore him back to his castle in mute sorrow; while his daughter at once wept for her brother, and endeavoured to mitigate and soothe the despair of her father. But this was impossible;

the old man's only tie to life was rent rudely asunder, and his heart had broken with it. The death of his son had no part in his sorrow: if he thought of him at all, it was as the degenerate boy, through whom the honour of his country and clan had been lost, and he died in the course of three days, never even mentioning his name, but pouring out unintermitted lamentations for the loss of his noble sword.

I conceive, that the moment when the disabled chief was roused into a last exertion by the agony of the moment is favourable to the object of a painter. He might obtain the full advantage of contrasting the form of the rugged old man, in the extremity of furious despair, with the softness and beauty of the female form. The fatal field might be thrown into perspective, so as to give full effect to these two principal figures, and with the single explanation, that the piece represented a soldier beholding his son slain, and the honour of his country lost, the picture would be sufficiently intelligible at the first glance. If it was thought necessary to show more clearly the nature of the conflict, it might be indicated by the pennon of Saint George being displayed at one end of the lists, and that of Saint Andrew at the other.

I remain, sir,
Your obedient servant,
The Author Of Waverley

Roger Dodsworth
The Reanimated Englishman
Mary Shelley

IT MAY BE REMEMBERED, that on the fourth of July last, a paragraph appeared in the papers importing that Dr. Hotham, of Northumberland, returning from Italy, over Mount St. Gothard, a score or two of years ago, had dug out from under an avalanche, in the neighbourhood of the mountain, a human being whose animation had been suspended by the action of the frost. Upon the application of the usual remedies, the patient was resuscitated, and discovered himself to be Mr. Dodsworth, the son of the antiquary Dodsworth, who perished in the reign of Charles I. He was thirty-seven years of age at the time of his inhumation, which had taken place as he was returning from Italy, in 1654. It was added that as soon as he was sufficiently recovered he would return to England, under the protection of his preserver. We have since heard no more of him, and various plans for public benefit, which have started in philanthropic minds on reading the statement, have already returned to their pristine nothingness. The antiquarian society had eaten their way to several votes for medals, and had already begun, in idea, to consider what prices it could afford to offer for Mr. Dodsworth's old clothes, and to conjecture what treasures in the way of pamphlet, old song, or autographic letter his pockets might contain. Poems from all quarters, of all kinds, elegiac, congratulatory, burlesque and allegoric, were half written. Mr. Godwin had suspended for the sake of such authentic information the history of the Commonwealth he had just begun. It is hard not only that the world should be baulked of these destined gifts from the talents of the country, but also that it should be promised and then deprived of a new subject of romantic wonder and scientific interest. A novel idea is worth much in the commonplace routine of life, but a new fact, an astonishment, a miracle, a palpable wandering from the course of things into apparent impossibilities, is a circumstance to which the imagination must cling with delight, and we say again that it is hard, very hard, that Mr. Dodsworth refuses to appear, and that the believers in his resuscitation are forced to undergo the sarcasms and triumphant arguments of those sceptics who always keep on the safe side of the hedge.

Now we do not believe that any contradiction or impossibility is attached to the adventures of this youthful antique. Animation (I believe physiologists agree) can as easily be suspended for an hundred or two years, as for as many seconds. A body hermetically sealed up by the frost, is of necessity preserved in its pristine entireness. That which is totally secluded from the action of external agency, can neither have any thing added to nor taken away from it: no decay can take place, for something can never become nothing; under the influence of that state of being which we call death, change but not annihilation removes from our sight the corporeal atoma; the earth receives sustenance from them, the air is fed by them, each element takes its own, thus seizing forcible repayment of what it had lent. But the elements that hovered round Mr. Dodsworth's icy shroud had no power to overcome the obstacle it presented. No zephyr could gather a hair from his head, nor could the influence of dewy night or genial morn penetrate his more than adamantine panoply. The story of the Seven Sleepers rests on a miraculous interposition – they slept. Mr. Dodsworth did not sleep; his breast never heaved, his pulses were stopped; death had his finger pressed on his lips which no breath might pass. He has removed it now, the grim shadow is vanquished, and stands wondering. His victim has cast from him the frosty spell, and arises as perfect a man as he had lain down an hundred and fifty years before. We have eagerly desired to be furnished with some particulars of his first conversations, and the mode in which he has learnt to adapt himself to his new scene of life. But since facts are denied to us, let us be permitted to indulge in conjecture. What his first words were may be guessed from the expressions used by people exposed to shorter accidents of the like nature. But as his powers return, the plot thickens. His dress had already excited Doctor Hotham's astonishment – the peaked beard – the love locks – the frill, which, until it was thawed, stood stiff under the mingled influence of starch and frost; his dress fashioned like that of one of Vandyke's portraits, or (a more familiar similitude) Mr. Sapio's costume in Winter's Opera of the Oracle, his pointed shoes – all spoke of other times. The curiosity of his preserver was keenly awake, that of Mr. Dodsworth was about to be roused. But to be enabled to conjecture with any degree of likelihood the tenor of his first inquiries, we must endeavour to make out what part he played in his former life. He lived at the most interesting period of English History – he was lost to the world when Oliver Cromwell had arrived at the summit of his ambition, and in the eyes of all Europe the commonwealth of England appeared so established as to endure for ever. Charles I was dead; Charles II was an outcast, a beggar, bankrupt even in hope. Mr. Dodsworth's father, the antiquary, received a salary from the republican general, Lord Fairfax, who was himself a great lover of antiquities, and died the very year that his son went to his long, but not unending sleep, a curious coincidence this, for it would seem that our frost-preserved friend was returning to England on his father's death, to claim probably his inheritance – how short lived are human views! Where now is Mr. Dodsworth's patrimony? Where his co-heirs, executors, and fellow legatees? His protracted absence has, we should suppose, given the present possessors to his estate – the world's chronology is an hundred and seventy years older since he seceded from the busy scene, hands after hands have tilled his acres, and then become clods beneath them; we may be permitted to doubt whether one single particle of their surface is individually the same as those which were to have been his – the youthful soil would of itself reject the antique clay of its claimant.

Mr. Dodsworth, if we may judge from the circumstance of his being abroad, was no zealous commonwealth's man, yet his having chosen Italy as the country in which to make his tour and his projected return to England on his father's death, renders it probable that he was no violent loyalist. One of those men he seems to be (or to have been) who did not follow Cato's advice as recorded in the Pharsalia; a party, if to be of no party admits of such a term, which Dante recommends us utterly to despise, and which not unseldom falls between the two stools, a seat on either of which is so carefully avoided. Still Mr. Dodsworth could hardly fail to feel anxious for the latest news from his native country at so critical a period; his absence might have put his own property in jeopardy; we may imagine therefore that after his limbs had felt the cheerful return of circulation, and after he had refreshed himself with such of earth's products as from all analogy he never could have hoped to live to eat, after he had been told from what peril he had been rescued, and said a prayer thereon which even appeared enormously long to Dr. Hotham – we may imagine, we say, that his first question would be: "if any news had arrived lately from England?"

"I had letters yesterday," Dr. Hotham may well be supposed to reply.

"Indeed," cries Mr. Dodsworth, "and pray, sir, has any change for better or worse occurred in that poor distracted country?"

Dr. Hotham suspects a Radical, and coldly replies: "Why, sir, it would be difficult to say in what its distraction consists. People talk of starving manufacturers, bankruptcies, and the fall of the Joint Stock Companies – excrescences these, excrescences which will attach themselves to a state of full health. England, in fact, was never in a more prosperous condition."

Mr. Dodsworth now more than suspects the Republican, and, with what we have supposed to be his accustomed caution, sinks for awhile his loyalty, and in a moderate tone asks: "Do our governors look with careless eyes upon the symptoms of over-health?"

"Our governors," answers his preserver, "if you mean our ministry, are only too alive to temporary embarrassment." (We beg Doctor Hotham's pardon if we wrong him in making him a high Tory; such a quality appertains to our pure anticipated cognition of a Doctor, and such is the only cognizance that we have of this gentleman.) "It were to be wished that they showed themselves more firm – the king, God bless him!"

"Sir!" exclaims Mr. Dodsworth.

Doctor Hotham continues, not aware of the excessive astonishment exhibited by his patient: "The king, God bless him, spares immense sums from his privy purse for the relief of his subjects, and his example has been imitated by all the aristocracy and wealth of England."

"The King!" ejaculates Mr. Dodsworth.

"Yes, sir," emphatically rejoins his preserver; "the king, and I am happy to say that the prejudices that so unhappily and unwarrantably possessed the English people with regard to his Majesty are now, with a few" (with added severity) "and I may say contemptible exceptions, exchanged for dutiful love and such reverence as his talents, virtues, and paternal care deserve."

"Dear sir, you delight me," replies Mr. Dodsworth, while his loyalty late a tiny bud suddenly expands into full flower; "yet I hardly understand; the change is so sudden; and the man – Charles Stuart, King Charles, I may now call him, his murder is I trust execrated as it deserves?"

Dr. Hotham put his hand on the pulse of his patient – he feared an access of delirium from such a wandering from the subject. The pulse was calm, and Mr. Dodsworth continued: "That unfortunate martyr looking down from heaven is, I trust, appeased by the reverence paid to his name and the prayers dedicated to his memory. No sentiment, I think I may venture to assert, is so general in England as the compassion and love in which the memory of that hapless monarch is held?"

"And his son, who now reigns? –"

"Surely, sir, you forget; no son; that of course is impossible. No descendant of his fills the English throne, now worthily occupied by the house of Hanover. The despicable race of the Stuarts, long outcast and wandering, is now extinct, and the last days of the last Pretender to the crown of that family justified in the eyes of the world the sentence which ejected it from the kingdom for ever."

Such must have been Mr. Dodsworth's first lesson in politics. Soon, to the wonder of the preserver and preserved, the real state of the case must have been revealed; for a time, the strange and tremendous circumstance of his long trance may have threatened the wits of Mr. Dodsworth with a total overthrow. He had, as he crossed Mount Saint Gothard, mourned a father – now every human being he had ever seen is 'lapped in lead,' is dust, each voice he had ever heard is mute. The very sound of the English tongue is changed, as his experience in conversation with Dr. Hotham assures him. Empires, religions, races of men, have probably sprung up or faded; his own patrimony (the thought is idle, yet, without it, how can he live?) is sunk into the thirsty gulf that gapes ever greedy to swallow the past; his learning, his acquirements, are probably obsolete; with a bitter smile he thinks to himself, I must take to my father's profession, and turn antiquary. The familiar objects, thoughts, and habits of my boyhood, are now antiquities. He wonders where the hundred and sixty folio volumes of MS. that his father had compiled, and which, as a lad, he had regarded with religious reverence, now are – where – ah, where? His favourite play-mate, the friend of his later years, his destined and lovely bride, tears long frozen are uncongealed, and flow down his young old cheeks.

But we do not wish to be pathetic; surely since the days of the patriarchs, no fair lady had her death mourned by her lover so many years after it had taken place. Necessity, tyrant of the world, in some degree reconciles Mr. Dodsworth to his fate. At first he is persuaded that the later generation of man is much deteriorated from his contemporaries; they are neither so tall, so handsome, nor so intelligent. Then by degrees he begins to doubt his first impression. The ideas that had taken possession of his brain before his accident, and which had been frozen up for so many years, begin to thaw and dissolve away, making room for others. He dresses himself in the modern style, and does not object much to anything except the neck-cloth and hard-boarded hat. He admires the texture of his shoes and stockings, and looks with admiration on a small Genevese watch, which he often consults, as if he were not yet assured that time had made progress in its accustomed manner, and as if he should find on its dial plate ocular demonstration that he had exchanged his thirty-seventh year for his two hundredth and upwards, and had left A.D. 1654 far behind to find himself suddenly a beholder of the ways of men in this enlightened nineteenth century. His curiosity is insatiable; when he reads, his eyes cannot purvey fast enough to his mind, and every now and then he lights upon some inexplicable passage, some discovery and knowledge familiar to us, but undreamed of in his days, that throws him into wonder and interminable reverie. Indeed, he may be supposed to pass much of his time in that state, now and then interrupting himself with a royalist song against old Noll and the Roundheads, breaking off suddenly, and looking round fearfully to see who were his auditors, and on beholding the modern appearance of his friend the Doctor, sighing to think that it is no longer of import to any, whether he sing a cavalier catch or a puritanic psalm.

It were an endless task to develop all the philosophic ideas to which Mr. Dodsworth's resuscitation naturally gives birth. We should like much to converse with this gentleman, and still more to observe the progress of his mind, and the change of his ideas in his very novel situation. If he be a sprightly youth, fond of the shows of the world, careless of the higher human pursuits, he may proceed summarily to cast into the shade all trace of his former life, and endeavour to merge himself at once into the stream of humanity now flowing. It would be curious enough to observe the mistakes he would make, and the medley of manners which would thus be produced. He may think to enter into active life, become whig or tory as his inclinations lead, and get a seat in the, even to him, once called chapel of St. Stephens. He may content himself with turning contemplative philosopher, and find sufficient food for his mind in tracing the march of the human intellect, the changes which have been wrought in the dispositions, desires, and powers of mankind. Will he be an advocate for perfectibility or deterioration? He must admire our manufactures, the progress of science, the diffusion of knowledge, and the fresh spirit of enterprise characteristic of our countrymen. Will he find any individuals to be compared to the glorious spirits of his day? Moderate in his views as we have supposed him to be, he will probably fall at once into the temporising tone of mind now so much in vogue. He will be pleased to find a calm in politics; he will greatly admire the ministry who have succeeded in conciliating almost all parties – to find peace where he left feud. The same character which he bore a couple of hundred years ago, will influence him now; he will still be the moderate, peaceful, unenthusiastic Mr. Dodsworth that he was in 1647.

For notwithstanding education and circumstances may suffice to direct and form the rough material of the mind, it cannot create, nor give intellect, noble aspiration, and energetic constancy where dullness, wavering of purpose, and grovelling desires, are stamped by nature. Entertaining this belief we have (to forget Mr. Dodsworth for awhile) often made conjectures how such and such heroes of antiquity would act, if they were reborn in these times: and then awakened fancy has gone on to imagine that some of them are reborn; that according to the theory explained by Virgil in his sixth *Aeneid,* every thousand years the dead return to life, and their souls endued with the same sensibilities and capacities as before, are turned naked of knowledge into this world, again to dress their skeleton powers in such habiliments as situation, education, and experience will furnish. Pythagoras, we are told, remembered many transmigrations of this sort, as having occurred to himself, though for a philosopher he made very little use of his anterior memories. It would prove an instructive school for kings and statesmen, and in fact for all human beings, called on as they are, to play their part on the stage of the world, could they remember what they had been. Thus we might obtain a glimpse of heaven and of hell, as, the secret of our former identity confined to our own bosoms, we winced or exulted in the blame or praise bestowed on our former selves. While the love of glory and posthumous reputation is as natural to man as his attachment to life itself, he must be, under such a state of things, tremblingly alive to the historic records of his honour or shame. The mild spirit of Fox would have been soothed by the recollection that he had played a worthy part as Marcus Antoninus – the former experiences of Alcibiades or even of the emasculated Steeny of James I. might have caused Sheridan to have refused to tread over again the same path of dazzling but fleeting brilliancy. The soul of our modern Corinna would have been purified and exalted by a consciousness that once it had given life to the form of Sappho. If at the present moment the witch, memory, were in a freak, to cause all the present generation to recollect that some ten centuries back they had been somebody else, would not several of our free thinking martyrs wonder to find that they had suffered as Christians under Domitian, while the judge as he passed sentence would suddenly become aware, that formerly he had condemned the saints of the early church to the torture, for not renouncing the religion he now upheld – nothing but benevolent actions and real goodness would come pure out of the ordeal. While it would be whimsical to perceive how some great men in parish affairs would strut under the consciousness that their hands had once held a sceptre, an honest artizan or pilfering domestic would find that he was little altered by being transformed into an idle noble or director of a joint stock company; in every way we may suppose that the humble would be exalted, and the noble and the proud would feel their stars and honours dwindle into baubles and child's play when they called to mind the lowly stations they had once occupied. If philosophical novels were in fashion, we conceive an excellent one might be written on the development of the same mind in various stations, in different periods of the world's history.

But to return to Mr. Dodsworth, and indeed with a few more words to bid him farewell. We entreat him no longer to bury himself in obscurity; or, if he modestly decline publicity, we beg him to make himself known personally to us. We have a thousand inquiries to make, doubts to clear up, facts to ascertain. If any fear that old habits and strangeness of appearance will make him ridiculous to those accustomed to associate with modern exquisites, we beg to assure him that we are not given to ridicule mere outward shows, and that worth and intrinsic excellence will always claim our respect.

This we say, if Mr. Dodsworth is alive. Perhaps he is again no more. Perhaps he opened his eyes only to shut them again more obstinately; perhaps his ancient clay could not thrive on the harvests of these latter days. After a little wonder; a little shuddering to find himself the dead alive – finding no affinity between himself and the present state of things – he has bidden once more an eternal farewell to the sun. Followed to his grave by his preserver and the wondering villagers, he may sleep the true death-sleep in the same valley where he so long reposed. Doctor Hotham may have erected a simple tablet over his twice-buried remains, inscribed –

To the Memory of R. Dodsworth,
An Englishman,
Born April 1, 1617; Died July 16, 1618; Aged 187

An inscription which, if it were preserved during any terrible convulsion that caused the world to begin its life again, would occasion many learned disquisitions and ingenious theories concerning a race which authentic records showed to have secured the privilege of attaining so vast an age.

Eli Whitney and the Cotton Djinn

Zach Shephard

ELI WHITNEY was not always a great inventor. Even the best of his early ideas failed to generate public interest, because no one needed weaponized cheddar or a sock that covers both feet. He had all the tools he needed to improve the world – a Yale education, free lodging with a friend and an abundance of physical resources – but without inspiration, he just couldn't come up with anything good.

Then came the day when he burned the handkerchief, and everything changed.

Eli, brainstorming alone in a shack on Catherine Greene's plantation, had just wasted his last piece of paper designing a harvester that couldn't possibly be efficient because yams aren't twelve feet long. It's for this reason that, when his next idea struck, the only available writing surface was the pair of handkerchiefs in his pocket.

On the square of red cloth Eli recorded his idea for a new type of banjo, which could churn butter more effectively than any banjo before it. He labeled his invention the slapwagon, which would make perfect sense if you could see the illustration.

Grinning at the thrill of discovery, Eli held the drawing out at arm's length. Upon review, he soon realized the slapwagon's fatal flaw: it was stupid.

"Worthless!" he said, and set the handkerchief on fire. He threw it to the dirt floor of the shack, where it promptly exploded.

From the cloth rose a pillar of smokeless fire, which shifted through various bestial shapes before solidifying into the form of a statuesque woman in purple, stomach-baring silks. Her skin was the color of lava, its texture that of rough tablecloth, and her eyes blazed like flame reflected in opal.

"Who dares?" she asked. "Who summons Mari, Lady of Fire, Wielder of the Eternal –"

The water struck her squarely in the face, soaking into the red cloth of her skin. Mari peeled open one eye, then the other, looking something less than jolly as her gaze fixed on Eli, who was still holding the empty bucket.

"Why," she said, "would you ever do that?"

"You said you were on fire."

"*Of* fire. *Of.*"

"Oh. I'm dreadfully sorry, then. Will you accept my apologies?"

Mari sighed. "Oh, I suppose so," she said, turning to the wall-mirror and finger-combing her long black hair. "After all, I'd hate to get off on the wrong foot. Tell me, darling, what's your name?"

"Eli. Eli Whitney."

"And how did you summon me, Eli Whitney?"

"I burned a handkerchief."

Mari stopped combing her hair. "A handkerchief? Yes …that does sound familiar. Do you happen to have another like it?"

Eli held up a black cloth.

"Oh, wonderful! Would you mind burning that one, too?"

Eli, eager to find an explanation for the seven-foot woman who'd materialized out of thin air, lit a match.

"Wait!" Mari said. She took the handkerchief, blew her nose into it and handed it back. "There we are. Carry on."

Eli lit the soiled handkerchief and tossed it to the floor. A familiar explosion followed, and when the flaming pillar stopped its shifting, a bare-chested, heavily muscled man with two small horns on his forehead stood beside Mari.

"Who calls me forth?" he asked. "Who calls upon Zumaj, Lord of the Shadowy Depths, Vanquisher of the Warrior-Kings, Keeper of the why the *hell* am I covered in snot?"

Zumaj held his arms to the sides, as if too disgusted to let his body touch itself. His skin, textured like Mari's and dark as an endless cave, was soaked.

"Eli, this is Zumaj. Zumaj, Eli."

Eli stepped forward to get a closer look at the pair. "This is remarkable," he said. "What are you?"

"We're djinn, silly."

"Djinn! Like from the Arabian tales! Do you grant wishes?"

"We've been known to dabble in miracle-making, in exchange for certain services. But before we get to any of that, I'd like to know more about those handkerchiefs. Where did you get them?"

"I bought them at the market, just the other day."

"From whom?"

"I don't recall the merchant's name – I'm new in town, just passing through on my way to a teaching job."

"Hm." Mari tapped her lips. "A teacher. I suppose that's all right."

Eli, not wanting to leave his wish-factories unimpressed, quickly updated his story.

"It's just a temporary position," he said. "What I really want is to be an inventor."

"An inventor!" Mari said. "That's *much* more interesting. Isn't that lovely, Zumaj?"

The darker djinni leaned away from Eli's curious hand, which was trying to touch one of his horns. "Yes," he said, sounding entirely unamused. "Lovely."

Mari clapped her hands. "It's settled, then! We'll do inventions. But we'll need some help. Eli, would you be interested in earning a few wishes?"

Eli's attention cut over to Mari. "Yes! I'd like that very much."

"Good," she said, draping her long red arm over his shoulders. "Now, let's talk details …"

* * *

In theory, Eli's rat-trap should have taken three hours to capture every rodent on the east side of the plantation. In practice, it only took forty minutes to kill two cats and incinerate a shed.

Eli splashed one last bucket of water onto the shed's smoldering remains. He sifted through the ashes, but found none of the rat parts Zumaj had tasked him with gathering. Too discouraged to start over right away, he took a break from that project and focused on Mari's needs for a time.

Eli headed into town to gather the materials on the djinni's list. Just before he reached the general store he felt a sudden tug on his jacket, which drew him forcefully into the empty space between buildings.

"I beg your pardon!" Eli said, as he was released with a shove. He turned to get a look at the brute who'd attacked him, only to find a five-foot woman with glittery green eyes and animal-hide clothing.

"I don't have much time, so I'll make this quick. Your name is Eli. You bought two handkerchiefs at the market recently. I need them, and you're going to give them to me."

"I'm sorry," Eli said, straightening his jacket, "but even if I wanted to, I couldn't help you." The woman leaned in close and sniffed him.

"Oh, hell," she said. "You've already burned them. I can smell Mari's stench all over you."

"You know Mari?"

"Better than I'd care to." The woman rubbed her forehead, muttering under her breath. "Okay. This is going to take longer than I thought. I'm going to have to tell you my name – promise me you won't panic."

Eli, having never experienced an aversion to obscure names in the past, confidently nodded.

The woman took a deep breath. "My name is Henrietta."

"Henrietta? Why would that –"

There was a sound like too-tight pants tearing over a too-plump rump, and in the next instant, Henrietta was a walrus.

Henrietta, with spiraled tusks like unicorn horns and a rainbow mane running down her back, regarded her left flipper.

"Oh, wonderful," she said. "That's just perfect."

Eli, far from panicking, leaned in for a closer look at the creature.

"Remarkable ..." He moved his hand toward Henrietta's tusk, but she flipper-slapped it away.

"Okay," she said, "I'm sure you want an explanation, so here's the short version: I'm cursed. If I don't tell strangers my name, they forget having ever met me. If I do, I temporarily change shapes."

"This is fascinating! I don't see why you were worried. I'm delighted to meet a ..." Eli gestured at Henrietta, searching for a word. "... Walricorn."

"Yes, well – we got lucky. This shape looks to be pretty tame. But now that I have your attention, let's talk djinn. I'm sure Mari and Zumaj have set you to a few tasks by now, yes?"

"They have. Though I must confess, I'm still not certain why they need me to gather such items."

"It's because they're planning to kill each other. Probably in a very elaborate fashion."

"Kill each other! But why?"

"Because that's the game they play. They've been playing it for as long as anyone can remember. Mari and Zumaj are immortal – their bodies may die every now and then, but they always come back. And when they do, they pass the time by finding new ways to end each other. We can't let that happen. There can't be a winner. They both need to die."

"I'm afraid I don't understand."

"The world of magic takes getting used to, I know. But look at me!" Henrietta flailed her flippers and body about, like she had an itch she couldn't reach. "You can't deny what your eyes are seeing."

"No, I don't deny it at all – I've seen enough magic today to be a believer. The thing I don't understand is why we can't let the djinn continue their game. If they're both consenting and they'll be resurrected anyway, where's the harm?"

"The harm comes from the winner having to wait a few decades for the loser's resurrection. When djinn get bored, they get into mischief."

"What kind of mischief?"

"The kind that involves death and destruction, and cursing innocent people." Henrietta spread her flippers, her rainbow mane ruffling. "Exhibit A."

Eli considered the woman's story. He shook his head.

"No," he said. "That can't be right. They promised me wishes."

"Of course they did. Because they want your help. This game of theirs is run by some pretty strict rules – they can't harm one another directly, which is why they're having you run errands. But you won't be getting any wishes after the day of their contest, Eli. The best you can hope for is a curse that doesn't make dating incredibly awkward."

Eli paced the alley. He didn't want to give up on those wishes. Despite his many failures, he really was a brilliant engineer – he could build any machine that came to mind, no matter how complex or likely to explode it was. Unfortunately, none of those machines was the world-changing device he aspired to produce. He had a creative block, which he was certain the wishes could fix.

"I'm sorry," he said, "but I only just met you. How do I know you're telling the truth? How do I know you're not the dangerous one here? I have no frame of reference for walricorns; maybe you're all thieves and killers."

"I am not a walricorn!" Henrietta shouted, flopping around like a walricorn. "I –". She paused, composing herself. "Okay, answer me this: what do the djinn have you collecting?"

"Mari needs some basic building supplies. Nothing unusual – all items that can be purchased from various shops around town."

"And what about Zumaj?"

"He …has me collecting rats." Eli quickly looked away.

"And?" Henrietta asked. "What else?"

"Well," Eli said, rubbing the back of his neck, "he did mention another ingredient, but he said it was optional. I don't *have* to collect a fresh human head."

Henrietta crossed her flippers over her chest, raising a rainbow eyebrow.

"I admit it sounds bad," Eli said. "But I don't suspect the djinn are as evil as you think."

"That's the greed talking. You want your wishes."

"And with them, I'll finally be able to make the world a better place." Eli straightened his posture, raised his chin and bowed. "It was a pleasure meeting you, Henrietta." He turned and exited the alley, knowing the walricorn would not follow him into public view.

"You need to think this through!" she shouted after him. "And once you have, you'll be hearing from me!"

* * *

Mari had selected the plantation's workshop as her base of operations, not only because its great size suited her needs, but because Eli had assured her total privacy: the workers tended to avoid that place, because no one wanted to be around when Eli resumed work on his Wasp-Agitation Device.

Eli entered the workshop with the bucket of metal spikes Mari had ordered, placing them on a crate as he marveled at the sight before him.

"My goodness!" he said. "You've been busy."

Mari stopped hammering on a machine she was building into the far wall. She approached Eli with a smile.

"Marvelous, don't you think? And are those my spikes? Lovely! This is all turning out so very well."

Eli circled the rectangular pit that took up most of the workshop's floor. A large wooden cylinder ran lengthwise through the middle, filling the majority of the pit.

"What's this for?" he asked.

"The event, silly. Did you get the rest of the materials?"

"They're outside. Mari, about this event ..."

"Which event? The one I specifically told you not to ask nosey questions about?"

"Yes, well – I'm just concerned for your safety, is all. Especially since the two of you are trying to kill one another."

Mari's eyes narrowed. "Who told you that?"

"No one," Eli said, picking at a loose shirt-thread. "But I'm an inventor, you know, and I can see the pieces of your event coming together, forming into an elaborate machine. It seems clear that you and Zumaj are planning a fight to the death."

Mari turned to examine the bucket of spikes. "You're right, of course. But don't worry about us. We've done this plenty of times throughout the centuries – we never stay dead long."

"That's certainly a relief. Still ..." Eli scratched the back of his head.

"Go on, darling."

"I just – it seems there are better things you could do with your immortality. You have an infinite supply of time, not to mention considerable strength and wit. With your tools you could invent machines, tend to the needy, write poems – you could change the world."

"Have you ever *tried* writing poetry? Good luck finding a rhyme for 'eviscerate' that fits the context of a love story. No, Eli, I will do none of those things. Your world-changing nonsense could never be as fulfilling as a good victory over Zumaj." She pointed her hammer at Eli. "And speaking of that big black behemoth, you should see if he needs any help – this won't be a fair contest if I'm monopolizing all your time. Run along, darling."

Eli crossed the plantation, hands in his pockets and heavy thoughts in his head. Before he knew it he was at the shack where he'd first summoned the djinn, which now served as Zumaj's headquarters.

The sack of dead rats Eli had dropped off earlier was no longer outside the door. He'd given up on capturing the vermin himself, and had instead acquired them from a local hotel owner who'd been lazy about cleaning his traps. The price had been very reasonable, because it turns out rat carcasses were not an expensive commodity in 1792.

Eli stepped inside the shack, its walls bright with sunlight seeping through the cracks. Zumaj sat on the floor, his hulking back toward Eli, with a pile of rat parts to one side and raven parts to the other.

Eli cleared his throat.

"Come in, mortal."

Eli circled Zumaj, seeing his first glimpse of the djinni's project.

"Oh, that's – that's some very nice work."

Zumaj pulled the thread tight and clipped it with his teeth, then stuck the needle into the cloth-flesh of his forearm. He held up his project, viewing it with a critical eye.

"Well?" he asked. "Tell me what you think, inventor."

"It's …I mean, it's certainly a …bird. Rat. Thing." Eli moved to get a better look at the abomination. "Very pretty, if that's what you're going for. Or not, if it isn't."

"Hmph." Zumaj removed the needle from his arm and resumed his work.

"I think it will be a fantastic tool for your event, if that's what you're asking. That thing surely has a decent chance of killing Mari."

Zumaj stopped stitching. "You know about the event?"

"I made some guesses. Mari confirmed."

"I see. Well, if you're worried that I'm not adhering to the theme, I would argue that biological inventions are still inventions. Now, come and sit. I need my legion prepared by tomorrow morning, and your aid is required."

For the next thirty minutes, Eli learned how to assemble unholy monstrosities from dead animal pieces. The process was equal parts educational and gross.

"I was wondering," Eli said as they worked, "have you ever considered doing something else with your immortality? Something that might benefit the world?"

"There is nothing else. Avenging my losses to Mari is all that matters."

"I see."

Eli finished his first abomination, which Zumaj animated and commanded to sprint to the other side of the shack. The bipedal creation ran in three big circles, tripped, and fell on its face.

"I see the problem," Eli said. "I took mismatched legs from the pile – they're not the same length. I'm sorry, but I'm afraid I've ruined this one."

"It's not ruined. The parts are interchangeable."

"Interchangeable?" Eli scratched his chin. "What a brilliant –"

A rat's leg hit him in the face, dropping into his lap.

"Use that one," Zumaj said. "Back to work."

* * *

By the next morning, Eli still hadn't figured out what to do about the djinn. On the one hand, his conversations with Mari and Zumaj had been eye-opening, and seemed to coincide with Henrietta's story about their evil nature. On the other hand, wishes.

Eli resolved to continue business as usual until he could decide on a course. It's for this reason that he went to Mari's workshop in the morning, only to find Henrietta in a giant birdcage in the corner.

Henrietta, human-formed once again, held a finger to her lips and beckoned Eli over. He jogged across the workshop, keeping an eye out for the absent Mari.

"Henrietta," he said, grimacing at her bruised cheek and split lip, "what are you doing here?"

"I came looking for you. I wanted to see if you'd found anything that would change your mind about the djinn." She gestured at her prison. "Is this proof enough?"

"I'm sorry – I never meant for you to be harmed. I should have known the djinn were cruel from the beginning, but I see the truth now. I'm getting you out of there."

"I'm afraid I can't allow that, darling."

Eli turned to see the towering form of Mari, standing just a few yards away. How a seven-foot woman with cherry-red skin had managed to sneak through the vastness of the workshop was anyone's guess, but there was probably some magic involved.

"I'd hoped this moment would never come," Mari said. "Or at least not until after my victory today. Do you have any idea how many of our wonderful competitions this one has ruined, Eli? In fact, I seem to recall her being responsible for a certain spell that turned me into a handkerchief."

"And I seem to recall *you* burning my village and killing my family."

"Did I? Hm. That must have been a good year for me – sounds like a victory celebration. You should be glad your family died for a noble cause."

Henrietta's spit landed just south of its mark, striking Mari below the eye. The djinni wiped herself clean with a forearm.

"Sometimes I wonder why I didn't kill you years ago," she said. "Then I remember what a delightful idea that curse was, and how much I enjoy knowing that you still suffer to this day. Once such a social creature, now unable to be remembered as anything but a strange beast ...How positively *lovely*."

"Please," Eli said, "let her go. You don't need to do this."

"I'm afraid I do, actually. Today's event must run smoothly, and that can't happen so long as this one's loose."

"What are you going to do with her?"

"I'm not certain. I'd like to hear Zumaj's opinion on the matter, which is why you're going to have him meet me in the western fields."

"I'm through running your errands."

"Come now, Eli – I can't seek him out myself. Catching a glimpse of his project before the event would be a blatant violation of the rules. And besides, you're in too deep at this point. If you don't do as I say, I'll kill this little darling, not to mention everyone you've ever loved. Here," Mari said, handing Eli a note. "This is a list of things I want you to accomplish while I'm meeting with Zumaj. I'll be checking your work when you're done. And if you finish early, do be sure to tidy up the places where Zumaj and I will be standing during the event; I'd hate for him to think I'm a slob."

Mari opened the cage, enveloped Henrietta with a large sack and slung the protesting prisoner over her shoulder. "Be back soon," she said. "The show starts at nine o'clock, sharp!"

* * *

After delivering Mari's message to Zumaj, Eli found himself with a second list of last-minute tasks. He only had a short time to work with, but managed to speed through the stitching on the abominations and prepare the workshop for the event. The djinn entered just as he finished sweeping.

"I've done everything you asked," he said. "Please don't harm her."

Mari put Henrietta, now bound and gagged, back into the cage. She then patrolled the workshop, checking the spinning gears on the machines she'd built into the walls, while Zumaj took Eli aside.

"My legion," he said. "They are prepared?"

Eli pulled the covering away from a crate, revealing the abominations inside.

"Good. This will be a day to be remembered, inventor. I see Mari's device in the floor, and don't suspect it is strong enough to end me. Prepare to celebrate in the name of Zumaj."

"Yes," Eli said, lifting his fist half-heartedly. "Zumaj. Woo."

Zumaj took the abominations to the far end of the workshop, where he started setting them up. Mari, halfway through her sweep of the area, came across the workshop's clock and sucked in a sharp breath.

"Eli!" she said. "Is that time right?"

"It should be. That clock's always run fine."

"Zumaj! Places!"

Mari ran to one end of the workshop and stood in the small red box Eli had painted on the floor. Zumaj stood in a similar box on the opposite end. Between them, running lengthwise through the workshop, was the pit containing the cylinder, which now had a number of spikes protruding from its curved surface.

Everyone, including the bird-rats, looked at the clock. A few seconds before nine, Mari smiled at Zumaj. "Good luck, darling."

"To you as well."

The clock chimed and the event began, Eli watching helplessly from the side.

Zumaj's legion waddled forth in their jerky, uncoordinated manner. Mari watched the cylinder, which was doing an excellent job of not moving at all.

"It's not spinning! Why isn't it spinning?"

Zumaj laughed. "Poor Mari. Was there an error in your calculations? Should we expect your machines to start functioning at the stroke of ten?"

"Even if my machines are late, at least they'll prove more useful than your little errors."

Zumaj looked at his legion. The bird-rats were supposed to be advancing on Mari, but were instead stumbling in circles.

"Inventor!" he yelled. "What is wrong with my creations?"

"It looks like a problem with their legs," Eli said. "Maybe you should check."

"I can't! Once the contest has started, I am forbidden from leaving this spot!"

Eli nodded. "I had a feeling that might be the case."

"Fool!" Mari said. "What have you done?"

Eli went to Mari and took the cage's key from her pocket. The djinni stood still as stone, not resisting.

"Explain yourself!" she said.

"I did a lot of thinking about your game while you were gone," Eli said, unlocking the door to Henrietta's cage. "It seemed odd that you would observe so many rules if the ultimate goal was simply to kill each other. Why not just get to the point and have it out? Why all this strange ritual? And then I realized: you do it this way because you have to. You do it because, like Henrietta, you're cursed.

"I probably wouldn't have made the connection if I hadn't known about Henrietta's condition," Eli continued, cutting his ally's bonds. "But I saw definite similarities between her curse and your game, which led me to a realization: they're both machines. They both have rules – mechanical parts, essentially – that dictate their functions. So in order to ruin your game, I took the approach I'd take in stopping any machine: sabotage."

Just then, the cylinder in the pit began its rotations.

"Oh," Eli said, checking his pocket watch. "It's now nine. I changed the clock while you were gone. I wasn't certain it would help, but you'd seemed very adamant about starting on time, and the cardinal rule of sabotaging a machine you don't understand is to break anything that seems important."

"You're a fool," Mari said. "I may be off to a late start, but that doesn't matter. My machines will end Zumaj, and once he's gone and I've won, I'll no longer be bound to this place."

A wooden beam that had been spring-loaded against the wall snapped out like a sideways catapult, swinging in an arc intended to strike Zumaj's back and knock him into the pit. It narrowly missed, grazing the djinni's arm.

"I should also mention," Eli said, "that the other reason I changed your start-time was so you wouldn't have a chance to inspect everything properly." He pointed at Zumaj's feet. "I painted your boxes a few feet to the side of where your note instructed."

"Mari!" Zumaj said. "Do something!"

Eli had Henrietta stand behind Mari, then positioned himself behind Zumaj. All the while, traps sprung on the walls, ineffectively striking the air around Zumaj.

"They can't move their feet to resist," Eli yelled to Henrietta over the sounds of the workshop, "but they're still awfully big, so we're going to have to put our weight into it. Ready?"

"Ready!"

"One …"

"No!" Mari said.

"Two …"

"You can't do this!"

"Three!"

Eli and Henrietta pushed their shoulders into the backsides of the djinn, who had conveniently high centers of gravity. Mari and Zumaj fell simultaneously into the spinning cylinder, whose spikes pulled them through a slotted sheet of metal and started shredding their cloth flesh from the legs up.

"Curse you, Eli Whitney!" Mari yelled, her lower half sucked into the death-trap, the rest of her torso following quickly. "May you never find profit as an inventor! May you never –"

And then she was gone, along with Zumaj. All that remained was the separated threads of their flesh, taking another trip around the cylinder.

As the last of the wall-traps finished springing, Eli took up his broom and swept Zumaj's legion into the cylinder pit. He wiped the sweat from his brow and leaned on the broom handle as Henrietta approached.

"What now?" he asked.

"Now I collect their threads and lock them away somewhere safe."

"Will that keep them from returning?"

"They'll find a way back, like they always do. But this might keep them sleeping long enough to forget about you." She tilted her head to the side. "What about you? Where do you go from here?"

"I suppose I continue on to my teaching job. I'm not thrilled by the idea, but –"

"Oh …my …*Lord*."

Eli and Henrietta turned to the doorway. Standing there with a basket against her hip was Catherine Greene, the owner of the plantation and Eli's gracious hostess. She advanced, marveling at the contraptions on the walls.

"Catherine," Eli said, kicking a stray bird's wing into the cylinder pit before she could notice. "What are you doing here?"

"I was picking up some cotton from one of the workers, and thought I heard a commotion …" She leaned over the pit, looking curiously at the still-spinning cylinder. "What is this thing?"

"It's …why, it's my latest invention, of course! Look!" Eli grabbed a handful of cotton from Catherine's basket and tossed it into the pit. He tried not to show his surprise when he realized the spinning spikes had instantly separated the cotton fibers from their seeds.

"Eli! It's marvelous!"

"Yes, well – this is just a prototype. The final version will be much smaller."

"You're going to be rich! I'll go tell Phineas right away!"

Catherine hurried off. Eli turned to Henrietta, smiling.

"Cancel that order for the teaching job," he said, hooking his thumbs in his suspenders and sticking his chest out. "I'm going to be *rich*."

And that's how Eli Whitney, creator of the cotton gin and pioneer of the interchangeable-parts manufacturing system, finally found his inspiration. Although his inventions would go on to forever change the world of industry, he never did get rich.

Dressing Mr. Featherbottom

Amy Sisson

THE FIRST TIME AnnaBella Frostwich put makeshift clothing on her companion, Mr. Featherbottom, her mother thought nothing of it. Anna was only three years old, and small children naturally treated their companions as playthings, almost like the porcelain baby dolls that had gone out of fashion at the end of the last century. But by the time children reached school age, they understood that companions were more than mere toys; they served as playmates, teachers, chauffeurs, and chaperones. In spite of their ubiquitous presence at every level of society, however, there simply was no reason to dress them. Companions did not feel the cold, and their brass and copper plating did not require covering to maintain modesty, after all.

But unlike other children, AnnaBella did not outgrow her habit of dressing Mr. Featherbottom. In fact, by the time she was seven, she was becoming an accomplished little seamstress, and had turned Mr. Featherbottom into a facsimile of a fashionable young 'gentleman' Each time he initiated a growth phase, using spare parts from the local companion co-operative to lengthen his limbs and maintain a commensurate size with Anna, she created a new wardrobe for him, covering his metal body with a green seersucker jacket and trousers, or perhaps a gabardine suit for rainy days. As Anna's skills did not extend to shoemaking, and her own outgrown shoes would have looked silly on him, Mr. Featherbottom's metal feet stuck out from the bottom of his trousers rather comically, but otherwise he seemed quite dignified.

Mrs. Frostwich did not know what to do about her daughter's propensity. It was not *wrong*, precisely, to dress one's companion, just as it was not *wrong* that the newly created Mr. Featherbottom had chosen a male identity and an unusually formal name for himself upon Anna's birth. It was just very *odd*.

One day, Mrs. Frostwich happened upon Anna playing with a remnant of white lace that the little girl had found in the household rag bag. Humming and singing little snatches of songs, Anna used a headband to anchor the lace to her head as a makeshift veil. Mr. Featherbottom sat by patiently. In addition to a dark gray walking suit, he wore an expertly tied dove-grey cravat and a matching top hat, which Anna had begged from her father's valet.

Anna appropriated a small bunch of artificial flowers from a nearby vase and held them towards Mr. Featherbottom, sing-songing, "Oh, Mister F, will you marry me?, Uh-huh, uh-huh. Mister F, will you marry me? And when shall the wedding be?' Uh-huh, uh-huh."

"I should be delighted, Miss AnnaBella," Mr. Featherbottom said, standing up and doffing his hat. Anna giggled and proceeded to hum a loud wedding march as the two promenaded around the perimeter of the room.

Later, Mrs. Frostwich discussed the matter with her own companion, Geraldine, who unfortunately didn't have much to say. She then tried Mr. Frostwich, both expecting and receiving his customary response ("I'm sure you can manage it, my dear"). Finally, not knowing to whom else she could turn, she made an appointment to see Dr. Hughes, who had attended the family since Mrs. Frostwich's own girlhood.

"I really don't see any harm in AnnaBella dressing her companion, Mrs. Frostwich," Dr. Hughes said with a reassuring smile. "Do you, Jacoby?"

The doctor's companion, sitting unobtrusively nearby, shook his head. As with most medical companions, the majority of Jacoby's body was comprised not of brass and copper, but rather of surgery-grade composite steel, so that he could withstand frequent sterilization and assist Dr. Hughes without undue risk of infecting human patients. Jacoby's spotless metal torso gleamed yet was not flashy, lending him an air of understated efficiency and trustworthiness.

"It's unusual but not unheard of," Jacoby said, inclining his head and addressing Mrs. Frostwich in clipped yet pleasant metallic tones. "There have been a number of reports of children dressing their companions well beyond the play-acting stage. In fact, some of those children eventually grow up to become seamstresses, tailors, or even fashion designers. If Mr. Featherbottom himself doesn't object, it seems likely that he has noticed her talent and is subtly encouraging her to develop those skills."

"But the wedding veil ...?" Mrs. Frostwich trailed off. She'd been unsure whether to bring it up, but she'd found herself blurting it out to Dr. Hughes as soon as she'd arrived.

"Just exercising her imagination, I'm sure," said Dr. Hughes. "It makes perfect sense, since AnnaBella is so interested in clothing. I've always suspected," he continued with a chuckle, "that weddings are simply an excuse for the ladies to buy new clothes, wouldn't you agree? I'm sure AnnaBella is more interested in dressing as a pretend-bride than in actually getting married."

Mrs. Frostwich felt somewhat reassured. Perhaps she should even ask her husband to arrange extra drawing lessons for Anna, who might yet turn out to be a prodigy rather than an oddity. There was a certain prestige in having a child pursue artistic endeavors in this dawning industrial age, and fashion design seemed to incorporate the best of both worlds: it was an art form, yet it was practical *and* potentially lucrative. Mrs. Frostwich imagined herself at the center of an admiring throng of her peers at a future Gardening Society luncheon.

From that point on, Mrs. Frostwich took an almost perverse pride in describing Mr. Featherbottom's latest ensembles to her friends during their afternoon visits, and remarking upon the precision of the stitches and other fine details that Anna incorporated into her work. She even allowed Anna to adorn Geraldine with a few small accessories on their days out. But underneath, the devoted mother still wondered whether Anna's eccentricities were quite ...*quite*.

* * *

When AnnaBella was 22, she graduated with honors from the New Yorke Institute of Fashion, taking home the Weetwood Prize based on her thesis collection. As the winner, AnnaBella was scheduled to give the last student showing in the Institute's event at the New Yorke Spring Fashion Week Extravaganza.

The decision to give AnnaBella the award had not been without controversy. During her four years at the Institute, other students had partially followed her example by giving their companions occasional accessories to match their own designs. But Anna dressed Mr. Featherbottom every single day, in full rigging right down to his custom-made shoes. Her idiosyncrasy, argued some of the more conservative faculty members, might ultimately reflect poorly on the Institute, which was still struggling to achieve legitimacy in the eyes of the more-established fashion academies in Paris and London.

In the end, however, even those professors had to admit that talent such as AnnaBella's did not come along frequently. During the weeks leading up to the event, AnnaBella had shown her advisors an array of costumes that many of them secretly wished they had conceived themselves. Some of the faculty even wondered whether AnnaBella's collection would help make the stodgy European and British houses finally sit up and take notice.

It was therefore a shock when AnnaBella's first models appeared on the runway. Unlike in the dress rehearsal, the models were now accompanied by their fully dressed companions, each of whom wore a simplified, more practical version of their human's ensemble. Anna's *coup de maître* likely would not have succeeded had the backstage tent been less chaotic, but of course Anna had been counting on that, and by the time the faculty realized what was happening, it was too late.

The first shocked titters from the audience quickly gave way to rising murmurs of excitement and a few of chagrin. Journalists' companions took notes and made quick sketches under the direction of their humans, while society wives relished the thought of all the new shopping they would get to do. The few reluctant husbands in attendance mentally reviewed their bank account balances and sighed. And even the older, more jaded designers perked up, imagining the upswing in demand that this as-yet-unknown AnnaBella Frostwich was creating right in front of their eyes.

* * *

Six months later, AnnaBella held an exclusive luncheon for a dozen of the most influential fashion columnists in New Yorke, at which she made the not-unexpected announcement that she was launching her own fashion line, backed by the banking house of Taylor & Sons. No, the surprising part was not the company itself, but rather the company name. Everyone had assumed that AnnaBella would take advantage of her distinctive first name, the perfect mononym to adorn a designer label.

"Can't you just hear it, darling? 'I'm wearing the latest AnnaBella!' ", Mrs. Frostwich had said to her daughter. "Simply *everyone* would know your name."

"I know it has a nice ring, Mother, and I do love my name, but it's not right for the company," Anna replied absently, as she pinned up an elaborate skirt hem sporting row after row of seed pearls. Mrs. Frostwich, watching, fervently hoped that Anna would not be run out of town for allowing her models' *ankles* to show.

"But darling –" she said.

"Mrs. Frostwich," said Mr. Featherbottom. He was standing on the dais, wearing the skirt upon which Anna sewed, as the hour was late and the in-house models had already gone home. "We wondered if you would be so kind as to help us settle on the company's trademark, which we'll introduce at the luncheon. We've narrowed it down to these three possibilities," he went on, leaning over to pick up a folder from a nearby table.

"Stand still, Mr. F!" said Anna through a mouthful of pins.

"– and we simply must have your opinion before we can make a final decision," he went on. "In fact, Anna thought that you might be willing to serve as our Consulting Advisor – we'll have cards made up for you, of course, and there will be any number of social functions that we'll need your help in planning."

Mrs. Frostwich was so delighted with this idea that she completely forgot the question of the company's name. A Consulting Advisor! *That* would be something to tell Mrs. Compton, the current President of the Gardening Society, who made cutting little criticisms to one so politely that it often took half an hour to realize that one had been insulted.

At the announcement luncheon, AnnaBella spoke from the front of the flower-bedecked banquet room that they had rented at the Crestwicke Hotel. The podium at which she stood was emblazoned with a circular trademark containing a beautifully scripted letter "F" in dark green, entwined with its own mirrored image in a lighter shade. The guests sat at two large round tables while their companions, a few of whom were dressed, sat in a row of chairs lined up against the back wall. Models, trailed by their matching companions, circulated in a slow figure eight pattern around the two tables, pausing to twirl at appropriate intervals.

"Ladies," AnnaBella said. "It gives me great pleasure to introduce you to Mr. Featherbottom, who is not only my companion but also my partner in this venture. We hope you are as excited as we are to witness the birth of our new company –" she paused dramatically – "Frostwich & Featherbottom."

* * *

When AnnaBella was 57 years old, she and Mr. Featherbottom retired, announcing that the firm of Frostwich & Featherbottom would continue under the auspices of Leanna Bowton and her companion Charlotte, who had been with the company for nine years. Although Anna could no longer keep up the frantic pace demanded by the always-changing fashion industry, she still possessed a gentle loveliness that continued to attract suitors, with whom she maintained friendly but platonic relationships. The society pages, which had long since ceased speculating about whether Anna would ever marry, briefly revived their interest in her love life, only to realize that retirement did not seem to indicate any propensity on Anna's part to 'settle down.'

Mr. Featherbottom, naturally, remained by Anna's side. His body had taken on a dignified patina that was only a shade darker than before, yet somehow conveyed a sense of aging that was as graceful as Anna's. He had taken to carrying a cane, even though he did not need it, and could often be seen strolling slowly with Anna in the park on warm afternoons.

When AnnaBella Frostwich died at age 63, a stoic Mr. Featherbottom assisted the funeral director's companion, Wallace, in laying out her body for the service. Mr. Featherbottom had brought Anna's favorite afternoon gown of light green georgette edged with cream lace, and Wallace tinted her cheeks with a pale pink rouge. As always, Anna was the picture of elegance.

When the service was over, Mr. Featherbottom waited until the last guest had departed, then sat on a chair he placed next to the casket. Wallace stood near the doorway, unsure whether to stay or leave. He watched as Mr. Featherbottom touched Anna's cheek and then lovingly rearranged her hands, which clutched a lace handkerchief over her midsection.

Finally Mr. Featherbottom stood, but he still did not leave. Instead, he slowly removed his coal-black mourning suit and crisp white shirt. Wallace, unaccustomed to seeing other companions without clothing, did not know how to react. Mr. Featherbottom folded each garment neatly, tucking them along the inside edges of the casket. He placed his shoes at the bottom, near Anna's feet, and then straightened up to his full height. Turning towards Wallace, he gestured toward the casket, indicating that he was ready.

Wallace, accustomed to observing the small details required by his profession, could not help but notice Mr. Featherbottom's left hand. One of the fingers had a slightly raised band, as might result from a too-hasty solder repair. It seemed out of place compared to the companion's otherwise immaculate appearance, but perhaps Miss Frostwich's illness had demanded all of Mr. Featherbottom's attention in recent months.

As Wallace moved to close the casket lid, he paused. The ring that Miss Frostwich was wearing -- hadn't it been on her right hand rather than her left? Involuntarily, he looked back at Mr. Featherbottom.

Without a word, Mr. Featherbottom inclined his head, then turned and made his way to the front entrance of the funeral home. In spite of his unclothed state, his gait was as dignified as ever.

Wallace knew that due to AnnaBella Frostwich's lack of direct heirs, Mr. Featherbottom would report to a companion co-operative to decide his own future: either service to an adult who had lost his or her companion in an accident, or complete dismantling, so that his own parts could be passed along to the next generation of companions. Wallace felt fairly certain which option Mr. Featherbottom would choose.

The Touchstone

Robert Louis Stevenson

THE KING was a man that stood well before the world; his smile was sweet as clover, but his soul withinsides was as little as a pea. He had two sons; and the younger son was a boy after his heart, but the elder was one whom he feared. It befell one morning that the drum sounded in the dun before it was yet day; and the King rode with his two sons, and a brave array behind them. They rode two hours, and came to the foot of a brown mountain that was very steep.

"Where do we ride?" said the elder son.

"Across this brown mountain," said the King, and smiled to himself.

"My father knows what he is doing," said the younger son.

And they rode two hours more, and came to the sides of a black river that was wondrous deep.

"And where do we ride?" asked the elder son.

"Over this black river," said the King, and smiled to himself.

"My father knows what he is doing," said the younger son.

And they rode all that day, and about the time of the sunsetting came to the side of a lake, where was a great dun.

"It is here we ride," said the King; "to a King's house, and a priest's, and a house where you will learn much."

At the gates of the dun, the King who was a priest met them; and he was a grave man, and beside him stood his daughter, and she was as fair as the morn, and one that smiled and looked down.

"These are my two sons," said the first King.

"And here is my daughter," said the King who was a priest.

"She is a wonderful fine maid," said the first King, "and I like her manner of smiling,"

"They are wonderful well-grown lads," said the second, "and I like their gravity."

And then the two Kings looked at each other, and said, "The thing may come about".

And in the meanwhile the two lads looked upon the maid, and the one grew pale and the other red; and the maid looked upon the ground smiling.

"Here is the maid that I shall marry," said the elder. "For I think she smiled upon me."

But the younger plucked his father by the sleeve. "Father," said he, "a word in your ear. If I find favour in your sight, might not I wed this maid, for I think she smiles upon me?"

"A word in yours," said the King his father. "Waiting is good hunting, and when the teeth are shut the tongue is at home."

Now they were come into the dun, and feasted; and this was a great house, so that the lads were astonished; and the King that was a priest sat at the end of the board and was silent, so that the lads were filled with reverence; and the maid served them smiling with downcast eyes, so that their hearts were enlarged.

Before it was day, the elder son arose, and he found the maid at her weaving, for she was a diligent girl. "Maid," quoth he, "I would fain marry you."

"You must speak with my father," said she, and she looked upon the ground smiling, and became like the rose.

"Her heart is with me," said the elder son, and he went down to the lake and sang.

A little after came the younger son. "Maid," quoth he, "if our fathers were agreed, I would like well to marry you."

"You can speak to my father," said she; and looked upon the ground, and smiled and grew like the rose.

"She is a dutiful daughter," said the younger son, "she will make an obedient wife." And then he thought, "What shall I do?" and he remembered the King her father was a priest; so he went into the temple, and sacrificed a weasel and a hare.

Presently the news got about; and the two lads and the first King were called into the presence of the King who was a priest, where he sat upon the high seat.

"Little I reck of gear," said the King who was a priest, "and little of power. For we live here among the shadow of things, and the heart is sick of seeing them. And we stay here in the wind like raiment drying, and the heart is weary of the wind. But one thing I love, and that is truth; and for one thing will I give my daughter, and that is the trial stone. For in the light of that stone the seeming goes, and the being shows, and all things besides are worthless. Therefore, lads, if ye would wed my daughter, out foot, and bring me the stone of touch, for that is the price of her."

"A word in your ear," said the younger son to his father. "I think we do very well without this stone."

"A word in yours," said the father. "I am of your way of thinking; but when the teeth are shut the tongue is at home." And he smiled to the King that was a priest.

But the elder son got to his feet, and called the King that was a priest by the name of father. "For whether I marry the maid or no, I will call you by that word for the love of your wisdom; and even now I will ride forth and search the world for the stone of touch." So he said farewell, and rode into the world.

"I think I will go, too," said the younger son, "if I can have your leave. For my heart goes out to the maid."

"You will ride home with me," said his father.

So they rode home, and when they came to the dun, the King had his son into his treasury. "Here," said he, "is the touchstone which shows truth; for there is no truth but plain truth; and if you will look in this, you will see yourself as you are."

And the younger son looked in it, and saw his face as it were the face of a beardless youth, and he was well enough pleased; for the thing was a piece of a mirror.

"Here is no such great thing to make a work about," said he; "but if it will get me the maid I shall never complain. But what a fool is my brother to ride into the world, and the thing all the while at home!"

So they rode back to the other dun, and showed the mirror to the King that was a priest; and when he had looked in it, and seen himself like a King, and his house like a King's house, and all things like themselves, he cried out and blessed God. "For now I know," said he, "there is no truth but the plain truth; and I am a King indeed, although my heart misgave me." And he pulled down his temple, and built a new one; and then the younger son was married to the maid.

In the meantime the elder son rode into the world to find the touchstone of the trial of truth; and whenever he came to a place of habitation, he would ask the men if they had heard of it. And in every place the men answered: "Not only have we heard of it, but we alone, of all men, possess the thing itself, and it hangs in the side of our chimney to this day". Then would the elder son be glad, and beg for a sight of it. And sometimes it would be a piece of mirror, that showed the seeming of things; and then he would say, "This can never be, for there should be more than seeming". And sometimes it would be a lump of coal, which showed nothing; and then he would say, "This can never be, for at least there is the seeming". And sometimes it would be a touchstone indeed, beautiful in hue, adorned with polishing, the light inhabiting its sides; and when he found this, he would beg the thing, and the persons of that place would give it him, for all men were very generous of that gift; so that at the last he had his wallet full of them, and they chinked together when he rode; and when he halted by the side of the way he would take them out and try them, till his head turned like the sails upon a windmill.

"A murrain upon this business!" said the elder son, "for I perceive no end to it. Here I have the red, and here the blue and the green; and to me they seem all excellent, and yet shame each other. A murrain on the trade! If it were not for the King that is a priest and whom I have called my father, and if it were not for the fair maid of the dun that makes my mouth to sing and my heart enlarge, I would even tumble them all into the salt sea, and go home and be a King like other folk."

But he was like the hunter that has seen a stag upon a mountain, so that the night may fall, and the fire be kindled, and the lights shine in his house; but desire of that stag is single in his bosom.

Now after many years the elder son came upon the sides of the salt sea; and it was night, and a savage place, and the clamour of the sea was loud. There he was aware of a house, and a man that sat there by the light of a candle, for he had no fire. Now the elder son came in to him, and the man gave him water to drink, for he had no bread; and wagged his head when he was spoken to, for he had no words.

"Have you the touchstone of truth?" asked the elder son and when the man had wagged his head, "I might have known that," cried the elder son. "I have here a wallet full of them!" And with that he laughed, although his heart was weary.

And with that the man laughed too, and with the fuff of his laughter the candle went out.

"Sleep," said the man, "for now I think you have come far enough; and your quest is ended, and my candle is out."

Now when the morning came, the man gave him a clear pebble in his hand, and it had no beauty and no colour; and the elder son looked upon it scornfully and shook his head; and he went away, for it seemed a small affair to him.

All that day he rode, and his mind was quiet, and the desire of the chase allayed. "How if this poor pebble be the touchstone, after all?" said he: and he got down from his horse, and emptied forth his wallet by the side of the way. Now, in the light of each other, all the touchstones lost their hue and fire, and withered like stars at morning; but in the light of the pebble, their beauty remained, only the pebble was the most bright. And the elder son smote upon his brow. "How if this be the truth?" he cried, "that all are a little true?" And he took the pebble, and turned its light upon the heavens, and they deepened about him like the pit; and he turned it on the hills, and the hills were cold and rugged, but life ran in their sides so that his own life bounded; and he turned it on the dust, and he beheld the dust with joy and terror; and he turned it on himself, and kneeled down and prayed.

"Now, thanks be to God," said the elder son, "I have found the touchstone; and now I may turn my reins, and ride home to the King and to the maid of the dun that makes my mouth to sing and my heart enlarge."

Now when he came to the dun, he saw children playing by the gate where the King had met him in the old days; and this stayed his pleasure, for he thought in his heart, "It is here my children should be playing". And when he came into the hall, there was his brother on the high seat and the maid beside him; and at that his anger rose, for he thought in his heart, "It is I that should be sitting there, and the maid beside me".

"Who are you?" said his brother. "And what make you in the dun?"

"I am your elder brother," he replied. "And I am come to marry the maid, for I have brought the touchstone of truth."

Then the younger brother laughed aloud. "Why," said he, "I found the touchstone years ago, and married the maid, and there are our children playing at the gate."

Now at this the elder brother grew as gray as the dawn. "I pray you have dealt justly," said he, "for I perceive my life is lost."

"Justly?" quoth the younger brother. "It becomes you ill, that are a restless man and a runagate, to doubt my justice, or the King my father's, that are sedentary folk and known in the land."

"Nay," said the elder brother, "you have all else, have patience also; and suffer me to say the world is full of touchstones, and it appears not easily which is true."

"I have no shame of mine," said the younger brother. "There it is, and look in it."

So the elder brother looked in the mirror, and he was sore amazed; for he was an old man, and his hair was white upon his head; and he sat down in the hall and wept aloud.

"Now," said the younger brother, "see what a fool's part you have played, that ran over all the world to seek what was lying in our father's treasury, and came back an old carle for the dogs to bark at, and without chick or child. And I that was dutiful and wise sit here crowned with virtues and pleasures, and happy in the light of my hearth."

"Methinks you have a cruel tongue," said the elder brother; and he pulled out the clear pebble and turned its light on his brother; and behold the man was lying, his soul was shrunk into the smallness of a pea, and his heart was a bag of little fears like scorpions, and love was dead in his bosom. And at that the elder brother cried out aloud, and turned the light of the pebble on the maid, and, lo! She was but a mask of a woman, and withinsides she was quite dead, and she smiled as a clock ticks, and knew not wherefore.

"Oh, well," said the elder brother, "I perceive there is both good and bad. So fare ye all as well as ye may in the dun; but I will go forth into the world with my pebble in my pocket."

Vortaal Hunt

Brian Trent

PERSONAL DIARY ENTRY 115

WE ARE leaving to kill the Vortaal at last.

It's been fifteen hundred days since father's hunting party departed on its herd of shellephants, their copper tusks glinting by the lamps of their eyes. The village was proud of father. He sat atop the carriage of the largest mechanical beast, and between the cheering crowd and the noise of the shellephant herd, I was half-thinking my young ears would bleed. Still I watched him go, until the sight of the hunting party had dwindled into the mist and twisting bramble of the *jangala*.

Father was gone, but he sent his mission reports to us every few hours. Our village gathered around the transmitter – a shrine dedicated to Banka Mundi, her many arms acting as signal receivers for the hunting party's transmissions.

We listened to father's report of their trek into the mysterious country north, through the polyp groves and hills that undulate like the mythical python. We listened to his breathless transmission of how the shellephants had stomped through the barricades of the Valiant village …and how they continued their march towards the first great chasm.

We listened to his strained, gasping report of how he had been wounded in a firefight with the soldiers of Valiant. How nearly the entire hunting party was killed in a desperate battle between metal monsters and winged garuda-men bearing steel-and-steam-driven wings to swoop down upon them.

And then, the reports stopped coming.

I remember my terror, staring at the tranquil face of Banka Mundi and wishing her arms would catch another transmission from father. Was he still alive? Had he managed to descend the first chasm to the bottom, evading Valiant soldiers as he went? Had he reached the second chasm, and then the third and final chasm after that …the one leading down into the green rock where the tunnels of the Vortaal waited? The damnable thing dwells so far down, the journey would be difficult enough without the soldiers of Valiance harassing incursions every step of the way.

I refused food and sleep, waiting for an update from father. I prayed to all the old gods for his victory and safe return.

And then, at long last, he sent an update:

"I have reached the bottom of the third chasm. I have attained the tunnels where the Vortaal lives."

Our village cheered, renewed by the strength in my father's voice, his certainty of victory. With his message, he had sent a visual of this deepest set of tunnels – allowing us to fill in the gaps of our maps.

It was hours later when he sent a final, cryptic message:

"It can't be killed."

I've had years to reflect on why father uttered those words.

We never heard from him after that. Some believe that Valiance hunters found him at last. Perhaps, but how does that explain his final utterance? I don't think father could have been forced into saying something so demoralizing, so crazy. He had attained the tunnels! He *must* have reached the lair of the Vortaal!

And it must have killed him.

I love you father.

I wish you could see the man I have grown into. How the villagers who once cursed me for being born without legs now praise me and wish good fortune and prayers upon my mission.

Yes, I am joining the new hunting party. My sniper skills were never in doubt – even the elders admit I am the most gifted marksman they remember. But being born with emaciated, useless legs – which in another era might have reduced me to begging in the lost cities – meant that my skills were of little use in the battles with the enemy village of Valiance. I couldn't run into battle, after all. Couldn't accompany a hunting party unless carried by another.

Well, the ingenious tinkerers of Dhawan have built me legs out of repurposed copper and brass, spring-coiled pistons and pulleys. The materials salvaged from the ancient ships now means that I can walk.

Ironic, since walking will be only the merest portion of this mission.

I am going on the hunt, to attempt success where father's group failed. We are going without shellephants or fanfare. We are attempting a secret infiltration, not an all-out war. And I am accompanied by my brother Achal, by scout Kamal, and of course, by Huntress Harshadi. Dhawan's greatest minds have refined our strategy. We will not lumber forward into the villages of Valiance on great, noisy, steam-driven monsters.

No. This time, we will fly to the chasm, and will drop down with the mist, and will reach the tunnels of the Vortaal. And I will walk those tunnels on my metal legs.

And this time, we will kill the great monster.

We will kill the Vortaal.

* * *

PERSONAL DIARY ENTRY 116

They strapped me into the wing-harness, fitting the mask over my face, the goggles over my eyes. Father would say I look like a bird, and he would show me pictures of what birds looked like back in the old days. A bird with coppery legs.

My fellow hunters also were fitted with the harness, mask, and wings of the garuda-class flight-suit. The villagers did not cheer this time. Our village is only a few miles downhill from the sentry posts of Valiance. We will give them no warning that we are coming. No one knows why the missions keep failing, but I think it has a lot to do with betrayal. Valiance keeps a watchful eye on us. Our two colonies have been enemies for as long as anyone remembers. They outnumber us, their scattered farmsteads dotting this relentlessly hilly country, and their patrols are always on the lookout for new incursions from the Dhawan side of the border.

Would be nice if our two sides could join forces against the Vortaal.
Would be nice if they didn't worship the damnable thing.

* * *

PERSONAL DIARY ENTRY 117

I am flying like a falcon in the old stories!

My hunting party gathered in a circle and we each twisted the dial on our suit chestplates, releasing the water into the fuel-chamber, building up steam until I could feel the power of the garuda-suit vibrating around me. Our leader, Huntress Harshadi, wanted to time our flight with mist-down, as she is wary of enemy sentries seeing us take to the skies. At her signal, we each pulled the cord on our suits, and the wings from our backpacks became a blur bordering on the invisible. One by one, we rocketed up into the sky.

It is impossible to see anything in the mist – an advantage and peril.

For this reason, the inventors at Dhawan outfitted our suits with a veiny overlay of tubes that can mix phosphorous into the steam, coming out as greenish exhaust. Just a flicker, enough to keep us flying in formation – as if the Diwali festival was being held in the dark green sky. If only father could have seen me! The descending and ascending mist cool against the little bit of exposed skin around my masks.

My brother Achal was the first to dip below the mist and to conduct surveillance on the chasm. We waited together, like a ring of glowing fireflies hovering in the mist, and he returned to us with grim news:

Valiance has doubled their watchtowers since father's failed expedition. There are eight towers now, perched all around the chasm edge. Snipers in each of them. Achal's sharp eyes got a glimpse of high caliber rifles. Weapons that are as good as ours.

Huntress Harshadi floated near me in the mist, her goggled face looking grim in the backsplash of shadows. "The mist will be dropping soon," she told us. "We will wait, and drop with it straight down the chasm," Then her gloved hand touched mine and she said, "Take care with what you carry."

I nodded to her, bobbing up and down in the mist, the furious beating of my wings causing the mist to swirl out in freakish, remarkable freakish spirals.

What I carried was something better than the rifles and pulse-bows that my father's hunting party had taken with them. Better even than Achal's wrist-grapple that can snap out like a cobra from the old stories.

Before we set out, the Dhawan elders gave something special into my safekeeping. An old weapon. A *ship* weapon, plucked of the metal carcass and stuffed into *my* backpack. The elders feel that the time is right. Before we set out, our party ringed it, linked hands and prayed over it. For my part, I tried fighting back my tears at the incredible honor.

The elders think that maybe father's rifle was insufficient to kill the monster. They believe that accounts for his final message.

But that won't be a problem now. As long as we can get to the lair ...

The weapon I was given is like something out of the *Mahabarata*. A weapon that can kill anything.

* * *

PERSONAL DIARY ENTRY 118

A very close call.

At mistdown, we dropped towards the chasm. The watchtowers of Valiance were cloaked in the mist, affording us the cover we needed to begin our descent.

When we reached the chasm, however, we bounced into something springy and resistant. A net! Valiance had stretched a black net across the vastness of the chasm!

At once, iron bells began to clang, reacting to the impact we had made in the barrier. Cries of alarm went out around us.

"Cut through it!" Huntress Harshadi barked, and without waiting she snapped open her serrated blade from her wrist and began to saw at the ropy mesh beneath us. The bells rang more urgently.

"Huntress," I managed to say. "The bells must be attached to each strand! We're betraying our position by –"

A shot whispered past us, then another. The net began to shake even more violently, and suddenly I saw a Valiant soldier rushing up behind my brother through the mist, his dark shape like one of those spiders from the old stories. Achal, the imbecile, never even realized he was in danger.

Harshadi raised her cross-bow and put a bolt into his throat.

It was the first death I'd ever witnessed. The soldier's bulging eyes staring at us, as if he couldn't believe he had been shot. He fell backwards, his corpse bouncing lightly on the netting.

The huntress knelt and sawed the rest of the way through the netting; the strands frayed and snapped. As bullets whined around us and other soldiers began converging on our position, we dropped through the breach and fell into blackness. I activated my wings in mid-fall, and floated downward, downward, ever downward. Above us, flashlights lanced the gloom, searching for the intruders.

We reached the crater bottom. Retracting our wings, we hurried into the nearest tunnel on foot. Making our way to the second chasm.

They know we're here now.

Time is against us.

* * *

PERSONAL DIARY ENTRY 119

I'm not going to sweat the death of that enemy soldier. For all I know, *his* father killed *my* father during the last hunt. And why? Because they worship a monster. Valiance is a lunatic colony with their petty altars and foolish traditions. Everyone knows that before the Vortaal came, humanity was united and powerful. Before it came, we lived in a world with other creatures and with blue skies and endless resources.

And no one can say precisely how the Vortaal destroyed the old civilizations. How humanity was once so mighty a civilization ...and how after the Vortaal came, we were now little more than beggars fighting over the little material and sustenance we could find.

How could anyone worship such a devil? With its death, humanity is avenged, and perhaps we can reclaim the old ways.

Why would Valiance oppose that?

They're insane. Killing the Vortaal won't mean the death of us all. I don't care how loudly they insist it would.

* * *

PERSONAL DIARY ENTRY 120

We're out of steam – literally.

Our approach through the mist, our descent into the first chasm, has depleted the fuel-chamber of our garuda-suits unless we can find new sources of water to replenish them. That shouldn't be difficult – everyone knows you only need to dig into the ground or tunnel walls a few meters and you'll be rewarded with plenty of liquid. That's not the source of our concern.

Our concern is that we have now reached the second chasm, and we can't just fly to its bottom. We have to climb down by hand and foot.

It's not like we didn't suspect this would happen. Huntress Harshadi showed us how to twist the dials around our ankle and wrist-greaves to cause crampons to spike out from the armor. My copper legs were built with hooks, allowing me to find instant purchase on the green walls and descend rapidly. Achal laughed at the sight of his boot spikes, and he kept twisting the dial back and forth, making the spikes seem to dance, until Harshadi told him to 'stop acting like a fool'. I love my brother, but he is so often a fool.

We're climbing down the chasm wall now. It's slow going, but we're making progress.

* * *

PERSONAL DIARY ENTRY 121

Scout Kamal was killed.

We had reached the bottom of the chasm and two soldiers from Valiance were patrolling there. Kamal hopped off the wall, landing loudly on the squishy ground, and they spun around and blew him away. Achal, Harshadi, and myself were still on the chasm wall, and Achal got to use his wrist-grapple – shooting it out like a whip that knocked the enemy soldiers on their asses.

I leapt off the wall – a leap no one else could have made and survived – and landed hard on my metal legs. The soldiers barely had time to cry out in surprise when I shot them where they lay.

Then I rushed to Kamal, hoping that perhaps his garuda-suit had deflected the shots. And in fact, they had …but his exposed face was hit and he was bleeding out, choking and dying.

As the life sputtered out of him, he looked at me and said, "Kill it for all of us. Kill it for your father."

I will, Kamal.

I'll carve all our names into the thing's face.

If it even has a face.

What does the Vortaal even look like?

* * *

PERSONAL DIARY ENTRY 122

We reached the third and final chasm. Down there are the tunnels that lead to the Vortaal. We must be at the place where father transmitted his penultimate message.

Once again, we're manually descending. There are Valiance stations everywhere below us, hewn into the slimy green rock, with stairs and spotlights and armed guards; I dialed up my goggles to maximum zoom and counted soldier after soldier after soldier. At two dozen, I stopped counting.

Harshadi told me and my brother that our descent must be timed to avoid the spotlights. Easy for her to say.

Transmitting this message now, along with all previous entries. Know this: We're on the last leg of the journey.

* * *

PERSONAL DIARY ENTRY 123

Two things.

First: We made it the bottom of the chasm.

This was no easy feat, as Valiance patrols kept shining their spotlights into the darkness to look for evidence of incursion. It was Huntress Harshadi who finally insisted that it was too dangerous, that we needed to chisel out a wet burrow into the chasm wall to hide in until the enemy relaxes its guard. Hours passed while we sat there; I even used the time to scoop up the running liquid around us to refill a little bit of my suit fuel-chamber. Finally, as the hours stretched on without any sight of incursion, the spotlights clicked off. We resumed our descent.

And that takes me to the second thing:

Achal is dead.

We were all soaked from our burrowing into the chasm, and Achal's hand must have slipped on the wall. He fell the whole way and we found his shattered body at the bottom. My brother never screamed.

That's courage. A scream would have boomed in this echo chamber, brought Valiance down on us. But he let himself fall quietly.

I'm going to kill the Vortaal for you and father, Achal. I'm going to make this sacrifice worth it. Dhawan will live and prosper.

I swear it.

* * *

PERSONAL DIARY ENTRY 124

Harshadi and I reached the bottom of the chasm. I'm scared.

No sign of enemy soldiers down here, but I think I can *hear* the Vortaal. The tunnels ahead of us are shaking with the sound of its thundering footsteps. The thing must be … must be *huge*.

Dhawan has pictures of large animals from the Lost World of Earth. But this Vortaal must be absolutely gigantic. My hands are shaking as I type this on my suit-display. What the hell can be so immense as to make such a sound? The spring-coils in my legs hum with the vibration.

I'm so afraid.

The only thing that comforts me is the old weapon. The words on its casing give me strength:

> *BLUESPACE REPUBLIC*
> *SEVENTH FLEET*
> *IPCS DHAWAM*
>
> *!WARNING!*
> *WARHEAD CASING*
> *PENNING-MALMBERG CONTAINMENT*
> *DO NOT PUNCTURE*

* * *

PERSONAL DIARY ENTRY 125

Huntress Harshadi and I have decided to arm the old weapon.

We're exactly where father must have been in his final moments. We need to be ready, in case the thing is about to burst from the darkness ahead.

* * *

PERSONAL DIARY ENTRY 126

The Vortaal must be right around the bend. The tunnels are shuddering with the sound of it moving about.

I just can't believe the size of the thing, for it to be making so much noise. And it doesn't ever rest! It just keeps thundering about, pounding the tunnels in some kind of ceaseless rage that is beyond my comprehension.

* * *

PERSONAL DIARY ENTRY 127

We're looking at the Vortaal.

I …

I don't know what to say.

Huntress Harshadi insists we still have to kill it, but even she sounds unsure. We find ourselves unable to do anything but stare.

No one told us.

I don't think anyone in Dhawan really knew.

Don't think they would believe it anyway.

* * *

PERSONAL DIARY ENTRY 128

I had to kill her.

Huntress Harshadi tried wrestling the old weapon away from me. Said we had a sacred duty to complete our mission, that it wasn't up to us to question our orders, that no matter what, the Vortaal has to die.

When I disagreed, she attacked me. The very artificial legs I've been given gave me the leverage to defend myself against her assault. I pushed back against her, begging her to stop. In the middle of the scuffle …

I'm so sorry, Huntress.

It's just me now, the last surviving member of the team. And I'm sitting here, staring up at the Vortaal …realizing now what must have happened to my ancestors, to all our ancestors. *Father was right. It can't be killed.*

Sure, I could detonate the ship weapon, and I have little doubt that the resulting explosion would tear this thing to pieces. But I can't. I *won't*.

Because Valiance was correct all along. If the Vortaal dies, we all die.

It is a monster, yes. Large enough to destroy the old fleets and topple spacefaring humanity. Larger than anyone could ever have imagined.

This thing that's pounding and thudding in front of me …

…is…

…its heart.

A Drama in the Air

Jules Verne

IN THE MONTH of September, 185–, I arrived at Frankfort-on-the-Maine. My passage through the principal German cities had been brilliantly marked by balloon ascents; but as yet no German had accompanied me in my car, and the fine experiments made at Paris by M.M. Green, Eugene Godard, and Poitevin had not tempted the grave Teutons to essay aerial voyages.

But scarcely had the news of my approaching ascent spread through Frankfort, than three of the principal citizens begged the favour of being allowed to ascend with me. Two days afterwards we were to start from the Place de la Comédie. I began at once to get my balloon ready. It was of silk, prepared with gutta percha, a substance impermeable by acids or gasses; and its volume, which was three thousand cubic yards, enabled it to ascend to the loftiest heights.

The day of the ascent was that of the great September fair, which attracts so many people to Frankfort. Lighting gas, of a perfect quality and of great lifting power, had been furnished to me in excellent condition, and about eleven o'clock the balloon was filled; but only three-quarters filled, – an indispensable precaution, for, as one rises, the atmosphere diminishes in density, and the fluid enclosed within the balloon, acquiring more elasticity, might burst its sides. My calculations had furnished me with exactly the quantity of gas necessary to carry up my companions and myself.

We were to start at noon. The impatient crowd which pressed around the enclosed space, filling the enclosed square, overflowing into the contiguous streets, and covering the houses from the ground-floor to the slated gables, presented a striking scene. The high winds of the preceding days had subsided. An oppressive heat fell from the cloudless sky. Scarcely a breath animated the atmosphere. In such weather, one might descend again upon the very spot whence he had risen.

I carried three hundred pounds of ballast in bags; the car, quite round, four feet in diameter, was comfortably arranged; the hempen cords which supported it stretched symmetrically over the upper hemisphere of the balloon; the compass was in place, the barometer suspended in the circle which united the supporting cords, and the anchor carefully put in order. All was now ready for the ascent.

Among those who pressed around the enclosure, I remarked a young man with a pale face and agitated features. The sight of him impressed me. He was an eager spectator of my ascents, whom I had already met in several German cities. With an uneasy air, he closely watched the curious machine, as it lay motionless a few feet above the ground; and he remained silent among those about him.

Twelve o'clock came. The moment had arrived, but my travelling companions did not appear.

I sent to their houses, and learnt that one had left for Hamburg, another for Vienna, and the third for London. Their courage had failed them at the moment of undertaking one of those excursions which, thanks to the ability of living aeronauts, are free from all danger. As they formed, in some sort, a part of the programme of the day, the fear had seized them that they might be forced to execute it faithfully, and they had fled far from the scene at the instant when the balloon was being filled. Their courage was evidently the inverse ratio of their speed – in decamping.

The multitude, half deceived, showed not a little ill-humour. I did not hesitate to ascend alone. In order to re-establish the equilibrium between the specific gravity of the balloon and the weight which had thus proved wanting, I replaced my companions by more sacks of sand, and got into the car. The twelve men who held the balloon by twelve cords fastened to the equatorial circle, let them slip a little between their fingers, and the balloon rose several feet higher. There was not a breath of wind, and the atmosphere was so leaden that it seemed to forbid the ascent.

"Is everything ready?" I cried.

The men put themselves in readiness. A last glance told me that I might go.

"Attention!"

There was a movement in the crowd, which seemed to be invading the enclosure.

"Let go!"

The balloon rose slowly, but I experienced a shock which threw me to the bottom of the car.

When I got up, I found myself face to face with an unexpected fellow-voyager, – the pale young man.

"Monsieur, I salute you," said he, with the utmost coolness.

"By what right –"

"Am I here? By the right which the impossibility of your getting rid of me confers."

I was amazed! His calmness put me out of countenance, and I had nothing to reply. I looked at the intruder, but he took no notice of my astonishment.

"Does my weight disarrange your equilibrium, monsieur?" he asked. "You will permit me –"

And without waiting for my consent, he relieved the balloon of two bags, which he threw into space.

"Monsieur," said I, taking the only course now possible, "you have come; very well, you will remain; but to me alone belongs the management of the balloon."

"Monsieur," said he, "your urbanity is French all over: it comes from my own country. I morally press the hand you refuse me. Make all precautions, and act as seems best to you. I will wait till you have done –"

"For what?"

"To talk with you."

The barometer had fallen to twenty-six inches. We were nearly six hundred yards above the city; but nothing betrayed the horizontal displacement of the balloon, for the mass of air in which it is enclosed goes forward with it. A sort of confused glow enveloped the objects spread out under us, and unfortunately obscured their outline.

I examined my companion afresh.

He was a man of thirty years, simply clad. The sharpness of his features betrayed an indomitable energy, and he seemed very muscular. Indifferent to the astonishment he created, he remained motionless, trying to distinguish the objects which were vaguely confused below us.

"Miserable mist!" said he, after a few moments.

I did not reply.

"You owe me a grudge?" he went on. "Bah! I could not pay for my journey, and it was necessary to take you by surprise."

"Nobody asks you to descend, monsieur!"

"Eh, do you not know, then, that the same thing happened to the Counts of Laurencin and Dampierre, when they ascended at Lyons, on the 15th of January, 1784? A young merchant, named Fontaine, scaled the gallery, at the risk of capsizing the machine. He accomplished the journey, and nobody died of it!"

"Once on the ground, we will have an explanation," replied I, piqued at the light tone in which he spoke.

"Bah! Do not let us think of our return."

"Do you think, then, that I shall not hasten to descend?"

"Descend!" said he, in surprise. "Descend? Let us begin by first ascending."

And before I could prevent it, two more bags had been thrown over the car, without even having been emptied.

"Monsieur!" cried I, in a rage.

"I know your ability," replied the unknown quietly, "and your fine ascents are famous. But if Experience is the sister of Practice, she is also a cousin of Theory, and I have studied the aerial art long. It has got into my head!" he added sadly, falling into a silent reverie.

The balloon, having risen some distance farther, now became stationary. The unknown consulted the barometer, and said –

"Here we are, at eight hundred yards. Men are like insects. See! I think we should always contemplate them from this height, to judge correctly of their proportions. The Place de la Comédie is transformed into an immense ant-hill. Observe the crowd which is gathered on the quays; and the mountains also get smaller and smaller. We are over the Cathedral. The Main is only a line, cutting the city in two, and the bridge seems a thread thrown between the two banks of the river."

The atmosphere became somewhat chilly.

"There is nothing I would not do for you, my host," said the unknown. "If you are cold, I will take off my coat and lend it to you."

"Thanks," said I dryly.

"Bah! Necessity makes law. Give me your hand. I am your fellow-countryman; you will learn something in my company, and my conversation will indemnify you for the trouble I have given you."

I sat down, without replying, at the opposite extremity of the car. The young man had taken a voluminous manuscript from his great-coat. It was an essay on ballooning.

"I possess," said he, "the most curious collection of engravings and caricatures extant concerning aerial manias. How people admired and scoffed at the same time at this precious discovery! We are happily no longer in the age in which Montgolfier tried to make artificial clouds with steam, or a gas having electrical properties, produced by the combustion of moist straw and chopped-up wool."

"Do you wish to depreciate the talent of the inventors?" I asked, for I had resolved to enter into the adventure. "Was it not good to have proved by experience the possibility of rising in the air?"

"Ah, monsieur, who denies the glory of the first aerial navigators? It required immense courage to rise by means of those frail envelopes which only contained heated air. But I ask you, has the aerial science made great progress since Blanchard's ascensions, that is, since nearly a century ago? Look here, monsieur."

The unknown took an engraving from his portfolio.

"Here," said he, "is the first aerial voyage undertaken by Pilâtre des Rosiers and the Marquis d'Arlandes, four months after the discovery of balloons. Louis XVI refused to consent to the venture, and two men who were condemned to death were the first to attempt the aerial ascent. Pilâtre des Rosiers became indignant at this injustice, and, by means of intrigues, obtained permission to make the experiment. The car, which renders the management easy, had not then been invented, and a circular gallery was placed around the lower and contracted part of the Montgolfier balloon. The two aeronauts must then remain motionless at each extremity of this gallery, for the moist straw which filled it forbade them all motion. A chafing-dish with fire was suspended below the orifice of the balloon; when the aeronauts wished to rise, they threw straw upon this brazier, at the risk of setting fire to the balloon, and the air, more heated, gave it fresh ascending power. The two bold travellers rose, on the 21st of November, 1783, from the Muette Gardens, which the dauphin had put at their disposal. The balloon went up majestically, passed over the Isle of Swans, crossed the Seine at the Conference barrier, and, drifting between the dome of the Invalides and the Military School, approached the Church of Saint Sulpice. Then the aeronauts added to the fire, crossed the Boulevard, and descended beyond the Enfer barrier. As it touched the soil, the balloon collapsed, and for a few moments buried Pilâtre des Rosiers under its folds."

"Unlucky augury," I said, interested in the story, which affected me nearly.

"An augury of the catastrophe which was later to cost this unfortunate man his life," replied the unknown sadly. "Have you never experienced anything like it?"

"Never."

"Bah! Misfortunes sometimes occur unforeshadowed!" added my companion.

He then remained silent.

Meanwhile we were advancing southward, and Frankfort had already passed from beneath us.

"Perhaps we shall have a storm," said the young man.

"We shall descend before that," I replied.

"Indeed! It is better to ascend. We shall escape it more surely."

And two more bags of sand were hurled into space.

The balloon rose rapidly, and stopped at twelve hundred yards. I became colder; and yet the sun's rays, falling upon the surface, expanded the gas within, and gave it a greater ascending force.

"Fear nothing," said the unknown. "We have still three thousand five hundred fathoms of breathing air. Besides, do not trouble yourself about what I do."

I would have risen, but a vigorous hand held me to my seat.

"Your name?" I asked.

"My name? What matters it to you?"

"I demand your name!"

"My name is Erostratus or Empedocles, whichever you choose!"

This reply was far from reassuring.

The unknown, besides, talked with such strange coolness that I anxiously asked myself whom I had to deal with.

"Monsieur," he continued, "nothing original has been imagined since the physicist Charles. Four months after the discovery of balloons, this able man had invented the valve, which permits the gas to escape when the balloon is too full, or when you wish to descend; the car, which aids the management of the machine; the netting, which holds the envelope of the balloon, and divides the weight over its whole surface; the ballast, which enables you to ascend, and to choose the place of your landing; the India-rubber coating, which renders the tissue impermeable; the barometer, which shows the height attained. Lastly, Charles used hydrogen, which, fourteen times lighter than air, permits you to penetrate to the highest atmospheric regions, and does not expose you to the dangers of a combustion in the air. On the 1st of December, 1783, three hundred thousand spectators were crowded around the Tuileries. Charles rose, and the soldiers presented arms to him. He travelled nine leagues in the air, conducting his balloon with an ability not surpassed by modern aeronauts. The king awarded him a pension of two thousand livres; for then they encouraged new inventions."

The unknown now seemed to be under the influence of considerable agitation.

"Monsieur," he resumed, "I have studied this, and I am convinced that the first aeronauts guided their balloons. Without speaking of Blanchard, whose assertions may be received with doubt, Guyton-Morveaux, by the aid of oars and rudder, made his machine answer to the helm, and take the direction he determined on. More recently, M. Julien, a watchmaker, made some convincing experiments at the Hippodrome, in Paris; for, by a special mechanism, his aerial apparatus, oblong in form, went visibly against the wind. It occurred to M. Petin to place four hydrogen balloons together; and, by means of sails hung horizontally and partly folded, he hopes to be able to disturb the equilibrium, and, thus inclining the apparatus, to convey it in an oblique direction. They speak, also, of forces to overcome the resistance of currents, – for instance, the screw; but the screw, working on a moveable centre, will give no result. I, monsieur, have discovered the only means of guiding balloons; and no academy has come to my aid, no city has filled up subscriptions for me, no government has thought fit to listen to me! It is infamous!"

The unknown gesticulated fiercely, and the car underwent violent oscillations. I had much trouble in calming him.

Meanwhile the balloon had entered a more rapid current, and we advanced south, at fifteen hundred yards above the earth.

"See, there is Darmstadt," said my companion, leaning over the car. "Do you perceive the château? Not very distinctly, eh? What would you have? The heat of the storm makes the outline of objects waver, and you must have a skilled eye to recognize localities."

"Are you certain it is Darmstadt?" I asked.

"I am sure of it. We are now six leagues from Frankfort."

"Then we must descend."

"Descend! You would not go down, on the steeples," said the unknown, with a chuckle.

"No, but in the suburbs of the city."

"Well, let us avoid the steeples!"

So speaking, my companion seized some bags of ballast. I hastened to prevent him; but he overthrew me with one hand, and the unballasted balloon ascended to two thousand yards.

"Rest easy," said he, "and do not forget that Brioschi, Biot, Gay-Lussac, Bixio, and Barral ascended to still greater heights to make their scientific experiments."

"Monsieur, we must descend," I resumed, trying to persuade him by gentleness. "The storm is gathering around us. It would be more prudent –"

"Bah! We will mount higher than the storm, and then we shall no longer fear it!" cried my companion. "What is nobler than to overlook the clouds which oppress the earth?

Is it not an honour thus to navigate on aerial billows? The greatest men have travelled as we are doing. The Marchioness and Countess de Montalembert, the Countess of Podenas, Mademoiselle la Garde, the Marquis de Montalembert, rose from the Faubourg Saint-Antoine for these unknown regions, and the Duke de Chartres exhibited much skill and presence of mind in his ascent on the 15th of July, 1784. At Lyons, the Counts of Laurencin and Dampierre; at Nantes, M. de Luynes; at Bordeaux, D'Arbelet des Granges; in Italy, the Chevalier Andreani; in our own time, the Duke of Brunswick, – have all left the traces of their glory in the air. To equal these great personages, we must penetrate still higher than they into the celestial depths! To approach the infinite is to comprehend it!"

The rarefaction of the air was fast expanding the hydrogen in the balloon, and I saw its lower part, purposely left empty, swell out, so that it was absolutely necessary to open the valve; but my companion did not seem to intend that I should manage the balloon as I wished. I then resolved to pull the valve cord secretly, as he was excitedly talking; for I feared to guess with whom I had to deal. It would have been too horrible! It was nearly a quarter before one. We had been gone forty minutes from Frankfort; heavy clouds were coming against the wind from the south, and seemed about to burst upon us.

"Have you lost all hope of succeeding in your project?" I asked with anxious interest.

"All hope!" exclaimed the unknown in a low voice. "Wounded by slights and caricatures, these asses' kicks have finished me! It is the eternal punishment reserved for innovators! Look at these caricatures of all periods, of which my portfolio is full."

While my companion was fumbling with his papers, I had seized the valve-cord without his perceiving it. I feared, however, that he might hear the hissing noise, like a water-course, which the gas makes in escaping.

"How many jokes were made about the Abbé Miolan!" said he. "He was to go up with Janninet and Bredin. During the filling their balloon caught fire, and the ignorant populace tore it in pieces! Then this caricature of 'curious animals' appeared, giving each of them a punning nickname."

I pulled the valve-cord, and the barometer began to ascend. It was time. Some far-off rumblings were heard in the south.

"Here is another engraving," resumed the unknown, not suspecting what I was doing. "It is an immense balloon carrying a ship, strong castles, houses, and so on. The caricaturists did not suspect that their follies would one day become truths. It is complete, this large vessel. On the left is its helm, with the pilot's box; at the prow are pleasure-houses, an immense organ, and a cannon to call the attention of the inhabitants of the earth or the moon; above the poop there are the observatory and the balloon long-boat; in the equatorial circle, the army barrack; on the left, the funnel; then the upper galleries for promenading, sails, pinions; below, the cafés and general storehouse. Observe this pompous announcement: 'Invented for the happiness of the human race, this globe will depart at once for the ports of the Levant, and on its return the programme of its voyages to the two poles and the extreme west will be announced. No one need furnish himself with anything; everything is foreseen, and all will prosper. There will be a uniform price for all places of destination, but it will be the same for the most distant countries of our hemisphere – that is to say, a thousand louis for one of any of the said journeys. And it must be confessed that this sum is very moderate, when the speed, comfort, and arrangements which will be enjoyed on the balloon are considered – arrangements which are not to be found on land, while on the balloon each passenger may consult his own habits and tastes. This is so true that in the same place some will be dancing, others standing;

some will be enjoying delicacies; others fasting. Whoever desires the society of wits may satisfy himself; whoever is stupid may find stupid people to keep him company. Thus pleasure will be the soul of the aerial company.' All this provoked laughter; but before long, if I am not cut off, they will see it all realized."

We were visibly descending. He did not perceive it!

"This kind of 'game at balloons,' " he resumed, spreading out before me some of the engravings of his valuable collection, "this game contains the entire history of the aerostatic art. It is used by elevated minds, and is played with dice and counters, with whatever stakes you like, to be paid or received according to where the player arrives."

"Why," said I, "you seem to have studied the science of aerostation profoundly."

"Yes, monsieur, yes! From Phaethon, Icarus, Architas, I have searched for, examined, learnt everything. I could render immense services to the world in this art, if God granted me life. But that will not be!"

"Why?"

"Because my name is Empedocles, or Erostratus."

Meanwhile, the balloon was happily approaching the earth; but when one is falling, the danger is as great at a hundred feet as at five thousand.

"Do you recall the battle of Fleurus?" resumed my companion, whose face became more and more animated. "It was at that battle that Contello, by order of the Government, organized a company of balloonists. At the siege of Manbenge General Jourdan derived so much service from this new method of observation that Contello ascended twice a day with the general himself. The communications between the aeronaut and his agents who held the balloon were made by means of small white, red, and yellow flags. Often the gun and cannon shot were directed upon the balloon when he ascended, but without result. When General Jourdan was preparing to invest Charleroi, Contello went into the vicinity, ascended from the plain of Jumet, and continued his observations for seven or eight hours with General Morlot, and this no doubt aided in giving us the victory of Fleurus. General Jourdan publicly acknowledged the help which the aeronautical observations had afforded him. Well, despite the services rendered on that occasion and during the Belgian campaign, the year which had seen the beginning of the military career of balloons saw also its end. The school of Meudon, founded by the Government, was closed by Buonaparte on his return from Egypt. And now, what can you expect from the newborn infant? as Franklin said. The infant was born alive; it should not be stifled!"

The unknown bowed his head in his hands, and reflected for some moments; then raising his head, he said, –

"Despite my prohibition, monsieur, you have opened the valve."

I dropped the cord.

"Happily," he resumed, "we have still three hundred pounds of ballast."

"What is your purpose?" said I.

"Have you ever crossed the seas?" he asked.

I turned pale.

"It is unfortunate," he went on, "that we are being driven towards the Adriatic. That is only a stream; but higher up we may find other currents."

And, without taking any notice of me, he threw over several bags of sand; then, in a menacing voice, he said, –

"I let you open the valve because the expansion of the gas threatened to burst the balloon; but do not do it again!"

Then he went on as follows:

"You remember the voyage of Blanchard and Jeffries from Dover to Calais? It was magnificent! On the 7th of January, 1785, there being a north-west wind, their balloon was inflated with gas on the Dover coast. A mistake of equilibrium, just as they were ascending, forced them to throw out their ballast so that they might not go down again, and they only kept thirty pounds. It was too little; for, as the wind did not freshen, they only advanced very slowly towards the French coast. Besides, the permeability of the tissue served to reduce the inflation little by little, and in an hour and a half the aeronauts perceived that they were descending.

" 'What shall we do?' said Jeffries.

" 'We are only one quarter of the way over,' replied Blanchard, 'and very low down. On rising, we shall perhaps meet more favourable winds.'

" 'Let us throw out the rest of the sand.'

"The balloon acquired some ascending force, but it soon began to descend again. Towards the middle of the transit the aeronauts threw over their books and tools. A quarter of an hour after, Blanchard said to Jeffries, –

" 'The barometer?'

" 'It is going up! We are lost, and yet there is the French coast.'

"A loud noise was heard.

" 'Has the balloon burst?' asked Jeffries.

" 'No. The loss of the gas has reduced the inflation of the lower part of the balloon. But we are still descending. We are lost! Out with everything useless!'

"Provisions, oars, and rudder were thrown into the sea. The aeronauts were only one hundred yards high.

" 'We are going up again,' said the doctor.

" 'No. It is the spurt caused by the diminution of the weight, and not a ship in sight, not a bark on the horizon! To the sea with our clothing!'

"The unfortunates stripped themselves, but the balloon continued to descend.

" 'Blanchard,' said Jeffries, 'you should have made this voyage alone; you consented to take me; I will sacrifice myself! I am going to throw myself into the water, and the balloon, relieved of my weight, will mount again.'

" 'No, no! It is frightful!'

"The balloon became less and less inflated, and as it doubled up its concavity pressed the gas against the sides, and hastened its downward course.

" 'Adieu, my friend,' said the doctor. 'God preserve you!'

"He was about to throw himself over, when Blanchard held him back.

" 'There is one more chance,' said he. 'We can cut the cords which hold the car, and cling to the net! Perhaps the balloon will rise. Let us hold ourselves ready. But – the barometer is going down! The wind is freshening! We are saved!'

"The aeronauts perceived Calais. Their joy was delirious. A few moments more, and they had fallen in the forest of Guines. I do not doubt," added the unknown, "that, under similar circumstances, you would have followed Doctor Jeffries' example!"

The clouds rolled in glittering masses beneath us. The balloon threw large shadows on this heap of clouds, and was surrounded as by an aureola. The thunder rumbled below the car. All this was terrifying.

"Let us descend!" I cried.

"Descend, when the sun is up there, waiting for us? Out with more bags!"

And more than fifty pounds of ballast were cast over.

At a height of three thousand five hundred yards we remained stationary.

The unknown talked unceasingly. I was in a state of complete prostration, while he seemed to be in his element.

"With a good wind, we shall go far," he cried. "In the Antilles there are currents of air which have a speed of a hundred leagues an hour. When Napoleon was crowned, Garnerin sent up a balloon with coloured lamps, at eleven o'clock at night. The wind was blowing north-north-west. The next morning, at daybreak, the inhabitants of Rome greeted its passage over the dome of St. Peter's. We shall go farther and higher!"

I scarcely heard him. Everything whirled around me. An opening appeared in the clouds.

"See that city," said the unknown. "It is Spires!"

I leaned over the car and perceived a small blackish mass. It was Spires. The Rhine, which is so large, seemed an unrolled ribbon. The sky was a deep blue over our heads. The birds had long abandoned us, for in that rarefied air they could not have flown. We were alone in space, and I in presence of this unknown!

"It is useless for you to know whither I am leading you," he said, as he threw the compass among the clouds. "Ah! A fall is a grand thing! You know that but few victims of ballooning are to be reckoned, from Pilâtre des Rosiers to Lieutenant Gale, and that the accidents have always been the result of imprudence. Pilâtre des Rosiers set out with Romain of Boulogne, on the 13th of June, 1785. To his gas balloon he had affixed a Montgolfier apparatus of hot air, so as to dispense, no doubt, with the necessity of losing gas or throwing out ballast. It was putting a torch under a powder-barrel. When they had ascended four hundred yards, and were taken by opposing winds, they were driven over the open sea. Pilâtre, in order to descend, essayed to open the valve, but the valve-cord became entangled in the balloon, and tore it so badly that it became empty in an instant. It fell upon the Montgolfier apparatus, overturned it, and dragged down the unfortunates, who were soon shattered to pieces! It is frightful, is it not?"

I could only reply, "For pity's sake, let us descend!"

The clouds gathered around us on every side, and dreadful detonations, which reverberated in the cavity of the balloon, took place beneath us.

"You provoke me," cried the unknown, "and you shall no longer know whether we are rising or falling!"

The barometer went the way of the compass, accompanied by several more bags of sand. We must have been 5000 yards high. Some icicles had already attached themselves to the sides of the car, and a kind of fine snow seemed to penetrate to my very bones. Meanwhile a frightful tempest was raging under us, but we were above it.

"Do not be afraid," said the unknown. "It is only the imprudent who are lost. Olivari, who perished at Orleans, rose in a paper 'Montgolfier;' his car, suspended below the chafing-dish, and ballasted with combustible materials, caught fire; Olivari fell, and was killed! Mosment rose, at Lille, on a light tray; an oscillation disturbed his equilibrium; Mosment fell, and was killed! Bittorf, at Mannheim, saw his balloon catch fire in the air; and he, too, fell, and was killed! Harris rose in a badly constructed balloon, the valve of which was too large and would not shut; Harris fell, and was killed! Sadler, deprived of ballast by his long sojourn in the air, was dragged over the town of Boston and dashed against the chimneys; Sadler fell, and was killed! Cokling descended with a convex parachute which he pretended to have perfected; Cokling fell, and was killed! Well, I love them, these victims of their own imprudence, and I shall die as they did. Higher! Still higher!"

All the phantoms of this necrology passed before my eyes. The rarefaction of the air and the sun's rays added to the expansion of the gas, and the balloon continued to mount. I tried mechanically to open the valve, but the unknown cut the cord several feet above my head. I was lost!

"Did you see Madame Blanchard fall?" said he. "I saw her; yes, I! I was at Tivoli on the 6th of July, 1819. Madame Blanchard rose in a small sized balloon, to avoid the expense of filling, and she was forced to entirely inflate it. The gas leaked out below, and left a regular train of hydrogen in its path. She carried with her a sort of pyrotechnic aureola, suspended below her car by a wire, which she was to set off in the air. This she had done many times before. On this day she also carried up a small parachute ballasted by a firework contrivance, that would go off in a shower of silver. She was to start this contrivance after having lighted it with a port-fire made on purpose. She set out; the night was gloomy. At the moment of lighting her fireworks she was so imprudent as to pass the taper under the column of hydrogen which was leaking from the balloon. My eyes were fixed upon her. Suddenly an unexpected gleam lit up the darkness. I thought she was preparing a surprise. The light flashed out, suddenly disappeared and reappeared, and gave the summit of the balloon the shape of an immense jet of ignited gas. This sinister glow shed itself over the Boulevard and the whole Montmartre quarter. Then I saw the unhappy woman rise, try twice to close the appendage of the balloon, so as to put out the fire, then sit down in her car and try to guide her descent; for she did not fall. The combustion of the gas lasted for several minutes. The balloon, becoming gradually less, continued to descend, but it was not a fall. The wind blew from the north-west and drove it towards Paris. There were then some large gardens just by the house No. 16, Rue de Provence. Madame Blanchard essayed to fall there without danger: but the balloon and the car struck on the roof of the house with a light shock. 'Save me!' cried the wretched woman. I got into the street at this moment. The car slid along the roof, and encountered an iron cramp. At this concussion, Madame Blanchard was thrown out of her car and precipitated upon the pavement. She was killed!"

These stories froze me with horror. The unknown was standing with bare head, dishevelled hair, haggard eyes!

There was no longer any illusion possible. I at last recognized the horrible truth. I was in the presence of a madman!

He threw out the rest of the ballast, and we must have now reached a height of at least nine thousand yards. Blood spurted from my nose and mouth!

"Who are nobler than the martyrs of science?" cried the lunatic. "They are canonized by posterity."

But I no longer heard him. He looked about him, and, bending down to my ear, muttered, –

"And have you forgotten Zambecarri's catastrophe? Listen. On the 7th of October, 1804, the clouds seemed to lift a little. On the preceding days, the wind and rain had not ceased; but the announced ascension of Zambecarri could not be postponed. His enemies were already bantering him. It was necessary to ascend, to save the science and himself from becoming a public jest. It was at Boulogne. No one helped him to inflate his balloon.

"He rose at midnight, accompanied by Andreoli and Grossetti. The balloon mounted slowly, for it had been perforated by the rain, and the gas was leaking out. The three intrepid aeronauts could only observe the state of the barometer by aid of a dark lantern. Zambecarri had eaten nothing for twenty-four hours. Grossetti was also fasting.

" 'My friends,' said Zambecarri, 'I am overcome by cold, and exhausted. I am dying.'

"He fell inanimate in the gallery. It was the same with Grossetti. Andreoli alone remained conscious. After long efforts, he succeeded in reviving Zambecarri.

" 'What news? Whither are we going? How is the wind? What time is it?'

" 'It is two o'clock.'

" 'Where is the compass?'

" 'Upset!'

" 'Great God! The lantern has gone out!'

" 'It cannot burn in this rarefied air,' said Zambecarri.

"The moon had not risen, and the atmosphere was plunged in murky darkness.

" 'I am cold, Andreoli. What shall I do?'

"They slowly descended through a layer of whitish clouds.

" 'Sh!' said Andreoli. 'Do you hear?'

" 'What?' asked Zambecarri.

" 'A strange noise.'

" 'You are mistaken.'

" 'No.'

"Consider these travellers, in the middle of the night, listening to that unaccountable noise! Are they going to knock against a tower? Are they about to be precipitated on the roofs?

" 'Do you hear? One would say it was the noise of the sea.'

" 'Impossible!'

" 'It is the groaning of the waves!'

" 'It is true.'

" 'Light! Light!'

"After five fruitless attempts, Andreoli succeeded in obtaining light. It was three o'clock.

"The voice of violent waves was heard. They were almost touching the surface of the sea!

" 'We are lost!' cried Zambecarri, seizing a large bag of sand.

" 'Help!' cried Andreoli.

"The car touched the water, and the waves came up to their breasts.

" 'Throw out the instruments, clothes, money!'

"The aeronauts completely stripped themselves. The balloon, relieved, rose with frightful rapidity. Zambecarri was taken with vomiting. Grossetti bled profusely. The unfortunate men could not speak, so short was their breathing. They were taken with cold, and they were soon crusted over with ice. The moon looked as red as blood.

"After traversing the high regions for a half-hour, the balloon again fell into the sea. It was four in the morning. They were half submerged in the water, and the balloon dragged them along, as if under sail, for several hours.

"At daybreak they found themselves opposite Pesaro, four miles from the coast. They were about to reach it, when a gale blew them back into the open sea. They were lost! The frightened boats fled at their approach. Happily, a more intelligent boatman accosted them, hoisted them on board, and they landed at Ferrada.

"A frightful journey, was it not? But Zambecarri was a brave and energetic man. Scarcely recovered from his sufferings, he resumed his ascensions. During one of them he struck against a tree; his spirit-lamp was broken on his clothes; he was enveloped in fire, his balloon began to catch the flames, and he came down half consumed.

"At last, on the 21st of September, 1812, he made another ascension at Boulogne. The balloon clung to a tree, and his lamp again set it on fire. Zambecarri fell, and was killed! And in presence of these facts, we would still hesitate! No. The higher we go, the more glorious will be our death!"

The balloon being now entirely relieved of ballast and of all it contained, we were carried to an enormous height. It vibrated in the atmosphere. The least noise resounded in the vaults of heaven. Our globe, the only object which caught my view in immensity, seemed ready to be annihilated, and above us the depths of the starry skies were lost in thick darkness.

I saw my companion rise up before me.

"The hour is come!" he said. "We must die. We are rejected of men. They despise us. Let us crush them!"

"Mercy!" I cried.

"Let us cut these cords! Let this car be abandoned in space. The attractive force will change its direction, and we shall approach the sun!"

Despair galvanized me. I threw myself upon the madman, we struggled together, and a terrible conflict took place. But I was thrown down, and while he held me under his knee, the madman was cutting the cords of the car.

"One!" he cried.

"My God!"

"Two! Three!"

I made a superhuman effort, rose up, and violently repulsed the madman.

"Four!"

The car fell, but I instinctively clung to the cords and hoisted myself into the meshes of the netting.

The madman disappeared in space!

The balloon was raised to an immeasurable height. A horrible cracking was heard. The gas, too much dilated, had burst the balloon. I shut my eyes –

Some instants after, a damp warmth revived me. I was in the midst of clouds on fire. The balloon turned over with dizzy velocity. Taken by the wind, it made a hundred leagues an hour in a horizontal course, the lightning flashing around it.

Meanwhile my fall was not a very rapid one. When I opened my eyes, I saw the country. I was two miles from the sea, and the tempest was driving me violently towards it, when an abrupt shock forced me to loosen my hold. My hands opened, a cord slipped swiftly between my fingers, and I found myself on the solid earth!

It was the cord of the anchor, which, sweeping along the surface of the ground, was caught in a crevice; and my balloon, unballasted for the last time, careered off to lose itself beyond the sea.

When I came to myself, I was in bed in a peasant's cottage, at Harderwick, a village of La Gueldre, fifteen leagues from Amsterdam, on the shores of the Zuyder-Zee.

A miracle had saved my life, but my voyage had been a series of imprudences, committed by a lunatic, and I had not been able to prevent them.

May this terrible narrative, though instructing those who read it, not discourage the explorers of the air.

Master Zacharius

Jules Verne

Chapter I
A Winter Night

THE CITY of Geneva lies at the west end of the lake of the same name. The Rhone, which passes through the town at the outlet of the lake, divides it into two sections, and is itself divided in the centre of the city by an island placed in mid-stream. A topographical feature like this is often found in the great depôts of commerce and industry. No doubt the first inhabitants were influenced by the easy means of transport which the swift currents of the rivers offered them – those "roads which walk along of their own accord," as Pascal puts it. In the case of the Rhone, it would be the road that ran along.

Before new and regular buildings were constructed on this island, which was enclosed like a Dutch galley in the middle of the river, the curious mass of houses, piled one on the other, presented a delightfully confused *coup-d'oeil*. The small area of the island had compelled some of the buildings to be perched, as it were, on the piles, which were entangled in the rough currents of the river. The huge beams, blackened by time, and worn by the water, seemed like the claws of an enormous crab, and presented a fantastic appearance. The little yellow streams, which were like cobwebs stretched amid this ancient foundation, quivered in the darkness, as if they had been the leaves of some old oak forest, while the river engulfed in this forest of piles, foamed and roared most mournfully.

One of the houses of the island was striking for its curiously aged appearance. It was the dwelling of the old clockmaker, Master Zacharius, whose household consisted of his daughter Gerande, Aubert Thun, his apprentice, and his old servant Scholastique.

There was no man in Geneva to compare in interest with this Zacharius. His age was past finding out. Not the oldest inhabitant of the town could tell for how long his thin, pointed head had shaken above his shoulders, nor the day when, for the first time, he had walked through the streets, with his long white locks floating in the wind. The man did not live; he vibrated like the pendulum of his clocks. His spare and cadaverous figure was always clothed in dark colours. Like the pictures of Leonardo di Vinci, he was sketched in black.

Gerande had the pleasantest room in the whole house, whence, through a narrow window, she had the inspiriting view of the snowy peaks of Jura; but the bedroom and workshop of the old man were a kind of cavern close on to the water, the floor of which rested on the piles.

From time immemorial Master Zacharius had never come out except at meal times, and when he went to regulate the different clocks of the town. He passed the rest of his time at his bench, which was covered with numerous clockwork instruments, most of which he had invented himself. For he was a clever man; his works were valued in all France and Germany.

The best workers in Geneva readily recognized his superiority, and showed that he was an honour to the town, by saying, "To him belongs the glory of having invented the escapement." In fact, the birth of true clock-work dates from the invention which the talents of Zacharius had discovered not many years before.

After he had worked hard for a long time, Zacharius would slowly put his tools away, cover up the delicate pieces that he had been adjusting with glasses, and stop the active wheel of his lathe; then he would raise a trapdoor constructed in the floor of his workshop, and, stooping down, used to inhale for hours together the thick vapours of the Rhone, as it dashed along under his eyes.

One winter's night the old servant Scholastique served the supper, which, according to old custom, she and the young mechanic shared with their master. Master Zacharius did not eat, though the food carefully prepared for him was offered him in a handsome blue and white dish. He scarcely answered the sweet words of Gerande, who evidently noticed her father's silence, and even the clatter of Scholastique herself no more struck his ear than the roar of the river, to which he paid no attention.

After the silent meal, the old clockmaker left the table without embracing his daughter, or saying his usual "Goodnight" to all. He left by the narrow door leading to his den, and the staircase groaned under his heavy footsteps as he went down.

Gerande, Aubert, and Scholastique sat for some minutes without speaking. On this evening the weather was dull; the clouds dragged heavily on the Alps, and threatened rain; the severe climate of Switzerland made one feel sad, while the south wind swept round the house, and whistled ominously.

"My dear young lady," said Scholastique, at last, "do you know that our master has been out of sorts for several days? Holy Virgin! I know he has had no appetite, because his words stick in his inside, and it would take a very clever devil to drag even one out of him."

"My father has some secret cause of trouble, that I cannot even guess," replied Gerande, as a sad anxiety spread over her face.

"Mademoiselle, don't let such sadness fill your heart. You know the strange habits of Master Zacharius. Who can read his secret thoughts in his face? No doubt some fatigue has overcome him, but tomorrow he will have forgotten it, and be very sorry to have given his daughter pain."

It was Aubert who spoke thus, looking into Gerande's lovely eyes. Aubert was the first apprentice whom Master Zacharius had ever admitted to the intimacy of his labours, for he appreciated his intelligence, discretion, and goodness of heart; and this young man had attached himself to Gerande with the earnest devotion natural to a noble nature.

Gerande was eighteen years of age. Her oval face recalled that of the artless Madonnas whom veneration still displays at the street corners of the antique towns of Brittany. Her eyes betrayed an infinite simplicity. One would love her as the sweetest realization of a poet's dream. Her apparel was of modest colours, and the white linen which was folded about her shoulders had the tint and perfume peculiar to the linen of the church. She led a mystical existence in Geneva, which had not as yet been delivered over to the dryness of Calvinism.

While, night and morning, she read her Latin prayers in her iron-clasped missal, Gerande had also discovered a hidden sentiment in Aubert Thun's heart, and comprehended what a profound devotion the young workman had for her. Indeed, the whole world in his eyes was condensed into this old clockmaker's house, and he passed all his time near the young girl, when he left her father's workshop, after his work was over.

Old Scholastique saw all this, but said nothing. Her loquacity exhausted itself in preference on the evils of the times, and the little worries of the household. Nobody tried to stop its course. It was with her as with the musical snuff-boxes which they made at Geneva; once wound up, you must break them before you will prevent their playing all their airs through.

Finding Gerande absorbed in a melancholy silence, Scholastique left her old wooden chair, fixed a taper on the end of a candlestick, lit it, and placed it near a small waxen Virgin, sheltered in her niche of stone. It was the family custom to kneel before this protecting Madonna of the domestic hearth, and to beg her kindly watchfulness during the coming night; but on this evening Gerande remained silent in her seat.

"Well, well, dear demoiselle," said the astonished Scholastique, "supper is over, and it is time to go to bed. Why do you tire your eyes by sitting up late? Ah, Holy Virgin! It's much better to sleep, and to get a little comfort from happy dreams! In these detestable times in which we live, who can promise herself a fortunate day?"

"Ought we not to send for a doctor for my father?" asked Gerande.

"A doctor!" cried the old domestic. "Has Master Zacharius ever listened to their fancies and pompous sayings? He might accept medicines for the watches, but not for the body!"

"What shall we do?" murmured Gerande. "Has he gone to work, or to rest?"

"Gerande," answered Aubert softly, "some mental trouble annoys your father, that is all."

"Do you know what it is, Aubert?"

"Perhaps, Gerande"

"Tell us, then," cried Scholastique eagerly, economically extinguishing her taper.

"For several days, Gerande," said the young apprentice, "something absolutely incomprehensible has been going on. All the watches which your father has made and sold for some years have suddenly stopped. Very many of them have been brought back to him. He has carefully taken them to pieces; the springs were in good condition, and the wheels well set. He has put them together yet more carefully; but, despite his skill, they will not go."

"The devil's in it!" cried Scholastique.

"Why say you so?" asked Gerande. "It seems very natural to me. Nothing lasts for ever in this world. The infinite cannot be fashioned by the hands of men."

"It is none the less true," returned Aubert, "that there is in this something very mysterious and extraordinary. I have myself been helping Master Zacharius to search for the cause of this derangement of his watches; but I have not been able to find it, and more than once I have let my tools fall from my hands in despair."

"But why undertake so vain a task?" resumed Scholastique. "Is it natural that a little copper instrument should go of itself, and mark the hours? We ought to have kept to the sun-dial!"

"You will not talk thus, Scholastique," said Aubert, "when you learn that the sun-dial was invented by Cain."

"Good heavens! What are you telling me?"

"Do you think," asked Gerande simply, "that we might pray to God to give life to my father's watches?"

"Without doubt," replied Aubert.

"Good! They will be useless prayers," muttered the old servant, "but Heaven will pardon them for their good intent."

The taper was relighted. Scholastique, Gerande, and Aubert knelt down together upon the tiles of the room. The young girl prayed for her mother's soul, for a blessing for the night, for travellers and prisoners, for the good and the wicked, and more earnestly than all for the unknown misfortunes of her father.

Then the three devout souls rose with some confidence in their hearts, because they had laid their sorrow on the bosom of God.

Aubert repaired to his own room; Gerande sat pensively by the window, whilst the last lights were disappearing from the city streets; and Scholastique, having poured a little water on the flickering embers, and shut the two enormous bolts on the door, threw herself upon her bed, where she was soon dreaming that she was dying of fright.

Meanwhile the terrors of this winter's night had increased. Sometimes, with the whirlpools of the river, the wind engulfed itself among the piles, and the whole house shivered and shook; but the young girl, absorbed in her sadness, thought only of her father. After hearing what Aubert told her, the malady of Master Zacharius took fantastic proportions in her mind; and it seemed to her as if his existence, so dear to her, having become purely mechanical, no longer moved on its worn-out pivots without effort.

Suddenly the penthouse shutter, shaken by the squall, struck against the window of the room. Gerande shuddered and started up without understanding the cause of the noise which thus disturbed her reverie. When she became a little calmer she opened the sash. The clouds had burst, and a torrent-like rain pattered on the surrounding roofs. The young girl leaned out of the window to draw to the shutter shaken by the wind, but she feared to do so. It seemed to her that the rain and the river, confounding their tumultuous waters, were submerging the frail house, the planks of which creaked in every direction. She would have flown from her chamber, but she saw below the flickering of a light which appeared to come from Master Zacharius's retreat, and in one of those momentary calms during which the elements keep a sudden silence, her ear caught plaintive sounds. She tried to shut her window, but could not. The wind violently repelled her, like a thief who was breaking into a dwelling.

Gerande thought she would go mad with terror. What was her father doing? She opened the door, and it escaped from her hands, and slammed loudly with the force of the tempest. Gerande then found herself in the dark supper-room, succeeded in gaining, on tiptoe, the staircase which led to her father's shop, and pale and fainting, glided down.

The old watchmaker was upright in the middle of the room, which resounded with the roaring of the river. His bristling hair gave him a sinister aspect. He was talking and gesticulating, without seeing or hearing anything. Gerande stood still on the threshold.

"It is death!" said Master Zacharius, in a hollow voice; "it is death! Why should I live longer, now that I have dispersed my existence over the earth? For I, Master, Zacharius, am really the creator of all the watches that I have fashioned! It is a part of my very soul that I have shut up in each of these cases of iron, silver, or gold! Every time that one of these accursed watches stops, I feel my heart cease beating, for I have regulated them with its pulsations!"

As he spoke in this strange way, the old man cast his eyes on his bench. There lay all the pieces of a watch that he had carefully taken apart. He took up a sort of hollow cylinder, called a barrel, in which the spring is enclosed, and removed the steel spiral, but instead of relaxing itself, according to the laws of its elasticity, it remained coiled on itself like a sleeping viper. It seemed knotted, like impotent old men whose blood has long been congealed. Master Zacharius vainly essayed to uncoil it with his thin fingers, the outlines of which were exaggerated on the wall; but he tried in vain, and soon, with a terrible cry of anguish and rage, he threw it through the trapdoor into the boiling Rhone.

Gerande, her feet riveted to the floor, stood breathless and motionless. She wished to approach her father, but could not. Giddy hallucinations took possession of her. Suddenly she heard, in the shade, a voice murmur in her ears, –

"Gerande, dear Gerande! Grief still keeps you awake. Go in again, I beg of you; the night is cold."

"Aubert!" whispered the young girl. "You!"

"Ought I not to be troubled by what troubles you?"

These soft words sent the blood back into the young girl's heart. She leaned on Aubert's arm, and said to him, –

"My father is very ill, Aubert! You alone can cure him, for this disorder of the mind would not yield to his daughter's consolings. His mind is attacked by a very natural delusion, and in working with him, repairing the watches, you will bring him back to reason. Aubert," she continued, "it is not true, is it, that his life is mixed up with that of his watches?"

Aubert did not reply.

"But is my father's a trade condemned by God?" asked Gerande, trembling.

"I know not," returned the apprentice, warming the cold hands of the girl with his own. "But go back to your room, my poor Gerande, and with sleep recover hope!"

Gerande slowly returned to her chamber, and remained there till daylight, without sleep closing her eyelids. Meanwhile, Master Zacharius, always mute and motionless, gazed at the river as it rolled turbulently at his feet.

Chapter II
The Pride of Science

THE SEVERITY of the Geneva merchant in business matters has become proverbial. He is rigidly honourable, and excessively just. What must, then, have been the shame of Master Zacharius, when he saw these watches, which he had so carefully constructed, returning to him from every direction?

It was certain that these watches had suddenly stopped, and without any apparent reason. The wheels were in a good condition and firmly fixed, but the springs had lost all elasticity. Vainly did the watchmaker try to replace them; the wheels remained motionless. These unaccountable derangements were greatly to the old man's discredit. His noble inventions had many times brought upon him suspicions of sorcery, which now seemed confirmed. These rumours reached Gerande, and she often trembled for her father, when she saw malicious glances directed towards him.

Yet on the morning after this night of anguish, Master Zacharius seemed to resume work with some confidence. The morning sun inspired him with some courage. Aubert hastened to join him in the shop, and received an affable "Good day."

"I am better," said the old man. "I don't know what strange pains in the head attacked me yesterday, but the sun has quite chased them away, with the clouds of the night."

"In faith, master," returned Aubert, "I don't like the night for either of us!"

"And thou art right, Aubert. If you ever become a great man, you will understand that day is as necessary to you as food. A great savant should be always ready to receive the homage of his fellow-men."

"Master, it seems to me that the pride of science has possessed you."

"Pride, Aubert! Destroy my past, annihilate my present, dissipate my future, and then it will be permitted to me to live in obscurity! Poor boy, who comprehends not the sublime things to which my art is wholly devoted! Art thou not but a tool in my hands?"

"Yet. Master Zacharius," resumed Aubert, "I have more than once merited your praise for the manner in which I adjusted the most delicate parts of your watches and clocks."

"No doubt, Aubert; thou art a good workman, such as I love; but when thou workest, thou thinkest thou hast in thy hands but copper, silver, gold; thou dost not perceive these metals, which my genius animates, palpitating like living flesh! So that thou wilt not die, with the death of thy works!"

Master Zacharius remained silent after these words; but Aubert essayed to keep up the conversation.

"Indeed, master," said he, "I love to see you work so unceasingly! You will be ready for the festival of our corporation, for I see that the work on this crystal watch is going forward famously."

"No doubt, Aubert," cried the old watchmaker, "and it will be no slight honour for me to have been able to cut and shape the crystal to the durability of a diamond! Ah, Louis Berghem did well to perfect the art of diamond-cutting, which has enabled me to polish and pierce the hardest stones!"

Master Zacharius was holding several small watch pieces of cut crystal, and of exquisite workmanship. The wheels, pivots, and case of the watch were of the same material, and he had employed remarkable skill in this very difficult task.

"Would it not be fine," said he, his face flushing, "to see this watch palpitating beneath its transparent envelope, and to be able to count the beatings of its heart?"

"I will wager, sir," replied the young apprentice, "that it will not vary a second in a year."

"And you would wager on a certainty! Have I not imparted to it all that is purest of myself? And does my heart vary? My heart, I say?"

Aubert did not dare to lift his eyes to his master's face.

"Tell me frankly," said the old man sadly. "Have you never taken me for a madman? Do you not think me sometimes subject to dangerous folly? Yes; is it not so? In my daughter's eyes and yours, I have often read my condemnation. Oh!" he cried, as if in pain, "to be misunderstood by those whom one most loves in the world! But I will prove victoriously to thee, Aubert, that I am right! Do not shake thy head, for thou wilt be astounded. The day on which thou understandest how to listen to and comprehend me, thou wilt see that I have discovered the secrets of existence, the secrets of the mysterious union of the soul with the body!"

As he spoke thus, Master Zacharius appeared superb in his vanity. His eyes glittered with a supernatural fire, and his pride illumined every feature. And truly, if ever vanity was excusable, it was that of Master Zacharius!

The watchmaking art, indeed, down to his time, had remained almost in its infancy. From the day when Plato, four centuries before the Christian era, invented the night watch, a sort of clepsydra which indicated the hours of the night by the sound and playing of a flute, the science had continued nearly stationary. The masters paid more attention to the arts than to mechanics, and it was the period of beautiful watches of iron, copper, wood, silver, which were richly engraved, like one of Cellini's ewers. They made a masterpiece of chasing, which measured time imperfectly, but was still a masterpiece. When the artist's imagination was not directed to the perfection of modeling, it set to work to create clocks with moving figures and melodious sounds, whose appearance took all attention. Besides, who troubled himself, in those days, with regulating the advance of time? The delays of the law were not as yet invented; the physical and astronomical sciences had not as yet established their calculations on scrupulously exact measurements; there were neither establishments which were shut at a given hour, nor trains which departed at a precise moment. In the evening the curfew bell sounded; and at night the hours were cried amid the universal silence. Certainly people did not live so long, if existence is measured by the amount of business done; but they lived better. The mind was enriched with the noble sentiments born of the contemplation of *chefs-d'oeuvré*. They built a church in two centuries, a painter painted but few pictures in the course of his life, a poet only composed one great work; but these were so many masterpieces for after-ages to appreciate.

When the exact sciences began at last to make some progress, watch and clock making followed in their path, though it was always arrested by an insurmountable difficulty, the regular and continuous measurement of time.

It was in the midst of this stagnation that Master Zacharius invented the escapement, which enabled him to obtain a mathematical regularity by submitting the movement of the pendulum to a sustained force. This invention had turned the old man's head. Pride, swelling in his heart, like mercury in the thermometer, had attained the height of transcendent folly. By analogy he had allowed himself to be drawn to materialistic conclusions, and as he constructed his watches, he fancied that he had discovered the secrets of the union of the soul with the body.

Thus, on this day, perceiving that Aubert listened to him attentively, he said to him in a tone of simple conviction, "Dost thou know what life is, my child? Hast thou comprehended the action of those springs which produce existence? Hast thou examined thyself? No. And yet, with the eyes of science, thou mightest have seen the intimate relation which exists between God's work and my own; for it is from his creature that I have copied the combinations of the wheels of my clocks."

"Master," replied Aubert eagerly, "can you compare a copper or steel machine with that breath of God which is called the soul, which animates our bodies as the breeze stirs the flowers? What mechanism could be so adjusted as to inspire us with thought?"

"That is not the question," responded Master Zacharius gently, but with all the obstinacy of a blind man walking towards an abyss. "In order to understand me, thou must recall the purpose of the escapement which I have invented. When I saw the irregular working of clocks, I understood that the movements shut up in them did not suffice, and that it was necessary to submit them to the regularity of some independent force. I then thought that the balance wheel might accomplish this, and I succeeded in regulating the movement! Now, was it not a sublime idea that came to me, to return to it its lost force by the action of the clock itself, which it was charged with regulating?"

Aubert made a sign of assent.

"Now, Aubert," continued the old man, growing animated, "cast thine eyes upon thyself! Dost thou not understand that there are two distinct forces in us, that of the soul and that of the body – that is, a movement and a regulator? The soul is the principle of life; that is, then, the movement. Whether it is produced by a weight, by a spring, or by an immaterial influence, it is none the less in the heart. But without the body this movement would be unequal, irregular, impossible! Thus the body regulates the soul, and, like the balance wheel, it is submitted to regular oscillations. And this is so true, that one falls ill when one's drink, food, sleep – in a word, the functions of the body – are not properly regulated; just as in my watches the soul renders to the body the force lost by its oscillations.

Well, what produces this intimate union between soul and body, if not a marvellous escapement, by which the wheels of the one work into the wheels of the other? This is what I have discovered and applied; and there are no longer any secrets for me in this life, which is, after all, only an ingenious mechanism!"

Master Zacharius looked sublime in this hallucination, which carried him to the ultimate mysteries of the Infinite. But his daughter Gerande, standing on the threshold of the door, had heard all. She rushed into her father's arms, and he pressed her convulsively to his breast.

"What is the matter with thee, my daughter?" he asked.

"If I had only a spring here," said she, putting her hand on her heart, "I would not love you as I do, father."

Master Zacharius looked intently at Gerande, and did not reply. Suddenly he uttered a cry, carried his hand eagerly to his heart, and fell fainting on his old leathern chair.

"Father, what is the matter?"

"Help!" cried Aubert. "Scholastique!"

But Scholastique did not come at once. Some one was knocking at the front door; she had gone to open it, and when she returned to the shop, before she could open her mouth, the old watchmaker, having recovered his senses, spoke:

"I divine, my old Scholastique, that you bring me still another of those accursed watches which have stopped."

"Lord, it is true enough!" replied Scholastique, handing a watch to Aubert.

"My heart could not be mistaken!" said the old man, with a sigh.

Meanwhile Aubert carefully wound up the watch, but it would not go.

Chapter III
A Strange Visit

Poor Gerande would have lost her life with that of her father, had it not been for the thought of Aubert, who still attached her to the world.

The old watchmaker was, little by little, passing away. His faculties evidently grew more feeble, as he concentrated them on a single thought. By a sad association of ideas, he referred everything to his monomania, and a human existence seemed to have departed from him, to give place to the extra-natural existence of the intermediate powers. Moreover, certain malicious rivals revived the sinister rumours which had spread concerning his labours.

The news of the strange derangements which his watches betrayed had a prodigious effect upon the master clockmakers of Geneva. What signified this sudden paralysis of their wheels, and why these strange relations which they seemed to have with the old man's life? These were the kind of mysteries which people never contemplate without a secret terror. In the various classes of the town, from the apprentice to the great lord who used the watches of the old horologist, there was no one who could not himself judge of the singularity of the fact. The citizens wished, but in vain, to get to see Master Zacharius. He fell very ill; and this enabled his daughter to withdraw him from those incessant visits which had degenerated into reproaches and recriminations.

Medicines and physicians were powerless in presence of this organic wasting away, the cause of which could not be discovered. It sometimes seemed as if the old man's heart had ceased to beat; then the pulsations were resumed with an alarming irregularity.

A custom existed in those days of publicly exhibiting the works of the masters. The heads of the various corporations sought to distinguish themselves by the novelty or the perfection of their productions; and it was among these that the condition of Master Zacharius excited the most lively, because most interested, commiseration. His rivals pitied him the more willingly because they feared him the less. They never forgot the old man's success, when he exhibited his magnificent clocks with moving figures, his repeaters, which provoked general admiration, and commanded such high prices in the cities of France, Switzerland, and Germany.

Meanwhile, thanks to the constant and tender care of Gerande and Aubert, his strength seemed to return a little; and in the tranquillity in which his convalescence left him, he succeeded in detaching himself from the thoughts which had absorbed him. As soon as he could walk, his daughter lured him away from the house, which was still besieged with dissatisfied customers. Aubert remained in the shop, vainly adjusting and readjusting the rebel watches; and the poor boy, completely mystified, sometimes covered his face with his hands, fearful that he, like his master, might go mad.

Gerande led her father towards the more pleasant promenades of the town. With his arm resting on hers, she conducted him sometimes through the quarter of Saint Antoine, the view from which extends towards the Cologny hill, and over the lake; on fine mornings they caught sight of the gigantic peaks of Mount Buet against the horizon. Gerande pointed out these spots to her father, who had well-nigh forgotten even their names. His memory wandered; and he took a childish interest in learning anew what had passed from his mind. Master Zacharius leaned upon his daughter; and the two heads, one white as snow and the other covered with rich golden tresses, met in the same ray of sunlight.

So it came about that the old watchmaker at last perceived that he was not alone in the world. As he looked upon his young and lovely daughter, and on himself old and broken, he reflected that after his death she would be left alone without support. Many of the young mechanics of Geneva had already sought to win Gerande's love; but none of them had succeeded in gaining access to the impenetrable retreat of the watchmaker's household. It was natural, then, that during this lucid interval, the old man's choice should fall on Aubert Thun. Once struck with this thought, he remarked to himself that this young couple had been brought up with the same ideas and the same beliefs; and the oscillations of their hearts seemed to him, as he said one day to Scholastique, "isochronous."

The old servant, literally delighted with the word, though she did not understand it, swore by her holy patron saint that the whole town should hear it within a quarter of an hour. Master Zacharius found it difficult to calm her; but made her promise to keep on this subject a silence which she never was known to observe.

So, though Gerande and Aubert were ignorant of it, all Geneva was soon talking of their speedy union. But it happened also that, while the worthy folk were gossiping, a strange chuckle was often heard, and a voice saying, "Gerande will not wed Aubert."

If the talkers turned round, they found themselves facing a little old man who was quite a stranger to them.

How old was this singular being? No one could have told. People conjectured that he must have existed for several centuries, and that was all. His big flat head rested upon shoulders the width of which was equal to the height of his body; this was not above three feet. This personage would have made a good figure to support a pendulum, for the dial would have naturally been placed on his face, and the balance-wheel would have oscillated at its ease in his chest. His nose might readily have been taken for the style of a sun-dial, for it was narrow and sharp; his teeth, far apart, resembled the cogs of a wheel, and ground themselves between his lips; his voice had the metallic sound of a bell, and you could hear his heart beat like the tick of a clock. This little man, whose arms moved like the hands on a dial, walked with jerks, without ever turning round. If any one followed him, it was found that he walked a league an hour, and that his course was nearly circular.

This strange being had not long been seen wandering, or rather circulating, around the town; but it had already been observed that, every day, at the moment when the sun passed the meridian, he stopped before the Cathedral of Saint Pierre, and resumed his course after the twelve strokes of noon had sounded. Excepting at this precise moment, he seemed to become a part of all the conversations in which the old watchmaker was talked of; and people asked each other, in terror, what relation could exist between him and Master Zacharius. It was remarked, too, that he never lost sight of the old man and his daughter while they were taking their promenades.

One day Gerande perceived this monster looking at her with a hideous smile. She clung to her father with a frightened motion.

"What is the matter, my Gerande?" asked Master Zacharius.

"I do not know," replied the young girl.

"But thou art changed, my child. Art thou going to fall ill in thy turn? Ah, well," he added, with a sad smile, "then I must take care of thee, and I will do it tenderly."

"O father, it will be nothing. I am cold, and I imagine that it is –"

"What, Gerande?"

"The presence of that man, who always follows us," she replied in a low tone.

Master Zacharius turned towards the little old man.

"Faith, he goes well," said he, with a satisfied air, "for it is just four o'clock. Fear nothing, my child; it is not a man, it is a clock!"

Gerande looked at her father in terror. How could Master Zacharius read the hour on this strange creature's visage?

"By-the-bye," continued the old watchmaker, paying no further attention to the matter, "I have not seen Aubert for several days."

"He has not left us, however, father," said Gerande, whose thoughts turned into a gentler channel.

"What is he doing then?"

"He is working."

"Ah!" cried the old man. "He is at work repairing my watches, is he not? But he will never succeed; for it is not repair they need, but a resurrection!"

Gerande remained silent.

"I must know," added the old man, "if they have brought back any more of those accursed watches upon which the Devil has sent this epidemic!"

After these words Master Zacharius fell into complete silence, till he knocked at the door of his house, and for the first time since his convalescence descended to his shop, while Gerande sadly repaired to her chamber.

Just as Master Zacharius crossed the threshold of his shop, one of the many clocks suspended on the wall struck five o'clock. Usually the bells of these clocks – admirably regulated as they were – struck simultaneously, and this rejoiced the old man's heart; but on this day the bells struck one after another, so that for a quarter of an hour the ear was deafened by the successive noises. Master Zacharius suffered acutely; he could not remain still, but went from one clock to the other, and beat the time to them, like a conductor who no longer has control over his musicians.

When the last had ceased striking, the door of the shop opened, and Master Zacharius shuddered from head to foot to see before him the little old man, who looked fixedly at him and said, –

"Master, may I not speak with you a few moments?"

"Who are you?" asked the watchmaker abruptly.

"A colleague. It is my business to regulate the sun."

"Ah, you regulate the sun?" replied Master Zacharius eagerly, without wincing. "I can scarcely compliment you upon it. Your sun goes badly, and in order to make ourselves agree with it, we have to keep putting our clocks forward so much or back so much."

"And by the cloven foot," cried this weird personage, "you are right, my master! My sun does not always mark noon at the same moment as your clocks; but some day it will be known that this is because of the inequality of the earth's transfer, and a mean noon will be invented which will regulate this irregularity!"

"Shall I live till then?" asked the old man, with glistening eyes.

"Without doubt," replied the little old man, laughing. "Can you believe that you will ever die?"

"Alas! I am very ill now."

"Ah, let us talk of that. By Beelzebub! that will lead to just what I wish to speak to you about."

Saying this, the strange being leaped upon the old leather chair, and carried his legs one under the other, after the fashion of the bones which the painters of funeral hangings cross beneath death's heads. Then he resumed, in an ironical tone, –

"Let us see, Master Zacharius, what is going on in this good town of Geneva? They say that your health is failing, that your watches have need of a doctor!"

"Ah, do you believe that there is an intimate relation between their existence and mine?" cried Master Zacharius.

"Why, I imagine that these watches have faults, even vices. If these wantons do not preserve a regular conduct, it is right that they should bear the consequences of their irregularity. It seems to me that they have need of reforming a little!"

"What do you call faults?" asked Master Zacharius, reddening at the sarcastic tone in which these words were uttered. "Have they not a right to be proud of their origin?"

"Not too proud, not too proud," replied the little old man. "They bear a celebrated name, and an illustrious signature is graven on their cases, it is true, and theirs is the exclusive privilege of being introduced among the noblest families; but for some time they have got out of order, and you can do nothing in the matter, Master Zacharius; and the stupidest apprentice in Geneva could prove it to you!"

"To me, to me, – Master Zacharius!" cried the old man, with a flush of outraged pride.

"To you, Master Zacharius, – you, who cannot restore life to your watches!"

"But it is because I have a fever, and so have they also!" replied the old man, as a cold sweat broke out upon him.

"Very well, they will die with you, since you cannot impart a little elasticity to their springs."

"Die! No, for you yourself have said it! I cannot die, – I, the first watchmaker in the world; I, who, by means of these pieces and diverse wheels, have been able to regulate the movement with absolute precision! Have I not subjected time to exact laws, and can I not dispose of it like a despot? Before a sublime genius had arranged these wandering hours regularly, in what vast uncertainty was human destiny plunged? At what certain moment could the acts of life be connected with each other? But you, man or devil, whatever you may be, have never considered the magnificence of my art, which calls every science to its aid! No, no! I, Master Zacharius, cannot die, for, as I have regulated time, time would end with me! It would return to the infinite, whence my genius has rescued it, and it would lose itself irreparably in the abyss of nothingness! No, I can no more die than the Creator of this universe, that submitted to His laws! I have become His equal, and I have partaken of His power! If God has created eternity, Master Zacharius has created time!"

The old watchmaker now resembled the fallen angel, defiant in the presence of the Creator. The little old man gazed at him, and even seemed to breathe into him this impious transport.

"Well said, master," he replied. "Beelzebub had less right than you to compare himself with God! Your glory must not perish! So your servant here desires to give you the method of controlling these rebellious watches."

"What is it? What is it?" cried Master Zacharius.

"You shall know on the day after that on which you have given me your daughter's hand."

"My Gerande?"

"Herself!"

"My daughter's heart is not free," replied Master Zacharius, who seemed neither astonished nor shocked at the strange demand.

"Bah! She is not the least beautiful of watches; but she will end by stopping also –"

"My daughter, – my Gerande! No!"

"Well, return to your watches, Master Zacharius. Adjust and readjust them. Get ready the marriage of your daughter and your apprentice. Temper your springs with your best steel. Bless Aubert and the pretty Gerande. But remember, your watches will never go, and Gerande will not wed Aubert!"

Thereupon the little old man disappeared, but not so quickly that Master Zacharius could not hear six o'clock strike in his breast.

Chapter IV
The Church of Saint Pierre

MEANWHILE Master Zacharius became more feeble in mind and body every day. An unusual excitement, indeed, impelled him to continue his work more eagerly than ever, nor could his daughter entice him from it.

His pride was still more aroused after the crisis to which his strange visitor had hurried him so treacherously, and he resolved to overcome, by the force of genius, the malign influence which weighed upon his work and himself. He first repaired to the various clocks of the town which were confided to his care. He made sure, by a scrupulous examination, that the wheels were in good condition, the pivots firm, the weights exactly balanced. Every part, even to the bells, was examined with the minute attention of a physician studying the breast of a patient. Nothing indicated that these clocks were on the point of being affected by inactivity.

Gerande and Aubert often accompanied the old man on these visits. He would no doubt have been pleased to see them eager to go with him, and certainly he would not have been so much absorbed in his approaching end, had he thought that his existence was to be prolonged by that of these cherished ones, and had he understood that something of the life of a father always remains in his children.

The old watchmaker, on returning home, resumed his labours with feverish zeal. Though persuaded that he would not succeed, it yet seemed to him impossible that this could be so, and he unceasingly took to pieces the watches which were brought to his shop, and put them together again.

Aubert tortured his mind in vain to discover the causes of the evil.

"Master," said he, "this can only come from the wear of the pivots and gearing."

"Do you want, then, to kill me, little by little?" replied Master Zacharius passionately. "Are these watches child's work? Was it lest I should hurt my fingers that I worked the surface of these copper pieces in the lathe? Have I not forged these pieces of copper myself, so as to obtain a greater strength? Are not these springs tempered to a rare perfection? Could anybody have used finer oils than mine? You must yourself agree that it is impossible, and you avow, in short, that the devil is in it!"

From morning till night discontented purchasers besieged the house, and they got access to the old watchmaker himself, who knew not which of them to listen to.

"This watch loses, and I cannot succeed in regulating it," said one.

"This," said another, "is absolutely obstinate, and stands still, as did Joshua's sun."

"If it is true," said most of them, "that your health has an influence on that of your watches, Master Zacharius, get well as soon as possible."

The old man gazed at these people with haggard eyes, and only replied by shaking his head, or by a few sad words, –

"Wait till the first fine weather, my friends. The season is coming which revives existence in wearied bodies. We want the sun to warm us all!"

"A fine thing, if my watches are to be ill through the winter!" said one of the most angry. "Do you know, Master Zacharius, that your name is inscribed in full on their faces? By the Virgin, you do little honour to your signature!"

It happened at last that the old man, abashed by these reproaches, took some pieces of gold from his old trunk, and began to buy back the damaged watches. At news of this, the customers came in a crowd, and the poor watchmaker's money fast melted away; but his honesty remained intact. Gerande warmly praised his delicacy, which was leading him straight towards ruin; and Aubert soon offered his own savings to his master.

"What will become of my daughter?" said Master Zacharius, clinging now and then in the shipwreck to his paternal love.

Aubert dared not answer that he was full of hope for the future, and of deep devotion to Gerande. Master Zacharius would have that day called him his son-in-law, and thus refuted the sad prophecy, which still buzzed in his ears, –

"Gerande will not wed Aubert."

By this plan the watchmaker at last succeeded in entirely despoiling himself. His antique vases passed into the hands of strangers; he deprived himself of the richly-carved panels which adorned the walls of his house; some primitive pictures of the early Flemish painters soon ceased to please his daughter's eyes, and everything, even the precious tools that his genius had invented, were sold to indemnify the clamorous customers.

Scholastique alone refused to listen to reason on the subject; but her efforts failed to prevent the unwelcome visitors from reaching her master, and from soon departing with some valuable object. Then her chattering was heard in all the streets of the neighbourhood, where she had long been known. She eagerly denied the rumours of sorcery and magic on the part of Master Zacharius, which gained currency; but as at bottom she was persuaded of their truth, she said her prayers over and over again to redeem her pious falsehoods.

It had been noticed that for some time the old watchmaker had neglected his religious duties. Time was, when he had accompanied Gerande to church, and had seemed to find in prayer the intellectual charm which it imparts to thoughtful minds, since it is the most sublime exercise of the imagination. This voluntary neglect of holy practices, added to the secret habits of his life, had in some sort confirmed the accusations leveled against his labours. So, with the double purpose of drawing her father back to God, and to the world, Gerande resolved to call religion to her aid. She thought that it might give some vitality to his dying soul; but the dogmas of faith and humility had to combat, in the soul of Master Zacharius, an insurmountable pride, and came into collision with that vanity of science which connects everything with itself, without rising to the infinite source whence first principles flow.

It was under these circumstances that the young girl undertook her father's conversion; and her influence was so effective that the old watchmaker promised to attend high mass at the cathedral on the following Sunday. Gerande was in an ecstasy, as if heaven had opened to her view. Old Scholastique could not contain her joy, and at last found irrefutable arguments' against the gossiping tongues which accused her master of impiety. She spoke of it to her neighbours, her friends, her enemies, to those whom she knew not as well as to those whom she knew.

"In faith, we scarcely believe what you tell us, dame Scholastique," they replied; "Master Zacharius has always acted in concert with the devil!"

"You haven't counted, then," replied the old servant, "the fine bells which strike for my master's clocks? How many times they have struck the hours of prayer and the mass!"

"No doubt," they would reply. "But has he not invented machines which go all by themselves, and which actually do the work of a real man?"

"Could a child of the devil," exclaimed dame Scholastique wrathfully, "have executed the fine iron clock of the château of Andernatt, which the town of Geneva was not rich enough to buy? A pious motto appeared at each hour, and a Christian who obeyed them, would have gone straight to Paradise! Is that the work of the devil?"

This masterpiece, made twenty years before, had carried Master Zacharius's fame to its acme; but even then there had been accusations of sorcery against him. But at least the old man's visit to the Cathedral ought to reduce malicious tongues to silence.

Master Zacharius, having doubtless forgotten the promise made to his daughter, had returned to his shop. After being convinced of his powerlessness to give life to his watches, he resolved to try if he could not make some new ones. He abandoned all those useless works, and devoted himself to the completion of the crystal watch, which he intended to be his masterpiece; but in vain did he use his most perfect tools, and employ rubies and diamonds for resisting friction. The watch fell from his hands the first time that he attempted to wind it up!

The old man concealed this circumstance from every one, even from his daughter; but from that time his health rapidly declined. There were only the last oscillations of a pendulum, which goes slower when nothing restores its original force. It seemed as if the laws of gravity, acting directly upon him, were dragging him irresistibly down to the grave.

The Sunday so ardently anticipated by Gerande at last arrived. The weather was fine, and the temperature inspiriting. The people of Geneva were passing quietly through the streets, gaily chatting about the return of spring. Gerande, tenderly taking the old man's arm, directed her steps towards the cathedral, while Scholastique followed behind with the prayer-books. People looked curiously at them as they passed. The old watchmaker permitted himself to be led like a child, or rather like a blind man. The faithful of Saint Pierre were almost frightened when they saw him cross the threshold, and shrank back at his approach.

The chants of high mass were already resounding through the church. Gerande went to her accustomed bench, and kneeled with profound and simple reverence. Master Zacharius remained standing upright beside her.

The ceremonies continued with the majestic solemnity of that faithful age, but the old man had no faith. He did not implore the pity of Heaven with cries of anguish of the 'Kyrie;' he did not, with the 'Gloria in Excelsis,' sing the splendours of the heavenly heights; the reading of the Testament did not draw him from his materialistic reverie, and he forgot to join in the homage of the 'Credo.' This proud old man remained motionless, as insensible and silent as a stone statue; and even at the solemn moment when the bell announced the miracle of transubstantiation, he did not bow his head, but gazed directly at the sacred host which the priest raised above the heads of the faithful. Gerande looked at her father, and a flood of tears moistened her missal. At this moment the clock of Saint Pierre struck half-past eleven. Master Zacharius turned quickly towards this ancient clock which still spoke. It seemed to him as if its face was gazing steadily at him; the figures of the hours shone as if they had been engraved in lines of fire, and the hands shot forth electric sparks from their sharp points.

The mass ended. It was customary for the 'Angelus' to be said at noon, and the priests, before leaving the altar, waited for the clock to strike the hour of twelve. In a few moments this prayer would ascend to the feet of the Virgin.

But suddenly a harsh noise was heard. Master Zacharius uttered a piercing cry.

The large hand of the clock, having reached twelve, had abruptly stopped, and the clock did not strike the hour.

Gerande hastened to her father's aid. He had fallen down motionless, and they carried him outside the church.

"It is the death-blow!" murmured Gerande, sobbing.

When he had been borne home, Master Zacharius lay upon his bed utterly crushed. Life seemed only to still exist on the surface of his body, like the last whiffs of smoke about a lamp just extinguished. When he came to his senses, Aubert and Gerande were leaning over him. In these last moments the future took in his eyes the shape of the present. He saw his daughter alone, without a protector.

"My son," said he to Aubert, "I give my daughter to thee."

So saying, he stretched out his hands towards his two children, who were thus united at his deathbed.

But soon Master Zacharius lifted himself up in a paroxysm of rage. The words of the little old man recurred to his mind.

"I do not wish to die!" he cried; "I cannot die! I, Master Zacharius, ought not to die! My books – my accounts! –"

With these words he sprang from his bed towards a book in which the names of his customers and the articles which had been sold to them were inscribed. He seized it and rapidly turned over its leaves, and his emaciated finger fixed itself on one of the pages.

"There!" he cried, "there! This old iron clock, sold to Pittonaccio! It is the only one that has not been returned to me! It still exists – it goes – it lives! Ah, I wish for it – I must find it! I will take such care of it that death will no longer seek me!"

And he fainted away.

Aubert and Gerande knelt by the old man's bedside and prayed together.

Chapter V
The Hour of Death

SEVERAL DAYS passed, and Master Zacharius, though almost dead, rose from his bed and returned to active life under a supernatural excitement. He lived by pride. But Gerande did not deceive herself; her father's body and soul were for ever lost.

The old man got together his last remaining resources, without thought of those who were dependent upon him. He betrayed an incredible energy, walking, ferreting about, and mumbling strange, incomprehensible words.

One morning Gerande went down to his shop. Master Zacharius was not there. She waited for him all day. Master Zacharius did not return.

Gerande wept bitterly, but her father did not reappear.

Aubert searched everywhere through the town, and soon came to the sad conviction that the old man had left it.

"Let us find my father!" cried Gerande, when the young apprentice told her this sad news.

"Where can he be?" Aubert asked himself.

An inspiration suddenly came to his mind. He remembered the last words which Master Zacharius had spoken. The old man only lived now in the old iron clock that had not been returned! Master Zacharius must have gone in search of it.

Aubert spoke of this to Gerande.

"Let us look at my father's book," she replied.

They descended to the shop. The book was open on the bench. All the watches or clocks made by the old man, and which had been returned to him because they were out of order, were stricken out excepting one:

"Sold to M. Pittonaccio, an iron clock, with bell and moving figures; sent to his château at Andernatt."

It was this "moral" clock of which Scholastique had spoken with so much enthusiasm.

"My father is there!" cried Gerande.

"Let us hasten thither," replied Aubert. "We may still save him!"

"Not for this life," murmured Gerande, "but at least for the other."

"By the mercy of God, Gerande! The château of Andernatt stands in the gorge of the 'Dents-du-Midi' twenty hours from Geneva. Let us go!"

That very evening Aubert and Gerande, followed by the old servant, set out on foot by the road which skirts Lake Leman. They accomplished five leagues during the night, stopping neither at Bessinge nor at Ermance, where rises the famous château of the Mayors. They with difficulty forded the torrent of the Dranse, and everywhere they went they inquired for Master Zacharius, and were soon convinced that they were on his track.

The next morning, at daybreak, having passed Thonon, they reached Evian, whence the Swiss territory may be seen extended over twelve leagues. But the two betrothed did not even perceive the enchanting prospect. They went straight forward, urged on by a supernatural force. Aubert, leaning on a knotty stick, offered his arm alternately to Gerande and to Scholastique, and he made the greatest efforts to sustain his companions. All three talked of their sorrow, of their hopes, and thus passed along the beautiful road by the water-side, and across the narrow plateau which unites the borders of the lake with the heights of the Chalais. They soon reached Bouveret, where the Rhone enters the Lake of Geneva.

On leaving this town they diverged from the lake, and their weariness increased amid these mountain districts. Vionnaz, Chesset, Collombay, half lost villages, were soon left behind. Meanwhile their knees shook, their feet were lacerated by the sharp points which covered the ground like a brushwood of granite – but no trace of Master Zacharius!

He must be found, however, and the two young people did not seek repose either in the isolated hamlets or at the château of Monthay, which, with its dependencies, formed the appanage of Margaret of Savoy. At last, late in the day, and half dead with fatigue, they reached the hermitage of Notre-Dame-du-Sex, which is situated at the base of the Dents-du-Midi, six hundred feet above the Rhone.

The hermit received the three wanderers as night was falling. They could not have gone another step, and here they must needs rest.

The hermit could give them no news of Master Zacharius. They could scarcely hope to find him still living amid these sad solitudes. The night was dark, the wind howled amid the mountains, and the avalanches roared down from the summits of the broken crags.

Aubert and Gerande, crouching before the hermit's hearth, told him their melancholy tale. Their mantles, covered with snow, were drying in a corner; and without, the hermit's dog barked lugubriously, and mingled his voice with that of the tempest.

"Pride," said the hermit to his guests, "has destroyed an angel created for good. It is the stumbling-block against which the destinies of man strike. You cannot reason with pride, the principal of all the vices, since, by its very nature, the proud man refuses to listen to it. It only remains, then, to pray for your father!"

All four knelt down, when the barking of the dog redoubled, and some one knocked at the door of the hermitage.

"Open, in the devil's name!"

The door yielded under the blows, and a dishevelled, haggard, ill-clothed man appeared.

"My father!" cried Gerande.

It was Master Zacharius.

"Where am I?" said he. "In eternity! Time is ended – the hours no longer strike – the hands have stopped!"

"Father!" returned Gerande, with so piteous an emotion that the old man seemed to return to the world of the living.

"Thou here, Gerande?" he cried; "and thou, Aubert? Ah, my dear betrothed ones, you are going to be married in our old church!"

"Father," said Gerande, seizing him by the arm, "come home to Geneva, – come with us!"

The old man tore away from his daughter's embrace and hurried towards the door, on the threshold of which the snow was falling in large flakes.

"Do not abandon your children!" cried Aubert.

"Why return," replied the old man sadly, "to those places which my life has already quitted, and where a part of myself is for ever buried?"

"Your soul is not dead," said the hermit solemnly.

"My soul? O no, – its wheels are good! I perceive it beating regularly –"

"Your soul is immaterial, – your soul is immortal!" replied the hermit sternly.

"Yes – like my glory! But it is shut up in the château of Andernatt, and I wish to see it again!"

The hermit crossed himself; Scholastique became almost inanimate. Aubert held Gerande in his arms.

"The château of Andernatt is inhabited by one who is lost," said the hermit, "one who does not salute the cross of my hermitage."

"My father, go not thither!"

"I want my soul! My soul is mine –"

"Hold him! Hold my father!" cried Gerande.

But the old man had leaped across the threshold, and plunged into the night, crying, "Mine, mine, my soul!"

Gerande, Aubert, and Scholastique hastened after him. They went by difficult paths, across which Master Zacharius sped like a tempest, urged by an irresistible force. The snow raged around them, and mingled its white flakes with the froth of the swollen torrents.

As they passed the chapel erected in memory of the massacre of the Theban legion, they hurriedly crossed themselves. Master Zacharius was not to be seen.

At last the village of Evionnaz appeared in the midst of this sterile region. The hardest heart would have been moved to see this hamlet, lost among these horrible solitudes. The old man sped on, and plunged into the deepest gorge of the Dents-du-Midi, which pierce the sky with their sharp peaks.

Soon a ruin, old and gloomy as the rocks at its base, rose before him.

"It is there – there!" he cried, hastening his pace still more frantically.

The château of Andernatt was a ruin even then. A thick, crumbling tower rose above it, and seemed to menace with its downfall the old gables which reared themselves below. The vast piles of jagged stones were gloomy to look on. Several dark halls appeared amid the debris, with caved-in ceilings, now become the abode of vipers.

A low and narrow postern, opening upon a ditch choked with rubbish, gave access to the château. Who had dwelt there none knew. No doubt some margrave, half lord, half brigand, had sojourned in it; to the margrave had succeeded bandits or counterfeit coiners, who had been hanged on the scene of their crime. The legend went that, on winter nights, Satan came to lead his diabolical dances on the slope of the deep gorges in which the shadow of these ruins was engulfed.

But Master Zacharius was not dismayed by their sinister aspect. He reached the postern. No one forbade him to pass. A spacious and gloomy court presented itself to his eyes; no one forbade him to cross it. He passed along the kind of inclined plane which conducted to one of the long corridors, whose arches seemed to banish daylight from beneath their heavy springings. His advance was unresisted. Gerande, Aubert, and Scholastique closely followed him.

Master Zacharius, as if guided by an irresistible hand, seemed sure of his way, and strode along with rapid step. He reached an old worm-eaten door, which fell before his blows, whilst the bats described oblique circles around his head.

An immense hall, better preserved than the rest, was soon reached. High sculptured panels, on which serpents, ghouls, and other strange figures seemed to disport themselves confusedly, covered its walls. Several long and narrow windows, like loopholes, shivered beneath the bursts of the tempest.

Master Zacharius, on reaching the middle of this hall, uttered a cry of joy.

On an iron support, fastened to the wall, stood the clock in which now resided his entire life. This unequalled masterpiece represented an ancient Roman church, with buttresses of wrought iron, with its heavy bell-tower, where there was a complete chime for the anthem of the day, the 'Angelus,' the mass, vespers, compline, and the benediction. Above the church door, which opened at the hour of the services, was placed a 'rose,' in the centre of which two hands moved, and the archivault of which reproduced the twelve hours of the face sculptured in relief. Between the door and the rose, just as Scholastique had said, a maxim, relative to the employment of every moment of the day, appeared on a copper plate. Master Zacharius had once regulated this succession of devices with a really Christian solicitude; the hours of prayer, of work, of repast, of recreation, and of repose, followed each other according to the religious discipline, and were to infallibly insure salvation to him who scrupulously observed their commands.

Master Zacharius, intoxicated with joy, went forward to take possession of the clock, when a frightful roar of laughter resounded behind him.

He turned, and by the light of a smoky lamp recognized the little old man of Geneva.

"You here?" cried he.

Gerande was afraid. She drew closer to Aubert.

"Good day, Master Zacharius," said the monster.

"Who are you?"

"Signor Pittonaccio, at your service! You have come to give me your daughter! You have remembered my words, 'Gerande will not wed Aubert.' "

The young apprentice rushed upon Pittonaccio, who escaped from him like a shadow.

"Stop, Aubert!" cried Master Zacharius.

"Goodnight," said Pittonaccio, and he disappeared.

"My father, let us fly from this hateful place!" cried Gerande. "My father!"

Master Zacharius was no longer there. He was pursuing the phantom of Pittonaccio across the rickety corridors. Scholastique, Gerande, and Aubert remained, speechless and fainting, in the large gloomy hall. The young girl had fallen upon a stone seat; the old servant knelt beside her, and prayed; Aubert remained erect, watching his betrothed. Pale lights wandered in the darkness, and the silence was only broken by the movements of the little animals which live in old wood, and the noise of which marks the hours of 'death watch.'

When daylight came, they ventured upon the endless staircase which wound beneath these ruined masses; for two hours they wandered thus without meeting a living soul, and hearing only a far-off echo responding to their cries. Sometimes they found themselves buried a hundred feet below the ground, and sometimes they reached places whence they could overlook the wild mountains.

Chance brought them at last back again to the vast hall, which had sheltered them during this night of anguish. It was no longer empty. Master Zacharius and Pittonaccio were talking there together, the one upright and rigid as a corpse, the other crouching over a marble table.

Master Zacharius, when he perceived Gerande, went forward and took her by the hand, and led her towards Pittonaccio, saying, "Behold your lord and master, my daughter. Gerande, behold your husband!"

Gerande shuddered from head to foot.

"Never!" cried Aubert, "For she is my betrothed."

"Never!" responded Gerande, like a plaintive echo.

Pittonaccio began to laugh.

"You wish me to die, then!" exclaimed the old man. "There, in that clock, the last which goes of all which have gone from my hands, my life is shut up; and this man tells me, 'When I have thy daughter, this clock shall belong to thee.' And this man will not rewind it. He can break it, and plunge me into chaos. Ah, my daughter, you no longer love me!"

"My father!" murmured Gerande, recovering consciousness.

"If you knew what I have suffered, far away from this principle of my existence!" resumed the old man. "Perhaps no one looked after this timepiece. Perhaps its springs were left to wear out, its wheels to get clogged. But now, in my own hands, I can nourish this health so dear, for I must not die, – I, the great watchmaker of Geneva. Look, my daughter, how these hands advance with certain step. See, five o'clock is about to strike. Listen well, and look at the maxim which is about to be revealed."

Five o'clock struck with a noise which resounded sadly in Gerande's soul, and these words appeared in red letters: *You Must Eat of the Fruits of the Tree Of Science.*

Aubert and Gerande looked at each other stupefied. These were no longer the pious sayings of the Catholic watchmaker. The breath of Satan must have passed over it. But Zacharius paid no attention to this, and resumed –

"Dost thou hear, my Gerande? I live, I still live! Listen to my breathing, – see the blood circulating in my veins! No, thou wouldst not kill thy father, and thou wilt accept this man for thy husband, so that I may become immortal, and at last attain the power of God!"

At these blasphemous words old Scholastique crossed herself, and Pittonaccio laughed aloud with joy.

"And then, Gerande, thou wilt be happy with him. See this man, – he is Time! Thy existence will be regulated with absolute precision. Gerande, since I gave thee life, give life to thy father!"

"Gerande," murmured Aubert, "I am thy betrothed."

"He is my father!" replied Gerande, fainting.

"She is thine!" said Master Zacharius. "Pittonaccio, them wilt keep thy promise!"

"Here is the key of the clock," replied the horrible man.

Master Zacharius seized the long key, which resembled an uncoiled snake, and ran to the clock, which he hastened to wind up with fantastic rapidity. The creaking of the spring jarred upon the nerves. The old watchmaker wound and wound the key, without stopping a moment, and it seemed as if the movement were beyond his control. He wound more and more quickly, with strange contortions, until he fell from sheer weariness.

"There, it is wound up for a century!" he cried.

Aubert rushed from the hall as if he were mad. After long wandering, he found the outlet of the hateful château, and hastened into the open air. He returned to the hermitage of Notre-Dame-du-Sex, and talked so despairingly to the holy recluse, that the latter consented to return with him to the château of Andernatt.

If, during these hours of anguish, Gerande had not wept, it was because her tears were exhausted.

Master Zacharius had not left the hall. He ran every moment to listen to the regular beating of the old clock.

Meanwhile the clock had struck, and to Scholastique's great terror, these words had appeared on the silver face: – *Man Ought To Become The Equal Of God.*

The old man had not only not been shocked by these impious maxims, but read them deliriously, and flattered himself with thoughts of pride, whilst Pittonaccio kept close by him.

The marriage-contract was to be signed at midnight. Gerande, almost unconscious, saw or heard nothing. The silence was only broken by the old man's words, and the chuckling of Pittonaccio.

Eleven o'clock struck. Master Zacharius shuddered, and read in a loud voice: "MAN SHOULD BE THE SLAVE OF SCIENCE, AND SACRIFICE TO IT RELATIVES AND FAMILY."

"Yes!" he cried, "there is nothing but science in this world!"

The hands slipped over the face of the clock with the hiss of a serpent, and the pendulum beat with accelerated strokes.

Master Zacharius no longer spoke. He had fallen to the floor, his throat rattled, and from his oppressed bosom came only these half-broken words: "Life – science!"

The scene had now two new witnesses, the hermit and Aubert. Master Zacharius lay upon the floor; Gerande was praying beside him, more dead than alive.

Of a sudden a dry, hard noise was heard, which preceded the strike.

Master Zacharius sprang up.

"Midnight!" he cried.

The hermit stretched out his hand towards the old clock, – and midnight did not sound.

Master Zacharius uttered a terrible cry, which must have been heard in hell, when these words appeared: '*Who Ever Shall Attempt to Make Himself the Equal of God, Shall be For Ever Damned!*'

The old clock burst with a noise like thunder, and the spring, escaping, leaped across the hall with a thousand fantastic contortions; the old man rose, ran after it, trying in vain to seize it, and exclaiming, "My soul, – my soul!"

The spring bounded before him, first on one side, then on the other, and he could not reach it.

At last Pittonaccio seized it, and, uttering a horrible blasphemy, ingulfed himself in the earth.

Master Zacharius fell backwards. He was dead.

The old watchmaker was buried in the midst of the peaks of Andernatt.

Then Aubert and Gerande returned to Geneva, and during the long life which God accorded to them, they made it a duty to redeem by prayer the soul of the castaway of science.

Biographies & Sources

Andrew Bourelle
Little Healers
(First Publication)
American author Andrew Bourelle has published science fiction, fantasy, horror, mystery, and literary short stories in a variety of journals, including *Hobart*, *Isthmus*, *Kestrel*, *Jabberwock Review*, *Prime Number Magazine*, *Thin Air*, *Weave* and *Whitefish Review*, as well as fiction anthologies, such as *The Best American Mystery Stories, Corrupts Absolutely: Dark Metahuman Fiction* and *Law and Disorder: Stories of Conflict and Crime*. He is the co-author, with James Patterson, of the novella *The Pretender*, which is featured in the collection *Triple Threat*. Bourelle lives in New Mexico with his wife and two children.

John Buchan
The Grove of Ashtaroth
(Originally published in *Blackwood's Magazine*, 1910)
John Buchan (1875–1940) was born in Perth, Scotland. He trained as a barrister, though his working life went on to span several sectors, including publishing, politics and war correspondence. He wrote solidly during this time, producing a number of short stories and novels, as well as historical and biographical works. He is perhaps best known for his thriller *The Thirty-Nine Steps*. Most of his horror stories are influenced by the wild and strange places he experienced during his time as a government administrator in South Africa. In 1935, Buchan was made Governor-General of Canada, and lived there until his death.

Beth Cato
Moon Skin
(First Publication)
Beth Cato hails from Hanford, California, but currently writes and bakes cookies in a lair west of Phoenix, Arizona. She shares the household with a hockey-loving husband, a numbers-obsessed son, and a cat the size of a canned ham. Beth is the author of the steampunk fantasy *Clockwork Dagger* series from Harper Voyager, which includes her Nebula-nominated novella *Wings of Sorrow and Bone*. Her newest novel, *Breath of Earth*, is set in a steampunk alternate history 1906 San Francisco. Follow her at BethCato.com and on Twitter at @BethCato.

Robert W. Chambers
The Demoiselle d'Ys
(Originally published in *The King in Yellow*, F. Tennyson Neely, 1895)
Robert William Chambers (1865–1933) was born in Brooklyn, New York. He started his career publishing illustrations in magazines like *Life, Truth* and *Vogue* before abruptly turning his attention strictly to fiction. He produced works in numerous genres including historical, romance, fantasy, science fiction and horror. Everett Franklin Bleiler, a respected

scholar of science fiction and fantasy literature, described *The King in Yellow* as one of the most important works of American supernatural fiction.

L. Maria Child
Hilda Silfverling: A Fantasy
(Originally published in *The Columbian Magazine*, 1845)
Lydia Maria Child (1802–80) was born in Medford, Massachusetts. She received her education first at home, then a local dame school and later a women's seminary. She established herself as a social reformer – advocating abolition, women's rights and Native American rights. These themes were explored through much of her writing as she published novels, journals and domestic advice books. She spent the 1840s and 1850s writing for numerous periodicals and newspapers as well as producing a variety of short stories addressing the issues of slavery and promoting the emancipation of slaves and their incorporation into American society.

Amanda C. Davis
Dear George, Love Margaret
(Originally Published in *Sci-Fi Romance Quarterly*, 2015)
Amanda C. Davis lives in Pennsylvania, where she writes dark fantasy, light horror and the very softest science fiction. Her work has appeared in dozens of magazines and anthologies, and was collected in 2013 along with her sister Megan Engelhardt's work in *Wolves and Witches: A Fairy Tale Collection* from World Weaver Press. She has an engineering degree and an obsession with baking the perfect macaron. She tweets enthusiastically as @davisac1. You can find out more about her and read more of her work at www.amandacdavis.com.

Daniel J. Davis
Pax Mechanica
(First Publication)
Daniel J. Davis is a longtime lover of the heroic fantasy and steampunk genres. He attributes the former to his discovery of David Gemmell in his late teens, and he blames the latter on the children's editions of H.G. Wells and Jules Verne in the elementary school library. He lives in North Carolina, USA, where his wife listens to him ramble about alternate histories and make-believe worlds. Daniel's other stories have appeared in *Writers of the Future Volume 31*, *Urban Fantasy Magazine* and *Unidentified Funny Objects 5*. He also blogs at danieljdavisblogs.wordpress.com.

Jennifer Dornan-Fish
Fire to Set the Blood
(First Publication)
Jennifer Dornan-Fish has a Ph.D. in anthropology and is a professor by day, writer by night. She has also been a private investigator, K9 Wilderness Search and Rescue unit, dog walker, ditch digger, photographer, social justice activist and video game writer. Her short fiction has appeared in *Daily Science Fiction*, *Interzone* and elsewhere. A dual Irish/American citizen, she has also lived in Senegal, Belize, the UK and Micronesia. She now lives in the Bay Area with her husband and son. You can follow her writing at dornan-fish.com.

Arthur Conan Doyle
The Horror of the Heights
(Originally Published in *The Strand Magazine*, 1913)
Arthur Conan Doyle (1859–1930) was born in Edinburgh, Scotland, and became a well-known writer, poet and physician. As a medical student he was so impressed by his professor's powers of deduction that he was inspired to create the illustrious and much-loved figure Sherlock Holmes. In contrast to this scientific background, however, Doyle became increasingly interested in spiritualism, leaving him keen to explore fantastical elements in his stories. Paired with his talent for storytelling he wrote great tales of terror, such as 'The Horror of the Heights' and 'The Leather Funnel'. Doyle's vibrant and remarkable characters have breathed life into all of his stories, engaging readers throughout the decades.

Spencer Ellsworth
The Fires of Mercy
(Originally Published in *Beneath Ceaseless Skies*, 2015)
Spencer Ellsworth has been writing since he learned how. His work has been published in and is forthcoming at Tor.com, *Lightspeed Magazine*, *Beneath Ceaseless Skies*, *Michael Moorcock's New Worlds Magazine* and many other places. His space opera trilogy *Starfire* will be released by Tor.com in 2017. Spencer lives in Bellingham, Washington, with his wife and three children. He works as a teacher and administrator at a tribal college on a Native American reservation, and also blogs and posts homemade punk rock at spencerellsworth.com and twitters @spencimus.

David Jón Fuller
Sisters
(First Publication)
David Jón Fuller was born and raised in Winnipeg, MB and has also lived in Edmonton, AB and Reykjavík, Iceland. His short stories have appeared in *Long Hidden: Speculative Fiction From the Margins of History*; *Tesseracts 18: Wrestling With Gods*; *Kneeling in the Silver Light: Stories From The Great War*; *Insignia: Chinese Fantasy Stories*; *No Shit, There I Was*; and *On Spec*. He studied theatre at the University of Winnipeg, and Icelandic language and literature at the University of Iceland. He speaks French and Icelandic as second languages, and has also studied Latin and Anishinaabemowin.

Friedrich de la Motte Fouqué
Undine
(Originally published by Hitzig, 1811)
Friedrich de la Motte Fouqué (1777–1843) was a German novelist and playwright born in Brandenburg an der Havel to a family of aristocratic descent. In 1794 he joined the army to participate in the Rhine campaign but dedicated the rest of his life to his literature after he met scholar and critic August Wilhelm Schlegel, who influenced much of his poetry. Many of his works were influenced by Scandinavian myths and he often promoted the ideals of chivalry through them. *Undine* is perhaps his best-known work, a fairy tale like story that acts as his most enduring success.

George Griffith
The Raid of Le Vengeur
(Originally published in *Pearson's Magazine*, 1901)
George Griffith (1857–1906) was a British science fiction writer, journalist and explorer, also occasionally writing under the pseudonym of Levin Carmac. He frequently published works in pulp and pre-science fiction magazines including *Pearson's Weekly* and *Pearson's Magazine*. His works often featured prescient elements of aerial battleships, themes focused on utopia, world domination, apocalyptic visions, parallel worlds, lost worlds, and immortality. Despite being overshadowed in success by H.G. Wells, it was ultimately Griffith's work that provided the model for what became the steampunk genre.

Edward Everett Hale
The Man Without a Country
(Originally published in *The Atlantic Monthly*, 1863)
Edward Everett Hale (1822–1909) was born in Boston, Massachusetts and worked as a writer, historian and Unitarian minister. He entered Harvard at age 13, graduating second in his class and teaching at Boston Latin School for two years. He embarked on a career in journalism for a few years at his father's *Boston Daily Advertiser* and held multiple teaching positions while studying theology to prepare for the ministry. During this time he wrote several short stories and addressed various social issues through his writing tracts, such as slavery and educational reform. Through this Hale garnered much respect for his tolerant views.

Kelly A. Harmon
Advantage on the Kingdom of the Shore
(First Publication)
Kelly A. Harmon is an award-winning journalist and author, and a member of Science Fiction & Fantasy Writers of America. A Baltimore native, she writes the *Charm City Darkness* series, which includes the novels *Stoned in Charm City*, *A Favor for a Fiend* and *A Blue Collar Proposition*. Her stories can be found in many anthologies, including *Triangulation: Dark Glass*, *Hellebore and Rue* and *Deep Cuts: Mayhem, Menace and Misery*. Kelly is a former newspaper reporter and editor, and now edits for Pole to Pole Publishing. For more information, visit her at kellyaharmon.com, facebook.com/Kelly-A-Harmon1 or twitter.com/kellyaharmon.

Nathaniel Hawthorne
The Artist of the Beautiful
(Originally Published in *United States Magazine and Democratic Review*, 1844)
P.'s Correspondence
(Originally Published in *United States Magazine and Democratic Review*, 1845)
The prominent American writer Nathaniel Hawthorne (1804–64) was born in Salem, Massachusetts. His most famous novel *The Scarlet Letter* helped him to become established as a writer in the 1850s. Most of his works were influenced by his friends Ralph Waldo Emerson and Herman Melville, as well as by his extended financial struggles. Hawthorne's works often incorporated a dark romanticism that focused on the evil and sin of humanity. Some of his most famous stories detailed supernatural presences or occurrences, as in his The *House of the Seven Gables* and the short story collection *Twice Told Tales*.

E.T.A. Hoffmann
The Sandman
(First Published in *Nachtstücke*, Aufbau-Verlag, 1816)
E.T.A. Hoffmann (1776–1822) was a musician and a painter as well as a successful writer. Born in Germany and raised by his uncle, Hoffmann followed a legal career until his interests drew him to composing operas and ballets. He began to write richly imaginative stories that helped secure his reputation as an influential figure during the German Romantic movement, with many of his tales inspiring stage adaptations, such as *The Nutcracker* and *Coppélia*. Hoffmann's chilling tale 'The Sandman' has influenced many, including Neil Gaiman, whose popular graphic novel series *Sandman* also features a character who steals people's eyes.

Liam Hogan
Spectrum
(First Publication)
Liam Hogan was abandoned in a library at the tender age of three, only to emerge blinking into the sunlight many years later, with a head full of words and an aversion to loud noises. He's the host of the award-winning monthly literary event, Liars' League, and the winner of Quantum Shorts 2015 and Sci-Fest LA's Roswell Award 2016. His steampunk stories appear in Leap Books' *Beware the Little White Rabbit* #Alice150 anthology, in *Steampunk Trails II* and in Witty Bard's *Of Airships & Automatons*. He lives in London, tweets at @LiamJHogan and dreams in Dewey Decimals. Find out more at: happyendingnotguaranteed.blogspot.co.uk.

Robert E. Howard
Skulls in the Stars
(Originally Published in *Weird Tales*, 1929)
Robert Ervin Howard (1906–36) was born in Peaster, Texas. An intellectual and athletic man, Howard wrote within the genres of westerns, historical and horror fiction, and is credited with having formed the subgenre within fantasy known as 'Sword and Sorcery'. His novella *Pigeons from Hell*, which Stephen King quotes as the one of the finest horror stories of the century, exemplifies his dark yet realistic style. Howard's work is strongly associated with the pulp magazine *Weird Tales*, in which he published many horror and fantasy stories, including those featuring the character Conan the Cimmerian and Solomon Kane.

Washington Irving
Rip Van Winkle
(Originally Published in *The Sketch Book of Geoffrey Crayon, Gent.*, 1819)
Washington Irving (1783–1859) was a famous American author, essayist, biographer and historian born in New York City. He was influenced by his private education and law school studies to begin writing essays for periodicals. Travelling and working all over the globe, Irving established a name for himself with his successful short stories 'Rip Van Winkle' and 'The Legend of Sleepy Hollow'. These works in particular reflected the mischievous and adventurous behaviour of his childhood. Years later, Irving lived in Spain as a US Ambassador. He returned to America towards the end of life, where he wrote several successful historical and biographical works including a five-volume biography of George Washington.

S.T. Joshi

Foreword: Swords & Steam Short Stories

S. T. Joshi is the author of *The Weird Tale* (1990), *The Modern Weird Tale* (2001), and *Unutterable Horror: A History of Supernatural Fiction* (2012). His award-winning biography *H.P. Lovecraft: A Life* (1996) was later expanded as *I Am Providence: The Life and Times of H.P. Lovecraft* (2010). He has prepared editions of the work of Arthur Machen, Lord Dunsany, Algernon Blackwood, M.R. James, Ambrose Bierce, Clark Ashton Smith, and other classic authors of weird fiction, as well as the anthology *American Supernatural Tales* (2007).

Percival Leigh

The Aerial Burglar

(Originally published in *The Comic Album: A Book for Every Table*, 1844)

Percival Leigh (1813–89) was an English comic writer born in Haddington. He studied medicine at St Bartholomew's before abandoning this profession to engage in a writing career. Soon after the formation of *Punch* he joined its staff and contributed to it regularly until his death. As an amateur actor he also worked with Dickens in his 1845 presentation of *Every Man in his Humour* and his medical training allowed him to help Dickens by writing on science in layman's terms. 'The Aerial Burglar' is thought to be the first ever Steampunk short story.

B.C. Matthews

The Crime of a Windcatcher

(First Publication)

B.C. Matthews hails from the rural farmlands of Northern California, where she still eats the best tomatoes grown in the world. She is published in *On the Premises: Changes Issue #27*, *Triangulation: Lost Voices*, *Spark: A Creative Anthology VII* and an anthology of Lovecraftian romance, *Eldritch Embraces*. She currently battles scientists at a laboratory by day, and finds sleep-deprived moments to tend to her reptile herd at night, leading her to pen many stories involving dragons and mad scientists. You can find her online at www.bcmatthews.blogspot.com.

Angus McIntyre

War Mage

(First Publication)

Angus McIntyre was born in London and now lives in New York, where he mistreats computers for a living. He writes about spaceships, monsters, bad choices and what it means to be human. His short fiction has appeared in the anthology *Mission: Tomorrow*, in *Black Candies* magazine and on the BoingBoing website. More of his writing will appear soon in the anthology *Humanity 2.0* and in the magazine *Abyss & Apex*. He is a graduate of the 2013 Clarion UCSD Writer's Workshop. Find out more on his website: angus.pw.

A. Merritt

Three Lines of Old French

(Originally published in *All-Story Weekly*, 1919)

Abraham Merritt (1884–1943) was born in Beverly, New Jersey. A writer of science fiction as well as an inductee to the Science Fiction and Fantasy Hall of Fame, Merritt wrote characteristic pulp fiction themes of lost civilization, monsters and treacherous villains. Many of his short stories and novels were published in *Argosy All-Story Weekly*. His most famous novels are perhaps *Burn Witch Burn*, *The Ship Ishtar* and *Dwellers in the Mirage*. His writing was known for its excessive descriptive detail as well as the immense creativity of the alternative worlds he created.

Dan Micklethwaite
Pen Dragons
(First Publication)
Dan Micklethwaite is a freelance writer and novelist based in the north of England. His short fiction spans several genres and has featured in various international publications, including *AE Science Fiction*, *Unsung Stories*, *Metaphorosis* and Meerkat Press's *Love Hurts* anthology. He won the Magic Oxygen 6-Word Story Competition 2015, and claimed 2nd Prize in The Short Story Competition 2015. His debut novel, *The Less than Perfect Legend of Donna Creosote*, was released in July 2016 through the award-winning independent publisher Bluemoose Books. For more information, follow him on Twitter @Dan_M_writer.

Edward Page Mitchell
The Clock that Went Backward
(Originally published in *The New York Sun,* 1881)
Pioneer of the science fiction genre, American author Edward Page Mitchell (1852–1927) was a short story writer and editor for *The Sun* newspaper in New York. His work featured predominantly in *The Sun*, and most of his stories were published anonymously. His story 'The Clock That Went Backward', which is a contender for the first time-travel story and predates H.G. Wells's *The Time Machine*, was also published anonymously in *The Sun* and Mitchell wasn't revealed as the author until 40 years after his death.

Edgar Allan Poe
The Unparalleled Adventure of One Hans Pfaall
(Originally published in *Southern Literary Messenger*, 1835)
The versatile writer Edgar Allan Poe (1809–1849) was born in Boston, Massachusetts. Poe is extremely well known as an influential author, poet, editor and literary critic that wrote during the American Romantic Movement. Poe is generally considered the inventor of the detective fiction genre, and his works are famously filled with terror, mystery, death and hauntings. Some of his better-known works include his poems 'The Raven' and 'Annabel Lee', and the short stories 'The Tell Tale Heart' and 'The Fall of the House of Usher'. The dark, mystifying characters of his tales have captured the public's imagination and reflect the struggling, poverty-stricken lifestyle he lived his whole life.

Howard Pyle
The Winning of a Sword
(Originally published in *Part II of The Story of King Arthur and His Knights*, Charles Scribner's Sons, 1903)
Howard Pyle (1853–1911) was born in Wilmington, Delaware. As well as working as an author he was also a teacher and prolific illustrator. He often wrote and illustrated his own stories, and some of his notable works include *The Merry Adventures of Robin*

Hood and *The Story of King Arthur and His Knights*. The stories that captivated him were fairy tales, fables and adventure tales; and he is sometimes called the father of American illustration.

Victoria Sandbrook
Taking Care of Business
(First Publication)
Victoria Sandbrook is a fantasy writer, freelance editor, and Viable Paradise XVIII graduate. She is an avid hiker, sometimes knitter, long-form talker and initiate baker. She is often found loitering around libraries. She spends most of her days attempting to wrangle a ferocious, destructive, jubilant tiny human. Victoria, her husband and their daughter live in Brockton, Massachusetts. She reviews books and shares writerly nonsense at victoriasandbrook.com and on Twitter at @vsandbrook. This is her first publication.

Walter Scott
My Aunt Margaret's Mirror
(Originally published in *The Keepsake for 1828*)
Death of the Laird's Jock
(Originally published in *The Keepsake for 1828*)
Walter Scott (1771–1832) was born in Edinburgh, Scotland and was a historical novelist, poet and biographer. He was fascinated by the oral traditions of the Scottish Borders and later developed an interest in German Romanticism and Gothic novels. Scott is often credited with inventing the modern historical novel, and is known for such works as *Ivanhoe* and *Rob Roy*. His first novel, *Waverley,* was published anonymously along with the rest of his fictional works. Those familiar with the internationally celebrated poet though, would come to recognize these stories as Scott's due to his unique narrative style.

Mary Shelley
Roger Dodsworth: The Reanimated Englishman
(Originally published in *Yesterday and to-day*, Cyrus Redding, 1863)
Mary Shelley (1797–1851) was born in London, England. Encouraged to write at a young age by her father, William Godwin, who was a journalist, philosopher and novelist, Shelley became an essayist, biographer, short story writer and novelist. She is famous for her horror novel *Frankenstein: or The Modern Prometheus*, and for being married to the poet Percy Bysshe Shelley. Suffering many traumatic events and widowed early on in her life, she worked hard to support herself and her son through several publications, such as her apocalyptic novel *The Last Man*.

Zach Shephard
Eli Whitney and the Cotton Djinn
(Originally appeared in *Intergalactic Medicine Show #42*, 2014)
Zach Shephard lives in Enumclaw, Washington, where he occasionally writes fantasy stories based entirely on stupid puns. His fiction has appeared in places like *Galaxy's Edge*, *Intergalactic Medicine Show*, *Weird Tales* and the *Unidentified Funny Objects* anthology series. He never would have started writing if not for Roger Zelazny, and he hasn't washed any part of his body since being in the same room as Neil Gaiman. For a complete list of his published stories, check out zachshephard.com.

Amy Sisson
Dressing Mr. Featherbottom
(Originally Published in *Robotica*, 2015)
Amy Sisson is a writer, reviewer and librarian currently living in Houston, Texas. Previously, her short stories have appeared in *Strange Horizons, Lady Churchill's Rosebud Wristlet* and several licensed *Star Trek* anthologies from Pocket Books. In January 2015, she began working on a goal to read at least one short story every day of the year, and to date has read over two million words of short fiction. She blogs about her favorite stories each month at amysisson.com.

Robert Louis Stevenson
The Touchstone
(Originally published in *Fables*, Charles Scribner's Sons, 1896)
Robert Louis Stevenson (1850–94) was born in Edinburgh, Scotland. He became a well-known novelist, poet and travel writer, publishing the famous works *Treasure Island, Kidnapped* and *The Strange Case of Dr Jekyll and Mr Hyde*. All of his works were highly admired by many other artists, as he was a literary celebrity during his lifetime. Travelling a lot for health reasons and because of his family's business, Stevenson ended up writing many of his journeys into his stories and wrote works mainly related to children's literature and the horror genre.

Brian Trent
Vortaal Hunt
(First Publication)
Brian Trent's dark fantasy and science-fiction work appears in a wide array of publications including *Analog, Fantasy & Science Fiction, Cosmos, Daily Science Fiction, Nature, Apex, Galaxy's Edge, Pseudopod, Escape Pod* and numerous year's best anthologies. His story 'Shortcuts' appears in Flame Tree Publishing's *Science Fiction Short Stories*. His literary influences are varied, and his interests include technology, classical history, and sociology – particularly the interplay between all three. Trent lives in New England, where he is a novelist, poet, and screenwriter. He can be found online at www.briantrent.com.

Jules Verne
A Drama in the Air
(Originally published in *Musée des Familles*, 1851)
Master Zacharius
(Originally published in *Musée des Familles*, 1854)
Jules Verne (1828–1905) was born in Nantes, France. As a novelist, poet and playwright, he wrote adventure novels and had a big impact on the science fiction genre, as well as providig inspiration for later Steampunk authors. Along with H.G. Wells, Verne is considered to be one of the founding fathers of science fiction. His most famous adventure novels formed the series *Voyages Extraordinaires*, and include *Journey to the Centre of the Earth* and *Twenty Thousand Leagues Under the Sea*. His stories continue to be popular today, and Verne ranks as the most translated science fiction author to date, with his works often reprinted and adapted for film.

Flame Tree Publishing

New & Classic Writing

Flame Tree's Gothic Fantasy books offer a carefully curated series of new titles, each with combinations of original and classic writing:

Chilling Horror Short Stories
Chilling Ghost Short Stories
Science Fiction Short Stories
Murder Mayhem Short Stories
Crime & Mystery Short Stories
Swords & Steam Short Stories
Dystopia Utopia Short Stories

Available from all good bookstores, wordwide, and online at:
flametreepublishing.com

GOTHIC FANTASY

For our books, calendars, blog
and latest special offers please see:
flametreepublishing.com